'TIS THE SEASON

VARIATIONS INSPIRED BY JANE AUSTEN'S CHRISTMAS

SUSAN ADRIANI JAN ASHTON JULIE COOPER
AMY D'ORAZIO JENETTA JAMES
KARALYNNE MACKRORY LUCY MARIN
ELIZABETH RASCHE MARY SMYTHE

Quills & Quartos
PUBLISHING

Edited by: Jan Ashton, Julie Cooper, Beth Flintoft, Katie Jackson, Kristi Rawley, Justine Rivard and Debra Anne Watson

Cover Design by Lesley Worrell

ISBN 978-1-956613-09-4

TABLE OF CONTENTS

"This is quite the season indeed for friendly meetings! At Christmas every body invites their friends about them, and people think little of even the worst weather."

— Mr Elton, Emma

HEART ENOUGH

AMY D'ORAZIO

There are very few of us who have heart enough to be really in love without encouragement.

— *Charlotte Lucas, Pride & Prejudice, Chapter 6*

chapter one

A LACK OF ENCOURAGEMENT

December 1812

THROUGHOUT THE MONTHS OF JANE'S ENGAGEMENT, Elizabeth had been plagued by one dreadful thought: *I want to be happy for her more than I truly* am *happy for her.*

Could there be any greater proof that she was indeed a most selfish and unfeeling girl? To envy, so bitterly, the happiness of a most beloved sister, the same sister whose joy she had once so bitterly defended to *him*? Yes, she was not only selfish; she was reckless, capricious, and silly as well. But Elizabeth could not help herself, no matter how she tried. She was jealous; she wanted Jane's happiness for herself.

By appearances, Elizabeth had contrived to be all that a glad-hearted bridesmaid ought to be in the weeks of Jane's engagement. She spent hours tirelessly discussing trousseau and wedding tours. She consented —enthusiastically—to a gown in calamine blue silk because Jane said it suited her. It did not suit her, in fact, but as it was almost the precise shade of Bingley's eyes, she could understand her sister's preference.

Elizabeth had engaged in no less than four arguments, ranging from energetic to vitriolic, on the absence of fish from the wedding meal. Jane could not abide either the taste or smell of fish; Elizabeth felt it perfectly reasonable that her sister should not wish to have the hated odour lingering over her wedding breakfast. Mrs Bennet, however, believed that a wedding breakfast which aspired to any degree of elegance whatsoever simply must have fish. Both Jane and her mother came to tears about it at one time or another, but Elizabeth was steadfast in support of her sister.

Outward appearances notwithstanding, inside she felt nothing but loss—loss of Jane, loss of *him*, loss of what should have been. *He* had been supposed to return from London ten days from when he had departed Netherfield Park. That was above two months ago. She supposed that, were it not for his friend's wedding, she might never have seen him again.

The night before the wedding, Elizabeth took herself up to the bedchamber she had shared with her sister since she was too young to know. *One last night to share with Jane,* she thought.

Over the last weeks, the room had grown close with half-packed trunks, bonnets, buttons, and fabrics strewn all about, but now the room felt bare. All of Jane's belongings had been taken to Netherfield where they were carefully put in their correct places by Jane's new maid. *Only three miles away,* Elizabeth reminded herself. *A brisk walk, no more.*

It was a strange feeling, hollowed out and emptied, like the bedchamber itself…yet it was as it should be. A woman was meant to leave home and be with her husband. Elizabeth had never imagined how it would be when it was she who was left behind.

Elizabeth had gone to the closet, intending to retrieve her nightgown, as Jane entered. "Already enjoying all the extra room you have for your possessions, Lizzy?"

"Hardly." Elizabeth withdrew the gown and closed the closet door, a lump suddenly obstructing her throat. She did not turn around, unsure of herself, but Jane must have sensed something. She came up behind her sister and wrapped her arms around her.

"I feel it too," she whispered. "It shall not be this way again."

Elizabeth shook her head. "No, it shall not." With a deep breath, she turned to Jane with a smile. "How many plans and schemes and dreams these walls have known!"

In the hall, Kitty began an argument with Mary, and Jane and Elizabeth exchanged a look, rolling their eyes at one another. "This room has been our refuge," Jane said, her tone undeniably wistful. "As much as I wish to be Mrs Bingley, I find it is not so easy to cease being Miss Bennet. Silly, is it not? It is always expected of a lady, and I have stayed home longer than most."

"Expecting something does not necessarily make it easy." Elizabeth reassured her with a smile. "But come now—will you brush my hair? One last time. I promise I shall not complain if you tug."

"You always complain, and I never tug," Jane retorted, but gladly she took up the brush and, with practised hands, undid her sister's pins and plaits. Elizabeth sat under her deft care, enjoying being tended to.

The house grew silent around them; while Jane brushed, they listened to Mrs Bennet's querulous laments die off, followed by the gradual quieting of Kitty and Mary. Then, the sisters doused the lamp, curled up in Elizabeth's bed, which Jane always protested was larger, and commenced one last night of sisterly secret-sharing.

As Jane recounted the horrors of Mrs Bennet's wedding-night speech, Elizabeth thought she might be ill. "The act itself does not shock me as much as imagining our own father and mother—"

"I beg you say no more!" Jane groaned. "I cannot comprehend…no, such a vision could not be borne."

"You seem remarkably less nervous about it than I might have imagined," Elizabeth said.

"I am dreadfully nervous," Jane replied, yet with an air of serenity that belied her words. The glow from the fire was just enough that Elizabeth could see the ease in her countenance. "But I am sure I have nothing to fear from Charles. He is so very good to me."

As it seemed that Jane might run off on a speech extolling the virtues of Bingley, all which Elizabeth had heard many times over, she hastened to interject. "You nearly fainted when you overheard Aunt Philips telling the story of her wedding night!"

"I did, that is true," Jane admitted with a little laugh. "Quite silly of me."

"Was it?"

"Was it what?"

"Was it silly of you?" Elizabeth pressed. "I think it perfectly reasonable to have some anxiety for that which is unknown."

"There is nothing to it, I am sure. Any pain must certainly be of short duration."

"You seem quite certain," Elizabeth said, and this observation caused Jane to turn onto her back, carefully avoiding her sister's eye. "Jane!"

"Oh Lizzy, do not, pray do not…" This was said among giggles and an attempt to pull Elizabeth's sheet over her face.

"Jane, have you and Bingley…?" Elizabeth paused a moment, thinking she might have heard some noise from the hall. Such a moment to have an errant sister burst in! Fortunately, it was not, but Elizabeth lowered her voice to a whisper to ask, "Did Bingley ask you to…?"

"No," Jane said firmly.

"No?"

Elizabeth watched her sister nibble her lip a moment before admitting, "I asked him."

"What!" The word was shrieked loudly, and both ladies immediately threw themselves into the posture of deep sleep, just in case their mother stirred herself to seek out the source of the noise.

When no such interference arrived, Jane turned and whispered, "I did not wish to spend my wedding day fearful and anxious so I…I asked him. He was most obliging."

"I should imagine he was!"

The sisters fell into stifled laughter, holding the sheet to their faces and choking and gasping their mirth. Elizabeth came perilously close to rolling right off the bed from gleeful convulsions, and was still wiping tears of laughter from her eyes when Jane said, "So you know my secret…will you tell me yours?"

"Secret?" Elizabeth took a deep breath designed to calm herself. "I have no secrets from you."

"Ah, but you do." Jane rolled over, resting her head in one hand and peering at Elizabeth. "Whatever became of Mr Darcy?"

The effect of that question felt like a dash of cold water across Elizabeth's face. Immediately sobered, she found herself grateful for the shadows which she hoped hid her expression. "Nothing became of him. He is at Netherfield, no doubt drinking to Bingley's final night as a bachelor."

Mr Darcy had arrived late that day, ostensibly due to some sort of business. How lucky it was to be a man, able to avoid anything at all simply by conjuring up some pressing matter of business! He had missed the dinner at Netherfield thrown in Jane's honour. Was it the distaste he held for all Bennets that kept him away? Or, more painfully…was it the thought of seeing her?

"I think it most peculiar that a man who would do so much for our poor sister—"

"He felt a responsibility on account of his history with Wickham," Elizabeth interjected hurriedly.

"—a man who loved you so ardently for so long, went away without making anything of it."

Elizabeth wondered if Jane could see her shrug. "These things go off sometimes."

"There is much we have misunderstood about Mr Darcy's character, but I am confident that he is not capricious."

"No, he is not," Elizabeth agreed. Tentatively she added, "I daresay his family must have prevailed upon him."

"Why do you think so?"

Elizabeth laid in quiet contemplation of her canopy a moment before saying, "I have never told you of the particulars of Lady Catherine's visit to us."

"No, but Mama did. She said her ladyship brought us a letter from Charlotte."

"No." Elizabeth chuckled weakly. "Mama wished to believe that more than it was actually true. Lady Catherine's purpose was to warn me from pursuing her nephew."

Lady Catherine de Bourgh had called at Longbourn in the first week of October, about a week after Jane had become engaged. She had been arrogant, rude, and disapproving of all she saw, and her manners to Mrs Bennet were nothing short of abominable. To even think of it now made Elizabeth ill with equal parts shame and indignation.

"We walked out, over into our little wilderness near the road, and she began to upbraid me, saying that she had been made aware of a rumour—one that she supposed I had put about myself—that I would be soon betrothed to her nephew." Elizabeth said it lightly, wanting to show how amusing and inconsequential it all was, although she knew she fooled no one and certainly not Jane.

"Who would have told her that?"

"I cannot say for certain. I imagine it went from the Lucases to Charlotte and then Charlotte to her husband. No doubt Mr Collins thought it his duty to inform his benefactor. Lady Catherine said it would be a grave insult to Mr Darcy to imagine there was any truth in it."

"Yet she came here anyway?"

"Yes, despite the obvious untruth of it, it nevertheless alarmed her enough that she felt compelled to wait upon me and hear me deny it myself."

"Oh Lizzy." Jane sighed and reached over to find her hand in the darkness. "How perfectly terrible. I hope you were not dreadfully impertinent to her. I daresay a person of rank must be afforded due respect even if they are not doing credit to that rank."

"She thought I was impertinent, to be sure."

"Do you not think that her calling here could only confirm the rumours of an alliance between you and her nephew? She would never have come to us otherwise."

"That is true." Elizabeth sighed remembering that day, the faint warmth of an October sun on her face and the cold disappointment that Mr Darcy had departed for London in her heart. "I was as forbearing to her as I could possibly be. Quite civil."

"But what did you say? What did she say?"

"Oh..." Elizabeth shifted uncomfortably. "She wished to know if I was engaged to Mr Darcy. I said I was not, very politely. When she asked if I comprehended the basis of these falsehoods, I said I could not. Then I said that I supposed one marriage in the offing compelled my neighbours to imagine there ought to be two. I told her that Mr Darcy and I had danced together at Netherfield in the autumn, and it likely made people imagine there was more to it."

"What did she say to that?"

"She delivered an impassioned speech about her daughter and Mr Darcy—how they were both descended from the same noble lineage, and how they had been formed for one another and promised in marriage since they were in the cradle. I told her I had already heard of that, even before I came to Kent."

"That was all?"

"Yes, for I...I did not wish to vex her, vexatious as she was. For Mr Darcy's sake, it seemed most prudent to retain her good opinion of me, inasmuch as I could, and I believe she went away satisfied."

It was maddening to Elizabeth that she could not read the expression in her sister's eyes in the darkness.

At last, in her naturally mild way, Jane said, "I am surprised, Lizzy."

"Surprised that I was civil?"

"Surprised that you pretended there was nothing between you."

"By that time, there might not have been, as attested by how he behaved at Longbourn! I had no notion by then of what was in his head or his heart. He was decidedly grave and silent when he called here with Bingley, and when they came to dine, I scarcely had two words from him that night. Then he went back to London without a word to me, or our father, and simply left it to Bingley to give his regards. There was no sense in distressing his aunt for what seemed to be coming 'round to nothing."

Jane was silent.

"What good could come in risking insult to such a lady? She already thinks me a poorly educated country savage, why earn her ire? That would certainly not endear me to him."

"How was it when she left?" Jane asked, turning her head towards the canopy. "You were polite and denied any connexion between you and Mr Darcy? Thus, she received her satisfaction and went away?"

The lump returned to Elizabeth's throat, and she swallowed hard against it. Yes, it had been easily proffered, this notion that there was nothing between Mr Darcy and her, for by that time she could no longer be certain of him. All expectation, all hope, seemed in vain, even if she hardly knew why.

"She appeared content with my responses."

The two ladies were silent a few moments until Jane said, "Charles and I have considered it, of course. He thought your connexion with Mr Darcy was certain while I believed it rather unlikely. My opinion, however, was founded on my recollection of your initial dislike of the gentleman. I knew you eventually liked him better, but I had no notion that your feelings extended to..."

To ardent love. Elizabeth could not speak it. She dashed at the tear that slipped down her cheek. "Bingley's opinion was likely altered when he saw us reunited at Pemberley, before...before Lydia."

"You have never really told me the whole story. There was too much else to occupy us in the days after—our worries about her and what was to come."

Elizabeth could hardly bear to talk of it now, those brief, glorious days in Derbyshire, although she would treasure them for the rest of her life. Presently, they were too sweetly painful to remember, but surely time would mend that.

"My feelings are quite the opposite of what they once were," she said with soft certitude. "I was wrong, utterly mistaken, in my first understanding of him, and once I realised his true nature, how good and honourable and...well, it was easy enough to develop sincere esteem for him after that."

Jane squeezed Elizabeth's hand beneath the coverlet and gently asked, "Are you in love with him?"

Elizabeth hesitated, for she wished to answer her sister with equanimity; soon enough she realised equanimity was impossible. "I am," Elizabeth admitted hoarsely. "I am terribly afraid that I am."

"Oh Lizzy." A sigh of deep sorrow came from beside her. "Yet you told his aunt it was all nothing! What a moment for your courage to fail you!"

This rankled a bit. "It was not so much a failure of courage as it was a triumph of wisdom."

"Only think of how he must have felt on hearing her account of it!"

"I daresay he never even knew of it."

"Surely he must have. Lady Catherine was undoubtedly pleased with herself for taking the matter into her hands and must have felt it her duty to tell him of the rumour."

A prickle of unease spread over Elizabeth's skin. She had presumed that the reassurances she offered to Lady Catherine would be sufficient to see an end to the matter. She expected that her polite denials would placate her ladyship's indignation and, hopefully, make her forget all about it.

But Jane was right. Lady Catherine would have told her nephew of the rumour, as well as the ease with which she had conquered it.

"Impertinence to his relations would surely not have recommended me to him."

"That is true," Jane agreed through a yawn. "But he knows that for people whom you really love, you will stop at nothing to defend them. And he knows that you do not suffer foolishness. Your indifference, your ability to be civil to his aunt must have surely told him your heart remained your own."

Dismay wound Elizabeth's stomach into a knot. *My heart unattached? Could there be anything further from the truth?* "My only wish on that dreadful day was to appease her ladyship into silence. I believed that if I did, she would speak no ill of me to him!"

Elizabeth had no reply from Jane; her sister had fallen asleep, quickly and completely as she always did. It was likely for the best; it would not do for the bride to be pale and tired on her long-awaited wedding day.

She could see now what a vain wish it was, to imagine appeasing Lady Catherine, but even so, her spoken wishes were by no means the whole of it.

Some part of her had been afraid. Not of Lady Catherine herself, for even in her attempt to be fearsome, Elizabeth knew she was merely an old woman who despised not having her way. By then Elizabeth knew very well that Darcy did not think himself bound to Miss de Bourgh.

No, she had been afraid of *him,* afraid his heart had grown cold, or that his sense had at last overcome his sensibilities. She was connected to his worst enemy, for heaven's sake! Of all the degradations she offered him, brother to that scoundrel had to be the worst.

He had been so silent, so grave at their last meeting, and had offered nothing at all in the way of encouragement to her. She could no longer depend on his admiration.

Elizabeth eased herself out of her bed and removed to sleep in Jane's bed, whispering, "Good night, sweet sister."

Her own repose was a long time off. Her mind was plagued now, overcome by thoughts of what might have been. She remembered once saying to him that her courage always rose with every attempt to intimidate her—but he had not wished to intimidate her, had he? He had delved right into the very heart of her, and that had frightened her more than anything and sent her courage skittering.

And now my courage and I are alone and unloved.

So much wasted time. How easy it all seemed for most people! They met, they liked one another, they danced a few dances, he asked a question, she gave a proper reply, and it was done. No months spent pining and repining, no hate turned to love, no eloping sisters, and no meddlesome aunts.

The question now was what she should do about it. She was surer than ever that his late arrival was done to avoid discourse with her. But there was tomorrow. Jane's wedding might be the last chance she had to remedy the confusion and heartache between them, even if plain talk and boldness were required to do it.

Yes, she was resolved. Tomorrow, everything would be put to rights.

chapter two

THE EXPECTATION OF A WEDDING

Elizabeth had never really known what the phrase 'male beauty' meant until the day she first saw Mr Darcy. She had always believed it meant pleasingly arranged hair, or good height; possibly something to do with the air with which he carried himself.

But then, October last, she saw Mr Darcy walk in, with the other habitué of Netherfield, at the assembly in Meryton. Their party arrived during 'Lady Charlotte's Fancy', and though she knew that dance as well as she knew how to walk, Elizabeth missed a step when she beheld him. Male beauty; he had it in abundance. She felt a flush heat her body that had nothing to do with her exertions.

She cared not that he was rich—indeed, in that moment, she was unaware. Her mind was not formed to reckon a person's rank by examining attire and jewellery and all the other nuances that somehow enabled Society to ascertain a person's worth at thirty paces.

What she did care about was that he had a fine noble countenance, a tall, athletic bearing, and lips that made her want to learn what kissing was about. Scandalous thoughts indeed!

Enchanted, she imagined what it would be like to kiss those lips right until the very moment he had opened them and rudely refused to stand up with her, then said she was not handsome enough to tempt him.

Now, more than a twelvemonth later, she still had not grown used to his appearance. It made her heart leap and stutter to see him, standing outside the church with Mr Hurst. More handsome than ever, she thought, her eyes hungrily moving over his countenance.

Astonishing, really, how a man could look so refined, yet have that air of wildness about him—though perhaps it was only her recollection of the time she came upon him at Pemberley that made her think so. Elizabeth permitted her eyes to linger on him, feeling equal parts pleasure and pain in the beholding.

It was an exceedingly wintry day for what was in truth late autumn, and Elizabeth shivered as soon as the carriage door was opened. She was first to step out and was pleased beyond anything that he came to help her down. "I thank you," she murmured, peeping up at him from around the edge of her bonnet, but his attention had already turned to her mother.

When everyone was out of the carriage, he said, with perfect composure and civility, "Ladies, you are all looking quite lovely. Miss Bennet, my friend is an exceptionally fortunate man."

Mrs Bennet twittered and blushed while Jane and Elizabeth thanked him, and Elizabeth noted, with no little discomfort, that he was careful not to meet her eye. But the time for being demure had long since passed, and she needed to be the coquette, at least a little. "Mr Darcy?"

He appeared startled to be addressed so directly by her, and she smiled, eager to put him at ease, perhaps even tease a little. "You did not join us last night for dinner."

"Forgive me, no. I was late in leaving town and arrived just as the party was ended." He smiled genially, looking for all the world like he had missed nothing of consequence to him.

Elizabeth pressed on. "How did you leave Miss Darcy? I do hope she is well?"

"She remains at Pemberley until Christmas," he replied. "But in her last letter, she urged me to give you her regards."

Elizabeth murmured her appreciation, but there was not time for more. They had by then entered the church, and the moment had arrived to witness those dear to them binding their lives to one another.

It was as perfect as any wedding could be. Jane was blushing and lovely, and Bingley was nearly bursting with pride and delight. When they gazed at each other, the love between them was almost too much; such tenderness of feeling was to be envied, and Elizabeth did envy them both.

While Jane stood basking in the worshipful gaze of her beloved, Elizabeth grew increasingly anxious, yearning for a look, a secret smile, or anything of the sort from Mr Darcy. She received none.

Throughout the ceremony, Mr Darcy stood in an upright posture, his countenance calm, complaisant, and wholly unreadable. No one who saw him could ever imagine that he had once uttered words of love to her, or the substance of the arguments between them. Maybe he could no longer imagine them himself.

Never before had she understood better Jane's admonitions on the cruelty of civility. Elizabeth would have preferred he be angry, or hateful to her, or even showed her cold disdain, because this tepid amiability was the absolute worst treatment she could ever imagine. It hurt, his newfound congenial manners.

Elizabeth had duties to attend to at Jane's breakfast. Jane travelled the mile to Longbourn in her husband's carriage—a mile that appeared to require an unduly long time to peregrinate—while Elizabeth, along with the rest of the Bennets, returned in the family landau to see that the servants had everything as it ought to have been. Naturally they had, and so she was left to amble about, fretting about seeing him again.

At length, Jane and Bingley arrived to many cheers and well wishes. Longbourn had never been so full; despite the chill of the day, people spilled out into the garden, seeking refuge from the moist heat of those packed into the drawing rooms. It was not a surprise; everyone liked both husband and wife and was eager to see them established as one of the principal families of the district.

"Do you need me for anything?" Elizabeth asked when at last she was able to press through the crowd and reach her sister's side.

Jane could scarcely take her eyes from Bingley long enough to shake her head. Elizabeth smiled fondly at her and then reached up to her sister's hair, tucking in a particularly damning tress that had fallen. Then she asked her new brother, "Shall I fix you a drink, sir? Something to eat?"

"Eat?" Bingley asked dreamily, as if he had no idea what she was talking about.

"A glass of wine? Shall I get you one?"

"No, thank you, I am…" His attention and his footsteps drifted away from Elizabeth simultaneously. Elizabeth shook her head fondly at the pair of them.

Very well. I have done as I ought, and now am free to tend to my own concerns.

Gathering her courage, she set forth to find him and speak to him. He was not in the room where she was, and so she went room to room, finding him in the small back parlour which was less populated than the others but still full. Elizabeth had recalled his fondness for coffee—he drank it in copious amounts at nearly every gathering she had ever attended with him—and so had brought with her a cup for him. She hoped she had fixed it as he liked, with just a little milk and one heaping spoon of sugar.

He was facing the window and did not turn when she approached. "Sir?"

The sound of her voice made him jerk and whirl about. Instinct made him recover quickly into a truncated bow that almost struck her arm, stretched as it was to offer him coffee. She yanked her arm back at the last moment, and some of the coffee splashed over the edge.

"Excuse me," he said stiffly. "I did not mean to—"

"No, no, I...you did not have any coffee," Elizabeth explained, her discomfort amplified by his obvious dismay. "I thought you might like—"

"I stopped drinking it," he replied abruptly. "It gives me headaches."

"Oh...well." Elizabeth looked down at the foolish cup and then had no idea what to do with it. They were standing by the window with nowhere to dispose of it, this stupid attempt at rapprochement. Wishing it gone, she decided she would drink it herself, though she despised coffee. "More for me, then," she said with a brave smile.

She took a generous gulp that scalded her tongue and made her gasp. For a terrible moment, she thought she might choke, but she pushed it down, feeling all the dreadful consciousness of his steady gaze upon her.

The incident rendered her unable to speak for several long moments; in the face of it, Mr Darcy was induced to speak. "I hope your sister is satisfied with the day?"

Elizabeth was still left with the urge to cough, but she determinedly denied it, grinning madly in an attempt to appear easy. "As she is ending it as Mrs Bingley, I daresay her chief sources of delight have not failed her."

He chuckled. "Bingley is likewise pleased, I am sure."

The strained silence came again between them. From the other room, Elizabeth heard a loud conversation, her mother's voice rising above the din. Mrs Bennet was holding forth on having such wonderful sons-in-law as Bingley and Wickham, and Elizabeth winced. Hoping to distract him from any possible overhearings, she enquired, "Will you be remaining at Netherfield for long?"

"Alas, I must return to town today. I shall likely leave fairly soon."

Elizabeth thought it a great feat of self-control that she did not exclaim her dismay aloud. "You must take a bit of wedding cake with you for Miss Darcy, then," she said. "A young lady likes to put it under her pillow, to dream of her husband."

"She undoubtedly would like that very much, but alas, she will have to do without it. As I had said previously, she is—"

"At Pemberley. Forgive me, yes, you did say so. I forgot."

"No matter," he said. "In any case, she will not be in town until a day or so after Christmas, when my aunt and uncle bring her."

In this, Elizabeth saw her opportunity. Forming her resolution, she sallied forth. "Then surely you must stay! To be alone at Christmas is a dreadful thing! Bingley and my sister would surely be pleased to have you at Netherfield and then you could join us all at Sir William Lucas's party. He holds it every year to celebrate the Festive Season, and there are punch and sweetmeats and dancing, of course, and Sir William likes to go about holding a bough with mistletoe over—"

Mr Darcy glanced away and shifted on his feet, and his clear discomfort made Elizabeth realise how brazen she was. *What must he think of me, carrying on in such a way? Inviting him to Bingley's house? Mistletoe? Good heavens, what have I become?*

"What I mean to say," Elizabeth said with an embarrassed half-laugh, "is that I am certain your friend would enjoy the opportunity to host you and have you join with him in the festivities of the season. They are simple pleasures but decidedly better than being alone?"

"In fact, I shall not be alone." Mr Darcy's gaze was now fixed on his own feet. "My aunt, Lady Catherine, and my cousin will join me."

"Forgive me," Elizabeth gabbled wildly—and too loudly. "Such presumptions! You will have a splendid time with them, I am sure. Please accept my well wishes for the season and the new year and extend the same to her ladyship and Miss de Bourgh."

He raised his eyes then, and Elizabeth was struck by what appeared to be remorse within them. Remorse? Regret? Whatever it was, she could not comprehend it and more than anything wanted to flee it. Thus, she excused herself and turned back, hastening out of the room, the coffee swashing and spilling over her hand as she moved with quick paces across the room and down the hall, nearly collapsing with relief when she saw Jane beckoning her.

"Lizzy," she said, her blue eyes urgent. "Lizzy, come with me."

With a demure smile to those around her, Jane glided from the room, bestowing one final angelic smile on her new husband before they left. Elizabeth followed her towards the back stair, setting the coffee cup down on the way.

Jane was walking with uncommon rapidity, and Elizabeth matched her pace, the two ladies hastening up the stairs and into a bedchamber.

Jane carefully closed the door behind them before turning and reaching to take her sister's hands in her grasp. "Charles just told me something I thought you should know, much though it grieves me to tell you."

A prickle of alarm touched Elizabeth's heart. "What is it?"

"Lizzy, he is engaged."

Elizabeth sank onto the edge of the bed, fearing she knew even before she asked, "Who?"

Jane's sorrowful look and downturned mouth were answer enough, yet Elizabeth required confirmation. "N-not...you do not mean to say Mr Darcy is...is..."

"He proposed to his cousin," Jane said quietly. "To Miss de Bourgh."

In retrospect, Elizabeth thought she should have gasped or cried or fainted, but she did none of those. A deep chill swept over her, and she wrapped her arms around her body, allowing her eyes to fall on Jane's slender left hand—the hand on which Bingley's ring now resided. The only syllable she uttered was "Oh."

"Charles is not certain exactly when it happened, though he does believe it was rather recent."

Elizabeth could think of nothing rational to say. She could only hug herself tight and silently scream, *No!*

At length, Jane offered, "He does not love her."

Elizabeth laughed weakly. "I should hope he does, otherwise they are due for a long, sad life together."

"Charles thinks it is an enormous mistake. He is grieved on his friend's behalf. Miss Darcy is none too pleased either."

"I am sorry to hear it," Elizabeth said. "At least we may hope Lady Catherine's joy is complete."

"Lizzy—"

"Well, one cannot undo that which is done," Elizabeth said briskly. She straightened her shoulders and rose from the bed. "I must go help our mother. Do you need anything?"

"Lizzy, stop. Talk to me. I know how this must upset you."

"No, no, I cannot allow my romantic tribulations to mar your happy day. Go to your husband."

"I cannot leave you when I—"

"Jane. Go." Elizabeth forced a smile to her face. "Please go. All will be well. I just need a few minutes to myself."

With a kiss on her sister's cheek and a few worried glances behind her, Jane eventually did as she was bid. As soon as she did, Elizabeth sank back onto the bed feeling weak and nauseated and bitterly cold. The tears did not come immediately, but when they did, they were copious. Elizabeth shoved her face into a pillow to suppress the sounds of her sobs, praying no one downstairs heard her and not caring if she suffocated to death.

At length she realised she must go back down, loath as she was to see him again. She forced herself to rise and go to the washstand, wiping her face with a cool, wet cloth that did very little to repair her appearance. There was nothing for it, though; she had been absent too long.

Downstairs once again, she soon found that she need not have concerned herself; Mr Darcy was already gone.

chapter three

A GREAT ESCAPE

Christmas 1812

ELIZABETH FOUND NO JOY IN THE FESTIVE SEASON. AS SHE had long been an avid practitioner of all the delights of Christmas, she was disappointed, but in the face of all else, it had less consequence. She did not attend Sir William Lucas's party, though it would be the first occasion attended by the newly married Bingleys. She simply could not summon sufficient cheer, and heaven forfend Sir William hold his mistletoe bough aloft over her head!

Indeed, the nearest she came to enjoying Christmas was the day when she sat at Oakham Mount, utterly alone and gazing at nothing. Somewhere in the midst of her time there, it began to snow. Her thoughts fell away as she watched it fall in persistent sheets. The landscape was first pale and grey but soon became covered in white. The ghostly pallor was oddly comforting, although the moment she comprehended it, she also realised she ought to get back to the house. Her skirts were cold and damp, and her pelisse was not chosen to withstand a wintry tempest. *Perhaps if I come down with a fever, it will burn Mr Darcy right out of my brain.*

It was an agreeable notion, but it did not come to pass. Elizabeth could not even summon up a snivel.

Mr and Mrs Gardiner arrived with their children on the twenty-third. Elizabeth could see her dear aunt was concerned with how she found her. She was thinner, and her ennui was plain to any who knew her, but she did her best to reassure.

"That is the disadvantage of organising someone else's wedding," she said with a smile. "All the trouble with none of the exhilaration."

Mrs Gardiner smiled faintly, but her brow remained creased every time she beheld her niece.

On Christmas Eve, Elizabeth sat on the sofa at her aunt Philips's house for a small family party, made larger this year by one. Mary played the pianoforte, Jane and Bingley sent about as much good cheer as they could, and Mrs Bennet spoke loudly and at length about how determined she was to see Elizabeth married in the new year. Elizabeth could not hear all they said, but the few phrases she did hear— 'not getting any prettier' and 'must learn to check her tongue' and 'perhaps the Lucas boy'—made her feel she heard enough. She excused herself to go home, walking the mile to Longbourn and locking the door behind her when she reached her bedchamber.

Elizabeth woke on Christmas morning feeling much as she had any other day recently. She rose and was dressed; they walked to church for the service. Then the Bennets, Gardiners, Philipses, and now Bingleys commenced their standing tradition—a little game they played whereby each had been assigned to choose a gift for someone else secretly. Without being seen, the participants were to place the gifts on a table in the drawing room, and the gift-giver would be revealed after dinner.

Elizabeth's person that year was her father; he had been an easy enough task, as he only ever wished for a book and usually announced the title of the one he wanted sometime in November. The book had arrived in Mr Hatchard's a fortnight past, and Mr Bennet smiled widely when he saw the tome.

"*Literary Anecdotes of the 18th Century*," he said with such pleasure that even Elizabeth felt it. "I daresay you will know where to find me, then."

Cries of dismay rose, and he raised his hands. "Very well, very well. If you must have me, I shall remain, but after dinner, no one must trouble me!"

When it was Elizabeth's turn to see her gift, she was surprised to receive a lace cap. "What is this?" she asked, looking around the room. Kitty, in the corner, was nearly overcome by giggles and could not immediately reply.

"I daresay it must have been meant for me," Jane said hurriedly. "A cap for a married lady..."

"Or a spinster!" Kitty cried, laughing wildly. "It was Lydia's idea. She wrote and dared me to do it. Is it not a fine joke!"

"Yes," Elizabeth replied, forcing herself to grin and give a little chuckle. "Quite amusing."

Mrs Bennet leant over in her chair to take it from her daughter's hands. "Very fine lace, Kitty! Well done!"

A spinster's cap. Elizabeth shook her head. Her young sisters would see how it was soon enough.

But if Kitty's thoughtlessness provided her some amusement, it rebounded to Elizabeth's benefit as well. Mrs Gardiner approached her the next day with an invitation. "Come back with us. I understand you had planned to be in London with Jane for the Season, yes? So, you will come early and be with us awhile."

"Do not think it so bad for me here," Elizabeth told her. "I do miss Jane, as much for her kindness as her good sense, but I am not unhappy at home."

"Of course," Mrs Gardiner agreed smoothly. "But we always long for time with you, you know that. This is not an invitation of pity."

Would he be in London? A year ago she would have been certain not to find him on Gracechurch Street, but he was friends with Mr Gardiner now. She even believed he might have business interests with her uncle. Would it be worse to stay at Longbourn and think endlessly of what would never be? Or to enjoy a change of scene and society and risk seeing him?

A change was needed, Elizabeth decided, and if there was risk, she would take it.

One morning in January, Elizabeth entered her aunt's breakfast room to find Mrs Gardiner awaiting her. "Good morning, Lizzy."

"Good morning, Aunt." Elizabeth sat and poured herself some coffee. She had developed a strange liking for the bitter brew, though she did require a bit more sugar than Mr Darcy did. There was something about holding the steaming cup in her hands on a cold day that was soothing.

"How would you like to do some shopping today?" Mrs Gardiner asked her. "Your uncle and I are invited to a dinner party next week at the home of Lady Berkeley, and I thought some new accoutrements might be in order."

Elizabeth smiled wanly at her, even as every feeling within her revolted against the notion. Shopping? Indeed, no.

London had proved a more dangerous place than expected. Elizabeth lived in fear of seeing Mr Darcy—seeing him accompanying Miss de Bourgh was a horror she dared not even contemplate. Every time there was a caller, she feared it was him. Every tall man on the street made her heart plunge into her boots, and each time she heard a deep voice speaking behind her, she wanted to run.

Knowing that he likely wished to avoid her afforded some consolation; the chance that the perverseness of fate would throw them together in Cheapside was slim. But if she went off to the shops, the odds increased measurably.

"I do not think I need anything right now," she replied, then applied herself to the careful buttering of a slice of toast.

Mrs Gardiner laughed. "You are a singular young lady, Lizzy! What has need to do with shopping? Come now, I shall not hear a refusal." Elizabeth could do nothing but acquiesce.

They set off to Pall Mall in the mid-morning, and within a short time, Mrs Gardiner had all she needed and turned her attention to Elizabeth. "That primrose superfine would make up rather well for you, my dear. Allow me to buy it for you."

Elizabeth protested, but her aunt would not hear of it and soon had purchased the muslin as well as some netting for an overdress. She suspected it was likely her aunt's design all along and so kept her protests brief, settling for a thank you kiss on Mrs Gardiner's cheek.

It was while the fabric was being measured out for them that Lady Berkeley entered the shop. She was a handsome woman in her sixth decade who had recently come out of mourning. Her late husband had been friends with, and a business partner with, Mr Gardiner, and he and his wife had developed a fondness for the Gardiners despite their difference in rank. Elizabeth was predisposed to like the lady for that alone.

"Mrs Gardiner!" she cried delightedly. "How good to find you here. And who is this pretty young woman with you?"

Elizabeth swiftly decided that she liked Lady Berkeley very much indeed. She had sense and good breeding, and even cursory conversation was enough to learn that the amiable lady was also well-read.

"So," she said eventually. "You must be here for the enjoyments of the Season."

"In some manner of speaking," Elizabeth agreed. "My sister is recently married, and she and my new brother have taken a house in Harley Street—"

"That she might throw you before all of his friends, and see who might do for you. Ah yes, the way of the civilised world."

Elizabeth could not help herself; she emitted a soft groan at the idea of Jane and Bingley matchmaking for her. It made her ladyship laugh.

"You do not wish to be paraded about, is that it? Well, my dear, there is only one way to escape it, and that is to beat them at their own game. See if you can find your own husband before they arrive in town."

Elizabeth could not hide her feelings—the quick burst of pain that always beset her whenever thoughts of husbands or Mr Darcy arose. Lady Berkeley noticed, or it appeared she had, but she said nothing of it. With a wink and a nod, and entreaties to Mrs Gardiner to come early to her party, Lady Berkeley was off.

"How was the party?" Elizabeth asked her aunt the next morning. "You were out very late!"

"Aye, that we were," Mrs Gardiner said with a rueful laugh. "I thought your uncle might fall asleep standing while we were awaiting the carriage to be brought 'round! But we enjoyed ourselves enormously. Lady Berkeley is off to Italy for a while, and those who had gone already were full of stories and advice for her."

Mrs Gardiner described all that her friend intended to see and do; Elizabeth had to own that it all sounded rather enchanting.

"...and now she wants only for someone to travel with her. Some gently bred young lady, preferably one who—"

"Would she take me, do you think?" The words popped out of Elizabeth's mouth almost before she knew her own mind.

"You?" Mrs Gardiner paused with a spoonful of porridge halfway up to her mouth. Slowly she lowered it. "Surely not."

"Why not? I have always yearned to travel."

"Yes, but why would you need a situation? You do not need the employment."

"No, but I do need the escape," Elizabeth admitted. "Please, Aunt? Allow me to write to her."

Mrs Gardiner sighed. "I have not wanted to pry..."

"You know most of it already, I am sure." Elizabeth struggled to appear sanguine.

"Knowing something is not to be confused with understanding it! All that he did for Lydia—it was certainly not done on *her* behalf! I could see how he looked at you, and—"

"Aunt. Please." Elizabeth could no longer bear to dwell on her past with Mr Darcy. "May I have her ladyship's direction?"

With that, Mrs Gardiner was silenced, though she stared at her niece with sympathetic eyes for far too long. At length, she rose and left the room a moment, returning with Lady Berkeley's card. Elizabeth sent a note not a quarter of an hour later, and an hour after that, she was summoned to the lady's home.

Lady Berkeley received Elizabeth in her dressing room, an elaborate chamber with a multitude of mirrors, Pomona green wall coverings, and an enormous fur rug in the middle of it. It was uselessly fine—like the lady herself—but Elizabeth rather liked it. She took a seat on an overstuffed velvet chaise lounge that sat beneath a large portrait of a pug with a ribbon around its neck.

Lady Berkeley had been delighted to receive Elizabeth's note. "What I need is a travelling companion—someone to make up a card table and shop with and perhaps run an errand now and again. Not a nurse! I am in perfect health, no matter what my son-in-law thinks."

"I am glad to hear it. I am able enough for those with a trifling cold, but anything more serious is entirely beyond me."

"Then we understand each other. Oh, you will find Italy captivating. I am exceedingly fond of it myself, though I have not been since my wedding trip. It is all quite different there—in Italy, a woman can walk down the street without everyone thinking she's trying to whore herself. Then again, a lot of them are, and bless them for it!"

She laughed, loud and vulgar with no attempt to cover her mouth.

"England is different, of course. A lady simply cannot go about without a friend. So you come along, we will see some sights and have some adventures together, but mostly it's just me and the girls having all the fun we could not have when we were young. I am not there to mind you, and you are not there to mind me. Do you understand?"

Elizabeth smiled and nodded. Lady Berkeley then went on to ask her whether she played, whether she sang, and if she enjoyed drawing. Almost as an afterthought, she asked if Elizabeth spoke Italian.

"I do," Elizabeth said. "My father is very fond of languages and taught me many of them. We will have to see if the accent holds up on the Continent, but I shall not see us lost in Rome or anything of the like."

Lady Berkeley nodded firmly, her bright eyes showing her satisfaction. "I had a very good feeling about you, Miss Bennet. I think the pair of us will do splendidly together."

Elizabeth agreed, and after some time spent speaking of plans, she departed, her step lighter and her vision clearer than they had been in some time.

In truth, she cared very little for the reasons why Lady Berkeley and her friends went to Italy or what they planned to do. She was simply eager to be out in the world—out of Hertfordshire, out of London, away from her mother, away from Jane's plans and schemes...but most of all, away from Mr Darcy.

chapter four

SILENCED FOREVER

JANE LEARNT OF HER SISTER'S INTENTIONS BY LETTER, AS did the rest of the Bennets, and she brought the full force of her disapproval with her to London in February.

"What is this silliness about Italy?" she said almost before Elizabeth was in the room. "You cannot go to Italy, for we planned to take you out around London! Do you not wish to see the Season?"

Jane made a sweet domestic picture—despite the highly unusual frown on her face—sitting in her drawing room in front of a warm fire and stitching away at some little garment. Elizabeth smiled, wondering if Jane had something to hope for. If so, she had not confided in her about it, but the couple had only been married for two months—no doubt it was far too early for anything but wishes.

Elizabeth moved slowly to the chair opposite her sister and sat. "Undoubtedly, the delights of the Season will wait for another time. An unexpected opportunity came to me and—"

"You cannot just run off to Italy!"

"I can, Jane, and I will," Elizabeth said with gentle insistence. "I need to."

"What do you mean, you *need* to? What you *need* to do is stay here and meet gentlemen...and fall in love with one of them, perhaps. You are not getting any younger, you know. You simply *must* stay in town.

Charles will introduce you to his friends, and I am certain that among them you will find—"

"A husband?"

"Well…yes. That is the hope, is it not?"

"No," Elizabeth replied. "That is not my hope. Not right now."

Jane raised her head from her needlework. "Lizzy, please do not tease me. I know you must want a husband and your own home."

"Yes, a husband and a home and children, and then once the children are born I fuss about until my children are married, and then, once my children are married, I content myself with worrying about *their* children marrying, on and on until I die." Elizabeth spread her arms. "Is it so wrong that I wish to see something of the world first?"

Jane laughed. "It is hardly as grim as all of that. You only think this way because of your…recent disappointment."

That was how they had come to refer to Mr Darcy: her 'recent disappointment'.

"Surely you do not intend to remain a spinster forever?"

"Kitty thinks I do," Elizabeth replied.

"Hang Kitty. That was a poor trick."

"I did not care…not really," Elizabeth said, her elder sister's vehemence bringing a smile to her lips. It had stung, to be sure, but Kitty knew nothing of Mr Darcy, and only meant it as a joke. Taking care to speak with good humour, she added, "I will admit that the notion of marriage is less interesting once the man you love ends as someone else's husband."

"You are heartbroken."

Jane's solicitude was almost too much—nay, it was too much—to bear.

"I daresay I am. And what better place to recover than the Continent?"

"But you must not give up—"

Elizabeth leant forward, entreating her sister to understand her. "We were raised in such a small way, Jane. I want to meet people who are different. I want to taste unusual food and see a variety of paintings and carvings and—"

"London has dozens of art galleries!" Jane cried.

"—learn new languages, hear new music…I want to soak in the world and all its peculiarities."

"You can do that with a husband," Jane replied primly.

"But how many do? Once the business of marriage and family sets in, who can really run about like that? Mr Darcy has done me a favour.

He has broken my heart, but from that broken heart emerged a new mind. Marriage is not all there is for me. I shall go off and feast from the table of the world."

Jane did not respond. Elizabeth's mind was made up, and she knew Jane understood enough of her stubborn nature to know she would adhere to her plan.

"How long will you be gone?" Jane asked, sounding a bit plaintive.

Elizabeth paused a moment. Here was the truth she had not admitted to even her mother, or Mrs Gardiner, but in the face of a direct question, she knew she must be honest. "A year," she said quietly. "Perhaps a bit more."

"So long?" Tears welled up in Jane's eyes. "It seems too much."

Privately Elizabeth wondered if it would be long enough. "You know how it must be. He is Bingley's intimate; I am sure you have already met with them in town—"

"If you do not wish it, then we will not accept the invitations that—"

"No, no! I hardly wish for Bingley to estrange himself from his friend on my account! But the thought of being thrown together in company with them is unbearable to me. Perhaps when I return, I will be able to meet him with equanimity. Pray promise me one thing, Jane?"

"Anything, of course."

"Please do not mention him in your letters. Not a syllable, I beg you. I want him to be set aside."

To this supplication, Jane gave her word.

It was the end of the discussion for that day, but Elizabeth did not fool herself. She anticipated many more such conversations designed to make her see reason, to keep her in London, and to re-settle her mind on the object of matrimony.

Indeed, some such conversation was had, but her family understood the battle had been lost. And Elizabeth turned her mind to travel, doing her valiant best to keep Mr Darcy from the chief seat in her thoughts.

The busyness of preparation proved her best means of distracting herself, and she threw herself into it with alacrity. Lady Berkeley scolded her for undertaking too much, but she discerned that she had the older lady's esteem when she would return from Bond Street with a particular necessity for her.

"Miss Bennet, I see already what an uncommon treasure I have found," she said at last one day. And Elizabeth took her pleasure in this, along with the assurance that she could, and would, find contentment.

She never saw him, and because she did not, she came to believe she would not. And then, one terrible day, she did.

She had gone with Jane to Oxford Street on a pleasant-enough day for February—the pallid sunshine doing all it could to warm the city—and suddenly, there he was. With her.

When she recognised them, her knees buckled a little, and every impulse urged her to escape before they saw her. "Jane," she said, tugging on her sister's arm. "Here. Lace."

Jane had not seen them—thankfully, for she did insist on greeting positively anyone with whom she had any degree of acquaintance—and so easily followed her sister's dart into Haywards & Carters. While Jane exclaimed over lengths of lace, Elizabeth tried to calm herself, pressing one hand to her chest as she nodded and made the correct noises over the embellishments Jane showed her.

She proved to have chosen poorly for her sanctuary. Moments later, a tinkle of the little bell that hung on the door told her others had entered the shop, and somehow she knew, even before she turned, that it would be them.

Becoming engaged to her cousin had done nothing to improve Miss Anne de Bourgh's appearance or disposition. She appeared, as she had before, sickly and cross, and she did not exert herself to put anyone at ease, least of all her intended husband who stood before Jane and Elizabeth looking as if he had been recently struck by lightning.

"Mr Darcy, Miss de Bourgh," Elizabeth said. "I have not yet had the opportunity to congratulate you, so pray let me do so now. My best wishes for your happiness."

Miss de Bourgh muttered some disinterested reply, and Mr Darcy thanked her. Then there was silence, but as the couple before them did not seem inclined to continue on their way, Elizabeth spoke. "The weather has made for a pleasant day, has it not?"

They all agreed that it had, then Mr Darcy said, "You were not with your sister and Bingley at the Morleighs' dinner two nights ago. Were you unwell?"

"She had a headache," Jane offered a trifle too loudly.

At this, Miss de Bourgh was enlivened and began to speak energetically about the afflictions and maladies she had suffered of late. Elizabeth and Jane made sympathetic frowns and exclamations of 'oh my dear' as appeared to be expected of them.

All the while, Mr Darcy stood nearby, unhappy and silent. Elizabeth watched him from the corner of her eye and felt some sympathy for him. This would be his life—this dreary, colourless creature with her complaints. She hoped the lady's fortune and property would be enough to compensate him for it, then scolded herself for such an uncharitable thought.

When Miss de Bourgh was done, Jane turned to Elizabeth and, with a pointed look, said, "Lizzy, I am expected at home soon."

"Of course." Elizabeth smiled and offered the most sedate farewell she could manage, then followed Jane out of the shop.

"You did very well," Jane said as soon as the carriage was moving.

Elizabeth sighed and pressed herself back against the squabs. She had thought it rather absurd that they took a carriage for a distance shorter than they used to walk into Meryton, but Jane had a new landau, purchased for her by Bingley as a wedding gift. Now Elizabeth was grateful for the quick privacy it afforded.

"You see now why I am eager to go away," she said. "No matter how I appeared, I assure you every moment was torment. I could not decide whether I was most angry or pitying or sad. It commingled to produce a dreadful state."

In the end, it was her sorrow that won out. As soon as she was safely tucked away in her bedchamber on Harley Street, she wept, holding her shawl over her face so that no one would hear. How happy they might have been! And how foolish it was that neither had had heart enough to overcome the obstacles contrived by pride and irresolution!

A knock on the door interrupted her. Susan, a young upstairs maid, entered with a card—a finely wrought, elegant gentleman's calling card. Mr Darcy was in the parlour.

"For me?" Elizabeth asked her. "He must be here for Mr Bingley."

"No, ma'am, he said specifically for you, and that Mr Bingley had given him leave to call."

"I cannot receive him," Elizabeth protested. "I am…" Surely Susan could see she was in no fit state to see anyone?

She rose and went to the dressing table, but one glimpse told her immediately that it would not do. Her hair had become a blowsy tangle, and her red-rimmed eyes were swollen to twice their customary size in her pale countenance. "Tell him I am ill," she implored. "Tell him I cannot see anyone today."

"Very well." Susan left, only to return a few minutes later. "Mr Darcy says he will wait as long as is needed but insists that he see you."

"Pray tell him I cannot—"

"Please, Miss Bennet," she interjected. "He offered me a crown to ask you and another if I am successful in bringing you to him."

"What?" Elizabeth exclaimed. "You are surely in jest!"

Susan pulled the crown from her pocket and held it out, lowering her eyes but failing to hide her enthusiasm for the unexpected riches. "I can help you tidy up, if you would like."

Nothing changes, does it? He has always been unafraid to sprinkle his fortune about to obtain what he wants. With a resigned sigh, Elizabeth said, "Very well. Do as you must."

Susan did her best with her face and hair, but Elizabeth thought she still looked a fright when she descended into Jane's parlour a quarter of an hour later. Susan entered behind her, beaming when Mr Darcy handed her the promised coin.

"You may go, Susan," Elizabeth said to her.

Susan hesitated so Elizabeth reassured her, "Mr Darcy is very nearly a married man, so you have nothing to worry about. You may leave the door open a little." Susan retreated, leaving them alone with the door wide ajar.

As it had been in the shop, seeing him brought both pain and pleasure, along with a dreadful burst of nerves. For some reason, his words —*I ardently admire and love you*—rang into her head the instant she saw him, and much as she wanted to, she could not get them out.

"Twice in one day?" Elizabeth offered a trembling smile that strived for confidence. "This is an unexpected pleasure, sir."

She sat then before her knocking knees gave way. Mr Darcy took the seat directly across from her, looking at her intently.

There was little to be said that had not already been said scarcely an hour prior. He had called, evidently with some purpose, and she stayed quiet, silently urging him to state that purpose. At last, with a slight clearing of his throat, he said, "I understand you are going to Italy."

"I am." Elizabeth was required to clear her throat too. "With Lady Berkeley. She is a friend of my aunt and needed a companion for the journey."

"When will you return?"

Elizabeth shrugged. "A year or two…or ten? Our plans, such as I know them, are not yet fixed. I am at her ladyship's pleasure."

His dark eyes, heavy with some emotion she would not dare to name, traced her countenance. It almost made her blush, so she turned her head to the side, fixing her gaze on a garish Meissen potpourri vase that Miss Bingley had given Jane for the wedding. Hideous thing, she knew not if it had been a kindness or a slight, but Jane displayed it, nevertheless.

"Why?"

"Why?" Surprised, she looked back at him. "I have always wished to travel, to expand my education, perhaps become proficient in—"

"Elizabeth." He leant forward, his hand almost reaching for her but then pulling back. *"Why?"*

His eyes were so dark they nearly burnt her, and she was forced to swallow hard. "I want to see the world," she said, her voice emerging small and much less certain than it was before.

"Do you not…?" His voice broke, and he paused to reset himself. "I believed that you wished for marriage, a home and family of your own."

"And so I do," she said. "But…but for now, my life will take a little turn."

His stare was unwavering and unnerving. She dropped her eyes to his cravat, watching the pin that held the snowy folds in place move up and down in time with his breathing. Breathing fast, she noted, and it was this evidence of some slight discomposure on his part that made her sigh and admit to him, "Obviously my…my recent *affaires de coeur* have not…circumstances have…surely you, of all people, can understand why I wish to get away."

"Get away from…?"

Elizabeth could not answer.

"What are you running from, Elizabeth?"

It was the way he said her name that did it. Her name, her *given* name, sounded so intimate coming from his lips, so rich and deep. She heard him say *Elizabeth* and knew somewhere within him there was still love for her, no matter how hopeless such love would be.

She met his eyes and whispered, "You."

In the prolonged pause that followed, she fancied he could see everything, all her hopes and longings and fears—fears which had, unfortunately, all come true. She had loved and lost.

Impulsively, she stretched her hand towards him and he, though surprised, took it. "I wish, most ardently, that you will be happy, but I would be a liar if I did not admit that I cannot bear to watch it."

He dropped her hand and was on his feet in a trice. He walked several quick paces to the window, then spun and came back to loom before her. "What are you saying?" he demanded.

She could not reply with anything but a bowed head. He fell back into his chair, the weight of their mistakes seeming to sink them both. There was a long silence until, by unspoken agreement, their eyes met. Mr Darcy was first to speak.

"I thought you must surely despise me for what had befallen your sister."

"Despise you? You own my deepest gratitude."

"I never wished for your gratitude."

"It was not gratitude for you that changed my heart."

He deserved to know this much, did he not? Or was she being cruel to tell him now when all was in vain?

"Your letter to me had already made many of my prejudices fall away

—indeed, I was ashamed by how little I knew of you and how silly I had been. Then when we met at Pemberley, you were so kind, so gracious... when I saw the man you truly were, I could not stop myself from..."

Elizabeth shook her head. It was no time for that confession. "But then you came to Longbourn with Bingley, and you were so grave, so silent."

"Had I felt less, I might have said more."

"I thought your feelings and wishes had changed. Surely every feeling within you would revolt at the notion of Wickham as a brother-in-law!"

"Why do you think I had him sent so far off? Yes, I dislike the idea, but certainly not enough to turn me from you. But when Lady Catherine told me of her call on you at Longbourn—"

"I believed I would do best not to vex her," she said. "I wished only to placate her and send her on her way."

"From her account, I believed your heart remained untouched," he said. "I knew that you no longer disliked me, but I believed that you could never love me."

"It was a mistake," Elizabeth admitted as sorrow overwhelmed her senses. "I allowed her to think there was nothing between us so that she would not go to you—not attempt to persuade you against me. It was foolish, and I regretted it as soon as I understood what I had done."

"It left me without hope," he said in a soft tone that did nothing to belie his anguish. "I thought, by then, that if I asked you again to marry me, you would likely consent. I wondered if I could bear being with you while knowing that you did not, *would not* love me...when I love you so deeply."

Love. He loved her still, and it shattered her heart to hear him say so.

"Nevertheless, I believed I could bear it. I spent many long nights wrestling with the notion, but then...but then one day I realised a dreadful truth."

It was his turn now to stare at the carpet beneath his feet, his head resting in one hand.

"You are such a naturally loving person, I imagined that if you could not love me, your heart would, at length, turn to another man."

"What!" Elizabeth exclaimed. "Surely you do not think that I—"

He shook his head. "No, no. I do not mean it as a slight on your character. I merely mean that your heart...your heart is made to love. And even though I knew you would be a dutiful wife...duty is not what I want, certainly not from you."

Another painful silence fell while Elizabeth, and she imagined he too, considered how once again, misunderstandings had confounded them. It made her sigh heavily.

"Is that when you decided to propose to Miss de Bourgh?"

When he raised his head, his eyes were hollow and bleak. "I wished to remove all temptation."

"You proposed to her to stop yourself from proposing to me?"

He nodded.

Elizabeth rose and went to look at the fire, placing one hand on the mantel to steady herself. They were the victims of the most wretched perversion of circumstance.

She heard his footsteps crossing the room to stand behind her. "You and I have never had our timing right," she said.

He stood too close to her; she could feel the warmth of him, and it required all her fortitude not to allow herself to lean back into his embrace. She thought she felt his hand whisper along her spine—a light, glancing touch—but perhaps it was her imagination.

In a low tone, he asked, "Do you love me?"

"Please do not ask me that. It cannot signify…not now."

"But do you? I must know."

"Mr Darcy, only harm can come from me saying the words."

"Do you love me?"

Elizabeth turned to him, silently begging him to stop. "You belong to another, Mr Darcy. There is no purpose in me saying words that can only make matters more difficult for us both."

"My affections and wishes are unchanged," he said, his voice quietly urgent. "But one word from you will silence me on the subject forever."

She raised her hand, lightly touching his cravat. "Then I shall give you the one word which holds sway in this matter—not a word, rather, but a name…Anne."

"Anne." He drew in a breath that obviously pained him. "Is there nothing to be done?"

"The thing I love most about you is the very thing that makes it all impossible," she said. It was the closest she would come to telling him all that was in her heart. "I shall go to Italy, and you shall get married and raise a family. That is all we can do."

"I do not think I can," he whispered.

"You can." She nodded, trying to give him the encouragement she had failed to give before. "And please—do all you can to be happy with her. You deserve happiness, and I beg you not to forswear what you might find with her for the sake of a few trifling memories of me."

For a moment, they shared a silent communion together where each came to comprehend what was their unfortunate truth. He then took her hands and raised them to his lips, kissing them tenderly before nodding his farewell and leaving her.

chapter five

RETURNS & REUNIONS

December 1814

IT WAS A TRUE SHOCK TO HER SYSTEM, AFTER THE SUNNY days and temperate climate of Italy, to return to the grey skies and cold weather of England in winter, but she was glad to do it. How much she had missed her family and friends! Time had transformed the circumstances for many of them. Jane was a mother, as was Lydia, and Mary had wed Mr Philips's clerk. Charlotte Collins had one son and presently suspected there might be another, and Mr Bingley had found an estate in Derbyshire for their growing family.

But no less significant were the changes in her. The months spent on the Continent had materially altered her, and Elizabeth believed it was all for the better. She was now, she hoped, a lady of sense and some education; she had lived in the world, and acquired the polish associated with such experience. Her mode of dress had been vastly improved —indeed, she realised now how very countrified she had once looked— and her manners too had been altered. She had been a silly and impertinent creature, certain she knew so much when, in fact, she had known rather little and understood even less.

She no longer chafed against the restrictions of fortune and sex; the world was as it was. There was no sense in being miserable about conditions one could not change, and she was resolved to thrive no matter what was laid before her.

At Lady Berkeley's side, she had learnt more than she ever could have imagined. Art, history, language—yes, much had been seen and done. The education she had gleaned reading from books was nothing to what she gained absorbing herself in a new world rich in culture and heritage. Lady Berkeley had given her something she would never lose, and she was infinitely grateful to the older lady. Theirs was a true affinity; Lady Berkeley had even gone so far as to invite Elizabeth to live with her 'until you marry', and Elizabeth was considering it. She did not think she wished to go to Derbyshire with Jane and Bingley; town life seemed much more agreeable to her now.

More importantly, Elizabeth had learnt a great deal about herself. She came to realise that no matter how far one goes, heartbreak travels right alongside. She finally accepted that true love is nearly impossible to forget; however, it was also undeniable that the affliction is not fatal. She had loved and she had lost, but it did not break her. She had regained her joy in Italy, and her humour was restored; she even thought, sometimes, that making a marriage would not wholly disgust her. After all, she wanted children, now more than ever, and a husband would be required for that.

It was with no little trepidation that Elizabeth arrived on Jane's threshold. Not the house on Harley Street now—that had been only a season's lease. The Bingleys were now on Brook Street, just off Grosvenor Square and, she thought, quite near Mr and Mrs Darcy. It did not merit consideration, she reminded herself often. They were married now and perhaps had a child as well.

"Lizzy? Lizzy!" The lady of the house came rushing into the vestibule with the skip of a schoolgirl, laughing and crying and reaching for hugs and kisses, and Elizabeth returned them gladly, pulling Jane's body tight against hers and abandoning all dignity immediately. Bingley was not far behind his wife and claimed the privilege of a brother, hugging her as his wife had and kissing her on the cheek.

"Come meet our Stephen!" Jane cried out, and Elizabeth was taken into the nursery to find a round, blue-eyed little cherub who was happily engaged in attempting to eat his own feet. "Oh!" Elizabeth cried out, softening at the very sight of him. "May I?"

At Jane's nod, she picked him up and settled him on her hip. He immediately tried to grab her earbobs and, failing that, began to tug at the hair on her temples while she tickled his belly and kissed his sweet cheeks. "We will be best friends, you and I," she murmured to him. "I shall keep sweets in my apron pockets only for you, and when your parents are being unreasonable, you will come to me to straighten the situation."

To this promise, young Stephen gurgled and cooed.

"You look very well there, Lizzy," said Jane. "And now that you are done adventuring, perhaps eager to get one of your own?"

Elizabeth laughed. "Well done, Jane. You waited almost a quarter of an hour before mentioning that I ought to marry and have a family."

At this Jane laughed, then urged Elizabeth to join her in the drawing room for some refreshment and conversation.

"I have been told," said Bingley, "that I must absent myself awhile so the sisterly confidences are not inhibited by my presence. Thus, I will be off to my club and see you both for dinner? Or am I unwelcome in my own home for even longer than that?"

They all laughed at his put-upon expression while Jane reassured him that dinner would do, and soon after the two sisters were sitting before a warm fire, steaming chocolates in their hands and an assortment of breads and cheese before them.

Elizabeth sighed looking around her. Jane was ever fond of Christmas, and her home bore witness to that. There were boughs of holly and little arrangements of pinecones and berries set about, and even the hall had been arrayed in a manner fit for a ball. "The house is lovely, Jane."

"There is something special about Christmas, is there not?" Jane sighed contentedly. "It was my dearest wish to see you home for it this year—last year felt very strange without you!"

"Christmas is a wonderful time to come home, is it not?" Elizabeth agreed. "I confess I had grown impatient to be here. We thought it would be November, but the weather impeded our progress."

The two ladies chatted for a time while Jane told her all the latest news—their Uncle Philips had sustained a bout of apoplexy, Aunt Gardiner was again increasing, and their mother had suffered a cold for most of the autumn. "A trifling cold," Jane assured her. "She needs to see another daughter married off so she can think of something besides her own health for a time."

"Well, there's always Kitty, is there not?" Elizabeth teased. "You need not always look at me for these prospects."

"You have been gone a year and a half, and Kitty had it all in that time. You are due." Jane leant forward then, her eyes gleaming with anticipation. "Now, you have heard all my gossip, and I am eager to hear yours. You simply must tell me about Mr Dillard."

"Dillard?" Elizabeth nearly laughed aloud. Mr Dillard was the nephew and travelling companion of one of Lady Berkeley's friends. He was a beautifully coiffed man, and his clothes were like nothing she had ever seen in London, and certainly not in Hertfordshire. She wondered at times how his seams did not simply give way, for though he was tall and almost painfully slender, he wore his attire as if it were painted on him. He also enjoyed jewellery and had even pierced one ear in which he wore, always, a large emerald.

Elizabeth had asked him once why the emerald, and only the emerald, and he had replied, "Because diamonds are dull and the emerald makes my eyes look more blue."

"There is very little to say about Mr Dillard except that I enjoyed his company a great deal and thought he was very useful when it came to choosing new gowns for me. You can thank him for this gown I have on now; the whole of it was his idea."

"It suits you very well," Jane admitted. "But from your letters, it sounded as if the two of you were nearly inseparable!"

"Aye, that is true, we were, and I daresay you should expect to see a great deal of him now that we are both in London. But you must know—Mr Dillard is the sort of man for whom another gentleman's society will always be preferable to that of a lady." Elizabeth gave her sister a significant look. "He is not the marrying sort."

"Most men need to have time for their gentlemanly pursuits," Jane replied guilelessly. "It does not mean they have no intention to marry."

"In this case, I am afraid it does," Elizabeth said. "I speak of a very particular sort of gentlemanly pursuit, dear sister."

Jane stared at her for a moment, while Elizabeth sipped her tea and waited for comprehension to arrive. "Lizzy, no. I am sure you are wrong."

"How can you be sure I am wrong?" she asked, amused to see Jane blushing. "You have never even made the acquaintance of the gentleman."

"But it seemed you got on so well together! I expected some sort of announcement in every letter from you!"

"Yes, we do get on very well together, but for a different reason than you suppose. Every lady should be so fortunate to have a Mr Dillard. He offered all the advantages of a suitor with none of the bother of being courted in truth. It was positively delightful."

"I refuse to believe it. You really sounded as if you were in love with him!"

"You should know better by now, Jane. Had I been in love with him, you likely would have heard far *less* of him. No, Dillard is my friend, my dear friend, but neither I, nor any other lady, should expect any offers of marriage from him."

"You are trying to vex me, Lizzy."

"Indeed, I am not. He was a wonderful companion, and a true friend, and nothing more."

"But you must surely have had suitors in Italy? That man—in Naples, was it? He was English, you said."

"No," Elizabeth replied cheerily. "I mean, yes, he was English, but there was nothing to it. Nearly everyone thought I was engaged to Dillard, so thankfully the suitors kept their distance."

"Well, you cannot hide behind Mr Dillard now." Jane levelled a serious look at her. "I am determined to see you settled."

Elizabeth gave a quiet groan but smiled agreeably. "I might have expected as much."

"You are three-and-twenty now—"

"Oh, is that all? Four years until I am really on the shelf…perhaps I can wait another Season complete."

Jane frowned. "I hear it often from my mother how if I do not attend to this duty shortly—"

"You and Bingley might be forced to bear my society forever?" Elizabeth asked with a little laugh. "She is not entirely wrong, you know. I was not very eligible at twenty and can only grow less desirable with advancing age."

"Oh Lizzy." Jane sighed, her pretty brow creased with a mixture of amusement and annoyance.

"Forgive me, dearest…it has been too long since I have had the pleasure of teasing you," Elizabeth said in a conciliatory tone. "See here. It is not that I do not wish to marry, only that…I wish not for the interference of others in the matter. Whatever should happen will—"

"How can you say so? You, above all, know that five minutes one way or another—"

Elizabeth was shaking her head firmly halfway through the speech. "No. I have become persuaded that everything is as it should be. If I am unhappy in it now, it is only temporary, because my real, true happiness lies ahead. I am determined to forget the past and allow fate to come as it will."

Jane studied her closely. "Do you mean that?"

"With all my heart. Pray do not be a matchmaker for me. Allow me to shift for myself, and I promise I will not discredit you."

"Discredit me? I never thought you would, of course. I only wish to see you happy."

"And so shall I be—but in my own time and in my own way." Elizabeth patted her sister's hand. "But that is not to say I do not eagerly anticipate Christmas in London! Everything is happier at Christmas, is it not?"

Jane brightened. "Oh yes! What fun it will be—there are ever so many balls and concerts...even church is an affair, everyone there for Advent and dressed in their best attire!"

"It sounds marvellous," Elizabeth enthused. "How glad I am to be here to partake of it with you."

Jane considered it one of the first delights of the Festive Season to shop. Evidently the days of exchanged names and furtive gift-giving had been retired; Jane shopped for everyone, it seemed, and Elizabeth was mortified to find that her sisters, and Mrs Bennet as well, submitted lists of their wants.

Mr Bennet had, as well, his fond desires—all of which could be found, still, in a bookseller's shop—and Elizabeth was quick to take these suggestions for her own gift-giving purposes. "I spent hardly any of my own money in Italy and would much enjoy helping with our dear Papa's list."

"Dear Papa! How he has missed you! Yes, I think he would like to know you selected a book for him very well."

Jane had never been much in the habit of walking, and motherhood had not increased her stamina. By the time they were finished in Pall Mall and some shops nearby, she was ready to return home, though they had not, yet, been to the bookseller's.

"Go on without me," Elizabeth urged. "We are not a mile from the house, and I will walk back when I am finished."

"Elizabeth, it will look positively scandalous for you to walk home alone."

"So many are out and about with their own shopping, I daresay I can melt into the hordes with scarcely a notice," Elizabeth said. "Now do go; you make your coachman drive so slowly, I daresay I might be home before you anyway."

But Jane could not be so easy about it. Elizabeth thought, with some impatience, that she had navigated *il negozia* and *piazza* in Italy well enough to shop unescorted not a mile from home, but her sister would fret. So, she grudgingly accepted the footman assigned to tend her and set out into the charmingly crisp December air. Tiny crystals of snow drifted about obligingly, lending to the holiday cheer where she went, and she thought that everyone seemed to have a smile on their lips.

She entered the shop of a Mr Duckett; though his was not the largest, she rather liked the cosiness of it. She browsed the offerings for some time, seeing nearly all the books that Mr Bennet desired. It was difficult to know which to choose.

Amid her debate with herself over the choices, a gentleman entered the shop. It was none other than Mr Darcy.

Such scenarios were not uncommon. Elizabeth had seen men she mistook for Mr Darcy all over Italy, and once even in Switzerland. He haunted her throughout the Continent, but now that she was on English soil again, she recognised the likelihood that it truly was him and not some figment of her fancy.

She slid quietly around a shelf which allowed her to see him without being seen and studied him as he browsed the choices and at length selected a book. Mr Duckett offered his patrons a small group of overstuffed chairs and a roaring fire where they might sample the wares, and Mr Darcy availed himself of these comforts. He settled in, opened the book, and began to read.

With tiny, hidden glances, Elizabeth took him in while her mind weighed the advantages of fleeing from him versus greeting him. Would a proper lady even consider approaching a gentleman? Or was it impossibly brazen? She had not seen him for almost two years, but then again, with all that had passed between them, the usual civilities and strictures seemed stupid.

He is married now, perhaps even with a child. The thought was still echoing in her mind when she suddenly found herself standing in front of him, heart pounding and palms damp inside her gloves.

Darcy raised his eyes to her, blinking in the confused way people do when they have been absorbed in their books and are surprised to find themselves not in the worlds of their author's creations. In a trice, he was on his feet, his book landing at his side with a thud. "Miss Bennet!"

"Mr Darcy." She offered a curtsey to his bow. "How do you do? Allow me to wish you a happy Christmas."

"I am well. Um...happy Christmas to you as well. Have you been long back in England?"

"I returned just two days ago, sir."

His questions did not relent. "Are you returning to Italy? Or are you fixed here now? How is your family? Did you enjoy Italy? I daresay it agreed with you very well."

Elizabeth laughed at the tumult of words that spilled from his lips. "Italy was delightful, but I eventually found myself missing my home. An enormous advantage to travel—it makes one appreciate what was left behind that much more."

"I cannot disagree with that sentiment." After a brief hesitation, he indicated a chair opposite his, and she, after a glance at Mr Duckett, took it. Surely there was no impropriety in this? It was a public space.

"And how is…your family?" Try as she would, Elizabeth could not bring herself to say Mrs Darcy. *Not when it should have belonged to me. Not when it still brings a pang to my heart to think of it.*

"They are all very well," he replied. "My sister, I believe, will be very soon engaged. In fact, we are having a party on Christmas Eve, and I suspect it will happen there, if not before. You will come, I hope? Mrs Bingley should have received our invitation."

"Mrs Bingley has an abundance of schemes for us, though she has not made known the particulars to me," Elizabeth replied, which was in truth not a direct answer but good enough for now. "I am so glad to hear of Miss Darcy's good news. Do you approve of her young man?"

Mr Darcy brushed his trouser leg thoughtfully. "She is in love with him, and I find nothing to object to in him. Georgiana never wished for one of these society matches; a quiet life with a country parson will suit her well, I think."

A country parson's wife? This was surprising; Miss Darcy with her thirty thousand pounds and excellent connexions could have married someone titled, someone very wealthy. But Elizabeth could comprehend Mr Darcy very well, in both what he said and what he did not say. Having made a different choice for himself, he was good enough to encourage his sister to follow the directives of her heart.

"You are an excellent brother," she told him warmly. "How fortunate she is to have you."

He did not look up, but a faint smile warmed his countenance. "I have made many mistakes with her, to be sure, but I am proud of the lady she has become. She will do very well, I think, and be much happier away from town than she is in it."

Elizabeth watched the wistfulness flicker across his countenance. "You will miss her, I think. Or is the young man obliging enough to be situated near Pemberley?"

"Alas, no," said Mr Darcy with a chuckle. "He is in Kent."

Kent. Elizabeth was reminded that Mr Darcy had several great estates and extensive property over which he was master now.

"Ah! Well, just as good, then," she said. A silence fell over them then, and she held her tongue in it. Mr Darcy was staring at her in a way she knew very well. Two years ago, she might have been delighted by it, but much had changed. They could no longer share such looks.

To fill the void, Elizabeth began to rattle away about all she had seen and done in her months on the Continent. Mr Darcy had, of course, a multitude of his own tales to relate, and it was not long until the footman Jane had assigned to her began to poke his head in the shop and make awkward noises in her direction.

At last Elizabeth smiled at the poor man and said, "James, I am terribly rude to make you wait on me this way."

"No, miss, it's only that Mrs Bingley might begin to worry for your whereabouts."

"How right you are." Elizabeth rose immediately, as did Mr Darcy beside her. "It has been delightful to renew our acquaintance, sir. I hope this will be but the first of many such meetings."

"I would like that, too," he said with a smile. "And do know I shall plague Bingley to bring you to my party."

At this she could only laugh, with as much merriment as could be contrived, and wonder how marriage had inspired flirtation in him.

chapter six

A NIGHT AT THE OPERA

ELIZABETH LAY IN HER BED THAT NIGHT, TIRED BUT FAR from sleep. It was done now, the first meeting between them. She no longer had anything to fear and knew she could meet him as a common and indifferent acquaintance.

She had relived their conversation over and over again throughout the day. He had been anxious at first, and she had been too, but after a few moments, they had spoken easily, like true friends. It amazed her to recall how much she had liked to sit and talk to him, even when she quarrelled with him; there was a similarity in their minds and thinking that could not be denied. In some ways, she felt he understood her better than anyone ever had, even Jane.

Did he have that with his wife? Anne de Bourgh had rarely had much to say on anything but illnesses. Perhaps that had changed, or perhaps Darcy knew a side of her no one else did.

"Why do you think of such matters?" Elizabeth murmured into the darkness of her bedchamber. "He is her husband, and he ought to talk to her, share in her hopes and fears and wishes."

The ache that thought caused was considerable. Inasmuch as she enjoyed their little conversation in the book shop, Mrs Darcy had that sort of thing all day, every day. Did they lay awake at night together? Did she sit, cosy by a fire, tucked into his side while they laughed about this or that? Or did she allow him to hide in his study, indulging his more taciturn aspect?

What does it matter, Lizzy?

She could not eschew the truth. Her time in Italy had done much for her, but in one aim it had decidedly failed.

I am as much in love with him as ever I was.

She heaved an enormous sigh. *Who could have ever imagined that I should find myself in such a state! An impossible love—I should have imagined myself far too practical for such romantic nonsense, yet here I am, above two years now!*

She would stay away from him. There would be no Christmas Eve party for her. No, she would be too busy falling in love with someone else to trail after missed chances.

Gregory Andrew Dillard was a fine figure of a man. He was the grandson of the countess of Carberry and hailed originally from Chelmsford, which he decried as the 'dullest and most stupid place on earth'.

"The only thing really good about Chelmsford," he had informed Elizabeth, "is how easy it is to leave it."

His aunt, Mrs Augustus Dillard, was the dear friend of Lady Berkeley, and he came to Italy to keep her company and be sure she did not get herself into trouble; the lady's tendency to disregard the strictures of society had led her into more than one scrape in London. Indeed, once Elizabeth had met her, she could only wish she knew the entire family, for a more vivacious group she could not imagine.

Dillard had his own disregard for convention; he did not eat meat and mostly drank Madeira, though he decried being drunk as 'hopelessly common', saying 'any man who cannot hold onto his eminence while drinking is no man *I* would associate with'. He made Elizabeth laugh at a time when she least felt like laughing and enjoyed both conversations and walks that lasted for hours. They had discussed the subject of marriage within the first week of their acquaintance.

"I am not truly the marrying sort," Dillard told her. "For the sake of appearances, I could perhaps take a wife sometime, but she will need to content herself with my friendship and my fortune."

"I will take the friendship," Elizabeth replied. "But as for the rest, I am afraid it would not do. I should like some romance."

Of course, it was not until she had known him more that she truly understood what he meant, but by then it could not signify. Dillard was already quite dear to her and laughed uproariously when she told him she had only lately understood. They spoke then of his father's expectations for his son.

"My aunt—quite unlike dear Papa—is unflinching in the regard of the unconventional," he told her. "Even when the unconventional strongly savours of the criminal. Thus, I am here for my escape as well. Thankfully I am not to inherit; I have my mother's fortune, which I have increased into the realm of the considerable, and I am not yet thirty."

Upon their return, Dillard had decided he was not long for England; he had found the Italians far more to his liking and wished to travel to Greece.

Aside from his usefulness in allowing her to avoid unwanted suitors, Dillard was also adept in spotting gentlemen who might be worthy suitors. In London, he showed no signs of leaving his self-appointed commission on the Continent and invited Elizabeth to join him in his grandmother's box at the theatre. "It's Handel's *Messiah,*" he told her. "*De rigueur*, my girl. Wear your scarlet, and we will see if there are any promising young bucks around."

Jane, who still believed there was a chance that Dillard was merely misunderstood—and could, therefore, be secretly in love with her sister —was happy to relinquish Elizabeth into his care for an evening. So it was that Elizabeth found herself with Lady Carberry's party three days before Christmas.

Dillard was happily sharpening his claws on the haplessly unfashionable below them—while Elizabeth alternately shushed and giggled at him—when she saw Mr Darcy enter a box slightly closer to the middle than theirs. Her giggles died immediately as she feared she was about to see *them* together, husband and wife, the Darcys.

Such fears proved unfounded. Colonel Fitzwilliam came in behind him, escorting an older lady, splendid in cornflower blue satin and sapphires, who Elizabeth thought might be the colonel's mother, given her resemblance to him. But there was no lady on Mr Darcy's arm, or in the party. Mrs Darcy was not one to appear in public, it seemed; but, from her habits in Kent, Elizabeth supposed that should not surprise her.

"There is one for you!" Dillard poked her, somewhat painfully, in the back. "You have always seemed rather indifferent to a man in regimentals, but I never know when one might strike your fancy. This one is not much from the neck up, but the below-neck region makes do."

"I already know him—Colonel Fitzwilliam, youngest son of the Earl of Matlock," Elizabeth said with a little laugh. "I do not have enough money for him, though I do enjoy his society very well."

"Wants to be kept in style, does he? Well, what of the tall, proud-looking gentleman beside him? Mr Darcy, I think it is."

"Yes, it is Mr Darcy, but he already has a Mrs Darcy." Elizabeth gave Dillard a rueful smile. "You have that story already, although I think I had kept back the names."

"Ah, the substance of your regret. Yes, I do recall it, though you never admitted it was such an august personage." Dillard peered more closely. "I do not see any wife nearby."

"Mrs Darcy, if she is as she was, is in poor health. Likely she lives quietly."

Dillard nodded appreciatively. "I must own, when you are disappointed, you do it in style. Shall we go greet them? You never know, the colonel may have come into something of his own while you were away."

She had already met Mr Darcy once, and Elizabeth thought that meant she ought to be equal to doing it again—but somehow, she was not. "I do not think so," she said slowly.

"Oh! But perhaps she died!"

"Who?"

"Mrs Darcy," Dillard announced delightedly. "Women die in childbirth all the time. He might be a widower, particularly if, as you said, she is sickly."

Elizabeth shot him a censuring look. "You should not speak of her death with such a lack of feeling," she scolded.

"I do not know the lady, and her death could only benefit my friend," he said with a little sniff. "So yes, forgive me if I cannot imagine her death as anything but glad tidings."

Elizabeth rolled her eyes and gave him a little shove. "She is not dead—"

"She might be."

"We ought not speak of her as if she is!"

"Silly superstition," Dillard replied, but he did fall quiet.

Elizabeth did an excellent job of steadfastly disregarding Mr Darcy's presence throughout the performance, which was easy enough given the sublime nature of the music. She loved *Messiah*—she had seen it in Naples as well—and it was during the first part, when the chorus sang 'For Unto Us a Child is Born,' that she found herself leaning forward, rapt, and wholly engaged in what she saw, scarcely even breathing with her delight in the performance.

But sometime during it, she felt that peculiar sense of being watched. When it became too onerous to bear, she indulged herself in a glance towards Mr Darcy and was unsurprised to find him watching her.

His manners were so obvious it was shocking—he was very nearly turned away from the stage.

Disconcerted, she hurriedly looked back towards the stage, wondering what he was about. Though she determinedly did not look at him again, she felt still the weight of his stare.

Not long thereafter was an interlude, and Elizabeth remained seated, refusing Dillard's offer to escort her about. "I would rather sit," she murmured.

"Then I shall sit with you," he replied gallantly. "Lord knows, there is no one here I need to speak with."

They made idle conversation with Lady Carberry that mostly consisted of their impressions of the performances, and sometime during it, Mr Darcy and Colonel Fitzwilliam were admitted into the box.

Elizabeth rose, schooling herself to appear unaffected and not give him her particular notice. To her relief, Colonel Fitzwilliam was immediately into the breach, as always mannerly and amiable, and as friendly as if they had seen each other only days ago. "Miss Bennet! How good it is to see you!"

There were bows and curtseys all around, and Elizabeth fell into an easy conversation with the colonel, while Mr Darcy stood by looking as discontented as he ever had. But Lady Carberry soon drew him to her side—she had been acquainted with his mother and knew his Matlock relations—and left Elizabeth with the colonel.

Elizabeth saw readily that the colonel intended to play the flirt, but she did not think anything of it. He had warned her off any expectation of him years ago, and she recognised now that he simply enjoyed flirting. So, with impunity did she tease and flirt with him in reply, enjoying the pleasures of admiration and relieved not to suffer Mr Darcy's stares.

"We have settled it, then," he said at last. "You owe me a dance the next time we are together at a ball."

"Which might well be never," Elizabeth replied lightly. "After all, I have known you many months now, and we have never been at a ball together."

"Miss Bennet, I am so exceedingly determined to collect on this debt," he announced, "that I shall bodily drag you to the next ball I attend if I need to." Such a proclamation made Elizabeth laugh merrily, which drew Mr Darcy's eye to them. Surprisingly, she saw that his discontent had deepened into outright vexation.

With scarcely a word, he went to the far edge of the box and stared down at the floor. The colonel could no longer see him, for Mr Darcy was behind him, but Elizabeth could and easily discerned from his stiff posture that he was angry.

What is wrong with him? He has a wife and should not begrudge his cousin some little flirtation with me, even if he did once have a design to marry me. He must know that it is all harmless, and even if it was not, it can be nothing to him.

But at the same time, she knew it was not so easy. Was this not the same reason she had fled England? To avoid seeing him with someone else? Elizabeth realised then that inasmuch as her time in Italy had not erased him from her heart, perhaps it had not yet erased her from his heart either.

"May I call on you?" Colonel Fitzwilliam asked as the bell sounded that signalled the second act would soon begin.

"I should be delighted if you did," she replied warmly, noting that, over the colonel's shoulder, Mr Darcy had exited the box with no farewell and no look back.

One of the finest advantages of the house on Brook Street, in Elizabeth's estimation, was its nearness to the park, and since returning to London, she availed herself of daily walks within it. She learnt quickly her sister's habit of taking her breakfast in her bedchamber and began to steal from the house early enough to avoid both Jane's notice and an accompanying footman.

A light snow had fallen the night prior, and Elizabeth took pleasure in the unbroken purity of the park lawn. Children ran about in it, trying to play games that required more snow than was had, but it was still a distinct pleasure to behold. Elizabeth watched them for some time before realising she was not alone.

She turned to see Mr Darcy nearby. He walked forward the moment he saw her. "I wondered if you might keep to your habit of an early morning walk."

"I do," she said. "As much as I can."

"And how did you enjoy *Messiah* last night?"

"Very well indeed. Did you as well?"

"I did."

He was subdued, standing there, his countenance, like hers, aimed at the playing children. She wondered if he was imagining the time when his own child would play among them, but perhaps his child was yet unborn. It did not seem the time to ask.

"I owe you an apology for last night—when we came to see you in Lady Carberry's box. I was…it was not as I intended."

Elizabeth flashed a smile at him as she shook her head. "Think nothing of that."

He gave a quick nod, and Elizabeth noticed that he was gripping his walking stick rather tightly. It occurred to her that he was *still* angry, but the reason of that anger eluded her. Yes, she might comprehend that the shadows of a tender feeling remained within him; nevertheless, he surely could not be angry that she received the attentions of other men. Did he not wish to see her happy, as she had wished for him so many months past?

The Elizabeth of old might have taken offence to that sort of presumption, but age and experience had imparted more temperance and even some bit of wisdom to her. Elizabeth did sympathise with him and could overlook his pique enough to offer some consolation for the wounds which afflicted them both.

"Shall we walk?" she asked him, and on his nod, they struck off down the path.

"I have heard it said," she began, "that friendship is certainly the finest balm for the pangs of disappointed love."

Mr Darcy wore a guarded expression when she glanced up at his countenance. "Perhaps it is," he allowed. "But I confess I do not understand—"

"It is not in my nature to be so bold as this," Elizabeth said with a little smile. "And perhaps it is not ladylike of me to speak so frankly…I have been among the Italians too long, speaking with open honesty has begun to seem more natural to me than all this fan waving and eyelash fluttering I am supposed to do."

He chuckled but still seemed faintly wary. "It is certainly far less likely to lead to misunderstanding."

"Precisely! And I do not want there to be any misunderstanding between us. I only want to say to you that…that…" Elizabeth paused a moment—no one said, after all, that open honesty was easy—and then forged ahead. "I want you to know that I…I like you. After all that has gone between us, I know how very much I admire your…your temperament and your wit. And so, I wish to offer you my friendship, for as much as you will have it."

When she gathered enough courage to look up at him again, she saw him staring down at her with what appeared to be bewilderment. Clarification seemed to be required, thus she continued.

"All the tumult of our past, all the ups and the downs have…they have mellowed, I suppose you could say, into a true regard. That is to say, I have the highest respect for your character, your honour…I enjoy talking to you. What I mean to say is that I hope that we may be, at long last, friends—good friends, even."

He stopped walking and thus so did she. She turned to face him, seeing his eyebrows raised on his forehead. Was it surprise or doubt that created such an expression on him? She could not tell.

"Friends?"

She nodded. "There is nothing else for us, is there?"

"Friendship." He said it as if the word tasted sour to him. "You wish to be my friend."

"I do indeed," she said earnestly. "I would be exceedingly honoured to count myself among your friends."

They were still and silent for several terribly long minutes. Behind them the children frisked and capered, their shouts having grown dim but still audible.

Mr Darcy turned his head to the side for a moment, and she saw his jaw clench tightly. She had not a moment to understand the meaning of that before he burst out, "Friends? No, Elizabeth, we will *never* be friends."

Elizabeth took a step back when he rounded, staring at her with burning eyes and barely concealed fury. But she had faced his ire before, and it would not quail her now. "What? Surely you do not refuse me?"

"You ask too much of me," he said, his voice low with rage. "Far too much. If you think I shall be your friend while you gad about London, being the belle of the ball—"

"How dare you!" Elizabeth cried out. "When have I ever said I wish to gad about any place?"

"I cannot do it," he spat. "I cannot and simply shall not."

"Then it seems all intercourse between us has reached its end," Elizabeth retorted. "Why prolong the misery in this association?"

He stopped then and stared at her, and for a brief moment, Elizabeth had the mad notion that he was going to kiss her. He did not, and she was relieved—she would have had to slap him, and she did not want to do that.

Instead, he spun on his heel and walked away from her as rapidly as his long legs could carry him.

Elizabeth was left to get herself back to Brook Street with her eyes stinging and her stomach churning with repressed sorrow—then to run into the house, past her startled sister, and up the stairs, to fling herself across her bed and to yet again spill out her tears for the cause of Mr Darcy.

chapter seven

SUCH A MEETING

HAVING HAD SUCH A MEETING, ELIZABETH COULD NOT HAVE imagined going to a party at his home, but it was Christmas Eve and to forgo it would have been unimaginable. In any case, Jane and Bingley might have felt compelled to remain back with her or, worse, would ask questions of her, and either of those possibilities would be insupportable.

Miss Caroline Bingley had become Mrs Caroline Edmonds during Elizabeth's absence. Mr and Mrs Edmonds came to town for a fortnight and arrived that morning in eager anticipation of town parties and festivities of the season.

It required only a short period of time to discern that while Mr and Mrs Edmonds were not precisely unhappy, neither were they in love. In half an hour in Jane's drawing room, Elizabeth scarcely heard more than 'how do you do' intoned sombrely from the gentleman. Edmonds was tall, dark-eyed, reserved, and—from the look of Mrs Edmonds's jewels—wealthy. In short, Elizabeth deduced he was the next best thing that Miss Bingley could have acquired to pretend she was marrying Mr Darcy.

Though Elizabeth's past with Miss Bingley did not bear fond remembrance, she felt a sort of kinship with her. Like herself, Caroline Bingley had suffered disappointed hopes from Mr Darcy; however, she had chosen to marry a substitute while Elizabeth ran off to the Continent.

"I have scarcely seen Mr Darcy since my marriage," Mrs Edmonds twittered as she availed herself of the bottles of French scent on Elizabeth's dressing table. She had come into Elizabeth's dressing room with the stated purpose of 'greeting her as old friends ought' but had instead begun to rifle through Elizabeth's gowns and accessories brought back from Italy. Elizabeth did not entirely mind; it was a pleasure to have her envy rather than her scorn. "I do not think he is much in town. Have you seen him?"

"I have," Elizabeth replied. "Several times, in fact."

"How did he seem?" she asked. Elizabeth thought it a strange question but did not think of it overmuch.

"Much as he always has been."

"He has been holed up at Pemberley for above a twelvemonth," Mrs Edmonds informed her. "Quite the recluse. I daresay this is the first he has been back in town for some months."

Elizabeth watched with some astonishment as Mrs Edmonds applied a third layer of scent from a different bottle. "You know, in Italy they say, *'indossare un profumo per invogliare'*—wear your perfume to entice."

"What is that supposed to mean?" She tossed Elizabeth a look while she smelled a fourth scent.

"It means they should not be able to smell you at ten paces," Elizabeth replied with a little smile.

Mrs Edmonds smirked but forbore to apply a fourth scent. "I cannot help myself! They are all quite delicious, Eliza. Italy surely shook the mud right off you."

"I daresay it did."

"And your name has been paired with Mr Dillard quite a lot... anything there?"

Elizabeth laughed and said, "Nothing at all. He intends to go back to Italy, perhaps Greece. He found the life there quite agreeable."

"I daresay I would as well, if only Edmonds would take me." She pouted. "Well, it will be to you to entice tonight. The rest of us have all settled where we could."

"I am all anticipation," Elizabeth replied, though in truth it was more like dread. "I should like to see how Mrs Darcy arranges such gatherings; the last I knew her, she was more inclined towards a sickbed than a ballroom. I imagine them being hidden away at Pemberley was in deference to her wishes."

Caroline had set the perfume back down on the dressing table. "Mrs Darcy?" She raised one brow and gave Elizabeth a strange look. "Who on earth can you mean?"

Taken aback, Elizabeth replied, "I mean his wife, obviously." Then, with less certainty, she added, "The former Miss Anne de Bourgh."

"Oh, you have been away a long time." Mrs Edmonds laughed a throaty little chuckle. "Mr Darcy is not married."

"What?" Elizabeth gasped.

"It went off."

"Went off?" Elizabeth asked weakly. A peculiar spinning sensation afflicted her and made her reach for the chair beside her.

"I certainly hope you did not mention her. She was really too cruel to him. The family will not even speak to her now. Last I heard, she was off to spend time in Belgium or some such place."

"She was cruel?" Elizabeth was incapable of doing any more than echoing Miss Bingley's words.

"Oh, it was all so mortifying! The poor man, really...first she cried off, then she tried to blame him, said he had taken a mistress and she could not live with a man who was in love with his mistress."

"Surely not! How could she say such falsehoods of him?"

Caroline nodded sympathetically. "Indeed! Of all people! And while he denied that he had taken any mistress, he refused to deny that he loved another."

"H-he loved another?"

Caroline had returned to her perusal of Elizabeth's accoutrements. "Mm. And so, she threw him over. He did not love her, of course, but nevertheless, the embarrassment of... Where are you going?"

The last was a response to the fact that Elizabeth had lurched, unsteadily, towards the door. Her head swam with astonishment and dismay—*he is not married, he has never been married, is it once again too late for us*—and she knew only that she needed to go to him. Behind her, Mrs Edmonds was calling out, calling for a maid, saying, 'Bring help to Miss Bennet, she is swooning,' but the sounds of her voice died abruptly as Elizabeth flung the door closed behind her and ran down the stairs.

In a trice, Elizabeth was in the main vestibule, then shoving open the door and running out onto the street. Belatedly she recognised she was bare-headed and wore neither a pelisse nor gloves, but it was too late for that. She was in motion, and if she stopped and went back, she feared she might lose her nerve.

There was more snow, or something like half snow and half a spitting, icy rain. It made the roads a muck, but it kept people indoors so at least there were fewer about to witness this burst of madness. And all the while, her thoughts tormented her. *It is too late. Again.*

The words of Charlotte Lucas from years past echoed within her mind. *'There are very few of us who have heart enough to be really in love without encouragement.'* Nevertheless, Elizabeth had had heart enough to be in love, to remain in love, all this time, in the face of many discouragements—and so, she believed, had he. She could only pray that, once again, their timing and their misunderstandings would not defeat them. It had been too many long years for them; for once they should be able to be happy.

Elizabeth did not know this part of town well enough yet. She believed she knew where to find him, but then one street turned into another and panic set in. *Where am I? Where is he?*

She took a left turn, then a right turn. *Blast!* That should have been the park, but it was not and now she did not know where to turn.

The sleet came down harder, and her skirts soaked through as she scurried down another street, turning right and left wildly, her desperation mounting. Reason tried to assert itself—go home, meet him as a proper lady would—but it was prudence that had lost him to her once. She would not allow it again.

"Miss Bennet?" A carriage had drawn up next to her, and there he was, his dear face looking for all the world as if she had lost her mind. "Is something wrong?"

With a cry of feral animal relief, Elizabeth clambered into the carriage, the astonished coachman recovering his wits barely in time to reach a useless hand towards her.

Mr Darcy was, alas, not alone. Miss Darcy was wide-eyed and amazed across from him. Dear that she was, she swiftly slid to the side and patted her bench. "Sit here, Miss Bennet."

As her panic receded and her sensibilities stilled, she became mightily embarrassed. How wild and how silly to be scampering about, courting fever and making a fool of herself. "Excuse me," she said. "I hope I am not intruding."

"I hope everything is well?" Mr Darcy was the picture of concern. "Do you need a physician? Your sister and Bingley are not ill, I hope?"

"No one is ill," she said, shame making her quiet.

Miss Darcy was generous and sweet, taking her lap rugs and doing her best to dry and warm Elizabeth. "You are quite soaked through! Would you like us to return you to Mr Bingley's house?"

Numbly she shook her head, raising her eyes to look at the true object of her mission. "No, if it is not a terrible imposition, I need to speak to...to you, sir."

"To me?" Mr Darcy asked.

She nodded. "If you would grant me a few moments...I know you must be very busy with preparations for the party, and I shall not detain you."

"Of course," he said, then knocked on the ceiling to signal his coachman to drive on.

They arrived at his house minutes after that; Elizabeth's wild rambles had taken her to a point only a very short distance away. They showed her in, and Miss Darcy insisted on taking charge of her first. They retired to Miss Darcy's bedchamber, and summoned her maid Miss Oliver to see to Elizabeth's comfort.

Miss Oliver took one look at Elizabeth and summoned another maid called Sally to help, and soon Elizabeth was stripped to her petticoats and corset, her gown being held by the fire to dry while she herself received a vigorous towelling-off of both body and hair. Elizabeth submitted impatiently; having come to know her mind, she was eager to be about her business.

When she had been dried as best they could, her hair was rearranged with a pomade that smelt of roses, and she was wrapped in a clean, warm shawl. Then Sally took her to the study where Mr Darcy awaited her with a steaming mug of chocolate. The fire was blazing, and a chair was situated close to it; Elizabeth had no doubt that it was for her and went to stand beside it.

"Thank you, Sally, we will let you know if you are needed."

Sally—who was a timid creature unlikely to dare disobey anything the master said—abandoned her immediately. Elizabeth looked at him in amazement, only to be more shocked when he added, "And close the door, please."

Elizabeth was staring at him when he gestured to the chair. "Sit."

She did and then Mr Darcy astonished her further by kneeling in front of her. "What is this about?" he asked gently. "Has something happened to upset you?"

The kindliness of his tone nearly undid her. Her astonishment in his actions left, and in its place, her true purpose settled. She had to stare into her chocolate for a moment while willing herself to be sedate. "I heard some news today," she said in a wavering voice. "Mrs Edmonds told me you are not married."

"Mrs Edmonds? Oh, Bingley's sister."

Elizabeth nodded.

Nonplussed he asked, "Was this a surprise to you?"

"It was. When I left for Italy, you were engaged to Miss de Bourgh, so yes, I had assumed, on my return, that you were married."

"I see." Mr Darcy rose and took the poker from the stand beside the hearth, stabbing into the flames. "She cried off."

"I am sorry to hear that."

He shrugged, still not turning towards her. "It was for the best," he said. "It was purely an arrangement to satisfy our family. We would not have been happy. Indeed, I applaud her for having the courage to undo what never should have been done in the first place."

Elizabeth watched him a moment. He was handsome as ever; her own looks she dared not contemplate. She rose and took the step needed to be at his side, wrapping her hands around the mug of chocolate to keep them warm.

"I know that what I ought to do is...is wait. I should meet you at parties and balls and then I should hope you call on me. I should flutter my fan and smile behind my hand at you, but I am not going to do any of that." She drew one last fortifying breath. "Instead, I shall say only this—I love you. I loved you in Derbyshire, over two years ago, and I have never stopped loving you since. Neither time nor distance has changed anything about the way I feel."

He looked at her, his expression unreadable. She had shocked him into silence it seemed. After a moment, he said, "You said you wanted to be my friend. I understood it to mean you...you no longer cared for me, if indeed you ever had."

"No," she said amid a weak laugh. "Nothing could be further from the truth! I thought you a married man. I wished to tell you that, although we could not be lovers, I would always be your friend."

He reached towards her, entwining his fingers in the curls at her temple as his thumb stroked her cheek. "Both," he whispered. "I shall have both, if you will."

"I will," she said. "I will be your friend, your lover..." Elizabeth swallowed. "Your wife?"

A look of heartfelt delight came over his features, but he played at being severe. "Is this some Italian custom whereby a lady pronounces herself engaged to a man?"

Elizabeth laughed, feeling herself blush. "I cannot blame the Italians. I made an enormous mistake two years ago when I was not brave enough, had not heart enough, to let your aunt know how...how I felt about you. I could not allow it to happen again."

"Then allow me to say how ardently I admire and love you, the same —no, *more*...tenfold, one hundredfold more than I did the first time I proposed to you. And yes, I do beg you to become my wife."

"Yes," she said simply. "Yes."

Very deliberately, he took her mug of chocolate out of her hands and set it on the mantel. Then he took her hand, pulling her back towards the chair she had recently vacated. She scarcely had a moment to realise what he was about before he sat and pulled her onto his lap. For a long moment, he did nothing more than gaze at her. Then he touched his lips to hers—once, twice, and a third time before really kissing her—the true kiss of a lover and a husband.

chapter eight

TOO LARGE A PARTY

A KNOCK, QUIET AND HESITANT, CAUSED ELIZABETH TO LEAP to her feet. "A minute please," Darcy called out, while she righted her appearance and tried to imagine some way that the whole of it could look a lot less scandalous.

Darcy had no such concerns. Striding to the door, he opened it to reveal Georgiana standing there with no little diffidence, her face turned carefully to the side. "Um, Brother—"

"Congratulate me, Georgiana," he said. "Miss Bennet has just agreed to be my wife."

Embarrassment was forgotten as Georgiana uttered a cry of pure delight and nearly flew into the room where she pulled Elizabeth into a strong clasp. "Oh! I knew it! I knew that it must end this way, the wisest and best way of all!"

"Dear girl." Elizabeth smiled and hugged her soon-to-be sister, then kissed her on the cheek. "My only regret is that it seems I shall take the name Darcy just as you give it up."

"Perhaps," said Darcy, "I ought to refuse consent to Ritson, so Georgiana may enjoy the sister she always wished to have."

At this Georgiana's eyes flew wide, and her mouth dropped agape, but then she was smiling even more than before. "Brother, you are teasing again. I began to think that part of you, so newly awakened with Miss Bennet's acquaintance, had gone forever."

"So did I," said Darcy. "But thankfully—all has come back again."

"Jane, there is a matter of some curiosity to me," Elizabeth said some hours later, back at Brook Street. The party she had longed to eschew only that morning was now a chief source of eager delight, and she wished she could hurry the preparations along, to bring upon them the night. Jane's maid was preparing her a bath, but in the meantime, Elizabeth had some words for her sister.

"What is it?"

"I learnt today that Mr Darcy is not married."

"Did you think he was?" Jane asked sweetly.

"Yes," said Elizabeth in a matching tone. "Because he was engaged when I left and none of my acquaintance saw fit to write to me and tell me it had gone off."

Jane was sitting at her dressing table, going through her jewellery and selecting what she would wear. With a smile, she handed Elizabeth a gorgeous gold bracelet inlaid with emeralds and pearls. "This will do very well for you, I think."

"And so it shall. Nevertheless, why did you never tell me he had not married her?"

"You told me I should not write to you of him—"

"Because I believed you would be telling me of *them*! Had I known that it had come to nothing—"

"—and then he ran off to Pemberley, and you seemed to have regained your former spirits and even, I believed, fallen in love with Mr Dillard."

"How many times can I explain to you that—"

"I know, I know." Jane waved her protestations off. "The news of Mr Darcy appeared to be of little consequence, as if whatever had gone between you had suffered its natural demise."

"But since I have returned?" Elizabeth pressed. "What about that?"

"If you will recall, in one of the first conversations we had, the very day of your return, you said you were persuaded that all had ended exactly as it ought, and that you were determined to forget the past. I believed you in earnest!"

"And so I was," Elizabeth said with a sigh. Defeated, once again, by her own foolish presumptions and pert opinions.

But while their felicity had suffered some delay, it could not be denied that their ardour for one another had not dimmed; in fact, it might have increased. Would she have wished to forgo the time she had on the Continent? Possibly not. In any case, things had done as they did, and there was no sense in repining what might have been. She only needed to know the felicity that she had now.

Sitting on her sister's chaise, with Jane once again engaged in the task of selecting jewellery, Elizabeth permitted herself to smile, thinking of him and all she had to look forward to. Her fingertips drifted towards her lips, recalling the feel of his lips on hers.

"You will see him tonight, of course," Jane said, peering at her sister over her shoulder.

"I know." Elizabeth only hesitated a moment before saying, "I have seen him already, in fact."

"Already since your return? When?"

"Several times, in fact. In the bookshop some days ago, then at the opera, and in the park. And then, most importantly, I saw him today at his house."

"Lizzy!" Jane whirled around on her seat. "You went to his house?"

Elizabeth nodded.

"And did what? Really, Lizzy, you cannot carry on in some wild way simply because you have been abroad. This is English soil now, and a lady is expected to—"

"Jane." Elizabeth stilled her sister's admonishments with a look. "He loves me still, and we…we are engaged."

Jane's eyes flew wide, and she pressed her hands to her mouth, then she rose and flung herself at her younger sister, hugging her tightly. "Are you happy? I am so very happy for you!"

"In truth, I can scarcely believe it just yet. So much joy after so many months of unhappiness—it is too incredible. But I think I am growing accustomed to it by the minute."

The party of Bingleys arrived at Darcy House just as the first flush of guests had gone in. Bingley got out first and handed out his wife; Mr and Mrs Edmonds were next to leave the carriage.

Elizabeth reached out her hand, expecting to find Bingley or a footman ready to assist her, but instead, there was Darcy. "Are you not greeting your guests?" she teased him.

"Yes," he said with an intent look. "You are my guest—for a short time, in any case, until we can make this your home as much as mine—and I am greeting you."

Although Elizabeth had been there only hours earlier, the house had been transformed into a Christmas wonderland—ribbons and pine boughs in abundance; the scent of spiced oranges and vanilla in the air; and all the footmen wearing ruby-hued velvet waistcoats.

Elizabeth wore a dark green gown in silk gauze with an overskirt that gathered up into rosettes. She thought it became the season admirably and had hoped he would as well. It seemed he did, for nearly as soon as she gave her pelisse to the waiting footman, Darcy leant in and murmured, "Beautiful, my love."

"Do you like it?"

"It is the handsomest gown I have seen, by far," he said. "But I suspect that is mostly due to the superior beauty of the lady within it."

She blushed, looking down, but he would not have it. "Allow me to have the pleasure of staring at my bride."

"What is this?" Bingley had, unbeknownst to them, drawn near enough to overhear. "Bride? What do you say, Darcy?"

"Jane did not tell you?" Elizabeth asked.

"Tell me what?"

"Charles, um, Mr Darcy asked me to marry him today, and I have accepted him." Elizabeth nearly laughed at the expression on her brother-in-law's face at such news. He looked between them, plainly bewildered, then scratched his head where his hat had lately been.

"But...but we only just arrived. Dash it all if you do not work quickly, Darcy!"

"Yes, like a flash of lightning," Darcy replied drily. "A flash of lightning which began three years ago."

Elizabeth laughed merrily as Darcy offered his arm. She took it, and they went into the party.

There were not a hundred people in attendance, sizeable compared to her days in Hertfordshire, but not one of the London crushes she used to read of. She danced first with Darcy—he had been supposed to open it with Georgiana, but by then Georgiana's young man had spoken, had been accepted, and had wished to open it with his bride. Mr Darcy, of course, did not object to the alteration in scheme.

It amazed her to learn that the waltz had been danced at Almack's; it amazed her even more to find that Mr Darcy expected to dance it with her.

"This was surely not your original plan for the first dance?" she asked him.

"Certainly not. But knowing I would be able to open with you required an alteration in the scheme; indeed, I would not dance it with anyone but you."

He took her in his arms, ready for the start of it, and she, not unpractised, positioned herself comfortably. "Alas, I have danced it before, but only with Dillard, in Rome."

"You have a taste for being on the Continent now," he said a little wistfully. "I only wish I had shown it to you."

"I wish you had too," she told him—which eased him a little—and added, "but mayhap we shall go together sometime?"

"A wedding trip, perhaps?" His eyes warmed at the notion of it, even as they began to waltz, turning and twirling. "But you have not told me when we will marry."

"Told you?" She laughed, already breathless and exhilarated from the dance.

"Name the day," he said. "The day when I may have you as my own."

Elizabeth considered it for a moment, then said, "What is your preference?"

With a smile and an endearing look, he said, "Thursday."

"Thursday?" She laughed, gleeful and surprised and happy. "As in...*this* Thursday? The twenty-ninth?"

"The fifth day of Christmas," he said. "The day of gold rings."

"That is perfect," she said decisively. "Thursday it is."

"Will your family come?" he asked. "It is rather sudden, to be sure."

"They are already due in London to see the Gardiners," Elizabeth said. "But do you not require time for marriage articles and the like?"

"They were drawn up some time ago," he confessed, looking a little sad. "In '12. I need only some small alterations for them."

"I wish we had married then," she told him.

"Then you would not have had your adventures abroad."

"Instead, I would have had you," she replied. "But one cannot repine the twists and turns that brought us to this moment, only be glad that, at last, we are here. And let us make a quick business of it and go on to our own adventures."

They were all together, then, on Christmas Day—Bennets and Bingleys and Gardiners. They met at church for the Christmas Day service, and if they were surprised to find Mr Darcy and his sister waiting for them, they counted it something to do with his friendship with Bingley and forgot it.

At Brook Street, after church, a fine breakfast was laid and they sat down to it, noisy and jolly and festive. Mr Bennet was first to tire of the din and rose, announcing his intention to retire to Bingley's seldom-used and mostly empty book room. Darcy rose to accompany him. The two men were absent minutes before a footman came to summon Elizabeth to attend them.

She entered the room to find Mr Bennet staring at Darcy in astonishment. "Lizzy," he said. "Come in, my girl, for Mr Darcy has just told me some rather fantastical news."

"Fantastical?" Elizabeth walked into the room, going to a chair that her beloved indicated in front of him. He stood beside her, resting his hand on the back. "I cannot credit that. Mr Darcy speaks the truth."

"You cannot know what he said."

With an upward glance at Darcy, Elizabeth said, "I believe I know the better part of it."

"You are twenty-three now, I suppose you know your own mind in these things."

"Not only my mind," Elizabeth said earnestly. "I know my heart as well, and it is for him. I love him, Papa, and I beg you grant us your blessing, for we have endured trials enough already."

"Sir," Darcy interjected, "I have loved Elizabeth for three years now. What seems the work of a moment has been, in truth, long coming, and now that our happiness is within reach, we wish that we might not suffer further delay."

To this Mr Bennet had no reply. He regarded them thoughtfully for a moment and then, with no further objection or expression of wit, he said, "Who am I to stand in the way of young love?"

"Thank you, Papa," Elizabeth said. They went to him then, and Elizabeth kissed his cheek and Darcy shook his hand; and thereby was it settled.

"Send your mother to me," Mr Bennet instructed Elizabeth as she left with Darcy. "I will do my best to absorb as much of her felicity as I can before releasing her back into the general company."

The rest of the group, those who remained ignorant, was given the glad tidings while Mr and Mrs Bennet conferred in the other room. Then did they all come together again, and many congratulations and well wishes did flow among them.

And as simple as that, it was done; they married days later at St George's—Elizabeth in a dress of palest pink superfine muslin with Darcy handsome beside her in a grey morning suit.

"Will any Christmas ever be so wonderful, do you think?" Elizabeth asked her new husband as they stood, later that day in the vestibule of Darcy House.

"Yes," he replied with a joyful smile. "In my estimation, they will all be just as wonderful now and always. Happy Christmas, Mrs Darcy."

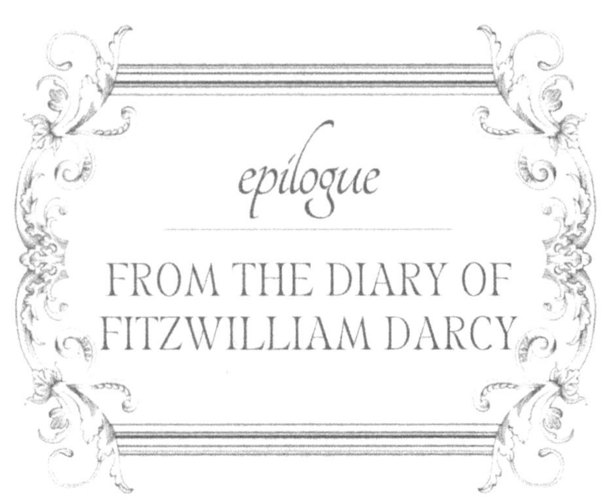

epilogue

FROM THE DIARY OF FITZWILLIAM DARCY

Pemberley, Christmas 1811

I HAD HOPED, RATHER THAN BELIEVED, THAT BEING AT Pemberley might relieve these accursed longings I have for her. Alas, though it has been a month complete, she haunts me as much as ever she did. Would that the gift I received this year be some measure of peace! Some respite, some release from the infernal hold she has on me!

The strangest fancy overtook me last week. I could imagine Miss E here, doing as my mother once did and draping the house in fir boughs and berries, putting scent in the air and bringing merriment to the hearts of all. We have not, since Mother's death, been much of a mind for such nonsense. Our dear father could not countenance it, knowing how fond she was of the Christmastide festivities. Something tells me that Miss E would certainly wish to resurrect such traditions, once she had command of the house...which will never happen.

Blast! I must endeavour to remind myself that though she commands my heart, she cannot be, ever, in command of my house. She cannot be my wife. It is impossible in every way.

And yet, despite every rational argument against it, it feels right. She belongs here, at some Pemberley in my imagination, and though I comprehend the sheer folly in thinking of it, on today, Christmas Day, my gift to myself shall be to indulge my fancy. For today only, I shall let the spectre of Miss E roam free in my heart and mind and home.

One last day to think of such foolishness and then I will put her from my mind forever.

Rosings Park, Christmas 1812

Christmas at Rosings Park is a dark, quiet affair; the hibernal solstice is no friend to those at the whim of a wealthy woman who refuses to burn candles. The expense, she says, is not to be borne, proclaiming it wasteful. So we are, from mid-afternoon on, shrouded in gloom, wanting for conversation, and wishing there was someone to play the pianoforte. Collins comes to us to make up a fourth of the card table some evenings. It must surely be a sign of my desperation that I have begun to enjoy his society. At least he speaks, even if nearly all of what he says is foolish.

And this shall be my life.

I cannot help but think what might have happened had I only the patience to… No. Such regrets cannot be permitted. I had known her above a year, and for that year enjoyed torment, uncertainty, and misunderstanding; perhaps it has all settled as it should have done.

Anne and I have set a date; we shall marry after Ascot. Lady Catherine abhors the notion of such delay, but I have, at least, the small comfort of my betrothed's preference being like mine. Why she is not more eager to see it done I cannot say, but so it is.

My birthday is one week away, and I shall be nine-and-twenty. Only nine-and-twenty, despite feeling decades older. Lady Catherine has already told me she thinks it vain puffery to celebrate birthdays, not that I have ever sought as much. It was Mrs Reynolds's practice to make a custard pudding with wine sauce for me, not that I ever wished to discourage her. I daresay it will be there to make the occasion of turning thirty…unless Anne insists we are again at Rosings for the Christmastide. Likely she will.

The bright spot in this decidedly cheerless sojourn is that Georgiana has made the acquaintance of a gentleman she much admires. Mr Ritson is perhaps not the best suitor for her—he is the third son of Sir Edgar Ritson of Stowe Manor—but he has some fortune from his mother's people, and he is very kind to her. Georgiana has blossomed under his regard. We shall see if anything comes of it.

At least Bingley is happy, or so I assume. I received a letter from Mrs Bingley, wishing me all the best for Christmas and in the coming year. I confess it was a relief to have some readable missive from that quarter, and hope that Mrs Bingley will undertake writing all of Bingley's future correspondence with me.

Alas, she said nothing of her sister.

Pemberley, Christmas 1813

Having revisited last year's entry, I can say that, above all, I am glad to be again at Pemberley this Christmas and even more so to have evaded the imprudent obligation into which I had feverishly and foolishly leapt.

That is not to say that it has been without some chastening at the hands of Society. Georgiana chose to decamp from town with me in late May, having had enough of the whispers and looks. I do not think anyone thought it surprising that Anne and I were marrying only to suit our families, but once rumours of a mistress began to circulate, it was above enough.

Of course, like all the best gossip, there was some grain of truth in it. They said I had a mistress and that it was her I loved, not Anne. My beloved is not my mistress, nor shall she ever be, but neither is she Anne, and to that end, there was truth enough in rumour to end the arrangement.

She remains on the Continent; I have no notion whether Bingley has told her that I remain unwed, or if it would matter to her now. I wish to believe it would, but perhaps her tender feelings for me are now gone. Her name has been linked with one of her travel companions, Mr Dillard; he sounds like a macaroni to me, but I doubt I could approve of any man who was linked to her, save myself.

Bingley has been little help in providing information about her. The man who once sought my directive above even his own has surged ahead of me; he is a husband and a father and has little time or inclination to devote to the lovelorn state of an old friend. I cannot blame him of course and, indeed, I am glad for him. I merely wish he would tell me when she might return, and if she has fallen in love with another; I should vastly prefer he would tell me without me having to ask him.

I have by now a weekly correspondence with Mr Ritson so I must assume that the scandal surrounding her brother has not materially altered Georgiana's prospects with that gentleman. I confess, though I had not wished to allow her to be engaged until she was eighteen, I may permit it if only to relieve myself of the obligation of reading and replying to his infernal letters! He dangled a bit in the last, seeming wishful for an invitation to Pemberley, but I did not offer one. He may come to us in town; we shall be there soon enough.

London, Christmas 1814

Though it was my intention to remain at Pemberley through January, I returned to town at the end of November, all on the strength of one dreadfully blotched sentence from a letter sent to me by Bingley. The letter had contained mostly matters of business—he will move to Derbyshire soon and has allowed my advice and assistance in that venture—but at the end said, merely, "I daresay Elizabeth will require apartments there as well."

It was enough, more than enough to waken all feeling for her within me—not that such feeling ever truly slumbered. It dozed, fitfully, on occasion, but roared to life at any bell of laughter or flash of eye that reminded me of her.

I intend it to be a proper Christmas. Darcy House shall be decorated in the manner that my mother once did it, for if somehow, some way she sees it, I wish it to be enchanting for her. If I might contrive her to be at Pemberley…but no. Darcy House will do. I shall create for her a house that has every bit of the romance of the Festive Season and hope she will see it.

She came upon me quite serendipitously in a book shop, and although caught unaware, I believed I had acquitted myself well enough. But then, even then—when I was determined to put an end to such miseries between us—confusion arose on our meetings over the next days. She thought me married; I thought her indifferent. Thank God we were, both of us, in error! Christmas Eve brought us to one mind with one another, allowing us to quickly come to the place we ought to have been all along.

I am, in every way, the happiest of men, and it is a joy that rests deep within me; I know now what contentment means, and what it means to have, at last, the other half of your heart united within you. She will be mine, and in less time than I might ever have dreamt possible. I am ever fond of the Festive Season, but from this day forward, I believe I shall become a most ardent devotee. It has been said hearts are opened at Christmas, and I can surely attest to that.

Pemberley, Christmas 1815

Have I been ever happy before? Have I loved? I thought I had, but a fullness of joy such as this has not been known to me. My wife has given me a gift this year that will never be again equalled.

I am to be a father.

A strange thing to behold a woman who bears your child. I found myself awash in tenderness for her, overwhelmed by love for her, and filled with a desire to protect her that was nearly nauseating in magnitude. She was not, at the moment, in any evident danger, yet I wished to vanquish any potential for unpleasantness or strife.

She referred to him as my son; in truth, I care little for what form the blessing takes. A daughter will please me just as well.

She sat on my lap, and I put my hands on her, willing the child to stretch or kick itself into my perception, but it was not to be so. It might be some weeks before those pleasures are known to more than the child's mother, but I can wait. There is probably some danger in too much delight at once, and I would not wish to expire now when all source of sublime happiness is laid before me.

I once did wonder, most ridiculously, whether I had heart sufficient to love anyone as much as I love Elizabeth. Having not before known the depth of feeling I have for my wife, it seemed rather impossible.

But the truth is known to me now; I have heart enough today for Elizabeth and my child and anticipate having yet more tomorrow—and still more after that, should we be blessed with a brother or sister for this child some other happy day.

But there is time enough for such greed later; today I am content, happy in knowing there is heart enough for my growing family and love in abundance for all.

The End

About the Author

Amy D'Orazio is a longtime devotee of Jane Austen and fiction related to her characters. She currently lives in Pittsburgh with her husband and daughters, as well as three Jack Russell terriers who often make appearances (in a human form) in her books.

Also by Amy D'Orazio

A Fine Joke
A Lady's Reputation
A Short Period of Exquisite Felicity
A Wilful Misunderstanding
Of a Sunday Evening
So Material a Change
The Best Part of Love
The Mysteries of Pemberley

A YULETIDE DREAM

JULIE COOPER

"My troublous dreams this night doth make me sad."

— King Lear, Henry VI Part II

December 19, 1811

To begin with, it was Sir William Lucas to whom Darcy owed his first of many unwelcome discoveries. Bingley, with typical recklessness, had incited a general expectation of *marriage* by his prolific attentions towards Miss Bennet of Longbourn. Truthfully, and until Sir William's displeasing disclosures, Darcy had hardly noticed Bingley's partiality. He had been too obsessed with his mighty attempts to disregard the pull and provocations of the pretty, perceptive next-eldest Bennet sister.

Darcy's wrestle had been caused by his second unpleasant discovery: an interest, then an admiration, and, finally, an...was *adoration* too strong a word? When he rose from his bed eagerly, because the day's interactions might include her? When he took an excessive interest in her concerns? When he felt humiliated, for her sake, as her cousin, her younger sisters, her mother, even her father at times exposed themselves with ridiculous and intemperate behaviour?

No. Adoration was too mild, affection too trifling. He had watched her only this evening at Lucas Lodge, at yet another Christmas festivity he had not wished to attend, listening as she baited Miss Bingley in a teasing so subtle, her victim had no idea when she stepped into the trap of foolish declaration. Kindly, however, Miss Elizabeth had not enlightened her; only the sparkle in her eyes bespoke her amusement, allowing her opponent to retain all her coveted self-importance.

His mortification was complete: he was in love.

He could only imagine the responses of his relations if he attempted to explain his preference for her above all others. *'Who is her mother? Who are her uncles and aunts? What is her fortune?'* They would not long remain ignorant of the Bennets' condition in life. Their expectations would be disappointed—and while he never had any intention of marrying Anne de Bourgh, he had at least hoped that her mother should not be able to say a word of objection when he presented his bride—because said bride was to be the epitome of beauty, birth, and fortune. His pride demanded it.

Leave here! he lectured himself. *Leave before the countryside begins speaking of* you *and her with the same certainty as Bingley and Miss Bennet!* Had he not singled out Miss Elizabeth with his attentions more than once? Was it not becoming more and more difficult to pretend an indifference he did not feel? Why had he remained in this dull village, on the thin excuse of determining whether or not Miss Jane Bennet actually *cared* for his friend? What would it matter if she did? Regardless, the moment he had been certain Miss Bennet's affections were *not* engaged, he ought to have fled, taking Bingley with him.

His ruminations were suddenly interrupted by the arrival of the last person he ever expected to meet in Netherfield's library: Miss Bingley. She did not admire books, only that he owned so many of them. He stood at once, giving her a brief bow, then raised one brow in enquiry.

"I apologise for disturbing you," she said rather breathlessly. But then, she could not possibly be in the habit of intruding, alone, upon gentlemen in their private recesses, and was doubtless embarrassed. "I determined that I must speak to you at the earliest opportunity—regarding my brother."

"Your brother?" he asked, though he could almost guess what she would next say.

"Yes. As much as it grieves me to admit, I fear he believes himself in love with the sly and shrewd Miss Jane Bennet. It defies all rational thinking, but you know how easily his affections are bestowed. When do you leave to join Miss Darcy in London?"

Yet another imprudence on his part. Georgiana had begged him to come home to Pemberley for Christmas; instead, he had convinced *her* to journey to London, where he intended to meet her. She had departed for town only today, so would not arrive there until the twenty-third of December. All so that he could remain where he was for a few days longer.

He had indulged his fascination with Miss Elizabeth by attending one entertainment after another in this country village, all of them inferior to London's prospects, and only worth the while for those brief moments when he could watch for her, listen to her, be near her. He ought to have left yesterday. Or last week. He ought never to have come at all.

"Tomorrow, most likely," he made himself say.

"Oh, Mr Darcy, will you not convince my brother that we *all* must go? Surely, once we are in town, with its attendant delights, he will forget this foolish infatuation! As his friend, I beg you to save him from himself! I do not think I exaggerate the danger."

No, she did not, and Bingley was not its only casualty. "I will speak to him, and will do my best to encourage his departure. Once we are in London, common sense must surely prevail."

Once away in London, Darcy mused, *a gentleman's imagined love must rapidly jump to distant admiration; the leap from admiration to apathy ought to require but a moment. Oughtn't it?*

It was a simple matter to convince Bingley to spend Christmas in London. All Darcy had to do was to say that he truly wished for him to go—Bingley was always accommodating. He pretended not to notice his friend's backward glances as the carriage wheeled away. Determinedly, he made none of his own. Between him and Miss Bingley, they could help Bingley see the impossibility—the grave error—of ever returning to this place.

He *ought* to have felt relief. He *should* have been thankful for the quick escape. Instead, as they reached the familiar bustle and noise of London, he felt nothing but the heavy weight of gloom. Nevertheless, he manfully stayed his course. Once all were settled, he invited Bingley for a private conversation in his study. There, he explained all he had observed of Miss Bennet—that her open, cheerful manners were as pleasant towards Bingley as they were towards Sir William Lucas.

However, there were no sidelong glances or longing stares. She was a woman being pressured by her mother to net herself a husband, so of course she would never discourage him—but *his* feelings were one-sided. Darcy's explanations continued as the light in Bingley's eyes dimmed and all joy fled.

It was a necessary evil! he told himself. *As his friend, I could do no less!* But the weight of the dreadful duty continued to plague him long after Bingley took himself off to his brother Hurst's London abode.

Darcy's third disagreeable discovery came at Georgiana's arrival in London. His sister had always been quiet and shy. Now, however, she was almost silent. She stared at her feet or her hands in her lap rather than meeting his eye. She could not be drawn out. He spoke with her companion, who was departing for a brief holiday to visit relations; Mrs Annesley assured him it was a temporary condition she would soon outgrow. *He* remained uncertain, feeling all the helplessness of the situation—and a good deal of annoyance at himself for allowing the companion to leave her charge at such a delicate time.

Diffident, sweet Georgiana had lost all her confidence. Once more, George Wickham had taken something precious and left only ruins behind.

TWO

"To die, to sleep—to sleep perchance to dream: ay, there's the rub, for in that sleep of death what dreams may come when we have shuffled off this mortal coil, must give us pause."

— *Hamlet, Hamlet Act 3*

December 23, 1811

Darcy sat in his London home's music room while his sister played the Christmas melodies he had suggested. Georgiana was remarkably talented, but in those notes he could hear her sorrow; she played *The Coventry Carol* as if it were a dirge.

Morton tapped upon the door, and the music ceased abruptly with his entrance.

"An express for you, sir."

He took the missive from his butler, brow furrowed. It was from his uncle, Earl of Matlock. Breaking the seal, he read it. And gaped at the contents.

"Brother? Is anything the matter? You look pale."

He glanced up from the writing on the page. "It is Lady Catherine." He swallowed. "She is dead. An apoplexy."

"Dead? It seems quite impossible."

It was not, perhaps, a usual response to the death of a near relation, but Darcy understood his sister's meaning. While neither of them was, nor could be, consumed by grief at the news, Lady Catherine de Bourgh had seemed an indomitable, immoveable fixture in both their lives. For all the times she had driven him mad with the frustration of her constant urgings in her daughter Anne's direction—no matter how often he informed his aunt, in no uncertain terms, that the match was impossible—he *had* cared for her; he visited her regularly, endured her self-importance and endless fascination with minutiae. In looks, she was very like his mother, even if not quite so pretty or refined. It was a great shock.

"What of Anne?" his sister asked, and he sighed. Anne was doubtless devastated by this loss.

"She will go to Matlock for the nonce, our uncle says. He would like me to overlook Rosings Park and settle affairs there."

It was not all his uncle had said.

You ought to think carefully on this, Darcy. Rosings Park and all it encompasses could be yours. Of course, I would like Anne for Richard, but the girl prefers you, and her wishes ought to be considered.

The thought of marrying Anne had never been a tempting one. But how much of his distaste had been the notion of dancing constant attendance on Anne's difficult mother? Anne was sickly and cross, but she was also retiring and uncomplicated. She got on well enough with his sister; Georgiana would have no issue with a closer connexion. And then there was the estate.

Darcy had always taken a deep interest in Rosings Park. It was vast, full of undeveloped potential, and his aunt had resisted nearly all of his best suggestions for improving it. The earl was warning him as plainly as he could—*act now, or the estate will go to Richard.*

"Ought we to put out the black crape?" Georgiana asked, interrupting his musings.

Would Darcy House go into full mourning, with a hatchment and black ribbon on the door? No. No, they would not. His aunt had died in Kent, not London, and Georgiana was sombre enough without decking her in black and grey. Lady Matlock might express a different opinion, but for now he would avoid too dismal a display.

"Black gloves only, I think. And of course, I shall not go out so much." It was wrong, undoubtedly, that he was pleased to have an excuse to avoid the flood of invitations that would surely arrive, once it was known he was in town.

His sister nodded, then begged to be excused on the pretext of writing to her cousin.

For the rest of the day, a deluge of rain kept callers at bay. Darcy locked himself in his study, ostensibly to ponder the needs of Rosings, but really to consider what he ought to do with his future. What, truly, was best?

The thought of being husband to Anne was revolting. But could he force his feelings to change? His own parents' marriage—which he believed to have been a happy one—was arranged by their respective families to enhance the wealth and prestige of their respective houses. He had been taught, almost from his cradle, to fulfil his duties to both his antecedents and his progeny. It was why he could not allow himself to consider Elizabeth.

Elizabeth. He had endeavoured to disregard her, to forget her vivacity, her wit, her fine character—developed, somehow, despite the ridiculous creatures surrounding her. He tried not to consider how wonderful a sister she would be for Georgiana, how her *joie de vivre* would encourage the too-solemn younger lady. He sought to forget the fine, perfectly respectable birth of her father, in favour of remembering who would inherit her family properties upon that father's death. He struggled against the dreams haunting him each night—the dream of Elizabeth waltzing in his arms; the dream of seeing Elizabeth by moonlight; the dream of kissing her—*No!* He flung himself away from his desk, the papers he was supposedly examining drifting haphazardly to the floor.

There was so little acceptable to remember! Should he foster a family connexion to William Collins, the obsequious and ridiculous vicar who had held the living for Lady Catherine? Should he expose dear Georgiana to the other more coquettish and less well-mannered daughters of Mr Bennet? Should the Darcy heir go visiting to Elizabeth's relations in *Cheapside*? He shuddered to think of it. It was not to be borne.

All told, it was a long and depressing day, followed by a nearly silent dinner.

At least the rain kept the carollers away.

THREE

"Why, thou hast put him in such a dream, that when the image of it leaves him, he must run mad."

— *Sir Toby Belch, Twelfth Night, Act 2*

Darcy lay in his bed, staring up at the canopy. He was warm, well-fed, comfortable, and tired. So why would sleep not come? He had decided to—nay, *commanded*—himself that he put aside all thoughts of the future. He had brought out, from his vault, his mother's pearl necklace and bracelet set to be presented to Georgiana on Christmas Day, spending time over a little note expressing his hope that she would one day grow to be such a woman as their mother had been.

And then he lay still, willing a restful sleep to finally carry him into oblivion.

However, what happened next was neither restful nor slumberous. Rather, there came the sound of…of wood or stone scraping, metals clanking, followed by the discordant notes of a pianoforte. He shot bolt upright in bed, and the noise stopped. By the light of the fire, he peered carefully around him, wary and alert. He did not think he had imagined the sounds; he was quite certain he had been the furthest thing from dozing. But perhaps it was a noise from another part of the house—an intruder? He swung his legs over the side of the mattress, preparing to rise and light a candle, that he might investigate.

A sudden clattering at his chamber door arrested his attention. It was the sound of...dishes rattling? Grunting? The hairs at his nape prickled. The door, of its own volition, opened. He grabbed the heavy candlestick at his bedside, prepared to wield it as a weapon.

But there, unmistakably standing in the doorway in the glow of what *must* have been candlelight, though he could not see any candle, was the last person in the world he might have expected—Lady Catherine de Bourgh.

"Aunt?" he said tentatively. "There–there...has been some mistake. I–I heard you were dead. I am so—"

"There *has* been a mistake," she announced regally. "Grave, momentous errors have been perpetrated. I am here to see that they are corrected." With that, and much to his continued astonishment, she pushed her way into his bedchamber, dragging behind her what looked to be the chimney-piece from Rosings' finest drawing room. How it fit through his door, he could not have said. Grabbing the banyan hanging on the hook near his bed, he shrugged it on, even as he chided himself that he was, plainly, in the throes of a vivid dream and need only await his own awakening.

"As you are aware, it was the favourite wish of both your mother and myself that you marry Anne. From your infancy, we have made your destiny known. You, Fitzwilliam, were formed for my daugh—" She broke off mid-word, swivelling her head to look behind her at something—or *someone?*—he could neither see nor hear.

"I am making my point!" she disputed, with some irritation, to whomever—or *whatever*—she spoke. She turned back to him, taking a few steps closer. Or rather, she attempted to. Along with the chimney-piece, she appeared to be dragging a pianoforte, a set of elbow chairs, stacks of Sèvres porcelain, an ornately ostentatious jewel cabinet, and a massive, hideously gilded chamber pot. How she moved at all, he could not say, but she finally managed to wedge her way farther into his room.

"As I was saying," she began, but he could not keep from interrupting.

"Forgive me, my lady, but why are you chained to your furnishings?"

She rolled her eyes. "There are, evidently, *rules*—which *somebody* might have *bothered* to explain *earlier*," she said, with a quick glare directed towards the invisible personage behind her, "which dictate certain advantages or disadvantages in the world to come, of which I was *wholly* unaware—"

Again, she appeared to be receiving interruptions and reprimands from beyond, then impatiently turned back to him. "Yes, yes, endless sermons of 'where your treasure is, there will your heart be also,' and who takes these ideas *literally*, I ask you?"

"Do you mean Holy Scripture?" Darcy queried, incredulous, but noting that, however ridiculous this dream, his aunt remained very true to character. There must be a means of awakening himself, and it was surely past time to do so. But first, he simply *had* to ask the most perplexing question of the many occurring to him.

"But why the marble chimney-piece?"

"Because it *weighs* eight hundred pounds," she replied with a disdainful sniff. She glanced again over her shoulder. "And *somebody* possesses a very *warped* sense of justice."

"Perhaps you ought to say what you were, um, sent here to say," Darcy said, pinching himself without any successful disappearance of this strange dream-incarnation of his aunt.

"Not so hasty! I will not be interrupted. Hear me in silence. You have been considering marriage, but your obligations to your family and your name—some of them imposed by me—have prevented you. Is this not true?"

"Marriage! This is fantastic! Who told you this?" Darcy sputtered.

Something in his aunt's expression turned sly. "Would you admit, then, that I have *never* discouraged you from following your noblest inclinations, your finest feelings, your…heart, so to speak?"

This, Darcy thought, *is too much of a stretch, even for a dream*. And since it *must* be merely his imagination gone awry, for once he would speak honestly to her. "Oh, so you have developed a sudden interest in my heart? Perhaps death has truly altered your opinions, my lady. What difference did my *heart* make when you beseeched, browbeat, and badgered Anne to consider me as her betrothed, telling the same to all your acquaintance, exposing me to the censure of the world for caprice and instability and her to its derision for disappointed hopes? Where was your sympathy then?"

"Pardon me for having the best interests of my daughter in mind! Do not pretend she has nothing to offer you." Again, she turned to look behind her as if listening. She cleared her throat. "Nevertheless. Your happiness is important…exceedingly important. More important than earthly treasures."

"It is?" Darcy could not help but ask. "More important than descendants and deportment, riches and relations?"

She hesitated. "You would not, of course, wish to bring any discredit upon your young sister."

No; no, of course I would not. Would disgrace *be the end result of such an alliance, however?* For the first time, he seriously considered the question, as he had never before allowed himself to even *think* it, and spoke aloud at least one of his conclusions. "But in marrying Elizabeth Bennet, I would surely gain access to such extraordinary resources of happiness as must truly help Georgiana find hers as well."

Lady Catherine began speaking rapidly. "To be divided by the upstart pretensions of a young woman without family, connexions, or fortune is not to be borne. Honour, decorum, prudence, nay, interest, forbid you from quitting your native sphere and entering into an engagement, ruining your destiny and Anne's—"

Her voice cut off abruptly, her lips still moving, but no words emerging. Darcy could have sworn he heard a heavy sigh. Without warning, the entire apparition disappeared.

For some time, he only stood where he was, bewildered. *I must be asleep, yet I cannot waken. What should one do when a dream behaves in such an irrational manner? I have always been temperate. Could I have hit my head somehow?*

He pinched himself again, wincing at the pain, but nothing changed. "Never mind it," he said aloud. *I am only dreaming that I am pinching myself. In the way of ridiculous dreams, this one is a reminder from my rational brain of those truths I could not perceive while awake. I cannot love Anne de Bourgh, but what is love? Can it be love if I disappoint all the expectations of my entire family? Marrying to please myself without consideration of my bride's family and fortune would brand me a selfish and even foolish being to future generations of Darcys. I shall forget such reckless and imprudent inclinations as love, return to my bed, and dream myself back into a more peaceful slumber.*

With that, he sat back upon his mattress…but he did not remove his banyan or take up his coverlet. Instead, he rested against his pillows and thought with some incredulity upon the vision, doing his best to convince himself that it was all nonsense and to quash the wellspring of hope that consideration of such a future had wrought within his breast.

After several minutes of self-lecturing, he felt his tension easing. It was just and understandable that he was feeling unsettled, and wild dreams were a usual outcome of such shocking news as the death of Lady Catherine, of his worries for Bingley and for Georgiana, even of the distress of fleeing Hertfordshire under a cloud of almost-disgrace. He was an eminently practical man, just as practical as his aunt was silly. He had been plagued by guilt all day long, for neglecting to act in the way Lady Catherine and his parents would have wished in offering for his cousin. No wonder he had, momentarily, mistakenly fallen into an imaginative delusion.

Most of all, he was deeply fatigued, almost to the point of insensibility. He pulled back the linens at last, preparing to lie down, when another light appeared in his room, which continued to increase until the chamber was lighter than at noonday. With real distress, he looked into it, expecting Lady Catherine again and wondering for his own sanity.

But it was not his aunt, though the resemblance was apparent. Lady Anne Darcy stood looking at him, still as lovely—ethereal, even—as he remembered. Nonetheless, a melancholy unfamiliar to his memories was obvious upon her visage. To his recollection, her normal aspect had always been lively, smiling, and sanguine. A pit of dread lodged in his belly as he wondered whether this new sorrow was all due to him—and the choices he had failed to make.

"I wish to awaken now," he demanded. Nothing changed, and his mother's apparition only silently watched him. At least she did not appear to be sporting furnishings, musical instruments, or dinnerware. Defiantly, he spoke his thoughts aloud. "I am simply imagining this. It has been a distressing, dreadfully depressing day, and I am out of my head. At least, I am thus momentarily afflicted. I shall lie down now, fall asleep, and awaken in the morning much recovered. If you are the portion of my imagination bent upon lecturing me regarding the folly of taking a wife such as Elizabeth Bennet, you need not bother. I have already disregarded the notion, and will drop the acquaintance entirely."

"Well, Fitzwilliam," the figure replied, "that will make your situation at present more pitiable, but it will have no effect on *me*." She spoke with that exact touch of wry impatience he remembered from his youth, whenever he was slow to recognise what she wished of him. Just as then, he felt the old yearning to please her, to do whatever she wanted in order to ensure her happiness.

He scrambled to his feet. "Mother," he said, and she...brightened. He could not describe it any other way. Suddenly—delusion or dream or apparition, *anything*—he wanted nothing more than to speak to her, as he had wanted to so many times since her unexpected, untimely death in childbed. Unfortunately, he also remembered how tongue-tied he so often became in her presence, and how little he wished to appear foolish or unsophisticated before her. With his father, estate business had forged a common language. Father had spent endless hours patiently instructing him, and as Fitzwilliam did his best to absorb it all and offer as much intelligent contribution as possible, he had earned his father's gratifying approval. But he had been too young when his mother died; she ever remained the lovely, elegant figure perched upon the pedestal of old memory, and he had never learnt to be easy with her.

"Come with me," she said, holding out her hand. Without hesitation, he took it.

Suddenly, he found himself hurtling through time and space at a dizzyingly rapid speed. Stars loomed overhead, his stomach pitched, and he feared he would be sick. With a hard jolt, he landed in a church pew.

Incredibly, he recognised the building as the village church in Lambton, but the old one that burnt to the ground in '04. With amazement, he realised he was a boy again, perhaps six years of age, sitting stiffly on the bench between his parents, hardly daring to move. And though he looked upon the scene with his adult mind, he was merely a hidden bystander, with the thoughts and behaviours of his six-year-old self as apparent to him as if he relived the moment.

Nor did it take him long to recognise the event; it was the village school's annual pageant performed on Christmas Eve. Mrs Tilbury, the stick-thin schoolmistress, herded her charges to the front, two by two. Since some of them were dressed as sheep and assorted other barnyard animals, she appeared as a female Noah driving her flocks onto the ark.

His adult self could spot all the flaws in costuming—ragged angels, moth-bitten lambs, and a diminutive Joseph beside a much taller Mary. The casting of the holy couple became obvious when it grew apparent that the part of baby Jesus was played by a real infant, who was none too fond of his starring role. To Fitzwilliam's younger self, however, it appeared the epitome of one word: fun.

There were two solos, one duet, and one recitation before the dénouement—the eldest boy intoning the story of an overcrowded inn, a suffering mother, and the promise of divine love, clothed in flesh and come to earth in the lowliest of circumstances. Each of the children moved forward more or less in good time with the recital, alongside heavenly hosts, frightened shepherds, kingly boys bearing gifts, and a valiant, youthful Mary quieting an infant's cry. Even his adult self recognised the simple beauty of it; these humble actors were, in truth, perfectly wonderful in their roles, despite a fussing baby, an angel with only one wing, and wise men kicking and elbowing each other until reproved by the stern frown and threatening brow of their teacher.

But he saw something else as well: the growing enthusiasm within his six-year-old self—the imagination brewing and bubbling beneath his composed exterior. *Stop!* he wanted to cry. *Do not think what you are think-*

ing! But of course, he could not stop it. He was a mere spectator to his past, and could only watch as the youthful Fitzwilliam continued to imagine and plan.

He stood silently beside his parents as they solemnly thanked the performers, complimented their presentation, urged them to listen conscientiously to their teacher, and to be good children. Until that point, Darcy had not paid any attention to the sea of faces surrounding them, but of course the mothers and fathers were all in the packed pews, seemingly frozen in place. That was always the way of it—the villagers would not be easy until the Darcys took their finely clothed, censorious selves away. With the wisdom of age, he realised that they saw all the same flaws in the performance that he noticed, and that his presence with his parents had stolen some of their enjoyment of it. Instead of being free to feel pride in their little angels and kings, they had to imagine what criticisms the Darcys must be pronouncing—judgmental, disapproving witnesses to youthful misbehaviours and shabby costumes.

But his youthful self only felt the disappointment of missing out on whatever festivities had been prepared for those who remained, as he followed his father and mother out of the church. Everyone stood stiffly quiet as they departed.

His parents walked swiftly towards their waiting carriage, but he lingered, looking over his shoulder. Already he could hear the sounds of merriment, now that the Darcys were no longer there to dampen their enthusiasm. George had boasted of the carolling, treats, punch, and gaiety that would shortly follow, once the Darcys were out of the way of it all. An estate's steward was not, evidently, an obstacle to happiness—unlike its owner.

"Fitzwilliam," called his father, and he hurried towards the carriage.

For the entire return journey to Pemberley, the idea grew within his young brain. If the Lambton cottagers and Pemberley's tenants could put on such a marvellous performance, why, only think what the Darcys could do! He was certain his mother had magnificent satins, furs, and silks for the robes of angels and kings. Perhaps the servants would even *want* to join the nativity, if they could dress in such splendid garb. But his parents were murmuring quietly to each other, and he dared not interrupt. In fact, they had pulled into the Pemberley drive without a single opportunity presenting itself for him to request anything.

"I do hope the Wentworths have hired superior musicians to their last entertainment," he heard his mother say, and his heart sank. He had utterly forgotten that his parents planned to attend some party or other this evening. A small part of him understood them to be unlikely to agree even had they *not* been going out, but he was utterly captivated by the romance of his *grand idea*. How could they disagree with its brilliance? Moreover, he had witnessed his parents' entertainments from behind the upper stairwell in the past, and they always appeared rather dull. Perhaps they had never before *thought* of such an excellent amusement! Perhaps they would be delighted by its novelty!

Inside Pemberley's vast entry, his mother bent to kiss his cheek, the signal that he should take himself off to the nursery. It was now or never.

"Father, Mother, I wonder whether we could put on our own pageant tonight," he began.

When they frowned, he hastened to explain.

"We wouldn't have all the parts, but Susannah would help, and you could be Mary and Joseph, and I could be the innkeeper," he offered eagerly. "Except, I would say, 'Of *course* you can enter, and take my own bed.' It's changing the story, but that could explain why we don't have all the animals. And Mrs Frost, the stablemaster's wife, has an infant she would loan, I am sure, for she says she is always tired and wishing for a rest from him. We could borrow some hay from Mr Frost, and I promise to clean up every bit of it after we finish. I am a very good reader. I could also play the part of the wise men, and we could pretend —Mother, we could use your jewellery for gold, frankincense, and myrrh."

His parents exchanged glances, and he knew they were thinking of polite ways to refuse him. He increased the rapidity of his speech.

"Or you could play the wise kings, and you could wear your tiara, Mother. You look so beautiful in it. You could be a wise queen. I am certain the Holy Family would not mind."

His father cleared his throat. "Son, your mother and I have accepted an invitation for this evening. We are expected at the Wentworths'. It would be remarkably ill-mannered for us to fail to attend after we gave our word, would it not?"

"We don't have to get a real baby. My stuffed bear, if it were wrapped in swaddling clothes, would serve. And I would play the shepherd parts, while you, Father, narrated. This is my 'sore afraid' face," Fitzwilliam continued, widening his eyes and waggling his brows in desperate demonstration. "You love to read. Or we could take turns."

To this day, Darcy had no notion why the idea of a nativity pageant had meant so much to him. Perhaps he had been entranced by the Christmas story, and the concept of a God not eager to pounce upon his every error, but instead a new-born infant, lower than everyone. Lower, even, than a little boy who sometimes forgot to be *gentlemanly*, who must always be an *heir*, and who must somehow learn to shoulder the vastness that was Pemberley and protect everyone in it.

Or perhaps he had simply been very lonely.

"But please!" he begged, as his mother shook her head impatiently. "Please! I promise not to ask for anything again, ever! Just this once!"

Hope filled him as he saw signs that his father was softening, if not towards the pageant, at least enough to offer some sort of compromise. His mother saw it, too.

"Fitzwilliam Sébastien Spencer Darcy, this is what comes of associating with villagers! Stables! Shepherds! We will never attend the school's pageant again if *this* is the ill-bred sort of behaviour it inspires! Your father *told* you we have commitments elsewhere. You would have us embarrassed before the entire household, and all because you want to play at–at *innkeeping*!"

She said it as though he had begged to run naked through the streets of Lambton. It was the *Christmas story*! In that moment, it seemed as though she hated him, and he was filled with a reckless, impetuous fury. "That's a lie! You are unfair! I *hate* being a Darcy, and I hate—"

He was not allowed to finish the sentence. His father grabbed him by the arm, towed him into his study, lectured him on the proper way to speak to his lady mother and the respect due his family name, followed by receiving his first—and, thankfully, his last—caning.

He had been sent to his room without supper, but his backside hurt too much to inspire any appetite, regardless. Gingerly, he crept to the nursery, only to discover that Susannah was not there, having been permitted to go to the village Yuletide celebrations. Her sullen younger sister, Nan, plainly peeved at being forced to miss the festivities, was there to sit with him instead.

In his misery, he did not know whether he could bear her hostility. And he did not wish *anyone* to see him cry. It had been difficult enough to prevent sobbing before his father; he would be unable to hold back his tears for much longer.

"You could go and be with your family," he offered Nan humbly. "I will go to my bed now, I promise, and I will not leave it."

"That would be a fine way for my family to lose our places here, wouldn't it?" she snapped. "There's not to be a tray for you, I hear. Be a good boy, then, and do go to sleep."

He limped to his bed, pulled the covers up over his head, and tried to weep as quietly as possible.

Darcy opened his eyes. He was back, somehow—thankfully without the dizzying journey—in his own room, as his adult self. His cheeks were wet. He stood before his mother once more.

"Thank you for rehearsing one of the most humiliating episodes of my youth," he said coolly, utterly embarrassed. His posterior smarted with phantom pain, still.

She smiled sadly. "I have witnessed it a hundred times, now," she said. "Over and over again, from the view of your little eyes. Your eagerness. Your perfect trust in us, as mother and father, who should have cherished and nurtured you. All destroyed in one utterly selfish moment."

Darcy looked at her with consternation. "Surely not. For one thing, you certainly never laid a hand upon me. If I were to dwell in resentment, it would doubtless be aimed at my father; I can assure you I do not. For another, I like to believe I never repeated my foolishness."

She sighed. "Your father felt guilty as the devil," she went on, as though he had not spoken. "He never apologised to you, for it was not done. But he went out of his way to pay you more attention, to try and compensate for his loss of temper and subsequent poor behaviour. He took you sledding, I believe, as soon as you could sit without undue discomfort. He vowed never again to respond with violence, and he never did. And he had a miserable time at the Wentworths' party, it goes without saying."

"Father was all that was good," Darcy said stiffly.

"He is," she agreed. "I, however, proceeded to enjoy myself at the Wentworths' and never gave the incident much thought. If it crossed my mind at all, it was with justification. You had attempted to interrupt my important plans, you see. You had expressed anger towards me and accused me of injustice. You were disrespectful."

"I believe I learnt from my mistakes," Darcy replied, even more stiffly.

"Oh, you did. You learnt extraordinarily well. You grew more silent, and more dutiful. You weighed every word before you spoke it, and seldom expressed your true feelings, however unhappy. You certainly never asked us to play with you again."

"Naturally, I outgrew such notions, ma'am."

"You were six!" she cried. "The Wentworths' party was a senseless, stupid reason for beating our only child, and I did not see it! I am so very sorry!"

Darcy, keenly uncomfortable, bowed. "Please do not distress yourself, my lady. It was all forgotten, I promise."

Her eyes closed, and she sighed again. "Of course. I knew an apology would be futile. That six-year-old little boy has been gone for a long while, and it was to him I owed it. I did not see all of what I ought to have seen in the time I had with you, but I want you to understand, now, that the example I set for you was often a foolish one. I wish I could undo so much."

"I am sure I do not wish for you to waste a moment's regret upon any childishness of mine," he said sincerely, distressed by the thought of her feeling a failure. He had always loved and esteemed her, although unable to easily express it. She had had powerful notions of duty, and the fact that there was a school at all was due to her influence and many contributions. But she was not finished.

"I was a selfish being all my life, in practice, at least. I taught you what was right—but I did not teach you to correct your temper. You were given good principles, but left to follow them in pride and conceit. I, especially, allowed, encouraged, and exhibited a near constant example of selfishness and arrogance. Because I cared for none beyond my own family circle, because I thought meanly of all the rest of the world, of their sense and worth compared with our own, it is only natural that you should do the same now."

He grimaced at this description that showed neither of them in a very favourable light. "You were an excellent mother and a perfect mistress to Pemberley, and of course I wish for my future wife to be your equal in both birth and intelligence. But finding such a person has been difficult; I am ill qualified to recommend myself to those unknown to me. I certainly have not the talent, which some people possess, of conversing easily with those I have never seen before. I cannot catch their tone of conversation, or appear interested in their concerns, as I often see done."

His mother, to his surprise, began reciting Shakespeare. "'When, in disgrace with fortune and men's eyes, I all alone beweep my outcast state, And trouble deaf heaven with my bootless cries, And look upon myself and curse my fate'?" She phrased the sonnet as a question; her tone of wry impatience had returned.

The devil of it was, she was not wrong; he lived a blessed existence granted by wealth and privilege, and ought to have put himself forward in duty to his progeny and his sister well before this. Darcy sighed. "It is a hard lesson you have been, er, sent here to teach," he said, bowing again. "By you, I have been properly humbled. You are correct, of course. I have not taken the trouble."

She smiled sadly. "You have always been so very much like your father," she said. "A good man. The very best of men." The edges of the light surrounding her began to darken.

"Wait! Mother!" he cried. Dream or not, he had never been able to say a final farewell! There was so much left unsaid, so many words they had yet to speak. The light paused momentarily, but he was tongue-tied again—without, as he had just bemoaned, any skill for reviving the conversation. "Good-bye," he managed, and felt stupid when the room fell to sudden darkness once again.

Lighting a candle, Darcy began pacing. What had it meant? Or did it mean nothing? Surely it was all a figment of his imagination, triggered somehow by his aunt's unexpected demise! But how could he have crafted such a vision of his mother? He had not lied—he had entirely forgotten the youthful incident. There must be some rationale for his brain reminding him of it, but he could not think what it could be. As he had explained to...to the *hallucination,* if he were to feel resentment, it ought to have been directed at his father! And he did not! His father had not been perfect, of course, as the very memory showed. He hoped to never respond so harshly towards a child, no matter the provocation.

His love for me was certain, regardless. I knew it.

Could it be...could his conscience be responding to some overlooked flaw or consequence of behaviour? Had he failed to perceive something—something important, something regrettable? Had he wronged someone and failed to notice...or care?

His mind fixed upon a memory, of a place he had not wanted to be, and all the people he had not wished to be in company with...and the ungentlemanly words he had offered.

'She is tolerable, but not handsome enough to tempt me; and I am in no humour at present to give consequence to young ladies who are slighted by other men. You had better return to your partner and enjoy her smiles, for you are wasting your time with me.'

He had known Miss Elizabeth heard him. Simply because he had been full of resentment at the time—impelled to attend an assembly when he was vexed and distraught by his sister's situation and in no mood for enjoyment—he had felt justified in lashing out, to both his friend and anyone unlucky enough to be within range of his voice.

Of course, it was not long afterwards that he thought the lady he had so boldly declared barely 'tolerable' to be the handsomest lady of his acquaintance.

He had assumed, because he had paid her some attention after the incident, that she would realise he had not meant for her to take the insult personally. He had assumed that asking her to dance at the ball at

Netherfield was a signal to her that she was, absolutely, handsome enough to tempt him.

I did not apologise. Not ever. Even if she did not take the insult personally, she was surely owed an apology.

Yet he knew Wickham had been speaking with her, the misbegotten scoundrel saying who-knew-what lies. And what had he done to prevent Wickham from wreaking his usual havoc upon the people of Meryton—knowing, as he certainly did, the man's propensity for vicious behaviours? *Nothing*. Not once had he made any effort whatsoever to correct or mitigate Wickham's influence. He had overheard Mrs Bennet's ill opinion of himself and had not cared, because he thought her ridiculous. She was not refined, true, but that only meant she would not hide her opinions behind a mannerly masquerade.

The Bennet ladies have nothing to fear from Wickham! he comforted himself. *They are too well born to molest, and too poor to be victimised by schemes such as Georgiana endured.*

But they *were* pretty and convivial and…sheltered.

He sat upon his bed, head in his hands, scrubbing his face. Even if he was overtired, distraught, and dreaming, he could not deny his recent selfish, ungentlemanly conduct. Perhaps he could find some means of placing a letter into Miss Elizabeth's hands? An apology, with a warning? He had no doubt that an explanation shared in confidence was safe in her care.

But was such an apology good enough? It might protect his reputation in *her* eyes, to be sure. Nevertheless, could others be at risk? By informing only her, was he not still behaving selfishly? Miss Elizabeth could never shield her community from such a villain, especially with information given in utmost confidentiality.

Sighing, he lay back amongst the pillows, thinking of the names of those he must correspond with to disclose at least *some* evidence of Wickham's nefarious character. Sir William Lucas, Mr Bennet, Mr Goulding, certainly. Perhaps Philips? The thought of exposing himself, if not his sister, as the dupe of such as Wickham before these men made him groan. He could only imagine Sir William's effusions, Mr Bennet's smirk, and Philips's too-interested questions. A deep yet unfamiliar emotion—a brew of wounded pride, fatigue, frustration, and even hurt at his unreasonable, unacknowledged, unattainable love for Elizabeth—swept through him in a wave.

"I wish I had never gone to Hertfordshire, to Netherfield, to Meryton, and never met any of the Bennets at all!" he cried aloud.

The sound of a throat clearing caught his attention, and he looked up sharply.

There, in a long, black robe, stood a figure much resembling Mr William Collins, the heir of Longbourn and lately the vicar of Hunsford parish. It bowed very low.

"Your wish is my command," said the Collins-like spectre. "I beg your pardon for not having offered my services earlier."

Darcy closed his eyes. The deranged dream had degenerated into a night terror.

FOUR

"If we shadows have offended, think but this and all is mended, that you have but slumber'd here, while these visions did appear. And this weak and idle theme, no more yielding but a dream."

— *Puck, A Midsummer Night's Dream*

THE STRANGEST THING ABOUT THE APPARITION WEARING Collins's face was its silence. When Darcy opened his eyes once again, the entity only stood there, staring. Perhaps it was not *truly* Collins—it was not like he had scrutinised the man's appearance. Certainly he could not remember a time when the rector missed an opportunity for sycophantic fawning, excessive flattery, or ridiculous opinions. His aunt had deeply enjoyed such toadying reverence; he despised it, and despised Collins with a virulent aversion.

Of course at this moment, when he was questioning everything, he must needs question his abhorrence of the vicar, as well.

His first interaction with the man had been at the ball at Netherfield, when Collins had pushed his way forward and demanded to introduce himself. It was rude, of course, which was distasteful, but naturally—and especially in crowded venues—others had made themselves known to him with equivalent presumption and received a good deal more tolerance.

It might have been the way he had paired his name so freely with the Bennets, while ensuring Darcy recognised the connexion between himself and his aunt—trading on both. And yet, a certain amount of social climbing was always understandable. In the case of Bingley, he had taken Darcy for a model of gentlemanly behaviour as well as a friend, and—not to mince words—had used their friendship to elevate his family. What was the difference, truly?

Bingley would do anything for me and mine. Perhaps, in the beginning, he would not have been so loyal, but he had wanted a genuine connexion, and strove to practise the type of friendship he wished to receive from Darcy.

Genuine. That was the word for Bingley. Collins had wanted the respect and the connexion upon the basis of whom he knew and his thin ties of blood to mere acquaintance. He expected nothing of himself in exchange, except for his efforts in advancing his own introduction.

If I found myself penniless tomorrow, Bingley would still take me in, while Collins would drop the acquaintance as quickly as possible. It was ample justification for his dislike.

Of course, Bingley's youngest sister would do the same, and I tolerate her. Darcy sighed yet again. But the Collins-like apparition was pointing to a door of his chambers, as if he should leave his room.

Darcy's instinct was to pull the covers over his head and ignore the whole thing. Certainly, the temptation to do so was strong. Unfortunately, though half-afraid he had descended into madness, he feared even more that he had somehow lost himself—his very identity. This evening, while making ready for bed, he had been convinced of the world and his place in it. In the course of these irrational dreams, the foundations of those beliefs, set in stone for so long, had cracked. It seemed vital, somehow, to examine the fissures more carefully; if he did not—as fanciful and foolish as it sounded—he might always wonder whether he could ever think himself a gentleman again.

Thus, he acted as the spectre seemed to demand, opening the door and walking through it. And found himself not in his dressing room, as he ought to be, but in a large room wholly unfamiliar to him.

It was also loud, with the noises of popping corks, boisterous speech, and raucous laughter assaulting his ears. A party of some sort, then. The people were all strangers to him; many were more finely clothed than others, but the sight of the skimpily clad women told him that this was not the sort of party where he would find ladies of quality in attendance. The room's *décor* was the type that showed all rich, velvety reds and glistening golds in candlelight, but in the bright light of day would appear seedy and vulgar. Most likely a brothel—and not one of the more discreet ones.

His first thought was to dash right back out again—this was *not* the place he wished to be caught dressed only in his banyan—but the door through which he had entered was now a wall of red-flocked paper, exhibiting a lewd portrait. Collins was nowhere to be seen. Nevertheless, no one seemed to notice Darcy. While they did not precisely *walk* through him, they *looked* through him as if he were not there.

There must be a connexion to his life somehow, as ill as the thought might be. And then he saw her.

Lydia Bennet stood not three feet from him, laughing loudly, a glass of wine in her hand. She wore a gaudy, revealing dress, and her familiarity with those surrounding her made it clear that she was no stranger to this establishment. In his shock and horror, he completely forgot his lack of clothing and desire to remain unnoticed, striding directly to her.

"Lydia Bennet, you will come with me at once!" he ordered sternly. "Let us leave this place *immediately*."

She did not respond in any way—only laughed at a remark from one of the other men. In fact, none of her circle seemed to hear him or pay him any mind. He tried to grasp her arm, but directly found himself several feet away.

"I propose a toast!" shouted a corpulent man near the stairs. He wore striped breeches that appeared ready to split at the seams, topped by an ugly purple tailcoat.

"To wine and women, song and laughter, and never a thought for the morning after!"

"Hear, hear," chorused the other patrons, raising their glasses.

"To a happy Christmas and a prosperous 1815!"

"Hear, hear!" cried the crowd. "To 1815!"

1815? Darcy thought, taken aback. It was not yet even 1812! Again, he drew nearer to Lydia. This time he examined her more closely; she was still quite young, but there was a coarseness to her features that had not been there the last time he had seen her, perhaps the result of heavy applications of rouge and face powder. Her hair was lank and oily; she held her glass out to be refilled, laughing stridently. It was no stretch to imagine her aged an additional three years—truthfully, she looked as though she had aged more than three.

"Lydia, my sweet flower!" called a voice from behind him, and Darcy stiffened. He knew that voice—oh yes, he did. George Wickham sauntered in, placing an arm about her, resting his hand most familiarly upon her person.

"George!" Lydia said, smiling eagerly up at him with a puppyish sort of adoration.

"You despicable cur! Take your hands off her!" Darcy shouted, but no one heard him or responded. His own hands fisted in frustration.

Wickham kissed her quite ardently upon the lips, to a chorus of catcalls and whistles. "Merry Christmas, dearest pet," he replied fondly, adoringly. And then he whispered something in her ear.

Her expression fell, and she looked up at him pleadingly.

His face, in return, was implacable, uncompromising.

With a heavy sigh, she gulped down her wine, then sauntered over to the corpulent man in purple and took his arm. He grinned, his smile full of rotten and missing teeth, and pulled her none-too-gently up the stairs.

Darcy stood with his mouth agape. This was unpalatable, unbelievable, unacceptable! He wanted to stop it all, but though he tried to follow, his feet were prevented from making forward progress. George Wickham did not even glance after her, embracing instead another of the women present.

"This cannot be happening," Darcy muttered.

"Oh, but it can," replied the unctuous, oily voice of the phantom Collins from a few feet away. "Be assured, my dear sir, that I most sincerely sympathise with you in your present distress, which must be of the bitterest kind—to know that a person whom you once condescended to acknowledge should be guilty of this licentiousness of behaviour."

"Cannot you see, you supercilious oaf? She is completely under that villain's thumb! I do not know where her parents are, but—"

"They have thrown her off," he said with a smug sort of pity. "Alas, her death would have been a blessing. But of course, they pretend."

Darcy narrowed his eyes and made a threatening move towards the vicar, but suddenly, Collins was gone, as was the brothel. Another door stood before him instead, and Darcy walked through it most reluctantly.

But it was a quiet study he entered this time. A man, his back to Darcy, sat writing at a desk by the light of several candles. He was dressed prosperously, and a healthy fire burnt at his hearth. The furnishings were tasteful and masculine; the room's occupant dipped his pen into the inkwell and wrote another line before setting it down with a sigh. Cautiously, Darcy approached him.

"Bingley?" he asked with some surprise. The man possessed silvering hair at his temples, appearing perhaps forty years of age. Still handsome, there was a solemnity etched upon his features, the exact opposite of Darcy's gregarious friend. But of course, Bingley—for it was, indeed, him—neither heard nor saw him.

Darcy peered over at the letter Bingley had been writing, noting the date—December 24th, 1826. Unfortunately, his friend's handwriting had not much improved over the years; Darcy squinted at the rest of the letter, trying to make it out.

But translating Bingley's hieroglyphics proved unnecessary. From his pocket, Bingley removed a miniature encased in a gold locket and set it, opened, on the desk before him.

Why does Bingley possess a miniature portrait of Jane Bennet? Had he married the girl after all?

And then, Bingley commenced reading aloud.

"To my dearest angel," he began, causing Darcy to immediately search for a means of escape. Whether addressing a wife or no, whatever his friend was about to say was deeply personal. But there was nowhere to go; neither was there any sign of the phantom vicar. He tried covering his ears, but he found no reprieve from Bingley's resonating voice.

Evidently, Darcy was here to eavesdrop, and eavesdrop he would.

"It has been many years since I saw you last, but I think of you often...almost daily," Bingley continued. "It is a relief, I admit, on those days which are so busy that my mind cannot dwell upon you for any length, and yet there is a sorrow in it, as well. I am damned for missing you, and damned for being prevented from doing so—there is no pleasing Charles Bingley, is there?"

He paused for a moment, shaking his head, and Darcy wondered... had the eldest Bennet sister died? Had Charles married her, defying friends and family, only to lose her? But Bingley was speaking again.

"I hope your life is uniformly happy and without troubles. I hope you are extremely satisfied in your motherhood and numerous friendships."

Not dead, then. At least Elizabeth does not bear that *burden of grief.* Would Elizabeth's name be mentioned now, in this unusual letter? And why would Bingley write it in the first place? It was hardly proper for him to send such a thing to a married woman who was no relation.

"I admit that I have not always been so magnanimous. When I wrote to you last year, I know I railed against the man who is your children's father, the children of mine you would not bear. I suppose I drank too much at dinner, and wasted my one indulgence to this unrequited love, my annual Christmas letter to you, on jealousy and despair. I promise, I drank only water tonight so I would not malign you so again. How could I? If you were never my bride, it is only my own fault. I know you must have awaited my return. But I listened to the reasonings of my sisters, and I failed you. I simply was not confident enough in myself; I met you perhaps a year or so too soon. But my heart, once truly given, could never stray. It is yours, though you no longer need nor want it. I could never marry another; I cannot seem to get out of the habit of belonging to you."

Fifteen years later and he still regrets her! This cannot *be real!*

"I know you have heard this all before. I am not clever, am I? If I could turn back time, I would come for you. Since I cannot, I watch over you from afar. I dare not approach you in any manner, but my man of business frequents your husband's shop on occasion, ensuring all is well as best he can. He reports that the premises appear prosperous, for which I am thankful. However, if it became obvious that there was need or want—well, I would help. Somehow, I would find a way to aid you, and be grateful I could."

"Sentinel of Jane Bennet's husband's business? Preposterous!" Darcy cried aloud, now standing directly in front of his friend, resting his hands on Bingley's desk. But his own heart whispered a shockingly agreeable thought: *I could watch over Elizabeth, at least enough to ensure she does not ever suffer from poverty or want*. He pushed the notion away. This was madness!

"Your husband does not deserve you, of course," Bingley continued on, insensible to any interruption. "Not that any man could, but he does not even try, which is the hardest to bear of all. To know he has a gracious and lovely angel on his arm as the mother of his children, yet is disloyal to you—I cannot fathom it. My friend, Darcy, has explained many times why it would be wrong to interfere, but the only true reason keeping me from it is the pain it would cause you. Perhaps you do not know, and remain blissfully ignorant of his indiscretions. I pray it is so."

Darcy looked into his friend's eyes; they held a world of sorrow. At that moment, he grew certain—absolutely certain—that Bingley would never post this letter.

"I wish you the happiest of Christmases, my love, this year, ever, and always. From the bottom of my empty heart, I regret your loss, made especially bitter by my own culpability in losing you. I only tell you once a year now, instead of daily or weekly. However, my affections remain unchanged. They are ever yours, as am I."

Heaving a great sigh, he sanded the letter, as though it could matter whether the ink smeared. Carefully, precisely, he folded it, stood, and walked towards the hearth.

"I wish...I wish Darcy had met you, just one time, so he would know how priceless you are. I cannot help but think he would have *urged* me to marry you, had he met you even once."

Darcy straightened. What was this? He had been in company with Miss Bennet many times. Surely this was wholly a fantasy, a dream, with *nothing* of reality to it?

Bingley took a last look at the letter, placed a kiss upon it, and threw it into the flames. One tear slid down his cheek, then another.

"This was not my fault," Darcy said aloud.

"Oh, no, certainly it was not," the phantom vicar replied, startling Darcy with his sudden reappearance. "You wished for a world in which you had never met any of the Bennets, and I have done my best to show it to you. I am ever your servant."

Darcy took a deep breath of relief.

"Of course, however, you cannot deny that you have been the principal, if not the only means of dividing them from each other in the *present*, involving them both in misery of the acutest kind." He steepled his fingers, his tone pontificating. "Perhaps your friend is simply not formed for happiness, no matter his circumstance, and you have merely enacted a sort of divine execution of it."

"I *thought* I acted in his best interests!" Darcy countered. "Miss Bennet certainly showed no sign that her heart was engaged. A man ought never to pursue a connexion of unequal affections."

"I have the highest opinion in the world of your excellent judgment in all matters within the scope of your understanding," the phantom said obsequiously, bowing, while his expression assumed a maddeningly condescending mien. "Permit me to say, however, that there must be a wide difference between the perception of minds and hearts amongst the laity and those of the clergy. A little show of unwillingness *is* a ladylike indication of regard. The usual practice of elegant females is to increase our love by suspense. One must never assume a lady is serious in her rejection when a greater mind has determined the advantages. It is the height of coquetry and charm."

Darcy could only look at him with a restrained sort of wonder. The vicar must be a constant source of entertainment to one such as Elizabeth's father, who most enjoyed poking fun at those least likely to detect any mockery. As for himself, he had discovered at least one true inducement for his inherent disgust of the man: his belief that women were *incapable* of any true expression of emotion. His accusations of female coquetry were awkward at best, sinister at worst, and certainly not the manner of a gentleman. And yet…

He found himself searching his memory for a time when Miss Elizabeth had *welcomed* his company—*any* expression of delight or even warmth. She was, of course, a warm and delightful person, but had any of it been directed especially towards himself? Unfortunately, though he had studied intently for any sign of Miss Bennet's regard for Bingley, he had significantly failed to search for clues as to whether Miss Elizabeth held any regard for *him*. He had only assumed—assumed her circumstance in life meant she would *have* to love him, should he bother to love her.

He had paid so little attention. However, if *Wickham* had been watching, he most certainly would have detected Darcy's eye upon Miss Elizabeth. Had he not been jealous of her defence of the churl, when she had spoken of him during their one dance? He had excused her for it, of course—she could not be expected to know his enemy's lies. But that was the problem, was it not? Miss Elizabeth was far too sensible to make away with an impoverished soldier. Yet, if her sympathies had been stirred against himself, she was too upright in character to simply excuse Fitzwilliam Darcy without any explanation.

Was she to believe in his goodness merely because *Miss Bingley* claimed it to be so?

It was all too much. This madness needed to stop, before a dreadful bitterness of spirit consumed him.

"I have had quite enough," Darcy pronounced. "Pray return me to my own chambers."

But the phantom only looked down his nose. "Pardon me for neglecting a compliance, which on every other demand shall be my constant resolution, though in the case before us I consider myself more fitted to decide on what is best than any gentleman, however learned."

Infuriating fool! Darcy turned away from the vicarly apparition and from Bingley, giving them both his back. Everything he had viewed this night had wrought painful havoc with his understanding, and now he was the helpless prisoner of a ghastly guide. A creeping fear began to overtake him. All of his 'visitors' this eve had been dead ones…well, he supposed he did not know for a fact that the vicar of Hunsford parsonage was dead, but he certainly might be.

Could I have died as well? Perhaps in my sleep, between one breath and the next, as my father did, without sign or warning? Horrifying as the thought was, he was determined to know the truth.

"Have I died, and your presence is a judgment upon me?"

The odious vicar laughed, a peculiar, high-pitched sort of giggle that did nothing to reassure his listener. "It is particularly incumbent on those who never change their opinion, to be secure of judging properly at first."

Darcy swivelled sharply towards the vicar. "Who told you that? Miss

Elizabeth?" But he—*it?*— had vanished into thin air. Darcy looked over his shoulder towards Bingley, but he was gone as well.

There was a new door before him, however, and he hesitated. If he would not walk through it, would this…dream or vision or illusion end? Or would he?

Grimacing, he pushed his way forward.

It was a fine parlour, the furnishings of highest quality, if a bit overdecorated. There, on an ornately gilded settee, sat Elizabeth Bennet, a sewing basket by her side. Head bent, she stitched a delicate linen with an intricate pattern of ivory on white.

How he knew it was *her*, he could not say. Though he had not yet seen her face, he knew she was no longer young. A neat cap covered her dark hair, but escaping curls were dusted with grey, and the fingers carefully handling the fabric bore some marks of aging. Even so, know her he did, and he knew she was beautiful, still.

She looked up then and proved it—her fine eyes, large and slightly atilt; her lips, perfectly shaped; her chin, ever determined. In her late forties, perhaps, she was nevertheless handsome, for hers was a beauty that would never fade. His heart caught in his throat as her eyes met his…but hers slid past him to something or someone behind him.

Was he to see her husband, the fortunate man who had won her heart, her respect, her hand? Or a sweet, dark-haired granddaughter, coming to sit beside her grandmama?

Instead, a tiny woman, stick-thin, entered. Her face was inscrutable and wrinkled like a dried apple—she could have been a century old. Elizabeth hurried to her side. The woman regally gave Elizabeth her arm, allowing her to guide her into a chair. Elizabeth busied herself positioning her footstool and quietly asking whether she wished for a tea tray, which was refused. She returned to her seat in the ensuing silence.

Elizabeth did not take up the sewing she had set aside. Hands folded neatly in her lap, she simply observed the other woman. After about ten minutes, the smaller woman murmured something in such a low voice that, despite the quietness of the room, Darcy failed to hear. Elizabeth rose, rearranged the screen to the woman's satisfaction, and resumed her seat once more, folding her hands again upon her lap.

And that was all. Darcy was utterly perplexed. While he could happily, he discovered, gaze upon Elizabeth Bennet for a dozen years without growing bored, the utter stillness was the opposite of her nature. For her, tramping merrily across woods and fields, reading a good book and discussing it with another, or—as she had been when he entered—stitching some pretty needlework, were her usual occupations. She was an excellent and witty conversationalist, gregarious and convivial without volubility. This studied taciturnity was incredible, and certainly must have been difficult for one formerly so energetic.

"Miss Elizabeth, please, tell me how you have fared," Darcy begged. But neither woman heard. After a time, he simply sat on the settee beside her. Although to his observation, the cushion compressed with his weight, and he was so near he could feel the heat from her body, she, plainly, had no idea of his presence.

He was uncertain how to proceed. If neither would talk, there seemed little else to be discovered. And so, he...simply sat. Had someone told him that he would so easily and gladly agree to remain beside another in silence, without acknowledgement, without knowing how long it might be before he could leave or speak, he might have called them foolish. But he had thought he would never see Elizabeth again, and though he longed to hear her voice, he had *missed* her. No longer could he remember why it had seemed so urgent to distance himself from her. Rather, it had been an honour and privilege to be counted within her circle of acquaintance.

I have been stupid. Stupid and short-sighted. Blind.

After many minutes of observation, however, he determined that Elizabeth was not quite so still, and certainly not as at ease, as he had first believed. Though her hands were folded in her lap, her knuckles were white as she squeezed them together. Her eyes blinked rapidly, as if she restrained tears.

"What is the matter, dearest?" he asked gently, even knowing she could not hear him. She waited there with an almost desperate inertia as the minutes ticked slowly by. Finally, a clock somewhere struck eight chimes. As if it were a signal, Elizabeth stood and moved the tiny lady's footstool, then helped her to her feet.

"Miss de Bourgh," she said quietly. "I wonder whether you would permit me to take myself to London on the early post tomorrow to visit my sister Jane, to be returned by evening. Dawson will be here, of course, and I would be back to Rosings by dinner. As you might remember, I have been unable to see my family in over a year, due to your last illness. For the day only."

Anne? This tiny, ancient figure was Anne? Why, she was his own age! Even if Elizabeth were fifty years, Anne would be fifty-seven—aging, certainly, but not in her dotage. Had a lifetime of potions and pills ruined her health? Of course, she had never had much health to speak of. And Elizabeth—dearest, loveliest Elizabeth—was her *companion*? The best woman in England had replaced Ida Jenkinson?

While he had been thinking these incredulous thoughts, Elizabeth waited patiently for Anne's reply. The tension in her shoulders and the lift of her chin showed the depth of her concern for what it would be.

"Abandon me for your sister's company if you must, but do not bother returning if you do. Mrs Jenkinson's youngest niece has written again. She has been pestering me for a position this age. I shall send someone to the village to fetch her in the morning."

For one moment, and one moment only, he saw Elizabeth's despair. And then it vanished, her answer as smooth as if nothing had ever occurred to distress her.

"There is no need for it, Miss de Bourgh. Of course I shall not go if you do not wish it. Oh, and your cousin, the earl, has sent another letter, asking to be permitted a short visit. He and his wife are in town, and hope you will allow them to come, for even a brief call, on Christmas Day." She spoke evenly, no hint of her disappointment in her well-modulated tone—yet he knew she adored her sister. To sacrifice all visitation for a *year,* perhaps more?

How long had it taken her to learn to hide any hint of feeling?

"You know I do not see my family. It is out of the question."

What was this?

"Very good, ma'am. I will write your answer to the earl."

"There has been entirely too much chatter this evening. It has given me a megrim. Call Dawson to bring my tonic before you retire."

Elizabeth curtseyed, nodded, and trailed her out of the room.

Darcy could only remain where he was in open-mouthed astonishment. Apparently, silence was a requirement of his cousin's employ. Rather, not a total silence, but a complete subservience, without benefit of ladylike occupations, such as sewing, allowed in her presence. Was Elizabeth not even given a half-day off, without threat of losing her position? Anne's family—which included himself, no doubt—was not permitted to visit? Was *anyone*? Did she wait upon his sickly, fractious cousin without company or entertainment of any kind? Plainly, she had waited all day to ask her meagre favour, only to be refused. Did she weep now in her lonely bed? Why would Elizabeth remain in such dreadful circumstances?

There was only one answer. Miss Elizabeth's father must have died; her mother's fears of the hedgerows had been realised. Elizabeth *must* have had offers—she was too intelligent, too desirable not to have. No, she had accepted this position because it met other needs. Anne must pay—and pay exceedingly well—for such attendance from such a person. If Mrs Bennet yet lived, or any sisters remained unwed, Elizabeth's pay would be stretched to include whatever necessities her family required. Perhaps Anne even enjoyed keeping Elizabeth—who, though in many ways her peer, was her exact opposite, possessing every gift fate had failed to bestow in her own case—thus imprisoned and dependent.

He felt sickened.

"Collins!" he yelled. "Collins!"

And there the vicar sat, in the overstuffed chair so recently vacated by Anne de Bourgh, his face a study in innocence.

"What is this?" Darcy shouted. "Who are you? *Why you?*"

"I consider the clerical office as equal in point of consideration and comprehension with the highest rank in the kingdom. You must therefore allow me to follow the dictates of my conscience on this occasion, which leads me to perform what I look on as a point of duty."

"You talk and you talk," Darcy interpolated bitterly, "but with every word spoken, you say less."

"It is required of every man," the vicar continued as if unaware of the interruption, his tone pontificating, "that the spirit within him should walk abroad amongst his fellow men and travel far and wide, and if that spirit goes not forth in life, it shrivels, it shrinks, it withers. I have permitted you to witness those with whom you would *not* share your better self. You *might* have shared, might even have turned those experiences to happiness, theirs or perhaps your own. I am *your* spirit, a haughty figure of pride and conceit only *you* could have created. Your contempt for me is obvious, and yet—though sick of civility, deference, and officious attention—you snub and reject the first person refusing to pay that approbation which so disgusts you."

Darcy's fists clenched in rage and frustration. "What nonsense! Courtesy of *you*, I have witnessed a grim future in which the Bennets never met me! But they *have* met me! You know they have! I demand you show me what has changed!"

For a moment, the phantom vicar only looked at him, his expression both imperious and impassive. But at last, he spoke. "Why, nothing has changed at all, good sir," he replied coolly. "*You did not stay.*"

And he vanished.

It was with a sense of near anguish that Darcy wondered what awful scenes he would next behold.

However, and much to his great relief, he suddenly found himself within a reassuringly familiar passageway at Pemberley—just before the door of the gold salon. It was his least favourite of the many parlours in the great house, but he had never had it redone because it had been his mother's especial favourite. The door was ajar, and he gladly walked through it, grateful to be in a recognisable location.

The room was large and ornately decorated in gilt and shades of gold. *Not gaudy,* he thought, staring at it critically, *but rather uselessly fine; there is nothing welcoming or comfortable, and those chairs are the very devil if one must sit for any length of time.* A man and woman were seated before the fire, their backs to him, one on either side of the hearth like a matched set of bookends. He could not tell who they were, only that they were elderly, judging by their silvered hair.

The man stood, walking forward to lean against the chimney-piece, and Darcy's heart leapt in his chest. "Father!" he cried aloud. Of course, he ought to have expected no answer—and he did not, truly—but he gazed upon him with moistened eyes. Here was the man he had, for so long, honoured and revered. Also, this time, in this vision, Darcy was no silly six-year-old, locked into the memories and actions of his childish self.

And yet, there was something…off. The man appeared to be an inch or two taller than Father, for one thing. For another, his father's hair had been thinning in those final years, and this man's hair was thick, still, with a bit of curl. Then the man looked directly at him, and it was like looking into the mirror at an older version of himself. It *was* himself, perhaps forty years hence.

"I have accepted the invitation to the Cavanaugh ball," said the woman, whose face was still hidden from him. "I shall buy a new dress for the affair, as Lady Markham is sure to attend, and her pride in her dressmaker is too, too ridiculous. Madame Marchand is quite superior in every respect, and her laces are directly from the Loire Valley, you know. Why, I could not believe Sir Henry complimented her ladyship's ensemble so baldly, when everyone knows she merely copied the marchioness's pattern with an inferior fabric."

In this manner, the woman rattled on. Darcy studied his elder self curiously. His eyes were…empty. He pretended to mind the woman's words in a jaded, world-weary sort of manner, although it was obvious most of his attention resided elsewhere. However, he did nothing to take charge of the situation or attempt to turn the conversation. Plainly, no answer was required to any of these insipid observations, nor did he attempt any, not even a grunt of agreement or disapproval.

The topic of fashion being exorcised, the woman moved on to the doings of her neighbours. "It is said that Mr Ringleton is fascinated by the sister of his nephew's wife. I never could understand what he sees in Mrs Ringleton, when he could have married anyone." In blunt terms, she gave an intimate recital of the 'facts' of their marriage as she understood them, including several no one ought ever to have said aloud.

"Stop her from speaking!" he shouted at himself. "Whether true or false, it is all appalling, demeaning, and unfortunate!" But his elder self simply stood there, propped by the hearth like a fire iron.

Perhaps I have gone deaf, he thought with a forlorn sense of hope as she continued to spew vitriol and venom, foolishness and folly.

"Fitzwilliam, are you listening to me? I asked you whether you sent your regrets to Lord Butterfield. You cannot possibly go hunting on the weekend of Sir Percy's fete."

"Yes, madam," he replied. Since the woman had not shouted to make herself heard, he must conclude that he was indeed aware of her prattle.

The truth was obvious: he had become, simply, irrelevant.

This, then, was the summit and summary of his personal life—all of it lived with some jewel of the *ton*, her head empty of anything of importance. Had she entrapped him with her arts and allurements? Had he been tempted by her fortune and connexions? And, most of all, did he know her now, or would he be able to recognise her elderly self? He could change, at least, this much of his future, could he not?

Taking a deep breath, he strode to a position where he could see her face. And stopped short.

He would, most likely, recognise Caroline Bingley were she a hundred—she had always been handsome, and was stately in appearance, still.

But he had *never* had any feeling for her, no attraction beyond a basic appreciation of face and figure, and no desire, *ever*, to join her life with his.

Why had he done this thing? What possible reason could he have had for marrying a woman with whom he shared no affection, no liking, or any deeper emotion—and what was more, no possible chance of it ever kindling?

The answer came to him between one breath and the next.

He had not cared, because his heart was dead. The organ that beat in his chest might function, but there was no feeling, no depth, no sensitivity, no compassion nor vitality within the blood it carried to his body. And he knew, with every fibre of his being, just who was responsible for murdering it.

He had killed it himself.

FIVE

"If it be thus to dream, still let me sleep!"

— *Sebastian, Twelfth Night Act 4*

Arthur Pennywithers had valeted with Fitzwilliam Darcy for over five years, and had never been dissatisfied with his position. Mr Darcy was neither unpleasant nor unkind, a liberal employer who treated him fairly. Beyond this, being both agreeably fine-looking and of considerable stature, Mr Darcy looked well in whatever attire was chosen for him—a definite credit to Arthur's standing.

In the last several days, however, Arthur had cause for concern. Circles beneath his employer's eyes bespoke sleepless nights, and his attention to detail—always superior—suffered. As he entered his master's bedchamber at dawn's early light, he hoped to find him resting peacefully.

At first, he believed the wish fulfilled. However, abruptly, Mr Darcy sat straight up in bed, gasping, his eyes wild; without warning, he nearly leapt from the mattress, swivelling round as if being attacked from all sides. As Pennywithers looked on in some dismay, his employer ran to the mirror, peering within as if he expected to see a different face, scrubbing his hands through his sleep-mussed hair.

"I believe you are a bit young to be concerned about your hair colour, sir," he offered.

Mr Darcy jumped a little, but upon recognition, asked frantically, "What day is it?"

Plainly, some awful dream had disoriented him. "Tuesday, sir."

"What date? What year?"

This response showed worse than the effects of a simple dream. Perhaps he had contracted a fever?

"Are you feeling well, sir? Ought I to call the apothecary?"

"Please, man, answer the question."

Arthur could not help the rise of his brows—or the slight sarcasm—inspired by his master's fervour. "It is the twenty-fourth of December, year of our Lord eighteen hundred eleven."

Then, completely beyond any expectation, Mr Darcy…chuckled. He was not, and never had been, a chuckling sort of fellow.

"Excellent! Astonishing! I have not missed it. The dreams have done it all in one night. Or was it angels? Of course it was—they can do what they like. Send word to Miss Darcy, if you would—we shall be making a journey to Hertfordshire. She should dress warmly." But then his face fell. "Oh—rather—Pennywithers, do you have family in town?"

Arthur's alarm grew at this unusual stream of volubility from his solemn employer. "I–I have a brother, sir."

"I wish to go to Hertfordshire—and at once. Bingley will travel with us as well, I believe. However, I completely understand if you need time. Time to spend with your family, that is. You and Miss Darcy's maid will take the brougham but may wait a few days to follow us. I am certain we can make do without you for a short while, until your Christmas celebrations are past."

At this shocking offer, Arthur wondered how expeditiously the family physician might be summoned. He could only imagine what Miss Darcy's maid, the indefatigable Alice, would say to leaving her charge to 'make do'. "I am afraid I do not understand you, sir."

"It is Christmas Eve, Pennywithers! What is to understand?" He clapped the valet on the shoulders. "And a new day! A new, wonderful and fortunate day!"

"I knew you ought not to have ridden yesterday. You have taken a chill. I shall call the physician." He played his trump card. "You would not like for Miss Darcy to catch whatever it is that ails you."

But Mr Darcy only chuckled again. "Pennywithers, my good man, there is nothing in the world so irresistibly contagious as laughter and good humour. I *pray* I am catching and *she* is infected! And yourself, as well!"

What had happened to the grave, somewhat dull and fastidious gentleman—who rarely smiled and never laughed—whom he had put to bed the night before? It took some moments for Pennywithers to recover enough to reply, but there was never any doubt in his mind as to what his answer would be.

"My brother's is a bachelor household, sir, and cannot be depended upon for much in the way of Christmas festivities. I will accompany you wherever you decide to go, if it pleases."

"Yes, sir. 'Tis naught but a bit of damp, sir, and 'appy I am to do it, and anything else ye've a mind to 'ave fetched today! Thank ye, sir!" The footman practically danced out the door in his eagerness to accomplish the requested errand, although the weather was something more than 'a bit of damp'. Darcy felt somewhat guilty about sending his people out into it, even though he had provided extra compensation for the trouble. Besides which, the entire household had received their Christmas stipends a day early—with an additional guinea besides—and thus the general mood could be described as remarkably cheerful, despite the expresses to be sent, trunks to be packed, and the Darcy vehicles to be made ready for immediate travel.

Darcy had never been wished such enthusiastic 'Merry Christmas!' salutations in all his life, and he was gladdened by it. Still, as his sister walked slowly towards him down the spiral staircase, he was somewhat uncertain what to say to her. The phantom dreams—*spirits?*—of the night before had never revealed any of his sister's future; he had no idea what he ought to do. He only knew he must lead with his heart.

"Happy Christmas, my dear sister," he said, as soon as she reached him.

"It is not yet Christmas Day," she said, plainly puzzled by his mood.

"It is not so much the day, as the reason for it," he replied, handing her the jewellery box containing their mother's precious pearls. "A present for you, dearest." He had destroyed the note written the day before, exchanging it for another saying only 'I know our mother loved you, and would have been honoured to see you wear these. You are a credit to us both.'

She took the box, read the note with tear-filled eyes, viewed the pearls with admiration, and clutched them to her, thanking him profusely. Yet, her attitude of perplexity clearly remained. "What is this

I hear about a journey to Hertfordshire?" she asked quietly, once they sat alone together in the gold parlour.

He did not answer her immediately, peering around at the formality and fineness of the room. The cushions were stiff and uncomfortable; one did not dare slouch. It reminded him of the gold salon at Pemberley. "You know, I feel we should redecorate this parlour. Something brighter, more welcoming. I think yellow instead of gold, with simpler, more comfortable furnishings."

His sister shook her head, and finally, after days of hardly speaking at all, expressed her bewilderment. "I have never seen you in such a state, Brother. Alice and Pennywithers are in a packing frenzy. Not only are you more cheerful than I have ever before noted, but you have been distributing guineas as if they were roasted chestnuts! And now, you talk of redecorating?" She coloured at her own words, plainly regretting her candour. "I beg your pardon. It is only I have never seen you take an interest in furnishings, and though you have always been generous… much more quietly so."

He smiled. "What your brother has been is a great fool, and he wishes, very much, to attempt to undo some of the tangle he has made of his life while staying at Bingley's leased estate, Netherfield Park."

Her brows rose. "I cannot believe you were ever foolish in your life, even when a child."

"I am certain I had a good deal more sense as a child than I have demonstrated in recent years. The realisation has made me reconsider many things, and hence I have asked for a good deal of extra effort from many, at a time when I usually ask little. Thus, a few extra coins," he replied, shrugging.

"Much more than a few. And I have always thought you the epitome of what every gentleman should be," she protested loyally.

He gazed at her fondly. "Were you under the mistaken impression that I am a perfect being, destined for sainthood? Perhaps I do have a short way to go before being canonised." He laughed, while her expression grew ever more baffled at this teasing. He never teased. He was resolved to tease her at least once per day until she could match Miss Elizabeth for insouciance, but, taking pity on her apparent alarm, he clasped her hand in his.

"I do need to go, dearest, and at once. I would not like to leave you in London, and I sincerely hope you will accompany me, but I must warn you—George Wickham is in Meryton, the area to which I travel."

"Oh no!" she whispered, paling.

"Oh yes. You will not see him, not if I can prevent it. But go, I must, even so. Can you be brave and come with me? Please?"

Thus it was that Georgiana Darcy found herself heading out on a cold winter's day towards the location of the one man on earth whom she had hoped to never see nor hear of again. Her brother's mood was both confounding and disconcerting, but she could not leave him to do alone whatever it was that he felt must be done—he had never before begged for her company.

After he had secured her agreement, he had gone to Mr Hurst's town house to speak to Mr Bingley; whatever he had said there had caused *that* gentleman so much agitation that he could not even bring himself to ride in their carriage, despite the frigid temperatures.

"I do hope the weather will not worsen," she said quietly, as she lost sight of Mr Bingley's figure on horseback. "I would not like him to take a chill."

"Mr Bingley's hopes are high enough to thaw him through a snowstorm," her brother replied, unconcerned. "If only I were as certain of a warm reception."

She finally noticed it then—beneath his unusually cheerful exterior, a very real discomposure of spirits, and she brought herself to question him.

"Will you tell me what troubles you, Fitzwilliam? What…foolishness you spoke of, that you feel you must put right?"

It was usual for him to discount such enquiries—and she could certainly not think of a time when he had ever confided any troubles to *her*. She could barely believe she had summoned the temerity to ask. But to her surprise, he regarded her seriously.

"My natural inclination is to be a selfish man," he said, forestalling her protest with a quickly raised hand. "I have been in the habit of caring little for any beyond my own acquaintance, frequently devaluing the sense and worth of others. That habit did not change, even when I met someone…extraordinary. Someone whose family circumstances are not as comfortable as ours, yet who looks at life with superior sense, humour, and liveliness. It did not change, although she is everything I could want in my life's companion—everything I could want for you, in a sister."

"You are in *love*?" she asked, astonished.

"I am, I trust," he replied seriously. "However, I have not behaved as a man in love ought."

"I will not believe it possible that you could act wrongly. I cannot fathom it."

He patted her hand. "I appreciate your loyalty, dear sister. But no, I tell you truly. I informed you that Wickham is there—stationed with his regiment in Meryton, the nearest village to Netherfield. As you can imagine, there is no good feeling between us, and he has set out to do what damage he can to my reputation. What lies, specifically, he has spread about me, I know not, but that he *has* spoken them is certain. Of course, I would never expose you by revealing his unworthy behaviour towards you, but I also thought it beneath me to confront *anything* he said. What is more, he has made himself a friend to my…my beloved and her family, while I have never bothered to try to establish a connexion of any kind. I left the county without warning her father of the shades in Wickham's character. Mr Bennet has five daughters, without any fortune to tempt an honourable proposal from the reprobate. I mean to correct his standing with them, at least."

Georgiana sat transfixed with amazement at this confession. She could not, however, blame Fitzwilliam for ignoring George, even in the face of attempts to besmirch his honour. "It is understandable that you should refuse to speak of such a villain."

"Not when others could be hurt by my silence."

"That is all you mean to do? Warn them? Will you not court the lady?" she dared ask him.

"I cannot, not yet, I fear," he replied soberly. "I am afraid that I have given no good impression of my own character. For now, I will inform Mr Bennet of the snake in the grass—without involving your name, I promise. Mr Bingley is determined to ask for the hand of his eldest daughter, Miss Jane Bennet. It is to be hoped that I will have opportunities in the future to lessen her sister's ill opinion of me and show, by every civility in my power, that I understand how to please a woman worthy of being pleased."

He smiled at her then, with a full and genuine affection, losing the furrow between his brows. "I hope that I can overcome the worst of my mistakes. But even if I have ruined my chances, I can see my course. She shall never be left in doubt of my friendship." He reached across again to clasp her hands. "Do you not see, my sweet sister? Today is a new day. All of the preceding ones are forever in the past, and our mistakes are gone with them. We shall make others, of course, but upon every awakening to a new sunrise, we gain a new opportunity. Another chance to change, to grow, to learn, even if only a tiny bit. To make things better for those around us, even if we cannot make things better, quite yet, for ourselves."

"My past mistakes are heavy indeed," she said, biting her lip.

He shook his head. "I disagree, most emphatically, but what *I* think does not matter. If you wish to give that churl more of your attention, more of your sorrow, and more of your precious heart, I cannot stop you. I will only pray that, in time, you will learn to look upon the past only as it gives you pleasure to do so, coming to see yourself as I see you: lovely, intelligent, good-humoured Georgiana Darcy, who has entirely too much sense to squander another moment on regrets."

And then he winked at her. Winked!

❋

They barely stayed at Netherfield long enough to change their travel clothing. Mr Bingley, who had, of course, arrived first, was beyond anxious to present himself at Longbourn.

One of the morning's earliest couriers had fortunately been sent to Netherfield's housekeeper, Mrs Nicholls, who had everything in readiness. Thanks to Darcy's largesse, it was also an extremely merry household, offering many expressions of gratitude—all of which were waved off by the giver.

Once arrived at Longbourn and introductions completed, the small group was greeted enthusiastically by the mother, loudly by the two youngest, decorously by the three eldest, and acerbically by the father.

His newfound humility rendered the rather overwhelmingly jubilant greetings from Mrs Bennet easily borne. She was Elizabeth's mother, and deserving of his best behaviour. Somewhat more difficult to bear was her habit of spilling out everything inside her head for the edification of her listeners.

"It is a long time, Mr Bingley, since you went away," she cried. "I began to be afraid you would never come back again. Miss Bingley did say you meant to quit the place entirely, but I was certain she must be mistaken, for you agreed to come for dinner, and you would not forget. You remember, of course, Miss Bennet. I am sure you see how little altered she is since you were last here—her complexion so brilliant, her eyes so extraordinary."

This time, however, Darcy caught how Miss Bennet, her cheeks pinkening, immediately retreated into herself.

How stupid I have been! he thought. *She does not dare show* any *affectionate display, for fear of worsening her mother's enthusiastic outpourings*.

"I do not think there is a prettier girl in the country, though I *am* her mother!" Mrs Bennet continued. "I see the flaws in my daughters for what they are. Lizzy's nose wants character, and her teeth are nothing out of the common way, as I am certain you have noticed. Whereas Jane—"

But that his beloved should be publicly criticised was not to be tolerated from anyone, parent or not. Despite his embarrassment and what would doubtless be hers, his tongue could not be restrained. "For my own part, it is many weeks since I have considered Miss Elizabeth as unequalled, in appearance or deportment, by any lady of my acquaintance."

The room fell utterly silent. He glanced at Elizabeth who looked... flabbergasted. But the high spirits of Lydia Bennet came into usefulness as she giggled. "Next, Mama, you will be telling us that she is no better than Mary King, that nasty little freckled thing. Have you heard? She is gone down to her uncle in Liverpool!"

The whereabouts of Mary King was of great interest to Mrs Bennet and the next-youngest sister, while another Bennet sister—Mary, he thought—berated Miss Lydia for coarseness of expression. Amid the rather exuberant effusions that followed, he noticed Mr Bennet did nothing to rein in his progeny, never mind his wife.

Darcy could not look at Elizabeth beyond the briefest of glances, however, for fear of what would be in his face—and on hers. His feelings were a maelstrom of emotion—vast relief, that his mistakes concerning her would not be permanent, followed by a deep sense of grief and guilt that he had not behaved as the man he knew he should have been, perhaps destroying forever any chance for atonement.

And joy, oh yes, that too. Joyfully admitting his love for her, if only to himself, had given him a clarity like naught else. He could not expect anything except contempt from her as yet—he *deserved* nothing better. But all future decisions were to be based upon a fundamental principle: What was best for Elizabeth? Which made his next actions simple, if not easy.

"Excuse me, sir. I wonder whether I might have a private word with you?"

Mr Bennet agreed, but they were barely behind the closed door of his book room before he manifested his negative assumptions.

"What is this, Mr Darcy? Having been unable to prevent your friend from exercising discretion, did you tag along to warn me of how censured, slighted, and despised my eldest daughter will be by everyone connected with him if I wilfully act against your inclinations?"

My reputation is even worse than I believed! Darcy thought with astonishment. It had been, perhaps, ill-mannered of Bennet to say it, but if this was the contempt in which he was held, he could hardly blame the man. It was more important than ever to inform him of the true source of danger.

"I assure you, sir, if Mr Bingley is able to win your daughter's regard, he will be the most fortunate of men. It is upon a different matter I must needs beg your attention."

Huffing, Mr Bennet waved him into the chair opposite his own desk. Unsurprisingly, he was not offered any refreshment.

"My attention is now yours," Bennet said formally, with no sign that his approval of Bingley's suit had any effect. "Pray tell me what so urgently requires it."

Darcy took a deep breath and began. "I am aware of rumours regarding my having injured Mr Wickham. I can only refute them by laying before you the whole of his connexion with my family. Of what he has particularly accused me, I am ignorant, but of the truth of what I shall relate, I can summon more than one witness of undoubted veracity." He then proceeded to explain such particulars of his father's bequest, Wickham's rejection of it, his subsequent payment for it, and Wickham's indignation when the living was thereafter refused his possession. Of course, he could not explain the revenge Wickham had attempted or the sorrow of his sister, and unfortunately, Mr Bennet felt no particular respect for his word.

"This appears to be a case of misunderstanding," Bennet proclaimed, plainly unwilling to give Darcy the benefit of any doubt.

"Was it misunderstanding when he took the money my father provided for him to further his education and spent it on wine and wenching? When he has left a trail of fatherless children in his wake, whether or not their mothers were willing? Ask your neighbours to whom he owes his markers! They will never see a penny returned."

"What is this? Surely not!"

Though he avoided bringing his sister's name into his earnest explanations, he related many other particulars. When he reached the end of such revelations as he could admit, Darcy scrubbed his hands through his hair, forcibly calming himself. "Mr Bennet, I can assist any who are hurt financially by him, but we both know there are injuries which can never be recompensed. I promise you, he is most capable of inflicting these wrongs. I apologise for bringing you such a sorry report during the Festive Season."

Mr Bennet only nodded. Darcy paused, and then, to that gentleman's great astonishment, confessed his hope of courting Miss Elizabeth. The notion had preoccupied him since his arrival. He had not lied to Georgiana; as things stood, it would be foolish to pursue Elizabeth, and much smarter to wait and hope time would reveal to her his true character. Yet, when he had seen her for the first time that morning, his heart had leapt within his chest, and he knew that given any opportunity, his feelings were unlikely to be repressed. It was only proper that he warn her father and beg his permission, if not his approval.

Of course, Mr Bennet was surprised and not overjoyed to hear of it. "I suppose I must give you my consent. You are the kind of man, indeed, to whom I should never dare refuse anything which you condescend to ask. But I warn you now, I shall advise her to think carefully on it. I know her disposition. I know that she could be neither happy nor respectable unless she truly esteems her husband. Riches can never compensate for misery."

It was a blow. Darcy absorbed it.

"I promise, sir, that unless I am certain she *could* care for me, I will not ask her to." He stood, offering a bow, and Bennet rose and returned the acknowledgement.

"Thank you, Mr Darcy," he said solemnly, his face expressionless.

Darcy departed with no idea whether Bennet would believe or discount his honest reports, or whether his reputation remained compromised. *Have these confessions been enough? What more could I have said? Or did I say too much?*

Georgiana had been the only one of the party not particularly eager to visit the bastion of the Bennets. She knew that Fitzwilliam would not require it of her, yet she was curious to see the woman 'worthy of being pleased'. His words—'*every awakening to a new sunrise, we gain a new opportunity*'—struck her again. She was certain that as of yesterday, he had still been disappointed in her. And yet, his note of this morning had been charity itself. Had their aunt's sudden death caused his sudden change of heart?

Longbourn was a pretty property, nicely situated, and while not at all modern, like Rosings Park or even Netherfield, it wore its age well. Mr Bingley's love for the golden-haired Miss Bennet was soon apparent, but it was no less obvious than Mrs Bennet's rather overwhelming admiration for him. Her brother somehow contrived to go away with Mr Bennet into the latter's book room, and Georgiana, feeling very bashful and out of place, tried to make herself as unnoticeable as possible. But she was not long left to her own devices.

"I have heard much of your talent at the pianoforte from Miss Bingley," Miss Elizabeth said, sitting beside her and smiling in a friendly manner.

Georgiana immediately coloured, for Miss Bingley could be so complimentary as to create an excessive expectation in any listeners who heard her fervour. "I am, um, perhaps, not so proficient as she, um, may have implied."

Miss Elizabeth grinned. "Oh, I am certain no one could be. You might be a prodigy and still not be as nimble-fingered as Miss Bingley claims. Nevertheless, I would be delighted to hear you play."

Georgiana could not resist Miss Elizabeth's smile, nor the relief she felt when they went together into another, much smaller parlour that held the instrument. It was quieter, and distanced from the gathered, more enthusiastic company in the larger drawing room.

"We keep the pianoforte in here so that my sister Mary may practise undisturbed," she explained, still smiling.

Georgiana found this a bit unusual. How could Mary entertain her family and guests with the instrument so far from any company? Nevertheless, she played a short piece for which she needed no music, and her audience of one was kindly complimentary, even asking her a question regarding a difficult passage and saying she had attempted it previously without success. Together they worked on it as a duet, and Georgiana almost forgot to be shy as Miss Elizabeth triumphantly declared a victory when they mastered it.

When Fitzwilliam had declared her 'unequalled, in appearance or deportment, by any lady of his acquaintance', she had been certain that Elizabeth *must* be the woman whom her brother admired, and whom he believed he had failed. In the moment he said it, Georgiana had been somewhat surprised. While Miss Elizabeth was pretty, she was not classically so, and not even so much as her sisters. Her mouth was wide rather than rosebud, her chin a bit sharp, her eyes large in her face, and her hair dark rather than golden. But now, after perhaps half an hour in her company, Georgiana was beginning to understand why he found her so pleasing.

Her smile was warm and genuine; she had immediately perceived Georgiana's shyness and set out to make her comfortable. Those large eyes sparkled with intelligence and good humour. It was so easy to be with her, even when easiness was not a talent one possessed!

I love my brother. He loves her. She is vulnerable to Wickham's lies, as was I. What is my pride in comparison?

"Miss Elizabeth," she began, unable to prevent the rather desperate pitch to her voice, "I saw there seemed to be a prettyish kind of a little wilderness on one side of your lawn. I know it is cold out, and I do apologise, but...I should be glad to take a turn in it, if you will favour me with your company?"

❄

Darcy emerged from the prolonged and difficult conversation with Mr Bennet feeling very subdued. It was such a shock, learning just how severely damaged his reputation in this community was, although he *should* have known it. *Could* have known it, had he bothered to pay attention. Worst of all, he was not completely certain he had been believed, although he had relayed numerous details—many humiliatingly personal—of Wickham's cruelties and viciousness, and even after giving Bennet the direction of his cousin, Colonel Fitzwilliam, so that he might have a witness of unarguable reputation with whom to verify Darcy's words.

At that moment, and to his surprise, his sister and Elizabeth entered the house from the large vestibule opposite him, obviously having just come in from the out of doors—their noses red and a footman collecting their wraps. Startled, he looked from one to the other. Georgiana smiled at him, fully, for the first time in recent memory. And Elizabeth...Elizabeth looked at him with such compassion, such kindness in her lovely eyes, that he immediately knew his sister's secrets were revealed. He did not know what to say or how to act.

But Elizabeth did. "I do hope you all will stay to dinner. Mama sets a fine table, which has been elevated to *extraordinary* in honour of Christmas Eve."

Darcy felt his own smile spreading across his face, suffusing his soul. "We accept your invitation, and with the deepest appreciation." He bowed. It was all he could do not to throw himself at her feet.

SIX

All days are nights to see till I see thee
And nights bright days when dreams do show me thee.

— *Shakespeare, Sonnet 43*

December 24, 1811

Lizzy hardly knew how to feel. Had anyone asked her yesterday whether she would enjoy sharing a meal with Mr Bingley's solemn houseguest, she would have laughed! Had she not giggled with Charlotte, titling him the 'Disapproving Detractor from Derbyshire'? Had she not lumped him in with Miss Bingley after that lady's horrid letter to Jane, wherein she blamed *him* for their sudden departure from Netherfield? Yet here he was at their noisy, merry dinner, receiving occasional sidelong glances from Mrs Bennet—who was, thankfully, just a bit too obsessed with poor Jane and Bingley to voice even an eighth of her hopefulness in his direction.

His sister—deemed 'proud' by that horrid Lieutenant Wickham—was touchingly sweet and terribly shy. Even now, she looked a bit overwhelmed as Kitty and Lydia peppered her with questions regarding her dressmaker, the latest London entertainments, and her opinions on gothic novels, hardly allowing her time to answer before they offered their own. Why had she chosen to reveal such secrets as she possessed to Lizzy?

Why had Mr Darcy declared her 'unequalled' before her entire family? Most likely, he thought her mother's open criticism coarse, and meant it as a kindly correction.

He could not have meant it in any other way! Had he not looked upon her, indeed all her family, with the most fervent disapproval? Did he not hate her? It seemed far too great of an about-turn to think of him as…as a *suitor*!

And yet, how differently did everything now appear in which he was concerned! Poor Miss Darcy, to have been subjected to such villainous treatment! Poor Mr Darcy, distraught as any caring brother and guardian would be, only to be further exposed to slander and disparagement by that same scoundrel!

Her father, who customarily used every opportunity to practise his wit upon visitors, had been silent and rather morose throughout the meal. Hopefully, he was now reconsidering his lackadaisical permissiveness towards her youngest sisters, and all suggestions pertaining to following the regiment once they departed the area would be vetoed.

After the ladies excused themselves from the dinner table, the gentlemen rejoined them in a gratifyingly short time. Elizabeth could not keep her gaze from drifting towards Mr Darcy, but he made no move to take a place beside her. Not that it would be easily done—in her mother's efforts to position Jane and Mr Bingley to her liking, she had stuffed Lizzy well-nigh into a corner between Kitty and Mary. Mr Darcy hovered protectively near his sister, saying little. Still, he returned her look once or twice, just often enough that she thought he *might* wish to at least exchange a word or two. Every time that she made an attempt to rearrange her own seating, however, her mother spoilt her plans, having her refill her cup, or her father's, or entreat Mrs Hill to bring more biscuits—was she purposely keeping her apart from him? Then she laughed at herself. Her mother would never consciously separate her from such an eligible male, even if she hated him. As she had already proven.

A wave of frustration followed. Why was it so difficult to learn what was in a man's heart? Of course, it had been simplicity itself to know Mr Collins; he wore his essence in plain sight, never disguising his avarice or his sense of self-importance. But she had been completely deceived by Lieutenant Wickham's false charms; why should she believe she had any insight whatsoever into the males of the species?

I cannot trust my own judgment. By leaving the room to speak to Mrs Hill, however, she had changed her position within it. Before she knew it, Mr Darcy stood directly before her.

"There is an evening service tonight, is there not? We would be pleased to drive you, if you care to attend."

Lizzy, her head just then full of puzzled musings on the nature of men, answered without thinking. "Oh, we have the sledge take us, two or three at a time—it is a family tradition, and not at all an efficient mode of travel."

"It sounds perfectly wonderful," he said—a little wistfully, she thought.

"Do you think so?" she asked, genuinely curious.

Thus it was that Lizzy found herself driving with Fitzwilliam Darcy, once considered the most staid and serious of gentlemen, in Longbourn's cutter-style sleigh to the Christmas Eve service, squeezed between him and Georgiana, with the siblings' delighted laughter ringing in the air as he—perhaps flaunting his excellent hand at the reins, just a bit—whisked them to the little church in Meryton.

It so happened that the evening featured a Christmas pageant performed by the village schoolchildren. Lizzy was filled with compassion for the harried schoolmistress when the goat escaped the stable yard scene, only to begin chewing on the particularly delicious wing of an angel—causing said angel to burst into tears until the angel's brother drove the goat away. The three kings in moth-eaten robes presented their gifts to a fretting infant, who, not caring particularly for frankincense and myrrh during what was doubtless his mealtime, set up a hue and cry fit to shout down a noticeably unconfident young narrator. Lizzy thought, perhaps, that the casting might have gone amiss, for mother Mary—the elder sister of said babe—could not have been more than nine years at most, and was completely unequal to the task of shushing him.

It appeared that his cries might bring the performance to an early finish. However, in a quick act of costuming, Lizzy flung her shawl over her head and joined the performers as a new character in the Holy Family: the baby Jesus's nurserymaid. Swiftly, she quieted the poor child, much to the relief of all.

Afterwards, however, Lizzy was feeling just a touch wary about the pageant's flaws and slightly self-conscious about her own participation in them, wondering whether the grand gentleman from London was in a mood to be critical. She waited until Sir William was finished bending his ear—although Mr Darcy asked after the health of Mr and Mrs Collins most politely, she thought, and appeared pleased enough to hear his positive reports—before broaching the topic.

"It does not feel like Christmas until the children portray the nativity," she explained, looking up at him to see his response while the teacher herded her noisy flocks towards the atrium where punch was being served, their parents trailing behind them. "And it is good to behave as children sometimes, and never better than at Christmas, when its mighty Founder was a child Himself."

But to her near surprise, Mr Darcy had nothing but praise for the entire entertainment and even her little part in salvaging it. "It has been the most wonderful performance I have ever seen," he declared with some strange emotion, taking her gloved hand within his own. "If I had my wish, I would come to this little church every Christmas Eve for the rest of my life, simply for the possibility of capturing its magic once again."

Which was the moment, of course, in which she began to fall in love. *Oh Lizzy, you do know how to pick them! If George Wickham was beneath you, this man is so far beyond your reach, you may as well ask for the moon!*

"You are laughing at me," she quietly accused, unable to believe he would not be. Her eyes widened when she realised that they were, at least briefly, alone in the nave.

He glanced about the empty sanctuary, then regarded her earnestly. "May I drive you back?" he asked. "I begged Bingley to see that my sister and yours all reached home safely. I received your father's permission to ask to see you home to Longbourn after the service." He smiled somewhat ruefully. "He said that he dared not refuse me, but he hoped that you might."

"You did? He did?" She felt her heart beginning to hammer and, in a sudden wave of embarrassment, looked at her feet. But she did not pull her hand away.

"I did," he said softly. "You must know...you *have* to know how ardently I admire you."

In her astonishment at this bold declaration, her gaze swiftly rose to meet his. "I had not the smallest idea, sir, I promise you. Until this precise moment, if anyone had told me you did, why...why, I would believe they were dreaming! And if I repeated such an idea to my neighbours, they would believe *I* was!"

For some peculiar reason, this sentiment made him laugh, its echoes sounding to the rafters. Lizzy could not help but notice he appeared particularly handsome when he was thus engaged, and then he grinned at her with what could only be called mischievousness.

"Come," he said coaxingly, turning towards the great double doors opening onto the street, urging her out into the frigid night. There were plenty of people about, laughing and talking. In fact, Mr Bingley was there with Jane, Georgiana, and Mary, near his vehicle across the lane, while her father had bestirred himself to come in the family carriage and was herding Mrs Bennet, Lydia, and Kitty into it. Lizzy also saw a good deal of interest from both family and villagers when they emerged together. The youth who Mr Darcy paid—quite handsomely, she had noted—to attend to their horse and sledge during the service was awaiting them only yards away.

Lizzy allowed him to tug her out of the church doorway, confused by his mood and his confessions. "Mr Darcy, everyone is watching! It will be thought you are—" Abruptly she broke off, for it felt foolhardy to say it aloud, despite his admission of admiration.

"Miss Elizabeth," he said, using a distinctly formal, stentorian voice that was probably loud enough to draw the attention of the entire village, "I beg you to grant me the favour of your escort to Longbourn."

She looked up at him with some chagrin, cheeks flushed and not with the cold, quickly dropping his hand. "I did not mean to imply that you ought to be making public any declarations."

"It is my dearest wish to do so," he replied promptly, even eagerly. "And your slightest preference, henceforth, shall be my command. If ever there is anything I might do to increase your happiness, you must only say so. Anything at all." He straightened, his expression growing more sombre. "Even if it is your wish that I remove myself altogether. If I have importuned or embarrassed you in any way, I apologise."

Could it be that he was...unsure of himself? Or at least, of how his suit might be received? As incredible as it seemed, she could not keep from smiling, remembering her own earlier self-admonitions. "I must confess myself surprised by your application—I did not expect it from you. It is even dangerous of you, perhaps, for you have no idea what my happiness requires. I wonder what you would say, for instance, if only this evening I admitted that I was longing for the moon?"

A long wooden crook, probably discarded by one of the young shepherds, stood leaning against the nearby church's sandstone wall. Mr Darcy plucked it up and pointed the hook's end skyward. "Naturally, then, I should capture it with my trusty staff and pull it down as a small gift for your pleasure and diversion. If the moon would be yours, my lady, you have but to ask," he said with a bow, wielding the crook with a flourish.

"I will take it," she replied, wondering at this new side to Mr Darcy, so opposite of the taciturn, critical being she had imagined him to be. Laughter bubbled within her. The surrounding snow brilliantly reflected the moonlight, and she tilted her face up to bathe in its glow. Turning back to him, she suddenly felt as powerful as Diana or Artemis or whichever goddess ruled the night sky. "And then what?"

"Why, I would melt it for you into a rich cordial for your evening dessert—it is astounding, I assure you, the difference a bit of moon makes for flavouring—and serve it any time you like. And of course, then, whenever you wish, moonbeams would surge from the tips of your fingers and your toes and the ends of your hair, and the world will not be able to take their eyes from you, or your beautiful moon-spun—"

"The world, in general, will have too much sense to join in. In my day, one simply asked the girl to marry him, instead of talking her to death."

They both whirled sharply in the direction of the speaker. Mr Bennet stood there, his most sardonic expression in full force.

"Papa!" Elizabeth cried, embarrassed.

Instead of responding to her father, however, Mr Darcy knelt before her in the dirty, slushy snow, not even appearing to notice or care for the ruination of his trousers. "Miss Elizabeth," he said, softly this time, and she knew he did not speak for the benefit of her father or the neighbourhood or anyone else except herself, "I realise I have not given you time to be certain of my character, or to show it to be a better one than you have any means of believing. If you will grant me the privilege of courting you, I promise to spend every day of the rest of my life attempting to prove myself worthy."

"Bah, more words. Youth is wasted on the young." Lizzy heard her father's sigh of impatience as he turned on his heel, but if Mr Darcy could so easily disregard him, she found she could as well. She held out her hands, and he searched her expression before he took them, rising up to look down upon her. The whole of *her* world watched, she knew, but she could not care, and plainly, neither did he.

"Be careful, Mr Darcy. You have promised me the moon, and now, your devotion. How you will outdo yourself tomorrow is quite beyond me."

He grinned, his dimple showing. But his expression intensified and sobered as his slitted gaze dropped to her lips; he appeared almost unbearably handsome in the moonlight. His voice, when he finally spoke, was deep and low. "Ah, but I have not yet kissed you, you see. There are many delightful surprises in store, I promise, if you will but agree to my suit."

A thrilling, near-giddy sensation overcame her at both his words and expression. "It is fortunate," said she, smiling up at him, "that I shall have *something* left to wish for. And perhaps you might have a dream or two yourself, I hope, that I can make come true as well?"

"Almost, I cannot breathe for hoping it," he murmured.

But the silent onlookers, plainly unable to ascertain any more of their conversation, were silent no longer. "What did she say?" called a jubilant-sounding Mr Bingley from across the lane.

"Yes, yes, what was her answer?" repeated many voices, Mrs Bennet's being one of the noisiest.

Mr Darcy turned to the expectant crowd. "Happy Christmas, Bingley! Happy Christmas, Georgiana! Happy Christmas, Bennet Family! Happy Christmas, Meryton! Happy Christmas to all, and to all a good night!" Both waving merrily, they quickly boarded the sledge and were soon lost to the sight of the questioning crowd.

Mr Darcy, it turned out, possessed another talent besides moon-capture and court-shipping—he could drive their cutter holding the reins in one hand whilst keeping one arm about her. She was dressed quite warmly—they both were—and there were woollen blankets besides, but still she snuggled in beside him so closely she could hear the steady beat of his heart. The bells of the harness tinkled in appreciative accompaniment.

He smiled down upon her, taking her breath away, and she found that, though in the certain possession of his warmest affection, and secure of her relations' consent, there was still something to be wished for. "I am afraid you heard only the smallest part of my mother's enthusiasm. You may want to stay at Netherfield until she has calmed, lest she insist upon you procuring a licence and at once."

"Rather, I shall encourage her and her effusions most warmly, to counter your father's disapproval."

Elizabeth hastened to explain. "He does not truly disapprove, you know. It is only he has little patience for romantic sentiment. I remember once explaining to him that certain harness bells held echoes of angel-song, and we could only hear them when an angel was released from a long sorrow. I do not even know why I thought it so, but it frustrated him endlessly when I could not be talked out of my childish belief. I do not think angels can *have* sorrows, do you?" She smiled at the memory, and he squeezed her affectionately.

"Why not? Does not Scripture say there 'must needs be an opposition in all things'? It is only great love that can instigate great grief. And I do not see why there must be an end, even in death, to any love so profound."

Lizzy looked up at him in some surprise. "You are a philosopher, sir! You shall never fear my father's wit. I daresay he will enjoy sparring with you. And...may I say how very happy I am that we are on the same side of this debate?" It was astounding, really, how comfortable she felt in expressing such feelings to a man who had seemed a distant, censorious stranger so short a time past. It also felt safe to confess flaws another man might never have overlooked.

"I ought never to have believed Lieutenant Wickham's claims," she admitted. "I cannot imagine why I was so easily misled. I apologise to you, most sincerely, for believing as I believed, and especially for repeating his words. Since speaking with your sister, I have reflected upon how little good reason I had for trusting his version of events so easily."

His arm tightened around her again. "I pray you forget it all," he said. "My own father believed in him, and even left him a legacy in his will, desiring that a certain living be given to him, once it was vacated."

"You mean, in the church?" she asked incredulously.

He nodded. "I knew it to be a mistake, and I thought he did as well, so with his agreement, I compensated him for it rather than grant the bequest. Of course, later he expected to receive it, regardless."

"Your sister explained that you had paid him quite handsomely for a legacy, but that he coveted her fortune as well. She said that he hates you and that he did everything in his power to turn her against you, telling her the most vicious lies. And also, that she is mortified every time she remembers how you felt obligated to prove to her, with signed documents, the dishonesty of his allegations. She cannot think how to make it up to you."

"There is nothing to atone for. She was but fifteen at the time and knew him only as a young child, which must be her excuse. She came to me, you know, when I visited her a day or two before the planned elopement, and confessed it all. She could never abide grieving or offending me, no matter what he said. I am proud of her, but I can see I must tell her so more often."

Lizzy smiled up at him. "She only wants a little more liveliness, and *that*—since you plan, I hope, to provide her a sister who is perhaps a bit spirited—your wife might teach her."

He smiled back so broadly that the whiteness of his teeth gleamed in the moonlight, and he tightened his arm about her again.

They drove through the dim snowy lanes, the winter moon as bright as any torch-glow—although the mare knew the way well enough to find her stable, even had the night been darker. This journey, unlike the one accomplished earlier in the company of Miss Darcy, was taken slowly, as they both revelled, she thought, in the newness of their connexion and the miracle of its discovery. In contrast to his earlier speeches, he was quiet as he brought the vehicle to a halt just before the lane leading up the hill to Longbourn.

"It occurs to me," he said, looking down at her with all seriousness, "that there is one thing I neglected to mention, above everything else—I do love you, you see. I ought to have begun with that."

"I was beginning to suspect something of the sort," she said impishly, arrested by his gaze.

He put both arms around her, not in an embrace, exactly, but more as if he could hardly believe it possible that he held her so near, and must touch her to confirm its reality. "I remember what you said, you know—of the efficacy of poetry in driving love away. If I am too mawkish, you must remind me. I fear I lose all sense with you beside me, battling the sonnets that do so constantly beset me whilst in your presence."

"We both have reason to think my opinions on romance not entirely unalterable. I only just confessed to imagining I have heard the sounds of angels."

He took her face within his gloved fingers. "I hope you never stop believing in angels *or* in romance. I will do everything I can to nourish your dreams and nurture passion between us. Not simply this night, but every future day, and all the nights to come. I hope you will allow me to recite you sonnets when our hair is silver and my eyesight dim. I promise, however, that I do know better than to compose any verses myself." Looking deeply into her eyes, he quoted:

"When, in disgrace with fortune and men's eyes,
I all alone beweep my outcast state
And trouble deaf heaven with my bootless cries
And look upon myself and curse my fate,
Wishing me like to one more rich in hope,
Featured like him, like him with friends possess'd,
Desiring this man's art and that man's scope,
With what I most enjoy contented least;
Yet in these thoughts myself almost despising,
Haply I think on thee, and then my state,
Like to the lark at break of day arising
From sullen earth, sings hymns at heaven's gate;
For thy sweet love remember'd such wealth brings
That then I scorn to change my state with kings."

Lizzy placed her hands over his own. "Oh! Not mawkish in the slightest! My feelings are now so widely different from what they once were. Promise me you will quote Shakespeare's sonnets whenever we are private enough for you to accept the consequences." And with a bravery she never could have fathomed just an hour before, she moved to touch her lips to his, expressing herself as sensibly and warmly as only a woman newly in love could be supposed to do.

"My dearest heart," he said, once he could speak again—which was not for some moments. "My only love." A snowflake drifted down and landed on his nose; she kissed it.

"Your nose is cold," she whispered.

He touched his forehead to hers. "Let us return to the warmth of Longbourn's fire, where we may plan the start of the rest of our lives together," he replied softly. After tucking the blanket more snugly around her, he took up the reins once more. And as he did so, a bell pealed, the reverberation more pure and sweet than any harness's jangling.

"Did you hear that chime?" she said. "That was it! The sound I once called angel-song! I have not heard it in ever so long, and I have not an idea from whence it originates. Some peculiar echo, I suppose."

"I did hear," he said confidently, urging the mare forward with an expert flick of the reins. "It is my opinion that it is the sound of an angel released from a long-held sorrow. In fact, I am absolutely certain of it."

She stretched up to place a kiss upon his cheek before snuggling back down once more into the shelter of his embrace. "I like so well that you are a romantic, too," she said. "I never would have dreamt it."

Mr Darcy only smiled.

The End
(or, The Beginning, depending upon how one looks at it)

About the Author

Julie Cooper, a California native, lives in the Central Valley with own Mr Darcy of nearly forty years. Her hobbies include bragging about her adorable grandchildren and showing pictures of them to anyone too polite or too slow to escape.

Also by Julie Cooper

Nameless
Seek Me: Georgiana's Story
Tempt Me
The Perfect Gentleman

IN THE SPIRIT INTENDED

JAN ASHTON

CHAPTER ONE

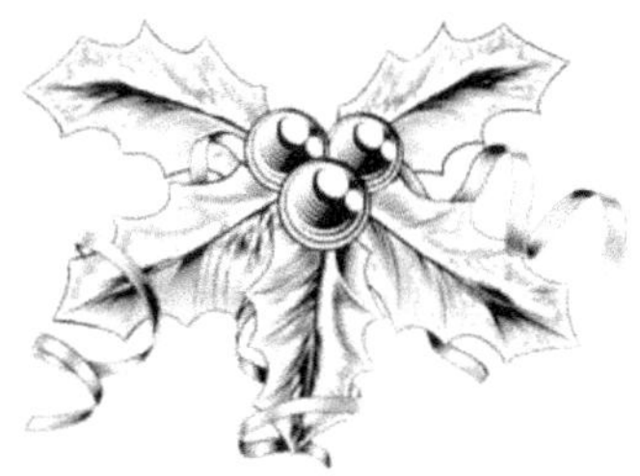

December 1813

THE SNOW, WHEN IT FINALLY ARRIVED, WAS A RELIEF. THE cold rain had turned to sleet, then to blessedly large flakes of snow. The sight gave Elizabeth Bennet a sense of comfort. Snow was a familiar part of Christmases in Hertfordshire. London had been muddy and grey until the northern winds blew in with cold and snow and laid a clean white blanket over the streets and roofs. She happily anticipated a pretty walk later in the afternoon, if only she would not be prevented from it.

"Lizzy!"

The warm voice of her second favourite male relation in London sounded from the hall. Elizabeth turned her attention from the parlour window and called out.

"Yes, Charles?"

Bingley strode quickly into the room, flashed a smile, and sat beside her on the blue divan. He held a flat box on his lap. "Jane is resting, and I have need of your opinion on her gift."

Elizabeth fought to contain her laughter. "Is this her Christmas gift, or just another of the gifts you give to her every second Wednesday and third Thursday?"

He drew a hand to his chest. "You wound me! And here I thought you my favourite sister."

This time she refrained from both laughter and words. No need to say aloud what either might be thinking when comparing her to Caroline or Louisa. Since Charles Bingley had become her brother a year earlier, they had grown dear to each other, each of them invested in the care and protection of the gentle, kind, and now achingly *enceinte* Jane Bingley. The warmth and joy the Bingleys felt in their marriage permeated the house on Bourdon Street, most particularly whenever Caroline absented herself to the Hursts' home a few streets away.

Elizabeth set aside her sewing and moved her attention back to the box, clearly from Aspley's.

"'Tis true that Christmas is on Saturday. What have you there for my favourite and most fortunate sister?"

Giving her a conspiratorial glance, Bingley looked around the room before opening the lid to reveal a diamond necklace with a large single pearl at its centre. It was beautiful and simple, ideal for Jane.

Bingley spoke in an eager voice. "You see the pearl? More can be attached later, one for each of our children. This is our first Christmas as man and wife, and our last without children gathered around the table."

Her brother's sentimentality nearly undid her, but Elizabeth managed to assure him it was lovely and oh so perfect before Bingley began to enthuse once more.

"Thank you again for staying with us rather than returning to Longbourn for Christmastide." Bingley smiled at her impishly. "I shall not enquire whether Caroline's choice to decamp to the country with the Hursts influenced your own decision, but Jane is not the only one who appreciates your company."

Though Elizabeth would miss the high spirits of her Gardiner cousins on Christmas Eve, and imagined they would yearn for the three Bennet sisters no longer at Longbourn, she could not regret her decision to remain in London. "I have had Christmas with my parents and sisters, aunts and uncles all of my life. How could I give up the opportunity to see how the happiest couple in the world celebrates their first Christmas? Not to mention, I am all anticipation for the arrival of your relations. If I am to believe the tales you and your sisters have told, your storied aunts should provide me with great amusement—at the expense of all of you!"

Bingley chuckled. "Indeed they shall! With no children of their own, Aunt Millie and Aunt Poppy are quite enthusiastic about our expected addition. And you know, I believe their eagerness to visit and my sisters' fervour to leave only rose when they received news of the others' plans!"

Elizabeth was in no doubt of either pair's motivation and had welcomed news of it. She gestured to the large sofa nearest the fire. "Jane is too kind and well-mannered to behave so badly, but I shall sit there, on her behalf, with an aunt on either side, and learn all of your secrets."

"You are as dangerous as Caroline, but much better natured."

They laughed quietly.

"I look forward to a wonderful reunion of family and friends for the Christmas season. Even Darcy shall be with us!" Bingley jumped up to return Jane's gift to its hiding place. He turned to Elizabeth, so amazed with his own happiness that he missed her shocked expression. "He sent a note this morning. 'Tis nearly a year since I have seen him—you recall how soon he left Meryton after the wedding—but he has arrived in town just in time for a merry holiday! What wonderful news!"

Elizabeth watched her brother's rapid exit from the room. While he looked as though he could jump in the air and kick his heels in glee, her own feelings were a jumble. *Mr Darcy is returned. Here, but a few streets away.*

Leaning her head back, she closed her eyes and took a deep breath. Almost immediately the image of his face when she last saw him rose in her mind.

He had been standing in the front hall at Longbourn, away from rooms smelling of brandy and bride cake and bursting with loud celebratory exclamations from her mother and neighbours, waiting to make his goodbyes to Bingley and Jane. He had spoken once to her all day, thanking her for the coffee she handed him; her hope for more was as desperate and fleeting as the sparks rising from the fire. When she walked towards him carrying Jane's cloak, clutching it tightly to keep herself steady, their eyes met only briefly and she detected no eagerness for conversation, only an impatience to be on with his business and be gone from the boisterous Bennets. She hugged her sister and new brother, and turned, certain he would do the same. Indeed, he was off to London the next morning, off to Pemberley the next, and away from her and memories of whatever had once chanced to happen.

The news that Mr Darcy was now in town for Christmas should not have surprised her; he could not stay away forever. He had a sister he cared for, and responsibilities for his estate and his tenants. No, it was his long absence, and the lack of news of him, that had consumed her thoughts. He had gone travelling; that much she knew. She suspected it was not the unreliable post that had led him to cease communication with Bingley, but his friend's connexion to her family and *their* connexion to the dishonourable Mr Wickham. Perhaps a year's duration —and some holiday spirit of forgiveness—was long enough for his disgust and resentment to ebb.

Was he still thinking ill of her? Or was it more likely that in his full and busy life, Mr Darcy never thought of, or scarcely remembered, the country girl he once professed to love?

It is of little difference to me. No matter what his feelings, or lack thereof, I am certain of my own happiness, she thought miserably.

When he had arrived in town three days earlier, Darcy ignored most of the cards and letters piled up on his desk. Anyone who mattered had known how to reach him directly, or through his solicitor or cousin, this past year.

Anyone but Elizabeth Bennet. She had not made the effort to speak to him, let alone look at him, when he returned to Meryton for Bingley's wedding to her sister more than a year ago. For two days, Elizabeth had scarcely looked in his direction. When she did meet his gaze, it was brief and awkward; she would colour deeply and quickly look away in barely disguised distress.

Why would she have any interest in where he had been since that time? What had happened with her? Bingley's few letters before Darcy left for Greece referred only to his happiness, his delight that Darcy had stood beside him at the wedding, and more on his own happiness, pleasure, and whatnot. Was Bingley's new bride as happy? Was her *sister* happy, and more importantly, pleased with him?

Is she happy now?

Darcy could not stand it, to know he *could* know if he could brave an enquiry as to the specific Bennet—the *only* Bennet—that he cared about.

Now, after more than six months away from England, he was home, and upon opening Bingley's invitation, he learned that answers were a mere ten-minute walk away. He must have some intelligence prior to agreeing to attend his friend's Christmas Eve festivities. Time away had eased the ache, but no amount of distance could fully heal the wound to his heart. Perhaps meeting Bingley and gaining an answer would grant him some beginning to...to what—an ending? A semblance of finality? Darcy refused to admit that the true goal of seeing Bingley was to learn whether Elizabeth had moved ahead with her life. A wonder such as she, introduced as she would have been to Bingley's friends and to others, could not go unmarried. Some man, someone whom Darcy hoped had seen her worth more clearly than he had and held her dear, would win her affection and treasure her as she deserved.

For months, he had prayed Elizabeth was content in whichever state she now lived—wed or unwed. But he hoped, perhaps more quietly and more fervently, that she remained unwed. Thinking of him, perhaps forgiving him. Her eyes had looked on him tenderly once, in the short time they had shared at Pemberley. Perhaps Bingley would tell him whether he could earn the chance to see that softness in her eyes once again.

Darcy owned he was unwilling to expose himself so soon to society by meeting Bingley at his club. After sending a note of his intention to pay a call, he set out on the nearly blindingly sunny winter morning to do so. It would be good to see Bingley. Darcy flexed his gloved hands as he walked along, nodding to those he recognised, which were few to none by the time he reached Bourdon Street.

Bingley's new address was only a few streets from Darcy House, but even at that small distance, the houses were smaller and more tightly set together. Still, thought Darcy as he walked along, his friend had done well for himself. A nice house, a nice wife. All was as it should be for a gentleman of means and happy disposition.

The Bingleys were established at a narrow brick-built flat-fronted townhouse; only its green door and canopy distinguished it from the identical houses flanking it. The joyful felicity Darcy anticipated within would distinguish it from many of the houses in town—at least if Miss Bingley now stayed with the Hursts. He raised his hand to the knocker, feeling a hesitant uncertainty—nearly reluctance—to gain answers to that which he had so long wondered; soon he would know Elizabeth's current situation and whatever path it meant for his future happiness.

God grant me strength, he whispered.

As it turned out, God answered at least his first hope. After an effusive handshake, a scolding for his poor attention to his letters, and demands to know all that had occurred on his travels, Bingley disclosed that Caroline and the Hursts were away in the country, attending Hurst's mother and sister in Surrey.

"We, of course, are not alone. Lizzy is with us."

The bell rang far sooner than Elizabeth had expected. Charles said Mr Darcy had sent a card, but did that mean he would soon follow it—here? She had thought she had at least a day to prepare her thoughts—

prepare herself, decide on a gown and a demeanour—before Mr Darcy appeared at Bourdon Street.

"Welcome, my friend!"

She could hear her brother's effusive greeting, the heavy steps of the two men as they embraced, or shook hands, and strolled off towards the study. *Thank you,* she mouthed silently.

"Lizzy? Are you well?"

Elizabeth looked up to find Jane peering at her, a look of concern in her tired expression. She smiled at her sister, whose pregnancy had been blessedly easy until this past week, when a flurry of preparations for their visitors had coincided with a seemingly quick expansion of her belly.

"Your well-being is of more immediate concern to me. I am merely in need of some exercise." Elizabeth glanced towards the window; its glass sparkled in the brilliant sunshine and large blocks of sunlight shone onto the rug where a grey and black cat lazed. "Figgy has found his bliss, I see."

Jane laughed. "A little more exercise would suit him well. Mrs Cooke says a maid claims to have seen a mouse yesterday."

"A little more exercise and fewer table scraps." Elizabeth leaned over to rub the feline's furry belly; she was rewarded with a purr. She looked up to see Jane resting her hand on her own midsection. "Coaxing a purr from your restless babe?"

Smiling wearily, Jane nodded. "Louisa is certain I am carrying a child just like its father. She remembers Charles as unable to sit still until he was in long pants."

"A serene babe would only worry you more." Elizabeth peered closely. "Although you would sleep better."

Her sister's silence was paired with a curious expression. Elizabeth waited with trepidation.

"Lizzy, I believe you heard Mr Darcy's arrival?" Jane's usual calm manner was replaced with some agitation; Elizabeth well knew the signs and frowned seeing her sister twist her fingers in her lap. "Charles is pleased his friend is back in country and delighted he accepted the invitation to spend the holidays here before going on to see his sister."

The holidays? How long will this visit last?

"Of course. Miss Darcy must miss him terribly," Elizabeth managed. The snows in Northamptonshire and Norfolk had been heavy and the winds further complicated travel; the roads could hardly stay cleared. "Mr Darcy will need a hardy sleigh to reach Derbyshire in time for Christmas. It is only a few days away."

"Indeed." Jane paused, her own unease clear. "I-I believe Charles hopes to persuade Mr Darcy to remain in town, to hear of his travels, to ask for his counsel on an estate, and to celebrate our happy news."

"Of course."

"Lizzy, we have not spoken of Mr Darcy, or your feelings about him, in nearly a year. Will his presence displease you? Do you wish to go to your rooms when Mr Darcy is here? Or shall Charles go to him at Darcy House? I do not—"

Elizabeth, far from being mortified, now felt herself give in to laughter at her dear sister's distress. "Jane! I am well. Truly, all is well with me. I have no tender feelings to protect in regards to Mr Darcy, and can rejoice for Charles that his friend is returned to him."

The relief with which her sister felt Elizabeth's word was unmistakable. "Thank goodness. With Caroline absent, Charles is eager to enjoy Mr Darcy's company here, in our home. He hopes to keep him entertained within our family circle until the New Year!"

CHAPTER TWO

'LIZZY IS WITH US.'

Of course she would be. Bingley had married Elizabeth Bennet's dearest sister. Naturally she would be attending them in London, likely desperate to flee her inane mother and spend time with her favourite relations.

His eyes flew briefly beyond the entryway, to the right of the hall where he assumed would be found a parlour or sitting room.

The question percolating at the front of his mind for months was now partially answered; Elizabeth was as yet unmarried and in residence with the Bingleys.

She is here. A room or two away from where I sit.

"Mrs Bingley is fortunate to have her favourite sister with her in town."

"Oh yes, especially since young Hurst was born in September—"

Darcy's eyebrows rose.

"Did you not receive my note?" cried Bingley. "Louisa and Hurst have a child! Bit of a surprise to us all, of course." He chuckled at Darcy's smirk. "The babe takes after his father in his love of long naps. He has a hearty appetite as well. I am told they keep two wet nurses at the house."

Darcy, still trying to sort out his feelings on the news of Elizabeth, could hardly digest this information or join Bingley in his jesting. He managed a small smile. "So Hurst has a son. Good for him and for your sister. I shall send a gift for young master Hurst."

"Brilliant! Fortunately for my sister—for both my sisters—he is an easy child. Louisa has done well with him, and Caroline is...is adjusting. Had she known you would join us, well, you know how that would go, old friend." Bingley patted him on the back. "Come, let us have a catch up before we join the ladies."

Darcy followed Bingley towards the only set of open doors along the corridor. "It is nothing to yours for books and paintings, but my study is a comfortable place," the younger man said proudly.

He sat Darcy down in a large green chair and gave him a quick inspection. Darcy felt some relief that his tanned skin, a remnant of his past months spent in Greece, concealed the heightened colour of excitement he had felt—still felt—upon hearing of Elizabeth's presence. He was grateful his friend's lips were more engaged than his eyes and ears. If Bingley had looked more closely, he would have seen Darcy's impatience and unease and his desperation to see Elizabeth—or escape her. Darcy swore he could hear her voice and smell her perfume, but as he had felt the same sensations for well-nigh a year now, he believed himself a fool. *She resides here, but she may not even be at home. She is likely shopping or paying calls.* Such thoughts calmed him.

"Truly, you look well, my friend. I wish to hear all about your travels and adventures—I am relieved you were not eaten up by tropical fevers or angry natives or poisoned plants or set upon by the French—"

Darcy chuckled, the ease he remembered from Bingley's company returning to him. "I was in no danger from savages whilst in Greece."

"Still, I am pleased you are returned to our shores, and that you are here in my house!"

"As am I. It looks to be a fine house." Darcy accepted a glass of brandy, enjoying the warmth it provided after his walk from Brook Street. "Your invitation was providential, as I had not thought to find you in town and the snow in the north has precluded my joining Georgiana at Matlock."

"I know you will miss your sister, but you shall celebrate the Yuletide with us, and journey north when the weather calms. Jane and Lizzy have decorated the house so wonderfully, as we shall have games and a merry feast on Christmas Eve."

Darcy noted the festive greenery and ribbon on the mantel. Much as he enjoyed the sights and sounds of the season, he had not occasioned to so openly celebrate it with decoration and merriment in his own home.

"The sins of English society, our dullness and restraint, stiffness and formality, are to be set aside?"

Bingley chuckled, an eyebrow waggling madly. "Ha, of course! I am eager to see Jane open her gift. It has some special sentiment, and—rude though it may be to say aloud—it will be pleasant not to have my sisters here voicing opinions on my taste."

He lifted his tumbler. "We are a joyful household here, my friend!"

Darcy nodded, settled in his chair, and tried to attend to Bingley's effusions about the house and his married status rather than listen for the voice or footstep of the lady he both feared and desired; he wondered whether she knew of his presence there, in the house where she now made her home.

"You have given up Netherfield?"

"A little distance between ourselves and Mrs Bennet was needed. She was at Netherfield every morning, and sometimes in the afternoon as well. It will not surprise you that Mr Bennet was amused by it."

"And rather relieved to have a quiet house to himself?"

Bingley's expression gave away his thoughts. He leaned forward and tapped his finger on the table. "Do you know that we could not host the neighbours at our home without Mrs Bennet also attending? Every bit of our business was known to her, and thus to many in Meryton."

"A woeful circumstance, Bingley, but not a surprising one. She had lost her two favourite daughters from Longbourn, and yet could celebrate the good fortune of the one still in the neighbourhood."

"We came here in February to enjoy the society, returning to Netherfield in June. Our absence had only made my mother-in-law's interest more keen. We came back to town in October, just after Louisa gave birth." Bingley grinned awkwardly.

"And the lease?"

"I plan to let it go."

Darcy sat back, mulling over what it meant for himself that his friend would no longer have an estate near his wife's family. It should mean little to him. He was not connected to the Bennet family, and although he had no real reason to think he would ever be, he had not set aside all hope.

"—and I will say there was some fortunate outcome to the difficulties in Hertfordshire as it drove Caroline to spend more time with Louisa."

Clearly Mrs Bingley wanted a friend and companion as she adjusted to her new position, and Bingley did not want Caroline to fill that role. Darcy suspected that while his friend might have forgiven his sisters for their contrivances and falsehood, he would do all he could to protect his wife and encourage her happiness and success.

Sensing it was finally his turn to speak, Darcy ventured a comment. "Mrs Bingley deserves the opportunity to enjoy her own home in peace without heed to the opinions of *any* of her relations. I am happy for her, and for you. You chose well, in your wife and in your home."

Bingley's pleasure in such praise spread a broad smile across his face. "I have missed you, old friend. I apologise for prattling on about my own happiness, and I do wish to hear all about your travels and adventures, and your reasons for leaving England and your friends, but Darcy, I have the most wonderful news to share, and then I shall get on with it and listen to you."

There was perhaps only one more form of good news Bingley could share, and Darcy braced himself.

"I am to be a father! And Jane a mother!"

"A child!"

"Yes! Imagine it! Married in January last and by February of the New Year, we shall be parents!"

Darcy immediately stood and held out his hand. Bingley rose and grasped it.

"Congratulations. You will be a wonderful father."

"Thank you." Bingley beamed, and pulled Darcy into a short embrace. "I am beyond joy."

It was a brief pat on the back, no more, but the gesture nearly undid Darcy. He had been away, living and travelling among strangers for so long, that such warmth felt foreign to him. He cleared his throat. "Mrs Bingley is a kind, gentle soul. She will be a wonderful mother."

"Oh, I must take you to Jane and you may tell her yourself!"

Before he knew it, Darcy had been spirited out the door and down the corridor into a bright drawing room overlooking the street. Jane Bingley sat on the sofa near the fire, a basket of threads and fabrics beside her. She was looking up at another lady—her back to them—who was holding up a small infant dress. Darcy could not see her face, but he would recognise the curve of her neck and the curl of her locks in his sleep. And her laugh, of course, which had kept him company on many of the lonely days of the past year.

"But Jane, how little it matters to a baby if her dress is longer on the left side than on the right. Only Mama and her aunt Caroline would notice. And see, the extra cloth is perfect for soaking up dribbles and spills!"

Elizabeth.

Bingley's excited voice broke through the spell. "Jane, Lizzy, look who has washed up on our doorstep, newly arrived from distant lands!"

"Mr Darcy." Mrs Bingley smiled up at him. "Welcome to our home, we are so pleased to have you here for Christmas."

He was unable to reply, for at that moment, Elizabeth lowered the dress and turned towards him. Her expression was welcoming, if not warm, but she was as pale as he was tanned. Pale with spots of red on her cheeks. Perhaps she was as embarrassed as he, at this moment.

"Hello, Mrs Bingley, Miss Bennet," he managed, nodding at each of the ladies. "I am pleased to see you again, and find you so well settled. I thank you for the invitation."

Mrs Bingley's serene countenance was lit with a warm smile. "Please, do come in. So much time has passed and I expect you have as much to tell us of the year you have spent, as Charles would like to tell you of his."

"Ours." Bingley's voice, besotted and reverent, corrected his wife gently.

A moment of silence ensued as the couple gazed at one another. The spell was broken when Elizabeth, seemingly coming to her senses, spoke in a laughing voice. "Do you see, Mr Darcy, what I and all the servants must put up with in this house? When not lost in the other's eyes, my brother and sister are busy with compliments, endearments, and loving gestures. There is no room for dissatisfaction, vexation, or ill humour."

"Lizzy," her sister scolded her affectionately. "You are rarely vexed at anyone and your only dissatisfaction is with your sewing."

"I notice you do not defend me from the charge of ill humour."

Darcy, amused, and more at ease than expected, observed the conversation. Elizabeth had not greeted him awkwardly or unwillingly, but immediately drawn him into the business of the Bingley household. *She is who she has always been, unaffected by time or my absence.*

Bingley strolled to his wife. "Any ill humour felt by you, myself, Mrs Cooke, or the housemaids was packed into Caroline's trunks last month, Lizzy."

Mrs Bingley looked abashed and hid her shocked smile, but Bingley's jest elicited gay laughter from Elizabeth before she recalled herself.

"Welcome, Mr Darcy. As you see, little has changed in your absence."

CHAPTER THREE

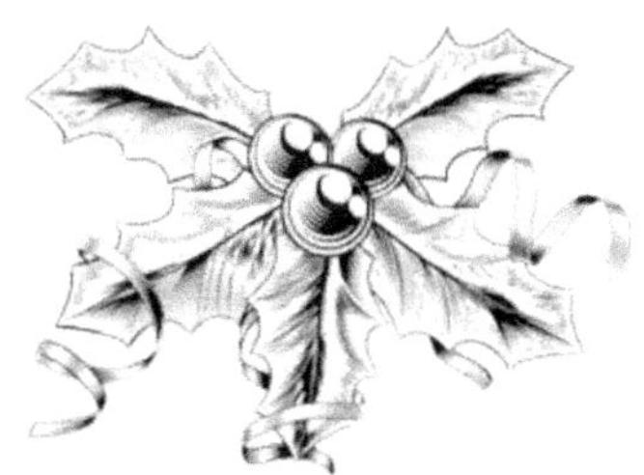

SHE WOULD REPRIMAND HERSELF LATER THAT EVENING, sitting on her bed, watching the candle burn down. To have mocked her sister and brother, pointed to her own poor behaviours, and told Mr Darcy how little his absence from their lives had been noticed! She was thoughtless and ill-mannered, and he—a man of the world made more worldly in the past year—had been all that was polite and well mannered. Had he been the man she once thought he was, he would not have rolled his eyes and joined his smile to their laughter.

But now, in this moment of laying eyes on the man who had proven himself to be not only the best man she had ever known but also the least foolish, Elizabeth felt herself tingling with nervous joy. He was more handsome than she recalled, his face lean and tan, his gaze as piercing and intelligent as before. He had been out in the world, pursuing passions and pleasures, taking in sights she had only read about; he had gained newfound experiences while her own world had expanded only from one suffocating and unhappy household to one overfull of bliss and amity. She was ashamed of her cranky spirits.

This is the season of joy and peace and I wish only to mock a house filled with both!

Mr Darcy, however, had every reason to be away from those who had caused him a hellish year. None of the Bennets had treated him well; she, Lydia and her mother were the worst of them. Lydia was ungrateful for his interference in her 'great romantic adventure', while Mrs Bennet resented the very attributes—pride, reserve and intelligence—that now most excited Elizabeth's admiration. He did not know nor likely care that her view of him had been altered. It had been too late a year ago, and it was far too late now.

How much did she owe him? Gratitude beyond measure. For all that he had assisted her family, no one else had ever done so much to alter her sense and understanding of herself. How deeply she regretted how that understanding had come about—she had been more sharp-tongued than sharp-witted, and ridiculously stubborn in thinking him cold and officious. Now she owed him the same consideration he had given her, and an openness to whatever he could possibly offer her now. Friendship at best, it seemed likely, but as he would soon learn, they would be connected as godmother and godfather to the Bingleys' child, no matter what might come in the future.

She did her best not to stare as Mr Darcy moved to the chair next to hers and Bingley took the chair nearest Jane.

Jane spoke first. "We are happy to welcome you to our home, sir. I am sorry the inclement weather precludes your return to your family."

"The weather has been fierce in the north, and the last letter I received from my sister ordered me to stay in London for my own safekeeping."

Elizabeth gave him a small smile. "Miss Darcy is a wise and loving adviser, sir. After so much time away, she cannot mind an extra se'nnight if it preserves your safety."

"She knows I am a man of common sense but one who is eager to see her. She is right to set aside emotion and remind me that I would give her similar orders to protect her welfare."

"We are of course pleased that you are able to be a frequent visitor to our home, and that you will share in the Christmastide festivities with us until you can journey north."

"Thank you, Mrs Bingley. How well it sounds to say that—*Mrs Bingley*—and how comfortable a home you have made here."

Elizabeth watched her sister and Mr Darcy begin a polite conversation about her time in town, her choices in wall coverings, and the plush comforts of the chairs. Bingley beamed, watching his beloved wife and his closest friend in such proximity, but Elizabeth felt only disquiet and a sense of what might have been had Jane and Mr Darcy had opportunity to know each other as brother and sister. Each had long since altered their opinion of the other, but had spent little time in company to truly appreciate and know one another. The fault, she knew, was her own.

Swallowing her pointless regret of the past, Elizabeth reapplied herself to the present when Bingley began prattling on about the house and its many advantages. She would be certain to mention the shelves in the closets, so as to have her share in the insipid conversation.

"And of course, we have Lizzy, who is Jane's greatest friend and companion. And nearly mine as well," Bingley added, grinning at Darcy. "You have abandoned me for nearly a year. I hope you will remain in country and meet your godson."

"Or goddaughter."

Darcy startled, whether more from Bingley's announcement that he would be the child's godfather or by Elizabeth's soft voice, teasing Bingley. He could not look at her, so he looked at his friend, who was smiling as though he could burst, his joy and excitement filling the room and shaming any man, woman, or potted plant that did not feel likewise. He swallowed, touched deeply by Bingley's trust in him. He had failed to understand the depth of his friend's feelings for Jane Bennet and arrogantly led him away from her, then hidden knowledge of her presence in London. And yet Bingley, son of a tradesman, had not only forgiven him, the grandson of a peer, but had asked his blessing. Now, after a year with little communication, Bingley requested that he, a man not related to him by blood or family tie, be godfather to his child. Darcy managed to ignore the sting in his eyes, nod his head, and affirm his gratitude and acceptance.

"You honour me," he replied, looking at Bingley and then to his wife, whose smile was at least as warm as her husband's. "It would be a privilege to serve in any capacity to such a child."

Appreciation and congratulations were exchanged and the room fell silent again as the Bingleys smiled at one another. Darcy could only envy such happiness while wondering how one as observant and witty as Elizabeth could stand it.

"I had thought to teach your ten children to play their instruments very ill and put on plays that would amuse only their parents—not be godmother to any," said Elizabeth in a voice with less levity and more sincerity than he had yet heard today. "Of course, I shall serve in any role, with any title of your choosing, and love this babe. How could any child of my sister and brother not be the most lovable and cheerful in all the world?"

"Indeed," Darcy managed to add, awed by her ability to say exactly that which he intended, had he ever owned the ability to speak with such gentle frankness.

His agreement seemed to please her, and Elizabeth smiled in that arch manner that had bewitched him from the beginning, before continuing. "Most happily, holding this honorific does give me the advantage of inciting all sorts of naughtiness. After all, nothing taught to a child by its godparent is considered wrong or mischievous."

"Lizzy!"

"It is true, Jane. I am certain I have read it in a book."

"But Lizzy—"

"Miss Bennet is correct," said Darcy. He felt Elizabeth's eyes, astonished and mirthful, shift back to him. "My own godfather was my father's cousin, a judge who chose to extend all his leniency in my direction. In spite of evidence to the contrary, such as muddy boots or cherry stains on my hands, my father was always dissuaded from punishment when my uncle was in residence with us."

"A great legal mind, no doubt of it," Bingley chuckled. "Would that he had stayed more often, how great would your mischief have grown?"

Darcy's expression sobered, and his reply, when it arrived a moment later, held a note of chagrin. "You forget that George Wickham was in residence at Pemberley. My own father was his godfather, and it was in his example that my own godfather found his model of beneficence."

"The Bennet family had no such traditions of godparents. A protector would have served me well for my own muddy skirts and cherry stains." Elizabeth turned to her sister. "You have been warned by myself and Mr Darcy, that we shall be at least as indulgent as you and Bingley. It is not too late if you prefer to choose Caroline for such a worthwhile role."

"Mr and Mrs Bennet must be pleased with your news," offered Darcy.

"You shall do very well, Lizzy." Mrs Bingley rolled her eyes at her sister before replying to Mr Darcy. "My mother enjoys babies and indulging small children, and although we have removed to London, I believe she will be constant with visits and gifts."

Bingley grinned. "She has yet to meet her first grandchild. The Wickhams were speedier to the bassinet, but they remain in Newcastle, I believe."

A child. Dear God, a child that actually bears Wickham's name and thus his legacy.

"They are never in town and have not been to Longbourn since their wedding," said Elizabeth hurriedly, as if to reassure him that he was safe from exposure to the couple.

"So much time has passed, so much has happened," Bingley exclaimed. "The nurseries are beginning to fill. Did I tell you Hurst's mother may not let them return to town, so thrilled was she with the birth of her first grandchild?"

"That is the wont of grandmothers and grandfathers." Darcy reached for the cup of tea Mrs Bingley had poured him a few minutes earlier. "And you, Miss Bennet? Your life has not been without its joys this year past?"

Elizabeth shrugged, an unusual gesture, he thought; her small smile did not reach her eyes. "I have been at ease, enjoying the happy fortune of a sister who made a good match. Of course, it is my lot to be the sensible, less compliant sister, and ensure household matters are resolved upon and the servants do not cheat."

Bingley grinned. "I am fortunate in my newest sister. Lizzy had been well occupied. She moved house with us to help Jane to adjust to her life as my wife and prepare our home for our child, counselled Mrs Collins with her daughter's birth..."

"Mr and Mrs Collins have welcomed a child?" *Everyone married and bearing children, while Elizabeth is filling time.*

"Yes," Elizabeth said slowly, in a tone that excited anticipation. "Catherine Maria Collins arrived in August."

Darcy bit back a laugh. "Lady Catherine must be pleased by their choice of name."

"I believe the honour is all due the child for choosing her sex, sir."

"Lizzy," Jane said quietly.

Darcy watched the mirth dim from her eyes as Elizabeth straightened. He recognised in her the behaviour of his own sister, nay himself, when in company with Lady Catherine. A quick glance at Mrs Bingley showed her to be satisfied with Elizabeth's return to more dutiful comportment. No one could doubt the affection between sisters but the change in their stations appeared to bring out their mother's disapproving side in one while stifling the humour in the other. Bingley had mentioned how much he enjoyed having Elizabeth as a sister living with them, and how much laughter he shared with her. Perhaps his wife was a little envious of their connexion—the warm and immediate friendship Elizabeth made with everyone she encountered?

How is it so easy with her, here in company? Is she often able to exercise her wit, or is she, as she said, acting as the sensible one—a lonely role for her.

"I admit to having set aside recent letters from my aunt. If she had shared the Collinses' happy news, I am ignorant of it." Darcy smiled at Elizabeth and her sister. "I am compelled to action, and will address that situation today. Next to a roaring fire, in case her words have the usual effect on my peace." He was pleased when Elizabeth shared his smile and he saw the sparkle return to her eyes.

"A year has passed and Mr Darcy now knows all about how we have got through it. A wedding, a house, a baby to come, a ball or two. I should think he has been too reticent," Elizabeth said lightly before glancing at the man himself. "I recall his talent for telling stories."

He gave her a bemused look, but she detected some relief as well. Clearly, he was unaccustomed to a household of suffocating happiness and joyful agreement on all matters. She wished only to shift the conversation away from its most uncomfortable moments; when Bingley had mentioned the Wickhams, Mr Darcy's ease disappeared. It was as if a checklist of embarrassments was being ticked off—her mother, Lydia and her husband...she had feared what was yet to come. Her father's resentment that she had chosen to live with Jane? Or would Bingley mention that Kitty's suitor was yet another man *she* had rejected?

"Of course we must hear from Darcy," Bingley cried. "He has been travelling, and I have been remiss in demanding his stories. We have much to catch up on while I have commanded all the air in the room with my own happy news."

Mr Darcy smiled. "You have much news to tell, my friend."

Bingley grinned and turned his gaze on Jane. Elizabeth, accustomed to being forgotten in the sort of besotted, numbing happiness that permeated the Bingley home, looked at Mr Darcy when the silence became uncomfortable and said, "Have you not one dreadful tale to share?"

He did indeed, and mentioned his travels to attend his estates in Ireland and Wales before sailing to Greece with a university friend. Elizabeth hung on his words as he described the heat, beauty and rugged climbs of Delphi and Athens, the glory of the Parthenon, and the clay beaches of Santorini. His descriptions filled her head with images of him in shirtsleeves, clambering up rocks and mountains, drinking wine in the Greek countryside. Never had she heard him so loquacious on any subject but Pemberley.

It was clear he was not regretting her, nor dwelling on the past; it was unlikely he had even thought of her during his time away. Mr Darcy had tended his estates, then gone off and busied himself with a world she would never experience. She could not regret her time with Jane and Bingley, but it was not what she had truly wished for.

Adventuring, not pining. He was not thinking of me. Marble goddesses and tavernas filled his days.

A slight gasp from Jane startled her. Elizabeth had been so caught up in the stories, she had not noticed her sister had fallen asleep. A deep blush suffused her cheeks, one Elizabeth thought might be equal to the flush of excitement she felt on her own face.

"I am sorry for my rudeness, Mr Darcy," Jane said in a mortified voice. "I find myself tired at this time nearly every day."

Bingley gave her a soft smile. "My saintly wife bears much to carry our child."

"No, no. I apologise, I went on too long." Mr Darcy stood. "I must go. I have an appointment with my solicitor and must first return to my home."

"But you shall keep your promise to join us for all of our Christmas festivities, Mr Darcy?" Jane spoke with some urgency.

Elizabeth felt all the surprise, again, at his assent. The Mr Darcy she remembered would dig his way to Derbyshire to see his sister, especially when it had been half a year since they were last together. While he would not have to suffer the attentions of the absent Miss Bingley, she had believed her own presence might be unbearable to him. But he reiterated his agreement.

"I would be honoured."

"Brilliant!" Bingley rose to escort his friend out. "You are walking home as well, Darcy? Have you lost your carriage in a card game?"

"I assure you all is well with my stables. As you know, my house is but a short distance away and nothing restores one's holiday spirits more than a stroll in December's bracing air."

Mr Darcy looked at Bingley as he spoke, but Elizabeth felt his reply was meant for her and said brightly, "Be it a town or country walk, I would agree."

Bingley guffawed. "Of course you would. If given the chance, Lizzy would walk everywhere. We must keep our eye upon her, or my poor cattle would rarely know exercise now that Caroline is off with the Hursts." He patted his friend's shoulder and led him from the room.

Elizabeth let out a breath as the two men disappeared through the doorway. She had not known how she and Mr Darcy would receive one another upon meeting again; she was relieved that rather than a chance encounter, each had had at least a few minutes' awareness of the other separately before being brought together. Was Mr Darcy surprised she was in residence with the Bingleys? While he had been polite and courteous, and had conversed far more easily than expected, he had shown no real interest in her. Of course, why should he? She was nothing to him now. She was a lady he had once liked well enough to offer for, one whom he had shown his estate and introduced to his sister, and whose complaints had led him to encourage Bingley's return to Netherfield. But he had barely spoken to her then, and hardly again at the wedding. His interest in her had shifted, moved on, if not to another lady, then to goddesses carved in stone.

"Lizzy, you do not mind that I invited Mr Darcy to Christmas, do you? It will not be too awkward for you?"

Jane's anxious tone gave her back her sense of calm, and she turned to her sister. "It would be more awkward for Mr Darcy to find himself at a crowded inn, trapped by snow to the north and the south, and sharing his Christmas pudding with strangers. Of course he is welcomed here, Jane. All are welcome on Christmas, although I would prefer he not bring his aunt, Lady Catherine."

CHAPTER FOUR

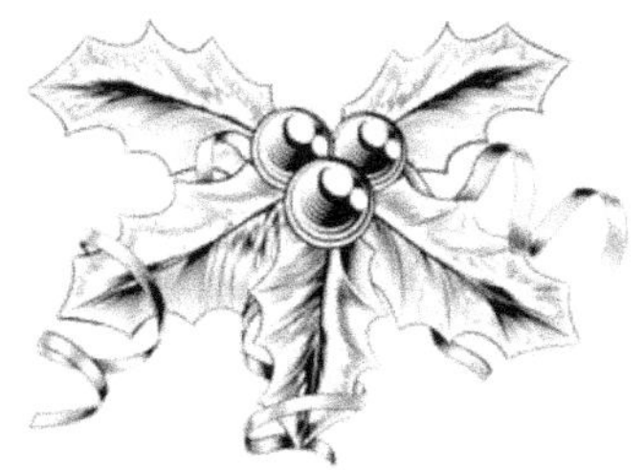

DARCY TOSSED HIS GLOVES ONTO THE TABLE AND STALKED to his study. He had walked triple the distance between his home and Bingley's, going round corner after corner in his efforts to think over the events of the past two hours and cool the overwarm feeling prickling his skin since Bingley had said Elizabeth was there, in his home, perhaps only a room or two away.

And then there she was.

Her beauty was unaltered, her mind as lively and engaged as ever. She made light of awkward moments, she smiled and laughed. But her spirit seemed dimmed, her energies directed towards caring for her sister and heeding the tone set in a house headed by a brother still finding his way and overreaching in his need for order and peace. There was no conversation of deep topics; Mrs Bingley, even when in full health, preferred a gentle atmosphere, where only pleasantness and niceties could be exchanged. Such kind people, but it was a stifling atmosphere for a lady of Elizabeth's intelligence and curiosity. Even Caroline would have been helpful in providing a sharp wit and intellect for sparring.

'If given the chance, Lizzy would walk everywhere.' If given the chance? Was Bingley asserting himself more as guardian than brother? Reining in Elizabeth's natural desire for activity in order to protect her and to ensure his wife's sensitivities were not disturbed?

Her own sensibilities to others—her skill in company—were unchanged. Her kind heart, lent to her elder sister once again, had recognised his discomfort when speaking of Wickham. He had been unsure of her thoughts on the man, her brother even longer than Bingley had been; but she saw his feelings, cloaked as they were, and had shifted the conversation. Did she know he saw it? That he knew what she had done?

He stopped his pacing and sat down at his desk. It was not as empty as he had hoped. Although his solicitor and stewards had done yeoman's work on his estate business, there were many affairs he still needed to address. He reached for his pen and pulled a half-written letter from underneath his blotter.

My plans remain uncertain, my dear. The snow which so amuses you and your cousins at Matlock will soon arrive in London, but sleet, its less welcome cousin, comes tomorrow. After months in the warmth of Greece, your brother has not forgotten how to traverse the worst of snowstorms, but I fear risking the men and horses put to the task of driving me to Derbyshire.

He crossed out the first line—his plans now felt much more certain—and, determined, to post the letter today, put pen to paper.

I was gladdened today to find Charles Bingley and his wife at home, and spent a happy afternoon in conversation there. The Hursts and Caroline Bingley are in the country at present; the Hursts welcomed a son, Marcus, in the autumn. Miss Elizabeth Bennet is in residence to keep company with Mrs Bingley, the former Jane Bennet, who will deliver their first child in the New Year. She is as you remember, charming and intelligent, and is helpful to Mrs Bingley as she nears her confinement. It is a happy household, and with the weather at odds with my hopes, I believe I may spare you worry and remain in town for Christmas with them.

Would you mind so terribly if your brother dawdles a bit, if he is able to procure you sheet music and ribbons and novels he will pretend not to first read? With hope for better weather and improved roads, I shall join you before the New Year. Mr Wright informs me that Pemberley's sleigh is polished and its skids are waxed. I expect you to be our driver come January.

Your laggard but always loving brother,
FD

Elizabeth was frowning at the sad state of the weather the following afternoon, but her mood was greatly livened by the company within the house. Bingley's great aunts from Scarborough had arrived, the two kind ladies who had been his chief correspondents when he was away at school after the deaths of his parents.

She had met Bingley's aunts—Miss Yates and the long-widowed Mrs Wilmot—only once prior, when they had shared few thoughts that were not outrageous, humorous, or embarrassing—most particularly to Caroline. Mrs Wilmot, or Aunt Millie, was especially opinionated, but it was her sister, Aunt Poppy—"Charlie could never pronounce Penelope," she would boast of her intimate acquaintance with her nephew—who often sparkled in pointing out the obvious.

With their fondness for conversation and Christmas traditions, they made a spirited addition to the household. Full of opinions on puddings and pregnancies, both insisted they still could wield a needle and thread to create berry garlands, and peppered Elizabeth and Jane with questions on Bennet family traditions.

They had been chased to London by rain, making their two-day journey more exciting than expected. But it was the snow behind it, the snow that had blanketed much of the north and kept Mr Darcy in town, that was the focus of Elizabeth's fascination, and she admitted, her gratitude.

But by dinner, more snow had arrived. The sight was worrisome, for if the weather worsened, Brother Bingley would feel obligated to insist any scenery be viewed from within a carriage, and she dearly hoped permission for a rare walk come morning. London had been muddy and grey until the northern winds blew in with cold and snow and laid a clean swathing over the streets and roofs. Elizabeth insisted to herself she thought only of the streets and skies. It was not that Mr Darcy's arrival had brightened the town or brought its beauty back in sharp relief; no, that would be too convenient an explanation for why her outlook on the holidays had shifted. But she was not insensible of the pleasure she took in his company, and was quietly delighted he had come to dinner.

"You are enjoying the snow, Miss Bennet?"

She looked up to find Mr Darcy's eyes resting on her; the dining room was lit not only by candles but by the newly brightened evening landscape outside. "I am," she replied, straightening under the intensity of his gaze. "I recognise the snow impedes your travel north, but I find the white blanket gives the city a sense of newness and clarity."

"Clarity, you say? I call it dangerous!" cried Miss Yates, waving her ear trumpet. "Some of us lack the rubber bones and plump bottoms of youth!"

Elizabeth nearly burst out laughing; Bingley had no such restraint. "Aunt Poppy!"

"I would not have you think me insensitive to the woes and dangers winter poses to many of my countrymen and women," said Mr Darcy. "Not all are fortunate to have a warm hearth and safe haven from the cold."

"Nor are all fortunate to have a warm bed with a warm husband or wife." Mrs Wilmot sighed. "It is not that I question the choice of Louisa and her husband to have their son's first Christmas with his grandmother, but with so much joy and mistletoe, it is a shame we have but one married couple amongst us to enjoy it."

"And no little moppets to climb on our laps and beg hugs and candy." Miss Yates looked pointedly at Jane. "Would that we had rubber left enough to bounce them."

Mr Darcy's cough covered the unfortunate squeak of laughter that finally emerged from Elizabeth. Bingley complimented the potatoes and the clatter of forks on plates filled the air until a brief lull in conversation was broken by Mrs Wilmot.

"You must take care of that cough, Mr Darcy. Sickness lurks in the winter winds, and we shan't wish to catch whatever has caught you."

"Mr Darcy is a gentleman in the best of health." Elizabeth's solemn statement was offset by the twitching of her lips. "I have on good authority he is never ill, and is too honourable to pass along any sickness."

Mr Darcy looked amused while Bingley chuckled. "*Caroline* is indeed the font of all Darcy-related praises. But my friend here *is* likely too well-behaved to ever be ill, or to let anyone know if he so much as sneezes." Bingley shrugged and drained his wineglass, oblivious to the incredulous look given him by Mr Darcy.

"Bingley, you have often told me my expression too closely resembles that of a man struck by a megrim."

"Megrims are a terrible affliction, especially for a young man with such a handsome face." Miss Yates sighed heavily. "Biliousness does not choose those who deserve it. Would that it did."

Mrs Wilmot snorted quietly and turned her attention towards Elizabeth with an observation prompting everyone else to look as well. "You there, Miss Bennet. You are a clever girl. Pretty as well."

"Has she no husband?"

"No, Sister, that is why she is referred to as Miss Bennet."

Miss Yates polished off her third glass of wine. "She should have a husband. She could not be much more than twenty and if not soon wed, she will begin the slow putrefaction. Look at Caroline. At three and twenty, her teeth are rotting and her countenance is beset with peevish creases."

Her sister agreed. "A woman needs a husband, if not for happiness, then for comfort and children."

Unwilling to be mortified at her own future decay and deeply amused at the image of Miss Bingley now affixed in her mind, Elizabeth brought her hand to her lips to stifle a laugh. Finally in control of her amusement, she looked between the two ladies and leaned closer to Mrs Wilmot. "You speak from the experience of a happy marriage then? I see that your face is fixed in a merry way."

"Ah, yes. A short period of bliss followed by an age of sorrows." She waved away Elizabeth's immediate and regretful apology. "No, my dear. Five years of joyful amity is far better than many have in a marriage of thirty."

Miss Yates spoke up. "My visage is neither fixed nor unpleasant, for I have enjoyed solitude and the frequent company of my dear nephew, Charlie. His sisters, too," she added after a short pause. She smiled and deep dimples emerged. "And of course, my darling animals."

Elizabeth recalled that this was the lady, complained about by Caroline and nearly worshipped by Charles, who had taken in and nursed lost birds, baby rabbits, orphaned hedgehogs, and a lamed fox kit. Her affection for Miss Yates grew, particularly as her witty opinions had relieved her mind from thinking about the man sitting just across the table, listening to every word of the exchange.

"My efforts have gone to the wild and unfortunate creatures of the forest ever since my first pup was killed by a hunter aiming for a rabbit. Since that day, in memory of Lancelot, I have cared for rabbits and their forest brethren and forsworn eating the flesh of any living creature."

The lady seemed not to notice when the attention of every guest was directed at her plate. No serving of pheasant or roasted beef adorned it; instead it was laden with cheeses, fruits, potatoes, and vegetables. A strange self-consciousness came over Elizabeth, and perhaps the others, for the table fell quite silent.

"You are a Pythagorean?"

Mr Darcy's deep voice pierced the air. Elizabeth looked up to find him smiling kindly at the elderly lady.

"I am indeed," Miss Yates replied, a bit stridently at this notice from the handsome young man across the table. "For nigh on these past thirty years."

"I admire your steadfastness, madam. Such adherence to principles is a virtue."

"Hear, hear," cried Bingley, waving a forkful of potatoes for emphasis. He added, somewhat abashedly, "Although I do enjoy my beef and bacon. And fish and a tasty partridge or chicken."

"Bingley is too kind and welcoming to turn away from anything our cook offers," Elizabeth explained.

"My husband does boast a strong appetite. Every dish is a favourite," said Jane.

"My wife is kind to ensure my favourites are always available, even if her own appetite is less than before," Bingley replied quickly. "This shall be our first Christmas as husband and wife. A special pudding, perhaps, to celebrate!"

His aunts smiled warmly before their attention shifted. "What say you, Miss Bennet?" Mrs Wilmot queried. "You should like to be married?"

"I fear I shall be far too occupied as indulgent aunt to my sister and brother's ten children. Jane and Charles are far too pleasing, however. Of course, their children will be as perfect and happy as they, until my visage reflects only vexation and I become known as the grumpy auntie."

"Such a thing is not possible," said with a Bingley smile.

"No, it is not," Mr Darcy agreed quietly.

"You say that only because Caroline will always be less accommodating than I." She clapped a hand over her mouth, mortified by her outburst.

Bingley's grin burst into a loud guffaw. "You are more polite than I, Lizzy. There is no other contender for the title of 'grumpy auntie' than my sister. We are fortunate that she will gain experience with young Marcus."

"Louisa may wish to exchange sisters," said Mrs Wilmot.

Bingley chuckled. "Hurst has oft proposed the idea."

"Charles."

Elizabeth glanced at Jane, wishing she would worry less for propriety and enjoy the warm camaraderie fostered when family could find humour in one another's foibles. Happy as marriage had made her sister, impending motherhood had made her tired and more anxious than ever for a peaceful house.

Mrs Wilmot turned to Mr Darcy. "Sir, shall you remain in town for amusements? My sister and I so love a good game or two, especially when handsome, unmarried men play with us. Do you not agree, Miss Bennet?"

Perhaps she could laugh at Mr Darcy's stunned expression much later, but at present, Elizabeth's own mortification could only match his. "I enjoy games with anyone, be they my young cousins or my neighbours," she managed to say. "If you find advantage in such diversions by partnering with or competing against handsome, unmarried men, you must explain your strategy to all of us. My brother can no longer benefit or protect himself, but Mr Darcy deserves full knowledge of your schemes."

Bingley chuckled and Mrs Wilmot tittered. "With such a clever mind as yours, Miss Bennet, I believe *you* must be my partner in any amusement!"

CHAPTER FIVE

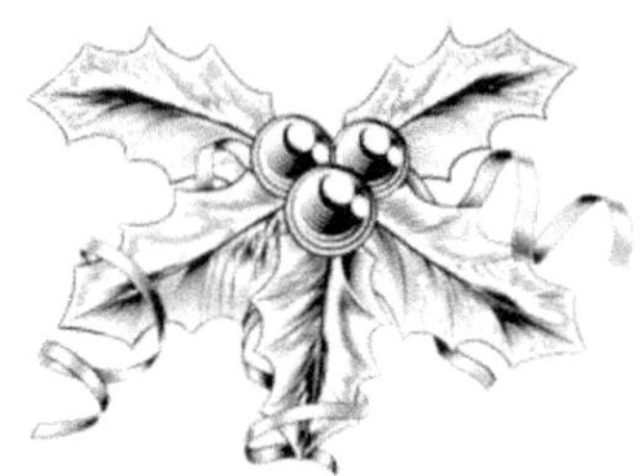

WITH SUCH A SMALL PARTY, A SEPARATION OF SEXES WAS hardly needed; the older ladies were fatigued by their travels, as well as the good wine and spirited conversation, and retired early. Jane was soon to follow but Elizabeth lingered in the front sitting room. Darcy, although eager to return home before the snow was to his knees, joined Bingley for a brandy.

"You have determined to give up Netherfield. So your child—it will be born in town?" At Bingley's firm nod, Darcy continued. "You will host Mrs Bennet here?"

A smile flickered across Bingley's face. "Mr Bennet has promised me he can spare his wife for no more than a fortnight, and the Gardiners are all that is gracious. We have but two spare guest chambers, after all. Caroline maintains her rooms, Lizzy has hers, and the nursery of course." He sipped his brandy. "Come, Darcy! Are you not impressed at how thorough I have been in my planning?"

Darcy did indeed admire his friend's newly forged decisiveness. "I am."

Bingley smiled and popped a chocolate in his mouth.

"Are you to remain here in town?"

"I should like to settle in the country, of course, and some distance between us and Meryton would be advantageous. I have long admired Pemberley."

"It is not for sale."

"Mayhap there is an estate near it. Derbyshire is fine country—"

"And three days' journey from Meryton, in fine weather." Darcy sat back in his chair, glancing at the smug expression on Bingley's countenance. "Your mind is sharper than when I saw you last. Is it marriage or the knowledge that you soon will be a father that has so altered your perspective?" He knew the answer, of course, but was generous enough to indulge his friend a few minutes expounding on the joys of being husband to 'the most wonderful angel in all of England'.

Finally, mindful that their glasses were empty and his wife awaited him, Bingley sighed. "Derbyshire is indeed some distance. Jane would not like to take Lizzy too far away from her own opportunities to make a match."

"She is with you to keep her sister company. Does she seek a husband? Why is she not married? Has she sworn off the idea?"

"I am her brother and cannot claim to know her heart or what events have occurred outside my knowledge. She has had at least two proposals."

Darcy froze. "Two?"

"Oh yes, you knew of the first, I think. That cousin of the Bennets, Mr Collins, was not a good fit for Lizzy's temperament, and went on to marry the eldest Lucas girl. She was older than Louisa, so it was a good match for her."

"The Collinses have been established at Hunsford, Lady Catherine's parsonage, for well past a year. When did he propose marriage to Miss Bennet?"

Bingley rolled his eyes and reached for another chocolate. "Do try one, these are quite good."

Darcy demurred and waited for the other man to savour the sweet and provide him the information so critical to his well-being.

"It was two years ago, after we had closed Netherfield and gone to London. Dark days for everyone, and poor Lizzy had to defend herself from Mrs Bennet's efforts to force her to marry Collins, what with him being Longbourn's heir and all. It was Mr Bennet who refused the idea of such a match, and Collins went off and proposed to Miss Lucas just like that."

"Just like that," Darcy repeated, shocked to learn his proposal at Hunsford was Elizabeth's second; briefly, he wondered whether Collins received a similarly blistering refusal. "Without either admiration or love, he jumped from one lady's refusal to another in matrimony in a moment."

"He saw an opportunity for happiness. He wanted a wife."

"As you see it." Darcy rolled his eyes. "And the other? The other proposal?"

Bingley fixed him with a look. "You take an uncommon interest in Lizzy's romantic history."

"Hardly romantic history. The lady is unlikely to volunteer details of how her time has been spent the year I have been gone, and as she is your wife's sister, I wish not to stumble about in conversation and insult her. As is my wont, you know."

"Ha, well, clearly other men find my favourite sister quite tolerable." Bingley ignored Darcy's glower. "Last spring, it was a clerk of her uncle's that took a fancy to Lizzy."

"Mr Gardiner?"

"No, back in Meryton. Mr Philips's law clerk, Shawcross. Rather jovial for the law, I thought, but clever underneath all his bluster. He grew sweet on Lizzy but she refused him last spring, and he is now settled on Catherine. I am in rare agreement with Caroline in her opinion that the men Lizzy refuses are beneath her, but they find contentment with her friends and sisters. It is an odd thing, as if Elizabeth knows who better suits her suitors."

Bingley laughed at his own cleverness, irritating Darcy even beyond what he had felt the past few minutes. He bit back his immediate response to such an absurd declaration. He could admit to feeling himself beneath Elizabeth in understanding and wit, but *he* would find no contentment with any woman connected to her. Not even had she a twin sister; Elizabeth Bennet was singular in every way.

Shaking off his thoughts, Darcy smiled guilelessly at his friend. "And what is the meaning of such an observation as it pertains to your marriage to Miss Bennet's favourite sister? Is there anything you wish to confide to me—?"

"No, do not dare joke on this matter! As you well know, Jane was always my heart's first desire and she is all I could wish for in a wife," cried Bingley, his eyes steeled against any insult to his angel. "I like Lizzy a great deal but she is too intelligent and too independent for any of her suitors. Mr Bennet is not a father who keeps close rein on his daughters. Jane and Mary were content at home, Catherine blew as the wind or as Lydia inclined her. But Lizzy is different."

She is better.

"Lizzy has such a keen mind and interest in all things. She chafes at my insistence on a chaperon or footman to escort her on her walks and errands."

"You seek to temper her independence?" Darcy could scarcely keep his outrage from his voice.

"Elizabeth is my sister. I am responsible for her safekeeping. The neighbourhood is a safe one, but often she goes to the park and into less familiar neighbourhoods. Caroline has tested me in her own way, but Lizzy must have some boundaries to allow Jane her peace of mind."

Darcy had been overjoyed by the liveliness in Elizabeth's conversation and the bright look of fascination in her eyes as he spoke of his travels. How interested she had been! How often had he imagined her at his side at he walked the ruined temples and fragrant gardens in Greece? She would be a far worthier companion on such an excursion than any man he could name. He felt great frustration for her, suppressing her own needs to those of a brother and sister who would be happy wherever they were placed, but never seek out more than the comfort at hand.

"Elizabeth is not a lady who likes to be ordered about. Not by you, her father, or by any man. Is that not why she has refused so many proposals?"

Bingley stared at him. "Two...not so many. And when did you begin to call my sister by her Christian name?"

Darcy reached for the tray of chocolates. "These do look rather good."

A few minutes later, after donning his coat and hat, he pulled his scarf from his pocket and waved off the elderly butler. Slowly looking around the entry hall, emptied but for a small pile of boxes, he noticed Elizabeth's half-boots sitting underneath the bench, dry, alert and at the ready for her next sojourn to London's streets and parks if 'given the chance'. A red muff lay beside them. He could imagine how she charmed the house's servants, providing such a contrast to Miss Bingley's petty strictures and Mrs Bingley's serene restraint. His mind lost in thought, his fingers loosened their grip on the silken fabric and the cloth fell beside Elizabeth's left boot. The sound of laughter from down the corridor stirred him from his reverie and clearing his throat, he reached for the doorknob and slipped out.

CHAPTER SIX

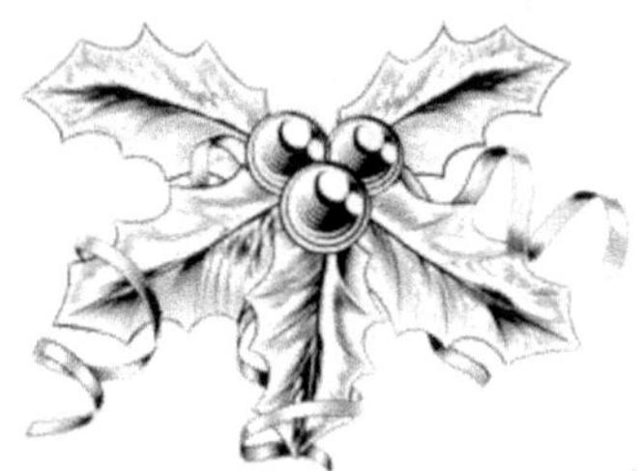

"CAN'T YOU QUIET THAT CHILD? 'E'S BEEN WAILING FOR THE past hour!"

The exhausted young woman shifted the writhing bundle in her arms and glared at the worn, angry man sitting across from her in the crowded carriage. She began to reply, but instead turned her head to her baby and traced a soothing finger over his red, unhappy face.

The old woman beside her stirred. "Is he hungry or in need of a cleaning?" She smiled underneath her thick woollen wraps. "I had three myself, all hardy lads now. Give him to me, dear. I know a song or two to help settle the sweet thing."

She tucked her scarf over the infant and took him from his mother's arms. A strong gust rattled the carriage, bringing an icy blast of wind through the unsealed windows and door. "Close your eyes a while, miss. We shall reach London in no time at all."

Darcy paced across his chambers. He could not sleep. Not after nearly two days spent under the same roof as Elizabeth Bennet. The same Elizabeth Bennet who had turned him away, and likely would have again, had turned away another man? Three proposals in total? Who was this third man? It was bad enough to stand in company with a man like Mr

Collins, but yet another had sought her hand and again spurned, quickly pursued another?

He leaned his forehead against the windowpane. Was he the only one who saw her true value? No man worthy of Elizabeth Bennet could spin away and swiftly settle for another lady! These men had waited hours, weeks! He had waited well over a year and had not considered, nay noticed, another lady.

The walk to his home from the Bingleys should have helped him shake off his stupor. He had sought the bracing cold winds that stung his face, waking him to the bittersweet reality that was now his: he was trapped in London for Christmas with Elizabeth Bennet. He had once dreamt of being trapped with her, huddled in the warmth of their marriage bed, passing the hours talking, learning about each other, making the other laugh, reading, loving each other. Instead, after months spent in the warm embrace of Greece's sun, endeavouring with some success not to think about the lady, he was mired with her in the bitter cold of Mayfair.

But we have shared a laugh, he told himself. *And exchanged glances of amusement at the exhortations of Bingley and his aunts.*

She does not hate me. She is not indifferent to me. She may not love me, but I believe she finds me tolerable company.

The weather was not improving; the snows had moved south and would remain for at least two more days. He would be with his friends —with *her*—for Christmas Day, and would not be able to travel until at least the Monday following.

Christmas had been a quiet day of reflection for him the past few years. If at Pemberley, as he preferred, he and Georgiana often joined their family at Matlock for a few days. Poor weather or unhappy spirits had occasioned them to be home alone, or to spend the holiday in London to enjoy the shopping and shows. They had never spent a Christmas apart—not even last year, when he left Bingley's wedding to return to her in London.

At least Georgiana was in good company with her aunt and uncle. Richard would provide a dose of frivolity and fun, and his older brother and his wife had an infant daughter Darcy had yet to meet but who had enchanted his sister. It seemed there was a wife and a child for every man, even Wickham.

His scowl disappeared at the sound of church bells. It was nearly Christmas, the day to celebrate the birth of the Christ child, and he was wallowing in envy and remorse. He was young, healthy—and contrary to certain declarations made at his expense—perfectly capable of sneezing in company if circumstance necessitated. He was wealthy and intelligent, his manners had improved, and he was fated by the heavens —and Mother Nature—to spend the next few days with the woman he loved.

He had known he would never be indifferent to her charms, but he had hoped to have at least quelled his susceptibility to the attraction. Outgrown, outlasted his love for her. He was a fool. He would always love her. He could not walk away and begin another year without trying to win her. If she was still averse to him, he could hasten to his sister and be done.

God rest ye, merry gentleman, he laughed softly to himself. *Let nothing you dismay.*

Elizabeth was a sound sleeper, and it was only the howling December winds and the tapping noises beyond her door that stirred her. The high-pitched noise increased in volume as she sat up, but it was the sound of her name breaking through as the source of the screech that brought her to her feet. She reached for her thick dressing gown and slippers and stumbled in the dark towards the door.

"Jane?" she called out, fearful that her elder sister was in distress. But it was not Jane who replied.

"Lizzy? Lizzy!"

"Lydia?!" *Here?*

Wide awake now, her spirits sinking as shock thrummed through her, Elizabeth hurried downstairs to find her youngest sister, wrapped in a snow-splattered coat, surrounded by Bingley, Stokes, and Mrs Cooke. She averted her eyes from their state of dress—all, like her, clad in robes and gowns and slippers—and stared at Lydia and the wailing infant in the basket at her feet.

"Hello, Lizzy! Come meet your nephew!"

Her sister had come without Mr Wickham, perhaps the most favourable aspect Elizabeth could find in the entire situation. In most circumstances, a babe was a blessing; in this, however, shock and trepidation warred with the joy Elizabeth should feel at meeting her sister's child. Her nephew was unharmed by the ordeal of travelling; he remained in that deep sleep known only to babies and cats, and Elizabeth was content to wait until the dawn came for his eyes to open and reveal which of his parents he most resembled.

Lydia appeared amused by their dazed expressions and proved loquacious on the odours and foibles of her fellow passengers on the post. Of Mr Wickham, she had less to say. 'Business with his commanding officer' was not an answer Elizabeth could find satisfactory.

Once she had shaken off the snow and handed off her son to Jane, Lydia sat in the middle of the large sofa and prepared to regale the stunned but sleepy household with her tale.

"This is a pretty room, Jane. So comfortable and warm," she said, eyeing the roaring fire built quickly by the footmen. "I am famished! Will your kitchen bring me some cake and chocolate?" Pleased by Jane's assurance that a tray was being prepared, Lydia proceeded with her announcement. "I am to astonish Mama, bringing her the most wonderful Christmas surprise."

Elizabeth fought the urge to scold her youngest sister for her heedless thinking. "If she or Papa does not suffer apoplexy at the slight of you arriving alone, in a snowstorm."

"She and Papa will be overjoyed to meet their grandchild," Jane said, sighing as the infant gurgled in her arms.

"Well, yes, but me as well!" Lydia smirked before providing her audience with a loud, elaborate sigh. "Much as I have missed Mama, I am certain she has regretted my absence even more."

Jane continued to gaze at the babe, her finger softly stroking his pink cheek as he slept. Bingley looked as though he were half drunk with the angelic image, although Elizabeth suspected her brother was merely half asleep.

Where Elizabeth and Bingley found beauty, Lydia found humour. "You are glowing, Jane. Your babe shall not arrive for a month at least and your crib sits empty while I have the babe to use it. Pray you have some clean cloths? Poor Freddie has been swaddled tightly for better than a day."

"The Bingley family crib—" Elizabeth began, before her incredulous reply was interrupted.

"We are of course pleased to have you with us." Bingley gazed blearily at Lydia. "The nursery is not yet furnished fully but we shall make up something for the babe. With Caroline gone, you will be accommodated in her rooms."

"Miss Bingley has wed? Surely not! She—"

Elizabeth lay a calming hand on her sister's. "Miss Bingley is in Surrey with the Hursts."

Lydia smirked her understanding. "It will be a fine joke for her to return and find me in her bed!"

More than a year of marriage and six months as a mother had done nothing to alter her behaviour. Her cheeks were as plump and her laugh as loud as it had been last year, when she brought her husband to Longbourn. Elizabeth's heart softened. Her own life may have been uneventful over the same period, but her youngest sister had become a mother and tended to the birth of her son. She reached towards Jane and, raising her eyebrows in silent request, took the bundled infant from her arms. He looked as any other babe; fubsy and pink, with a cherubic face, dark lashes, and as yet, nary a hair on his head. Innocence personified, even if he was the son of a wicked man. She ran a finger along the baby's cheek.

"Mr Wickham will not join you in London? Will he come to Longbourn for you?"

"Of course, Lizzy. My husband is a busy and important man. He was lately in Brighton, in the large encampments there, though why anyone would wish to be by the sea in the dead of winter is ridiculous. 'Tis a soldier's life," she said, laughing. "He shall join me at Longbourn in a few days to celebrate Christmas. I so missed it last year."

Elizabeth glanced at Jane. The Gardiners and their four children, as well as Aunt Gardiner's recently widowed elder sister and her daughter, already claimed all of Longbourn's guest chambers. She should send a note to warn her father of her sister's unexpected arrival. Lydia could read her expression and protested the idea.

"No, Lizzy! It is to be a surprise!"

The door opened and Miss Yates toddled in.

"Charlie, I heard a noise," she cried. "Is it the French? Have they reached Mayfair?"

Elizabeth could not decide whether to laugh at the question or at the befuddled expression on Bingley's face.

"Well?"

Elizabeth placed the baby in Jane's arms and rose to comfort the distraught lady. "It is not the French invading us, it is my sister, Mrs Lydia Wickham."

The older woman squinted at the faces staring up at her. "Another of your sisters? Is she one of the good ones?"

Lydia snorted, more amused than affronted. "I am more than good, I am one of the married ones."

"Ah yes," said Miss Yates, lowering herself to the seat across from Lydia. "The youngest sister, wed to a soldier of some sort. Were you beset by the French? Did he send you to us here so he could go fight them?"

Lydia looked at her sisters, clearly uncertain whether she was speaking to a mad woman.

"My sister's husband, Lieutenant Wickham, had business in the south but will join her at Longbourn, my father's estate in Hertfordshire."

Miss Yates did not reply to Elizabeth's explanation. Her attention had been captured by the sleeping bundle in Jane's arms.

"Charlie! Your wife has had the babe! How hale you look, Jane! 'Tis early, is it not?"

CHAPTER SEVEN

If snow was likely to slow the letter Elizabeth penned to her father, alerting him to Lydia's anticipated arrival two days hence, she was even less able to warn Mr Darcy about the Bingleys' unexpected visitor. Fortunately, Lydia was a late sleeper and was surrounded by sisters and servants eager to care for her son, providing Jane and Elizabeth the opportunity to discuss the situation.

Elizabeth had been up far too late thinking on Mr Darcy when her first moments of sleep had been interrupted by Lydia's arrival. Another hour or two of conversation and settling in the new visitors and calming down a high-spirited Miss Yates had gotten her to her bed only an hour before dawn. When she arrived at the breakfast table to find only Jane, her fatigue and worry showed in her eyes and in her speech. She fixed a plate and sat down wearily across from her sister.

"I rarely find you alone at breakfast. Is Bingley gone to the kitchen to demand more bacon and jams?"

"He was here earlier, and wished to do some business and return before the house was awake. He worries I will be taxed by Lydia and Freddie."

"Your husband is mired in a houseful of women, and mindful of the demands and difficulties inherent in certain of us." Elizabeth buttered a piece of toast she was not certain she would eat; a walk outside in the bracing cold would remedy her fatigue more thoroughly than would even a delicious breakfast, but Jane had already been upset enough for one day. "He is a good man, attentive to your needs and wishes. However, I am less kind. I believe Lydia thinks her visit is a delightful surprise fashioned for the pleasure of all of us."

Jane laid aside her napkin. "Little Freddie appears well, does he not? He is not turned six months, Lizzy. Why would Lydia travel such a distance, in such weather, alone, with an infant?"

"Because she wished to, Jane. What Lydia wants, Lydia gets." And she had gotten what she wanted, Elizabeth thought, albeit with a limited span of happiness and security. A cavalier husband who had not provided her a real home, who would send his wife and infant child on the post to London, not even confirming their safe arrival at the Bingleys' home, let alone making certain they reached town. Mr Darcy had gone to great lengths and personal expense to ensure Lydia was safely married and Wickham could not bother to guarantee his family's welfare. She was ashamed, again, at her sister's foolishness and her father's inaction, but her thoughts centred on Mr Darcy. *How did he bear it? How will be bear seeing Lydia—and that man's child—here?*

"Lizzy, do not be angry. All is well. No harm came to our sister and nephew, and our parents will be so pleased to have them for Christmas Day."

"You do not worry for Lydia and her son? This careless life holds dangers for them."

"I prefer to think well of Mr Wickham for wishing his wife to be with her family rather than alone at an inn or encampment. Lydia has not been to Longbourn or seen our parents in nearly a year. It is a gift for them to spend some weeks together."

"Weeks, though? How can Mr Wickham be absent from his duties for such a time?" Elizabeth stabbed a slice of poached pear with her fork.

"Lydia said if Mr Wickham does not arrive in time for Christmas, he will join her after the New Year," Jane said, laying a hand on her midsection. "How terrible it must be for a father to be separated from his child at such a time."

He has abandoned her. If not forever, he has decided she is a burden and sent her away so he can make merry elsewhere.

"How much the separation was by choice or by force is the truer issue. I am happy to see my sister, but I worry that motherhood has not made her wiser."

Jane shifted in her chair. "Be that as it may, I believe young Frederick Wickham's cries are stirring this little one. The babe is kicking me."

Elizabeth smiled, watching the warm glow spread across Jane's face, already softened by the pounds she had gained in service to nurturing the child she carried. Jane's contentment should be enough to placate her worries. Lydia had made her choice—a bad one—and all her family could do now was support and care for her and her son.

"I understand Bingley's joy in seeing Mr Darcy again, but I should like to spare him from meeting Lydia."

Jane looked at her, incredulous. "Mr Darcy is our friend, but Lydia is our sister. He can make his own choice—to remain with us for Christmas dinner or to stay away." She lifted her teacup to her lips. "I do not think he will stay away. Although Mr Darcy may not be pleased with Lydia's company, he is more than pleased to be in yours, and I think you realise it. Why else are your cheeks nearly as red as holly berries when he looks at you?"

"Mr Bingley is here, sir."

Darcy looked up, startled. His knocker was off, but Hobson was wise enough to know if anyone could be admitted anyway, it was Bingley. Still, at half past ten, it was quite early for Bingley.

His friend breezed through the doorway into the breakfast parlour. "I say, Darcy, your poor servants. Not a bit of holly or ribbon to be found in this house! Are you so heartless as to deprive them of merrymaking?"

Bingley winked at him and took a seat at the table.

"You are welcomed to see the pine boughs and ribboned bells below stairs, Bingley, but unlike you, I have given those of my people with families the week to go home and celebrate. Only Hobson, Parsons, Mrs Rutter, the cook, and a maid or two are in residence. Are you come here to nettle me on my alleged parsimony or to steal a bite of eggs and rolls?"

Bingley looked chagrined. "No, indeed. Well, perhaps some jam and one of those French rolls." He reached across the table and prepared a small plate before accepting a cup of coffee from a footman. "I am here to provide you a warning. Lizzy is of the opinion—"

Incredulous, Darcy heard no more. "You are warning me off your sister?"

Bingley looked perplexed. "Should I? Which sister—Lizzy or Caroline?" He laughed.

Darcy paused to sip his coffee and regain his bearings. "What is this warning, then?"

"Lydia. Mrs Wickham. She arrived at our door last night, just off the stage coach, I believe."

Darcy stared, unblinking. "Is she alone?"

"No, I mean yes—Wickham is not with her, apparently indispensable at his post or some such thing. But she has brought their son, an infant of some five months. She plans to surprise Mr and Mrs Bennet," he added around a mouthful of bread. "I know—madness, yes?

"Has Wickham abandoned her?"

"Lydia says he means to follow in a day or so and meet her at Longbourn. He has been lately in Brighton."

"Brighton?" Darcy's thoughts raced. What was in Brighton? The army maintained a significant presence there, but Colonel Fitzwilliam kept an eye on Wickham's doings and had said nothing of the dastard being posted to Brighton. His mind went to the worst scenario: smuggling. Or desertion. Or—

Bingley yawned loudly. "Pardon me. Lydia surprised us with her arrival only hours ago. Knowing your dislike of Wickham, I did not wish you to be surprised. I-*we* were uncertain you would wish to join us for the day or two that Lydia is with us. And as we have only recently been reunited, I hope you will abide by your plan to join us for Christmas."

"I would not wish to distress you and Mrs Bingley by absenting myself. Nor do I wish to be alone in a dull, cold house, as I have given the servants the day off."

"You will join us. Brilliant. Your company is desired by more than myself and Mrs Bingley. Lizzy has been enlivened by your presence, and by that of my aunts. We shall make a merry party." Bingley chuckled as he lifted a heaping spoonful of jam to his roll. "Whatever her faults, no one can say Lydia is not a jolly addition to any room she enters."

Darcy nodded, less aware of the breadcrumbs Bingley was dropping mindlessly on his plate than he was on the crumbs of information his friend appeared to be dropping deliberately. He was near certain Bingley was speaking for Elizabeth as well.

Lydia Wickham, in residence with the Bingleys. Perfect. The pangs of anger at what her husband had wrought on the Bennets and his own sister and countless others had dulled; now his concern centred on the outcome—a young wife and mother, barely more than a girl, who appeared to have been abandoned by the cur.

And Elizabeth, already tending to one sister's needs, now concerned with another and worse still, thrust back into the living memory of all that had first wounded their understanding of one another. Darcy had done what he could for Lydia Bennet; the moment he heard of her 'elopement' from Brighton, he had raced to town to extract her from Wickham. The dazed effrontery she had affected, the rumpled bed, the duration of their stay in that hovel...he had patched together a wedding for them. And here was the happy ending? Wickham, back in Brighton? Lydia, sent off to London with a babe in tow? Could Elizabeth forgive him? Could he forgive himself? He must. They had been apart a year, and he saw, as before, his future, his life, was with this beautiful, contrary woman with the heart-stopping eyes.

He stepped out his front door, took a deep breath, and climbed into his carriage. He would do a little shopping, clear his head, before venturing to tea at Bingley's house. The air was clean, the skies blue, and the neighbourhood was full of cheerful passers-by. Truly, he thought, it was no wonder that the Bingleys had yet another surprise visitor. It was Christmastide, after all. A time for families to gather, even if they had to travel great distances to celebrate together. Of course, *he* had expended great energy to return to England for the holiday—he had crossed an ocean in rough seas, for goodness' sake. And if his efforts to reach his family had sputtered when he discovered Elizabeth Bennet living within a few minutes' walk, unwed and unpromised, inclement weather made for a convenient excuse to stay in town. No one by the name of Wickham would chase him off this time. Whatever change Elizabeth had not yet seen in him, or had forgotten after the brief time they shared at Pemberley, he could show her now by exhibiting the friendly manners he had practised.

CHAPTER EIGHT

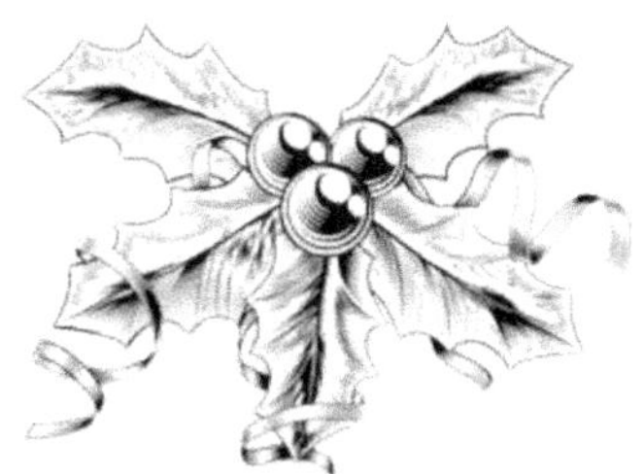

"Oh, it is so festive here, Jane! You have strung the berries and the holly and greens are so pretty." Lydia looked up. "But I have seen no kissing bough! Are you and Bingley such a married couple that you see no need for frivolity? When Wickham and I have such a house, we will throw merry parties and dinners, and hang kissing boughs in every room—even when it is not the Christmas season!"

Miss Yates leaned closer with her ear trumpet. "You are a lively sort, Mrs Wickham."

"One should always have cause for liveliness, madam." Lydia's dimples emerged as she gave the elderly women a broad smile before gesturing to the rest of the table. "You see, I am a married lady and mama to the dearest boy in the world, but I have not lost my joy."

"This is the time for joy," Mrs Wilmot said. "And 'tis your son's first Christmas, as well."

"Oh yes," Lydia said. "That is why I wish to go to Longbourn, so that Frederick could be part of all the festivities."

"Mama and Papa will be pleased to have you home for Christmas," Jane smiled.

Mrs Wilmot nodded her agreement. "Aye, he is their grandson, but a mite young for sweets and games and dancing."

"I would be pleased to dance with my nephew, no matter his inability to walk or eat cake," Elizabeth said to the amusement of all.

Bingley sighed happily. "Jane has mentioned much gaiety during Christmas at Longbourn. I am sorry to have taken her away from such events this season."

"And last!" cried Lydia. "You wed her and took her off to Netherfield for much of the holiday!

"Um, yes I did. But you, dear sister, were absent as well."

Lydia appeared thoughtful, even a bit melancholy, prompting Elizabeth to realise her youngest sister was homesick, and in fact yearning for her family during the happy Christmas season.

"It was my first Christmas without one of Lizzy's pantomimes! She writes such funny little plays for the children, and Kitty and Jane and I create costumes and such, while Mary plays the music." Lydia turned to Elizabeth excitedly. "Do come to Longbourn with me! We shall have such a merry time!"

"We shall have a merry time today, and send you off with gifts and kisses tomorrow, Lyddie. And you shall lead the fun at Longbourn, and tell stories and write plays for our cousins."

"It shall not be the same Yuletide."

"It had best not be! Last year's goose is well rotted now," Bingley laughed.

Elizabeth's smile at her brother's joke faded as she watched him stride to the doorway to greet Mr Darcy. Her breath caught as she watched him sweep a lock of his dark hair off his forehead. When they had first met two years ago, she had persuaded herself that she was indifferent to his looks, that Wickham was his superior in appearance and character. How wrong, how shallow she had been, denying the truth because of a slight given by a man with every reason to be uncomfortable with his friend's urging him to dance. An overheard insult, taken to extremes. How often had she or her father made a joke at another's expense? How often did her father continue to do so while exercising no control over his own family? And what had been the result? The Bingleys, and she, removed here to London. With Mr Darcy and Lydia. She could laugh at the irony if it were not so painful.

She turned back to her sister. "This Christmas is the same as the last in that we celebrate and sing. But you can make new traditions, try new games, and give and receive new gifts. You can teach all of this to your son."

A moment later, Elizabeth realised Mr Darcy was standing in front of Lydia. She detected no animus or regret for having to be in company with the wife of his most wretched friend. Instead, he bowed, and in a kind voice, said,

"Good afternoon, Mrs Wickham. Congratulations on the birth of your son."

"And of course I had to be swifter than my cousins, and landed hard on the ice. Two fingers were broken. I have skated only twice since that day." Bingley's expression showed how well he recalled the pain of that long-ago afternoon. His wife looked down at his hand, her soft expression full of concern for an injury some fifteen years' past.

"The true damage has been passed on to those receiving his correspondence," quipped Darcy.

"You wound me! In this, the season of holiday cheer and love!"

Mrs Wilmot reached over the small table between them and patted Bingley's knee. "Your friend is accurate, Nephew. You have a very poor hand. My eyes tire and my head spins trying to read your letters. It is unfortunate, as your news is always welcome, and far more cheerful, than that of many of our other relations."

Mrs Wickham laughed. "Lizzy's letters are cheerful but she has so many to write, her letters can be hurried. Mary's letters go half-read. Her penmanship is as dull and staid as her news."

Darcy refrained from rolling his eyes. The girl was married and a mother, and still showed no restraint in polite company. He sipped his tea and smiled, mindful of exhibiting a more generous spirit in Mrs Wickham's presence than she merited; her sisters, however, deserved all civility and understanding.

Miss Yates appeared to find Elizabeth's sister a fascinating creature. "You are the youngest of five daughters, Mrs Wickham?"

"I am the youngest of my sisters and the first married!" She leaned closer to Miss Yates and whispered in a manner that commanded notice, "I was fortunate to have caught the attentions of a handsome man while in my prime. My sister Mary shall remain an unsought spinster like Miss Bingley. She has had no proposals, but Lizzy is pestered with them from pesky men."

Darcy stared down at his near empty cup, focusing his attention on a small scar on his wrist. He had done his best, asking after Lydia Wickham's health, and that of her son; he had enquired as to his name and likeness and parried her dumbfounded response upon learning he had gone to Greece. 'Why go look at dusty old ruins and rocks when you have an estate like Pemberley,' she had cried. 'Had we known you were gone, George—who was raised there—and I could have run things in your absence!'

No, he could be polite but he could not enjoy her company; a year wed to Wickham had only coarsened her manners.

"Lydia! Miss Bingley, Mary and I neither deserve nor wish for your opinion on our private matters. No gentleman should be mocked for the courage it takes to propose marriage to a lady."

Astonished, Darcy looked up and found Elizabeth, her cheeks pinked by mortification, staring with evident vexation at her sister. He tilted his head, trying to capture her gaze but she evaded his scrutiny.

"But Lizzy—first the odious Mr Collins, and then the eager Mr Shawcross!" She looked around the room, happy to enthral her audience. "As soon as he could lift his head from my uncle's lawbooks, he set off in pursuit of Lizzy."

"Lydia, that is not how it was with Mr Shawcross—" Mrs Bingley began.

Darcy was hardly listening; Elizabeth had met his eyes. He gave her a small smile, the kind of soft, awkward smile he recalled sharing with her when they walked together at Pemberley. She returned it, and shrugged in resignation as her youngest sister went on, preening in the full attention of her company. Miss Yates leaned closer, clearly keen for details of a tragic love story.

"La, once Lizzy had her say and broke his heart, poor Mr Shawcross was turned towards Kitty. A much more willing prospect for him, although Kitty must endure the future wrinkles round his eyes and brow from reading all that fine print!"

"Wrinkles and creases tell the tale of one's felicity," offered Miss Yates. "Or so I understand it to be with my worries over my creatures."

Bingley supplied a soft, polite chuckle before complimenting his aunt's jolly warmth and assuming blame for a few of her worry lines.

Mrs Wickham was not yet done with her need to remain the room's centre of attention. "You should laugh as well, Lizzy, for you have lost your best chance for a husband. Now all you have is to be nursemaid to Jane and her babies."

Enough, Darcy thought to himself. He tore his gaze from Elizabeth and turned to Mrs Wickham.

"Your sister—both of your sisters—are fortunate to be in company together and enjoy the care and companionship they provide one another. Mrs Bingley has spent a full year settling in as my friend's wife and as mistress of his house. I have only just arrived in town myself, and during my travels, missed the close bonds of family and trusted friends, for they are the greatest treasure God can give to us. Any man privileged enough to win the esteem and affection of Miss Bennet would be the most fortunate, nay happiest, man in the world."

Darcy sat back, seemingly oblivious to the stares and blushes fixed on the faces around him. He had practically declared himself but felt no embarrassment or awkwardness; it was fury and indignation that fuelled his stoic expression. Lydia Wickham was not different, not improved from the girl who had been Lydia Bennet. She had changed not a whit, but remained brash, ridiculous, and completely uncaring of the feelings of others. If he was more generous, he might think her lonely and overly exuberant to be in company, but her insults to Elizabeth denied him such compassion.

"Hear, hear, my friend," cried Bingley, raising his wineglass and clearly relieved to have had the conversation directed towards happier topics. "To the joys of friends and family, this Christmas season and many more to come!"

Darcy nodded and held up his own glass. He felt Elizabeth's presence, her thoughts and judgment of his words, all around him, and he knew her attention was fixed on him. Was she angered by his words, practically shaming her sister? Was she angered that he had spoken so imprudently of her, as if a prize to be won by a suitor? Darcy allowed his gaze to drift over to her. She was pale, but her eyes were bright with mischief. Her lips quirked as she leaned in his direction, saying quietly,

"I have had the pleasure of your acquaintance long enough to know that you find great enjoyment in occasionally professing opinions which in fact are not your own."

CHAPTER NINE

ELIZABETH WATCHED MR DARCY'S EXPRESSION TURN TO astonishment, then mirth.

"I assure you, madam, my words and opinion are united."

Lydia was prattling on to Miss Yates and Jane was whispering to Bingley, but Elizabeth heard and saw nothing but Mr Darcy, smiling at her. She had no idea what to say; her thoughts were scattered yet stuck, and the quiet joy she felt was enough to content her.

The moment was broken when Mrs Wilmot waved her lace handkerchief and cleared her throat. "Mrs Wickham, do you know the story of the three sisters? Their father was too poor to afford dowries, so they had no hope of marriage. One night, St Nicholas dropped a purse of coins down the chimney into the house. The purse fell into a stocking that was put by the fire to dry. It was discovered in the morning and allowed the eldest daughter to marry.

"St Nicholas repeated the act and the second daughter was able to be married. The father was beside himself to discover who was so kindly giving money to his family. Night after night he kept watch by the fire, waiting for St Nicholas to return with money for the youngest daughter's dowry."

Lydia clapped her hands and laughed. "What a fine joke! To have money appear just like that in one's stocking! How my Wickham would enjoy such good fortune." Abruptly her giggles stopped. "Was there a trick? Did something terrible happen to the youngest daughter?"

Elizabeth stiffened and felt Mr Darcy's eyes brush over her.

"This is not a dreadful tale of comeuppance, Mrs Wickham. It is a story of Christmas kindness and tradition." Mrs Wilmot sniffed. "St Nicholas was caught by the father, whom he begged into remaining silent as he did not wish his good deeds to be known. However, no tale of such goodness, especially as it involves gold, can go untold and the story soon got out. From then on, and to this day, anyone receiving a gift owes thanks to St Nicholas."

Lydia gasped. "No matter the time of year?"

Miss Yates gave her an odd look. "No, you silly girl, at Christmastime."

"Father Christmas was kind enough to visit us as children." Bingley smiled softly at Jane. "He will visit our son or daughter next Christmas."

"I have a delicious idea. We must choose names and exchange gifts! Silly, whimsical gifts! With Mr Wickham away, I shall not have—"

"Lydia, you are to go to Longbourn! There will be gifts for you there."

Lydia was too pleased with her idea to be indignant. "Of course, and Freddie and I shall be the biggest gift of all for dear Mama. But do let's choose names amongst ourselves, and I shall collect my present when I return!"

Return?

"There is little time to shop, but my sister and I will have no problem producing additional gifts," said Mrs Wilmot, winking at Elizabeth. "Our luggage is full of surprises and we are quick with a needle."

Dubious looks were exchanged until Bingley grinned. "A splendid idea. We are a creative lot. I shall make it more of a challenge! I shall write down all the names in my 'very poor hand'."

Elizabeth watched as Bingley made a show of it, writing one name painfully slow and another with a hurried flourish. He was a happy man, but he was now at his happiest—a husband and expectant father, acting as host to his friends and family without fear of criticism from his sisters. Lydia was giggling with excitement, eagerly anticipating gifts and shopping in Meryton. The morning post had brought letters from Mrs Bennet and Mary, which proved the roads were cleared at least that far north. Mr Darcy may not be able to travel to Derbyshire, but the house's most distracting and demanding guest would move on in the Bingleys' carriage, to surprise her parents, sisters, and the Gardiners. How Elizabeth hoped her own letter would reach her father; his surprise would be lessened if he knew Lydia was so near. Certainly she anticipated her own great relief when the carriage pulled away. She tried not to think what she would feel if the weather continued to improve and the snows melted in the north.

The sounds of tearing paper pulled her from her thoughts and she joined the others watching Bingley drop the pieces into the silver bowl on the side table.

"That is only six pieces, and we are a party of seven!"

"We will be a party of six for Christmas, Lydia. But I shall send a present with you to open, and some small things for the children as well."

It appeared to Elizabeth that Jane's offer appeased Lydia, who frowned briefly but at least refrained from stomping her foot before speaking. "That is a fine idea, but you must tell me of all the silly presents that are exchanged. And do let's have some games and dancing tonight."

Glancing at the man standing beside her, Elizabeth pressed her lips together, and in a low voice light with chagrined amusement, said, "Mr Darcy, I apologise for what just occurred, what has occurred in the past, and what shall undoubtedly occur in the future."

His eyes wrinkled as he smiled. "There is no need. Truly."

"But how will you bear it? I should not blame you if you would prefer to find yourself obliged to a previous engagement somewhere else this evening."

"I am not such a coward," he said with a smile. "However, I admit that when Lady Catherine last visited London, I found much to do in Warwickshire."

"Pressing business matters, of course," she said, her smile widening.

"But it is Christmas, and Mrs Wickham is your family, and I cannot visit my own. She is joyous to be with her sisters. I recall lively dinners at Longbourn, far livelier than those of my own family. I would prefer to forge onward and suffer whatever blushes and embarrassments lay ahead."

"We are well assured, then."

"Everyone must choose names," came a shrill cry from Lydia. "I will peek to ensure no one picks their own name."

Elizabeth and Jane, accustomed to the imperiousness common to their mother and youngest sister and at ease indulging it for a short time, exchanged a familiar look.

Lydia dipped her hand in the bowl, stirring it quickly before holding up a piece of the folded paper. She handed it to Mrs Wilmot, who opened it and squinted closely at the name written on it.

"Oh my."

The bowl clanged again as Lydia's ring hit its side. "Miss Yates." Elizabeth watched as Lydia, smiling slyly, placed one of the papers in Jane's hand. The final two slips were given to the two gentlemen; Bingley opened his and chuckled. When Mr Darcy glanced at the name on his paper, his eyes darted to Lydia, then to the carpet.

Curious, Elizabeth unfolded her own paper and read the scrawled name.

Darcy

Shortly thereafter they went in to dinner. As Mr Darcy was obliged to escort Bingley's aunts, Elizabeth walked in with Lydia. She often felt herself under his scrutiny during the meal, his eyes seeming always upon her when she glanced in his direction. Here as well, Lydia, Bingley and his aunts carried the conversation; Elizabeth did her best to ignore the silliest comments and steer conversation away from mention of Lydia's husband, the unfairness of their financial deprivation, and whether a betrothal contract made in the cradle with a duke's daughter was a wise plan for young Frederick Wickham.

Conversation inevitably turned to the weather. With the snows slowing in the north, it appeared Lydia's travels to Hertfordshire would be unencumbered by ice-grooved roads. Such assurances mattered little to Jane, whose worries as to the safety of Lydia's journey, despite current conditions, prompted Lydia to make clear her demands.

"Bingley," she said shrilly, "your carriage is of the best design, is it not? Poor Freddie suffered so on our journey here. It was not only the cold and the smells, but the carriage was so poorly sprung, it was quite the challenge to hold onto him as we bounced!"

"Of course—"

Bingley's reply was interrupted by Mr Darcy's firm voice. "My carriage possesses especially good wheels and my team is sturdy and fast, Mrs Wickham. You and your son will travel in ease."

Elizabeth and Bingley looked at him, amazed. "Darcy?" said the latter.

"My cattle are superior to yours, Bingley, and in need of some exercise before we journey to Matlock." Mr Darcy turned to Lydia and nodded. "Mrs Wickham and her son must travel in comfort and warmth. May I offer you my carriage for your journey?"

"Thank you, Mr Darcy. That is very kind." Lydia's voice lacked the coyness familiar to her sisters; indeed, she sounded shocked and sincere in her gratitude. Just as Elizabeth prepared her own reply of appreciation, Lydia added, "All of Meryton will see us arrive in the grand Darcy carriage. How astonished they will be. Imagine my parents' faces!"

"Shock is a dangerous thing, dear. My father died of apoplexy." Miss Yates sliced a piece of Stilton and lifted it on her knife for closer examination. "Christmas is a time for joy, not mourning."

Not even Lydia could reply to such advice, and the clatter of knives and forks and murmurings of people intent on enjoying their meal filled the quiet. A sort of giddiness rose in Elizabeth as she considered the last half an hour. She was surrounded by ridiculous people—kind, thoughtful, clever, ridiculous people. She was certain Lydia had made sure to give her the slip of paper with Mr Darcy's name and likely had given her name to him, and he—the kindest of them in bearing all that was insufferable and infuriating—was taking care of her sister. Again. She shook her head in disbelief of his goodness.

'Any man privileged enough to win the esteem and affection of Miss Bennet would be the most fortunate, nay happiest, man in the world.' What could he mean by it? Did he praise her simply as a means to reprove Lydia? Yet he had denied, to her, that he was teasing or insincere.

'My words and opinion are united.'

He was all that was good, and whether he cared or not, she would endeavour to find a way to show him the esteem she felt. He deserved to know.

"Lizzy? Are you wool-gathering?"

Startled, Elizabeth turned her attention to Jane, gazing at her with a warm expression.

"I asked if you recalled our childhood games in the snow."

Her sister's question unleashed a memory in Elizabeth. "Oh yes," she replied. "The tunnels we would dig in the yard for Totters, our dog, and of course the snowball toss."

"Toss?" Jane laughed. "The snowballs that hit my dress and knocked off my bonnet were hardly 'tossed' by you, Lizzy! Only Mary and I adhered to the rules and tossed them. You, Papa, Kitty, and Lydia preferred to throw them as if they were weapons."

"How dare you?" laughed Bingley. "My angel!"

"Your *angel* liked nothing better than putting snow inside my collar."

"It was the one time, and quite well deserved," said a red-faced Jane.

"It was," Lydia agreed.

"Such actions are common in all families," said Mr Darcy. "It will not surprise you that my cousin Colonel Fitzwilliam was notorious for ambushing his brother and sister with snowballs, and thrusting snow down the collars of his classmates."

Bingley laughed. "No surprise at all that he showed early promise for a military career."

"Indeed, there is reason my uncle did not place him with the clergy."

"George once settled on the clergy for his career, and then was decided on the law." Lydia looked around the table as Elizabeth tensed; the smile had quickly disappeared from Mr Darcy's face and his hand stilled on the table as they awaited Lydia's next words.

"I am happy he is in such a distinguished uniform. I would not have liked seeing him dressed in wig and clerical robes, and the law is so very boring. Uncle Philips and Mr Shawcross never talk about criminals and adulterers and bigamists. It is all land disputes and wills and entails. Dull, dull, dull."

Mrs Wilmot made her agreement clear. "A man in uniform is a handsome sight, although it is character rather than red coat that decides true worth."

Elizabeth's lips quirked as the elderly lady continued.

"Yet to be the wife of a London solicitor has its merits. There is no dish so delicious as the tales told over the dinner table of a bigamist getting his comeuppance."

"*His* comeuppance?" Mr Darcy smiled. "You judge those of your own sex to be free of such behaviours?"

"I judge it far more difficult, sir, for a lady to have such ill intentions."

"Or freedom to pursue them," added Elizabeth.

"Point taken," he replied, meeting her gaze across the table. Lydia's shrill voice broke the moment.

"There is no shortage of ill-intentioned ladies bent on a husband in a red coat. George broke many hearts when he chose to marry me. And even fatherhood has not deterred some set on diverting him."

"His wife and son are diversion enough," offered Jane. "Young Frederick is such a dear."

Mrs Wilmot nodded sagely. "If Mr Wickham is half so lively and charming as his wife, the child is destined to be the delight of London when he is of age."

Lydia, pleased by such high praise of her husband and son, determined she must gaze on him in his bed. As the door closed behind her sister, Elizabeth was certain she was not the only person to breathe a sigh of relief.

CHAPTER TEN

Lydia slept until nearly eleven, but her son was awake far earlier. Her sisters, eager to better know their nephew, went to him in the nursery. The wallpapers had been put up a month earlier and the Bingley family crib, cleaned and placed just a week ago, held him securely.

"Do you mind, terribly, not having your child be the first?" Elizabeth asked, a little ashamed of how Lydia crowed about her son's temporary chamber and the ornate carvings in the wooden crib. She suspected Freddie Wickham did not usually sleep in anything nearly so fine.

"Charles and his sisters slept in this crib, and it is likely their cousins did as well. I am happy to give Freddie a warm bed." Jane's serenity slipped briefly when her voice lowered. "Some blankets and gowns were delivered this morning for her to take with her. I do not wish to give her those we have set aside for our child. She is careless with things, Lizzy. I cannot bear the thought of a blanket with our name sewn into it left behind in a posting inn. Am I so terribly selfish?"

"No, you are a wife and mother first. Lydia and Freddie will not go without."

"Lizzy, our sister is in need of a new coat as well."

"She may have my old one, for I am fortunate my favourite sister gave me a new coat on my birthday." Elizabeth smirked at Jane before gently running her fingers across the infant's few soft hairs. "He is a beautiful babe, sweet and innocent as all children are at this age. We can only hope he has more sense and goodness than either of his parents—or at least half as much as Baby Bingley will gain from *his* parents."

Jane attempted to hide her smile at her sister's teasing, before kissing the child and handing him to her lady's maid, eager to fuss over the baby and change him into a clean gown. "Lizzy, do you think Lydia is happy? We still do not know why she arrived alone and whether Mr Wickham will come to Longbourn in time for Christmas."

"We do not know whether he will arrive at all." Elizabeth scowled. "I have no faith in that man. How could he put his wife and infant on a post carriage? They travelled a full day in winter's worst—alone, with neither maid nor chaperon."

Whatever perils Jane could envision were quickly dispelled by happier thoughts. "They will be safe and warm on their journey to Longbourn. Mr Darcy was very kind to offer his carriage to Lydia."

"Most kind." Elizabeth moved towards the door.

"Charles is the best of men, Lizzy, but his friend is nearly as good." This time her smile, unseen by her sister, was full of playfulness.

Elizabeth busied herself writing notes to her parents and overseeing a basket for Lydia to take in the carriage. An hour later, yawning but fed and dressed, Lydia was effusive in her excitement to travel to Longbourn.

As Lydia puttered about, asking Jane what might be inside the hastily wrapped boxes with her name on the tags, Elizabeth stood in the hall. Her half-boots were worn but she felt quite festive in the merry red coat Jane had given her for her birthday. If only she could find the matching muff; it was nowhere to be found in her rooms. Bingley's generosity in allowing many servants to go to their families for the holidays had led to some late meals, mislaid items, and general confusion. Realising she had last worn it a day ago, Elizabeth opened the armoire in the entryway, where she found only a few rarely used umbrellas. Bending over to look under the chair where she had sat to remove her muddy boots, she laughed and reached for her muff, sitting on the floor with a cream-coloured scarf atop it. She soon realised the scarf was not one belonging to Bingley or Jane, but had a very distinctive 'FD' embroidered in its corner.

It took only a moment for her to act on instinct and raise the cloth to her nose. *Yes, it is his.*

As she stood wondering at the emotions provoked by his warm, spicy scent—emotions that had been stirred and intensified for two days when in his presence—the voices of her sisters came nearer.

"Mr Wickham must have a new watch! His old one went missing last spring in Newcastle."

Jane ignored her sister's cries. "We have packed blankets and woollen dresses for Freddie and a warmer coat for you, Sister. Come, Lizzy has been waiting for us."

Elizabeth tucked the scarf into her muff and clenched it tightly inside within her left fist. Certain her face was over-heated, she herded her sisters outside to the waiting carriages.

"Good morning, Miss Bennet. Mrs Bingley. Mrs Wickham."

Elizabeth whirled around to find Mr Darcy approaching from a few feet away.

"Mr Darcy! You find us on our way out."

He looked at her—curiously, she thought—as if he noticed it was not just her coat, but her cheeks, that were red. She felt her blush deepen.

"Yes, I arrived with my carriage. Are you prepared for your journey, Mrs Wickham?"

"Mr Darcy, you have not yet met Freddie, my son."

"I have not," he replied, bending to lift the basket holding the infant. "He is a handsome lad. He carries the venerable name of his grandfather, Frederick Wickham, a man of good character and intellect. May he grow to be as kind and steady as I remember him to be."

Lydia looked at him strangely. "George has never mentioned his father to me but says his mother was all that was good."

A gentle smile formed on his face. "As every son should say of his mother."

Elizabeth listened in silence. There was meaning behind Mr Darcy's words that Lydia could not grasp; she preferred only compliments for herself and her choices and Mr Darcy appeared determined to provide them in his own way. He could wish her sister and son well, not in spite of their connexion to his worst enemy, but *because* of what he knew of him—George Wickham, husband and father to innocents who deserved far better.

Mr Darcy handed Lydia and her son into the carriage, along with the basket of gifts, treats and letters for Longbourn. The wet nurse Jane had engaged followed.

Lydia leaned out the door of the carriage. "Be well, Jane! Freddie would like a boy cousin with whom to play!"

"Goodbye, Lydia! We shall see you soon!"

Mr Darcy shut the carriage door and tapped the roof. The three of them watched it roll down the street.

Elizabeth smiled, half in relief. "It was very kind of you to give Lydia use of your carriage, sir."

Mr Darcy shrugged. "It was my pleasure to assist her journey. It does, however, present an obstacle for me in completing my shopping. I am without my sturdiest carriage for a day or two, and I need to complete the task assigned me by Mrs Wickham. May I impose myself on your shopping party?"

His modest request was met with alacrity and soon Mr Darcy sat across from Elizabeth and Jane and her lady's maid in the Bingley conveyance.

When the carriage stopped by Hatchard's, he helped Elizabeth out and waved it on to her sister's destination.

They stood in the cold, staring at one another, for a long moment, until he again spoke. "I hope you do not mind that I accompany you? Your coat and muff liven a dreary day with cheerful holiday spirit. And," he added wryly, "I would like your assistance in choosing a gift."

Is he teasing me?

"You wish my assistance?" Whether Elizabeth's expression was as astonished as her tone was unclear, but at his nod, she quickly amended her reply. "I would have thought you had enough of marketplaces and shopping during your travels."

Mr Darcy was earnest in explaining himself. "While in Greece, I purchased gifts for my sister, aunt and uncle, but there is an item I wish to have engraved."

He began to lead her towards the shop when she stopped. "May we walk a little? I was unable to exercise yesterday and wish to breathe in winter's air. My brother is dear but extends his protective feelings towards Jane to me as well. His worries over the temperatures, the weather, the condition of the streets, the stray dogs, the temptations of a leafy path... Often I have wondered whether he heard too many stories of my childhood and is concerned I will climb a tree in Hyde Park and refuse to eat my peas."

"You dislike peas?"

"I did when I was six. I do like them now, and have always liked stray dogs. But I do not mean to complain! Living with my sister and her husband brings me great joy."

He nodded and as she took his arm, she asked quietly, "Might you tell me about the engraving?"

"I will confide in you," Mr Darcy said. "Bingley told me he wished to begin a library that would one day rival Pemberley's—"

"Pemberley? So ambitious! This is the wish of Bingley or his sister?"

His lips twitched in a small smile before replying. "He wishes for his children, and his children's children, to be great readers, as he has not been, and if not, at least be surrounded by great works of literature."

"'Tis a noble endeavour. Jane has many wonderful attributes and interests, but she is neither a great reader nor an imaginist in spinning tales."

Mr Darcy glanced at her, steering them past a family looking in a shop window. "You once claimed you were not a great reader. Will you also demur from the title of imaginist?"

"I am more guilty of imagining stories and regaling my cousins and sisters with farfetched tales of knights and pirates, naughty goats and foolish kings." She looked at him sideways. "Despise me if you dare."

"I admire you all the more for it. My sister would have been fortunate to hear your fantastic tales rather than those told by a much-older brother striving to recall stories from his own childhood or weaving them from his own limited imagination."

"We cannot all be jesters, sir. I am certain Miss Darcy found nothing wanting in your efforts. Nor will Bingley." Her eyebrows rose. "Have you purchased him some books? Were we not to exchange *whimsical* gifts?"

"Indeed, and I shall do so, but this is a wedding gift of sorts, grievously delayed by my travels. I hope to bolster his initial efforts and build his library with a small collection of volumes. He has been known to leave books unopened, but these he may admire, for they are distinguished with a book-plate marking them as property of the Bingley family."

"Oh, Miss Bingley has spoken often of the nameplates in the books you carry from your libraries. It is a splendid idea! Not only shall we all be witness to her admiration for your beneficence, but her brother will be so pleased!"

He smiled at her sly reference to her newest sister; Elizabeth realised they shared a mutual relief at Miss Bingley's absence this Yuletide season. "The design I have in mind is simple, vines framing *Ex Libris C.W. Bingley*, but it shall also include a small allusion to a creature that has long fascinated him."

"A tiger?"

He nodded.

"You are not only a thoughtful friend but a sly one, Mr Darcy. I believe it is the tiger's orange fur, so similar to the colour of Bingley's hair, that led to his admiration."

Mr Darcy's hearty chuckle washed over her, filling Elizabeth with a selfish pleasure; over these past two days, she had often made him laugh or smile and relished seeing the soft, handsome expression that overcame him when he did.

They walked a few more steps and came to a patch of grey mush, likely covering a patch of ice, that caused Elizabeth to lean more heavily on Mr Darcy's arm. He did not flinch, nor appear affected by the added pressure, nor did his footing ever appear at risk or unsure. He was sturdy, steady, a man to be trusted with any responsibility.

Once they were on firmer, drier ground, she turned to him. "You shall do well as a godfather. You have served admirably in a paternal role as guardian to your sister, and she is a fine young lady."

"Not always so admirably, as you know," he said grimly. "Much of the credit is due to her own resilience and character, similar to that of my mother." He looked at her. "You truly think yourself best suited as indulgent aunt to your sister's children? Not as a—?"

"As a mother?" She laughed quietly. "As you know from your encounters with my family, I have not been the model of propriety as an elder sister. Jane is all that is serene and gentle, and has long wished to be a mother. My own lack of patience with three younger sisters does not recommend my maternal abilities."

"I disagree," he nearly barked. "You are all a young lady should be, alive with wit and kindness and manners. Any child would be fortunate to have you as his mother."

A blush suffused her cheeks. "A child needs a father, and the paternal possibilities most recently presented to me were not what I wished for them."

He held up his hand. "Yes, Bingley and Mrs Wickham have been eager to mention your admirers and their proposals," he said quietly. "I must ask, are you so set against the institution of marriage or set against granting happiness to the male sex?"

"I have learnt a lesson, Mr Darcy. There is a gentleman meant for every lady, and a lady for every gentleman. The key is ensuring they meet, and that their timing is correct. All of these suitors have been fortunate in their time and place soon *after* meeting me. I am, perhaps, the impetus that lurches others towards happiness."

"Indeed you are."

CHAPTER ELEVEN

Christmas was a day away, but an afternoon spent in company with Elizabeth Bennet had already given Darcy perhaps the greatest gift he could imagine.

Camaraderie. Comfort. Friendship. There had been moments when he allowed himself to be carried away with his thoughts, to be the imaginist she said she was, and to think of how it could always be thus—walking London's streets arm in arm, laughing and talking. That moment when she had stumbled; if they had been anywhere private he would have been hard pressed not to sweep her into his arms and kiss her with all due feeling. Instead, he held her only more tightly and continued on as though nothing had changed, though his soul was on fire. She was, still and always, the most precious thing in the world to him.

He hoped she would know that tonight, when he presented her with his whimsical gift. He would explain it to her in full, prior to telling her of his true feelings and asking whether she could give him a last chance. She thought him a good, kind man. She thanked him for how he had acted with Lydia. Did she know—she seemed to know—about his role in her sister's wedding? Would that affect her answer? Had it affected her feelings? He was certain it was more than mere gratitude she felt for him. Tonight, he hoped he would know.

Bingley had invited a larger party to join them for a light dinner and games and dancing afterwards. Although Darcy did not look forward to sharing Elizabeth's company with Bingley's friends and neighbours, he could survive a round of bullet pudding if it meant an evening with her; he was fortunate she appeared of a similar eagerness for conversation with *him*.

Bingley's loud peal of laughter, echoed quickly by titters from Miss Yates, filled the drawing room. Elizabeth, seated at the opposite end of the room, felt Jane's eyes on her. She read concern in her sister's expression—worry perhaps that Elizabeth was caught in a too-serious conversation with Mr Darcy. She smiled, earning one from Jane in return, before turning back to him.

He leaned towards her, speaking in a low voice. "Women have an admirable ability to communicate silently with one another—through a look or a gesture—that we gentlemen never learn."

"Gentlemen have no need for it," Elizabeth replied, "but soundless conversation is necessary to ladies since custom and society impede our ability to speak directly."

"How so?" Mr Darcy's bemused expression made Elizabeth think of a confused little boy. Her heart fluttered and her thoughts flew away. How had she forgotten the ardent young man beneath his cool exterior? Had love changed her into this reticent, shy creature when in his presence?

"There are many things ladies are not allowed to say," she said, looking at him. "To each other, or in a roomful of others, or to gentlemen."

"I see."

"When feelings are difficult to convey in words, a look or nod must suffice. A sister who has shared her childhood bed and memories can read the meaning in such a physical expression."

A wistful but fleeting expression crossed his countenance. "Well as I know her, I am unable to fully understand my own sister's gestures and meanings, so I shall take *your* meaning and blame my sex."

"You have a vast span of years between you. You better understood her needs and thoughts when she was a child, and shall understand better when she is fully grown. These years, between childhood and adulthood, are fraught with confusion and misunderstandings."

He smiled at her but Elizabeth read disappointment in it. Once again, they had come close to a real conversation, and she had pulled them away from the precipice to discuss sisterly affection. Their own connexion had been fraught with confusion and misunderstanding! Could she not avoid such a reminder? *He does not know that I know what he did for my family. I must tell him, thank him. I must tell him how I see that he has not changed—did not need to change—but my feelings are so altered.*

It should not be so difficult to make herself vulnerable and make some overture to Mr Darcy; *he* had, once. And he was here, now, seemingly eager to be in her company again. She smiled, and was pleased when he returned it.

"All families have their own language," she began hesitantly. "But friends can as well. *We* are friends enough, perhaps our sensibilities are similar enough, that we can express thoughts that are novel to us or which others could find uncomfortable."

He nodded. "Yes, I think we are accomplished in this."

Elizabeth forged on. "But you must know, my feelings, when they are new or uncertain of their reception, are especially difficult to express. Comfortable as I am in your company, what I most wish to say is that my heart has been...my feelings have..."

Meeting his intense gaze, she suddenly became conscious of the question in his eyes—a burning look she realised she had put there—and she had to avert hers. A cough across the room recalled to her that others were present.

"I am mortified by my poor manners."

Mr Darcy did not answer immediately, but his whole attention was on her; Elizabeth blushed again.

"As I said," came his unexpected reply, "I would wish for more confidence between us, and as I have been the one sharing my thoughts, I would think it fair to see you share yours, although I must disagree as to your manners, which have long been impeccable."

"Thank you for your kindness to my sister," she blurted.

He blinked.

"From the beginning of our acquaintance, Lydia has been irksome in your presence and less than polite in your company and about you. Yet you have proven, time and again, to be a very good man, and have shown the true Christmas spirit in providing her with your own carriage. I-I believe I admire you more than any man I have ever known. My thanks cannot be suppressed. Thank you for all you have done for her, and for my family."

"I did it to ensure her comfort and safety on her journey, but make no mistake. The true reason for any kindness I show, and for any goodness in me, is you."

A heavy silence followed as a hundred questions flitted through her mind. Before she could sort out their precedence, or truly regain the sensibility needed to reply, her sister's voice broke through her thoughts.

Jane was too polite to interrupt; she usually entered a room or conversation quietly, gliding in on her cloud of goodness. But since Caroline had gone off and Bingley's aunts had arrived, Jane's voice had grown in both volume and authority.

"Lizzy, Mr Darcy—Charles wishes everyone to gather for the whimsies before the rest of the party arrives."

Elizabeth sighed. Bingley had invited friends and neighbours to celebrate Christmas Eve with singing and games; quieter festivities would continue on the morrow. Then it was church on Sunday, and Mr Darcy would leave Monday for Matlock. Would they have *any* opportunity to truly speak without interruption?

The party moved to the table in the room's centre. Bingley took a moment to revel in the gaily wrapped assortment of packages and boxes there. The largest was tall and oddly shaped; the smallest was a beribboned cylinder. With a mischievous grin, Bingley picked up the tube and glanced at the name written upon it. "My curiosity is wild for this one." He walked toward Elizabeth. "Here you are, dear Sister, a gift of Christmas whimsy for you."

She tapped it, prompting Miss Yates to call out her guess for the gift inside the wrapping. "It is a spyglass, no doubt. Quite useful for spotting poachers and lost creatures."

"And ships," her sister added.

Instead, Elizabeth pulled out a parchment map. "It is Wales." Confused, she peered more closely. "A map of Wales with a circle inked around a crossroads and directions to... *Gellu Aur*?"

"Golden Grove. It is my estate there."

Elizabeth felt the room's attention move between herself and Mr Darcy.

Bingley stood over her shoulder, staring at the paper. "A map? What does this mean, Darcy? Buried treasure? Is there an 'X' on it?"

"This gift lacks the spirit of whimsy," sniffed Mrs Wilmot.

Miss Yates peered closely. "Is the young man giving her his estate? I should like one as well."

Mr Darcy chuckled. "I believe the instruction was to present a gift in the spirit of good fun and goodwill. My gift to Miss Bennet is both." He crossed his arms and looked at Bingley. "You and Mrs Bingley shall be insufferably happy no matter your surroundings but I know Miss

Bennet to be a lady of active imagination and intellect who may wish some chance for exploration and new scenery. *Gellu Aur* is a beautiful property with lovely walking paths and views, and the most enviable gardens in the country. Miss Bennet is invited to go there and bring a party of friends and family at any time." He turned to Elizabeth. "I am rarely there, and of course would not intrude."

Elizabeth looked down at the map, almost unable to meet his eyes for fear of revealing her urgent inclination to hug him. She was violently shocked, but in a way that filled her heart. Without thinking, she wound the ribbon around her hand as she tried to calm herself to reply. "Oh my. This is the best sort of gift, sir. Good fun and good intentions, and so unexpected."

She looked up and smiled. "Thank you. It is too dear for me to laugh."

Bingley looked between them, his mind clearly shifting pieces of a puzzle he had not realised was near completion. "Well then, moving on. Lizzy, it is your turn to present a gift I hope may provide the rest of us some whimsy."

Elizabeth set down her gift on a chair and reached for a small, wrapped package. She handed it to Mr Darcy. "Happy Christmas."

He took it silently, untied the ribbon, and pulled off the paper.

"A book. Of course." He smiled and began to thumb through it, revealing blank pages within the covers.

"Perfect! A book without words! Well done, Lizzy!"

Mr Darcy glared at Bingley. "It is a journal, of course."

Elizabeth spoke quickly. "I do not mean to be presumptuous, but for you to provide us—me—with vivid and whimsical diversion. Your descriptions of your journeys and your views of the coast and the sea brought them to life in my mind. I may not have such a chance to travel, but Bingley said you would likely travel again."

Her fingers twisted the colourful ribbon she still held in her hands. "When we meet again, I hope to hear of your travels. I thought you might write down your impressions of the places you visit and share whimsical and adventurous tales of the seas and lands with us."

Mr Darcy's silent stillness began to alarm her and her voice faltered. He ran his fingers over the leather and, looking at her, said hoarsely, "Thank you. It is an inspired gift, and one I shall not only utilise, but treasure."

"Brilliant, Lizzy! A little too serious than the spirit of the idea, but—"

"It *is* quite silly, Charles, for we all know Mr Darcy cannot keep himself to but one book." Jane arched an eyebrow at her sister and gave her a knowing smile.

"Well done, Miss Bennet," called Mrs Wilmot. "Well done, indeed."

"It is not *my* idea of a whimsical gift," Miss Yates objected. "I thought we were to exchange only silly gifts. This is not going well at all."

"If you wish a silly gift, you must open up the one from me." Bingley walked to the table and picked up the oddly shaped package. He carried it to her, staggering in an exaggerated struggle over its heft. "For you, dear Aunt Poppy."

As the ladies gasped in anticipation, Elizabeth slipped out the door.

Darcy had caressed the leather face of that book as if it were the soft skin of her cheek. He had wanted to kiss her. To stake his claim to her right there, in front of her sister and Bingley and his aunts. A wish to travel? To leave her, now that he knew he still loved her and that she might possibly feel something similar in regards to him?

The warmth in her eyes, the quaver in her voice, had nearly undone him. He had been forced to look away, and desperate as he was not to lose the moment with her, Darcy was grateful when levity returned to the room. He looked up when he realised he could no longer hear Elizabeth's voice amongst the others.

He stood and moved quickly out to the hall. She was standing by the library, worrying a strip of cloth in her hands. Walking towards her, Darcy realised she was holding his scarf.

"I believe this may be yours." She lifted the scarf to him as he drew closer. "I apologise if you have taken a chill without it. The weave is so soft, I found myself thinking it would make a fine blanket for my nephew."

He stared down at the scarf but made no move to take it. "I would be pleased to give it to him."

"I believe you have given him, and my sister, quite enough."

Darcy took a breath. "She told you."

"I have known for nearly a year of how you arranged her wedding and saved her reputation and our family's. I wish I could have told you sooner." She let out a soft breath. "I was too embarrassed to speak to you at Jane's wedding. I was overfilled with feeling, and gratitude was the least of it."

"As was I," he whispered. "You gave me no encouragement, no sign that you thought me good, or—"

"Or that I regretted so badly misunderstanding you."

The hopeful expression in her eyes accompanying her words stirred the warmth in his chest into something large and overwhelming, "Did we not say that we were friends who could speak frankly to one another? Come," he said, taking her hand and leading her into Bingley's meagre library. "I will speak to you now."

Darcy led them to two chairs by the fire and laid a small box on the table between them. "Be it by chance or design, I am grateful for Mrs Wickham's role in enabling my gift to you."

Elizabeth looked at him, confused. "I have opened your gift."

He shook his head and pushed the package towards her. "This is another, bought for you some time ago. Please."

Hesitantly, she pulled silver paper from a small box, which when opened, led her to gasp. Inside lay a gold hair comb inlaid with looping vines dotted with small diamonds and rubies. She looked up at him with a stunned expression.

"Mr Darcy, I cannot accept such a gift! Surely this is meant for your sister."

He took her hands, cold and trembling, in his own. "No. When I saw it, nearly a year ago now, I thought only of you. Forgive me if I am presumptuous and misapprehend your feelings, but I must state my own, Elizabeth."

He leaned closer and spoke in a soft voice. "I do not wish to travel. I wish to be here, in this seat, or wherever you are."

Her smile, tremulous yet warm, encouraged him to go on.

"We have given each other the gifts of pushing away."

"Pushing away?" she repeated.

"As if I could desire you far away in Wales, if I could not be there to celebrate its beauties by your side. The journal is wonderful but I cannot accept it in the spirit intended." Briefly he closed his eyes, both desperately eager and fearful. "Elizabeth, I once was the last man in the world you would marry, but I wish to be the *only* man you could marry. I must tell you again how much I admire and love you, and ask, once more, and for the final time, I promise, if you would allow me to be your husband."

The tenderness and joy in her expression gave him hope before she spoke. "You dear man, I will allow you most anything, if you allow me to be your wife."

Elation and disbelief rushed through him. "Yes?"

"Yes."

CHAPTER TWELVE

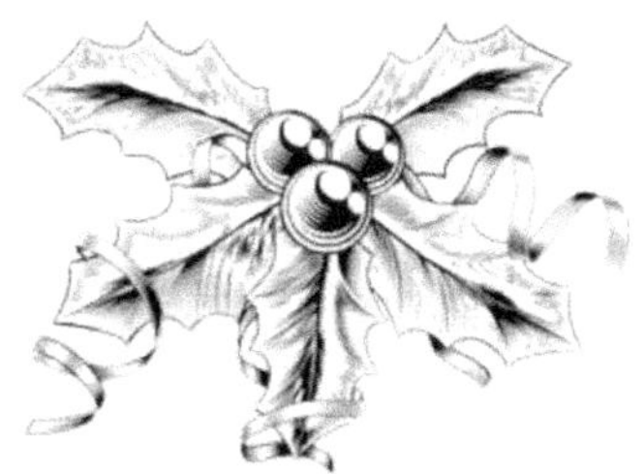

Elizabeth's eyes widened when he began to press fervent kisses upon her hand. The warmth of his ardour enveloped her and she bit her lip when his mouth moved to the side of her wrist. She lifted his chin so she could see him, and nearly swooned at the open joy and desire she found in his expression. Quickly Darcy stood and pulled her into his arms, and within a moment their lips met in a tender kiss. When they pulled apart after some minutes, he gazed at her through bright, lovestruck eyes and sighed.

"Do not tell Bingley, but I believe *we* shall be the happiest couple in the world," she whispered.

"Indeed," he said tenderly, "for in earning more than your friendship, I am the most fortunate of men."

She rested her head against his broad chest, overwhelmed by the quickness of it all after a full year of yearning wishes and self-recrimination. "I must learn to be content with being happier than I deserve."

"You, my dearest Elizabeth, deserve all that is good and wonderful in the world."

She laughed, feeling lighter in heart than she had in nearly two years. *How easy it is, now that we have spoken.* "Then you must indulge me. Where is the mistletoe ball and will you take me to it? I feel an immediate urge to take advantage of its purpose."

"I need no seasonal decoration to reward you," he murmured before kissing her soundly once again.

The noise of doors opening and closing and cheerful voices greeting one another returned them to themselves, although their blushes and brightened eyes rendered them less recognisable as the couple who had entered the room minutes earlier.

Darcy loosened his hold on her; unable to fully remove himself, he tenderly pushed strands of her hair back into place.

"Oh, how I must look."

"You look utterly beautiful, and rather well-kissed."

"Teasing man." Elizabeth shook her head, smiling happily at him before moving over to the mirrored mantel. Darcy watched her lift herself up on her toes to peer at her reflection and fix her hair. He imagined the jewelled comb in her tresses; he would tell her later, when they were married, perhaps on their wedding night, about the day he saw the original antiquity displayed in Greece, and thought how fine it would look in her umber curls. It gave a purpose to his time in Athens, to find a jeweller to craft the piece for him; it surely had been made for her and no one else.

Lost in thought, he startled when he felt her hands on him, adjusting his cravat and waistcoat. He looked down to see her smiling shyly up at him. "You must smooth your own hair, Mr Darcy. I fear that if I touch it, temptation may grow between us and I confess great curiosity about that strangely shaped gift for Miss Yates."

"It is a bird cage my great-uncle had constructed for his wife's pet peacock. The bird would not set foot in the thing and it has been sitting in the Darcy House attics since I was a boy. Bingley was at ends to find a gift on such short notice and I was grateful he seized on the idea when I mentioned it. His aunt will find it useful for her menagerie."

She laughed. "Thank goodness that Bingley, and Lydia, and my father and I—and perhaps half of London—have you to arrange things so well for us."

Darcy shrugged shyly, understanding that underneath her teasing was true admiration, and took her hand again to his lips. Her skin was so soft, her heart so generous and kind, her mind so fine and observant. He had noticed nothing of the other gifts; his attention had been solely on her and the words he longed to exchange. All his hopes and wishes had come to fruition. A year apart, and now two days reunited and betrothed. He would not have a lonely Christmas, nor a dull moment, ever again.

"Will you write to your father? I will stop at Longbourn on my way to Matlock to speak to him."

A shadow of disappointment swept briefly across her expression. "You must leave?"

"Not until Monday. We shall have three days here in London to enjoy Christmas. The walking paths are cleared in Hyde Park, and I wish for you to tour Darcy House."

"I should love anything to keep you in my company." She smiled sweetly. "Once again, Lydia owes you her gratitude, for if you went to my father any earlier, it would overshadow her surprise as my mother's finest Christmas gift."

Laughing, he said, "Our engagement will be treasured by Georgiana, for certainly nothing could be a greater gift than news that you shall be her sister, and my wife."

"Where is your amusing sister, Mrs Bingley?" came Miss Yates's shrill cry. "I wish to hear her thoughts on Charlie's new jester cap!"

He grinned down at her and offered his arm. "You have been summoned, Miss Bennet. Shall we?"

December 30

Elizabeth smoothed out Darcy's letter, delivered only hours ago yet already wrinkled from her multiple perusals, and read again her favourite passages.

> *As expected, your father was more surprised than pleased by your letter. That he was further vexed by my immediate application for his blessing would be a mild description of his bearing, but be at peace, my love. He has bestowed it, and wishes only to see you and ensure that you are indeed as felicitous as your letter claims. When my hearing returns to its usual state, I am certain I shall recall all of your mother's effusions of joyful shock at our news. Your sister Mary assures me that a generous supply of salts has been laid in, and that your father will be liberal with his brandy until Mrs Bennet's tranquillity is restored. I did not read the letter I carried to her, but your words have made her the proudest of mothers, perhaps even prouder than she has been with Mrs Wickham's homecoming.*
>
> *Your sister and Frederick are quite content at Longbourn. He is well*

attended to by all your family. Your father is especially eloquent on the joy of having another male in the house and has been seen bouncing the infant on his knee while reading poetry. I cannot report whether the child's tears were a result of boredom or indigestion, but it is clear he did not care for Wordsworth. Mrs Wickham has no plans to leave Longbourn in the next month, and thus your worries on that account, my love, must all be relieved. My offers to return her to London, Newcastle, or wherever Wickham may be residing were refused. Her husband will come to her, *she says, or never see her again. I think it likely he will come to fetch her as your clever sister has spirited away most of their money and all of their silver. Nevertheless, I shall have my cousin make enquiries into Wickham's true circumstances.*

By now, Elizabeth knew Darcy would be driving towards Matlock to celebrate Twelfth Night with his sister and cousins. He had been diligent in determining that the roads were clear; in fact, he was scrupulous enough about the weather to be the object of much teasing from Bingley, whose shock at their engagement was not equal to the Bennets, but nevertheless substantial. Jane was delighted, especially when Elizabeth assured her that she would remain by her side for the next two months, for the birth in London and then for the re-establishment of their lease at Netherfield through the summer.

Darcy had been persuasive, but it was Jane who wished to return to Hertfordshire and enjoy the comfort of family as she and Bingley christened their child and celebrated the wedding of her most beloved sister.

Her eyes fell back to the letter, and she admired Darcy's strong, steady hand. The words he wrote conveyed true feeling, and Elizabeth read them eagerly, and, in the spirit intended.

I am glad, my dearest, that pretty packages, even those containing the greatest treasures of my house, are secondary to what we most desire, for there are no words equal to the tenderness of heart I feel for you, and no gifts greater than what you have already given me: your own heart. The wisest, and the best, action I have ever done, is give you mine.

The End

About the Author

Jan Ashton didn't meet Jane Austen until she was in her late teens, but in a happy coincidence, she celebrates her birthday on the same day *Pride & Prejudice* was first published. A former journalist, she is a life member of the Jane Austen Society of North America, and co-founder of Quills & Quartos Publishing.

Also by Jan Ashton

A Searing Acquaintance
Mendacity & Mourning
One Minute More
Some Natural Importance
The Most Interesting Man in the World (*with Justine Rivard)*

STRANDED AT PEMBERLEY

JENETTA JAMES

chapter one

December 19, 1810

THE MOMENT BEFORE IT HAPPENED, EVERYTHING WAS perfect. The sun shone down upon our little party, though the air was bitter cold. My uncle Gardiner patted his belly, full from a hearty last breakfast in Lambton. My aunt commented on the winter crocuses by the side of the road. I had a cousin on each side to keep me warm. Rebecca, who was seven years of age, leaned her thick head of red curls against my shoulder and said, "When shall we reach Leicester, Lizzy?"

"Not yet a while," I whispered, and kissed the top of her head.

Veronica, aged five, was already asleep. Her face was pressed in upon the side of my chest in a manner that gave me to think I should move her slightly. The most splendid, frost-spangled country imaginable rolled by on each side. I was nineteen and thought myself the luckiest girl alive.

And then everything changed. An unexpected jolt, which became something more. A most dreadful, great crashing noise, followed by a scream. The faces of my relations were caught in horror. My whole being was thrown asunder, poor Rebecca beneath me and Veronica atop me, crying out, wailing. With a momentous thud, the carriage turned upon its side and I was certain that we should die. I felt rather than saw the horses rear and tumble. I heard the sound of glass breaking and my whole being shuddered, then became cold. I saw my uncle, his frock coat ripped on the side, and he was crying out "Marianne? Marianne!" A terrible shiver crept over me and yet I perspired as I can hardly say. Somehow, my hands found the children, each of them sobbing wildly.

The next moment, the coach boy, whose cheek and arm were bloody, began to scramble at the carriage door. Eventually he pulled it open. He pulled out Veronica first, with shaking hands. Then I clambered out, pulling Rebecca after me. There was a great cacophony of voices, names called out, shocked cries and the ghostly billows of our breath on the air. The coachman lay on the ground, moaning, his arm twisted oddly.

Veronica had a smear of the coach boy's blood upon her cloak, but I could see that she was unharmed. Rebecca, I feared for. She had been crushed beneath me and in the open air I traced my shaking hands over her head, her face, squeezed her arms, touched my palms on her chest, asking her, "Are you well? Are you injured? Do you have any pain?" I knelt on the ground before her, although she was grown tall. She answered me not, but her wide sad eyes fixed over my shoulder. They were filled with fright.

And then I became aware of the cries: frantic, anguished, unanswered.

"Mrs Gardiner? Ma'am? Can you hear me?"

"Marianne? Marianne! Can you move? Can you hear us?"

I turned, but when I went to stand, I fell into the muddy tracks left by our carriage and a dozen before it. I pushed myself up. Before me, the carriage remained on its side, surrounded by broken splinters of wood, a lost wheel, and the trunks which had cast off in the crash. The door out of which I had crawled was wide open and my uncle and the coach boy were leaning in.

Suddenly, I realised, that in all the babble, I had not heard my aunt's voice. I had not seen her. I went to cry out but no sound came. Forward, I went, by some unknown strength; when I got to him, my uncle turned to me, quite terrified. Although he was a large man, he seemed small, quivering, and helpless.

I found my voice. "Aunt! Aunt!" But it was useless. The coach boy moved aside and I took his place, peering inside.

My darling aunt laid still in a semi-circle on the floor of broken glass and mud and stone. Her sleeves were covered in blood and her raiment was like an angel's cape around her. Behind me, Veronica began to scream. Hurriedly, I cast off my winter cloak and found my way back inside the carriage, climbing in to be by my aunt's side. "Aunt? Can you hear me? Can you speak? Please speak!"

The only sounds were the cries of the others and the beating of my own heart. I knelt down beside her and placed my cheek beside her mouth. Relief swept through me at the delicate puff of warmth that I perceived. I looked up over my shoulder at my uncle's peering eyes. "She breathes, I can feel it." For a moment, he closed his eyes and I saw him mouth the words *'thank God'*.

I climbed from the carriage again, my movements jerky. I looked around, but saw nothing save rutted track and hedgerow, dry stone wall in the near distance, hills further off. There was a hint of a turning to the left, but I could not see it. I might have been anywhere on the earth.

"Where are we? What is this place?"

My uncle was leaning into the carriage again, speaking in low, soothing tones to my aunt. He did not even seem to hear me, but the coach boy was more responsive.

"Not five mile from Lambton, miss, I'm sure o' that. There's a big 'ouse just down that track. Else, it be back to Lambton. There ain't so much as a cottage on the road be'twixt. Shall I run back, miss?"

I looked at him, kneeling by the coachman, his shirt now completely covered in blood. The boy's face, like the driver's, was pale and grey. I should not have bet a shilling on him being able to reach the bend in the road.

"No, certainly not. It is much too far." A new wind swept across my face, so cold it almost burnt, as I surveyed the scene. My uncle had begun imploring my aunt again and the children were huddled together in misery. "Where is this big house?"

"Just down there, miss, you see that bend? Where the yew tree is?"

I saw it indeed, like a dead man's skeletal finger rising up from the ground, knotted and horrid.

"Do you know what the house is called? Who the family are?"

"No idea, miss, I'm a London boy. I ain't never been up 'ere save with the master."

"Very well." I removed my bonnet and threw it on the floor where my cloak lay. The boy and the coachman looked at me, questioningly.

"Please stay here and keep the party safe. I will be back as soon as may be." In the corner of my vision, Rebecca stood, as if she intended to accompany me, but I bade her stay with her sister.

My uncle called out to me, "Lizzy, whatever are you doing?"

But it was too late, I was gone.

I held up my skirts for the most part, to aid speed and ease. I had been known to run about at home, much to my mother's chagrin. But it had never been like this. It had been for devilment, for fun. I found the turn easily and began pounding down the track. It was icy, but there was enough mud and grit to steady my way and prevent me from landing on my bottom. Around me, the countryside opened up like a folded blanket, brown, fallow, empty of life, framed by leafless trees.

Still, I ran. After a time, I turned a corner and saw a house. I was too breathless, too desperate to look at the thing, but made for its threshold with all that I was worth. It took longer than I might have anticipated, and by the time I reached the great front door, I was gasping for breath, a most dreadful pain in my belly. I hammered upon the door with my clenched fist and almost fell when it was opened.

A whole array of persons appeared before me. Two footmen in livery came first, saying, "Miss? Can we help you? What is your business here?" Thereafter came an older lady in a green dress who frowned and asked me if I was well. Then a maid, who appeared to be my age, came running, screeching out, "Get her seated, get her seated!"

I would not sit; I did not have time. Behind me the wind from outside rushed in and tears, long held back, began in my eyes. More servants appeared, shouting out variously, 'Shut that door!', 'Whatever is afoot?', 'Run for Mr Pinkerton!', and 'Run for the master!'

I heard the sound of a door creaking down the hall, an old, heavy door from the noise of it. A man appeared, tall and frowning. He spoke, and every person, including me, turned to him.

"What is this?"

He had a voice that cut straight through all the clamour, all the bluster. It cut through me, too, but I could not be frightened, not after what had just happened.

A number of the others began to speak, but somehow I found the voice to be heard over them. "Please help. My uncle's carriage has turned over in the road. My aunt is grievously injured. And the coachman, too."

He stepped forward and all the others present stepped aside as though they were the chorus in a play, making way for him. His eyes fixed on me and I felt a sense of confusion. He looked me up and down but there was no emotion of any sort in his eyes.

"Where?"

"Just beyond the bend in the road. I ran here."

"You ran?" His eyes fixed me still.

"Yes. I should say it was about a mile."

A finely sliced moment of oddness took place. I was frozen *in situ*. Caught in an unknown hall, in an unknown house, before a community of complete strangers from whom I needed help. The man blinked before he spoke.

"Clark, send for Thomas to bring the carriage up. Fordham, bring my horse to the front and tell John to ride over too. Mrs Reynolds, send to the physician in Lambton and see to things here."

The lady in the green dress said 'yes, sir.' She then advanced upon me, removing her own shawl, moving to place it about me. "Now my dear, Miss.... Erm. Let us to the kitchens for a sweet drink."

She began to place her shawl about my shoulders, but I was sweltering already, the cold having been insufficient to overcome the heat of my exertions in getting here. I pushed it away. "No, but I thank you. I could not possibly. I must get back to my family."

Nothing could be more obvious to me than that fact. The tall man turned to me. "You stay here, miss, we will bring your family back."

One thousand horrors raced through my mind. What if my aunt was not recovered? What if she was worse? What if she worsened on the journey here? What of Rebecca and Veronica and my poor uncle and the coachman and his twisted arm? Even the coach boy may well have fainted, for all he had been bleeding and fighting it when I left.

I looked down at myself. My skirts were up to the knees in dirt and the front was ripped. Some blood, from the coach boy's hands, was on my sleeve. My hair was long out of its pins. But I was not injured. I was well and I may be wanted, needed, even. I would not stay.

"No, I cannot hear of it, I must go back to them. I will ride in the carriage or I can ride on a horse if you have one spare, or I can run."

The lady who had been called Mrs Reynolds looked aghast. "Sir, I think this young lady–"

"My uncle will be concerned for my safety. I ran here alone and without his permission."

"Your uncle can be assured that you are perfectly safe here. I will tell him that myself." The gentleman's voice was cool, steady, and assured. But he did not understand.

"I have young cousins, children, who are there. They will be fearful without me."

The man linked eyes with the lady in the green dress and waved his hand in a dismissing manner. "Very well, the girl may come if she wishes it."

He turned and vanished through the front door. The air seemed to go with him, and I felt the peculiar crisis of my situation afresh. He said I could come, but how was I to travel back there? Should I leap upon one of the horses that were presently fetched to the front of the house? Should I go as I had come, on my own two weary feet? The nameless souls of the house began moving about me with certainty and direction. A young man appeared at the door and whispered to the lady in green, who nodded. She turned to me. "Does the young lady wish to travel in the carriage? It is ready, Miss...?"

"Miss Bennet. I am sorry, I should have said. I am Miss Elizabeth Bennet."

She smiled and distressed as I was, and in a dreadful hurry, I saw the friendliness in her face. She said, "Pleased to meet you, Miss Bennet, although I wish the circumstances were better. I am Mrs Reynolds. I am the housekeeper here."

Swiftly, I agreed to get into the carriage, and was soon within a large comfortable carriage with a blank-faced girl and a pile of blankets hastily bundled in by a young man in a flat cap. The scene out of the window happened the reverse of how it had on the journey thither—the large house receded behind us, while the billowing fields cracked with ice on all sides reappeared. We travelled faster on the way back of course, but my experience of it was no less odd. The girl in the carriage spoke not a word and, exhausted, I did not press her.

Despite the increased speed, it was still slower than I would have liked until we came upon my family party. They remained much as I had left them but with the additions of the tall gentleman, his horse and two other men and their horses, all milling about. Rebecca and Veronica sat upon a log and clasped one another. My uncle was still by the broken carriage, his ashen face looking down in at where my aunt remained. I broke free of the carriage the moment it slowed to a stop and went to my uncle, but he hardly seemed to see me.

The tall man began barking instructions to his servants, and within a short time, my poor aunt was removed from the debris and loaded onto a flat panel to be put within the carriage I had arrived in. It was carefully but quickly done. I tried to help, but a young man in a green neckcloth said, "There's no need, miss." Therefore, I bit my lip and joined the children, whom I held close to my breast and in the strongest grip I could.

The same young man stepped down from the carriage and nodded to his master, whom I observed then exchanged some words with my uncle, although it seemed to me that it was mainly the man from Derbyshire who was doing the speaking. My uncle inclined his head; he may have said a few words, but he was far from himself. It was as though, in the accident, he and himself had been separated.

The tall man ceased his discussions with my uncle and turned. He looked to me and at that moment, Veronica rotated in my arms and began sobbing loudly into my belly. The man blinked and seemed to hesitate before stepping towards me, jerkily.

"Miss—um..."

"Miss Bennet, sir." Veronica continued her sobbing and I held her tighter to me.

"I am Mr Fitzwilliam Darcy. I am sorry we have not been properly introduced, but such is the manner of your family's appearance here, it cannot be helped. I have spoken with your uncle and I believe that he is suffering some manner of shock. Your aunt will be conveyed back in the carriage, I invite you and the children to also travel thus. Your uncle may sit with my coachman."

"Thank you."

"You and your family shall be made comfortable at Pemberley, and the physician has been sent for."

"Thank you. I am much obliged to you, sir. You do not know us at all."

"That is of no matter."

"Lizzy?" Rebecca had found her voice. "Shall Mama wake up?"

I turned to her, knowing that, like her sister, she needed some soothing. "I am sure she shall, Rebecca. And soon. We shall all pray and care for your mama, and I am sure that she shall regain her consciousness as soon as may be."

Mr Darcy touched his hat and moved away, before doubling back on himself.

"I—um—forgive me. You were not here when my men and I first arrived. Your aunt is not unconscious. Or at least, I do not believe that she is. I saw her open her eyes and speak very quietly. You may ask the physician, but I believe that she is now simply sleeping."

There was a ghost of a smile about his face as he touched his hat and made for his horse.

My heart seemed to warm and leap.

My aunt did not awake that night. She, and we, and our belongings that had been scattered about in the mud and ice, were transported back to the big house and installed in various comfortable rooms with assistance from waiting servants. The coach boy and coachman were likewise cared for, I was assured.

I tucked up my aunt beneath the yellow coverlet of a grand bed in an enormous room with a picture of an old lady, unknown to both of us, upon the wall. A girl came in to light a fire, and I sat for hours with its orange heat hitting my face. At some undefined moment, I came to, and the fire had burned down to a greyish red crackle. My face was pressed into the edge of my aunt's bed and my body ached most terribly from worry and sleeping in an ill position.

I blinked myself awake in the dark and checked my aunt. No change. Stealthily, I crept to the connecting door and stepped into the next room, where Rebecca and Veronica were obligingly and reassuringly asleep atop a colossal bed with a canopy above. I watched them for a moment and rubbed my eyes.

Leaving, I closed their door noiselessly and returned to the patient. Her breathing seemed even, but she had not moved.

There was a chaise longue in the corner of the room and a great tall window, sheathed in heavy curtains beyond that. I knelt on the cushions and moved the curtains apart. Outside, I saw nothing but an empty and seemingly endless black. There was not so much as a glimmer of light from the moon nor the slightest hint of illumination. Where the land stopped and the sky began, I could not say.

What had he called the place? *Pemberley*? The word came back to my mind, somewhat clouded. I had never heard of it. I knew nothing of the place, or of the people who called it home. I feared the future, both near and far, and my whole body was gripped by a sudden frightened melancholy. That was uncharacteristic of me—I was not formed for ill-humour—and I tried, in my mind, to cast it off. Without warning, my limbs seemed to fail me. My knees ached, my back hurt. I let the curtain drop. Soundlessly, I laid my head upon the cylindrical cushion of the chaise longue and slept.

chapter two

December 20, 1810

"WELL, I NEVER DID. WHAT A BUSINESS!"

Odd hands on my shoulder jerked me awake. My eyes opened to unfamiliar colours, sights—the smell of rose, a rough silk scratching my face. All at once, unwelcome light enveloped me and I sat up with haste. The whole scene came back to me in an instant, the dreadful events of the day prior recollecting themselves to me in a rush.

The girl who bustled behind me opening the curtains was the girl from the carriage the previous day. She tilted her head and spoke directly to me. "You never did sleep on there, did you, miss?"

"I am afraid I did." I smiled weakly. "But not by design. I did not want to leave Mrs Gardiner."

As I spoke, I rose and moved towards my aunt. A quick inspection found her just the same, and I turned my attention back to the young maid. "You came in the carriage with me, did you not?"

"Yes, miss."

"I am so sorry for my rudeness. You must think me quite ill-mannered. I was simply so worried."

The girl was adjusting blankets and neatening the bedside table as we spoke, and said, "It does you credit, miss."

I held out my hand to her and she paused in her ministrations, looking at it as though it were a bonnet that wanted mending.

"I am Elizabeth Bennet."

"Oh yes, Miss Bennet. All the staff have been told your name. Mr Darcy is the most charitable of gentlemen. A good master and a good host. Let that be your comfort."

I cannot say that her sentiments were obvious to me from the little I had seen of his bearing, but there it was. He was charitable, to be sure, but what could one do when a desperate, muddied stranger came to one's door begging aid for an injured aunt and terrified children?

"What is your name?"

"Annie, Miss Bennet. Nice to meet you."

During the course of that morning, I battled to keep her friendly smile in my mind. After opening the curtains and seeing to some linens in the corner, she left. I sat with my aunt for a time and spoke of little nothings. However, I saw not a shred of response from her.

Realising that I looked a fright and had limited time, I rushed to the room which had been allotted to me in order to straighten my appearance. The untouched bed in my own chamber seemed to taunt me, and I felt tired to the bone as I put on a serviceable blue day dress, taken from the top of my trunk. When I returned to my aunt's bedchamber, I found my uncle and a little man who clutched a leather case.

"Ah, Lizzy." My dear uncle croaked out the words. "This is the physician, Mr Fitch. Mr Fitch, my niece, Miss Bennet."

"Madam." He offered a small bow. "I came at first light, of course. One would never do less for a Darcy."

"A Darcy?" The words seemed to slip out of me, and then I recalled myself. "Oh, I am sorry. Of course. Mr Darcy is our host."

Mr Fitch's brow furrowed and he appeared to consider me. Lest he may be assessing me for Bedlam, I made great efforts to appear collected thereafter. The little physician roamed about my aunt's bed considering her and examining her at some length, muttering and exhaling noisily throughout. It seemed to go on forever and my uncle and I stood by watching in mutual mystification. Eventually, frustration moved me to speak.

"Mr Darcy thought that Mrs Gardiner may be sleeping. Do you think that can be true, sir, after all this time?"

"It can be true, and I do think it thus." He turned to my uncle. "Your wife, sir, has had a very nasty shock and possibly a blow to the head, although there is no mark, apart from a little bruising. She has, as you know, some cuts to the arm, but those are flesh wounds. Miss Bennet here has done an excellent job of dressing them, and I can see no reason for great concern there. Mrs Gardiner is running a slight fever at present."

"A fever?" I had not expected that word, and was suddenly fearful.

"Yes. Only very slight at the moment." He removed his eyeglasses and fastened his bag.

"I—"

He appeared to be preparing to leave, but the greatest question had not been addressed, still less answered.

"Mr Fitch, may I ask—when do you believe my aunt shall be fit to move?"

"That, I cannot possibly say, miss. When she wakes things may be clearer."

"*May* be clearer?"

"Yes. *May*."

"I see." I looked to my uncle, whose face appeared blank and impassive. "But—Are you able to say, for example, when she may travel? We were on the road south. We were going home when the accident took place."

"And where, may I ask, young lady, is home?"

"Mr and Mrs Gardiner live in London, sir. But my family home is in Hertfordshire, and that was where we were destined. For Christmas. It takes two days, but we had plenty of time. If we can get her to Hertfordshire, then my sisters and I can nurse her for as long as may be needed."

"Get her to *Hertfordshire*? For *Christmas*? My dear girl, I believe you have misunderstood the severity of your aunt's situation. I cannot say when she will be well enough to travel to another county, but it may not be for weeks or even months. At the present time, she should not be moved from this room."

A bud of nausea started in my belly. "I see. Of course. I shall attend to her here then, sir."

I glanced over at her. Her poor still body lay like a doll under the thick cover. My hand, on the edge of the bed, trembled.

"We cannot know the full extent of your aunt's injuries until her fever has passed," Mr Fitch said in a kindlier voice. "A fever must be treated with patience and close care and time, Miss Bennet. It cannot be remedied with worry, so I suggest you eschew that as far as you are able."

I managed a smile. "I will do my best, sir."

"Good, good," he said as he patted his belly. Having reassured us that he would be back in the morning and was available should he be needed before, he shook my uncle's hand and withdrew.

My uncle turned to me as the door closed. "Well, Lizzy, it seems that we must sit and wait." With that, he sank down on the chair beside my aunt's bed and appeared to lose himself in contemplation of her.

Consideration for his feelings, and the discovery that rather than being in bed as I suspected, Rebecca and Veronica were up and abroad playing without a chaperon, caused me to leave him.

Once out of the room in which I had spent so long, I found myself pacing, almost running down the waiting corridors. Our chambers were on a corridor flanked by doors and lined by a plush red carpet that was comfortable under my slippers. I turned a corner and there was another great corridor, much the same. In the distance, I heard clocks chiming, but I did not know the time.

Although I was tired, it was thrilling to be outside of the bedchamber. An array of portraits hung on the wall to one side, and I walked among them, wondering who they all were. Shortly, I came to a staircase and began to hope that I would recognise some aspect of the geography. I looked around, but it was hopeless. I did not recall any of this from the previous evening.

The staircase before me was a colossal great swirling creation, framed by yet more paintings and covered by the same deep red carpet I had been following for some time. Unlike the corridors, the stairwell was filled with light. Suddenly bathed in sunshine, I squinted. Standing at the top of the staircase, I considered the place afresh. From my vantage point, I could now see the door through which I had crashed only the previous day. But there had been so much happening, that I did not notice the surroundings. I had not noticed, for example, the black and white tiled floor, nor the tapestry—larger surely than the entire drawing room carpet at Longbourn—which hung upon the wall.

Inwardly, I smiled to myself. I should never be able to give enough description of this grand house to satisfy Mama, once she discovered our circumstance—that was a certainty. Hopeful of seeing a person who could direct me to the children, or discovering them myself, I made my way down the staircase. But there was nobody. My feet echoed about on the hard polished floor. There was nobody but me.

It was notably chillier on the ground floor and I drew my shawl tighter around me. Beneath the huge tapestry was a door, and it seemed to be as good a place as any to start my search for the others. I realised that I had lost some of the speed and easiness of my earlier running along the corridor. It was as though there was some manner of net around me. My movements became slow and careful. Still, I walked and walked. Wherever were the inhabitants of this house?

In an instant, I caught sight of a maid at the end of the corridor, carrying a pile of linens. She was far off, but just as I was about to speak, she vanished into a room.

Into the empty hall I spoke. "Has anyone seen my family? Two small children. Girls. Not naughty, just spirited. And could be anywhere here abouts?"

Silence came the reply. I began to wonder whether I should cease my wanderings inside, go back to the front door and try outside. Rebecca, for one, would likely have tried to get outside given the chance. Veronica's choice, I knew, would be to be curled up before a fire somewhere.

I peered into the first open room I came to. There was a fire, but it burned somewhat meanly, and was too small to heat the room, which was vast. The walls were lined with row upon row of books and there were a number of leather chairs. It was a library, but there was no reader within it.

I moved on and happily discovered the next room to be somewhat warmer. It was decorated in the most delicate greens and blues, and in the corner by the window stood the most beautiful pianoforte, opened up, as if expecting a person to play any moment. The fire had been laid wide and was throwing out a marvellous heat. On a table stood a vase of dried flowers, soft and velvety. I stepped into the room, gingerly; I could not resist. It was the first really lovely place that I had seen since my arrival here. I drifted a little further into the room and looked around. The instrument seemed to draw me in and I nearly gasped as I got closer. It was such a fine instrument, gleaming bright, fire light on one side, sunshine on the other. Suddenly I recalled home and playing carols for my sisters to sing, or practising a piece until Mama took to her bed in frustration.

Then, in the corridor, I heard what sounded like a door closing. Hopeful of some human contact I darted out, saying "Hello? Is anyone there?'" But when I got back to the hall, there was nobody. I exhaled and paused, wondering what I should do with myself. I would complete looking around this part of the house, and then try the garden. Thus decided, I moved with more purpose.

The next door was closed, but I opened it. I told myself that it could not be private, downstairs and situated with the music room and the library such as it was. With an effort, I pushed the door and went in. Upon beholding the room within, I did not 'nearly gasp'—I did gasp, loudly and honestly. The room was enormous, far larger than the others

I had seen. The floor beneath my feet was polished wood, the colour of honey and the ceiling was so high I could hardly credit it. A dozen windows ran along the side, most of them shuttered and with their curtains drawn across. There was just one from which the light flowed. Shutters and curtains had been opened and the winter sunshine poured in, lighting up a scene of the utmost strangeness. Items of furniture had been covered in great sheets and pushed against the walls. More sheets hung over paintings mounted on the walls. The fireplace was stone cold empty and the room itself bitter. Around the walls and hanging from the ceiling hung gold fittings, not a candle between them. The door did not slam behind me, but wedged open.

I moved to the middle and surveyed the place. I was shaking with cold now, but could not tear myself away. This was a ballroom, as sure as could be, although it was far grander than any I had seen, not to mention larger. The air smelt slightly musty. I could not account for lingering in this place, except to say that it fascinated me not a little. If my mother had a quarter of such a space, she would invite the families of three counties and my sisters would dance their legs clean off.

Suddenly from behind me, a voice said, "Miss Bennet?"

I spun around to see him framed in the doorway. "Mr Darcy!"

For all that it was perishing cold, I felt myself blush. "I am so sorry, sir, I was searching for my cousins. I did not realise until I came in that this room was shut up. I did not mean to pry. I am mortified—"

"No, no need to be concerned." He waved his hand in that way he had done the previous day. It was as though he imagined he could bat away any manner of challenge, any inconvenient thing at will. "It has been closed for some years now."

"Do you not care to dance, Mr Darcy?"

"I do not. Out of keeping with the spirit of my age, I know. But there it is."

"Um, I—"

"Let me close the shutter for you, Miss Bennet. It must have been very hard to open." With this he strode past me and begun forcing the great wooden contraption back into place and fastening it.

"I did not open it, sir. It was like that when I came in." Embarrassed and affronted all at once, I went to assist him. But he hardly seemed to notice.

"It is of no importance," he said as he turned.

"I—"

Suddenly, we were without the light from outside, and the room was dark as well as cold. Standing close, he was taller even than I had realised yesterday, and his face unreasonably fierce. What could he have to be so joyless about? Did he not live with every possible comfort, among people who admired him without reservation?

Having closed the shutter and turned to face me, he appeared agitated and began raking his fingers through his hair. I saw, very clearly, the impropriety of my situation, and although I sought to end it, an unseen force seemed to keep me in place. I had a sense of reaching beyond the life I had known and seeing something new, but I did not know what it was. After a moment, I came to my senses.

"I was searching for my cousins. They ran off to play when I was tending to Mrs Gardiner, and I am ashamed to admit that I have lost them."

The faintest hint of a smile crossed his face. "There is no shame in it. Come."

The last word was barked as he exited the room in long, quick paces. I did as I was bade and followed him, although he went at such a pace, I did not have time to close the door properly. Thereafter we stalked down various corridors, he in front, me behind, at a terrific speed. Was he trying to escape the strange proximity of the ballroom? Was he anxious to separate from my presence as soon as may be? I could not imagine, and began to find the sight of his frock-coated, speechless figure before me rather humorous.

Before long, we came to a door, which he opened. Outside glowed a lawn still more green than brown. The familiar yelp of playing children drifted in, and the unmistakable sound of Veronica laughing cut through the air. A sense of comfort stole over me. Mr Darcy gestured to me to go outside and, drawing my shawl around me, I did. Abruptly, and slightly unexpectedly, he did not follow.

The door closed with a certain sort of clunk and I was alone on a gravelly path overlooking a splendidly kept lawn surrounded on three sides by Pemberley's walls. Right in the middle, running in ever decreasing circles, were Rebecca and Veronica. "Lizzy!" they cried out and made for me, both colliding with my middle at the same time.

Thereafter the afternoon passed without incident. I played with the children for a time within the sheltered lawn, and when it became too cold to bear, we went back within doors. Mrs Reynolds informed us of some arrangements for their meals. It had been decided that the children would be fed an early supper and I would then put them to bed.

I returned to my aunt to reports that she had woken but fallen back into slumber. She was warm to the touch, but not warmer than before. Annie, who was changing sheets, assured me there was nothing to fear.

I hoped rather than believed her to be correct. I wrote letters to my family, seeking to inform them of events, without driving Longbourn into paroxysms of panic at the same time.

When the time came for dinner, I dutifully made my way to another grand room—a dining room on the other side of the house that surely could have seated one hundred people. In the event, it was just my uncle and I who sat down to dine. The food was delicious and everything arranged in a fine manner. But I found I could not eat a great deal. My belly churned and I pushed morsels around the plate without enthusiasm. My uncle was much the same, and I feared for him if my aunt did not make a quick recovery.

The time ached by. I had half expected Mr Darcy to appear, but he did not, and then it occurred to me that perhaps a truly grand gentleman would not wish to pass a meal with such people as us. Though Mr Gardiner was wealthy, his carriage did not have the marks of gentry or nobility; no doubt Mr Darcy believed he understood us. It was clear to me that he had an unusually high view of himself and perhaps, after the incident in the ballroom, he had seen enough of me.

When we had finished eating and liveried servants hovered about as if to complete their tasks, I squeezed my uncle's hand on the table. "I wrote to Mama and Papa today, Uncle. I shall write tomorrow as well. May I tell them that *you* are feeling a little better?"

Our eyes met and he smiled for perhaps the first time since the accident. "A little. You must not worry them overly, Lizzy. You are doing a sterling job, dear. It does not go unnoticed."

I kissed his forehead by way of reply. "I believe that I shall walk outside before retiring, should you like to join me?"

"Outside? In this weather? It is dreadful cold."

"Aye, but it is not wet. The children discovered a lovely lawn today and it is close. Shall I show you? We shall have some light from the house."

Hesitantly, he agreed and I traced my way to the door that Mr Darcy had shown me. My uncle gave me his arm and, shivering, we made our way around the gravelly path. There was just enough light from various windows to see.

"You see," I said, "there is always something invigorating about being in the dark. One sees the world in a whole new way."

"If you say so, Lizzy! You must not take a chill on top of everything else."

"I shall not take a chill—I am never ill, as you know. I believe we must make great strides to remain well in ourselves so that we can make Aunt well and take her home as soon as possible."

I looked hopefully at his half-lit face. I wanted him to say when he thought we may be able to leave, but he simply said, "Yes."

chapter three

December 22, 1810

THE ICY GRAVEL CRUNCHED BENEATH MY BOOTS AS I STRODE forth and the wind howled. Above my head, the sky was leaden, but I was determined to get out of doors. My aunt's condition was much the same, and Annie had insisted that she could watch both her and the children if I wished to go for a walk before Mr Fitch came.

Thus, I had donned my very warmest clothes and sturdiest boots and struck out hopefully. I knew the best ways out of the house now, and had swiftly found the doorway on to what I had learned was called the Chestnut Lawn, although there were no chestnuts to be seen. The cold was so biting, it made one scamper along, almost in an effort to escape it. The path had an incline and before long I felt the familiar comfort of my legs hurting gently and my heart pounding.

I reached a tree and paused, looking back. From this vantage, the house could be seen as, no doubt, it had been intended. Its façade was a great limestone monolith, a pale yellow which, I imagined, looked at its best in fine weather. Smoke plumed from dozens of chimneys and the windows were almost too many to count. Beyond, the landscape was by turns both gentle and brutal.

A sound came behind me and I turned.

"Miss Bennet." Mr Darcy was atop his horse, but dismounted after a moment. I bobbed a curtsey and he bowed to me.

"Are you quite well?" He looked at me, enquiringly.

"Very much so, sir. I was walking."

"Yes. I mean—I can see that." He had an agitated look that seemed to be always with him. "May I walk with you for a time? Are you going in this direction?"

He gestured to the way that he had just come. I nodded my assent and before I knew where I was, he was walking alongside me, holding his great braying stallion to the side.

For many minutes, we simply meandered, progressing in uneasy silence. I expected him to speak, but he did not. Churlishly, I began to hate him for having disturbed me in a contented reverie. After a time, I could bear it no longer. "You are out early, sir."

"Am I? It is my practice to ride out each morning. There are usually matters to be dealt with."

We continued to walk, ticking along like two bored clocks keeping slow time.

"And you, Miss Bennet? You are a keen walker?"

"Yes, very much so. Although, I must say that your terrain here in Derbyshire is not what I am used to. I am greatly challenged." I laughed, but he did not laugh back. I smarted, as I should not like to be taken for a person who laughs at their own jokes.

"Where are you from? Do your family also live in London, along with your aunt and uncle?"

"No, sir. My family resides in Hertfordshire."

"Ah, a fine country." He thought for a moment, then asked, "And you —what was it that brought your party to Derbyshire?"

"My aunt wished to visit a relation, a very elderly relation." I glanced up at him to see if he took my meaning. I was surprised to see a flash of recognition in his eyes. "She had been told that there was limited time and hence, we travelled at this time of the year, her relation being very dear to her."

"You would usually travel, when?"

"I cannot say that I have had the pleasure of travelling a great deal at any time of year. But usually, if I can, it is in the summer. I might be invited with my uncle and aunt to go on holiday here or there, such as they go."

"And what of your nearer family?"

A smile I knew to be wry came to my lips. "Oh, they do just as well at home. My mother struggles with the strains of distance and travel. And my dear father has never found a happier landscape than that of his own library."

"Mr Gardiner told me your father was a gentleman, but nothing further."

It was an odd comment, but I ploughed on. "I have four sisters who are satisfyingly envious—" I stopped myself. "Or rather, they were."

Surely they did not envy me this. I had a letter from Jane in my reticule, and another from Mary. It had stung my eyes to read both, and I longed to send them good news of our aunt.

Mr Darcy said nothing save for 'hmm'. He walked on still though, and I began to wonder whether or not he would ever leave me to myself. At length, he offered, "I observe that you are commendably caring towards your cousins."

"Yes, thank you. They are excellent children. And—of course, they are in some distress at present. They worry for their mother and miss their younger brothers, presently in the care of my family."

"Yes, of course." He said the words at astonishing speed, almost as though they were embarrassing to him. "Do they have a governess at home?"

"No, Rebecca attends school. And I believe that my uncle and aunt plan the same for Veronica."

"That is singular—school for younger girls, I mean. Although I understand that has become a fashion, and is growing more common."

"A fashion? Is that what you call a proper education, sir?"

"It is," he insisted. "For young ladies, it is."

"I should call it progress."

He smiled, maybe for the first time since I had met him. It was not an exuberant smile, but guarded, private. "Maybe the two are not mutually exclusive, Miss Bennet. I assume that you have received the education of a gentleman's daughter. There can be no honour in denying it to others on the basis of progress."

"Of course not. I would like for all ladies, high and low, to learn."

"And what method is better than a governess, in the home. Sometimes, the old ways are the best ways." His chin was raised altogether too high as he said this. "You must have had the same yourself."

"No, not at all," I said.

"Really? You surprise me. I did not understand there to be any of the new ladies' colleges in Hertfordshire. Were you sent away?"

"No," I admitted. "I was educated—insofar as the word can be used in this instance—at home. But I did not have a governess, nor do any of my younger sisters now. It was rather more ad hoc."

His face, which I glanced at, had tightened.

"Do I shock you?"

"Not at all. If you have lacked any manner of formal instruction, then it does not display itself. Nobody would ever be aware of anything lacking in you, Miss Bennet. Apart from maybe, some minor matters of deportment and clandestine turns of phrase, perhaps. Your social presentation belies any inadequacies of upbringing that you may have suffered."

"My father is a gentleman, sir, but not a wealthy man. These *inadequacies* to which you refer arise from that alone. Although I am obliged that you say they are not obvious."

He did not appear to hear my barb and said, "You cannot be so indifferent to the opinions of others."

"One can seek so to be."

"A hopeless endeavour. Surely you must see that."

We reached the peak of another hill as he said this, and the chill of the wind battered my face ferociously. I felt tired, although I was not so. I longed to get away from this unkind and harsh speaking man whom I hardly knew. Everything he had done for us must have arisen from some sense of duty alone, nothing more. He had as good as said that. His proximity to me now was a reminder of our odd compromised position. How I hated the thought of our debt to him. I could think of no person of my acquaintance whom I wished less to owe a debt of obligation.

I felt unequal to answering his question and so said, "I realise that time is pressing. I have been away for some time, and Annie—"

"Annie?"

"One of your upstairs maids, Annie. She must certainly have duties aside from watching my aunt and the children."

He fixed me with the most assessing stare and blinked, as though disbelieving. Something in his face told me that he did not intend to speak.

"Therefore, I believe that I must return to the house. It would not be fair for me to put upon her kindness."

"No, of course not."

With little ado, we turned course, and returned to the house in silence.

As we reached the Chestnut Lawn, he muttered, "If you will excuse me," or some such words, and was gone.

Suddenly, I felt able to breathe. Such an insufferable man! And what could he mean by waylaying me in this manner? The sight of his back vanishing was most welcome.

With my family in mind, I began to march with all speed towards the door. My time with Mr Darcy had thrown my mind asunder, but I tried to pretend otherwise. My fists clenched and I rubbed my eyes in the cold. How I wished to escape this place. As I strode towards the house, my eye was unexpectedly caught. A moment later, and I would not have seen, would have walked to the door unnoting. But I did see.

There was a woman standing at an upper floor window, looking down upon me. A young woman, but not a child, in a nightgown. With a flash of blonde hair hanging down, she was beautiful, but not dressed to be seen outside her chambers. It was an intimate sight, a picture I should not have seen.

No sooner had I observed her than she moved away from the frame, but she *had* been there; I was as sure of that as anything in this world. I stopped stock still and stared at the window, but she had vanished. My mind clouded with odd thoughts and confusions.

Who could that person be? Something in her bearing told me she was not a servant. We had met our host and some of his servants. No other person had been mentioned. No relations, no visiting friends. Nothing had been said about Mr Darcy having a wife.

I returned to my aunt's chamber and sat beside her all day aside from an hour when I played with the children. Annie had found some puzzles and games for them to play with and my heart glowed to see them getting on with the challenge, uncomplainingly. I gave them each an extra kiss on the nose at bedtime, for they were being remarkably good in difficult circumstances.

When I appeared for supper, a footman I had never before seen informed me that my uncle had decided to remain above stairs. His voice echoed about my head and I contemplated the great oak table, polished to a high shine, set for one. I wished to tell the man that I should much rather have a tray in my aunt's room, but I sensed that it was not permitted and, in any case, they had arranged things in this way already. I was not brought up to make unnecessary work for others. I tried to laugh but the air had gone out of me.

Crestfallen and fatigued, I sat where I was bade and speedily ate the dishes presented to me. Apart from servants, not a soul came in or went out. Straight before me hung an enormous picture of an old lady in a red dress, painted perhaps one hundred years ago. I wondered who she was and whether she had ever sat alone in this very room, wishing she were elsewhere. Silently, I battled an aching hollowness in my heart. I had never been anywhere so grand, but would have given anything to go home.

At last, it was over.

The footman pulled out my chair and I rose at just the right time, a skill I had both learned and perfected in this house.

"Thank you."

He nodded, softly. "There shall be tea in the music room for you shortly, Miss Bennet."

"I... Thank you." So, there it was: I was not yet permitted to retire. Languidly and without enthusiasm, I made a solitary progress to the music room. The room was much as it had been when I saw it before, but set for the evening. Great curtains had been drawn, and puddled on the floor in enormous extravagant heaps. Various chaise longues and chairs sat about with no occupants. The fire flickered beautifully, warming all and casting the most delicious light. The pianoforte was still open, just as before, and so inviting. I moved towards it, as though I were on a string, being slowly drawn on. But for some time, it was delight enough just to behold it. The bench was set exactly right, but I did not sit on it. My hand stroked the fine curve of the instrument.

At that moment, a different footman came in with a tray which he deposited on a small table; he bowed and left me alone once more. I did not particularly wish for anything on the tray, and although I thanked him, I had no real heart in it. I thought of my poor still aunt, of the lady at the window, and of the tightening face of Mr Darcy during our morning meeting. None of it was clear, none of it was a happy state of affairs.

I moved to the window and peeked between the curtains into the blank. The chill of outside hit my nose and I felt the same sense of disturbed foreboding that I had felt the first night. In some respects, it had grown worse. Where was I? And how should I leave with my family and my happiness and my own self intact?

Stop, Lizzy. A surge of defiance rose up inside me. I admonished myself, thoroughly, for pitying my position, when it might have been much worse. In my head, I sought to laugh at it.

With this in mind, I moved to the instrument, sat, and began to play.

Like many young ladies of indifferent talent and reasonable enthusiasm, I had a number of pieces I knew by heart. They were none of them difficult, still less impressive. But they gave me pleasure to play and I knew, to my unspoken satisfaction, that I could do perfectly good justice to them. I would usually play at home, for the ears of less than appreciative sisters, or occasionally at family or local gatherings with my parents and others. I had certainly never sat down at an instrument such as this. However, I soon found that it was not so very different or so very frightening. The keys were slightly softer to touch, and the pedals were not as loose as the pedals on our instrument at home. But none of that was of any importance. In moments, the music was gushing about me, reminding me of easier times. For the first time since arriving at

Pemberley, I began to unravel, and the strains of circumstance seemed to be falling away.

I was so engrossed that I did not hear the heavy, fast footprints running down the corridor until almost the moment that Mr Darcy, face darkened and brow furrowed, burst into the room. He appeared to me as though he were almost on the point of shouting, his mouth opened, but no sound came forth. He had no jacket on. My fingers, affrighted, slipped and produced a discordant sound, and I stood with a jolt.

"Miss Bennet—"

"Sir, forgive me, I—"

"How did you—"

"I am so sorry, sir. I have been playing your instrument, uninvited."

"Miss Bennet, I—"

"I was here alone, and I did not realise I would disturb anyone."

He had probably been thinking poorly of my playing, for from his words and demeanour it seemed he thought poorly of everything I did. Had he a generous thought towards me in his heart? If he did, he would not keep such a stony face.

He stepped into the room and raked a hand through his hair, as he seemed to do so often. He did not look at me.

My belly was sick with mortification and I felt a pain come in my head.

"There is no need for an apology. You mis—"

"Of course. Please forgive my trespass here, sir. I must return to Mrs Gardiner. I have lingered too long in any event." And in an instant, I tore out from behind the instrument, across the gilded room and before his disbelieving eyes, I ran away from him. After that, I continued to run, further and further, slipping slightly on the carpeted floor, the shallow stairs. My heart thudded most violently and my mind exploded with embarrassment and shame and confusion. He had looked so cross. I wished, quite desperately, for my aunt to be well and for us to go home.

As I reached the wing in which were our bedchambers, I paused, knowing that I had become breathless and was no longer presentable. I leaned my back against the wall and gathered my thoughts, straightened my clothing, steadied my breathing. I must go on as before, even though it would be hard, and I did not even know why.

I was about to move off when, without a warning, my aunt's chamber door opened and Annie appeared. Her expression was harried and she was rushing towards me.

"Miss! Please come quickly. I was just coming to find you. Your aunt has taken a turn for the worse."

chapter four

December 22-23, 1810

THE HEAT OF THE ROOM HIT ME AS SOON AS I ENTERED. THE fire licked about in an animalistic manner. My uncle, having removed his coat, paced about wiping his brow. Everything looked different and altogether more dangerous. In the centre of the room, my aunt's bed seemed enormous, like the ship depicted in Turner's *The Shipwreck* which she and I had seen together not so long ago. Her form, in its centre, was tiny, and writhing about dreadfully, sheets twisted, covers cast off. A bowl of water and a pile of linens lay on the floor.

Annie came in behind me.

"Oh Annie," I cried out.

"'Tis all right. We'll get her through it," she said, her placid demeanour soothing.

Tears pricked my eyes. To think that not moments ago I had been becoming missish about the vagaries of a man whom I hardly knew and playing upon a grand pianoforte like a lady of leisure and indulgence.

"It is positively roasting in here," I said. "We have to cool it down. Do we have plenty of water?"

"Yes, miss. Buckets of it."

"In that case, let us use this—" I picked up the used bowl of water from the floor "—to damp down the fire a bit."

She took the bowl from me and completed the task.

My aunt continued to roil around so painfully. Her face was white but glazed in sweat and each time I sought to hold her, she threw me off most violently. I lay flannels upon her brow and in calmer moments sought to spoon a tonic, given to me by Annie, into her mouth. Her eyes, when they opened, were glazed, too. For some periods, all too brief, she calmed and seemed to sleep. At other times, she was quite frantic, the fever no doubt producing wicked dreams in her mind. A stream of words issued from her, but they lacked any sort of order or coherence. I tried to acknowledge them whilst getting on with the task of caring for her. My uncle sat by the side of the bed appearing completely grief-struck in the cacophony of murmurings—'Rebecca', Veronica', 'John', 'Robert', 'my love', 'Oh Lizzy', 'Longbourn for Christmas' and 'where's the carriage?' These words she repeated over and over again, as though there were no end to it.

I stroked her face with shaking hand. "Calm, dear aunt. Calm. Do not worry for others, everyone is well. The girls are asleep, the boys safe at Longbourn. My mother, my father, they know you are unwell and only want you to get yourself better. Do not concern yourself about the carriage. Can you drink this?"

Periodically, Annie would appear with new bed linens, and she and I would change the sheet atop my aunt, moving as swiftly and as smoothly as possible in the circumstances. Annie taught me how to do it and after the fourth or fifth change, I believe I was quite proficient. Each sheet came off her sodden; her body beneath it clammy and agitated.

Thus we continued, interminably. I heard the clocks chiming, but could not say what the time was, my entire being having narrowed to the tortured wraith in the bed.

At my insistence and with my promise to wake him if there were any developments, my uncle retired to bed. The greatest, and possibly only mercy, was that the children continued to sleep in the next room. I did not know whether I was equal to the sight of them appearing and seeing their mother in such a state. Fortunately, that did not occur.

My hair fell out of the arrangement I had set it in that morning, but Annie tied it up again. She also procured a piece of bread for each of us and a cup of tea. We ate them together, sitting on the chaise longue. I had not realised that I was famished, but I was the moment I saw it.

"Annie, thank you for your efforts. They have been so great this evening." It had occurred to me then, as it had before, that she must have other duties which she was neglecting to help me and my aunt.

"You must allow me to speak with Mrs Reynolds, for I cannot have you getting into trouble for our sake."

"I won't get into trouble, miss. It was Mrs Reynolds what told me to help you."

That was odd. I could understand asking the doctor to attend—I heard Mr Darcy demanding that myself. But for a maid to be spared for us—that was so kind of Mrs Reynolds.

"You have been of such assistance. I should have been lost without you." I rose from where we had eaten and went to my aunt, laying my hand upon her arm. My aunt was presently at rest, and though still exceedingly hot, she seemed to lack the burning energy of before. "Do you think that she has cooled slightly?"

"Maybe so, though I don't like to speak too soon."

I stood at the end of my aunt's bed and rubbed my tired eyes, full of anguish.

Swish. Annie had risen and gone to the window, and in a deft and practiced sweep, pulled the curtains aside. Much to my astonishment, daylight flowed in and I blinked. It was that early sort of light that is fresh and creeping and in usual circumstances, life affirming. I looked down at my gown, water-spattered and rumpled. It was the same gown I had worn that evening to dine, to play the pianoforte uninvited, and to run away from Mr Darcy like a petulant child. I wore it still, but felt like a different person.

"How can it be morning, Annie?"

She laughed. "Very easily! The fever has lasted through the night, and still she battles it, the poor lady."

Annie then implored me to rest, to go to my own bedchamber for some hours of repose, but I could not leave. "When I am certain that the fever has broken, I may try to sleep, but otherwise, I cannot. She has always been so kind to me. She is the very best aunt a young lady could wish for. I feel so guilty that I was not here when this fever began raging so."

"Oh, no, you should not feel anything of that sort. Mrs Gardiner has not been left alone, and I was coming to fetch you when you appeared. I believe the cook likes to have guests to cook for, as Mr Darcy rarely entertains folk. She likes to show off a bit, if you know what I mean."

I smiled and thought of my own mother, whose table was always excellent. "Yes, I know just what you mean." Another thought occurred to me then. "Does Mr Darcy not entertain at Christmas? I might have thought that he would."

"Not these last few years. Shame really." She smiled but it did not quite reach her eyes and before I could ask more, she sprang up and started about a new round of tasks.

Then, two additional things happened which prevented us speaking further of Mr Darcy's social activities. Firstly, the children awoke and appeared in the bedchamber in their night clothes. Their wide eyes and the fact they held one another's hands showed their fright; they had easily observed that their mother looked different. However, though I myself was afraid and uncertain, I embraced them and reassured them as best I could. I believe they were comforted by it.

Shortly thereafter, my uncle and Mr Fitch appeared. Greetings were exchanged and I endeavoured to inform Mr Fitch as accurately as I could of what had taken place in the night. His brow furrowed as he listened to my recitation, and he then set about examining my aunt and speaking to her, trying to induce her to speak to him in return. The whole room ceased to breathe as she softly but clearly answered his questions.

"Mrs Gardiner, can you hear me?"

It took a moment but she replied, "Yes."

"Can you feel this?"

"Yes."

'Good, good. Now if you will, can you drink this please, Madam?"

Achingly slowly and with no little effort, my aunt's body was persuaded to lean forward and she sipped from the spoon in the physician's hand. This action was repeated several times until at last, she gave a little shake of her head. Mr Fitch, displaying hitherto unseen gentleness, assisted her back into a reclining position among the pillows, and turned to the room.

"Mrs Gardiner is still warm. However, I do believe that the fever has broken."

As soon as he said the words, there were various expressions of delight from those present. My uncle shook the man's hand and thanked him loudly. Annie and the children joined in the chorus. I found myself unable to speak and tears were welling up in my eyes, stinging, disturbing my vision. The whole room appeared suddenly as a watery mess.

"I shall visit again tomorrow. However, my advice is—" and he turned to me as he spoke, "—more of the same, Miss Bennet. More of the same. Very well done, young lady."

Salty tears streamed down my cheeks, unbidden as I tried to dash them away and appear composed.

"I also say, Miss Bennet, that persons who have not slept all night may *and should* now take an opportunity to rest themselves." With a nod, he added, "Doctor's orders."

There was a susurration of laughter from Annie and my uncle as he left the room. As matters were, my own relief, the exuberance of the children and the continuing need to tend my aunt conspired to prevent any sort of rest on my part. However, given all the circumstances, I did not mind.

A little later that morning, I wrote letters home to Longbourn in my aunt's chamber and once completed, prevailed upon Rebecca and Veronica to accompany me downstairs in order that they should be posted. They were enthusiastic and anticipating some adventure, found their coats and seemed almost to tumble down the stairs ahead of me. I was surprised to see Mrs Reynolds at the foot of the stairs.

"Ah, Miss Bennet."

"Mrs Reynolds, good morning."

"I understand that your aunt is a little better, having been unwell in the night?"

"She is improved, and I hope will continue to improve over the course of the day. She seems to be resting more peaceably now."

"I am so pleased to know that, and do hope that she continues to recover. You must be very worried."

I acknowledged her with a half-smile and a nod. "Thank you. It was a difficult night but we did all we could to bring her through it. I pray that it should continue."

Rebecca and Veronica had begun scampering about in the hall and were plainly desperate for a game. I encouraged them to go outside, with stern admonishments to stay close, and they went.

"I came down to ask about posting a letter, but I am so pleased to have seen you. I must express my thanks to you and the servants, Annie most particularly. My family have been so well assisted, and I fear that we have incommoded you greatly."

The lady smiled kindly. "No, no. Do not distress yourself. You have not incommoded us. It is a pleasure to see a few more faces about Pemberley. It is a big house, and it should not be almost emp– Forgive me, I speak out of turn. I must stop myself, lest I say more than I ought. Suffice to say that you have been very gracious guests, and all the household have such sympathy with you and your relations in these dreadful circumstances."

"That is terribly kind of all of you," I said with genuine pleasure. "Everyone here has been so wonderful to us."

"Well, it all comes from the master. He is the most charitable of men, a fine gentleman, and he would never leave people unattended who had an accident on Pemberley land. He would insist on the finest care possible for you."

My smile slipped a little. "Yes, of course. The road we were on—that is Pemberley land, is it?"

"Oh, yes. The Pemberley estate stretches for miles."

"It is a very beautiful part of the country. I am sorry that my first sight of it was while I was in such straits."

"I daresay there is no place finer in all of England." The lady swelled a bit, clearly feeling pride in the place. I wondered how long she had been here–she had an air of possession that was not unbecoming. "You may have a chance to go about walking now that your aunt is recovering. Indeed, I hope that you will and see as much of it as you can."

"Thank you. I shall try. I do not know when we shall be in a position to take Mrs Gardiner home, but I hope it will be soon. We must see what Mr Fitch's view is. Please know that we shall remove as soon as we can. I am conscious of your kindness, but do not wish to test it."

"You are not testing anything, not a bit." She had been holding some papers behind her back, but now presented them to me. I saw with some surprise that it was a pile of sheet music. "Now, that brings me to my purpose, which is to give you these. Mr Darcy understands from Mr Gardiner that you are an exemplary pianist. You may have seen that Pemberley has a fine instrument in the music room. I can show you if you like?"

"Oh!" I felt immediately flustered. "Thank you, but I am aware of where it is. It is quite the warmest room, and the loveliest, in the house. I have seen it already."

"You must feel at liberty to practise upon it whenever you wish. This is just a little of the music I collected up that you may wish to peruse."

The music was still in her hand, outstretched between us, and I reluctantly took it from her. "Thank you. I-I will very much enjoy looking at this. And trying to play, as long as it is not too difficult for me. I am afraid that my uncle may have exaggerated my talents to Mr Darcy. I have, alas, never taken as much trouble to practise as I ought."

Mrs Reynolds beamed. "You must play whenever you wish while you are here. The instrument is new to Pemberley and no doubt would enjoy the exercise."

I smiled at her little jest but still tried to demur. "I do not wish to monopolise the instrument. Mr Darcy himself may wish to play."

"Mr Darcy does not play, and in any case, it was he who explicitly asked me to convey this to you. He could not possibly object, no matter how much time you spent at it."

These pages were given on Mr Darcy's orders? My head fairly swam between my exhaustion and the contrariety of information being given to me. Who was this man, so charitable by proxy and so lauded by his servants?

With that, we said farewell and parted. Mrs Reynolds kindly took my letter and said she would see to it directly. I could hear her step vanishing down the hall as I leafed through the music. There were some lovely pieces, some familiar, others not. None of them looked impossibly difficult, although some I might prefer to practise without an audience.

I seemed to understand so little of what was occurring here. Mr Darcy had seemed unambiguously angry when he appeared in the music room, although further reflection forced me to recall that he had said, in truth, rather little. I tried to remember it clearly through the fog of my own fatigue and the events of the night. Whatever had happened, he was certainly being generous now in sending Mrs Reynolds to me with this message. I decided I should thank him in person and apologise for my behaviour.

Thus resolved, and having observed that the children were occupied in various capers and frisks on the lawn outside the tall window, I made for Mr Darcy's library.

I moved with haste, not wishing my cousins to be left unattended for too long, and because I was rushing, I did not hear the voices from within until I was at the door. By that time, overhearing was inescapable.

"I shall do no such thing."

That was Mr Darcy. He was not shouting but neither was he quiet.

"And what do you propose instead?" This from another voice, unknown to me. A man, and an agitated one seemingly.

A banging noise came from inside the room and I jumped. I was holding my breath. "Well? We must have a plan, Darcy. This cannot continue."

"I do have a plan," Mr Darcy asserted, the cool hauteur of his voice in direct contrast to that of his companion.

"And what is that, pray? To abandon her?"

"No."

There was a squeaking, like the sound of a cupboard being opened. I was painting pictures in my mind, although I knew that they were most likely mistaken.

"Shall you leave wrongs done to your family unavenged?" the unknown man demanded.

"No."

"Do you intend to ignore the best counsel of your entire family for the foreseeable future?"

After a short pause, Mr Darcy replied, "Quite possibly."

There were some unintelligible syllables that, though I knew not their meaning, I could discern represented the frustration of the speaker. "To—well I shall pass that on to my mother and my father. I am sure they shall be most gratified."

Mr Darcy did not respond immediately and there was a lull in the argument. Outside, I backed against the hall wall and waited in silence and awful fascination. I was perfectly well aware that I should not be there, and intended that I should move away as soon as may be.

And yet, I did not.

Then, they started again. Mr Darcy spoke first. "Do not tell them that. I would not want your parents to think that I am ignoring them or plan to do so. However, I will deal with my own household as I see fit."

"But I do have a say, Darcy. A legal say. And you know that. You cannot simply brush me, my wishes and concerns, aside. You *have* to do something about her."

Her? My hand rose to cover my mouth although I was not in danger of releasing anything more than a gasp of shock.

"Give it time," Mr Darcy replied.

"So that's your answer, is it? Just sit and do nothing."

Another banging sound came from the other side of the door, as if a book was dropped or something similar.

"Has it ever occurred to you to change tack? You will not act even now. You are happy to be walled up in this bloody mausoleum year on year."

"You know I would not hear that from any other man than you."

"I do know that," the other man replied. "But it is true."

"Perhaps it is. However, for now, I have heard all I wish to hear."

I heard then a sound of chairs scraping upon wood and the sounds of persons moving about within. Suddenly, unavoidably, I knew I must leave and be gone from sight. Clutching the sheet music in one hand and my skirts in the other, I ran as quickly and as softly as I could manage. I had just turned a corner, breathless and ashamed, when I heard the door open and the voices bid one another a starchy farewell.

❄

Truly exhausted, in every respect, I found Rebecca and Veronica on the Chestnut Lawn and ordered them to return to their mother's room with me. They complained a little about having to stop their frolics, but I was in no mood for a negotiation on the subject.

As I walked the children back inside, the two men's cross voices echoed about in my head along with a hundred questions I could not answer. The children and I, in an eerie and moody silence, had gone part-way up the stair when a strange man in regimentals passed beneath us, evidently on his way out. He had a face almost blistering with anger and stalked down the great stone steps, arms swinging. I should not have liked to be in his path.

"Who is that man, Lizzy?"

With a patient smile, I replied, "I cannot say, Rebecca. He looks like he is a soldier. Maybe he is an acquaintance of Mr Darcy."

"Tom Middler's father is a soldier, and he has the prettiest medals."

"Does he, indeed? Who is Tom Middler, dear?"

"A boy at church. He lives near us. Shall we be able to go home soon, do you think?"

I paused and turned to her. "Oh darling. I do hope so. But we cannot move your mama until it is safe for her. We want her to be well."

"We are never going to get to Uncle and Aunt Bennet for Christmas, are we?"

"No, I am afraid we are not. 'Tis a disappointment, I know. I am sorry, I thought you knew that." I smiled sympathetically. "Even if we left Pemberley now, we would still not arrive in time. But we will do our best to make it the best possible Christmas right here."

"Shall there be mince pies?" Rebecca asked, unsurprisingly. They were, I knew, her favourites.

"I am afraid I do not quite know what is available here, although I shall see what can be done. Will that do?" I smiled my most cheering smile and kissed Rebecca on her nose. She kissed me back.

"Yes, Lizzy."

Veronica, who had been largely ignoring our exchange, took my hand as we progressed up the stair. "Maybe the soldier is the lady's friend," she offered.

It took a moment for my mind, addled by tiredness and emotion and confusion, to absorb what she had said. "What lady do you mean?"

"The lady at the window," Veronica explained. "Rebecca and I have seen her three times now."

"All she does is stare out the window," Rebecca said.

"You must have seen Mrs Reynolds looking out at you. Or maybe it was Annie, or one of the other maids."

"No, we know Annie, we would not mistake her."

"And Mrs Reynolds is old," Veronica added with the brutal candour of a child. Rebecca hushed her at once. "Well, she is!"

"The lady is *not* a maid," Rebecca insisted. "I could tell."

"Well, I am afraid that I have no further suppositions to offer. Come, let us go see how your mama is doing."

December 24, 1810

My cousins sat on the window seat, their backs to the room as rain teemed down upon the pane in veritable rivers. "Lizzy?"

"Hmm?" I looked up from my place beside my aunt. I was attempting to brush out the ends of her hair while she slept. She had been awake and speaking with us for a full hour and Mr Fitch, who had appeared as usual that morning, had been most reassuring.

"'Tis Christmas Eve," Rebecca said.

"I know it is, dear heart."

"There are no decorations here," she replied. "Are we going to get a Yule Log? Everyone needs a Yule Log for good luck."

"I do not know. I do not think so."

There was nothing more I could say to this, for it was both true and disappointing. It was also incomprehensible to me. With so much woodland and beautiful trees and shrubs, why not bring some in to prepare the house for Christmas? The household seemed to shun the season and I could not account for it. Certainly a Yule Log would not have been too difficult to procure but it was not my place to insist upon it.

Rebecca continued. "What are we to do? The weather is abomible."

"Abominable."

"Yes, that."

"Have you played all of the games?"

"Ages ago. Twice," she said with a much-aggrieved air.

"Well then," I forced a brightness to my tone. "I wonder if there are any books for children in the library?" It was a suggestion I was loath to make, as I did not feel equal to going down there again after my last attempted excursion. "I could ask Annie to take you down there when she comes back."

"We don't want books, Lizzy! We want fun."

"Yes, fun!" Veronica echoed.

They had such charming faces, I could not resist it. And I sympathised too. Christmas was meant for revelry and joy, not sickrooms in strange places with stern strangers. "When Annie comes back to watch Mama, you two come with me. I have an idea."

Annie did indeed return, and with an exaggeratedly mischievous smile, I urged the children to follow me quietly. "Wherever are we going, Cousin Lizzy?" Both children pounded the stairs behind me without a care for noise.

"It is a surprise!"

We reached a short stubby sort of door, just as Annie had described, and went through it. There was then a corridor which was being used to store a quantity of fabric. We went along in single file and at the end, I came to the set of double doors I had been hunting. Confident and with a flourish, I pushed them open.

"Lizzy!" Rebecca gingerly stepped out from behind me and looked around. "What is it?"

Veronica gasped "Are there ghosts?"

"No ghosts, silly." I kissed the top of her head and squeezed her trembling shoulders. "This is a gallery. They were popular in grand houses in the olden days. This is the oldest part of the house, and it is not used anymore, so that is why it feels rather different."

The children looked about tentatively. The carpet was worn and a number of unframed pictures were propped against the wall. The curtains had such an old-fashioned appearance, I thought they must be a century old, if not more. It was completely different than the rest of Pemberley, but it had been here first.

"This is a curious place. What did people do in here in the olden days?"

"I believe that they would stroll about and have entertaining discussions, or...perhaps they used to play hoops and balls here!" I gave them a little wink and my most mischievous grin.

"Hoops and balls? In here?" They both looked incredulous and less impressed than I had anticipated. For myself, I was enthralled by the place. It had a musty and in some respects unattractive feeling; its care-worn appearance was so different from the rest of the house. It was far less grand and had plainly not been used for many a year. I wondered if Mr Darcy had ever even been in here.

"I want to play hide and seek," Rebecca announced. "Please? Ronnie and I will hide. Lizzy, you seek!"

"Very well, but do be careful." I covered my eyes with my hands, even though I had closed them and began to count. "One...two...three..."

"You have to count to twenty!" Rebecca cried, with Veronica echoing her.

"Why?"

"Because we don't know where we are. It is only fair."

Thus, I continued counting slowly to the sound of thumping feet and squeals and cries of 'get off my foot'. After a time, there was a click and the footsteps receded. I opened my eyes to see only the empty gallery.

"Coming to find you!"

Being a cluttered and disused room of enormous proportions, I spent far too long searching for them in the gallery itself. After a time, I concluded that for all the hiding possibilities, they were not there. The door at the other end of the gallery gave onto a square room with a number of doors, one of which I took onto a corridor. None of this part of the house appeared used at all and, absent any fires, it was fearfully cold. I shivered and a worm of worry started in my mind.

"Rebecca? Veronica? Where are you?"

Next came a bedroom, complete with ancient bed clothes and a thick layer of dust.

"Children? Rebecca?" I listened carefully for the tell-tale sounds of movement or repressed giggles, but heard nothing. I checked the wardrobe but it was empty. My heart began to thud painfully in my chest. "Where are you? You must come out. You have gone too far and I cannot find you in this house."

My palms grew clammy and my breath changed, quickening. Where was I? And where were they? How should I ever find them? In the middle distance, I heard a bang, like a door being closed forcefully. Without considering it further, I began to run in the direction it had come from. My slippers pounded along wooden floors and cast up dust behind me. Another door came into view and I made for it with all speed, calling out their names as I went. The handle moved easily and I crashed through.

I blinked, panicking afresh. I had come out onto a hall much like the part of the house in which our chambers were accommodated. Though it was not that part of the house, it looked much the same, with rich, thick red carpeted floor, candles, and paintings with gilded edges. I had run back into the modern Pemberley, the rich, beautiful perfect Pemberley of Mr Darcy. But I had left the children behind me somewhere. I marched down the hallway, hopeless of actually discovering them.

My voice had grown hoarse, but still I cried out at intervals, "Rebecca! Veronica! Come out at once!"

From behind me, there came a click and a swish. I spun around half hopeful, half terrified out of my wits, to find a young woman standing in a doorway. Immediately, I knew, it was the lady at the window, although on close inspection, she was little more than a girl. She was wearing only a nightgown, but it was most fine. Her hair was light and marked by great loose curls. Like her, it was undressed and simply hanging down over her shoulders.

The lady spoke first. "You are looking for those girls, I daresay? I am afraid I do not know where they are. They often play on the lawn outside. Should you like to come into my chambers and see if they are there now?"

I hesitated. She seemed so kind and guileless—and different. "Thank you. That is thoughtful, but I do not believe that they are out there. Not unless they have very fast legs." I smiled but she did not laugh.

"You see I was playing hide and seek with them. And they are better hiders than I am a seeker, I suppose. I am ashamed to say I have lost them."

"Why do you not come in anyway, and see if you see them?"

There was something so open in her expression and, extraordinary though it was, I followed her into the chamber. There I found a room of great warmth and comfort. A great high bed with a silk canopy, a dressing table as big as a pianoforte, crowned with a gilded mirror, strewn with books and rose petals and embroidery. A yellow-covered chaise longue was in a corner with a parasol tilted against the wall beside it. The sight of such a space made me feel like an intruder.

The girl moved to the window and pronounced immediately that they were not on the lawn. Turning she asked, "When did you last see them?"

"Um...when I closed my eyes in the gallery. I—"

I paused, as though trapped by a wire. There was a terrific gentleness about this young lady, and an openness. But I had a roiling sense of discomfort and a feeling that I was proximate to some manner of scandal or unhappiness.

"Yes? Do go on."

"Forgive me," I said to her. "I do not believe we have been introduced. And I believe that persons should be introduced, should they not? Even to unexpected hide and seek protagonists who appear at their chambers uninvited."

"I invited you in. I have seen you from the window," she insisted sweetly.

"As I have seen you as well. But I should still say at the outset that I am Miss Elizabeth Bennet and I am pleased to make your acquaintance." So saying, I curtseyed.

The girl returned my curtsey. "I am Miss Georgiana Darcy, and I am pleased to make your acquaintance as well."

My mouth opened to speak, but no words seemed available and so I simply smiled at her. After a time, I found my confidence. "And do you live here, Miss Darcy? I am sorry, you *did* say Miss, yes? Not Mrs?"

"Yes," she replied, looking suddenly suspicious. "*Miss* Darcy. I was born here at Pemberley and I do not believe I shall ever leave, not now."

"You are a relation of Mr Darcy?"

At this she laughed. "Well yes, of course. Mr Darcy is my brother."

A great weight, long hanging above my head, fell to the ground with a thump, leaving me uninjured.

"You are the niece of the poor people who had the carriage accident, are you not?"

"Yes, I am. How did you know?"

"I had it from the servants, and from my brother, who visits me every day, although he gets little thanks from me for it."

Though I wondered at her meaning, I felt the need to explain myself more fully. "We have been here for some days, and I am afraid to think of all the trouble we have caused your household."

"Oh, it is not my household, Miss Bennet."

"Is it not? But is your brother married?"

"No, he is not."

"Then are you not the lady of the house, Miss Darcy?"

"In a sense," she admitted. "And in a sense not. I do not believe that I am worthy of such a title, and in any case, I am only fifteen."

"Well, I am loath to cause more disturbance here. I am quite anxious for my young cousins. They might be anywhere in the house by now."

"You will need Mrs Reynolds or Mr Pinkerton to help you, then.

They are the people to mount a search expedition. Shall I ring for them?" She looked towards her bell pull.

I knew perfectly well that were she to ring it, somebody would be here in an instant. But by some unknown instinct, I suggested something else. "Miss Darcy, should you like to come downstairs with me and find some help?"

"Me? Now?"

I nodded. "I would be grateful to you. No doubt, having grown up in the house, you know well the nooks and crannies which are ideal for hiding."

Miss Darcy looked around her uncertainly. "I should need to dress."

"Should you like some assistance? I have four sisters and am quite used to such things. And with far less decorous persons than you."

"Four sisters?" At this she laughed. "I wish I had a sister."

She did in fact dress herself in very little time and we then proceeded together out of the beautiful room and towards the main part of the house. As we reached the top of the main staircase, Miss Darcy remarked, "My brother shall be awfully surprised. I had assured him that I would never leave my room again."

"Indeed?" I must have appeared disbelieving or confused, or maybe both, for she continued.

"I had in fact intended so to do. But I like you, Miss Bennet, and I like those little girls. I should not like to think of them lost. They might have run beyond their understanding of the house and become frightened."

Some minutes later, we arrived in the library and there followed a scene of supreme gratification.

Mr Darcy leaped from behind his desk with expressions of astonishment that I could not wholly comprehend. He seemed to be very amazed by the sight of her, which led me to wonder how long she had been closeted up in her bedchamber. I could not wonder for long, however, for there was still the matter of my lost cousins.

A footman rang the bell for further assistance as we related our tale of lost children, and before long a whole army of persons had appeared. Mr Darcy took charge, asking me, "And where did you start this game?"

"In the gallery, sir."

He stared down at me, asking, "The gallery?"

I did not like to say that Annie had suggested it as I did not wish to be responsible for her getting a scolding. "Yes."

"You do not know which door they left by?"

"No, I am afraid not. My eyes were closed, you see, counting."

He appeared to ignore this, neither upbraiding me for my lack of attention, nor laughing at it. Instead, he indicated that we, and the servants, should all begin in the gallery then fan out from there, calling the children's names as we went. "Do not fear, Miss Bennet, we shall find them soon enough."

As it was, he was perfectly right.

Rebecca and Veronica were discovered, within ten minutes of the search being commenced, two rooms away from the gallery, shivering and—in Veronica's case—sobbing wildly. I believe that they had been there above half an hour, and my heart beat with warmth and love when they each threw themselves into my person for an embrace. The search party rapidly dispersed, the servants to their various duties. By the time we returned to the library, it was just the children, Miss Darcy, Mr Darcy, and me.

Veronica, as it transpired, was fascinated by Miss Darcy, and beset her with questions about whether she was a princess and how long her hair was and what was her favourite pudding. It was so amusing to see the easiness with which they conversed on these subjects.

"Miss Bennet?" Mr Darcy's voice was a low rumbling counterpoint to Veronica's prattling.

"Sir?"

"I was surprised, to say the least, to see my sister appear this afternoon, almost upon your arm."

"I had gathered as much. I do not mean to pry into your family affairs, sir, but I must say that I have been pleased to meet her."

"The feeling must have been mutual, more so on her part even. Georgiana has been refusing to leave her chamber these four months. For reasons that I would wish to confide in you, if you are willing to hear them."

"Of course," I said, surprised. He wished to confide in me? "You honour me."

"It is not a tale for tonight, however. I am more than conscious that it is Christmas Eve."

"It was that observation, sir, that forwent the ill-fated hide and seek game," I admitted. "I should be quite happy to ignore the season entirely. With my aunt's state of health, I had already concluded that there would be no real festivities for us in any event."

"I should be very sorry if that were the case."

'There is no need to exert yourself on our account, for there is always next year. And I should far rather have my loved ones safe and well."

For some reason, he smiled at this. "My wider family consider me a miser and a recluse for not using Pemberley to greater advantage. There are no balls here, no great gatherings, or the like. I do not favour those sorts of things, generally. Or rather, the circumstances which might enable me to favour them have never transpired."

He looked towards me and I felt some rising heat under his stare, although I could not say why. "Maybe you should consider their views, sir. You have a fine ballroom in want of dancers."

"Yes. I am sorry about that. I believe that Georgiana had wandered down and opened the shutter during the night. I should not have suggested that you had. I had seen enough of you at that time to realise that you are not the sort of young lady to go about disarranging other people's homes at will."

At this I laughed outright. "You are right. I have many faults, but I am not given to that, I hope."

He laughed, and I believe it was the first time I observed his face in a relaxed, contented state. A certain twinkling light gave out from his eyes and the skin at his cheeks creased charmingly. How very different this was to how he had first appeared to me. I was forced to own that he was rather a handsome man.

He looked at me thoughtfully. "Your advice is well taken, though. I should like to make a small beginning."

"And what beginning is that?" I asked.

"Well, first of all, I intend, unless you suggest otherwise, that I should like to dine with you and your uncle this evening."

"It would be our honour."

"And, in the morning, I should be honoured if you and your uncle and the children would attend church with me?"

"Both of those sound very agreeable," I said. "I should very much enjoy your sister's company, if she can be prevailed upon to go with us as well."

Uncertainty crossed his face, but before he could demur, Miss Darcy turned and said, "Thank you Miss Bennet, I should like that very well indeed."

Thus, it was decided.

That evening, Annie suggested that she put the children to bed a little later than normal. While they sat up playing again with their toys, I dressed for dinner for the first time since our abrupt arrival. I had brought with me—and it was undamaged in the accident—a gown of Jane's, a blue superfine muslin, piped with white, which suited me well after my sister had altered its length. Annie dressed my hair and promised to sit with my aunt Gardiner, who by this time was much recovered in any event.

The experience was quite different to all of the previous evenings. Instead of silence, the room was filled with gentle laughter and chatter. The huge polished table, which had once seemed so deserted, came alive with a party of just four people agreeably engaged. On a couple of occasions, I caught Mr Darcy looking at me in a searching manner. I did not know quite what to make of this, but was determined to enjoy this little slice of conviviality. But for the most part, I was conversing with his sister or my uncle, or all of the company. I began to feel a sense of heady joy, of new things and old worries cast off.

I was most astonished when, after dinner, Annie arrived in the dining room with the children in tow. I had believed they were in bed, but they appeared to be excited and giggling. I hoped they had not created more mischief. "What is the meaning of this?" I asked.

"Lizzy, we have a surprise!" Veronica said. "Come, Papa, for you too!"

Rebecca was nearly dancing, she was so happy, and both of them reached for my hands, tugging at me as they pulled me towards the drawing room. I glanced over my shoulder to see Mr Darcy suppressing a grin as he helped his sister rise and follow after us all.

"Oh!" I cried out, unable to help myself when I arrived in the drawing room. The children and Annie had evidently been hard at work, tying up greenery and setting about little scenes of pinecones and berries in honour of the season. "How lovely!"

But that was not the end of it. Rebecca was bending backwards with excitement as she pointed towards the hearth. "A Yule Log! Mr Darcy got a Yule Log!"

"Indeed?" I turned towards him and found his eyes upon me. It was a peculiar moment, full of sensations I could hardly describe. Christmas spirit perhaps? "Sir, you are too good."

"Indeed you are," said my uncle warmly; and I saw then that he had some moisture in his eyes. He clapped Mr Darcy on the back and thanked him on behalf of the children.

"It was the least I could do," he demurred.

One of the footman came in then, bearing the charred remains of a Yule Log long past. Mr Darcy cast a look towards his sister and said, "These must be from the days when our mother was mistress of the house."

How good he is to her. I watched as the two Darcys knelt by the hearth. The log was prepared in accordance with tradition, being anointed in wine and wrapped in hazel twigs, and Mr Darcy called Rebecca to him, allowing her the honour of igniting it. Veronica had insisted that my uncle hold her, so that she might see over their heads and not miss any of the proceedings. It was altogether as festive as one could imagine us being.

When, later on, I ascended the stairs, first to check upon my aunt and thereupon to my own bed, I felt as though I were a caged bird, freed.

chapter six

December 25, 1810

"You look very fine, Lizzy. As well you know, I believe."

It was our Christmas miracle that Aunt Gardiner should be free of fever and able to speak with some clarity. She was sitting up in bed, and Annie fluffed a pillow behind her. My uncle and the children were already downstairs and I stood at the end of the bed in my cloak and bonnet, dressed for church.

"Thank you, Aunt. I believe we shall be back in an hour or two, and I shall come up directly. But it will be lovely to attend church in the village."

"Of course, dear. I assume you have not left the estate since the accident?"

I shook my head. "No. None of us have. There has been no opportunity. And when you were so unwell, no inducement, either."

I glanced out of the tall window to the winter sunshine striking upon the sodden fields and icy hedgerows. "I feel so happy this morning, Aunt. It is as though we have woken up under a different sky."

She laughed that knowing laugh habitual to her. "Well, I am pleased that you are happy. But I suggest that it is not the sky that is different. Maybe the way that you see it has changed?"

I gave her a sideways glance and did not answer that particular proposition. Suddenly recalling that the rest of the party was already assembled, and I did not wish to make us late, I kissed her head and sped down to the hallway. There I found my remaining family, along with Mr Darcy and Miss Darcy.

There were two carriages ordered to take us to church and my uncle travelled with Mr Darcy in one while Miss Darcy came in with me and the children in the other. When the coach boy shut the door on me, he said 'Merry Christmas, Miss' and I was overcome with festive joy and warm feelings.

At the church, which was in the next village of Kympton, we sat as guests in the Darcy family pews and afterwards were introduced to a number of local persons known to the Darcys. I found it interesting to see ladies and gentlemen, tenants and shopkeepers and clergymen alike, all queuing up to speak with us. I do not believe that I had ever met more new acquaintances in one place before, but it did not fatigue me. At last it was done, and we bundled back into the carriages and set a course for Pemberley.

There we found a marvellous table for our Christmas Day feast. I could hardly credit it, and indeed it was far more than the six of us could do service to. A great glazed boar's head sat upon a platter and there was goose and golden topped pies and many other wonderful things.

After eating all we could, Rebecca poked me on the arm. "Thank you for the pies, Lizzy."

"I did not procure the pies. I think you should thank Mrs Reynolds when you see her."

"I will," she announced, gladly consuming another one.

Later on, when all were sated from this great feast, we played a game of blind man's bluff in the drawing room. I suggested it, fearing that the children were becoming bored, but everybody appeared to enjoy themselves, even Mr Darcy, who consented to be blindfolded with alacrity. He made no complaint when each of the girls crashed into his fine hessians or snorted with laughter. I observed his face beneath the blindfold to have relaxed its composure, and although he appeared different than before, he was certainly no less handsome.

The festivities of the day also enabled me to spend time with Miss Darcy, which continued to be a happy but slightly odd experience. She and I walked arm in arm on the Chestnut Lawn with both children running around us. I was intrigued to learn of her upbringing at Pemberley, the deaths, in rapid succession, of her parents, only a few years previously, and her love of music and nature. Though I had known her only a short time, I felt a true affinity with her, and already felt the pang of separation though we were nowise ready to leave.

"I am so pleased that you came here. Before you came, I did not really have a friend," she confided.

"Oh, surely not, my dear. You have your brother and you have a wonderful household here."

"I know, but it is not the same as having a friend with whom to confide. Somebody who is alike in age to me—at least I have supposed you are. How old are you?"

"I am nineteen," Elizabeth replied. "My mother was married at my age and had a child, so sometimes I feel that it is not so young."

Miss Darcy nodded in understanding.

"My two youngest sisters are likely nearest to you in age. Lydia is fourteen and Kitty is almost sixteen."

"How nice to have so many sisters," she said, wistfully. "Do you think someday I could become acquainted with them too? How I should love that!"

I was about to tell Miss Darcy that if she had met my sisters, particularly my younger sisters, she may not be so ready to spend further time with them. However, that seemed churlish; in any event, Mr Darcy appeared and called out to us, forestalling further discussion on the matter.

"Miss Bennet, Georgiana!"

He had developed a sort of sauntering gait in the last day or so, and appeared so at ease compared to when we first met.

"I did not wish to break your company, but may I suggest some music?"

The sky, which had been darkening with clouds, was beginning to threaten rain in any case, so we all agreed it was time to go in. "Certainly, Brother. I shall be happy to play. And you, Miss Bennet? Will you favour us with some music?"

I hesitated, but said with a smile, "Yes, provided that my audience is not too exacting."

Georgiana laughed at this and then proceeded to initiate a game of chasing back to the house with Rebecca and Veronica. That left Mr Darcy and me slightly behind, and we walked in step languidly back to the door.

"You are your own, most exacting judge, Miss Bennet. I have heard you play, and there was nothing whatsoever wanting in it. You should not fear comparison with others or anything of that sort."

I glanced to him tentatively, trying to judge from his face what he meant to say. "Thank you, sir. Although you do surprise me."

"How so?"

"On the evening you found me playing, you did not appear best pleased. In fact, I took it into my head that you wished to admonish me."

He paused and I almost gave up hope of a reply when he spoke, softly. "I am sorry that you thought that. I took it that you had come to that sort of conclusion. But it was not intended. You see...It is a complicated tale, Miss Bennet. I hope that you will allow me—I hope that our acquaintance will allow me to tell you that story. However, suffice to say that I believed you to be my sister at the time. She and I had—we had a disagreement and I was angry in that moment. But it was not at you. As soon as I observed that the player was you, I—well, my displeasure changed. In fact, it evaporated."

I was silent, picking over that comment in my mind. We reached the door and the company of Miss Darcy and the little Gardiners, and therefore our discussion came to an end.

There were a couple of occasions during the rest of the day when I caught Mr Darcy looking in my direction. He seemed to be particularly aware of me, which stirred a strange feeling in my belly. When we took drinks in the drawing room, he was careful to ensure that I was comfortable. He opened doors for me with a sort of reverence that was also new. But when he and my uncle Gardiner sat down to discuss Napoleon and the war, I was quite astonished that he asked for my opinions. My own father, who has always encouraged me in reading and thinking, had never treated me thus in adult company outside of our family circle.

As had become customary, I sat with my aunt while she ate a small amount and drifted back to sleep. Thereafter, I put the girls into their bed and saw them safely to slumber. Rebecca spoke dreamily as she settled into her blankets, "Merry Christmas, Lizzy. Thank you, again for the pies."

Veronica was already asleep and having kissed each of their noses, I slipped out of the room.

The evening consisted of more music and quiet chatter over glasses of punch in the music room. At a point, my uncle announced that he should check upon his wife, and therefore he disappeared from the party. I played a duet with Miss Darcy and turned the pages for her when she played an awfully difficult piece by a French composer. She had, I observed, an excellent touch on the instrument and a real instinct for it. She drew to the conclusion beautifully.

"That was exquisite, Miss Darcy."

Mr Darcy, from his chair nearby, nodded his agreement.

"I do love it. I have another piece by the same composer, if I can only put my hands upon it," she said. She began rifling through a pile of sheet music casually left on a side table, but could not find it. "I think it must be in my chamber. I did take some music up there to consider. Oh bother."

"Perhaps you might play it for me tomorrow?" I suggested, not wishing her to put herself out.

"I should like very much to play it now! It is unusual, and I need the music. I believe I know just where to locate it. Excuse me just a moment." She moved to leave the room, which both alarmed and excited me.

"Shall I ring for somebody to fetch it?" asked Mr Darcy, apprehending my anxiety at being left alone in a room with him.

"There is no need. I shall be back directly." And with that, she nearly ran out of the room, leaving me alone with her brother.

There was a moment of shocked silence, and the air between us seemed to groan with the impropriety, the lack of ordinariness. I was still standing by the pianoforte and so moved slowly to take the chair near his.

Mr Darcy spoke, asking, "May I enquire after Mrs Gardiner?"

"My aunt is making an excellent recovery," I said. "Mr Fitch shall attend her tomorrow. He has given me to think that if she continues as she is, then maybe she could be fit for travel by Twelfth Night."

"That is excellent news. You must have missed your family, being kept here for the whole of the Christmas season."

"I do miss them, of course. However, it is more important that my aunt is well and the generosity that you have shown to us is so great—I hope you do not think that I overlook it."

"No, not at all," he said very seriously, "I doubt you overlook anything. However, I do not consider allowing a seriously injured lady and her family into my home when there is nowhere else they can go to be extremely generous. I am bound to say that I have done nothing that an ordinary Christian would not do, and I have, aside from your aunt's strife, of course, been very happy to have you here."

He emphasised these last words, as though they had added meaning. I did not know what to reply and so uttered only a soft 'thank you'.

Several minutes more elapsed with no sign nor sound of Georgiana's return. Mr Darcy mentioned it and again asked, "Should you like me to leave? I would not like you to be uncomfortable."

"No, sir, I assure you I am well." As I spoke, I suddenly realised that I had no wish for him to leave at all. The notion discomposed me and I began to rattle away to cover it. "That is not at all necessary. I am sure that Miss Darcy shall return very promptly. And in any case, a servant may walk in at any moment, and the door is wide open as well."

He smiled. "Yes. It is. If I were not so anxious to speak with you in private, I would certainly not put you in this position." He leaned forwards in his seat and his eyes fixed mine most unambiguously. They were a deep dark sort of hazelnut. "You see, my sister, who has always been of a flighty disposition, has had a deeply unfortunate and upsetting year."

"I am sad to hear it."

"Yes, well so was I. It is a long story and not improved in the retelling. But I feel that you need to know what has occurred. Because only then can you understand what has been happening around you since you have been here."

"I do not want you to feel that you must tell me private matters."

"I do not feel that I must, but rather, I wish to." Slowly and noisily, he exhaled and crossed his legs, as if considering where to begin. "You will realise that there are many hands on an estate such as this one. Hundreds of people whom one grows up with. Generations and generations can expect their lives to be entwined with an estate, and I strive to look after all of them. But one, particularly, has been a problem. A young man, whom both my sister and I grew up with and who was the son of our late father's steward. He has been entwined in our lives for many years. He was a friend to me once, and he knows us, as only people who know one another as children can. He deteriorated as he grew from boy to man, but I continued to protect him. I paid off debts and the like. I assisted in the avoidance of scandal. I would, of course, never have confided any of this to my sister."

I nodded. I could not imagine that my father or either of my uncles would, were they faced with such things, publish them to the female members of the family, either.

"So when, in the summer of this year, my sister was away at Ramsgate with her companion, this acquaintance contrived to be in her company, and she did not know to avoid it. It would seem that a premeditated plan of seduction was conducted with, unfortunately, the connivance of my sister's companion. In the course of the summer, my sister found herself in this man's company on any number of occasions. And in brief, because I cannot doubt that you understand the general direction of this narrative, she was persuaded to believe herself in love."

He paused, his expression grave as he looked at me searchingly. "You have met my sister, Miss Bennet. She has a certain innocence, and of course, she was just turned fifteen years of age at the time. In any case, she consented as a consequence of all this to an elopement. I do not believe that there was any real object other than her fortune, although even if he did love her, I would still regret the connexion most bitterly. As it was, I do not for a moment believe that he repaid my sister's infatuation or willingness to sacrifice her reputation with any sort of love."

I could see how painful Mr Darcy's recitation was for him, and I was shocked and repulsed by what had been done to his young sister. I wished him to know of my sympathies. "That is dreadful. How did Miss Darcy escape this unhappiness?"

He sighed heavily. "I am not sure that she has. She escaped the potential for forced marriage by latterly informing me of what was occurring. I went to Ramsgate with all speed and dissolved matters. I dismissed the companion, ended our association with the man, and brought my sister home to Pemberley, where she has remained ever since. Yet she has become melancholy in the extreme and has, for the most part, refused to leave her chambers."

"I see."

"Until recently, of course." His expression lightened a little when I gave him a small smile. "She has felt a sense of shame, fearing that the story will get out and she shall be tarnished by scandal forever more."

"But there is no reason that it shall, is there?"

"None at all. I paid off the man and it is not in his interests to speak of it. The companion will never be able to get another position if she takes to gossiping about her previous charges. So—in my mind at least—it is not a concern. I would like Georgiana to go about society in a normal manner. However she is, or rather was, unwilling, even despite being aware that other members of her family wished to have her committed to Bedlam."

Shocked, I gasped and raised a hand to my chest. "But surely it cannot be as bad as that."

He smiled gently. "No, it is not as bad as that. Those suggestions were only from the more excitable of her relations. And I would never have consented."

He tilted his head and raked his hand through his hair as he was inclined to do. "Miss Bennet. I very much credit you with the great change that has taken place in my sister."

"Me? Surely not."

"Yes. As I believe you know, Georgiana saw you from her window and was most interested in your comings and goings. I did not realise how lonely she had become, although I suppose that ought to have been obvious to me." He shook his head as if to clear some memory. "In any case, she had become interested in you from afar. And when she heard you, flesh and blood, right outside her chamber door, she leapt upon the opportunity to make your acquaintance. In doing so, she has somehow, returned to her old self."

"I do not know whether that is true. But it is very gratifying that Miss Darcy is feeling more in spirits," I said with all earnestness.

His eyes darted about, as if watching for something, fearing that this time would end soon. "I, too, have been most agreeably touched by your presence here. I hope that I do not say too much. If you are embarrassed or—you can stop me."

I said nothing but felt a powerful blush come to my face.

"I was impressed by you from your first moments here—"

"Surely not!" I laughed to think of my frightened, worried, unkempt appearance. "My distress, my wild appearance—these could not have been to my advantage!"

"But they were. You showed some presence of mind and grit and fortitude and clarity of thought that would evade most people. And warmth as well," he said quietly. "You are very warm and kind. I have been quite astonished by you at different times."

"That is astonishing to hear."

"It should not be. I—forgive me, but we have just a little time alone now and I…I cannot see the purpose in saying anything less than what I wish. I would very much like to call on you, at your home in Hertfordshire. I will assure you, and your father, that my intentions towards you are strictly honourable. Is that a sentiment which you can look kindly upon?"

I raised my eyes to him and leaned in slightly. "Yes, I believe I can."

A great smile suffused his face and reached his eyes with ease. "Excellent. I have matters to attend to in town at the end of January. If, as you expect, Mrs Gardiner shall be fit for travel within the next week or so, I could…"

"Yes." Suddenly I felt shy and lowered my eyes. "Yes, I see exactly what you mean. And I believe that will work perfectly."

"What will work perfectly?" came the sing-song voice of Miss Darcy as she re-entered the room clutching a sheaf of papers.

Mr Darcy looked as if he knew not what to say so I leapt in with, "Oh good! You have had success in finding your music. How wonderful. Shall I turn the pages for you?"

epilogue

MR DARCY WAS AS GOOD AS HIS WORD.

Our party departed from Pemberley on the eighth of January and took nearly a full week to reach Longbourn. My uncle was anxious that my aunt's health should not be taxed any further than was necessary, and so we had made more, and longer, stops than would usually be the case. When we reached Hertfordshire, the paroxysm of joy and relief and love that greeted us were quite overwhelming. All of my sisters sobbed along with little John and Robert, both so happy to see their mama and papa and sisters. Mama had, I learnt, herself become unwell with worry for us all—so much so that she had missed the Lucas's Twelfth Night ball in favour of being laid up in bed. Even Papa refrained from making poor jokes and greeted his sister Gardiner with true warmth and affection.

It was close to a full month before Mr and Mrs Gardiner and the children left for Town, by which time my aunt was quite restored to her usual spirits and good health.

Before their departure, on a sun-filled afternoon in the early part of February, Mr Darcy appeared to call. After taking Miss Darcy to visit her relations, he was travelling—so he said—to London, where he had business that would likely keep him engaged for some weeks. With the stated purpose of wishing to enquire after Mrs Gardiner and her party, he stopped at Longbourn. There he was introduced for the first time to my parents and each of my sisters as a new acquaintance who had come to be known in such strange and unpromising circumstances, but who was now firmly fixed as a kind and respectable gentleman of all our acquaintance. Matters could not have been organised in a more agreeable fashion by design.

Happily, my aunt Philips was having a card party that evening and Mr Darcy, who was staying at the inn in Meryton, was invited. He bore the interest of my family with great magnanimity and humour, more than an indifferent acquaintance may have thought he possessed, in fact.

On his journey back from town some weeks later, he called again, this time bringing along a friend. Mr Bingley was a jolly sort of gentleman and made it be known that he was interested in taking a local estate. Trips were made to observe Netherfield Park, which bordered Longbourn on one side, and appointments were placed with the landlords' agents. The gentleman declared that his sister, who was unmarried and kept house for him would 'utterly adore' the country. Therefore, he was subjected to a great deal of attention from local ladies young and old, for the duration of his stay. The visit of Mr Darcy and Mr Bingley coincided with the spring dance at the Meryton Assembly and so, of course, our family friends came with us.

Mr Darcy and I danced twice, to the great satisfaction of us and keen interest of nearly all my friends and neighbours. Thereafter there were other parties and dances and the like at which we contrived to meet.

On the occasion of a dinner at Longbourn, before Mr Darcy returned to Pemberley and when the flowers in the meadow were beginning their bloom, he disappeared into my father's study to put a proposition that had already been well received by me. We were married in June and returned to Pemberley in circumstances of great love and happiness.

My first Christmas as the mistress of the house was entirely different from the previous one. Nearly every room in the house was decorated and the Yule Log, dragged in on Christmas Eve, was alit with great ceremony and stayed alight as it should. The ballroom was opened up for a Twelfth Night ball, there were decorations brought into the house and arranged with great effort and industry.

The gentleman of Pemberley though, remained much as he had always been and a better, finer or more loving husband, I could never have hoped to find.

The End

About the Author

Jenetta James lives in London where she enjoys reading, writing and playing with her three children. She is also a practicing barrister.

Also by Jenetta James

Lover's Knot
The Elizabeth Papers
The Memory House: A Love Story in Two Acts
Suddenly Mrs Darcy

CHRISTMAS AT BLACKTHORN MANOR

LUCY MARIN

Chapter One

Mr Darcy! Elizabeth could not believe what her eyes were showing her. Never would she have imagined seeing him, of all men, walk through the door. Her eyes were fixed on his tall, handsome form. Her heart raced and her legs felt so weak that she did not know how she would be able to perform the customary curtsey. He regarded her, unmoving, his lips parted.

It had been above sixteen months since their last meeting that awful morning in Lambton when she had told him about Lydia's elopement.

The sound of a voice crying, "Miss Bennet! How wonderful to see you again," caused Elizabeth to swing her eyes to the left.

Oh my goodness, she thought. *Mr Bingley.* Looking back at Mr Darcy, she noticed the lady standing by his side. Elizabeth had no right to the relief she felt when she realised it was Miss Georgiana Darcy. Mr Darcy had turned to watch his friend and did not seem pleased. *He looks almost as he did when we first met.*

There was a laugh followed by her brother-in-law, Thomas, saying, "Mrs Ridley now. Jane, my dear, you know Mr Bingley?"

Elizabeth let her eyes drop to the carpet and held her breath for a moment to calm herself before having to participate in what would be unnecessary introductions but necessary explanations. *How can I bear to talk to him, let alone spend two weeks in his company?* Remembering Mr Bingley, she felt an added measure of dread.

"Mrs Ridley? I-I did not know…" Mr Bingley's brow furrowed almost as if it was inconceivable that Jane would be married.

What did he think would happen? Did he truly believe she would remain single for the rest of her life? They have not seen each other in above two years.

Their host, Mr Edward Ledbury, said, "They were married a few months ago. I was very glad when they agreed to spend the Festive Season at Blackthorn. It has given us a chance to know our new cousin and her sister, Miss Elizabeth Bennet. You have met?"

It was two days before Christmas. Elizabeth had been at Blackthorn Manor for a fortnight and had known from the outset that their party would grow larger. *Why did I not ask the names of their guests?* A shiver coursed through her. *At least then I would have been prepared—or I might have found an excuse to leave.*

Her thoughts slipped to the last time she had seen Mr Darcy. He had entered the parlour at the inn just as she finished reading Jane's letters which had carried the shocking news about Lydia. Distressed, Elizabeth had told him everything. He had left before the Gardiners returned, and she and her aunt and uncle had departed Lambton within two hours.

On their arrival at Longbourn, they had discovered that Mr Bennet was still in London, seeking Lydia and Mr Wickham. Mr Gardiner had promised to send him home, and he was as good as his word. Just as Elizabeth was abandoning the last shred of hope that the couple—and a way to save at least part of the family's reputation—would be found, an express had arrived for her father. When he showed it to her, she had been stunned into silence for a full five minutes. It was from Mr Wickham, asking for Mr Bennet's permission to marry Lydia.

> *Our original intention was to go to Scotland. However, I was obliged to remain in town longer than anticipated, and your daughter now professes a desire to do the deed here. With your written consent, I shall obtain a licence, and we shall be wed as soon as it can be arranged. Miss Lydia stays with an older lady of my acquaintance, Mrs Younge, who keeps a respectable establishment.*

Elizabeth had recognised the name from Mr Darcy's letter explaining his connexion to Mr Wickham. She very much doubted the situation was 'respectable' but would not burden her father with that news.

> *I suspect you have heard a great deal about debts &c., but I assure you it is all exaggerated. What little money I owed here and there, I have paid off, and I have purchased a commission in the regulars, in Colonel Clarke's regiment, which is quartered in Newcastle.*

Mr Wickham had asked for nothing from her father other than Lydia's share of Mrs Bennet's five thousand pounds, which her daughters stood to inherit on her death. Elizabeth could not believe he would take Lydia for so little and was convinced there was more to the story than he had disclosed.

As for his apparently-full purse, she assumed he had obtained the money through nefarious means, perhaps a stroke of good luck at the gaming tables.

Elizabeth forced her attention to the present when Mr Bingley greeted her.

"How do you do, Mr Bingley?"

"Excellent!" Looking over his shoulder, he continued, "Darcy, can you believe it? Here we find Miss Ben—er, Mrs Ridley and Miss Elizabeth."

James Ledbury, their host's younger brother, said, "It is a happy coincidence. We shall be a merry party without any of that awkwardness that comes from some of us not knowing the others."

Elizabeth almost laughed.

Mr and Miss Darcy stepped forward. After saying the proper words to the Ledburys and Ridleys, they faced Elizabeth.

Mr Darcy caught her eyes and bowed while murmuring, "Miss Bennet."

Elizabeth curtseyed. "Mr Darcy. Miss Darcy, how lovely to see you again."

Everything suggested the girl, who must be seventeen or eighteen by now, remained as painfully shy as she had been when they first met. She looked at her brother, blushed, and kept her gaze averted as she curtseyed.

Miss Harriet Ledbury encouraged everyone to sit, and they did. "Would you care for tea?" She looked first at Mr Darcy, then Mr Bingley, before returning her gaze to Mr Darcy. "Please, tell me what I can do for your comfort and that of your sister. Refreshments, or would you prefer to go to your rooms?"

Mr Darcy glanced at Georgiana. Addressing their hostess, he said, "I am afraid the journey has fatigued my sister. Perhaps it would be best if we rested for a while."

"Of course." Mr Ledbury jumped to his feet to ring for a servant. "Bingley, what is your preference?"

"Oh, uh," Mr Bingley looked between Miss Ledbury, Mr Darcy, and if Elizabeth was correct, Jane. "I suppose I should change."

James Ledbury said, "We would all need to retire to prepare for dinner soon in any case. We eat at half seven."

The butler entered the room, and Mr Ledbury issued his instructions. Elizabeth watched Mr Darcy's progress to the door and, a few minutes later, went with Jane and Thomas upstairs.

Thomas led them into the small, cosy sitting room the Ledburys had set aside for their use. Elizabeth much preferred it to the dark, formal withdrawing room they had just left. Jane and Thomas sat on the sofa, while Elizabeth went to the window that overlooked the courtyard. Half turned away from her companions, she asked if they had known who was to join them that day. All Elizabeth remembered being told was that a few of Mr Ledbury's friends would arrive closer to Christmas. She searched her memory for any clue she could have missed that it would be Mr Darcy, who, even after their long separation, still occupied her thoughts and heart.

Jane said, "Of course not. I would have told you."

"I knew," Thomas said. "Did I never mention their names? Of course, I did not know the two of you were acquainted with the Darcys and Mr Bingley, so I suppose I thought they would mean nothing to you. How do you know them?"

"Oh, it was a trifling thing," Jane said, shooting a glance at Elizabeth. "Mr Bingley leased Netherfield, the estate neighbouring Longbourn, two years ago. He was there perhaps two months, and naturally we saw him now and then. Mr Darcy stayed with him. I have never met Miss Darcy before."

Elizabeth sat in the soft armchair across from them. Jane's explanation concealed the depths of her friendship with Mr Bingley, but she understood. What husband wants to hear about his wife's former attachments? A prickle of unease nipped at her when Jane, with an expression that seemed almost wistful, looked away from Thomas.

"I understand Ledbury was at school with Darcy, and I later met Bingley through him. I have met Darcy a number of times over the years, though we are no more than acquaintances. Bingley, I have seen only occasionally." He scratched his jaw. "But now that I think about it, I seem to recall him saying something about an estate he had let and a lady he admired. Do you know who it was?"

Suspicion is not in his nature, Elizabeth thought. *If it was while he was at Netherfield, who else would it be other than Jane? He knows she is by far the most beautiful lady in the neighbourhood.*

Jane said, her voice a little sharp to Elizabeth's ear, "He may have lived at any number of estates since we knew him." She stood and strolled around the room, touching the paisley print on the walls and the decorations that adorned the mantel and tables.

When Thomas looked at Elizabeth, she offered him a quick smile. She liked him, as she had since the first time they had met. He was not as handsome or lively as Mr Bingley, but he was steadier, and she had no doubt that he loved Jane. Thomas was the heir to an estate in Northamptonshire. It was about the size of Longbourn, and, from what Elizabeth had seen, more competently managed. The couple had met through Mr Gardiner about eight months after Lydia's elopement. At the time, Jane said that she liked him, but that she would not allow her feelings to fully blossom until she was certain of his intentions. Left unsaid was that she had not been so cautious with Mr Bingley, and it had left her heartbroken.

Elizabeth had promised to go to Jane and Thomas for the Festive Season. When the invitation from Thomas's cousins had arrived, and, after being assured that she was welcomed, she had agreed to join them at Blackthorn Manor. Being at Longbourn held no appeal to Elizabeth. She had tasted the possibility of a different life when she was in Derbyshire, but had lost it, leaving her restless. It was difficult to be at home and see how little had changed despite their near ruination. Her father appeared relieved that the whole thing had ended well; any lesson he might have learnt from it was lost, except that he would not permit Kitty to go stay with the Wickhams, for which Elizabeth was thankful. Her mother liked to talk about her married daughters and scowled at Elizabeth as she lamented her lack of marital prospects. *If she only knew…*

Feeling a sudden need for solitude, Elizabeth leapt to her feet. "I believe I shall go to my room and read a little before dressing for dinner."

Darcy moved from the window in his bedchamber to one of the wing chairs near the fireplace. He dropped into it, its firmness feeling like a slap against his body, and ran his hands through his hair.

Elizabeth Bennet, here of all places.

A faint groan escaped his lips, and he slid down in the chair, extending his long legs in front of him and resting his chin on his chest. So much of the last two years had been spent battling his love for her. After his failed proposal in Kent, he had tried to forget her and had been foolish enough to believe he was succeeding—until the beautiful July afternoon he arrived at Pemberley to find her touring the grounds with her aunt and uncle. In an instant, he knew that he loved her as much as he ever had. Four wonderful days followed, and he had been growing more confident by the minute that she not only forgave him for the past, but also that she cared about him.

Then came the devastating news that Wickham, his old foe, had found a victim in her youngest sister. He cursed himself for not doing something, *anything*, to rob Wickham of the ability to injure people in the way that he had almost destroyed Darcy and Georgiana. His pride, his selfishness had led him to make so many mistakes, ones that had injured Elizabeth; losing her was the price he had paid for it.

Over the following weeks, he had come to accept that Elizabeth Bennet was lost to him forever.

Sixteen months. I must be the last person she wishes to see, yet now she must bear my company for the next two weeks, unless she and the Ridleys depart before Twelfth Night. Jane Bennet married, and to Ledbury's cousin. That is a piece of good news. Thank God it is not Elizabeth.

He sighed, sat up, and poured himself a glass of wine from the decanter on the walnut table beside his chair.

I shall have to find a way to tolerate the intolerable and make this as easy for her as it can be. If only I am strong enough not to seek her attention; I know she does not wish for mine.

Elizabeth was curled up under a rug on the settee in her bedchamber. She had tried to distract herself with reading, but it had not worked. How could she attend to anything when Mr Darcy was in the house, likely behind one of the doors that lined the corridor outside of her room? Did he ever think about her? Did he regret what they had lost? Feel relief that both he and Mr Bingley were spared the humiliation of being brothers to a man like Wickham?

The few days she had spent in Derbyshire were amongst the happiest of her life. How nervous she had been about visiting Pemberley! But since they had been assured that the Darcys were not in residence, she had agreed to accompany the Gardiners on a tour.

At the time, it seemed like the best decision I ever made. Seeing him, having the opportunity to know the man he truly is, meeting Miss Darcy— Oh, I cannot imagine a more pleasant interlude!

Mr Darcy had brought his sister to meet Elizabeth and the Gardiners the day after their unexpected encounter. The following day, she and Aunt Gardiner had called on Miss Darcy, while Uncle Gardiner went fishing with the gentlemen. They had remained with Miss Darcy for several hours, during half of which Elizabeth was also able to enjoy Mr Darcy's company. The next days had brought more time together, including a drive in the neighbourhood with both Darcys, a picnic at Pemberley, and dining together. Everything she had seen in him during those precious days had taught her to admire him and acknowledge that he suited her perfectly.

In the time it took to read two short letters from Jane, she had lost the promise of their future. It was the great regret of her life that she had been too proud to recognise his true character—and to see Wickham for the villain he was—before it was too late. If she had, Lydia would not now be married to a scoundrel, and Elizabeth would be wife to the best of men.

I do not know how I will bear having to see him, knowing how much he must hate finding me here and that he cannot want Miss Darcy to be in company with Wickham's sisters-in-law. I shall have to avoid them when I can, without being rude or obvious; the last thing any of us needs is for the Ledburys or Thomas to notice awkwardness between us. In two weeks, Jane, Thomas, and I will be gone. Surely, I can be strong enough for that long.

Chapter Two

THROUGHOUT DINNER, ELIZABETH FELT CONSTRAINED. SHE sat between James Ledbury and Jane, but Mr Darcy might as well have been on either side and across from her. His presence felt heavy. James Ledbury was his usual jovial self; he joked, encouraged her to eat more, asked if she was well when she said she was not hungry, told her tales of Christmases when he and his siblings were children, and made all manner of amusing comments. She could not deny that he was good company. Nevertheless, she was relieved when Miss Ledbury rose to lead the ladies out of the dining parlour.

In the withdrawing room, she joined Miss Darcy on a sofa. To Elizabeth, she looked apprehensive yet determined. She glanced at Elizabeth before lowering her eyes to her hands, which were clasped in her lap.

"I am happy to see you again, Miss Darcy," Elizabeth said.

Again, the girl peeked up, her blue eyes meeting Elizabeth's for just a second. Her voice was little more than a whisper when she said, "And I you."

Elizabeth smiled, hoping Miss Darcy would see it. "I understand your brother has known Mr Ledbury for years. Have you met the family before?"

Miss Darcy nodded. "O-only once or twice. They were very kind to include me in their invitation to my brother."

"As they were kind to extend their invitation to me. They wanted Mr Ridley and my sister to spend the Festive Season with them, and, when they were told that I had arranged to be with the Ridleys, insisted I come along. May I enquire after your family? As you may recall, I have met several of them—Lady Catherine, Miss de Bourgh, and Colonel Fitzwilliam. I hope they are all well."

Miss Darcy lifted her chin an inch or two and almost looked at Elizabeth. "They are. I have not seen my aunt or Anne in some time, but the colonel was at Pemberley in the autumn."

"I am glad to hear it. Will you tell me what new music you have learnt of late? I have taken the advice your aunt was so good as to give me when I was in Kent last year and have been practising more." With Jane no longer at Longbourn, playing the pianoforte was a welcome diversion from what she could only call loneliness.

As they spoke over the next ten or so minutes, Elizabeth was pleased to see Miss Darcy relax. When Jane and Miss Ledbury ended their conversation and sat with them, Miss Darcy was able to respond to their remarks with reasonable ease.

After the gentlemen joined them, Elizabeth excused herself when she saw Mr Darcy approaching. Knowing he did not wish for her company, she left brother and sister to talk. James Ridley immediately captured her attention, and she sat with him; Mr Bingley soon joined them.

"It is very good to see you again, Miss Bennet," he said.

He was as amiable as ever, and she responded in kind.

"What a coincidence to discover you all know each other," James Ledbury said. "That is a word I have heard more in the last five hours than in the previous five years, but it does suit the circumstances."

"My sister had not met Miss Darcy before," Elizabeth said, as if that made a material difference. She did not want the Ledburys to assume there was more friendship between them than there was. "It is above a year since I saw the Darcys and Mr Bingley, and even longer since my sister has."

James Ledbury gave her an odd look, eyebrows raised as if both curious and discerning. Elizabeth felt her cheeks begin to heat and turned to Mr Bingley.

"How are your sisters and Mr Hurst?"

"Very well," Mr Bingley said. "They are with Hurst's family for the Festive Season. Shropshire. I did not like to go with them, so here I am. And your, um, sisters and parents? They are well?"

Elizabeth said that they were and shared a little news about people he had met in Hertfordshire. She noticed that he glanced towards Jane more than once. She recalled that he had always admired Jane's beauty —what man did not?—and Jane looked particularly lovely this evening in a deep blue gown.

He said, "I had not heard that your elder sister was married. It was recent?"

"She and my cousin were married three months ago. Since it has been so long since you have seen them, your ignorance of the affair is not such a surprise," James Ledbury replied. "Will you play for us this evening, Miss Bennet, or would you prefer a night off from entertaining us? We could play cards or another game, or if you would like, I shall simply promise to devote myself to amusing you with my conversation."

Elizabeth found his speech verging on rude; it suggested that he wanted Mr Bingley gone. In truth, a part of her did, too, because she did not know what to say to him.

"Amusing conversation tonight, if you please," she said. "But I would not wish you to strain yourself. Feel free to call on reinforcements."

He laughed. "You wound me. I wish for nothing but your company, and you find that insufficient for your pleasure. Young ladies can be very hard, can they not, Mr Bingley?"

Mr Bingley, who had had his head twisted so that he was looking at Jane, Thomas, and Miss Ledbury, startled to hear his name. "Oh, yes, of course. If you will excuse me." He stood and, to no great surprise, joined the very people he had been so interested in.

Elizabeth asked James Ledbury what he knew of his siblings' arrangements for the next fortnight. She had heard it all from Miss Ledbury, but it would occupy him and demand little from her. While he spoke, she reflected on the two weeks she had already spent at Blackthorn Manor. From her earliest days, even hours, in the house, James Ledbury had singled her out. She did not take his flirting seriously; he wanted someone new to talk to. Like her, he was energetic, and they walked together in the house and outside, when the weather permitted. He was handsome in his own way, his golden hair tinged with red, his jaw square and strong, but he was nothing to Mr Darcy, whose dark looks she found more enticing. He lived in Leicester and was a barrister, work he said he enjoyed.

Elizabeth found her eyes drifting towards the Darcys more than they ought. At different times over the next half an hour, she saw them talk to Mr Ledbury and Thomas. After the latter left them, they whispered to each other, rose, and Mr Darcy announced that they were retiring for the night, blaming travel for their fatigue. Elizabeth watched them leave the room, her eyes lingering on the closed door until James Ledbury recalled her to their conversation by asking if she skated.

What was I thinking? Darcy asked himself as he paced in his bedchamber the following morning. The question had been his constant companion since the moment of their arrival. Ledbury's invitation had seemed opportune. He and Georgiana could avoid spending the holiday either alone at Pemberley or with Lady Catherine, and it would provide his sister with the chance to become more comfortable in company.

But I did not know she *would be here. To see James Ledbury with her— It is beyond intolerable!* The man acted as if he had known Elizabeth for months, not the two or three weeks Darcy believed she had been at Blackthorn Manor. Resting his forehead against the cold, damp glass of the window, he closed his eyes. He wished the best for her, yet he could not deny that he was relieved to discover that she had not married. Just the thought of her being another man's wife made him feel as if someone had reached into his chest and ripped out his heart.

Take hold of yourself, man! You are Fitzwilliam Darcy of Pemberley. Act like it, for yourself and for Georgiana. It is past time you go down to breakfast.

Two minutes later, he collected his sister to escort her downstairs, and they joined the others in the breakfast parlour. They were the last to arrive.

"Good morning, Miss Darcy, Darcy," Ledbury called. "I hope you found your rooms comfortable. We have just sat down."

"Mr Darcy, do take this seat," Miss Ledbury said, indicating the empty place to her left.

There was only one other empty place at the table—the one beside Elizabeth. She, the best woman he had ever met, smiled kindly at Georgiana. His sister seemed satisfied with the prospect of sitting beside Elizabeth, so he escorted her to her chair.

"I shall fix you a plate," he said in a low tone.

Georgiana nodded and whispered her thanks.

By the time Darcy had filled a plate with muffins, fruit, and baked eggs and turned away from the sideboard, Georgiana and Elizabeth were chatting. Throughout the meal, he occasionally turned his eyes to the two ladies, while not neglecting the one at his side. Miss Ledbury was pleasant, but he could not say what they talked about. Mr Ridley was at his other side, and he had much rather have talked to him. They had met previously, but Darcy knew little about him and was curious about the sort of man the former Jane Bennet had married. He hoped to discover that he was a good brother to Elizabeth.

When we were together in Derbyshire, everything I longed for was within my grasp; I could almost feel it in my hand. All I wanted was another day or two, which I had every reason to expect I would have. Then *I would have spoken, at least to ask if she would give me a chance to win her regard, even if she was not ready to accept an offer of marriage. Everything in her manner suggested she would say yes. Her ease when she called on Georgiana and when she and the Gardiners came to dinner, her attention to Georgiana, her looks to me. Even now, she is so good to my sister, so patient.*

After breakfast, the party went into the withdrawing room to discuss the day. Darcy sat with Georgiana and Miss Ledbury on a sofa. Across from him were Elizabeth, Mrs Ridley, and James Ledbury. Bingley was in a chair that placed him between Miss Ledbury and Mrs Ridley, and Ledbury and Mr Ridley stood.

Ledbury said, "It is Christmas Eve. What do you all think about going out to gather the greenery to decorate and that sort of thing? It is a fine day—not a cloud in the sky, and the sun makes the cold not feel so severe."

"The servants will collect some of the evergreens, but we can search for interesting bits to add," Miss Ledbury said. "We will need mistletoe for the kissing b—"

"No, we will not, Harriet," Ledbury interjected. "No kissing bough. Our parents disapproved of them, and I do not want any of that sort of temptation in the house, either. You will have other opportunities to flirt."

Miss Ledbury shrugged and twisted one of her curls around her finger.

James Ledbury's voice carried when he said, "Miss Bennet, you must accompany me. I know the best places to search for the sort of thing we need, and I promise you a fine walk in return. You see, I have learnt the way to your heart; I shall show you trees and even try to scare up a bird or small animal for your amusement."

She laughed. Darcy always liked it when she laughed, but that it was directed at another man made his fingers curl into fists.

"Am I so easy to understand, sir?" she asked.

"Oh, that you were!" James Ledbury feigned distress. "If you insist, we can admit a third to our party."

"Very good. James, you escort Miss Bennet and—" Ledbury paused to look around the room. "Miss Darcy, would you like to go with them, or do you prefer to remain with your brother?"

In the end, the party divided themselves into three groups. Bingley went with James Ledbury and Elizabeth, Miss Ledbury insisted Darcy and Georgiana walk with her, leaving Ledbury and the Ridleys.

❄

Elizabeth enjoyed the excursion, although she did not understand all the fuss about deciding who would walk with whom. They were hardly out of sight of the others. James Ledbury and Mr Bingley dove into a lively discussion about sport, and she gave herself over to appreciating the day. The ground was bare and hard; the lack of snow made it easy to walk wherever they liked, and they wandered through a grove at her request. The crispness in the air was as refreshing as a good night's sleep, and she watched the shadows of the bare branches bounce on the ground as a breeze whispered by. They collected little to contribute to the house decorations, but they did find hawthorn and laurel.

Back at the house, Elizabeth joined the other ladies to take tea, while Mr Ledbury led the gentlemen into his study for a different sort of warming beverage.

Miss Ledbury sat beside Elizabeth, leaving Jane and Miss Darcy to their own conversation. Watching them, Elizabeth saw that Miss Darcy seemed comfortable, which was not a surprise given Jane's sweet nature; she would be easy company for the younger lady.

Miss Ledbury and Elizabeth discussed the expedition for a few minutes before Miss Ledbury said, "I have not had a chance to talk to you since the Darcys and Mr Bingley arrived. How surprised we all were to discover that you knew each other! You must tell me all about your past acquaintance with them. I met Mr Darcy and Mr Bingley in town, of course, but only at soirées or balls, where it is impossible to truly get to know someone; I did not previously know Miss Darcy. You can tell me what the gentlemen like or do not like."

"Oh." Elizabeth's eyes darted around the room—to Jane and Miss Darcy, the portrait over the mantel, the remaining milky tea in the cup she held. "I cannot claim any such knowledge of them. Our-our acquaintance was brief and long ago."

Miss Ledbury leant closer. One of her curls—which seemed particularly mousy to Elizabeth at the moment—swung forward. "I do so want them to enjoy themselves, to see that…well, that I am an attentive hostess. Anything you can tell me would be so helpful. Does Mr Darcy have a favourite dish? Would he be offended if we played games in the evening? Mr Bingley seems like such an amiable gentleman that I am not as worried about impressing him."

Elizabeth sat back and licked her lips as she contemplated her response. She had a sudden memory of a conversation with Miss Ledbury the previous week. They had been sitting in this very room, and Miss Ledbury had talked about wanting to find a husband.

"I did not much care during my first Season," she had said. "I was too young to get married and wished to amuse myself. Last Season though…I own I was disappointed not to be betrothed by the time we removed to Blackthorn. I would be very well pleased if I am at least close to engaged before we return to town."

Elizabeth now realised that Miss Ledbury hoped to attach herself to one of her brother's friends. Amongst the gentlemen she had met while in Leicestershire, there had been none in whom Miss Ledbury had shown interest. *I could be mistaken, or-or she might prefer Mr Bingley, but please dear Lord, not Mr Darcy.* She should want Mr Darcy to find happiness in marriage, but it would be a terror to watch him fall in love with another woman.

Aloud, Elizabeth said, "I am afraid there really is nothing I can tell you that would be of assistance. Mr Bingley is amiable, as you said. Mr Darcy is… I found that it takes time and effort to understand him."

Miss Ledbury pinched her lips and tapped a finger on the side of her cup. Elizabeth swallowed the last of her tea and excused herself.

Wanting a few minutes to collect herself, Elizabeth remembered an errand she wanted to do and went to her bedchamber. She regretted it when, on her way back to the withdrawing room, she came face-to-face with Mr Darcy.

"Miss Bennet." He appeared as startled as she was by the encounter.

His eyes caught hers, and she felt instantly transfixed. She could not tell if her heart raced or stopped.

"I-I recalled a book I wanted to show your sister." Her voice sounded unsteady, and Elizabeth wanted to pinch herself so that she would stop being so ridiculous. "We talked about it last evening, and I thought she would enjoy it. Would you like to see what it is before I—" She held it out to him.

"No," he said. "I know you would not give her anything inappropriate for a girl of her age. How are you?"

For some reason, his question made her eyes burn, and she wanted to crumple to the ground and let her tears flow. She struggled to keep her voice steady. "I am well. And you?"

He gave an awkward nod rather than say anything. All the while, he kept staring at her. "And-and your sisters and parents?"

"They are healthy and much as they ever were."

They stood in silence for a long moment. Elizabeth tightened her grip on the book; she longed to touch him, just put a hand on his arm for a second or two, and feel his warmth and strength. The fingers of her free hand twitched as if reaching for him, and she curled them into a fist before she forgot herself and acted inappropriately.

Mr Darcy cleared his throat. "Mr Ridley seems like a good man."

She had to blink to clear her thoughts enough to reply. She swallowed heavily, hoping to clear the tightness in her throat. "He is. Jane was fortunate to meet him; I believe they are happy."

"And you? Are you happy?"

Something in his eyes changed. They became more intense, and she had the sensation that he was digging into her soul. She wanted to cry out that no, she had not been truly happy a single day since they parted, that she could never be happy without him in her life. Instead, she nodded, forced her eyes away from him, and said that she had forgotten something in her bedchamber. Turning, she then fled back to her room for a minute of solitude.

Chapter Three

Speaking to Elizabeth Bennet privately when they met in the hallway was a greater challenge than Darcy had expected it would be. It took all his restraint not to touch her hair, which looked so soft, or run his finger along the ridge of her cheekbone, or simply clasp her hand in his. When she had said she had a book to show Georgiana, his heart swelled so much, it stopped beating for a second. As he watched her walk back to her bedroom, he silently reprimanded himself.

Stop being a fool, man. It has been over a year. Whatever she may have felt for me ended long ago. No doubt it died as soon as she read about Wickham and her sister. I showed that I did not deserve her in Kent, and after that summer, between Wickham and Bingley— With a grunt, he straightened the cuffs of his coat and went downstairs.

The afternoon was spent decorating the house. The gentlemen allowed the ladies to lead the way; their task, and his especially as the tallest amongst them, was to place the greenery where they were told. The sweet scents of evergreen, rosemary, and laurel, now and again combined with apples or oranges, tickled his nose. Colourful ribbons, soft next to the rough vegetation, were laced through some arrangements.

Before retiring to dress for dinner, they lit the Yule Log. Darcy stood beside Georgiana and draped an arm across her shoulders. He was reminded of Christmases with his mother and father. Lady Anne Darcy had loved the Festive Season, and Pemberley had always been full of guests—including his cousins and other children so that he, too, had plenty of company—and gaiety. Georgiana was too young to remember what it had been like, since their mother had died when she was just three years old, but he did, and he indulged in a few minutes of melancholy. It did not help that Elizabeth was at Georgiana's other side.

Darcy went with Georgiana to her room. They sat in the delicate maple and brocade armchairs by the window, and he asked if she was enjoying herself and if she was comfortable with the ladies. He had known the party would be small and believed that would make it easier for his sister.

Georgiana nodded but kept her eyes lowered. He saw her bite her lip and waited patiently for her to speak.

At length, she said, "I felt awkward seeing Miss Bennet again. She left Lambton so suddenly last year. I had thought that..."

Darcy was relieved she did not finish her statement. He knew what she would say—she had expected him to marry Elizabeth. He had not told Georgiana the full story, but she knew Elizabeth's youngest sister had married George Wickham.

Georgiana continued, "She is so kind to me that I feel quite at ease with her. I think I shall like Mrs Ridley, and Miss Ledbury is very pleasant too."

"I am glad to hear the ladies are good company for you."

Again, she nodded and bit her lip; he would have to talk to Georgiana's companion about curing her of the habit.

"I think Miss Ledbury hopes that either you or Mr Bingley will..." She blushed.

"Take a romantic interest in her?" He had discerned as much from Ledbury's conversation. "Perhaps Bingley will. As far as I have seen, she is everything a young lady is expected to be, but she is not the one for me."

Georgiana lifted her head to look at him. He was certain from the expression on her face and in her bright blue eyes, so like their mother's, that she knew he still loved Elizabeth Bennet.

Elizabeth regarded her reflection in the dressing table mirror. She had just dismissed Jane's maid, Smith, who also attended her. She felt foolish and stupid after her encounter with Mr Darcy.

I was like a young girl, newly out and talking to a handsome gentleman for the first time. I will not make such a display again. I am two-and-twenty, and have enough life experience to be...stronger in the face of such a challenge. Indeed, the only proper response to the twists and turns of my acquaintance with Mr Darcy is to laugh.

To prove it, that is exactly what she did before changing her earrings to jade ones she believed better complemented the silvery satin of her gown. A knock on her door signalled that Jane and Thomas were waiting to escort her downstairs.

Christmas Eve was pleasant. There were no additional guests, but Elizabeth knew the Ledburys had arranged a party with their neighbours for the next day; she had helped Miss Ledbury with planning the menu and entertainments and such usual tasks.

The withdrawing room looked better with the new decorations, in Elizabeth's opinion. She often found the room too dark, especially in the evening, when the red walls seemed to absorb the candlelight. Now, the mantel and tables were adorned with vegetation that still looked alive, even though she knew it would fade in the coming days. She had suggested white ribbons and other bright bits and pieces, and she was happy with the effect.

The nine of them ate heartily and enjoyed sweet treats after dinner. They played cards and Miss Ledbury, Miss Darcy, and Elizabeth provided music. Elizabeth sang, but Miss Ledbury refused.

"Miss Bennet is so much better than I am. I am not so foolish as to give you cause to compare us." With that, she sent flirtatious smiles to Mr Darcy and Mr Bingley.

Mr Bingley obliged her by saying, "I refuse to believe you are anything other than the most charming of performers, Miss Ledbury!"

Elizabeth happened to be looking in Jane's direction as he spoke, and she thought she caught a scowl on her sister's face, but if so, it was quickly erased.

Do not be fanciful, she scolded herself. *Truly, if I do not reform my attitude, I shall go mad by Twelfth Night. Mr Bingley is nothing to Jane. She assured me of that long before she accepted Thomas. Tomorrow is Christmas—a day for joy. I will take advantage of it and keep my thoughts firmly rooted in the present, not the past and what might have been—for either Jane or myself.*

Elizabeth liked the church the Ledburys attended. The vicar spoke well, and the gothic edifice was architecturally interesting. On Christmas morning, a spirit of goodwill seemed to permeate the walls, and all around her, she saw nothing but happy people. Even Mr Darcy, sitting between his sister and Mr Bingley, seemed relaxed. Their eyes met several times, and she dared to offer him a small smile once, but other than pleasantries, they did not speak. Elizabeth knew it was for the best, but she yearned to hear his voice and look into his eyes.

Mr and Miss Ledbury had some dozen of their neighbours to spend the day at Blackthorn Manor. They arrived shortly after noon and were greeted by a luncheon. Elizabeth had met a few of them during her time with the Ledburys, but most of them were new to her, as they were to the Darcys and Mr Bingley. Miss Darcy looked at a loss with her brother busy with the gentlemen, and Elizabeth made sure to keep her close by as she conversed with several young ladies.

She is a sweet girl, but so shy, Elizabeth thought. *I understand Mr Darcy hopes she will become more comfortable in society, but she cannot simply be dropped into a group of people and made to sort out how to do it on her own. Yet if he were always beside her, she would have no reason to exert herself. What she needs is…* Elizabeth purposefully pushed away such reflections. If things had transpired differently, she might be Miss Darcy's sister-in-law, in which case it would be her role to ease her transition into society. If she was doing that now, it was only because it had to be done.

When they were alone for a moment, Miss Darcy, her voice hushed, said, "Thank you, Miss Bennet. I-it has always been difficult for me to know what to say to people I do not know well."

Elizabeth dared to give her forearm a quick, gentle squeeze. "You will find it easier with time and practise." She ignored the way Mr Darcy watched them. *I am glad he does not think so poorly of me that he objects to his sister spending time with me. At least, it appears he does not.*

Dinner consisted of everything one needed for a proper Christmas feast—roasted goose and beef and pork, Yorkshire puddings, gravy, mincemeat pies, vegetables and relishes, jellies, custards, and more. What Elizabeth ate was well-prepared, but there was such an abundance of food that it was impossible to taste it all. In her opinion, which she would keep to herself, there was *too* much, and it screamed of Miss Ledbury attempting to impress her potential husbands. *I suppose the servants will eat what we do not, and I am happy for them. They work hard, and Christmastide is a good time to reflect on and show appreciation for all they do for us.*

Elizabeth sat between two of the Ledburys' neighbours; they provided good conversation, and she had no complaints. Miss Darcy was beside her brother, which Elizabeth was glad to see. At Mr Darcy's other side was Miss Ledbury. Despite her attempts to engage him, Mr Darcy was more interested in speaking to his sister and the gentleman who sat across from him. Even knowing it was wrong, Elizabeth was relieved.

Down the table to the other side, Jane sat next to Mr Bingley. The pair chatted as if they were the best of friends, and Elizabeth's brow furrowed as she saw Jane smile and blush; she even laughed.

The meal ended with a traditional pudding. As it was presented, Miss Ledbury spoke so that the whole table heard her.

"I am happy to announce that the receipt is one that has been in my family for generations. My brothers and I have had it at Christmas our entire lives, have we not, Edward, James?" Without waiting for her brothers to comment, she said, "We observe many of the traditions of our parents, even though they are no longer with us. Family is so important, as is honouring the memory of those who came before us. Do you not agree, Mr Darcy?" She turned to him, her eyes wide and lips turned upwards. To Elizabeth, she seemed confident that it would be the start of a long and satisfying conversation. To avoid seeing it, Elizabeth turned to the lady beside her and asked which dish had been her favourite of the meal.

A moment later, James Ledbury, sitting beside Elizabeth's other neighbour, tapped her shoulder. She leant back to see what he wanted.

He winked and whispered, "My sister is on the hunt. I hope Darcy realises he is prey and, if he wishes to avoid being captured, knows to take cover. My brother would be just as pleased if Bingley is the one she catches. You know both men; which do you think would better suit Harriet?"

Elizabeth managed to chuckle and affect an unconcerned air. "I am sure I have no opinion on the matter."

After dinner, the entire party retired to the withdrawing room, the gentlemen deciding to forgo their time apart in light of the holiday. The room had been prepared for their merriment with additional candles and a buffet by one wall.

Mr Ledbury announced, "As you can see, we have biscuits, cakes, jellies, candies, marzipans, and fruits—everything you might want to celebrate the day and fill your bellies."

Miss Ledbury said, "There is more to come—pies, cold meats, and breads. Do enjoy the punch. It is our family's special receipt."

James Ledbury brought Elizabeth a cup before she decided she wanted one, and she felt a stab of annoyance with his continued attendance. *It was one thing when it was just the two of us, his siblings, and mine. There are others he would do well to talk to and whose company I might enjoy, especially tonight.*

She took a sip of the punch. It tasted strongly of orange and brandy and was too sweet for her; she wanted a little more spice too. *Oh, stop being so prickly!* Surreptitiously, she pinched her thigh. She could not account for her mood and was determined to enjoy the party. It was just the sort of thing she usually liked, especially after having no entertainment or company beyond the ordinary for months before coming to

Blackthorn Manor. Accordingly, when someone suggested a game of charades, she was the first to agree. When Mr Ledbury requested music, she played and sang Christmas carols and listened attentively as several of the other ladies sat down at the instrument. All the while, she was friendly with whoever happened to be by her side. What she did not do was allow her eyes to seek Mr Darcy or her mind to notice that he looked particularly handsome tonight in a green and gold waistcoat.

She wished she was as adept at ignoring Jane and Mr Bingley. Their conversation at dinner had evidently carried over to the withdrawing room, and Elizabeth seldom saw them outside of each other's company. Twice she saw Jane touch Mr Bingley's arm; once her hand had lingered longer than Elizabeth liked.

Joining them, she said, "What a delightful evening, is it not? How did you like your dinner? Does not Mrs Thompson play exceptionally well?" Mrs Thompson was the vicar's wife.

Elizabeth kept up a steady stream of questions and comments for almost ten minutes before she was interrupted by James Ledbury who called, "Miss Bennet, you must come settle the dispute my friend here" —he indicated the gentleman with him—"and I are having."

"Go on, Lizzy," Jane said.

The look in her eyes suggested she wished Elizabeth far away. Elizabeth went to James Ledbury with reluctance and a sick feeling in her stomach which had no relation to the rich food she had consumed.

Soon after that, Mrs Thompson offered to play so that those who wished to could dance. All the young people said that it was just what they wanted, and the furniture was quickly rearranged to provide enough space for the activity.

"You will dance with me, of course, Miss Bennet," James Ledbury said. "I would be mortally wounded if you stood up with another gentleman before me."

He grinned and laughed, and Elizabeth attempted to respond with the same light, easy manner he used. She had enjoyed spending time with him—*before* Mr Darcy's arrival. If she kept to her resolve not to think of the past, she might find the same pleasure again.

"We would not want that, sir. I humbly accept."

As they skipped and bounced through the lively dance, Elizabeth spied two other couples she did not especially like to see—Jane and Mr Bingley and Miss Ledbury and Mr Darcy. It made it difficult to keep her attention on her partner, but she asked him to tell her an amusing tale of a ball he had been to, and, during their time together, they traded several such anecdotes. It was almost enough to keep her from thinking about Mr Darcy.

Chapter Four

DARCY HAD BEEN TELLING THE TRUTH WHEN HE HAD TOLD Georgiana that he thought Harriet Ledbury was a proper young lady. He would even say that she seemed like a nice enough one. That did not stop him from finding her tedious. She had practically tethered herself to him most of the day. How he wished she would transfer her attentions to Bingley. Miss Ledbury would be an excellent match for him, in terms of fortune and connexions, and Bingley would appreciate her friendly manner.

Or he would if he were not so occupied with Mrs Ridley. What is *he doing? What* is *she thinking? And, while I am at it, why in blazes is Ridley not intervening?* He spotted Ridley in an animated conversation with Ledbury and another gentleman. *I can understand that he is happy to see his cousin again, but he ought to talk to Ledbury less and his wife more. I pray this behaviour is a matter of spirits made high by the holiday and too much punch.* He found the receipt overly strong and had already cautioned Georgiana to avoid it.

Even when Darcy went to speak to Georgiana or some other guest, Miss Ledbury remained by his side, demanding his attention.

"Oh Mr Darcy," she said in her worst transgression, "is there anything pleasanter than a country house party? Edward tells me that Pemberley is simply magnificent. How you shall hate to leave it when you are married, Miss Darcy, but such is a lady's lot, and, after all, making a new home of one's own can be very exciting, I am sure." She accompanied it with just such a look that he longed to issue a set down.

Darcy sighed and rubbed his temple, hoping no one noticed. He knew he was in a foul mood, and blamed his friend's behaviour and having to play charades—a game he particularly despised—but knew that the real reason was having to watch Elizabeth. He loved to see her liveliness and had missed seeing her smile and hearing her laugh. But he hated having to witness gentlemen, especially James Ledbury, flirting with her and—even worse—seeing her flirt in return. She seemed to like James Ledbury too much for his comfort, even though rationally he knew it would be an excellent match for her.

When the dancing started, Miss Ledbury, who continued to ignore her guests in favour of staying by his side, regarded him, a smile on her face, until he was forced to ask her.

Fluttering her eyes, she said, "I would be delighted, Mr Darcy," and took his arm before he offered it.

Seeing Elizabeth standing up with James Ledbury and Bingley with Mrs Ridley did not improve his mood. He could not say what he and Miss Ledbury spoke about; it was too commonplace, as had been most of their conversations, for him to remember any of it. When he felt his jaw ache, he knew he was clenching his teeth, which no doubt meant he was also scowling.

Which is no way to behave in company. Elizabeth taught me that with her reproofs about my manner in Meryton. Besides, Georgiana will notice, and it will distress her.

For the second dance, he partnered Georgiana and was able to relax.

"You played very well," he told her, referring to her turn at the pianoforte. "I did not realise you and Miss Bennet had practised a duet. When did you have time?"

Georgiana blushed. "Yesterday. I told her I did not think I could play in front of so many people, and she suggested it. She said I might find it easier to perform a second piece if we first did something together, and she was right. She is very sensible."

Darcy smiled. He could listen to Georgiana praise Elizabeth all day, but knew it would be better to change the topic. "Tell me what you have particularly liked about today."

When the dance allowed, they spoke about what they had done and speculated about how the Fitzwilliams and de Bourghs were getting along. Their aunt and uncle, the Earl and Countess of Romsley, along with their two sons and the eldest's wife and infant son, had gone to Rosings Park for the Festive Season.

Towards the end of the set, Darcy said, "If you would like to dance again, I will tell Bingley to ask you."

Georgiana bit her lip and nodded. Bingley was agreeable, and Darcy stood off to the side, sipping a glass of lemonade and watching them.

When a fourth and final dance was called for, Darcy succumbed to temptation and approached Elizabeth.

"Miss Bennet, will you do me the honour of dancing with me?"

When she looked at his proffered hand and seemed to hesitate, his heart sank into his slippers. But then she nodded. Her hand touched his, and he felt that familiar swelling in his chest. For a moment, he fantasised about closing his fingers around hers, her beautiful dark eyes meeting his, the curve of her lips teasing and enticing. He would pull her close, whisper words of love into her ear, and beg her to forgive him, to give him one last chance—

Shaking his head, he did as he ought and led her to the lines. Seeing that Elizabeth's attention was drawn into a corner of the room, he glanced that way and discovered that Bingley was, once again, standing with Mrs Ridley. He refused to concern himself with it, not when he could be talking to Elizabeth and rightfully claim her attention to himself for the next little while.

The music started, and they moved through the steps.

"Are you enjoying the party?" Darcy asked.

She produced a polite, stiff smile. "Very much. Are you?"

He nodded and, a minute or two later, said, "Do you stay much longer? I thought I understood you and Mr and Mrs Ridley would remain for Twelfth Night." *Please say yes.* It was difficult to see her, but he yearned for her company, and it did Georgiana good. A tiny voice in the recesses of his mind suggested that maybe, just maybe, she might pardon him for his past mistakes. If so, they could regain what they had had in Derbyshire. Rationally, he knew that such a hope was hardly worth admitting, especially in light of her frigid demeanour.

An odd expression flashed across her face. "We return to Northampton on the seventh."

"Bingley, Georgiana, and I leave the same day. Do the Ridleys go to town this winter?"

"I do not imagine so."

"Will you remain with them long?"

The dance separated them. When they were together again, she said, "My plans are not fixed. I might return to Longbourn or go to stay with my aunt and uncle which, I suppose, means I might be in town."

Darcy had liked the Gardiners a great deal. *I wonder if I ought to try to renew my acquaintance with them. I would like to, and if I did, and Elizabeth happened to be there… But to what purpose? I always must confront that question, as much as I do not like the answer.*

He said, "May I enquire after the Gardiners? I enjoyed meeting them."

Her eyes shot to his, though she soon looked away. "They are well, thank you. They were pleased to make your acquaintance, and Miss Darcy's."

They said nothing more, and, immediately after the dance was over, she curtseyed and went to her sister.

Soon after, the neighbours began to depart. Seeing that Georgiana was fatigued, he escorted her to her bedchamber, and retired for the night as well.

The following day was quiet for the ladies. Other than Mr Bingley, the gentlemen joined a fox hunt at a nearby estate. Elizabeth had not heard why Mr Bingley did not wish to go, and she saw little of him except when they met for luncheon in the early afternoon. She occupied herself writing letters to her mother, her sister Mary, and Charlotte Collins. She also spent time with Georgiana and assisted Miss Ledbury with several arrangements for the Twelfth Night ball being held at Blackthorn Manor.

In the late afternoon, Elizabeth sat in the sitting room she shared with the Ridleys, curled up in an armchair with a thick shawl across her shoulders. Staring at a clock on the fireplace mantel, her thoughts drifted to her dance with Mr Darcy. Every word he said, every look he gave her had to be studied. That he had asked her to stand up with him had surprised her. While she was tempted to say that his questions about her plans were a sign that he hoped she was soon departing, sparing him and Miss Darcy the shame of knowing her, she did not believe it.

Not of him, not of the man I knew in Derbyshire last year. He has done nothing to prevent his sister from spending time with me while we are both here. I suppose I should simply be thankful that he is willing to meet as…I cannot say friends, so let me say acquaintances. With Jane married to his friend's cousin, perhaps he expects we might see each other again, and it would be better if we could be on good terms.

Elizabeth sighed, stood, and went to look out the window. The day felt long, and Elizabeth was beginning to feel the want of activity. She had come upstairs because she preferred this parlour to the withdrawing room, and the other ladies were busy—Georgiana writing to her cousin, Jane resting in her bedchamber, and Miss Ledbury with household matters.

Perhaps I should go for a walk. It is cold, but if I keep a good pace, I shall be fine. I need not stay out long. Who is that? She narrowed her eyes in an effort to make out a couple walking in the gardens. *It cannot be, but I think…no, it certainly* is *Jane and Mr Bingley. Not an hour ago, she said she was—I must have misunderstood.*

Her body felt suddenly heavy. Elizabeth had told herself that Jane's attention to Mr Bingley the day before, really what had at times looked like flirting, had been a product of too much punch and excitement because it was Christmas and they were at a party. But now…

Aloud, she implored, "Oh Jane, take care."

It began to snow the evening of St Stephen's Day and continued overnight. At breakfast, Miss Ledbury suggested they go sleigh riding.

"Our groundskeeper says that it is the perfect time for it. We have a sleigh, you know, and Edward hired a second one so that we could all go at the same time. I am so glad that it snowed! It looks ever so pretty. Do you not agree, Miss Darcy?"

Georgiana glanced at Darcy and stammered, "Y-y-yes. V-very pretty."

Darcy said, "We have a sleigh at Pemberley. My sister and I both like to take advantage of pleasant winter days."

At dinner the previous day, Darcy had noticed that Miss Ledbury was paying more attention to his sister. He suspected it was an attempt to gain his interest. Bingley's sister Caroline had behaved in much the same manner for years. As much as he did not long for it, he wanted to draw Miss Ledbury's attention away from Georgiana, because it clearly made her uncomfortable. Darcy had been hesitant to leave her to go hunting, but she had insisted. During the outing, he had told Ledbury that he had no intentions of marrying soon, going so far as to hint that his interests lay elsewhere. Darcy trusted that Ledbury would tell his sister, who would then have the good sense to transfer her efforts to Bingley. It would serve the dual purpose of saving him from her flirting and keeping Bingley occupied and away from Mrs Ridley—with whom he was again talking. The pair, along with Elizabeth, was seated at the other end of the table. Elizabeth—looking particularly lovely in a long-sleeved sienna gown which made her skin glow—appeared to be trying to take part in their conversation.

Ledbury said, "We will have to divide into one group of four and one of five, unless there is anyone who does not wish to go?" Everyone was keen, and Ledbury continued, "Very good. Harriet, you and I can ride with Thomas, Mrs Ridley, and"—he looked around the table—"Mr Bingley. James, you will not mind being with Miss Bennet and the Darcys."

"That suits me well." James Ledbury smiled across at Elizabeth.

Darcy was pleased that she did not seem to notice; she was too busy studying her sister, a slight frown on her face.

"Oh, I do love a sleigh ride!" Miss Ledbury clapped her hands. "It is so...festive, and I am very glad we are going. But, Edward, I shall join Miss Darcy's party. I feel I have had very little opportunity to get to know her."

Ledbury shrugged and said something to Mr Ridley.

Darcy gritted his teeth. *Well, I shall just have to make the best of it. Elizabeth will be with us; that is all that truly matters. I wish...but I had my second chance. It would be too much to expect a third.*

In the end, Miss Ledbury and James Ledbury accompanied him, Georgiana, and Elizabeth as they drove around the park, by a copse, past a lake, and back again. It would have been perfect, had the Ledburys not been with them. Then, Elizabeth would have been having a lively debate with him, not James Ledbury. Then, when he looked across from him, he would see the two ladies he loved best in the world, not Harriet Ledbury. *Then, if it were just Georgiana, Elizabeth, and me, it would mean Elizabeth was mine. Good God, why is it that everything she says and does make me long for her more and more?*

He tried to be polite and listen to Miss Ledbury's prattle about how much she enjoyed country life and the feminine duties that came with it. *No doubt to impress on me what a good mistress she would make at Pemberley. Damn it, Ledbury, you were supposed to tell her she was wasting her time trying to attach me!* A snippet of Elizabeth's conversation caught his notice, and he turned his attention to her. She, James Ledbury, and Georgiana were talking about books.

"You are giving me too much credit," Elizabeth said. "I do like to read, but I seldom read extensively on any one topic. I had much rather learn about a wide variety of subjects, which might allow me to sound more intelligent than I am, but I am by no means an expert on anything. If you are looking for someone to admire in that regard, I give you Miss Darcy. I discovered just yesterday that she is an ardent student of botany and garden design."

Georgiana tried to demur, but Elizabeth said, "It may not be fashionable, but I believe ladies should not be ashamed to acknowledge that they have interests beyond the usual feminine accomplishments. I do not say we should ignore our duties as daughters, sisters, wives, mothers—whatever role we are assigned by life and circumstance—but if we have the ability and inclination to deepen our understanding of something that piques our curiosity, why should we not?"

"And your curiosity is aroused by a great many things, my dear Miss Bennet. That I find admirable," James Ledbury said.

"While I wish I had Miss Darcy's dedication to one subject. It does not mean she excludes developing an understanding of other important matters. That would not be praiseworthy. But we ought to talk about something else; I am embarrassing her. I apologise, Miss Darcy."

She smiled so sweetly, so genuinely at Georgiana, that he wanted to rip his heart out of his chest and hand it to her. She owned it already, and might as well have physical possession of it.

Miss Ledbury said, "How interesting. I adore a well-designed garden. Edward tells me that he has never seen finer ones that those at Pemberley." She continued along the same vein, but her attempts to make Georgiana say more than a few words—not that she gave her much opportunity to respond—were unsuccessful. James Ledbury continued his discussion with Elizabeth, who appeared to be frustrated with his attempts to show that he admired her mind.

Can he not see it? Darcy wondered. *The way she will not meet his eye, the tension around her mouth, the gentle arch of her right eyebrow. He does not understand her, and that alone means he does not deserve her.*

Darcy was not sorry when they returned to the house. He whisked Georgiana upstairs so that they could refresh themselves—and have a few minutes of quiet—before joining the rest of the party for refreshments.

The sleigh ride had been an agreeable diversion. The clouds had cleared, and Elizabeth enjoyed the feel of the cold winter air, mixed with the bright sun, on her face, while the rest of her was warm beneath layers of clothing and rugs. There was a certain beauty in the winter landscape that had always appealed to her—the starkness of trees free of their leaves, the contrast of evergreen against ice and snow, and the fresh scent that came with it.

James Ledbury's attentions had marred some of her pleasure. He was an amiable, respectable gentleman, and she knew he could afford a wife and family. She did not believe that his flirting meant he had serious intentions towards her. They had only known each other a few weeks, but she was convinced that she could not be happy with him. She might be a fool to reject even the possibility of a future as Mrs James Ledbury—her mother would doubtlessly say so, as might Jane—and she might feel differently had Mr Darcy not joined their party. But it would not be fair to any man to marry him when her heart and thoughts were full of another.

How I wish it had been only he, Miss Darcy, and I! We would have been our own little family had not Lydia—I know we would have been so happy. Miss Darcy is such a delightful girl. I would have loved to have her as my sister.

Elizabeth pressed her eyes closed and bowed her head, determined to banish such thoughts. Sighing, she opened her eyes and went to look out her bedchamber window.

I know I ought to avoid him—both of them, likely—but how can I? It would draw unwanted attention, and…and I am like a moth drawn to a flame where Mr Darcy is concerned. Will I ever conquer such feelings?

Chapter Five

AFTER DINNER ON THE TWENTY-EIGHTH, HARRIET LEDBURY suggested they play a game. Everyone was agreeable, and, after some debate, she succeeded in carrying her point and I Love my Love with an A was selected. Based on his stony expression, Elizabeth suspected Mr Darcy wished for a way to bow out of playing. When Mr Ledbury opened his mouth, perhaps to protest, Miss Ledbury shot him a quelling look. Somewhat to Elizabeth's surprise, because he seldom showed a disinclination to telling his sister what she could not do, he simply rolled his eyes and shrugged.

Mr Darcy said, "Georgiana, perhaps you would prefer to play the pianoforte for us? A little music would not be amiss."

Miss Darcy's relief showed in her enthusiastic nod. At once, she stood and went to the instrument.

Elizabeth had played the game before, and, as long as everyone treated it as a silly way to pass the time, she did not mind. This evening, she felt a frisson of discomfort, however, given the people involved, especially Jane and Mr Bingley. She had no wish to watch Miss Ledbury flirt with Mr Darcy any further, either.

They drew letters from a bowl, and Thomas, whose scrap of paper had a large ornate A on it, began.

He said, "I was rather hoping for B so I could take inspiration from my dear Jane, since we are not enough to reach J, but Mr Bingley has it. Let me see..."

While he considered his response, Elizabeth thought about how much she wished Mr Bingley had drawn the H. *Then perhaps he would have directed his response to Miss Ledbury. Oh, stop worrying about him, Lizzy. You have the D…*

Thomas said, "I have it. I love my love with an A because she is amusing. I hate her because she is adventurous. I took her to…Ascot, to the sign of the angel."

He smiled at Jane, and Elizabeth could not help remembering how often she had heard Mr Bingley refer to Jane as an angel; it made her want to groan. Jane returned her husband's smile, but to Elizabeth, it appeared forced.

"I treated her with apples," Thomas said, "and her name is Anne Anderson."

There was light applause when he finished. He bowed his head and said, "Mr Bingley, your turn."

Mr Bingley grinned. "Right. I love my love with a B because she is," he looked at Jane, "beautiful. I hate her because she is, um, betrothed."

That garnered a few chuckles, which Elizabeth was pleased to see. It meant he stopped staring at her sister. She glanced at Thomas to see if he had noticed, and saw that his eyes darted between Mr Bingley and Jane with what looked like curiosity, but he was soon distracted when Mr Ledbury whispered something to him.

Jane blushed and undertook a study of the room.

Mr Bingley scratched the back of his neck before continuing. "I took her to Bath, to the sign of the…bear. I treated her with buns, and her name is," he took a moment to look between Miss Ledbury and Jane, before finishing, "Beatrice," again he paused, this time to drop his eyes to his jacket, "Buttons." He grimaced. "Not very good, I am afraid. Someone else will have to come up with a clever response."

"I think it was charming, as long as you were thinking of the right lady when you said beautiful." Miss Ledbury smiled at him, dipping her chin so that she was in effect looking up at him, her eyes wide. The flirtatious expression made Elizabeth suspect her hostess had transferred her attentions from Mr Darcy to Mr Bingley, and she was glad of it.

Jane said, "I think you were very clever, far more than I will be."

Mr Bingley did not seem to know which way to look. Elizabeth wanted to scream, *To the one who is not married, you absurd man!*

She held her tongue.

Miss Ledbury loudly cleared her throat. "I am next. I have drawn inspiration from someone I know whose name starts with a C, but do not ask me whom, for I shall not say." She giggled, and Mr Bingley grinned. "I love my love with a C because he is charming." Miss Ledbury pouted before continuing, "I hate him because he is cruel. I took him to Cornwall, to the sign of the corn. I treated him with cake, and his name is Charles Clarke."

Charles Bingley clapped and cried, "Well done, Miss Ledbury!"

At the same moment, Jane said, "Oh no," and began to search for something on the floor.

"What is it, my dear?" Thomas asked.

"My bracelet. The clasp must be broken, and it fell off."

Mr Bingley and Thomas both leapt to assist her. Miss Ledbury regarded the trio with scepticism, and Elizabeth agreed with her. The bracelet was soon recovered, and Thomas tucked it into his pocket.

"I will bring it to a jeweller once we are home," he said.

Bright pink spots formed on Jane's cheeks. "Oh, no, I am sure that is not necessary. My maid or I shall be able to fix it." She held out her hand for it, but he did not appear to notice.

Mr Ledbury said, "Who is next?"

Elizabeth was too busy contemplating Jane's behaviour to respond. *Could it be that Jane regrets marrying Thomas now that she has seen Mr Bingley again? Impossible! Yet…*

It occurred to her that fretting about Jane kept her from thinking about Mr Darcy. Her eyes drifted towards him, and she discovered that he was watching her. Elizabeth found herself getting lost in his regard. He was the handsomest gentleman she had ever encountered, and there was something about his eyes when he looked at her that robbed her of her ability to think.

"Miss Bennet, I believe you have the D," Mr Ledbury said.

Elizabeth felt her cheeks flush, and she tightened her grip on the edges of her paisley-patterned shawl. "So I do." With a steadying breath, she recited, "I love my love with a D because he is delightful. I hate him because he is dead. I took him to Devon to the sign of the daisy. I treated him with dirt." Elizabeth heard a couple of chuckles, a noise of surprise, and someone repeat her last the word. She did not know who, because her eyes had once again fixed on Mr Darcy, who was watching her with a soft smile on his face. "And his name is Dan Delion."

Mr Darcy's smile broadened, and he appeared to be silently chuckling. That meant more to her than the louder sounds of appreciation for her light-hearted contribution to the game.

"You are clever, Miss Bennet," James Ledbury said. "I knew you had something in mind as soon as you said 'dead', and it was confirmed when you said 'dirt'."

"I did not," Miss Ledbury said. "I thought she had gone mad or had a very interesting story about an old beau I would insist she tell us. Did you know, Mr Bingley?"

Mr Bingley, whose attention had momentarily drifted to Jane, assured Miss Ledbury that he had not. "But I am not surprised. I remember this one time when she and her sister—"

Mr Darcy interjected, "Bingley."

When Mr Bingley looked at his friend, Mr Darcy gave a decided shake of his head. Elizabeth was relieved when Mr Bingley acquiesced. She was certain he was going to talk about the days she and Jane had stayed at Netherfield after Jane had taken ill while visiting Mrs Hurst and Miss Bingley. Thomas did not need to hear it. *I do not even know if he realises Jane had tender feelings for Mr Bingley. He must wonder...* Her brother-in-law, however, was again in conversation with Mr Ledbury. She knew they were good friends, but Thomas would do better to pay attention to his wife.

Miss Ledbury said, "Let us return to the game. I do adore it. Who is next? Who has E?"

Mr Darcy raised a finger, and Elizabeth found herself again trapped by his eyes until he gave a small cough. She looked away briefly but lifted her chin and watched him as he spoke, his voice an odd combination of trepidation and resignation. His eyes darted to and away from her repeatedly, causing her to blush.

"I love my love with an E because she is elegant. I hate her because she is elusive. I took her to Edale—"

"Edale?" James Ledbury interjected. "Is that a real place?"

The muscles in Mr Darcy's jaw tightened for a moment. "It is in Derbyshire."

"James," his sister scolded. "Pray continue, Mr Darcy."

"I took her to Edale to the sign of the eyebright. I treated her with elderberries, and her name is...Ellen Everton."

By the time he finished, he was again staring at Elizabeth, and she could not look away. *Was there a message I am supposed to understand? If so, I fail to... Oh, what a wretched game! I shall never consent to play it again.*

Fortunately, Jane spoke. "It is my turn. I have the F." She held up her piece of paper as proof. Thomas and Mr Ledbury stopped chatting, and Thomas turned to smile at his wife. "I love my love with an F because he is fine. I hate him because he is fickle. I took him to—oh, I cannot think of a place that starts with F." Thomas leant towards her and whispered in her ear, and she blurted, "Forest Gate."

Mr Bingley said he had never heard of Forest Gate, and Thomas explained that it was east of London. Elizabeth thought, *If nothing else, this game could provide a good geography lesson. I do not think that benefit outweighs the discomfort.*

"Go on, my dear," Thomas said to Jane, who offered him a polite smile.

"To the sign of the fox. I treated him with filberts, and his name is Frank Foster." She shrugged when she was finished.

James Ledbury sat forward and, with a grin, said, "My turn! I had hoped for a different letter."

He looked at Elizabeth, and one eye twitched just enough to be called a wink. She pretended not to notice. Since the Darcys and Mr Bingley had arrived, his manner towards her had become bolder, and she did not like it.

"But I have what I have," he continued. "Do not fret, Darcy. Even though your sister's name begins with a G, I know better than to incur your wrath by so much as teasing that she is my inspiration."

Mr Darcy treated him to a glare, which, in Elizabeth's opinion, he deserved.

"I love my love with a G because she is generous. I hate her because she is guarded. I took her to Gretna Green, to the sign of the goose. I treated her with gingerbread, and her name is—goodness, names beginning with G are rare, are they not? I shall have to take a cue from Miss Bennet and make up a clever one." Although he evidently expected her to favour him with a response, she remained silent, and he said, "And her name is Goldenrod Gorse."

Elizabeth heard Mr Darcy mutter a sarcastic, "Charming," that left her doing a quick count of the remaining people. With immense relief, she realised it was only Mr Ledbury. *If the game does not end with him, I shall make an excuse to retire.*

Mr Ledbury frowned. "Is it wrong to hope for a sudden emergency to call me away?"

Miss Ledbury huffed, and James Ledbury said, "Edward, be a good sport. We all did it."

Mr Ledbury's scowl deepened. "I will take my turn, but can we all agree to find a different game after this?" He shot a quelling look at his sister when she seemed prepared to protest. Mr Bingley looked disappointed, but no one else did.

Mr Ledbury spoke quickly, as though he had been thinking of his response all along and could not wait to finish. "I love my love with an H because she is healthy. I hate her because she is heavy. I took her to Halifax, to the sign of the hare. I treated her with ham, and her name is Helen Harper. There we go. I could use more tea, perhaps a little something to nibble on. Harriet?"

Mr Darcy practically sprang to his feet and went to the pianoforte. Elizabeth let her eyelids fall and stifled a sigh of relief.

Darcy tore at his neckcloth, throwing it onto the chair in his bedchamber as soon as it was no longer strangling him. His jacket was already there, his waistcoat unbuttoned. He felt like a caged animal, and he almost kicked the thick wood frame of the bed as he strode every inch of the room.

What was I thinking? E for elegant and elusive. Elizabeth the elegant. Elizabeth the elusive. I might as well have fallen at her feet right there and begged her to accept me!

He went to the window and thrust the heavy brocade drapes aside. *Stop it, man! She does not love you, does not even like you enough to marry you. Perhaps once…*

He pressed his forehead and hands against the cool glass and attempted to stave off the tears that burned at the back of his eyes. Several minutes later, he was calm enough to sit by the fire.

Dandelion. He chuckled at the memory and wished the others had treated the game with the same light-heartedness—himself included. Miss Ledbury's behaviour made him suspect Ledbury had finally told her she had no hope of being Mrs Darcy. She could not have been more obvious about her interest in Bingley, though Bingley seemed oblivious to it, and to the lady's charms.

What the devil is he thinking? He should not *be giving Mrs Ridley so much attention. Will I be forced to once again interfere in his relationship with the woman?*

With a groan, he slid down the chair and covered his eyes with his forearm. *What horror being here is! How I wish I could think of an excuse for Georgiana and I to leave.*

The next morning, Darcy manufactured a private interview with Bingley. They were in one of the smaller, disused parlours. With no fire lit, it was cold. Neither man sat.

"Why the devil are you paying so much attention to Mrs Ridley?" Darcy asked.

"What do you mean?" The laugh Bingley produced did not hide the knowledge of his guilt.

"Since the moment we arrived, it is almost as if we were back at

Netherfield Park. I have seen you flirting with Mrs Ridley again and again. I would be surprised if others have not noticed. They soon will if you do not desist. She is married, Bingley."

Bingley walked away from Darcy. He stopped by a table and began to rearrange the items on it. "She is an old friend. I enjoy her company."

"That is not how you are treating her. I say yet again, Bingley, she is *married*. You had your chance with her. You decided not to pursue it. Do you remember? I told you in the spring of twelve that, upon reflection, I believed I had judged her too harshly when I said she did not admire you, that perhaps she did not show her feelings to the world. You decided not to return to Hertfordshire. That summer, I confessed that I knew she had cared for you, likely still did, and had been in town that winter, but your sisters and I had hidden it from you. Do you recall what you said?"

Bingley made a half-hearted shrug, and Darcy continued, "I do. All the fond talk about your time in Meryton, all the memories seeing Miss Elizabeth recalled, vanished. You found it interesting, but so much time had passed. There was another lady you liked. You gave up your chance to reconcile with her and to discover if your feelings were genuine. To now devote yourself to her in this way is unseemly."

Turning to face Darcy, Bingley said, almost apologetically, "She is the loveliest lady I have ever met. So gentle. Ridley does not appreciate her as he ought."

Darcy felt his patience about to snap and curled his hands into fists. "Do you hear yourself? How do you think this ends? At best, hurt feelings—including Mr Ridley's, which could only damage her situation—at worst, gossip and scandal. You are too intelligent to let that happen. There are other people in the house; give them your attention, not a married lady."

"Do you mean Miss Ledbury? She is nothing compared to Jane, not in looks or temperament or—or in the feelings she evokes in me."

Darcy hung his head and sighed. "I am not saying you have to marry her, or even like her. If you cannot enjoy her company, there are others with whom you could spend your time. You hardly know James Ledbury, and I think you and he would get along well. Or Mr Ridley. Perhaps if you talked to him upon occasion, you might realise that he makes a very good husband for Mrs Ridley."

Bingley strode to the door. "Enough, Darcy. I am sorry you disapprove of my behaviour. You have told me. Let that be an end of it before we truly argue."

The sound of the door banging shut as Bingley left the room felt like a blow to Darcy's stomach. He rubbed his forehead and took a minute to talk himself into a better mood before going to find his sister.

THAT AFTERNOON, ELIZABETH STOOD IN THE WITHDRAWING room watching the Yule Log smoulder. She hoped it would remind her of the joy she usually felt at this time of year. It had been a trying morning after a disagreeable evening. After playing 'I love my love with an A', Mr Ledbury and Thomas had sat down to a game of chess. Mr Bingley talked to Jane and Miss Ledbury; Elizabeth had attempted to distract Jane, but she would not budge from her position. When James Ledbury had tried to engage Elizabeth in conversation, she had escaped —first by sitting with Miss Darcy at the pianoforte, then by finding a chair in a corner and burying her nose in a book until it was late enough to retire to her bedchamber.

She had just come from a terrible, disconcerting encounter with Jane. Elizabeth had felt compelled to speak to her about her manner towards Mr Bingley. The previous days were enough to excite her concern, and this morning, she had discovered Jane, her arm in Mr Bingley's and cheeks rosy, as they walked downstairs to join everyone in the breakfast parlour. They had been touring the gallery. After breakfast, while Thomas was riding with Edward and James Ledbury, Elizabeth had asked to speak with Jane in their sitting room.

"I have seen how much you enjoy renewing your acquaintance with Mr Bingley."

Before she could say more, Jane stood and began to walk around the room, although she had no clear purpose in mind. "I have. I see nothing wrong with it."

"To taking pleasure in seeing an old friend again? No. But, Jane—I hardly believe I am going to say this—"

"Then do not," Jane interjected.

"I feel I must. You are flirting with him. It is wildly inappropri—"

Jane turned to her, but her eyes did not meet Elizabeth's. "You have no idea what you are talking about, Lizzy."

Elizabeth stood so that she was not looking up at her sister. "I know what I have seen again and again since he arrived. You cannot deny that you do not act like you and he are nothing more than indifferent acquaintances. Anyone would suppose you and he were weeks, maybe just days, away from an understanding—or at least that you hoped so. You think that Thomas does not see, but after last night, I am convinced that he does. I thought you were happy with him. Before you accepted him, you told me you no longer had tender feelings for Mr Bingley."

Jane turned her back to Elizabeth and went to the window. Her fingers drummed on the glass as she looked outside.

"Jane?" Elizabeth asked when the silence between them stretched to over a minute.

"I truly loved him, and we never had the opportunity to..." Jane's voice was full of sorrow. "I do not know why he never returned. His sisters must have convinced him to give me up."

In Elizabeth's opinion, if Mr Bingley had genuinely loved Jane, nothing his sisters—or Mr Darcy—could have said would have kept him from seeking her out. "What about Thomas?"

"Marriage is not what I thought it would be. My husband...lacks passion. He is always so busy doing this or that for his father. My mother-in-law asks nothing of me, and I do not even have a child to occupy my time. Seeing Mr Bingley again, I know I would have been so much happier with him."

Elizabeth fell back into the chair, and she felt the blood drain out of her face. It took a moment before she trusted that her voice would not shake. "I am sorry that marriage is not what you expected, but it has only been three months. A period of adjustment is surely necessary."

With unexpected anger darkening her tone, Jane spun to face her and said, "What you know about it? You are not married. You have rejected the only two men who ever offered for you. Do you even know what it is like to be in love? I do!" She hit her chest with a fist. "I know what it is to love, know you are loved in return, and lose it. He *did* love me, Lizzy, I know he did, and he still has feelings for me, although we dare not speak of it."

There was no purpose to comparing her situation with Jane's, and Elizabeth remained silent about Mr Darcy. "If that is the case, then I am very sorry for both of you. But, Jane, it is impossible. Spending so much time with him cannot make the situation easier. It can only lead to gossip."

Jane's cheeks became red, and her jaw trembled enough that Elizabeth saw it despite the distance between them. Her sister shook her head. "In another ten days, we return to Northampton. He and I will be separated again, perhaps forever this time. I will take every minute of happiness I can in his company before then."

Having said this, Jane had left the room, leaving Elizabeth to bury her face in a cushion and growl out her frustration and fear.

Elizabeth had not known what to do with herself. Remaining alone invited her anxiety to take root in her thoughts, so she had sought company. In doing so, she found herself in the withdrawing room, gazing at the Yule Log. That it still burned, though faintly, so long after it was lit was supposed to be good luck.

At least we dine out this evening. I know I could use the distraction of other company, and I imagine I am not the only one. I can only hope Jane and Mr Bingley show some sense and behave appropriately.

The door opened. Looking over her shoulder, Elizabeth saw Mr Darcy. Turning back to the fireplace, she pressed her eyes closed. *He will go away again, having no desire to spend time with me unnecessarily. Goodness, I am in a melancholic mood, and at Christmastide of all times.*

Her ears expected to hear the door closing; instead, footsteps tickled them and—somehow—she felt him draw closer. Even with her eyes closed, she knew when he was beside her. She felt her body sway with longing to lean into him, to feel his arms around her. Jane thought Elizabeth did not know what it was to love, know you were loved in return, and lose it, but oh, Elizabeth did!

"Miss Bennet." Mr Darcy's voice was as soft as a caress.

Elizabeth opened her eyes and straightened her shoulders. "Mr Darcy. You find me contemplating the history of the Yule Log. Do you suppose today is the day it will stop smouldering? I know Mr Ledbury wishes to save a splinter of it for next year, but I fear it will be difficult to preserve any of it while also burning enough coal to keep us from freezing." What was left of the log was pushed to one side of the large hearth.

"I-I do not know." After a moment, he said, "How are you today?"

Elizabeth lips twitched into a quick smile. "I am well, thank you. I hope you can say the same."

He made a noise of agreement.

Grasping for something to say, and hardly knowing what was going to come out of her mouth, Elizabeth said, "I am alone, as you see. I thought I might find your sister or Miss Ledbury, but I ended up here.

There is something quite peaceful about watching it." She nodded at the fire.

"Georgiana is writing to the colonel. I do not know where Miss Ledbury is."

Elizabeth shrugged. "Attending to some household matter or another, I suppose."

"I told Georgiana about your response during the game last night. She found it very amusing, as did I."

After glancing at him, she wished she had not. *I suppose it was Jane's talk of love and allowing herself to enjoy Mr Bingley's company while she has it. Even if Mr Darcy were inclined to flirt with me, I could not behave in such a way, but—* But she loved him, and it was difficult to be so close to him yet know there was a gulf as wide as the ocean between them.

"I am glad." She cleared her throat before continuing, "It is not my favourite game, but if I am going to play it, I cannot treat it with seriousness."

"I do not like it," admitted Mr Darcy. "I never have, and yesterday did nothing to change my opinion of it, your witty response notwithstanding."

Elizabeth chuckled. "What say we join forces to ensure we play nothing but casino or whist from now on?" *Oh dear God, did I truly just say that? Join forces? Just when I thought about* not *flirting with him! What must he think?*

When he remained silent, Elizabeth wanted to cover her face with her hands and run away. She could think of nothing to say to ease the awkwardness.

At length, he said, "I wou—"

The rest of his statement was destined to remain a mystery. They were interrupted by Mr Ledbury.

"Ah, Darcy, there you are. I wanted to ask you something. Miss Bennet, I hope you are having a pleasant day."

Turning to face him, Elizabeth said that she was. "Have you just come in? What is the weather like? I was thinking about going for a walk."

Mr Ledbury said, "It is cold but not too cold for you, I believe. The paths through the gardens on the west side of the house are clear." To Mr Darcy, he added, "Miss Bennet had not been here a day before I discovered that she likes nothing better than a walk."

"Very true. I shall leave you to your conversation." Elizabeth inclined her head to both gentlemen and began to walk towards the door. She had not gone ten steps before Mr Darcy's voice stopped her.

"If you would like company, I am sure Georgiana would go with you. She is in her bedchamber and should be finished her letter by now."

Elizabeth met his eye for an instant. "Then I shall ask her."

His eyes were warm, and his lips turned upwards at the corner in that slight way that, once upon a time, she believed showed he felt genuine pleasure. Today, walking up the broad staircase, she convinced herself that she had imagined both.

Sitting across and down the table from Elizabeth while they dined with neighbours of the Ledburys, Darcy tried to attend to his dinner companions. He had never met either of them before, and, while they seemed pleasant enough, he found his foot tapping restlessly, and only the strictest of control kept him from being out-and-out rude. Elizabeth showed none of his discomfort; she even seemed to be enjoying herself, chatting easily with those around her, laughing upon occasion.

I wish I had remained at Blackthorn with Georgiana. Because his sister was not out, he had excused her from accompanying them. *If I had, I would not have to spend the night dreaming I was sitting next to Elizabeth, that her bright eyes were looking on me with such mirth, that her smiles were all for me.* At least James Ledbury was at the other end of the table from her.

Darcy's thoughts drifted to when he and Elizabeth had been alone that afternoon. If only he had had more time! What he would have done with it, he knew not, but at the very least, he would have talked to her more, added to his bank of remembrances of the only woman he would ever truly love. He wondered if reliving them over and over in the coming years would dampen their lustre, make them seem less special, if, with repetition, they would become banal.

It will never happen. She will always be the one lady with whom I could have found happiness. How could imagining her smiles when she looked at me in Derbyshire, or her laugh and teasing, ever fail to move me? Even today, the look of pleasure she gave me when I suggested she ask Georgiana to walk with her. Such a little thing, but I swear it meant something to her. Yet, in truth, I was thinking of myself, that I like the idea of them spending time together, almost as if they were the sisters I so wanted them to be.

Knowing Elizabeth was with Georgiana also meant that she would not be alone with James Ledbury. Even though he had not been at Blackthorn Manor a week, he had seen Elizabeth and James Ledbury walking together several times before breakfast. Once, Darcy had been on the point of flying down the stairs to join her because she appeared to be alone. Before he could turn away from the window of his bedchamber, though, James Ledbury had approached her, and the two of them had walked on together.

After dinner, there were cards and music, all of which kept him separated from Elizabeth. He was not sorry to see the evening end.

There was rather a shuffle when those of them bound for Blackthorn Manor walked out to the carriages. Darcy's chief wish was to keep Bingley away from Mrs Ridley. They had not sat together at dinner, but in the withdrawing room, Darcy had too often seen them together, first at cards, and then during the music. He did not want Elizabeth distressed by his friend's poor decisions. *Has she not been already? No, that was my fault. If I had told Bingley the entire story immediately instead of only hinting he return to Hertfordshire— But even by April, less than five months after he had last seen Jane Bennet—towards whom he had felt such a passion—it meant nothing to him that she might care for him. Perhaps I ought to have dragged him back to Netherfield. Clearly, all it takes to reignite his feelings is seeing her again.*

The result of what must have looked like a ridiculous commotion while eight adults decided who would go in which carriage was that Darcy succeeded in ensuring Bingley was with him and, to his delight, so were Elizabeth and Miss Ledbury.

Darcy held out his hand to help Elizabeth into the carriage, but she said, "Oh," and looked down at the ground as though she had dropped something. The consequence was that Miss Ledbury entered the carriage first.

Elizabeth offered him a brief smile as she held up a handkerchief. "Silly me." She rested her hand lightly in his as she stepped up.

Darcy elbowed Bingley, who was watching the other carriage pull away. When Bingley looked at him, he gestured that he wanted Bingley to go ahead of him. *This way he will be opposite Miss Ledbury, and I shall be able to gaze at Elizabeth—as much as the light permits—perhaps even talk to her.*

Two or three minutes into the drive, Darcy began to suspect that Elizabeth was as pleased with the arrangements as he was—at least as far as Bingley was concerned. He was certain he caught a smile of satisfaction on her face as she looked at their companions, and she did what she could to encourage conversation between Bingley and Miss Ledbury.

"Mr Bingley," she said, "did you know that Miss Ledbury is an accomplished painter? Have you seen any of her works? You would find them delightful." Another time, she mentioned Scarborough, saying that she had never been, but Miss Ledbury had, and she also introduced the topic of the Season and her certainty that they must have many acquaintances in common. It meant that, apart from Elizabeth's occasional statements to direct the conversation, the voices that were most heard were those of Miss Ledbury—seemingly pleased for any opportunity to talk and flirt with Bingley—and Bingley.

Oh, she is clever, he thought. *What a good opportunity to push those two together.*

Back at Blackthorn Manor, Darcy jumped out of the carriage so that he, not a servant, would have the pleasure of helping Elizabeth down. Bingley assisted Miss Ledbury, the pair still chatting about balls. Elizabeth regarded them, her eyes sparkling and smile broad. In a moment, she turned to him.

"Thank you, Mr Darcy. I believe I will retire immediately, so I shall also bid you good night."

Darcy bowed and wished he could take her hand, perhaps even kiss it. "Good night, Miss Bennet."

Chapter Seven

The next morning, Darcy did not see Elizabeth until he walked into the breakfast parlour. He frowned in disapproval when he saw Mrs Ridley and Bingley talking to each other and forced his features into a happier expression. He thought he caught a glimpse of Elizabeth watching them from across the table.

After the usual greetings, Elizabeth said, "We are a small party this morning, as you see. Mr Ledbury, his brother, and Thomas have gone to visit some old servants."

"I was a child, not more than five or six, when they retired from service, else *I* would have gone," Miss Ledbury said, an edge to her voice. "My brothers and cousin chose to ride, and I did not think it wise for me to attempt it in this cold. This sort of attention means so much to those people. Do you not agree, Mr Bingley?"

Bingley looked away from Mrs Ridley, his head jerking from person to person. "Eh? Oh, yes. Yes, of course."

Darcy felt like slapping him.

"So," Elizabeth said, speaking a little louder than necessary, "what shall we do this morning? Does anyone have anything particular in mind?"

When that topic failed to elicit much discussion, Darcy spoke about the previous evening. Elizabeth jumped into the subject with enthusiasm, and it was enough to stop Bingley and Mrs Ridley from ignoring the rest of them.

In the end, it was a busy day. Elizabeth and the other ladies attended a luncheon, and that evening, the whole party dined with friends of the Ledburys and joined them at a concert. Elizabeth was glad of the activity. She sensed a growing tension in the air amongst those at Blackthorn, though she knew it might just be between her sister and herself. Jane had said little more than was necessary to her since their conversation. She understood that her sister was vexed with her, but still felt she had been correct to caution Jane about her behaviour towards Mr Bingley. Elizabeth continued to do what she could to keep the pair apart and to encourage Mr Bingley to seek Miss Ledbury's company or that of the gentlemen. It appeared to be working, in part because—and she might be mistaken—Mr Darcy seemed to want to keep his friend separated from Jane as much as she did.

The next day, a week after Mr Bingley and the Darcys' arrival, began quietly, with everyone going off to pursue their individual activities after breakfast. Elizabeth had asked Jane what she was going to do, and Jane had shrugged; Elizabeth could only hope it did not involve a certain gentleman. She knew Mr and Miss Darcy were together and took the opportunity to finish a new book by Shelley she had borrowed from Mr Ledbury. He had encouraged her to treat the library as her own during her stay, and she had taken him at his word. As soon as she finished the last word, she left the comfort of the sitting room to return the volume and find a new one to read.

Her hand was still on the doorknob when she froze. Inside the library, by the window, stood Edward Ledbury and her brother-in-law. They were close together, Mr Ledbury's hand on Thomas's arm.

Thomas said, "I cannot believe it of her."

"Thomas—"

Mr Ledbury got no further. Elizabeth, her heart racing because she knew they must be speaking of Jane, had stepped backwards, intending to flee, but they caught sight of her.

"I beg your pardon." She held up the book. "I-I will return later."

The men spoke at the same time, Thomas saying her name, and Mr Ledbury encouraging her to stay, adding, "I must see to something."

Elizabeth stood to the side to give him room to pass through the doorway. Her mouth was dry, and she ran her tongue along her teeth, hoping it would help.

"Close the door, Lizzy. I want to have a word with you."

Elizabeth clutched the book to her chest and pulled her shawl more tightly around her body, telling herself it was just because she was cold. She would not meet his eye. "Oh?"

"About Jane."

Thomas began to pace, which only increased Elizabeth's desire to run away. Anger burned her insides—anger at Jane, Mr Bingley, and even Thomas for broaching the topic with her instead of his wife.

Thomas said, "When I met Mr Bingley previously, I recall him talking about an estate he had let and a lady he admired." He faced Elizabeth, who found herself swallowing heavily. "Was it Jane?"

How she wished she could say anything other than what she must; but lying would help none of them. "Yes. It was a long time ago. Until last week, they had not seen each other for more than two years."

He nodded his head three or four times and resumed his slow perusal of the room. "I wonder if marriage is what she expected it to be. If *I* am what she expected me to be. I love Jane, and I want her happiness. I believe we can be happy together, if that is what she wants. If I did not, I would not have pursued her."

I will not have this conversation with him. I will not interfere in their marriage. "I do not know what you wish me to say."

Elizabeth watched as Thomas, whose back was to her, shrugged. He was at the opposite end of the room when he turned to her. "Something reassuring, I suppose."

"You ought to direct your questions about her feelings to her."

"You and she are so close..."

"That does not mean I hold all of her secrets or that I understand her feelings." *Especially when they are about you and Mr Bingley.* "I cannot help you with this. If you will excuse me, Thomas."

With that, she returned to her bedchamber as quickly as possible, not to leave it until she was expected below stairs in a couple of hours.

All that evening—from the moment she joined the others in the withdrawing room, through dinner, and the hours afterwards—Elizabeth wanted nothing more than to be alone. Their party was enlarged by seven guests. While they awaited their arrival, Mr Ledbury commented on how busy they were.

"I spend very little time at Blackthorn Manor. The two or three months I am here, I feel it is incumbent on me to see as many neighbours as possible. And it is Yuletide; everyone expects a great deal of rushing around."

Miss Ledbury said, "You make yourself sound quite ancient, Edward! You are only thirty."

He grumbled, "Give it ten years and see if you are not as bored with it as I am."

Their brother laughed. "Ah, siblings. Delightful, are they not? I am afraid they are too different to ever understand each other. I, on the other hand, am a happy medium; I neither crave nor detest society. Do you not find me the most admirable Ledbury, Miss Bennet?"

Elizabeth made some vague reply.

The benefit of their being sixteen was that there were more distractions. Elizabeth observed Thomas watching Jane—and occasionally felt his gaze upon herself, as though she, too, had drawn his displeasure. She continued to do what she could to keep Jane away from Mr Bingley and encourage him to spend time with Miss Ledbury; avoid James Ledbury; and, resist the urge to devote herself to Mr Darcy, who, she was certain, spent too much time watching her. She was frustrated, annoyed, tired, and confused, and the result was a headache. While most of the party played cards, she sat with Miss Darcy, trying to participate in a conversation about music. After a quarter of an hour, Miss Darcy asked if she was well.

"E-excuse me for being so forward, but if you are not, I would not want you to feel you must continue to talk to me when you would rather be quiet."

Elizabeth smiled at her and patted her hand. "Thank you. I confess that I have a headache, and it is making me very tired."

"I am sorry to hear that," a deep voice behind her said.

It was Mr Darcy. She wanted to close her eyes and rest her head on his chest, feel his arms around her, perhaps let out a sob or two. She had noticed him distracting Mr Bingley several times when his attention appeared to be turning to Jane, and she wanted to thank him for it.

"Why do you not retire, Miss Bennet? You can slip away, and, if anyone asks, I will explain," he said. "I do not presume that Georgiana will enjoy my conversation as much as she does your—"

"Brother." Miss Darcy's cheeks flushed.

Elizabeth squeezed her hand. "I had no notion your brother could make such jokes. My sisters and I tease each other mercilessly. I suppose they would say it was I who teased them and not the other way around." She chuckled and was pleased when it seemed her words had eased the girl's embarrassment.

"Come, Miss Bennet," Mr Darcy said, holding out a hand to help her rise; she took it and stood. "I shall take your place beside Georgiana, and you can retire. Perhaps you would like Mrs Ridley to accompany you?"

Elizabeth met his eye and was certain she saw a recognition that she would ask Jane for assistance—not because she needed it, but as an excuse to have Jane leave the company, at least temporarily. Realising her hand was still in his, she quickly retracted it. "I shall ask her." To Miss Darcy, she added, "I hope we can resume our conversation tomorrow. Good night."

She went to Jane, who was sitting beside Thomas, who was speaking to James Ledbury. Elizabeth asked that she accompany her upstairs. Jane was reluctant to leave.

"Please, Jane, I have a terrible headache."

Jane's eyes flickered to where Mr Bingley sat beside Miss Ledbury at a card table; the pair were chatting and laughing. "Of course, Lizzy. I am not needed here."

Upstairs, Jane dutifully helped Elizabeth prepare for bed, sending the maid for peppermint oil with which to massage Elizabeth's temples. Elizabeth was sitting with her eyes closed, half-asleep, as Jane tended to her, when she heard Jane's soft voice.

"I have seen what you are doing with Mr Bingley, attempting to keep us apart. I do not blame you, Lizzy."

The tone of her voice matched her words, and Elizabeth grasped one of her sister's hands and kissed it. "I pray for you, Jane, and that you will find happiness with Thomas."

Jane gave a small laugh that was almost pitiable. "He asked me about Mr Bingley, and I had to tell him the truth. We argued. He says he forgives me for not telling him immediately. I never did confess that there had been another man I admired. He is still angry, or perhaps he is simply hurt."

"He will get past it." Elizabeth spoke with more assurance than she was currently able to feel. She hoped now that Thomas knew about Jane's former connexion to Mr Bingley, and they had talked about it, Jane would keep her distance from their old neighbour. Currently, she did not feel confident, which might be because of her poor health.

Jane sighed. "I hope so, and I hope I will have a child soon. That would make a difference, I believe. You know how much I have always longed to be a mother."

Elizabeth opened her eyes to a narrow slit—it was all she could manage—and said, "It has only been three months. Uncle and Aunt Gardiner did not have a child until they were married two years. Be patient, and I am sure you will have a baby. Thomas must surely want children too."

Jane nodded and offered her a faint smile as she resumed her efforts to reduce Elizabeth's headache. "He says he does, and he often speaks about what he will do with our children, where he wants to take them or what he wants to teach them. You are right, we have not been married long, and, although I find being his wife is not quite what I expected, I will…accustom myself to it. It is my duty."

Elizabeth embraced her sister, and the two of them clung to each other for a long moment before Jane insisted Elizabeth lie down. She fell asleep to the gentle sound of Jane humming a soothing tune.

Before breakfast the following day, Darcy was pleased to secure a moment alone with Elizabeth. He knew he should not seek such encounters, but the more time he spent in the same house with her, the less he could control his desire to be near her and have her attention devoted to him, even if it was just for a minute here and there.

He followed her into the library and found her standing by the window, the bright sunshine making it seem like she glowed. *A beacon, calling me to her, inexorably.* She heard him enter the room and watched as he walked towards her.

"Mr Darcy." She closed the book she was holding and let the hand which held the slim volume fall to her side.

He stopped a few feet away from her and thought how lovely she looked. She wore a long-sleeved, violet-and-cream-coloured gown and looked somehow warm and comfortable. "Are you feeling better this morning?"

"I am." She lifted her chin a little and kept her eyes on his almost as if she dared him to suggest she was unwell. *Or as though she finds talking to me difficult, and she is resolved not to show it.*

Even with that thought in mind, he could not simply wish her a good day and walk away, not so soon. "I…" He resisted the urge to lick his lips or fidget. "You have sometimes seemed…"

Her delicate eyebrows arched. "Please, speak plainly, Mr Darcy."

He dipped his chin in a single nod. "I believe you have noticed, as I have, that Bingley and your sister enjoy each other's company. I have spoken to him about it and am doing what I can to redirect his attention to Miss Ledbury. I suspect you are attempting to do the same."

Her shoulders seemed to relax, and she nodded.

"Good. Good. I hope that with the two of us working towards the same end, we will…"

"Be successful?" she offered when he could not find the words. "Whatever success looks like in such a case."

Confronted with her lovely face and bewitching eyes, he found himself babbling in a most unbecoming fashion. "Indeed. I think Bingley and Miss Ledbury are very well suited, and she would be an eligible match for him. I think even his sisters would approve. I do not know that anything will come of it, but at the very least, Bingley should take this opportunity to determine if he likes her rather than, well, flirting with your sister. He chose not to pursue her last year, and has no right to act towards her as anything other than an indifferent acquaintance now."

"What?"

Her clipped tone and round eyes made him stop and reflect on what he had said. *Which, it appears, was more than I had intended.*

"Mr Darcy, please explain yourself."

Darcy looked out of the window for a moment before telling her that he had twice hinted to Bingley that he should return to Hertfordshire—in the spring of 1812 and again that summer, at which time he had confessed everything to his friend. Both times, Bingley had shown no particular interest in renewing his acquaintance with the then Jane Bennet.

"Do you mean to say—? Mr Bingley's staying away had nothing to do with…with what I told you the last time we met in Lambton?"

There was a moment of silence before he said, "No."

"You hesitate?"

"It did not. He did not learn about her marriage until some time later, so no."

"You know that Lydia is married?"

Darcy nodded.

She furrowed her brow and tilted her head as she regarded him before saying, "Wickham wrote to my father not two weeks after they left Brighton, asking his permission. He said they had intended to go to Scotland, but then they decided to marry in town. He claimed his debts were exaggerated, he was able to pay them off, and, somehow, had enough to buy a commission in the regulars and marry a lady with no dowry. I assumed he had come by the money in a less-than respectable fashion."

He swallowed heavily and struggled to keep his voice steady. "I hope she is well."

Elizabeth scoffed. "Married to such a man? We do not write, but from what Jane and my mother say, she is satisfied."

"You do not sound convinced." Why, oh why, did they have to talk about the Wickhams?

"I am sure she is, but I doubt whether she deserves to be, or that her happiness will last for long. I am glad they married. It preserved Lydia's reputation and that of my sisters and myself, but I do not forget the truth. I apologise for burdening you with it as I did that morning. If you will excuse me, Mr Darcy."

With that, she practically ran from the room, leaving him standing alone and feeling bereft.

Chapter Eight

LATER THAT DAY, DARCY AGAIN FOUND HIMSELF IN THE library, this time with Bingley and James Ledbury. The ladies were in the withdrawing room; he did not know where Mr Ridley or Ledbury were. His attention wandered away from the conversation—something about James Ledbury's life as a barrister in Leicester—to his earlier one with Elizabeth. He was not sure what to make of it.

It did not sound like she blames me for either Bingley's failure to return to Netherfield or her younger sister's marriage, yet how could she not? But if she does not, then why— It did no good to go down that road, and he stopped himself before he went any further.

Regarding Bingley, now talking about growing up in Scarborough, he thought, *Mrs Ridley flirting with Bingley is surprising. Surely if she was happy with Ridley, she would not. I truly did not believe she cared for Bingley. As much as I allowed my—what did Elizabeth call it?—selfish disdain for others to twist my view of the Bennets, it was the conviction of Jane Bennet's indifference which most influenced my argument against her.*

By the time Elizabeth had assured him he was mistaken, it had been too late. Did that not prove that Bingley's attachment was never serious? Darcy compared himself to Bingley. Despite all the time he had been separated from Elizabeth, his love for her had never wavered, even as he told himself again and again that it was hopeless, and he needed to conquer it and forget what the future might have been.

Bingley leapt to his feet. "I must find Miss Ledbury and Miss Darcy. I promised them they could show me the gallery and try to teach me something about art. I fear it is a hopeless case—and so I have told them—but they insisted!"

He grinned and practically skipped out of the room. Darcy rolled his eyes and hoped James Ledbury had not seen.

"What can you tell me about him?" James Ledbury nodded to the door to show he meant Bingley. "I do not know him well, but as an older brother, I think I should."

Darcy regarded him as he took a drink from his wine glass. "He and Miss Ledbury hardly know each other. If something were to develop in that direction, you need have no concerns."

The other man cocked an eyebrow. "No…wandering eye, shall we say? I had wondered."

Bingley, you bloody idiot! And why, might I ask, am I *to answer for his behaviour?* He swallowed his bitter thoughts. "They are nothing but old friends who were surprised to see each other again after so long. They were never more than that. Mr Bennet's estate was the nearest neighbour to the one Bingley leased. We saw the Bennets frequently during the two months we were there."

Apparently, his explanation was not entirely satisfactory. James Ledbury pursed his lips and observed him for a moment before saying, "But Miss Bennet was not such good friends with him? I assume that is the case since neither she nor Mr Bingley single out the other."

If James Ledbury thought he would get Darcy to confess to anything he did not wish to reveal, he was mistaken. "The difference was with his sisters. They and Mrs Ridley became close, but they and Miss Bennet did not."

James Ledbury made a noise that seemed to denote understanding. He then said, "Miss Bennet is a remarkable young woman. I am very glad she joined the Ridleys in coming to Blackthorn."

It was all Darcy could do to not tell the man to keep his distance from her, that she was too good for him.

James Ledbury continued, "I imagine she would make someone a fine wife. Not me, I regret to say. Frankly, I believe she deserves better than I can offer her."

They stared at each other for a minute. Darcy then lifted his glass in a silent toast and decided that perhaps James Ledbury was not such a bad fellow after all.

On New Year's Eve, the Ledburys' vicar, his wife, and several other couples came to dinner. Throughout the meal and afterwards, Elizabeth could not look at Mr Darcy. She was so confused after their last conversation. He had confessed the truth to Mr Bingley! From what he had said, he had done so soon after their dreadful argument in Kent, even if he did not tell Mr Bingley about Jane being in town that winter until later.

He believed me and tried to correct his errors so far back as that. I know he had changed by the time we met in Derbyshire, but I did not realise he so soon gave credit to anything I said. I would not blame him had he not. I treated him so terribly—misjudged and abused him. How could it not raise him in her estimation even further? *I have even more reason to regret him now. Oh Lydia! Would you even care if you knew what your foolishness cost me?*

She could not blame Lydia alone; she ought to have known better, but their parents had spoilt her and failed to correct her behaviour. Elizabeth had warned her father that he should not allow Lydia to go to Brighton with Colonel and Mrs Forster, yet he had ignored her.

And we all bear the cost—Lydia most especially, doomed to life with such a man.

When the gentlemen joined the ladies in the withdrawing room, they decided to play games. Miss Darcy was not the only young person in attendance—the vicar's children, aged seventeen and eighteen were also there, which Elizabeth thought made it more pleasant for Miss Darcy. They played a rather rousing game of move-all. It led to a great deal of laughter, most of it brought on by the three Ledburys who excelled at cheating at it. Mr Ledbury admitted that it had been a favourite of theirs when they were children, and they developed a great deal of knowledge of the tricks to use to ensure victory. Elizabeth was breathless and her side ached by the time they decided they had had enough. The young people, joined by Miss Ledbury, her brother James, and Mr Bingley sat down to a game of commerce, while the others talked and otherwise amused themselves. Elizabeth remained close to Jane, not to keep her from Mr Bingley, but because her mood seemed subdued, especially each time she heard Mr Bingley's tenor voice showing how much fun he was having. Thomas appeared to be ignoring Jane, but without being overly obvious about it. Knowing about their argument, she supposed he was still angry.

Punishing her in such a way is not *the best idea,* Elizabeth reflected. *It might only make her like Mr Bingley more.*

The company left in time to arrive at their homes before midnight. At Blackthorn Manor, the family, their guests, and several servants gathered to usher out the old year and let the new one in. Elizabeth stood opposite Mr Darcy in the large circle they formed, and felt his eyes on her; it made her cheeks warm. She felt embarrassed, she might even say shy, which was unusual for her. Once the clock had chimed midnight,

Elizabeth turned to Miss Darcy, at her right, embraced her, and wished her the best of good luck for the year ahead.

Miss Darcy said, “I hope…I hope you find a great deal of happiness.”

Elizabeth smiled at her, then at Mr Darcy, who had come to stand beside his sister. As he bent to kiss Miss Darcy’s cheek, Elizabeth turned to Jane, who had approached, and hugged her tightly.

Elizabeth whispered, “I pray that eighteen-fourteen will be a wonderful year for you, my dearest sister. You know I shall always do whatever I can to ensure it is.”

“And I you, Lizzy.”

Thomas joined them, kissing first Jane’s, then Elizabeth’s cheeks. “Well ladies, what do you think this year will bring us? Perhaps a husband for Lizzy?”

His chuckle told her that he was teasing, but with Mr Darcy standing behind her, she wished he had held his tongue. She almost said, ‘Or a baby for you and Jane,’ but stopped herself in time. She suspected it would wound her sister.

Instead, she said, “I will settle for all of us, and the rest of our family, remaining healthy.”

The next quarter of an hour was spent wishing everyone a happy new year. Miss Ledbury had her arm linked with Mr Bingley’s, by whom she had stood at the turning of the years. Elizabeth thought it was bold of her, but her brothers were there to ensure propriety, and Mr Bingley was capable of finding a polite way to extricate himself if he wished. Her only regret was that it pained Jane; her delight was that it was Mr Bingley and not Mr Darcy.

As she lay in bed in the dark of her bedroom an hour later, Elizabeth wondered what the year would be like and where she would be to celebrate the end of it. Into the night, she murmured, “I have always been told that what happens on the first day of the year foretells what it will bring. Therefore, I will do one thing I know will bring me contentment; I shall write to Aunt Gardiner tomorrow and ask to stay with them. If I am fortunate, I shall be installed at Gracechurch Street by the end of the month, with no fixed date to return to Longbourn.”

Mrs Bennet insisted on talking about her ‘dear Mrs Wickham’ and lamenting how far away she was settled. Saying goodbye to Mr Darcy would be difficult enough. Being constantly reminded of the sister whose actions had forever separated them would make it worse.

There was an almost languid air in the house the next day, except for Miss Ledbury, who, to Elizabeth, seemed almost frenetic. After breakfast, as everyone else wandered off to quiet activities such as reading or writing letters, Miss Ledbury begged Elizabeth's assistance.

"The ball is just a few days away, and there is so much to do!" Miss Ledbury said. "I wish Edward did not insist on hosting so many parties! He does not have to arrange them, and has no idea how much effort they require. You do not mind, do you, Miss Bennet? If you are tired or...?" She regarded Elizabeth with a questioning yet hopeful look.

"I do not mind at all. I would be happy to help."

Miss Ledbury sighed. "Oh, thank you. Let us start with the invitations."

Early in Elizabeth's stay at Blackthorn, she had assisted Miss Ledbury with preparing the elegant invitations she had sent out for the Twelfth Night ball. A steady number of replies had been received, and Elizabeth discovered that Miss Ledbury had ignored them in favour of enjoying her guests, which she interpreted as 'flirting with either Mr Darcy or Mr Bingley'. Now, they recorded the responses to have an estimate of how many people would attend. After that, Miss Ledbury wanted her opinion on the menu for the supper and decorations for the rooms.

"I do not know why I am so anxious about it," Miss Ledbury admitted. "I am not accustomed to making arrangements such as this, it is true, but I have assisted others often enough that I know I am not forgetting anything vital. I want it to be perfect."

"I am certain it will be lovely." Elizabeth continued recording the changes they had decided to make to the supper.

Miss Ledbury was quiet for a moment, and when Elizabeth glanced at her, she discovered that her hostess appeared wistful. Elizabeth waited until she shook her head and recalled herself to the conversation.

"I beg your pardon, Miss Bennet. I wandered away from you." She picked up a pencil and began to tap it against the edge of the walnut table at which they sat. "I was thinking about gentlemen. You know what I hope; I would like to be married. Edward would like me to find a husband, although at times I think it very unfair. He is ten years older than I am, and James six, and neither of them feel they must be married soon."

"It is different for ladies," agreed Elizabeth. "I have never heard anyone tell a gentleman that he is approaching the years of danger or that he will soon be on the shelf."

Miss Ledbury gave Elizabeth's hand a quick squeeze. "I am not even that old, but I have had two Seasons already, and I know that the longer it takes, the less likely it is that I will attract a gentleman I would be happy to marry. The idea of having to settle for whomever will have me is…"

"Disagreeable." Elizabeth thought of her friend Charlotte, who had accepted the foolish Mr Collins in order to gain security and avoid being a burden on her parents and brothers. Would that be her fate in the end?

Miss Ledbury nodded. "The thing is…I quite like Mr Bingley." Her cheeks coloured, and she looked at her lap.

Elizabeth returned the pen to its holder and regarded her companion. A part of her was afraid she knew what Miss Ledbury wanted to ask, and she felt sick to her stomach. "Mr Bingley has always struck me as an amiable gentleman. He is very handsome, too, which I find is an essential quality in a man." She kept her tone light-hearted, hoping to avoid awkward questions.

Miss Ledbury looked at her and nibbled her lip before asking, "I wonder if his heart is as free as it should be. You understand what I am asking. I would rather not, but I must know."

Repressing the urge to sigh, Elizabeth considered her options. She could pretend that she had no idea what Miss Ledbury meant or be offended at what she was suggesting. *Or I could respond in as delicate a manner as possible and in a way that does not betray Jane. If I were in Miss Ledbury's position, I, too, would want to know the truth. How I wish I understood what Mr Darcy thinks and feels! But it might also add to my sorrow, so perhaps it is better to remain ignorant.*

Aloud she said, "I know of no other attachment, but, as you may recall, I had not seen him in sixteen months before he and the Darcys arrived. Perhaps one of your brothers might have a word with him?"

Miss Ledbury was again nibbling her lip; she nodded and seemed to contemplate Elizabeth's suggestion. "I shall ask James. Edward is not always…discreet."

"What is next?" Elizabeth asked, returning them to their work. The two of them kept at it until luncheon, when they joined the others.

Chapter Nine

THE BEST PART OF NEW YEAR'S DAY WAS GOING ICE SKATING. There was a stretch of stream on Ledbury's estate that was shallow enough that it was frozen solid. When he suggested the scheme as they ate luncheon, Darcy's eyes had immediately sought Elizabeth. With the long, cold Derbyshire winters, he and Georgiana often went skating or sleigh riding, as they had done the previous week, and he wondered if Elizabeth enjoyed such activities. It seemed to him that she would; she always appeared to have an abundance of energy and liked to be outside. Sure enough, her voice was one of the first to agree.

"I shall not go," Miss Ledbury said. "My brothers will tell you how clumsy I am when I skate."

"Oh, but you must!" Bingley insisted.

Bingley spent a minute trying to convince her, but she insisted she would remain behind, attend to several household matters, then walk down to watch them. Darcy saw that his friend was torn between staying with the lady and his desire to participate in the activity. That was fair enough, and Darcy was glad that Bingley had learnt to appreciate Miss Ledbury's company. What he did not like was seeing Bingley glance towards Mrs Ridley, especially after Mr Ridley said that he, too, would not go.

"I have letters I must write today. I ought to have done it already," he said.

"Must you?" Mrs Ridley asked.

He nodded. "I will walk down later if you are not back before I am finished. You go on and enjoy yourself, my dear. Make sure Lizzy does not do anything too daring, such as challenge Ledbury or James to a race. I warn you, Lizzy, they are both excellent ice skaters."

Elizabeth laughed and promised that she would behave. "I shall amuse myself and not risk being humiliated by those who must naturally be better at the sport than I am, if only because they are both so much larger than I am!"

Those who were going ice skating were soon changed into their warmest clothes, and, as a group, they walked down to the stream. The crunch of boots hitting the snowy path was accompanied by happy chatter. A clearing in the trees and brush that lined the stream gave them ready access to the frozen water. Willow branches hung low, and the sun glinted off the ice that weighed them down. Nearby logs, the snow brushed off them, provided places to sit and kept the scene charming and picturesque.

Darcy derived a great deal of pleasure from watching Elizabeth. She laughed, her eyes sparkled, and her cheeks were rosy. At first, she stayed beside her sister, but soon after Ledbury joined them, she knelt down, as if adjusting the laces on her skates, and waved at them to go on without her. Darcy was with James Ledbury and Georgiana.

"It looks like Miss Bennet might require assistance. I shall—" James Ledbury said, but he was too late; Georgiana had already dropped Darcy's arm to go to Elizabeth. Darcy felt his lips twitch upwards in satisfaction. Regardless of the man's words the other day—that he did not see Elizabeth as a wife for him—Darcy still preferred to keep the two apart.

For the next while, the seven of them glided along the ice, often coming together and breaking into groups. Darcy enjoyed the fresh, crisp air and exercise; it left him feeling invigorated. He stopped and stood by the side to watch Elizabeth and Georgiana. Elizabeth was a very good ice skater. She twirled around with Georgiana, their hands clasped, both of them laughing, sending puffs of steam up into the cold air.

Glancing at the others, he realised he missed an important change in pairings, as had Elizabeth. Bingley was with Mrs Ridley, her arm looped through his and their heads bent together. Mumbling something rude enough that he was glad no one heard him, he pushed away from the tree he had been leaning against and skated to them. His motion must have caught Elizabeth's attention, because no sooner had he caught up with Bingley and Mrs Ridley then she and Georgiana were there.

"Join us, Jane," Elizabeth cried. "Miss Darcy needs our advice about her gown for the ball."

She did not give her sister a chance to decline; she took her hand

and pulled her away. At the same time, Darcy nudged Bingley in a new direction. Ledbury was with them a moment later, his brother lagging behind him. James Ledbury met Darcy's eye, glanced at Bingley, and cocked an eyebrow. Having no answers for him, Darcy ignored the unspoken question.

Neither Miss Ledbury nor Mr Ridley appeared before they decided to return to the warmth of the withdrawing room. Elizabeth and Mrs Ridley walked just ahead of Darcy and Georgiana, the path admitting no more than two people. Elizabeth spoke almost the whole way to the house, though in a tone too low for him to hear. Mrs Ridley listened and nodded but said little if anything at all.

There, they were greeted with hot beverages and tarts and cakes. Elizabeth sat with Mr and Mrs Ridley on a sofa. She must have said five or ten words for each one either of the Ridleys did, and Darcy wondered if Mr Ridley had—at last—noticed his wife's preference for another man.

The sooner Bingley and Mrs Ridley are separated, the better, and yet... The end of the house party would bring about another separation, one he both dreaded and anticipated so that he could, once again, try to find a way to live his life without Elizabeth Bennet in it.

The next day passed easily. Darcy was with the gentlemen most of the day, while the ladies amused themselves. Georgiana told him that she, Mrs Ridley, and Elizabeth were helping with arrangements for the Twelfth Night ball, which included a great deal of discussion about what they would wear. Georgiana found it all very exciting. Although she was not out, they had agreed that she would attend but not dance, unless it was with him or Bingley.

After spending some time outdoors after breakfast, they found indoor occupations, from billiards to discussions of estate management and politics, local and national. Throughout it all, Darcy made sure that Bingley remained with them and did not find an excuse to join the ladies. Darcy also felt a pull in that direction. His excuse was a desire to see that Georgiana was well, but she was with Elizabeth, who would ensure Georgiana's well-being and comfort. Darcy's secret wish was to spend as much time with Elizabeth as possible; he had long since abandoned his initial plan to avoid her. The day of their departure was looming over his head like an anvil, and, at moments, he was not sure how he would endure having to say goodbye to her. He picked at every word she said to him, analysed each look searching for clues that her opinion of him had changed enough to give him hope. At times, he was certain he saw it, but he knew it was just a matter of him seeing what he wanted.

Late in the afternoon, James Ledbury excused himself, saying he had work to do. "I am back to Leicester in a few days, but the law does not wait. If I do not attend to some of this now, I shall be working fourteen-hour days for a fortnight, which, I assure you, is not nearly as much fun as it sounds!"

Ledbury and Mr Ridley went off to do something too; Darcy did not catch what Ledbury said and did not think it important. He had not realised how close the two men were. *But why not? After all, do I not count Fitzwilliam as my closest friend?* He and Colonel Fitzwilliam had been the best of friends since they were children.

Bingley suggested they play backgammon, and Darcy agreed.

"I played it with my father all the time," Bingley said. "It reminds me of him. Caroline used to play with me, until she decided it was not fashionable enough."

When Bingley laughed, Darcy was not sure why, but if it was at his sister's pretensions, he was in full accord.

"My grandfather taught me," Darcy said. "How long do the Hursts and Miss Bingley remain in the country?"

Bingley shrugged. "I imagine they will be in town by the middle of January. You know Caroline does not like to miss a day of London society. She is determined that this is the year she will find a husband." Bingley glanced at him and laughed again. "Do not fret, Darcy; she has given up hope that you will decide she is the perfect bride for you."

Darcy rolled his eyes.

Bingley chattered on. "I will never understand why young ladies are always so anxious about getting married. Oh, I know what you will say, so save your breath. Expectations, *et cetera*. They do not see that they make themselves less attractive by showing their desperation to the world. I suppose it does not help when they have parents or brothers who are rushing them to the altar. I never did that with my sisters. I would be very happy to see Caroline married, but I am not going to demand she accepts whichever man she can catch just to have her settled. It seems cruel. I know you would never treat Miss Darcy that way."

"I would not." If anything, he would discourage Georgiana from marrying unless she found a man she truly loved, who loved and valued her in return.

They played in silence for a few minutes, the only sound that of one or the other of them sipping their drink or the draughts hitting the board.

"Ledbury—the younger one—asked me about his sister," Bingley said. "I was not really sure what to say. Miss Ledbury is lovely. I suppose one could say she is everything a young lady ought to be. What do you think of her, Darcy?"

"She is very nice and would make the right man a fine wife."

Bingley contorted his features in a way that told Darcy he was thinking this over. A moment later, he sat back in his chair, the game forgotten. "Do you know, I would have thought it could be me. Perhaps she is. She is just the sort of girl I like. Lively, pretty, not so clever that I risk feeling stupid next to her. I leave those ladies to you." He chuckled. "You will not be surprised when I say that seeing Mrs Ridley again has, well, confused me."

Addled your wits, you mean. Darcy made a noise that could be taken as agreement or something less firm.

"I mean to say, I know you were right the other day. I was certain whatever I felt for her when we were in Hertfordshire was over. If I thought otherwise, I would have returned that spring or summer. A part of me thinks I was wrong not to."

"It is too late—" Darcy stopped speaking when Bingley nodded and waved a hand, brushing away the reminder.

"I know, I know. Any regrets I have should be kept to myself." He pulled his eyebrows together, making the tips of them stand up like a row of little spikes on his forehead. "I am not even convinced that I *do* regret her."

"Bingley, if you ever loved her—*genuinely* loved her—you would have returned, and you would not be questioning if you regretted not doing so. You find her attractive. It is understandable; she is a beautiful woman and has a sweet temper. But I do not believe your feelings have ever extended beyond that." *At least, I do not any longer—not since I first told you I was mistaken about her sentiments towards you.*

Bingley slowly nodded, picked up his glass of apricot wine—which Darcy found disgustingly sweet—and drained it. "I enjoy her company."

Darcy suppressed an urge to box Bingley's ears. "Be that as it may, do yourself, and especially Mrs Ridley, a favour and keep your distance. Do not go walking with her, do not sit next to her in the withdrawing room, do not ask her to dance at the ball. Treat her as the old acquaintance she is and as one who is married. As for Miss Ledbury, unless you are resolved against her, there is no harm in getting to know her better—as long as you are cautious with your behaviour so that you do not raise her or her brothers' expectations."

Darcy gave him a moment to consider his advice, then insisted they return to their game.

As the day drew to an end, Darcy sat with Elizabeth and Georgiana. The ladies had delighted the company—or at least him—with music, and he had escorted them to a sofa afterwards, intending to remain by Elizabeth's side as much as he could. The three of them spoke for a while; they said nothing beyond the ordinary, but it was agreeable and easy. Darcy neither knew nor cared what their companions did, so lost had he become in Elizabeth's fine eyes, lively conversation, and smiling countenance.

I shall pay for every moment of this pleasure in longing and melancholic reflections come the seventh, he told himself. *Yet I would not willingly give up a single instant of it.*

It was near midnight when Georgiana indicated she wished to retire. "It is getting quite late. I am afraid I am not used to such hours." She appeared almost embarrassed by her admission.

"There is no reason why you should be," Elizabeth said. "You will have time enough to stay up to see the dawn once you are out, but for my part, I prefer to greet the rising sun after a good night's sleep so that I might enjoy the peacefulness of the morning."

Darcy added, "I suspect the rest of us will soon retire too. Would you like me to escort you to your room?"

Georgiana looked appreciative, but shook her head. Darcy thought he saw her glance between him and Elizabeth, but the light was too dim to be certain. He prayed she was not hoping something would come from them seeing Elizabeth again. *If I had more sense, I would have removed us from Blackthorn as soon as I saw her. I did not think that she and Georgiana would become friends, and what that would do to Georgiana once we left.* And whatever he had told himself at the start of the visit, he had been drawn to Elizabeth and could not forego the opportunity to be with her once again.

"I shall see you in the morning," Elizabeth said to Georgiana. "Perhaps not until breakfast, however. I believe the weather will remain fair, and, as long as it is, I intend to take a long walk first thing." She laughed. "Even if I remained awake another three or four hours, which I assure you I will not, I will be up with the dawn. I shall take the road. I would rather trample through the park, but I will not, given the snow and ice."

With a final good night, Georgiana left them. Just as Darcy had predicted would happen, other people began to retire, too, beginning with Mrs Ridley, whom Elizabeth joined. He remained in the withdrawing room for another ten or fifteen minutes, not attending to the conversation but rather staring at the door through which Elizabeth had lately disappeared. Had she meant her talk of walking in the morning—going so far as to say where she would be—as a hint? Was it an invitation? Did she wish him to join her? As much as he told himself that, of course, she did not, he knew that, as the sun rose, he would be outside, waiting for her.

Chapter Ten

As Elizabeth prepared for her walk the next morning, she felt a fluttering in her stomach and chastised herself. When she had talked about her intention of going out before breakfast the night before, she had wanted Mr Darcy to know, hoping he would join her.

I should not have done so, she thought as she checked her reflection in the mirror and tucked an errant strand of hair under her hat. *But we will soon go our separate ways. Is it truly so wrong to want to enjoy his company while I can?*

She was not imposing herself on him. He need not seek her out if he did not want to talk to her. She even assured herself that it would be better if he did not, and all her fussing over how she looked was nothing short of absurd.

Walking along the road leading away from the manor, she reprimanded herself for walking slower than her usual gait and sped up. There was no sign of Mr Darcy—not a sound that could have been anyone other than a servant when she was inside or so much as a faint crunch of boot on stone or snow that did not come from her once she was outside.

I would do better to look about me and appreciate the environs. I wish there were fewer clouds, but I estimate a third of the sky is blue, and I shall be satisfied with that. There is no wind, for which I am glad, because it would make the morning too cold to remain outside long. From an aesthetic viewpoint, Mr Ledbury ought to have more evergreen shrubs and trees; it would add interest to the winter landscape.

Rounding a bend in the road, she gave an audible gasp and jumped when she saw a tall figure standing and looking across a white-blanketed field.

Mr Darcy turned at the noise. "Miss Bennet, I have startled you; I beg your pardon."

Elizabeth rested a hand over her heart, which was racing, and did her best not to grin like a fool. "There is no need, sir. I was wool-gathering."

She felt her cheeks heat as his eyes seemed to sweep over her, his lips forming a soft smile. He had come! Like her, he wanted to spend time together. While they could never be more than friends, they could at least have that for a few days longer. As she resumed walking, a smile was all the invitation she needed to offer for him to fall into step beside her. They said nothing for two or three minutes; Elizabeth was too pleased to see him, and she worried she would say too much.

Finally deciding his sister was a safe enough topic, she asked, "Is Miss Darcy finding her stay at Blackthorn agreeable? I understand she is trying to become more comfortable in company before her come out."

Mr Darcy had his hands clasped behind his back. His expression showed concern. "You might be better able to tell me. Georgiana does not find it easy to be with people she knows as little as she does the Ledburys. She says she is glad we came, is enjoying it, and that she is looking forward to the ball, but I am not convinced she would admit it if her feelings were the opposite. She does not want to displease me, which is generous of her, but how am I to know what to do for her if she hesitates to be frank with me?"

Elizabeth wished she had the right—or boldness—to rest a hand on his arm and offer him the comfort he evidently needed. "From what I have seen, she is doing very well, considering her shyness and youth. I believe you were right that this sort of party, where we are few, would be good experience for her."

He nodded, and a moment later said, "I know she takes great pleasure in your company."

Was she mistaken, or did his voice sound tentative? She could take it as proof that he meant to suggest that he, too, liked to spend time with her. *I shall take that knowledge and put it in my treasure box of memories. Despite all the reasons he should despise me, he does not. Oh Lydia, what you have cost me! What I cost myself by misjudging him.*

Aloud, Elizabeth said, "And I hers. She is a charming young lady, and you should be very proud of her."

"I am."

They fell silent until Elizabeth thought to ask where he and his sister would go next.

"Pemberley, at least until February or March," he said. "Lady Romsley, Colonel Fitzwilliam's mother, will want us to go to her in Worcestershire. She remains there until after Easter, although my uncle will be in town. I do not know if we shall, however. After that, we will be in London. Have you decided if you will remain with the Ridleys?"

Elizabeth shrugged. "I do not intend to. It would do them good to be alone. I should say, without me. They are hardly alone, living in the same house with Thomas's parents, but I understand they go to see friends in Devon or Cornwall."

"Bingley goes directly to town."

Their eyes met, and Elizabeth offered him a quick smile; they would both be pleased to know Mr Bingley and Jane were no longer together.

After another brief silence, they spoke of easier matters—what Leicestershire was like when it was not winter, how much they both liked the spring but preferred the autumn, and books and art. They wandered for longer than they should have, given the weather, but she said she was warm enough the several times he enquired about her comfort. In truth, she simply did not wish to end their time together sooner than necessary. She had him to herself—no one to interfere, no distractions for either one of them—and she wanted to take advantage of every possible minute.

At length, they knew they had to return to the house to join the others before their absence was remarked upon. They said no words of parting, but they did exchange a look that provided Elizabeth with yet another moment she would store away like a squirrel did nuts to pull out when it was most needed.

Elizabeth was already at the breakfast table when Mr Darcy entered the room.

"Darcy, there you are," Mr Ledbury cried. "I was looking for you earlier."

"Oh?" Mr Darcy looked unconcerned and said nothing further as he went to the sideboard.

Although Elizabeth tried not to show that she was attending to the conversation, she could not stop her eyes from darting towards him. She caught a glimpse of Miss Darcy looking between her and her brother, a pleased smile on her face. Elizabeth felt a sinking sensation in her stomach. Miss Darcy guessed she and Mr Darcy had been together. Elizabeth's behaviour had raised hopes that, when they did not come to pass, might injure the young lady, and she was ashamed of herself.

I will have to be more cautious. Surely, I can resist temptation for the next few days—for her sake, if not my own.

Forcing her thoughts away from Mr Darcy, Elizabeth gave her attention to what Mr Bingley, who sat beside her, was discussing with James Ledbury, who was across from him. She had the satisfaction of seeing Jane and Thomas in quiet conversation. Elizabeth caught Jane's eye and offered her a smile, which Jane returned. The previous afternoon, she had told Elizabeth that she had been right to caution her about her behaviour towards Mr Bingley.

Jane had said, "It was pleasant to… Well, it was a diversion, but it is over. I promise, Lizzy. Thomas is my husband, and I must make the best of it."

Elizabeth had clasped her hand and insisted, "You and he *can* be happy. He is a good man and loves you. Show him that your loyalty is to him."

Since then, Elizabeth had seen that Jane was doing her best to avoid Mr Bingley while remaining polite. She prayed that it continued and that, once in Northampton again, Jane and Thomas's relationship would improve.

As for me, I shall go to Gracechurch Street.

The Gardiners had never spoken to her about Mr Darcy. Intelligent and sympathetic as they were, they must have seen that she loved him. Elizabeth had told them enough so that they knew the connexion between Mr Darcy and Wickham had been severed long ago because of Wickham's dissolute habits. They were wise enough to realise that, while a man like Mr Darcy might decide to throw aside all expectations to marry the penniless daughter of a country gentleman whose relations were in trade, making himself brother-in-law to a man like Wickham was asking too much.

When I tell them Mr and Miss Darcy were here, they will understand my distress and provide me with the sanctuary I need until I can be myself again. I can ask no more of anyone.

Before retiring on the night of the fourth, Miss Ledbury suggested they visit Halfton, the nearest market town, the following day. It would allow them to escape the final push of preparations at Blackthorn Manor for the ball as the servants rushed around, cleaning and rearranging furniture. Everyone had been agreeable to the outing, and they set off after breakfast.

Elizabeth shared a carriage with Miss Ledbury, Mr Ledbury, and Mr

Bingley. Since Miss Ledbury devoted herself to Mr Bingley, who appeared a willing recipient of her attention, that left Elizabeth and Mr Ledbury to talk or not, and it was soon apparent that Mr Ledbury preferred to remain silent. Elizabeth watched the landscape as they drove the four miles between Blackthorn and the market town. They passed fields, one of which housed a flock of sheep, huddled together against the wind, or simply because they preferred it, and several well-tended cottages with plumes of smoke rising from their chimneys. The day was grey, but—according to Mr Ledbury's gardener—it was not likely to snow.

Halfton reminded Elizabeth of Meryton, which itself was like many other small towns she had seen on her travels.

And I am such a fool that I continue to think of Lambton as the most pleasant of them all. Why? Because it is close to Pemberley, and I have such fond memories of seeing Mr Darcy there. There were the times he called on her, the morning he and his sister collected her in an open carriage to take her on a tour of the neighbourhood, when they had walked together through the town, Mr and Mrs Gardiner behind them. She had felt so proud that afternoon, being by his side, watching him doff his hat when he was greeted by various townsfolk. The entire time, as they looked in shop windows or as he explained the significance of a building or statue, she had been suffused with warmth, excited to imagine that soon she would walk the same streets as his wife.

Today, let me stop my memories there and not remember what followed the next day.

The carriage came to a stop, which was the signal for Miss Ledbury to recall that she was not alone with Mr Bingley.

"You are very dull this morning, Edward," she said as she adjusted her velvet bonnet and tugged at her gloves. "I do not believe you said a single word to Miss Bennet the entire ride. Miss Bennet, I apologise for my brother."

But not for yourself? You, too, ignored me. It had not disturbed her; Miss Ledbury was taking every possible opportunity to know Mr Bingley better, which is what she ought to do, especially since Mr Bingley did not seem to object.

Mr Ledbury murmured an apology. "My mind is elsewhere, I am afraid."

Elizabeth smiled at her hostess and offered the same gesture to both gentlemen. "My eyes feasted on everything we passed, and I was well amused, I assure you."

"Nevertheless, I will ensure you have better company for the return journey. Now, let us enjoy what Halfton has to offer, shall we? A bit of shopping followed by refreshments at the inn."

They exited the carriage and joined the remainder of their party to discuss their plans. It was decided that the gentlemen, save Thomas, would visit the blacksmith's. Mr Ledbury claimed the man had invented a new tool he wished to show Mr Darcy, and his brother and Mr Bingley decided to go with them. Thomas would escort the ladies to the shop selling sundries, then wherever they wished to go. If they did not see each other first, the two groups would meet at the inn in an hour.

The shop was a more than adequate representative of its sort. The interior decoration was wisely light in colour—the walls and drapes and shelves all a pale cream and the window sufficiently large to let in an adequate amount of sunlight even on a cloudy day—and the proprietors stocked an interesting array of goods. Thomas attended Jane and Miss Ledbury, and Elizabeth went with Miss Darcy to look at ribbons. Miss Darcy hoped to find a purple one to go with the gown she intended to wear to the ball.

"I know I cannot dance, and I would not want to stand up with any gentleman I did not know," Miss Darcy said. "I would be too embarrassed. I shall have to eventually, but for now, I am happy to dance with my brother and then watch."

"I am sure you will have company as you sit out. Your brother, I know, is not fond of dancing, and, as unknown as I am here, I do not expect to have partners all night long."

Miss Darcy gave her a fleeting, sly look. "I believe Fitzwilliam likes to dance well enough when he has a partner he finds particularly agreeable. He will ask you for a set, I am certain of it."

Elizabeth smiled but said nothing. She did not want to encourage Miss Darcy to think her brother had any intentions towards her.

"He is the best of brothers," Miss Darcy continued a moment later. "So kind and patient with me. Lady Catherine tells me I am too old to still be so shy and that I ought to be anxious to come out and find a husband so that Fitzwilliam is no longer burdened with my care."

Elizabeth's fist tightened around a piece of lace she had picked up to examine. She longed to ask Lady Catherine if she felt burdened by having an unmarried daughter who was far older than Miss Darcy. "I apologise in advance for my rudeness, Miss Darcy, but that was a terrible thing for her to say to you. Not even the smallest part of me believes your brother views your situation in such a way. Neither do I believe he blames you for being shy. If anything, he would wish to make you comfortable in society, which—aside from any consideration of marriage—would be to your benefit. It would allow you to make more friends, find it easier to undertake charitable works and the like, and, yes, enjoy yourself at balls and other parties."

Miss Darcy gave her such a fond look that Elizabeth felt a crack form in her heart. It was bad enough that she continued to love Mr Darcy; now, she was in very real danger of loving his sister, if she did not already.

Miss Darcy repeated, "He is the best of brothers, the best of men. He has been very happy to see you again, as have I."

Scrambling for words, Elizabeth said, "I have been happy to see you too. These last two weeks have gone by very quickly. Just a few more days, and I go south while, if I understand correctly, you go north." She attempted cheerfulness, but gave it up as expecting too much from herself. When she saw a hint of lavender-coloured silk, she said, "Oh, I think I see just the thing for you."

With relief, Elizabeth was able to turn Miss Darcy's attention back to searching for ribbons. Before anything further could be said about Mr Darcy, she caught Jane's eye and sent her an imploring look. Jane joined them, and, after Miss Darcy found what she was looking for, they concluded their business and went on to explore Halfton's other shops.

Chapter Eleven

DARCY SURVEYED HIS REFLECTION IN THE STANDING MIRROR in his bedchamber. Having just dismissed his valet, he was alone.

It was, at last and too soon, Twelfth Night, the culmination of Yuletide celebrations. He, Georgiana, and the other guests had joined the Ledburys and their servants in clearing the house of all the festive decorations earlier in the day. Now, he was dressed for the ball. Running a hand over his freshly shaven jaw, he was exceedingly glad Ledbury had forbidden his sister from arranging a masquerade or anything more elaborate than the usual private country dance. Miss Ledbury had spent the past day rushing about in an effort to make sure everything was, in her words, 'perfect'. To his mind, the lady was worrying about it far more than it deserved.

Perhaps she is that sort of person who is never happy unless there is something to cause them anxiety. His less-charitable thought was that Miss Ledbury wished to show Bingley what an excellent wife she would be by demonstrating her ability to resolve last minute complications. *If that is so, she might wish to adopt a calmer manner!*

He sighed and scowled, knowing he was not being fair. Miss Ledbury was an agreeable young woman, and he would not be disappointed if she and Bingley formed an attachment.

"Well, old man," he muttered, "do you intend to stand here in this stupid manner, or will you do as you ought and find Georgiana and join the Ledburys? Twelve hours or thereabouts and we will be gone, away from Blackthorn, Christmastide behind us."

Elizabeth behind us. No more clandestine morning walks, no more sitting with her and Georgiana in the evenings, imagining the three of us are at Pemberley, no more hearing her laugh or seeing her smile.

With another sigh, he tugged at his waistcoat, turned away from his reflection, and headed for the door.

Miss Ledbury's arrangements were all very elegant and would not have looked out of place in town. Darcy thought the company was good too. He saw a few acquaintances, apart from those he had met over the last fortnight, and expected to be as pleased with the ball as he usually was with such affairs. That, at least, was his thought leading up to the start of the dancing. He had not asked any lady for the first set. The only one he wanted to stand up with was Elizabeth, but he would not make her uncomfortable by singling her out in such a fashion. He and Georgiana would dance the second or third set, and he would ask Miss Ledbury later in the evening.

As he and Georgiana stood with an older couple who knew their uncle, Lord Romsley, Darcy silently debated the wisdom of asking Elizabeth to dance at all. He wanted to; there was no doubt about it. But would he be able to stand across from her for half an hour or so, knowing this was the last evening they would have together and not embarrass himself by showing his feelings for the entire world to see? His eyes sought her out, soon finding her across the room. She stood with Mr Bingley, Miss Ledbury, and two young men Darcy did not know. It felt like someone squeezed his heart, to see how beautiful she looked. The rich blue fabric of her gown shimmered, and she wore pink flowers in her hair. Even from this distance, he was certain he could see the dusting of colour on her cheeks, and he almost felt himself inching nearer to her, ostensibly to see if the blooms had a pleasant scent, but truly just wishing to be as close to her as politeness allowed. He could feel the weight of her hand resting in his as he led her to the dance floor or to search for their friends or refreshments. She would turn her dark eyes on him, her soft lips upturned in a smile that was just for him.

Georgiana's voice recalled him to his companions. "I-I-I do not know. Brother?"

It took a moment to understand what they had been discussing and to give a reasonable response. After that, Darcy excused himself and his sister, and they went in search of something to drink.

A short while later, Ledbury caught up to them. Georgiana was talking with a lady they had met during their stay at Blackthorn—rather, she was listening to the woman talk—when Ledbury clapped him on the shoulder.

"Enjoying yourself, Darcy? Well, as much as you can. I know this sort of thing is not how you would choose to spend your time, as much as they are expected of us."

"Miss Ledbury has done an admirable job."

Ledbury nodded. "That she did. I think she started planning it the moment we decided to spend the Festive Season in the country. I wanted to thank you for coming and bringing Miss Darcy and Bingley. We have been a small party, but sometimes that is best, eh? I do not think it has been too tedious."

"Not at all. I know I speak for Georgiana as well when I say we have had a pleasant time."

"It helps that you were already acquainted with my cousin's wife and sister-in-law."

Darcy made a noise of agreement. The men looked over the crowd and remained silent for a minute until James Ledbury joined them. He wore a bright red waistcoat that would have given Darcy's valet an apoplexy. Darcy's dislike of it had nothing to do with having seen the man dancing with Elizabeth.

After saying the usual things about the ball, James Ledbury said, "Your friend is doing the pretty with Harriet tonight. I hope he knows what he is about."

Darcy lifted one shoulder and forced himself not to scowl. He was reminded of another ball at which he had danced with Elizabeth—and Bingley's behaviour towards another young lady that evening.

Ledbury said, "Stop fretting about Harriet. She wants a husband, and, in pursuing gentlemen with that goal in mind, she has to expect to face disappointment now and again."

James Ledbury stepped closer to his brother, and they began a hissed debate about how to manage their sister's life. Darcy tried not to listen, and was relieved when the lady with Georgiana excused herself and he and Georgiana could politely leave them to it.

"You should dance, Brother," Georgiana said.

"I shall ask Miss Ledbury later."

She bit her lips together before saying, "Will you not ask Miss Bennet for a set?"

Darcy looked beyond her, his eyes unseeing. The sound of the music, people chatting, and shoes hitting the wooden floor roared in his ears. He took in a deep breath and exhaled. "I do not know. I am glad you like her, Georgiana, but—" He gave a slight head shake.

Georgiana hung her head, visibly disappointed. Darcy knew she did not understand, but how could he explain everything that had happened with Elizabeth to his seventeen-year-old sister? Even Fitzwilliam did not know all of it.

"Come," he said, "let us find a waiter, one who has more of those little cakes. What do you say?"

Georgiana nodded and did her best to smile. He held out an arm to her, and, once her hand was wrapped around it, led her to another part of the ballroom.

Elizabeth curtseyed and smiled at her dance partner, a gentleman she had met early in her stay at Blackthorn Manor. He escorted her to Jane, and offered to get her something to drink, which she declined. He was pleasant enough company, but she was not sorry when he excused himself.

"Did you enjoy the dance?" asked Jane.

Elizabeth nodded. "And you? How did you pass the time?"

"I spoke to several ladies. Thomas was with me, but he remembered something he needed to ask Mr Ledbury. It is a lovely ball."

Jane looked wistful, and Elizabeth would not be surprised to learn that she was not sleeping well. There was a heaviness to her features, and she held herself too tightly.

Elizabeth said, "Are you looking forward to leaving tomorrow?"

Jane nodded. "I am. Are you determined to spend the winter with Aunt and Uncle Gardiner? You know I would gladly keep you with me."

Elizabeth squeezed her sister's hand. "I know, and I am. I think it best if you and Thomas have some time alone. But, Jane, I shall go to Northampton in an instant if you write and tell me you need me. Perhaps the two of you will go to town for a while, and we shall see each other there."

Again, Jane nodded. "I know you are right, Lizzy, but I will miss you."

"And I you. Let us not become maudlin; a ballroom is no place for such emotions."

Jane offered a tremulous smile and nodded. "Tell me who else you have stood up with. Has Mr Darcy asked you for a set?"

Elizabeth felt herself become pale and tears formed behind her eyes. She had been doing her best not to think about Mr Darcy all evening and wished Jane had not chosen this moment to ask about him, something she had not done once over the last fortnight. "I do not expect him to. You must recall that he is not fond of the activity."

Jane regarded her for a long moment. "Why do I think you have not told me everything about your connexion to Mr Darcy? I may have been…overly consumed with other matters of late, but I have the impression—"

Elizabeth interjected, "Let us speak of something else. It will be supper soon. I hope Miss Ledbury is satisfied with it. She was so anxious about the menu yesterday."

With an air of reluctance, Jane followed her lead, and the conversation was suitably bland for the next little while. They spoke to several other guests and were still together when Thomas returned to escort them into supper.

After supper, Elizabeth sat with Miss Darcy for a half an hour while Mr Darcy danced with Miss Ledbury. Miss Darcy claimed to be enjoying herself, but her spirits seemed a little depressed. Jane found them as the set was finished, and Elizabeth slipped away when she saw Mr Darcy's tall form approaching them.

She was startled when, as the interlude was ending, he found her and asked her to dance. He looked grave, and Elizabeth could not tell if he most wished she would accept or decline. All she could do was nod. She had spent the evening avoiding him, yet she could not deny that she wanted to be near him. Each time she looked across from her as the music played and she moved through the well-known steps of this or that dance, she had wished it was Mr Darcy, and not whichever gentleman was her partner, even when it was Thomas.

They took their places. Elizabeth straightened her spine and regarded him. He was always handsome. Even the night they had met at that long ago assembly in Meryton, she had been struck by his looks. Tonight, standing across from him, she wanted to drink in everything about him, etch his image into her memory, remember every detail—the way his neckcloth draped, how the light reflected off the silver thread in his waistcoat, the rich scent of his cologne.

They did not speak. Elizabeth was not sure she could force sound out of her mouth, even had she known what to say. Instead, they looked at each other. She was incapable of turning her eyes away from him, and it seemed that the same was true for him. As the dance continued and she somehow completed the movements without conscious thought, her heart grew heavier and more brittle until she could almost feel it shattering into tiny shards. Tomorrow, they would be separated.

I may never see him again. I cannot *see him again, whatever I must do to ensure it happens. It hurts too much, especially to see him look at me like this, as if he regrets—*

There was a softness in his eyes, a gentle pressure as his fingers closed around hers, the straight line his lips formed that suggested they were tightly pressed together, how his chin turned to follow her even when the dance separated them as if he could not bear to lose sight of her.

Mixed with her pain, Elizabeth felt a stab of anger. It was not fair of him to act as though he stilled cared for her. Somehow, she managed to make it through the dance, but with each step it became harder and harder. She felt tears pooling behind her eyes, and her chest rose and fell, her breaths shallow, until she was lightheaded. As soon as the last note struck, and without the usual curtsey, she spun around and walked away from him, desperate for a moment of privacy to regain her equanimity before she embarrassed herself. She did not care where she went —as long as it was far away from Mr Darcy.

Elizabeth's feet led her to the breakfast parlour, which she knew would be empty. It was cold, but she did not care. If anything, it would help to cool her emotions. Standing at the window, she watched the still, dark night. The faint noises of the ball reached her ears. A tear fell down her cheek; she brushed it away and sniffed.

Footsteps sounded behind her, followed by a deep voice saying, "Miss Bennet."

Elizabeth shook her head and pressed her eyes closed. "Please go away." Her voice sounded rough.

When he murmured, "Elizabeth," it felt like she was being pulled towards him, and another flash of anger surged through her gut, causing another tear to escape her eyes.

She spun around to face him. "How-how dare you? Do you have any idea what it is like for me to see you?"

Mr Darcy's brow furrowed as he stared back at her. "What it is like for *you*?"

"You made your choice, and I understand it. After Lydia's disgrace, with Wickham of all men, how could you—? I knew it was impossible. But to see you, to have you look at me that way."

His mouth was agape, the crease in his forehead deepening. "The choice *I* made? But…" He stepped towards her but remained six feet away. "*You* were the one who— I wrote to your father, but you—he—"

The blood rushed out of her cheeks and pooled in her stomach. For a moment, it seemed as if time stopped. When her mind managed to grasp the edge of what his words suggested, she demanded, "What? When? Why? Wh-what did you say to him?"

Mr Darcy took one more step towards her, his features mirroring the confusion she felt. "That autumn. I apologised for not doing more about Wickham sooner, and said that I was relieved everything had worked out as well as one could hope, under the circumstances. I told him that we had seen each other in Derbyshire, that if you, and he, would permit it, I would very much like to continue the acquaintance."

Elizabeth produced a sound that was part gasp, part sob. He had written? He had wanted to see her again?

Cautiously, as though he was afraid of her response, he asked, "You did not know?"

Elizabeth shook her head, and another tear or two fell down her face. She wiped them away. "You sent a letter to my father? You wanted to see me?" She had to be sure she understood; misunderstanding could be disastrous.

He nodded.

She closed her eyes for a minute and tried to dampen the near fury she felt as she understood what must have happened. When she was capable of speaking, she met his eyes. "It is likely still on his desk unread. Or, if he did open it, he thought it was a great joke, one he no doubt meant to share with me, but he forgot." She repeated, "You wanted to see me again?" Her voice quivered, and she knew she was close to losing control and sobbing.

Mr Darcy nodded again and took a small step closer. "I am almost afraid to ask. What would you have said had you known? Is it too late? Have I let my doubts and self-recriminations ruin my chances of ever having what I most want, what I dream of every day and night?"

Elizabeth's heart ached so much that she wanted to clench her chest. She could only shake her head and mouth the word 'no'. It was enough. He took another step in her direction, which left him close enough to claim her hand, though he did not.

"Will you—?" He stopped and swallowed. "C-could you possibly see your way to accepting me, to being my wife? Elizabeth, I…I do not have the words to tell you how dear you are to me, how ardently I love you."

As soon as the last three words were out of his mouth, she clasped his hand. A bubble of joy, all the greater in size for following so much despair, rose from her toes and through her body until it escaped as a laugh and grin. "Yes, yes, a thousand times yes. I love yo—"

He cut off her words with the most fervent of kisses.

Chapter Twelve

Darcy could not believe it. If he were not standing mere inches from Elizabeth, her hands in his, he would not. When they had been dancing, he could not stop himself from staring at her, his thoughts turning dark and brooding as he imagined having to say a polite adieu to her the next morning, hiding his affection and pretending it meant nothing to climb into his carriage and drive away from her. When she left him so unceremoniously, he had to follow. And then… Then everything had changed.

He pressed his lips to hers again, their kiss gentle, and rested his forehead against hers.

"I am afraid I am dreaming, as I have so often these last sixteen months," he whispered.

"Then I am as well, and I have never heard of two people sharing the same dream. The conclusion, my dear, dear Mr Darcy, is that this is reality." Like him, her words were soft, as was the laugh that followed.

"There is so much I must say to you, that we must discuss. I cannot bear the thought of sharing you with anyone else, not just yet."

She tightened her grip on his hands and smiled. When she suggested they stay where they were a little longer to give themselves the opportunity to talk, he agreed. First, he would go to the ballroom to check on Georgiana. Very likely, she had noticed his absence and was worried. Before he left, he lit several candles.

He was as quick as he could be about his errand and brought Elizabeth a thick shawl when he returned.

"Oh, thank you." She wrapped it around her shoulders.

Darcy led her to a chair and sat across from her, claiming her hands, which were cold. "Georgiana fetched it. I told her we needed to talk, that there had been some miscommunication between us."

Elizabeth, his dearest, beloved Elizabeth, laughed, and he rejoiced in the sound.

"That is an understatement." Glancing at the shawl, she continued, "I must conclude this is hers."

He nodded. "She has retired to her room. I walked her to it, and, when I told her where we were, she thought you would need it."

"She is such a lovely girl. I am already so fond of her. Indeed, the other day, I realised that I was growing to love her, which would only add to my heartbreak when we parted."

Darcy drew her hands to his mouth and kissed them. "Although I am a selfish being and want to marry you because I know it will bring me such joy, I have long known that you would make the most excellent sister for Georgiana."

They were silent for a moment. Darcy gazed at her, the flicker of the candlelight creating an intimate, calm atmosphere. Her lips formed a smile, and he had to restrain himself from kissing her again.

He said, "You can have no idea how many times I wished your letters from Longbourn had been delayed a day or two longer, just enough time for me to have found the courage to ask you to give me a chance to prove I was worthy of you."

"You did not need to. I had already decided that you were the best of men." In the teasing tone he adored, she added, "And the only man in the world I could ever marry."

He chuckled at the allusion to her rejection of him at Hunsford. It had been the worst day of his life, one marked by pain and humiliation, but now, having been assured of her love and desire to be his, it mattered not. Nevertheless, he felt his cheeks heat; he doubted he would ever not feel embarrassed by the dreadful showing he had made that day.

"I had hoped your feelings for me had improved. Those days in Derbyshire..." How could he possibly explain how wonderful they had been and how much they had meant to him.

"Oh yes, those days." Her voice was warm and rich with feeling. "I have held them in my heart as the happiest of my life. Until now."

Again, Darcy kissed her hands. He would rather kiss her lips, but—between the darkness, their solitude, and the relief of knowing his loneliness and heartache were at an end—did not trust himself. "We will have many more. I promise you that, my dearest, loveliest Elizabeth."

"And I vow to do everything in my power to help you keep that promise. I will see you as happy as I know you will make me." She tightened her grip on his hands for a moment before saying, "I have to know. Why did you not just come to Hertfordshire? Why write to my father instead?"

Darcy sighed and dropped his eyes to their joined hands. "In part, it was because, with Bingley having no wish to return to Netherfield, I had no easy excuse to be there. I might have overcome that, but I was certain you blamed me for your sister's marriage to Wickham and Bingley's failure to pursue Mrs Ridley. If I had explained some part of my past with Wickham, if I had not thought it beneath me to do so, if I had insisted Bingley go to Hertfordshire that spring or not waited so long to tell him everything— You would have been right to hate me for either. Together…" He shrugged.

"I never blamed you! Lydia, Wickham, and my parents alone are responsible. I believed you could not bear the thought of being connected to him. How could you, after how he treated you and Miss Darcy? As for Mr Bingley! If he could so easily forget Jane, then he was not the husband I would want for her. After how he has behaved here—and I do not excuse my sister's part in it—I know he is not. Had they gotten married, who is to say that he would not flirt with other ladies? That would have hurt her far more than his never returning to Netherfield."

In fairness to Bingley, who he considered a dear friend, he said, "I trust that, once he decides to marry, he will treat his wife as he ought. Despite his faults, he is a good man."

Elizabeth accepted his words with a nod. "But I do not want to talk about him or Jane or anyone else."

Darcy agreed, and, knowing they should not remain alone much longer, insisted they agree on their plans. They decided that he and Georgiana would accompany Elizabeth and the Ridleys to Northampton. From there, the three of them—Elizabeth, Georgiana, and he—would go on to Longbourn so that he could ask Mr Bennet's consent in person. At that time, they would choose a wedding date. Neither of them wanted a long betrothal.

"We have been separated long enough," she said. "Sixteen months! I cannot agree to any unnecessary delay."

"I would be a fool to want anything else, not when I have wanted you to be my wife for almost two years already. Now, my love, I am afraid we should return to the ballroom. I would be surprised if we have not been missed already."

Her shoulders slumped, and she sighed. "I know you are correct, but

I had much rather remain here with you. I have not felt so happy or peaceful in"—she chuckled—"sixteen months, I suppose."

He ran his thumbs over the smooth surface of her cheeks to brush away the remnants of her tears, then leant forward and kissed her before standing and pulling her to her feet. "Let us scandalise those who have nothing better to do than watch how others are behaving. We shall dance together again and not hide our smiles or laughs. I do not care if they see how happy, how overjoyed I am, and gossip about it to the world. I want to shout out the news."

Elizabeth laughed. "This is a new aspect to you, sir, and one of which I approve. We *are* happy. What care we for those who would seek to dampen our pleasure in this moment, one we deserve after so long? Those who love us will share in our joy. That is enough for me."

"And for me. When I left Kent—oh, how long ago that seems—I despaired. I never expected to see you again. Then you were there, in Derbyshire, at Pemberley. I cannot possibly describe what I felt to see you. No sooner had I assured myself that I expected nothing more than to show you that I had listened to your reproofs, that I was a better man than you had first known, then I began to have other hopes. It seemed that you would give me a second chance, and I knew I was the most fortunate man in the world. When you received word about your sister… It felt like my world collapsed all around me, not at first, perhaps, but as the weeks passed and I received no reply to my letter. Again, I never expected to see you again. For over a year now, I have tried to convince myself to put aside my love for you, the dreams I had of what our future could be. To find you here, in Leicestershire, staying in the same house? It seemed…unfair. Why must I be tortured in such a way? Were my sins so great?"

His hand was clasped between hers, and she held it to her chest. "Never! But none of that matters now. We have the future, *our* future to look forward to. In time, the pain of the past will be just that—the past." She smiled in just such a way that guaranteed he would give her anything she wanted. "Now, you promised me a dance, one in which we will throw caution to the wind and show everyone that we are the happiest couple in the world."

Her hand still in his, he extinguished the candles, dropped Georgiana's wrap on a chair, and led Elizabeth into their new life.

December 1814, Derbyshire

Darcy lifted the sleeping infant from Elizabeth's arms, placed a gentle kiss on his head, and took a moment to gaze at his precious, tiny features, now relaxed in sleep. At almost three weeks old, Alexander's skin was no longer mottled red, and he appeared more aware when he was awake, watching his parents and Aunt Georgiana sing and coo over him. Darcy handed his son to the nurse and hoped he would sleep for four, perhaps even five, hours. It would give Elizabeth a chance to rest. She insisted on feeding Alexander herself, at least until he was a little older. Darcy helped her out of the armchair she liked to use when she nursed their son and to the sofa where they could sit together. He draped a blanket on her lap and held her in his arms.

Elizabeth and Darcy had married in the middle of February. It had been a surprise to discover not two months later that they would be parents by the end of the year, but both had been delighted. They had lost enough time together. The Bennets had been surprised when Darcy and Georgiana had escorted Elizabeth to Longbourn after her time at Blackthorn Manor, and Mr Bennet had arched his eyebrows high on his forehead when Darcy sought his permission to marry Elizabeth. The resulting silence had stretched into what seemed like a quarter of an hour but was likely no more than half a minute.

After Darcy had told Elizabeth about her father's shock and disbelief, her features had hardened, and, despite his assurance that everything was well, she had gone into Mr Bennet's book room and demanded to know what had become of the letter Darcy had sent him in the autumn of 1812. Elizabeth had eventually discovered it, and several other unopened letters, buried beneath a stack of books and papers. It had not occurred to Darcy that she would have questions about it after she read it, but she did.

"I was struck by the date most of all," she had said. "You had very early knowledge of Lydia's marriage. How?"

He had had no choice but to confess what he had done. They were sitting in a small back parlour at Longbourn, and he kept his voice low, hoping that no one would overhear. "I went to town the day after you and the Gardiners left Lambton. I believed I had the best chance of finding them, being more familiar with Wickham's habits than I ever wished to be. I soon discovered them. Your sister would not leave him, as had been my initial hope, so I did the only other thing I could. I arranged their marriage. There, too, I failed. I intended to escort Mrs Wick—"

"Oh, please call her Lydia," Elizabeth had cried. "I hate to hear that name."

"Very well. I intended to escort Lydia to the Gardiners to await the wedding, but she refused and would not listen to anything I said. Had I presented myself better when I was at Netherfield— But you will say that is in the past. I saw her established apart from Wickham and sent a maid to stay with her and kept a guard on him to ensure the event went off as required."

"Why did you never tell the Gardiners or me, at least?"

"I did not want you beholden to me. I might have, had I received a reply to my letter."

She had thanked him and, when he asked, promised not to tell anyone. "I am astonished Lydia managed to keep the secret, but when they came to Longbourn, she was so full of her triumph at being the first of us to marry. I suppose she had already forgotten or chose not to remember that she owed her happiness to you."

Immediately after their wedding, Elizabeth and Darcy had returned to Pemberley with no intention of leaving anytime soon. The Gardiners had come to them in the summer, bringing their four children, and some of Darcy's family had visited in the autumn. The Ridleys, Mr Bennet, and Elizabeth's sister Mary were joining them the next day for the Festive Season and to meet the newest Darcy. Mrs Bennet had decided the trip was too long, and she and Miss Catherine had elected to remain at Longbourn. From what Elizabeth had told him, they were angry with her because she had vowed that the Wickhams would never be admitted to her or Darcy's company either in town or Derbyshire. Mrs Bennet had often spoken of her youngest daughter in Darcy's hearing. She assumed that 'dearest Lydia' would be invited to the wedding and began to hint about Darcy sending the Wickhams money to make the trip or—even better—sending one of his carriages for them. After one particularly unpleasant dinner, which had left Georgiana greatly distressed, Elizabeth had talked to her mother about it, and their relationship had yet to fully recover from the ensuing argument.

Darcy kissed Elizabeth's temple, and she sighed as she nestled closer to him, her head on his shoulder.

He said, "Do you realise, it was one year ago tomorrow that Georgiana, Bingley, and I arrived at Blackthorn Manor?"

Her voice was heavy with fatigue. "Mm. I was so confused and miserable to see you again. And elated. I wanted to rush into your arms." He chuckled, and she continued. "I think, seeing you, I felt that, finally, I was no longer alone. Yet, at the same time, I felt even more alone, more conscious of everything I had lost."

Again, Darcy kissed her, his lips falling on her hair, which smelled of rosemary. "I believe I understand. I told myself I should stay away from you, yet I encouraged Georgiana to seek your company. With each day that passed, my resolve weakened. I wanted to be near you, however little time we had before we went our separate ways again."

She made a noise of agreement. "There will be no such shocks tomorrow when our guests arrive."

"Thank God. It is enough that you have just had a baby. We do not need the distraction and frustration of people flirting with the wrong person—"

"Or those desperate to hide how much they love someone they believe they can never be with."

Again he chuckled, knowing she referred to the two of them, but also thinking about Bingley and Jane Ridley.

Suggesting her thoughts had gone in the same direction, Elizabeth said, "I hope Jane has good news to tell me. She was so hopeful that she was, at last, going to have a baby. I know she will be devastated if she was mistaken."

The news of Jane's suspicions had arrived the previous month. Before their wedding, Elizabeth had confided in him about Jane's unhappiness, which had been her excuse for her manner towards Bingley. Darcy had assured her that her sister would always be welcomed in their homes, should she need a refuge. Fortunately, the Ridleys appeared to have settled into their marriage. While they could not be said to be as happy as the Darcys, they did well enough.

The past year had seen another marriage—that of Miss Ledbury to a gentleman from Hampshire named Gilbert. Bingley remained a bachelor and seemed content.

"It will be a peaceful, happy Yuletide, my darling," Darcy said.

"The happiest ever. We are together, you, I, Georgiana, and now Alexander. I do love you, and our life together, so dearly."

"As do I," he murmured. "Hush. Rest now."

Darcy tightened his hold on his beloved Elizabeth and soon felt her body become limp as she slipped into sleep. A few minutes later, he carried her to bed.

The End

About the Author

Lucy Marin's lifelong admiration for Jane Austen began after first reading one of her novels as a teenager. She has been writing Austen variations for over ten years, publishing her first one, Being Mrs Darcy, in 2020.

Also by Lucy Marin

Being Mrs Darcy
Mr Darcy: A Man with a Plan
The Recovery of Fitzwilliam Darcy

CALL IT HOPE

SUSAN ADRIANI

You want nothing but patience; or give it a more fascinating name: call it hope.

— MRS DASHWOOD, SENSE & SENSIBILITY

CHAPTER 1

One half of the world cannot understand the pleasures of the other.

— EMMA WOODHOUSE, EMMA

SNOW SIFTED DOWN FROM THE DREARY DECEMBER SKY LIKE powdered sugar, coating everything in its path with downy white. When Darcy was a boy, small, fine flakes foretold a big snowfall, especially in Derbyshire, where the winters were not only colder than those in the south, but invariably harsher as well.

If only Darcy were in Derbyshire. Instead, he was in Kent, where the climate was warmer, the snow was wetter, and his temper was fouler for being trapped within the overbearing bosom of his family. Five days before Christmas, he and his Fitzwilliam relations arrived at Rosings Park, summoned there under the guise of some desperate scheme Lady Catherine had contrived to make his life an inconvenient hell. Had his sister Georgiana not been absolutely delighted by the prospect of their families staying on to spend the holiday together, Darcy would have quit the place at once and hied back to Pemberley, where there were pheasants to shoot and brandy to drink and no talk of carol singing or kissing boughs or Lady Metcalfe's ball.

With a long-suffering sigh, he scrutinised the park from the massive bay window in the library. Already, the ground was covered in several inches of snow, concealing the unevenness of the roads and the depth of the ruts. The temperature was dropping and soon everything would freeze, making the going not only arduous, but perilous. Darcy doubted his driver would make it as far as Hunsford Village within the next hour. Escaping to London would be impossible.

"There you are," said the exasperatingly cheerful voice of his cousin, Colonel Fitzwilliam. "I should have known I would find you in here, seeking refuge among Lady Catherine's mouldering old tomes."

Irritated as much with his cousin's carefree demeanour as he was with being discovered, Darcy made no reply.

As was often the case, the colonel was undeterred by silence. "Escape is futile," he said equitably, stretching his tall frame upon a tufted leather couch and folding his hands behind his head. "You will not make it halfway to Bromley before your carriage slides off the road and becomes stuck in a ditch. You had better remain here."

Darcy turned his back to the window and fixed him with a dour look. "You may say whatever you like of futility. A funeral procession is more diverting than Rosings Park."

"Codswallop," declared Fitzwilliam's elder brother, Viscount Emerson, as he wandered into the room. "There are plenty of diversions to be had at Rosings."

"I defy you to name one."

Emerson smirked. "There is a chambermaid on the upper floor I found extremely diverting during my last visit. If you remove that stick from your arse for two minutes together, she may be inclined to oblige you as well—perhaps twice."

Fitzwilliam's cough did little to conceal his bark of laughter. "In my experience, properly bedding a woman takes longer than two minutes. Whatever you have been doing, Arthur, you have clearly been doing it wrong."

Waving a dismissive hand, Emerson strolled to the sideboard and poured himself a large glass of sherry. "When you are married to a miserable, harping shrew who reviles congress even more than she reviles having a husband, you will comprehend my haste. Until Josephine begets a son, I shall have to continue running the gauntlet. The more expeditiously I do so, the better—or so I am told by my wife."

Darcy shook his head. "I will never understand why you were so insistent upon marrying a woman who hates you."

Swallowing a mouthful of sherry, Emerson shrugged. "Her connexions are excellent, she is reasonably attractive, has decent teeth, and came with eighty thousand pounds."

"And was such a sum worth the misery you inflict upon each other?

You are barely civil, and you reside in the guest wing of your own home."

Emerson raised his glass aloft. "For eighty thousand pounds, I would have married an ox and slept in the barn. Once she obliges me with an heir, Josephine and I intend to mark the occasion by thereafter residing in separate houses, preferably on opposite sides of the kingdom."

"Where you will live happily ever after, I presume."

"With a lovely, obliging Cyprian," the viscount replied, then drained his glass and promptly poured himself another.

Knowing Emerson, it was entirely likely he already had a mistress installed somewhere, or at the very least had one in mind. Darcy watched him guzzle half the sherry in his glass in a matter of seconds and said, "You had better pace yourself. It is not eleven o'clock. At this rate, you will be in your cups come noon."

"With my wife and her curtain lectures *and* Mother *and* Aunt Catherine all under the same roof, I would be a fool to remain sober. Speaking of Aunt Catherine, I suggest you start in on a bottle yourself. If you are on the cut, the old bat shall likely not want to deal with you, and your bachelorhood will remain intact, at least until you regain your sobriety. Come to think of it, avoid sobriety altogether."

Fitzwilliam rolled his eyes. "No one is asking you, Arthur. Suggesting Darcy drink himself into a stupor is a terrible idea. Mother would be livid, and Georgiana, distressed. As for Lady Catherine, she adores him. She barely lets him alone. If Darcy is foxed, his guard will be down, and his chances of being put in an untenable situation shall increase tenfold. Your plan is as unsound as it is idiotic."

Darcy was inclined to agree. He did not want to be caught unaware in the lion's den. A union with his doleful cousin would yield no pleasure, and likely no children. Unlike his overbearing aunt, he did not suffer the delusion that he and Anne were formed for each other. One only had to look at them to know they would never suit. Even so, he had attempted to broach the topic with Anne on countless occasions, but she promptly claimed a headache, quit the room, and sequestered herself in her bedchamber for days on end. Far from discouraged by her avoidance, Darcy had long hoped it was indicative of his own sentiments: that the idea of their marrying each other was so abhorrent it ought never to be mentioned.

Emerson sank onto a wingback chair upholstered with vile floral fabric. "Go ahead and stay sober, then. I was only trying to help."

"Do not," Darcy told him brusquely, "else I find myself leg-shackled to Anne without my knowledge and my name changed to de Bourgh."

Wisely, Fitzwilliam changed the subject. "I do not suppose either of you have seen Stephen this morning. He was supposed to meet me at the stable to tour the park at daybreak. There is an old hedgerow along the edge of the main pasture Lady Catherine's steward claims will need rebuilding before spring. I thought to have a look at it."

Darcy rolled his eyes.

As a third son, Stephen's prosperity hinged on distinguishing himself in a profession and marrying a woman with a substantial dowry. Instead of taking orders, or purchasing a commission, or finding a suitable wife, he appeared intent on distinguishing himself in other ways, all of them disreputable.

Darcy could only imagine the debauchery currently taking place under his aunt's roof. "Why you ever thought your brother would be keen to look at a hedgerow, especially at the crack of dawn, is anyone's guess. He was so foxed last night he could barely stand."

Emerson frowned. "The insolent little fop is probably tupping my chambermaid as we speak. He will likely make a day of it, then take a nap. I doubt we shall see him before supper."

The colonel ground the heels of his hands into his eyes and uttered an oath.

"He had better not wear her out," Emerson added petulantly, swirling his sherry in an absent fashion before gulping it down. He belched loudly and wiped his mouth with the ruffled cuff of his shirt sleeve. "I had planned to pay her a visit myself later, that is unless Darcy wants to partake of her favours first." He turned towards Darcy and said, "You could use a good tup. You are far too uptight."

An assignation with his aunt's chambermaid was without doubt the last thing Darcy wanted. He uttered a curt, "Absolutely not," then strode to the hearth, propped his forearms upon the mantel, and stared fixedly at the painting above the fireplace—a landscape done by one of his long dead ancestors. The composition was well executed, but it was not a prospect he recognised as being from Levens Hall, his uncle's seat in Cumbria, or any of their family's other holdings. In fact, the distant hills and fertile fields put him in mind of the country around Hertfordshire, which inevitably put him in mind of Elizabeth Bennet.

Darcy ran his hand over his mouth in annoyance. That he should suddenly have the misfortune of thinking of Elizabeth in one of the few rooms of his aunt's house she had not graced last spring while staying at the parsonage was not only inconvenient, but inexplicably painful. Eight months had passed, and still he ached for the life they might have had together had he not slighted her when they first met, or insulted her when he proposed marriage, or failed to warn her of the dangers George Wickham and his reprehensible habits posed to her sisters, her Hertfordshire neighbours, and to the world in general.

Somewhere behind him, Emerson droned on about God-only-knew-what as he poured himself his third glass of sherry and proceeded to consume it in very little time. If it were evening, Darcy would be sorely tempted to partake himself, if only to drown out Emerson's idiotic, puffed-up prattle.

Fishing his fob from his waistcoat pocket, he consulted his watch. It was a quarter past eleven o'clock. *Will this morning never end?*

"I am out of sherry," Emerson announced to the room. He sounded peevish and put out. "The old bat must have another decanter or two stashed somewhere. It is the only decent thing to be had at Rosings that isn't watered down..."

Ignoring him, Darcy abandoned the hearth and returned to the window, where he braced his arm against the casement and glowered at the snow-covered park. Save for Fitzwilliam and Georgiana, his mother's family and their eccentricities were tedious. He had not been at Rosings for one full day, and already his uncle, aunts, and cousins were grating on his nerves.

His thoughts returned to Elizabeth.

From the earliest days of their acquaintance her intelligence had impressed him, her playful disposition had charmed him, and her sweetness and solicitation for those she loved had endeared her to him. Duty and his family had summoned him to Kent, but Darcy wished he had summoned the courage to go to Netherfield instead. If he were to quit Rosings tomorrow and suddenly show up on Bingley's doorstep, begging for a room, would he be welcome?

Probably not.

Knowing he would never have been able to stand opposite Elizabeth in church and feign indifference to her—or sit beside her at the wedding breakfast or watch her speak animatedly with her neighbours while she avoided conversation with him—Darcy had declined attending Bingley's wedding to Jane Bennet the previous month.

"Balls," Emerson belched as he rifled through the sideboard, complaining about Lady Catherine being so cheap as to water down all the port in Kent.

Darcy recognised the distinct clink of crystal and the tell-tale splash of liquor as it was hastily poured into a glass.

A moment later, a sputtered, "God in heaven!" rang through the room, followed by a colourful string of curses. "Sacrilege! Mothers' milk is stronger than this weak swill!"

"It is a shame your constitution is not," Fitzwilliam told his brother blandly from the couch.

"Oh, shut it," Emerson muttered crossly. "There is nothing wrong with my constitution."

"With your head, then. You have always been incomparably slow on the uptake."

"Not nearly as slow as you. It is no wonder you have yet to oust Bonaparte from power, lazing about on the couch as you do…"

Darcy rubbed his forehead with his hand and attempted to tune out their bickering. He had long considered the manners of Elizabeth's two youngest sisters abhorrent, but they at least could claim the ignorance and caprice of youth as their excuse. His cousins were well above thirty, Cambridge educated, and had lived in the world. At this juncture, even Mrs Bennet's nonsensical observations were preferrable to Emerson's insipid quibbling!

Of course, whatever Elizabeth's mother lacked in discernment, she more than made up for by setting the finest table in Hertfordshire. The same could not be said for Lady Catherine. Mrs Bennet would never dream of watering down the port or the wine or the punch at Longbourn. Her suppers were eagerly anticipated and well attended by her friends. Her cook's pigeon pie and duck ragout were legendary. Darcy could only imagine what culinary heights might be achieved with a Christmas goose.

He exhaled in frustration. As exemplary the delights of Mrs Bennet's supper table were, they paled in comparison to the delights of her second eldest daughter. Should Darcy give into temptation and travel to Hertfordshire, the reception that awaited him at Longbourn would be awkward at best, mortifying at worst. Mr Bennet would be flippant, Mrs Bennet uncivil, and Miss Mary and Miss Catherine indifferent. Would Elizabeth be flippant, or uncivil, or indifferent to him as well? Would she endeavour to speak with him as she had at Pemberley, or would she go out of her way to avoid him now? Had Mrs Wickham's patched-up marriage brought her some measure of relief, or was she angry and mortified to have such a lasting, intimate connexion to such a despicable scoundrel?

Darcy hardly knew. He knew only that his love for Elizabeth had not diminished since he had first declared himself to her in April. Meeting her unexpectedly at Pemberley that summer had only increased his desire for her, as well as his sense of what he had truly lost when she had refused him.

"Richard," Emerson whined, sounding like an errant child as he kicked the sideboard door closed with his foot. "There is nothing of use to be found in this entire cupboard, only this watered-down swill. Tell me you have a flask strapped to your hip or your horse's arse or hidden away in a hedgerow somewhere. I am not nearly as foxed as the circumstances require."

Nor am I. Darcy laid his forehead against the glass and shut his eyes. His cousin and his appalling sense of self-entitlement were giving him a headache.

"You shall have to make do without your precious sherry, Arthur," Fitzwilliam informed him. "Neither I nor my horse have anything for you. Go take a nap in your room and sober up before Mother sees you, or worse—your wife."

"Damn my wife," Emerson muttered. "Damn women altogether." Miraculously, he did not argue—a sure sign he was well on his way to being in his cups. A moment later, the library door opened, then closed with a resounding bang as he quit the room.

Darcy opened his eyes.

Outside, the snow fell harder. The flakes were larger. The wide, manicured avenue that led to the lane that led to the parsonage had completely disappeared. Not a soul was about, not even the blackbirds. Darcy itched to don his greatcoat and forge a path through the snow-covered park until his nerves were settled and his mind was at ease; he doubted he would make it as far as the hall before Lady Catherine intercepted him. Another round of asinine castigations and impossible demands would follow. It mattered not how many times he told Lady Catherine he would not marry Anne; his aunt was not in the habit of being gainsaid. She was determined to have her way.

Resigning himself to his imprisonment, he remained where he was.

Eventually, Fitzwilliam abandoned the comfort of the couch and made his way to the window, stifling a yawn. "You are quiet. Are you well?"

Snowflakes clung to the windowpanes. They were bright and delicate and resembled lace. "Well enough," he muttered. "It was a long, insufferable journey from Derbyshire and the coaching inns offered no peace. It is nothing a night's repose will not remedy."

The last time he had seen Elizabeth she had worn a pretty muslin gown trimmed with lace. He had called upon her at the inn in Lambton, his head and his heart full of her, intending to renew his addresses; instead of hearing his proposal, Elizabeth had received the most dreadful news from home and burst into tears. Though he had no right, Darcy had comforted her, but upon hearing her youngest sister had eloped with Wickham, he was too horrified and furious to remain.

He had not seen Elizabeth since.

"Are you certain you only want sleep?" Fitzwilliam asked. "If there is something weighing on you…"

"I require nothing."

"Looking at you, that is difficult to believe. As it happens, I have a bottle of French brandy stashed in the old oak tree by the parsonage gate in the churchyard, courtesy of the Major General. If you breathe so much as one word of it to Arthur, I shall be forced to call you out. It is far too fine to waste on my brother's undiscriminating palate."

One corner of Darcy's mouth lifted. "Your secret is safe with me. Should your offer still stand, perhaps I will take you up on it later—when Lady Catherine and her intolerable demands have finally driven me to my wit's end."

Fitzwilliam made a show of consulting his watch. "So, another hour or two should do the trick."

"Just so."

Tucking his watch back into his pocket, he sighed. "You are a terrible liar, you know. You always have been."

Darcy passed a hand over his eyes. "Desist."

"That I shall never do. Regardless of whatever Arthur accuses me of, I am a tenacious devil."

"A Fitzwilliam family trait. Despite your tenacity, I am in no humour at present to indulge you."

"In my experience, you rarely are, but that has never stopped me from winkling all your secrets out of you in the past."

"You flatter yourself by assuming you are privy to all my secrets. In this case, I assure you are not."

"I see."

Darcy felt a rush of annoyance as he wondered exactly what it was that Fitzwilliam saw. His cousin knew nothing of what he suffered—no one knew. Darcy had kept his own counsel for the past year. Not once had he breathed a single word of his ardent love for Elizabeth Bennet, nor his appalling proposal, nor the crushing weight of his disappointment at her refusal to another soul. Even now, speaking of it—any of it—remained beyond his capabilities.

His head ached. His *heart* ached. The prospect of enduring another syllable of conversation was suddenly insupportable. Darcy required peace and solitude. Neither would be found at Rosings Park.

At length, Fitzwilliam ceded to his recalcitrance. "You have long desired my absence. I shall importune you no further this morning." He turned and made to leave, but paused when Darcy said gruffly:

"My mood is beastly. Forgive me."

"There is nothing to forgive. You are disinclined towards conversation at present, so I shall leave you to yourself. Should you desire a companion or a confidant, even a silent one, I am your servant."

Darcy raised his eyes to his cousin's. "You are far dearer to me than such a statement implies. Despite my stubbornness and intractability, there is no one's counsel, no one's friendship, I value more than yours."

Fitzwilliam laid his hand upon his shoulder and squeezed. "I know."

CHAPTER 2

> If adventures will not befall a young lady in her own village, she must seek them abroad.
>
> —Jane Austen, Northanger Abbey

Elizabeth had been in Kent for a week. She had shopped in the village. She had attended church. She had wandered through the woods and the park and the fields. She had even taken tea at Rosings not once but twice. Last evening, she had watched the convoy of fine carriages—six in total—rumble past the parsonage towards Rosings Park.

Now, all she saw was snow.

If Mr Collins would not suffer an apoplectic fit, Elizabeth would don her boots and pelisse, throw open the door, tilt her face to the sky, and catch the cold, lacy flakes on her tongue. She longed to leave her footsteps upon the pristine, white carpet blanketing the garden, and to hear her laughter resonate through the starkness and quiet of the brisk, winter air.

The idea of receiving a harsh chastisement from her cousin for exhibiting such unladylike behaviour so close to the condescension of Rosings Park prevented her from setting foot outside the house, even so far as the front gate. The servants at the parsonage were pleasant enough, but their loyalty was to their master. Even Charlotte's position as their mistress could not command their silence and discretion. Nothing happened within the parsonage walls that Mr Collins did not eventually learn of. Elizabeth was visiting Kent for Charlotte's sake as much as for her own. She determined she would give her cousin no cause to regret her presence in his home.

The little mantel clock in the front parlour chimed half past four o'clock. Soon the encroaching darkness would envelop the surrounding landscape, and travel between the village and the parsonage would be impossible, especially in Mr Collins's gig. Laying her needlework aside, Elizabeth rose from her comfortable chair by the fire and walked to the window. The lane was no longer discernible, nor the road, nor the path from the front garden to the door. An impressive amount of snow had fallen throughout the day. Even now, it seemed unlikely to let up anytime soon. Elizabeth expelled a weary breath. Charlotte and Mr Collins would not return that night.

She had started to turn away from the window when sudden movement near the churchyard gate caught her eye. Pressing her nose to the glass, she strained to better see the figure of a man striding through the snow towards the old oak tree in the waning light. He raised himself up on his toes and reached into the hollow, drew forth an object, and tucked it into his greatcoat pocket. It was then he happened to glance at the parsonage.

Elizabeth recognised him at once: Colonel Fitzwilliam.

So relieved was she to see a friendly face, she found herself throwing open the window without thought or care and calling to him, "Good evening, Colonel! Will you not come inside on this cold evening and warm yourself by the fire?"

"Miss Bennet!" he cried cheerfully, if not a tad bit sheepishly, and set off at once towards the house. "I had no idea of your being in Kent. Pray close the window or you shall take a chill. I will join you directly."

Elizabeth shut the window, secured the latch, rang for a fresh pot of tea, and stood before the fire in anticipation of her visitor. While she was not averse to solitude, neither was she a sedentary creature. Company—especially amicable company—was very welcome after passing the entire day alone.

Soon, the bell sounded, the maid answered the door, and Colonel Fitzwilliam was divested of his greatcoat and shown into the parlour with the tea things. Elizabeth curtseyed, but instead of issuing a formal bow, the colonel crossed the room, clasped both her hands, and greeted her with all the fondness and familiarity of a dear friend. "Miss Bennet, I cannot imagine a more pleasant surprise than meeting with you in the middle of all this bothersome snow! I trust you are well."

"I am very well, thank you, Colonel. I hope you will forgive my appalling lapse of manners. I confess I was so surprised and pleased to see you that I gave no thought at all to propriety! It is very good of you to oblige me by paying a visit at such a moment. The weather is frightful!"

The colonel laughed. "Very frightful, indeed! But surely, you and I need not stand upon ceremony."

Elizabeth smiled. "No, I daresay we need not." She indicated two chairs by the fire. "Will you not be seated?"

"I thank you," he said as she assessed the strength of the tea. "How are Mr and Mrs Collins? Will they be joining us? I should like to pay my respects."

"They were very well when I last saw them, sir, but you find me quite alone this evening. Mr and Mrs Collins went into the village early this morning before the weather turned to assist a family much in need. I fear there is no chance of their returning tonight."

He frowned. "You are alone? With only a few servants for company?"

"So, it would seem," she replied, handing him a cup of tea.

His forehead creased as he accepted it. "You cannot possibly remain here, Miss Bennet. An unmarried gentlewoman without protection—and in such wretched weather as this! It is neither prudent, nor proper."

A flush of heat suffused Elizabeth's countenance as she prepared her own tea. "I appreciate your concern, but I will manage well enough until Mr and Mrs Collins return tomorrow. The house is cosy and warm, and the weather, as you said, is so unpleasant no one save for yourself is about, not even Lady Catherine's woodsman."

"Assuming the Collinses are able to return tomorrow. The road to the village is buried by more than half a foot of snow! It could be days before the way is passable." He lowered his voice and glanced towards the door. "Can you say with any degree of certainty Mr Collins's servants are trustworthy? Would they keep you safe—would they protect you from harm at all costs?"

The colonel's words were sobering. For most of the day, Elizabeth's sole concern had been for her friend's safety; now, she felt a sharp prick of concern for her own. She doubted either of Mr Collins's servants would do more than was required of them under the circumstances.

As much as she hated to admit it, Colonel Fitzwilliam was correct—

being an unmarried lady, snowbound and alone save for two servants she did not know well and who owed her no fealty, was not an ideal situation in which to find herself. She licked her lips and said, "Be that as it may, I am far from home, sir. There is nowhere else for me to go."

"Nonsense," he insisted. "You must allow me to bring you to Rosings. There, you will find friends in abundance, and all the comforts of home."

Had Mr Collins not apprised her—repeatedly and in the most vociferous terms—of Lady Catherine's condemnation of Lydia's elopement and her indignation towards Mr Bennet for receiving the newlyweds at Longbourn, Elizabeth might have agreed. As she would be visiting Kent for a month complete, Elizabeth preferred to avoid incurring further censure. Thus far, she had been successful. Holding her tongue for an hour while Lady Catherine instructed her on proper comportment was easy enough; it was quite another matter to be expected to do so for an indeterminable length of time. "While I appreciate your concern and your generosity, Colonel, I would never dream of trespassing upon Lady Catherine's hospitality. I could not possibly impose upon her household when she already has guests to entertain."

Taking a sip of his tea, the colonel waved a dismissive hand. "It is no imposition at all, I assure you. Her ladyship's guests comprise an informal family party—namely my own dear relations. Certainly, I need not remind you how my aunt enjoys being of use to her neighbours! A gentlewoman of her acquaintance spending the night in an empty house is not to be borne, Miss Bennet. If I were to return to Rosings without you, there would be no escaping my aunt's displeasure."

Elizabeth, however, knew better. Clearly, Colonel Fitzwilliam knew nothing of her sister's infamy and her family's narrow escape from scandal. For that, she supposed she ought to be grateful to Lady Catherine. "Be that as it may, I am afraid I must decline."

Frowning, he set his teacup and saucer on the table, propped his forearms on his knees, and linked his fingers together. "While I own my aunt can be difficult and even unpleasant on occasion, no one currently in residence at Rosings will be easy knowing you have been left to shift for yourself. Neither would Mrs Collins for that matter. You are her dear friend. She could not possibly be satisfied with your remaining unprotected and alone in her absence. You must reconsider."

Elizabeth could well imagine Charlotte's concern for her, but Mr Collins would not want her to remove to Rosings and impose upon his patroness. "I am sorry, Colonel, but I cannot."

He regarded her with an inscrutable expression.

Like a child caught with her hand in the sweet jar, Elizabeth felt the urge to squirm under his unrelenting gaze. What was she thinking, throwing open the window and inviting him in? Since when had her comportment disintegrated to such a degree that she suddenly behaved as Lydia would, or Kitty? Mr Collins would learn of the colonel's visit—there was no avoiding that—but she hoped to keep the manner with which her impromptu invitation was issued to herself alone. She raised her teacup to her lips and silently berated herself for her thoughtlessness.

In the stillness of the room, the colonel's voice rang with an unmistakable air of authority. "It appears, Miss Bennet, you have left me no choice. Despite the seriousness of your present situation, you are determined to remain in the parsonage alone and unprotected. As a gentleman, I cannot accept that, and neither shall Darcy. Once he learns of your presence here—and your circumstances—he will likely set out from Rosings to fetch you himself, regardless of your stubbornness. So, you see, madam, your protests shall come to nothing. In the end, Darcy will insist upon having his way. We will see you at Rosings tonight."

Elizabeth heard nothing beyond Darcy's name. "Is Mr Darcy at Rosings?" she enquired in a slightly breathless voice. It was by sheer luck alone that she managed to maintain her grip on her cup and saucer. Both were quickly set upon the table. Clasping her hands on her lap, she endeavoured to calm her racing heart.

If only Darcy would come for her, but that had already proved an impossible hope. Elizabeth had waited months in anticipation of his return, only to be bitterly disappointed. No. Whether he was at Rosings or Pemberley or on the moon, Darcy would not come for her—not now that she was tied to a man he hated. He had not even come to Hertfordshire when Mr Bingley had married Jane.

The colonel smiled, seemingly oblivious to her distress. "Yes, Darcy is here, but I cannot say that he is pleased about it! He has had a bee in his bonnet since we arrived yesterday evening and Lady Catherine had the audacity to…" But whatever her ladyship had the audacity to do would remain a mystery. Chagrined, Colonel Fitzwilliam quietly cleared his throat. "Forgive me. I suppose the less said of my aunt's business with Darcy the better. In any case, I would wager a vast deal that seeing you again will improve his spirits tremendously."

Elizabeth sincerely doubted that would be the case, especially if Darcy currently found himself at odds with his aunt. "I cannot imagine our meeting would have such an effect upon Mr Darcy at present. I fear you mistake the matter, Colonel."

"Not at all, Miss Bennet. You and Darcy are old friends. He will be pleased to see you—beyond pleased. His sister, Georgiana, is also at Rosings. I believe you and she are acquainted as well."

"Yes," she admitted. "We met last summer when I visited Pemberley with my aunt and uncle. I found Miss Darcy to be a delightful young woman."

"Georgiana had much to say in your favour as well. No doubt she will enjoy renewing your acquaintance. I understand her disappointment was considerable when you left the country so unexpectedly."

With startling clarity, Elizabeth recalled the dark, agitated look on Darcy's countenance after she had revealed the whole of Lydia's impropriety to him in a moment of acute distress. He had all but leapt from his chair and paced to the window. His voice, as he demanded what had been done to attempt to recover her, was harsh. Just as she had that day in Lambton, Elizabeth averted her eyes to her lap and smoothed an imaginary crease in her gown. "I was very sorry to have disappointed Miss Darcy, but our leaving was unavoidable. Urgent family business called us back to Hertfordshire."

"And Darcy left for town soon after. The next day in fact. Georgiana was left with none but Bingley and his sisters for company, poor girl!"

"I am very sorry to hear that," she said, striving to keep her voice steady. "Miss Darcy must have felt her brother's absence keenly. From what I have witnessed, Mr Darcy's devotion to her is considerable, and her attachment to him as great. I imagine only the most pressing business would summon him from Miss Darcy's side at such a time."

The colonel scratched his head. "Indeed. It is unlike Darcy to leave Georgiana so suddenly, and even rarer for him to abandon her to the whims of his guests—especially Bingley's sisters! In any case, that is neither here nor there. We can speak further on the subject once you are settled at Rosings. I shall even give you leave to question Darcy about the business yourself if you dare, though I cannot guarantee he will be in any mood to explain himself tonight. He has had a particularly stressful day. My aunt, as you know, is determined to have her way in all things. I fear she has tried Darcy's patience exceedingly."

Hearing Darcy's temper had already been tried to its limits did nothing to ease Elizabeth's mind. He had been all that was gracious and welcoming when they had met at Pemberley; but Lydia—thoughtless, stupid Lydia—had not yet eloped with Mr Wickham, nor had Elizabeth been irreversibly bound to him through her sister's marriage—a marriage she had since learned had been orchestrated and financed, not by her Uncle Gardiner as her family had been led to believe, but entirely by Darcy.

Despite all he had done for her family, Elizabeth knew that if they were to meet again now, Darcy's black mood would only worsen. He had not, as she had so fervently hoped, come to the aid of her most foolish sister because he loved her still, but because he had failed to divulge Wickham's disreputable tendencies to the world. And because he had felt a heavy responsibility and a deep sense of duty to right that wrong.

Elizabeth was appalled to realise she was close to tears. Not wishing for the colonel to notice her discomposure, she turned her attention to the tea things and busied herself with refilling her cup. By the time she added cream and sugar and had taken a fortifying sip of tea, she had begun to feel mistress of herself once more, enough to say, "My removing to Rosings is unnecessary, Colonel. My cousin would not wish for me to impose upon your aunt, especially while your family is visiting for Christmas. In deference to his wishes, I shall remain here until he and Mrs Collins are come back. It is but one night. Their absence cannot be for long."

Giving her a stern look that brooked no opposition, Colonel Fitzwilliam shook his head. "That I cannot sanction, Miss Bennet. The weather is worsening as we speak. The longer we tarry, the less likely we are to have an easy journey, and I refuse to leave you alone with naught but the servants." He stood and extended his hand to her with the obvious intent of hastening her compliance. "I trust you will order your maid to pack your things while I return to Rosings and fetch the sleigh. I know you are fond of walking, but there is no chance of your walking all the way to Rosings in such weather. I will not take no for an answer. I will not abandon you, nor leave you without protection while your relations are from home. Either you come to Rosings, or I shall be forced to spend the night in this parlour arguing my point until you see reason."

Annoyed by her predicament and unable to see a way out of it, Elizabeth glanced helplessly at the window, where darkness had settled like a shroud over Hunsford. Beyond the curtains, she could discern nothing but a wall of blackness and falling snow.

She sighed.

Colonel Fitzwilliam had fought on the Continent. He had faced Bonaparte's army not once but twice. Clearly, he was unused to yielding to even the fiercest opposition. Unless she was prepared to argue with him until morning, there was nothing for her to do but capitulate. Pushing her frustration aside, she placed her hand in his and he assisted her as she rose from her chair. "Very well, sir. When you return, I will accompany you to Rosings. I thank you for your concern and for your gallantry."

He bowed to her. "You are most welcome. I will return for you within the hour. I will also recruit a chaperon. Darcy would never forgive me if I did not take prodigiously good care of you."

Elizabeth coloured deeply but made no reply, and the colonel took his leave.

CHAPTER 3

Time will generally lessen the interest of every attachment not within the daily circle.

— JOHN KNIGHTLEY, EMMA

"NO," LADY CATHERINE SNAPPED AT A HARRIED LOOKING servant. "Not the turnips, the potatoes! Leave the turnips where they are and fetch the potatoes at once. The potatoes must take their proper place beside the pickled eggs, otherwise the entire table will appear unbalanced. I cannot countenance having an unbalanced table and neither can Anne…"

Darcy rolled his eyes and reached for his wineglass. He doubted Anne was presently in any state to countenance anything. Should she manage to hold a fork correctly, he would be amazed. Anything more complicated was likely beyond her.

"Anne looks becoming this evening," her mother said to Darcy, "does she not?"

Anne looked drunk. He took a measured sip of watered-down wine and ignored her.

Across the table, Stephen snorted into his soup. He looked like hell.

Lord Carlisle scoffed. "The girl looks half in her cups, Catherine!"

"Henry," his wife hissed. "Do not start!"

Lady Catherine glared at him. "Anne is fatigued," she said with a disdainful sniff. "She has had a taxing day."

"She is drunk," the earl insisted, slapping his hand on the table for emphasis. "Drunk! Look at her, for God's sake. She has barely done more than blink since she stumbled into the dining room!"

"You are mistaken, Brother," said her ladyship coldly. "As usual." She spied another servant placing a heaping platter of mutton on the opposite end of the table and cried out, "You there! What do you think you are doing? Take that mutton away at once. It is dreadfully undercooked."

"Undercooked," Emerson muttered in annoyance. "The entire sheep is practically burnt to a crisp. We shall starve at this rate." He tossed his napkin onto the table, then reached for the decanter of wine, yanked the stopper off, and sniffed it. "Bah! Watered down, as usual...What a blasted waste." Despite his complaining, he poured a healthy measure of diluted wine into his glass and swallowed it down, then proceeded to pour himself another.

Emerson's wife, Lady Josephine, eyed her husband as distastefully as she had the platter of charred mutton. She looked as though she wanted to throw the entire haunch at his head.

"Darcy, where is Georgiana? Why has she not come down to dine? Is she indisposed?"

"To my knowledge," he said to Lady Catherine, "Georgiana is in excellent health." At least she had been when he had last seen her—donning her pelisse and fur muff as Fitzwilliam ushered her from the house with a cryptic smile on his face.

"This is most distressing!"

Darcy shrugged his shoulders and turned his attention to his soup, the most palatable offering on the table. *When Fitzwilliam returns, I shall beat him within an inch of his life for abandoning me. Then I will walk to the churchyard, retrieve his excellent brandy, and drink the bottle dry.*

"You know, if you had a wife—you know if you were married to Anne—you would not have to concern yourself with such things as indisposition. Anne would take Georgiana in hand—she is infinitely capable in that regard. I can think of no better sister for Georgiana and no better mistress for Pemberley. Anne will make you an excellent wife."

Regretting he did not take his supper in his rooms, Darcy exhaled in frustration and glanced furtively at Anne. For the moment, she remained upright, but appeared utterly transfixed by her reflection in a soup spoon. He had hoped he would find her reasonable for once; that he could speak with her seriously, present a united front against her mother, and put an end to this nonsense about a supposed engagement between them once and for all. Clearly, now was not an opportune moment.

"Anne," said her mother, "you will wear your gold silk with the olive embroidery to Lady Metcalfe's ball, and your cream silk with the pearl beadwork for your wedding. As Pemberley's future mistress, you ought to wear something befitting your station when you and Darcy exchange your vows in church."

Anne barely batted an eye, but Darcy's temper flared. "You speak out of turn, madam. As I have told you repeatedly since my arrival, I have no thoughts of matrimony at present."

"Nonsense!" Lady Catherine insisted. "You are nearly nine-and-twenty. It is time for you to do your duty and marry Anne. It is my dearest wish, as well as your mother's."

"But it does not follow it is mine."

"Your engagement has been well-known within our family for years! You must honour it! Cannot you see how Anne desires nothing more than to be your wife?"

In unison, all in the room turned to look at Anne.

"Tell him, Anne," her mother demanded. "Tell Darcy it has long been your dearest wish to marry him!"

Anne blinked at Lady Catherine for nearly a minute before slowly shifting her gaze to Darcy. Her complexion was heightened. Her eyes were glassy and round. "Darcy," she said in her soft, unduly serious voice. "It is my dearest wish to marry Jack Hastings. He is an excellent kisser." She giggled, then laughed outright as she slid from her chair onto the carpet.

Lady Catherine gaped at her in furious disbelief. She opened her mouth but was unable to utter more than a monosyllable before slumping forward into her soup.

Lord Carlisle turned to his wife in astonishment. "Who the devil is Jack Hastings!"

Darcy raised his wineglass to his mouth and drained the contents, then reached for the decanter to refill his glass. Over the last hour he had imbibed more than usual, yet, because of his aunt's penchant for diluting her liquor until it was worthless, remained infuriatingly sober.

The knob on his bedchamber door turned, then rattled, but the lock held firm. Darcy took another drink as the fire crackled and popped in the grate, sending a shower of bright sparks up the chimney.

"Darcy," said Fitzwilliam's muffled voice through the door. "Let me in."

Grateful it was not his uncle come to speak to him about Anne, he set his glass aside, rose from his chair, and crossed the room. After that ridiculous farce of a dinner and all it entailed, he had earned something stronger than watered-down wine. He turned the key in the lock and opened the door. "I am glad to see you are still in one piece," he told his cousin dryly. "You have been gone for hours."

Fitzwilliam smirked at him from the hall. A kissing bough was suspended from the ceiling above his head, likely at the behest of Lady Catherine. "Do I not get a kiss? A token of appreciation for venturing forth on such a cold winter's night?"

Rolling his eyes, Darcy waved him inside. "Please, no patronising remarks tonight. The entire day has been a misery." He shut the door and secured the lock. "You missed dinner by the way."

After divesting himself of his greatcoat and discarding it on a chair with his hat and gloves, Fitzwilliam surrendered the bottle of brandy. "I guessed as much. How was it?"

"A bloody nightmare," Darcy replied as he examined the bottle. "The mutton was overcooked, as were the potatoes, but the soup was decent. Anne, believe it or not, was completely foxed. Undeterred in the least by her daughter's insobriety, Lady Catherine persisted in promoting a union between us. We argued. Then Anne professed a desire to marry Jack Hastings instead."

"Jack Hastings," Fitzwilliam repeated incredulously. "You mean 'Handsome Jack'—the groom?"

"One and the same. Apparently, I am a dreadful cold fish, and Hastings is...the less said about what Hastings is the better."

"I suppose the whole family was present to bear witness to this spectacle?"

"And the servants," Darcy replied darkly. "I have never seen your father so livid, not even when your brother smuggled that courtesan into the house while the archbishop was taking tea in the drawing room with your grandmother."

"What of the others?"

"Your mother," said Darcy as he wiped sediment from the bottle and removed the cork, "was appalled. Lady Josephine was scandalised. Emerson was nonplussed, and Stephen laughed so hard he choked on a pickled egg. He was quickly set to rights with what appeared to be the entire contents of his hip flask. Had your father not been occupied with dismissing the servants, he would have boxed his ears."

Sighing, Fitzwilliam rubbed his brow. "He turned up. That is a small sort of accomplishment, I suppose."

"He looked completely disreputable and smelled even worse." Darcy retrieved two snifters and poured a generous helping of brandy for his cousin, then another for himself. "Thank you for indulging me."

Accepting his glass, Fitzwilliam raised it aloft and clinked it against Darcy's. "As I told you earlier, I am your servant. You have had a trying day."

"To say the least." Darcy took a measured swallow and savoured the rich, complex palette of flavours. The brandy was, in one word, exquisite. "How is Georgiana? I trust she is well?"

"Perfectly well," Fitzwilliam replied, "but you have yet to say anything of Lady Catherine. I imagine she was distressed by all that occurred, not to mention furious."

Darcy snorted as he absently swirled the amber liquid in his glass. "She fainted. The apothecary was called as a precaution. He is examining her now, but I doubt there is anything the matter with her. Once she regained consciousness, her first order of business was to resume her demands that I marry her daughter and save the family from scandal."

Fitzwilliam stared at him with something akin to alarm. "I certainly hope you told her no."

Darcy scoffed. "Of course I told her no. I had no interest in marrying Anne before—do you honestly think I would take her to wife now, after she has possibly lain with a groom?"

"I hardly know. You and your damned sense of familial duty…"

"I cannot possibly marry Anne," Darcy told him firmly, raising his glass to his lips and swallowing a large mouthful of brandy, "not now, or ever. This brandy is exceptional, by the way."

"I should hope so. I had a devil of a time getting it into England." Fitzwilliam took a generous sip from his own glass, then grinned. "I nearly forgot! You will never guess who is in Kent."

Darcy settled into a chair by the fire and crossed his ankles. "You had better tell me. Or not. I cannot say I particularly care at this point."

His cousin claimed the chair opposite with a look that clearly communicated his belief that Darcy would care very much. "The delightful Miss Bennet."

Darcy's glass was halfway to his mouth. He lowered it. Hearing Elizabeth's name was enough to make his pulse pound. That she was here, in Kent, was as incredible as it was inconceivable. "Miss Bennet is visiting the parsonage?" By some miracle, he managed to keep his voice even.

"She was. Now she is here, at Rosings. Installed in the bedchamber beside your sister's, to be specific. She is settling in as we speak."

Suddenly, the room felt too hot, too stuffy, and much too small. Darcy drained his glass and quickly rose to refill it. The bedchamber Miss Bennet was supposedly settling into was one he knew well. He had stayed in those rooms on countless occasions when Georgiana was a young girl and prone to having nightmares. He had slept in that very bed. Now, according to his cousin, Elizabeth would as well. He poured another measure of brandy into his glass and resisted the urge to gulp it down as he would a glass of water. As composedly as possible, he asked, "Why is she here?"

Fitzwilliam smirked at him. "Miss Bennet could hardly be made to sleep in the stable."

"Pray be serious. That is not what I meant."

"To my knowledge, the Collinses went into the village on a charitable mission this morning, where they were detained by the weather. As they took his gig," Fitzwilliam rolled his eyes, "they cannot return until the roads are passable. Save for two servants she barely knows, Miss Bennet found herself alone. Because I like her, and because it is the right thing to do, I insisted upon bringing her to Rosings for safekeeping. If you want to know why she is presently in Kent, I cannot say. You will have to ask her yourself."

Darcy stared at the glass in his hand with a grave countenance. The only sound in the room was the crackling of the fire. In that moment, he felt myriad emotions. He was thrilled, terrified, hopeful, and unnerved in equal measure, but he was also baffled. Why was Elizabeth not spending Christmas at Longbourn, or at Netherfield with the Bingleys? What could possibly have brought her to Hunsford? Mrs Collins was a dear friend, but there was no one in the world Elizabeth loved more than her eldest sister. When Mrs Bingley had fallen ill at Netherfield more than a year ago, Elizabeth had walked three miles in the aftermath of a rainstorm to nurse her. Darcy could not imagine her choosing to spend Christmas with the Collinses when Jane, her parents, and her two unmarried sisters were all in Hertfordshire.

"Have you nothing more to say on the subject?"

Darcy started at the sound of his cousin's voice. He had forgotten Fitzwilliam was even in the room. Setting his glass on the table, he walked to the hearth, where he drummed his fingers on the mantel. Finding no answers there, he strode to the window, where he pushed the drapes aside and propped his hands on his hips. The view afforded him nothing but darkness and falling snow.

"Darcy," his cousin prompted. "You are not unwell, surely?"

"I am perfectly well, only distracted."

"So I see. I had thought the prospect of renewing your friendship with Miss Bennet would please you. I cannot ever recall seeing you so smitten, so utterly charmed by a woman. I felt certain that you liked her more than any other lady of your acquaintance."

For the briefest moment, Darcy shut his eyes. He was so far beyond liking Elizabeth Bennet at this point it was absurd to pretend otherwise. His love for her was as immovable as it was constant, much like his regrets.

And she was here, now, at Rosings.

Darcy repressed an oath. How in the world was he to face her, after all that had come to pass, with any degree of equanimity? What could he possibly say to her that would ever make amends for Wickham seducing her fifteen-year-old sister? Even if Darcy did devise an appropriate apology, would Elizabeth wish to hear it? There was no privacy to be had at Rosings Park, and certainly no peace. His family would be present for every look, every breath, every moment of awkwardness and discomfiture between them. Lady Catherine was already displeased with him, but with Elizabeth in residence, she would become even more so. At best, she would demand his attention until he lost both his temper and his sanity. At worst, she would direct her vitriol towards Elizabeth with the express intent of reminding Darcy of her perceived inferiority in relation to Anne's. Anne, who, in a drunken stupor, claimed she wanted to marry a groom!

Across the room, Fitzwilliam shifted in his chair. "You are in love with Miss Bennet," he said with certainty. "That much is obvious. What I cannot understand is why her being here distresses you. Surely, after all this time—"

"It is not so simple," said Darcy, turning his back to the window. He shook his head with a self-deprecating twist of his mouth. "I will not insult your intelligence by denying that I do, in fact, hold Miss Bennet in a tender regard, but there are circumstances of which you are unaware. Circumstances that have likely altered her good opinion of me forever."

"What circumstances?" his cousin asked, wearing an expression of puzzlement as he leaned forward in his chair. "Of what do you speak?"

Darcy ran his hand over his mouth. Any explanation he thought to make died on his tongue. He dared not utter Wickham's name. It would likely choke him.

Taking pity on him, Fitzwilliam set his glass on the table, abandoned his chair, and crossed the room to stand beside him. "I do not say this to pry, or to force your confidence, but you must bring under regulation whatever it is that has you twisted up in knots. Whatever circumstances have created this gulf—be it real or perceived—between you and Miss Bennet, you must either confront them, or make your peace with them, but you cannot continue as you are. If you do nothing, you must know you will regret it—that you will regret *her*—for the rest of your life." He laid a hand on Darcy's shoulder. "Come," he said, and urged him back towards the fire. "Have some more brandy and tell me about Miss Bennet."

Together, they finished the bottle.

With Fitzwilliam's prompting, Darcy talked for half the night.

CHAPTER 4

One man's style must not be the rule of another's.

— Mr Knightley, Emma

"Do you approve of your rooms, Miss Bennet?"

Elizabeth offered Miss Darcy a diplomatic smile. "Lady Catherine has certainly gone to great lengths to ensure her guests are surrounded by every imaginable comfort. I daresay I shall sleep quite soundly tonight in such a stately bed." It was the best she could manage. In truth, the rooms she had been given were too much like the rest of the house—pretentious and ornate to the point of being vulgar.

Miss Darcy gingerly touched a figurine on the bedside table with her fingertip, an enormous porcelain peacock accented with an excess of gold leaf. Two facetted emeralds were inlaid for its eyes and less precious gems complemented its bright plumage. "My brother," she said, regarding the peacock with a frown, "once told me he found Rosings, and this room particularly, ostentatious and uselessly fine." She raised her eyes to Elizabeth's and blushed.

Instantly, Elizabeth thought of Pemberley, with its refined décor and simple but elegant furnishings. Everything in Rosings Park spoke of the perceived importance of its owner, and nothing of refinement and taste. Pemberley was a beloved ancestral home, not a nouveau riche showpiece. Of course, Lady Catherine's preferences would not be in accord with Darcy's. She repressed a smile. "Did he?"

Miss Darcy bit her lip. "He did. I hope my saying so has not offended you or caused you to think poorly of me, or my brother."

"Indeed, it has not," Elizabeth assured her. "Rest assured you are both safe."

"I am relieved to hear it," said the girl as the corners of her lips turned upward. "Forgive me, Miss Bennet. I am not usually so impertinent, but my cousin Richard reminded me you are my brother's dear friend and his, and that I have nothing to fear from you. Nor have I forgotten how very kind you were when we had the pleasure of meeting last summer in Derbyshire."

Elizabeth's heart skipped a beat upon hearing herself described as Darcy's 'dear friend'. She had been dear to him once, but her circumstances then were very different from what they were now. If Elizabeth were dear to him still, Darcy would have renewed his addresses long ago. If he still held her in a tender regard, he would have fetched her from the parsonage in Colonel Fitzwilliam's stead or greeted her upon her arrival at Rosings. He had done none of those things, and the reality of his disregard pained her.

Attempting to sound more cheerful than she presently felt, Elizabeth said, "You were gracious and kind yourself, and I am delighted to have an opportunity to renew our acquaintance. Perhaps, once I return to the parsonage, you would be so good as to consent to take tea with me one afternoon? Assuming your brother approves, of course." Even as she spoke the words, Elizabeth could not imagine Darcy would ever approve of his sister, who had once suffered Mr Wickham's lies and duplicity herself, calling on her at the parsonage, or anywhere else for that matter. She doubted he would approve of their proximity now, at Rosings.

Apparently, Miss Darcy's opinion on the subject differed greatly from Elizabeth's. "I have no doubt my brother would approve wholeheartedly. He has often told me how pleased he was to be granted such an extraordinary opportunity to have you visit with us at Pemberley. He esteems you so highly. He has for a long time—since he first met you in Hertfordshire. Whenever he wrote to me then, you were often mentioned in his letters."

Elizabeth stared at her in shock. When she had stayed at Netherfield to nurse Jane, Miss Bingley had much to say about the lengthiness of Darcy's letters to his sister and the elegance of his hand; but Elizabeth was at a loss as to what he could possibly have found to write about her. She had been awful to him then—obstinate, argumentative, and impertinent to the point of being uncivil. Somehow, she managed to say, "Mr Darcy mentioned me in his letters?"

"Many times. Was I wrong to tell you?"

"No," she stammered. "Not at all. I am only surprised to hear your brother related anything of me to you then, as he and I were not so well acquainted with one another until much later." She offered the girl what she hoped was a favourable smile. "Of course, it is perfectly natural for him to write to you of the people he meets and the places he sees in his travels. I am quite flattered he found me interesting enough to mention at all!"

Miss Darcy returned her smile. "I enjoyed hearing about you. I am sure Fitzwilliam had not written of you more than twice before I felt as though I knew you myself. I was so happy when he informed me you were staying in Lambton, and so excited and nervous when he told me you were looking forward to making my acquaintance." She took a few steps in Elizabeth's direction and wrapped her hand around an ornate bedpost. "When you left so suddenly, the loss of your society was deeply felt at Pemberley. I hope that all was well when you and Mr and Mrs Gardiner arrived home—that your family was in good health."

Elizabeth was moved by her sincerity; it was impossible not to be. The remembrance of the disappointment she felt that day when she realised she would not be able to keep her engagement with Miss Darcy was vivid, as was the despair of knowing their short acquaintance—and her acquaintance with Darcy—was likely at an end. "I was very sorry to leave Derbyshire without bidding you and your brother a proper farewell. My family are all in excellent health. In fact, my eldest sister is lately married to Mr Bingley. But you must tell me about your own family. Colonel Fitzwilliam has told me you and your relations are visiting Lady Catherine and Miss de Bourgh for Christmas."

"Oh, yes," said Miss Darcy, brightening at the mention of her family. "Our coming here was quite unexpected, but it is such a treat to see all my cousins together, especially at Christmastime. Uncle Carlisle's estate is even further north than our home in Derbyshire—at the north-western tip of Cumbria, beyond the lakes. It is a lovely place, as is Cousin Arthur's home in West Yorkshire, but Fitzwilliam and I prefer the untamed beauty of Pemberley to the manicured gardens of Levens Hall and Rosings Park and London."

"It appears we are of one mind, for I have never seen such beautiful grounds and woods as Pemberley's. In fact, I believe I may even prefer Pemberley's woods to Hertfordshire's, which boast some of the most wonderful paths and picturesque glens I have ever seen."

"I should like to visit Hertfordshire someday. Fitzwilliam told me how much he enjoyed exploring the country around Netherfield. From what I recall from his letters, he encountered you many times on his walks, and at Rosings, too, when you visited Mr and Mrs Collins last spring. I understand you are an avid walker."

Elizabeth was flooded with contrition as she recalled meeting Darcy on her sojourns through Rosings's grounds and woods, especially in the grove. She had cleverly—and mistakenly—believed she was warning him away from her favourite haunts by telling him how much they delighted her; instead, she had unwittingly encouraged his presence and his then unwanted suit. "Yes. I dearly love to be out of doors, even when the weather is gloomy and cold. I fear my poor mother does not know what to do with me, Miss Darcy. I am forever ruining my hems. It has long been a point of contention between us, for she is mortified someone might see me in such a state!"

"You must know my brother would hardly care." A gentle smile played upon Miss Darcy's mouth. "He would likely consider you to be as lovely wearing mud-stained petticoats as he would if you were wearing an elegant ball gown."

Miss Darcy's reference to her brother seeing Elizabeth's mud-soaked petticoats at Netherfield when she had nursed Jane mortified her. "Surely," she cried as a heated blush coloured her cheeks, "Mr Darcy has not mentioned that in his letters!"

"Please do not make yourself uneasy," Miss Darcy said in a rush, having the decency to blush herself. "The truth of the matter is that I have long wished to express my gratitude to you, Miss Bennet. Your love of nature and your enthusiasm for being out of doors have had such a profound effect upon my own happiness. Were it not for your adventuresome spirit, I doubt my brother would have granted me the freedom he has this past year. Where I was once cautioned against straying too far from the house, Fitzwilliam now encourages me to take long walks through the countryside—accompanied by a footman, of course. Like you," she said quietly but with considerable feeling, "I have found fresh air and exercise far more invigorating than taking a turn in a stuffy drawing room." She bowed her head as her fingers fidgeted with the lace trim on the sleeve of her gown. "It has done much for my peace of mind."

Elizabeth struggled to contain her astonishment. That her unfashionable country habits had inspired Darcy to encourage similar habits in his sister was as inconceivable to her as it was extraordinary. Again, Miss Bingley came to mind—proper, superior Miss Bingley, who relished declaring Miss Darcy one of the most accomplished and refined young ladies of her acquaintance. Whatever would she think of her friend now, boldly venturing beyond Pemberley's paved footpaths and into the wilds of Derbyshire—and with her brother's approbation! Elizabeth barely knew what to think herself.

The sharp succession of knocks that sounded upon the bedchamber door a moment later was jarring, enough to make both Elizabeth and Miss Darcy jump. Smoothing her skirts, Elizabeth's lips quirked upward as she met Miss Darcy's startled eyes. They laughed at their silliness, and Elizabeth crossed the room to answer the door.

A tall, elegant woman she had never before seen—but who she assumed must be Colonel Fitzwilliam's mother—awaited her in the hall. Sparing Elizabeth little more than a cursory glance, she stepped into the room as Elizabeth shut the door. "Georgiana," she said, "will you do me the honour of introducing me to your friend?"

Miss Darcy appeared both eager and happy to oblige her. When she had done, Lady Carlisle's pale blue eyes appraised Elizabeth from head to toe. "For once I see my son was not prone to exaggeration. You are as lovely in countenance and figure as he claimed."

"Thank you, ma'am," Elizabeth replied, more amused by the countess's direct manner than offended.

"My sister-in-law is currently indisposed, otherwise she would have seen to you herself. She is excessively attentive to such things. How do you like your rooms?"

Elizabeth could not be certain, but she thought she detected a flash of something in her eyes—a keen spark of diversion not dissimilar to what she had often seen in Colonel Fitzwilliam's expression on the occasions they had dined together at Rosings last spring. "Lady Catherine's generosity knows no bounds. I am sorry to hear she is presently unwell and hope her indisposition will be of short duration."

"That," said the countess with a cryptic turn of her mouth, "remains to be seen. If there is anything you require, simply ring for a servant and you will be attended to. Breakfast is at ten o'clock and is served in the breakfast parlour. Georgiana will show you where to go. As you are already acquainted with Lady Catherine, you must also know how highly she values punctuality. I urge you to be on time, Miss Bennet."

"Yes, your ladyship."

Lady Carlisle's eyes returned to Elizabeth's gown. While the style was flattering and the velvet ribbons trimming the sleeves and bodice were pretty, it was not an evening gown, but one designed for morning wear. Nor was it new or considered au courant among London's fashionable set; it certainly was not as fine as the gown Miss Darcy wore. Feeling the weight of her ladyship's gaze, Elizabeth raised her chin. The urge to be flippant and enquire whether she passed muster was difficult to resist, but it would not do to offend Darcy's aunt, nor would she wish to make Miss Darcy uncomfortable. She kept her impertinence to herself.

At length, the countess gave a haughty little sniff, but her voice when she spoke was kind. "My son has informed me you have no lady's maid to attend you, Miss Bennet. I shall send mine to you shortly, and again tomorrow morning at eight o'clock. Should you remain with us longer than that, I will arrange for a maid to attend you for the duration of your stay."

The thoughtfulness of the gesture startled Elizabeth. She had not expected to receive such a singular attention from any relation of Lady Catherine's, save for the few she already knew. She certainly had not expected such graciousness from Colonel Fitzwilliam's mother. "That is generous of you, Lady Carlisle, but I do not wish to inconvenience you."

The countess merely waved her hand in a dismissive fashion. "I assure you it is no inconvenience. In any case, we cannot possibly have you attending to your own toilette now, can we? Tell me, have you had your supper?"

"Yes, ma'am. Colonel Fitzwilliam and Miss Darcy were so good as to dine with me at the parsonage before we set out for Rosings."

"I am glad to hear it. Richard speaks well of you and has assured me that Darcy has long considered you one of the most intelligent, estimable ladies of his acquaintance. That is high praise from my exacting nephew, Miss Bennet. I have never known Darcy to pay such an extraordinary compliment to any lady, and I have known him all his life." The corners of her lips lifted, revealing the hint of a wry smile. "I believe you will prove an interesting addition to our little family party here at Rosings Park." Having said her piece, her ladyship bid Elizabeth a good night, inclined her head to her niece, and departed.

Expelling a breath that she had not realised she had been holding, Elizabeth returned Miss Darcy's bemused gaze and sagged onto the bed with a breathless little laugh.

"Who is Lady Birtwhistle?" Elizabeth asked Miss Darcy the following morning, taking care to keep her voice low. They were seated side by side at the breakfast table, spreading copious amounts of jam on their toast. Despite the mantel clock chiming half past ten o'clock, no one else was present. "I had thought it was Lady Metcalfe who was to give the Yule Ball tomorrow evening."

"Oh, it is," Miss Darcy replied as quietly, glancing towards the door.

"Lady Birtwhistle is her closest neighbour and oldest friend, but Lady Catherine cannot stand her. She has three daughters, all of whom have set their caps at Fitzwilliam, which vexes my aunt to no end. They will certainly be at Lady Metcalfe's ball, which I fear shall make for an unpleasant evening for my poor brother."

Frowning, Elizabeth wiped a smudge of jam from her fingers with her napkin. Despite Darcy's alleged dissatisfaction with the attentions of the Misses Birtwhistle, there would be other ladies at the ball—handsome, eligible ladies whose attentions Darcy may not wish to avoid; ladies whose youngest sisters had not run off with a scoundrel in the middle of the night. Tamping down her own dissatisfaction at the prospect, she cleared her throat. "And there are three of them, you say?"

"Three of what?" Colonel Fitzwilliam enquired as he entered the room whistling a lively Scotch air. He bowed to both ladies, then stooped to kiss his cousin on the cheek.

"Three Misses Birtwhistle," Miss Darcy replied solemnly.

The colonel winced. "I daresay your brother will not be pleased to see even one of them tomorrow evening, never mind all three. Nor can I say that I blame him. They are without doubt the most tiresome bunch of… ladies." Chagrined, he coughed into his fist and turned his attention to the sideboard, where he piled bacon and eggs on a plate. When he had done, he claimed a cup and filled it with coffee. "Tell me, Miss Bennet, how are you faring this fine morning? I trust that you slept well."

"Quite well, Colonel, I thank you."

"And the bed?" he asked as he made his way to the table. "Was it comfortable?"

"Indeed, it was," she replied over the rim of her teacup. "Very comfortable."

Grinning, he placed his plate on the table across from Elizabeth's and pulled out a chair. "That is precisely what Darcy always claimed as well! The room itself may be fitted up for a spectacular fop, but rest assured you will sleep like a babe in that bed, Miss Bennet."

Elizabeth flushed scarlet as she nearly choked on a mouthful of tea. Though Miss Darcy had shared her brother's opinion about the room and its décor the previous night, she had never once assumed it was because he had slept there himself. To distract herself from the provocative image of Mr Darcy in her bed, she took another measured sip from her cup and willed her flaming cheeks to cool.

"Are we discussing Stephen and his antics again, Richard?" a dull voice said from the doorway as Colonel Fitzwilliam tucked into his bacon. "It is too early by half." The owner of the voice, a well-turned-out gentleman in his late thirties who looked as though he preferred to be anywhere else, perked up when he noticed Elizabeth. "Well, well," he drawled, smoothing his hands over the lapels of his coat. "I do not believe I have the pleasure of being acquainted with this lovely creature. Georgiana, would you do the honours?"

Miss Darcy looked positively alarmed by his request. Elizabeth suspected it may have had something to do with the flirtatious gleam in the gentleman's eye, or perhaps his eccentric taste in waistcoats. The fabric from which his was constructed bore an alarming resemblance to the bright, tropical drapery adorning the windows in the upstairs hall. The corners of Elizabeth's lips lifted as she imagined an exclusive London tailor arguing with Lady Catherine's curtain maker over bolts of colourful, garish fabric.

Beside her, Colonel Fitzwilliam snorted inelegantly. "Spare us your false gallantry, Arthur. Miss Bennet is sharper than a rapier. She has likely already discerned your sad state of affairs for herself." Despite such a speech, he performed the introduction himself. "My dear Miss Bennet, allow me to present my brother, Viscount Emerson of Sallow Hall, West Yorkshire. Arthur, this is Miss Elizabeth Bennet of Longbourn in Hertfordshire."

Elizabeth rose from her chair and executed a brief but elegant curtsey. "It is a pleasure, my lord," she said, arching her brow slightly as she resumed her seat.

The viscount bowed to her. "The pleasure is mine, Miss Bennet." His smile was winsome, but it quickly turned to a frown once he espied his brother's smirking countenance. Straightening to his full height, he fixed the colonel with an imperious, disapproving look that would rival any of Lady Catherine's. "I see how it is, Richard. Despite your profession, you have no true respect for rank. Clearly, you are jealous I am first, while you must make your way in the world by playing hide and seek with Bonaparte."

"Clearly," Colonel Fitzwilliam countered, "you are delusional. Miss Bennet is a gentlewoman, and a great friend of Darcy's. I could hardly disrespect her by introducing *her* to the likes of *you.*"

"A friend of Darcy's, you say?" The viscount rubbed his chin as he regarded Elizabeth with a dubious expression. "Impossible. Darcy is far too fastidious and disinterested to have such a charming friend." He grinned. "Perhaps you would like to be my friend instead, Miss Bennet. I am not nearly so dull as Darcy, and I would pay you every civility in my power."

"Among other things," Colonel Fitzwilliam muttered. Before he could utter so much as another syllable, Miss Darcy turned her large, innocent, blue eyes on the viscount and said:

"How is your dear wife, Lady Josephine, faring this morning, Cousin Arthur? I do hope she is well."

Viscount Emerson's flirtatious expression turned petulant. "Et tu, Georgiana?" he asked as his brother snickered at him. "For such a lovely young lady, you have an appalling lack of sympathy for your elders. Unfeeling girl." He glowered at his brother, bowed gallantly to Elizabeth, gave Miss Darcy a saucy wink, and proceeded to the sideboard, where he bemoaned the lack of alcoholic libations with a dramatic flair even Sarah Siddons would envy.

Elizabeth endeavoured to conceal her amusement behind her napkin, with little effect.

The colonel looked at her and rolled his eyes. "Welcome to Rosings Park, Miss Bennet."

Surprizes are foolish things. The pleasure is not enhanced, and the inconvenience is often considerable.

— Mr Knightley, Emma

Darcy's head ached. To make matters worse, he had slept well past the breakfast hour, something he had not done since before he had reached his majority. As he made a valiant attempt to shed the brown coat that he wore in favour of his blue one, he repressed an oath of frustration. While the stylish, form-fitting garment flattered his figure, it was by no means designed with ease of removal in mind.

"Worth," he called to his valet, then winced as the sound of his own voice exacerbated the incessant pounding in his skull.

Worth appeared as though from thin air, effortlessly tugged the offending coat from his master's person, and assisted him as he donned the blue one. "Very fetching sir," he said in his even, dulcet tone, making a slight adjustment to the way the fabric lay across Darcy's shoulders.

"Thank you," Darcy murmured as he scrutinised his appearance in the mirror. Despite ten solid hours of sleep, he was exhausted, but thankfully no longer in his cups.

Damned Fitzwilliam and his illegal brandy. Such overindulgence was uncharacteristic of him, not to mention irresponsible, and the lingering effects—the fatigue, the dark circles beneath his eyes, and the harsh lines around his mouth—would do him no favours when he finally came face to face with Elizabeth.

Good God, I look nearly as disreputable as Stephen…

Groaning, Darcy dropped heavily onto a wingback chair, tugged at the knot in his cravat, and raked his hands through his hair, undermining a significant portion of his valet's efforts to make him presentable enough for company.

"Shall I retrieve the chamber pot, sir?" his man asked.

"No," Darcy told him. "I am well. I will summon you if I have need of anything else."

"As you wish, sir," Worth replied, and left as quietly and unobtrusively as he had come.

An hour later, Darcy stood on the precipice of a series of overgrown hedgerows that bordered Rosings Park's largest pasture. Save for a deer or two and a few birds, he passed his time there alone. It was the farthest parcel of land from the manor house and boasted a majestic view of the valley. The prospect was especially pleasant on a balmy summer morning, but it was December and therefore hardly warm enough to stand around in a dense snow-covered field contemplating his regrets and all that needed to be done to alleviate them.

The insistent crunch of snow drew his attention elsewhere.

Not twenty feet away, wearing an ambiguous expression, Colonel Fitzwilliam regarded him from astride one of Lady Catherine's horses. The air was cold, and his breath resembled a white cloud of vapour. "Whatever are you doing?" he asked Darcy, guiding his mount closer.

Darcy indicated the tangled, unkempt overgrowth and gnarled branches with a curt inclination of his head. "Mr Edmonton was correct. This hedgerow will need rebuilding. Sooner than later if this pasture is to be used to graze livestock come spring. There is significant damage to one large section along the high ridge, and a few less obvious breaches at various intervals along the lower ridge. If you like, we can look at them now." He reached for his horse's reins, but the exasperation in his cousin's voice gave him pause.

"Never mind about the hedgerow. It is freezing! Why on earth are you looking at hedgerows the day after a snowstorm? Breakfast was four hours ago. Not only did you miss it, but you also missed a perfect opportunity to speak with Miss Bennet."

Darcy averted his eyes. The moment he learned that Elizabeth was a guest in his aunt's house, neither his mind nor his nerves had given him a moment's peace; thus, his decision to seek the benefit of fresh air and exercise before seeking Elizabeth. He turned his attention to the reins in his hand and examined them for signs of wear. "I hardly know," he said. He doubted such an answer would satisfy his cousin.

It did not.

Fitzwilliam swung down from his saddle and secured his horse's reins to a limb thoroughly choked by vines. Tugging the collar of his greatcoat to his chin, he forged a path to Darcy through the snow. They stood in companionable silence for some time watching small winter birds—robins, redwings, and finches—flit from branch to branch. "You are hiding," he said at length. "It is beneath you, Darcy."

"And I suppose you have come to expedite my return. The last time I checked, you were a commanding officer of the Royal Army, not a dog dispatched to retrieve a pheasant."

"Obviously, you have forgotten that hunting down deserters is part and parcel of my profession," his cousin replied, rubbing his hands together to generate warmth.

Darcy snorted. "Since when does doing Lady Catherine's bidding carry the same distinction as executing an order from the Major General?"

"Not even the Major General would trifle with her ladyship when her mood is foul. You know I do not relish being idle."

Darcy could not disagree. "So long as you have employment—and the work is honourable—your mission hardly signifies."

Fitzwilliam rubbed his forehead with his hand. In that moment, he looked nearly as tired as Darcy felt. "I am not here by Lady Catherine's design. I came because I am concerned about you. Despite your being foxed last night, it is unlike you to miss breakfast, especially at Rosings."

"Rosings," Darcy muttered in annoyance, "has become a bane of my existence. I never should have come."

"Nevertheless, you are here for the time being. So is Miss Bennet for that matter." Fitzwilliam's lips quirked. "You will be pleased to know she is holding up well in your absence. Georgiana adores her, my mother and Josephine, believe it or not, have both been welcoming, and Arthur is thoroughly smitten, though whether Arthur's approbation is in your favour remains to be seen."

"Wonderful," Darcy muttered. "That is just what I need—interference from Emerson. Please tell me he was not drunk at the breakfast table."

"Hardly," Fitzwilliam said with a laugh, "though your sister pointedly asking after his wife when he was attempting to charm Miss Bennet likely made him wish for a pint or two of small beer with which to swallow his slice of humble pie."

The corners of Darcy's lips lifted infinitesimally. "Remind me to thank her later. What of Miss Bennet? What does she think of Emerson?"

"Rest assured, she knows what he is, just as she knows what you are."

The hint of a smile Darcy wore slipped from his face. "And what am I, in Miss Bennet's opinion?"

"A good man," his cousin said with steadfast conviction.

A brisk wind whipped through the trees, ruffling barren branches and sending errant snowflakes twirling into the air. Across the pasture, a flock of blackbirds took flight. Their loud, cacophonous cries echoed through the stillness and quiet of the afternoon.

A good man.

Was it true? he wondered. Did Elizabeth consider him to be a good man?

As far as Darcy was concerned, earning her good opinion had seemed incomprehensible after he had failed her in nearly every regard.

But what of Elizabeth's perception of the matter?

For the first time, Darcy dared to consider he may have been wrong. Not only had they not seen each other for many months, but age and experience had taught him that people in general possessed a tendency towards alteration in the wake of distressing circumstances.

It did not follow that everyone became altered for the worse.

Elizabeth was not formed for melancholy. Her nature was inherently warm and her heart unfailingly generous. She was compassionate. She was teasing and sweet. Surely, if anyone could find it within their heart to forgive him for concealing Wickham's profligate ways from the world and nearly ruining her family's good name in the process, it would be Elizabeth Bennet.

Perhaps the possibility of redemption was not lost to him, as he had believed. But the question remained: if he did manage to gain her forgiveness, could Elizabeth ever come to care for him—could she ever come to love him—if only a little?

There was but one way to find out.

Steeling himself, Darcy thrust his foot into his stirrup iron and mounted. "I have wasted enough time," he told his cousin. "Let us return to the house."

Upon his return, Darcy intended to order a hot bath before joining the ladies in whichever room they currently occupied, but the moment he entered the house he found himself accosted by Anne. Thankfully, she appeared to be sober, but there was a tiredness in her eyes and an anxiety apparent in her countenance that thickened the air around her like porridge. In a voice that was barely above a whisper, she insisted upon speaking to him without delay.

Against his better judgment, Darcy followed her down the hall, through several empty drawing rooms, and into the library, where he shut the door, ensuring they would not be seen by any family members or servants. The last thing he needed was for Lady Catherine to think he was proposing, or worse, for Emerson to think they were having an assignation.

As they stood beside the large window that overlooked the park, Anne folded her hands primly in front of her. Her face was pinched, her posture was stiff, and she seemed intent upon avoiding his eyes. Despite her insistence that she speak with him, she was taking a remarkably long time to do so.

Annoyed by her silence, Darcy tossed his hat and gloves onto a chair and removed his greatcoat. Anne glanced at him and blushed, then increased the distance between them by several feet. Darcy nearly rolled his eyes. Did she think he would remove his cravat and his coat next and ravage her?

Good Lord, what am I doing here? he wondered, turning towards the window with an abruptness that made Anne flinch. "I trust there is a point to your inviting me here, Anne, other than to admire the empty park."

Without further hesitation or ceremony, Anne blurted, "I cannot possibly marry you!"

Darcy faced her with a start. She had made a similar pronouncement the night before, but in a very different tone. Then, she had been drunk and giddy; now, she was as sober as he had ever seen her and had spoken in a rush, as though she had wanted nothing more than to expel the bitter taste of the words from her tongue.

She stood a little taller and lifted her chin. "I have an understanding. An understanding with another gentleman." She lowered her voice. "A gentleman of whom my mother cannot approve."

Darcy folded his arms across his chest. "You said as much last night," he remarked, trying and failing to keep his irritation with the entire business to himself. "Allow me to wish you joy, Cousin, for I harbour no doubts that you and Jack Hastings shall live a long and happy life together."

Anne made an indistinct choking sound. "Jack Hastings is a groom. I cannot possibly marry a groom. People will talk."

Darcy was barely able to keep his anger in check. "Then you ought not to have announced your desire to marry him within earshot of the servants! Hastings will likely lose his position, and your reputation and our family's respectability shall suffer for your appalling lack of discretion!"

To her credit, Anne appeared horrified. "Jack Hastings shall not lose his position," she replied with a veracity he had not expected. "My uncle has spoken to the servants. I suspect he paid them handsomely for their silence. In any case, he came to me afterward to...discuss the matter." Blushing furiously, she looked towards the window and stared at the park. "He knows the truth now," she said stoically, lifting her hand to trace an indistinct pattern upon the frosted pane with her fingertip.

"And what precisely is the truth, Anne?" Darcy demanded. "That Hastings is not, in actuality, the excellent kisser you claimed, and you have come to your senses based on that principle alone?"

"As far as I am concerned, Jack Hastings is not any kind of kisser! I have certainly never allowed him such liberties!" She covered her face with her hands and exhaled harshly, sniffling as she vigorously shook her head. "Oh! I do not know why I ever said such a thing yesterday! In truth, I have paid him little notice, other than to thank him whenever he had a carrot on hand to feed to my ponies!"

Darcy endeavoured to bring his temper under regulation. It would do him no good to have Anne reduced to a weeping, nonsensical mess. "It is well, then," he told her, tugging on his tailcoat as he effected an air of composure. "Hastings's position is safe, your reputation is safe, and neither you nor I shall ever agree to this farce of an arranged marriage your mother concocted. Pray tell her as much, and let us be done with this nonsense once and for all. I am tired of coming to this house and being browbeaten for failing to do that which your mother alone wants done." Believing that all discourse on the subject was now at an end, he bowed to her with the intent of quitting the room.

"It is not easy living in my mother's shadow," Anne told him, wiping tears from her eyes. Her voice was soft, but undeniably resentful as well. "Nor is it easy to live in yours. For years and years my mother has courted your interest and pushed me at you, and for what purpose? Certainly not because either of us desired the match. It was too much! Your being here now is too much!"

She exhaled harshly, inhaled a slow, measured breath, and continued in a more reasonable tone. "I was…not myself last night, Darcy. Owing to that—and a generous amount of Cook's sherry—I said some unfortunate things about Jack Hastings that never ought to have been said. But I never kissed him, nor do I think of kissing him. The only gentleman I have ever allowed such liberties—or shall ever allow such liberties—is my dear Thomas."

"Your 'dear Thomas'," Darcy repeated with increasing trepidation and more than a touch of irritation. "Exactly who is 'dear Thomas'?"

Anne merely blinked at him, apparently disinclined to divulge more than she already had.

Darcy repressed an oath, pursed his lips, and paced from the window to the hearth, from the hearth to the couch, and back to the window. He opened his mouth to speak, then, after thinking better of it, promptly shut it and resumed his agitated pacing before he could berate Anne for taking up with the undergardener, the apothecary's son, or one of more than a dozen servants in service within the manor house bearing the same name!

"It is Thomas Birtwhistle," Anne confessed after several minutes of watching him stride back and forth from one part of the room to another. She smoothed her hands over her skirts and glanced nervously at the door, which remained firmly shut. "We have been secretly engaged to each other for two years. It is him whom I wish to marry, and no other."

For a long moment, Darcy could do nothing more than stare at her in flagrant disbelief. That Anne had been secretly engaged to anyone for two years, never mind to the son of a woman Lady Catherine detested, was as confounding as it was incredible! To his knowledge, his cousin had few friends and fewer visitors. Lady Catherine either approved or disapproved of each one, and none were admitted without her stamp of approbation. Unless the weather was fine and she could drive her phaeton and ponies, Anne rarely left the house without her mother.

And yet she claimed to be engaged!

He shook his head in consternation. Clearly, his cousin had managed to arrange assignations of some sort with Thomas Birtwhistle, the clever, surprisingly sensible elder brother to three of the most infuriatingly persistent young women in Kent!

Despite having such sisters, Darcy knew there were worse men than Birtwhistle for Anne to have formed an understanding with. *Thank God she has not been having assignations with a groom!* He cleared his throat. "Does your mother know?" he enquired as composedly as possible.

The colour drained from Anne's countenance. "No!" she cried, glancing towards the door once more, then casting her eyes around the entire room, as though Lady Catherine might be lurking behind a bookcase, or beneath the couch, or a table. "Of course, she does not know. If I ever mentioned such a thing to my mother, she would ensure I never see Thomas again! You know he is a second son."

"Thomas Birtwhistle," Darcy replied calmly, "may be a second son, but he is hardly a pauper. He is in possession of an excellent living, not to mention he will receive a sizeable inheritance upon his mother's death. He does not drink to excess, he does not exceed his income, and he is not a philanderer or a heretic. He has devoted his life to doing the good work of the Lord. I daresay he would make you an admirable husband."

Anne's lips lifted in a smile, but it was a melancholy smile. "Thank you, but, on the subject of Thomas, my mother and I are not in accord. She detests Lady Birtwhistle with a passion, and Thomas and his sisters as well."

Darcy sighed and rubbed his forehead with his hand. "Lady Catherine detests Lady Birtwhistle because her daughters have all set their caps at me, Anne. Their interest undermines her own purpose. Do you not think her opinion might change if you were to tell her seriously, once and for all, that you have no desire to marry me?"

"It will not be enough. She is determined to have you for her son."

"Unfortunately for your mother, you and I have established that we do not have the inclination to wed each other, now or ever. There is nothing she can do to change our hearts. Surely, that must count for something."

Anne remained silent.

Darcy tried another tactic. "It is entirely likely your Mr Birtwhistle will attend Lady Metcalfe's ball tomorrow evening, you know."

Almost bashfully, Anne inclined her head. "He has asked me to reserve the first set for him, and the supper dance as well."

"And I assume you have granted them?"

"I have not," she said, averting her eyes to her hands. "I have yet to send him my answer. You know my mother will insist upon your opening the ball with me, Darcy, and—"

"I have absolutely no intention of obliging her," he told her with finality, thinking of how fervently he hoped to engage Elizabeth for those dances, should she remain a guest at Rosings for the occasion.

He extended his hand to her then, and Anne, with some hesitancy, drew closer to him and accepted it. With solemnity, he said, "A man deserves the honour of opening a ball with the woman he has chosen to spend his life with—the woman he cherishes and esteems above all others. It will likely cause Mr Birtwhistle considerable pain if you refuse his request. You are seven-and-twenty and an heiress. You have been of age for six years. You need not remain under your mother's thumb even one day longer if you do not wish it."

Anne's eyes filled with tears. "You are correct," she told him quietly but feelingly as she tightened her grip on his hand. "I cannot possibly refuse Thomas's request, especially for the sake of appeasing my mother and her impossible hopes. No more shall I hide what I feel from the world. No more shall I hide my dear Thomas." Anne raised her chin defiantly. "I am resolved, Cousin. I am resolved to act in the manner which will constitute my own happiness and that of my future husband, without reference to Mama, nor anyone so wholly connected to me."

The corners of Darcy's mouth turned upward, and Anne returned his smile with a breathless little burst of laughter he had not heard since they were children. Seeing her happiness, and knowing it stemmed from being free of him to begin her life with a man who loved her, made Darcy feel lighter as well. Though it was not his practice to make any overt gestures of gallantry to ladies other than Georgiana or Lady Carlisle, in that moment he raised Anne's hand to his lips and kissed it.

From across the room, a barely audible gasp alerted Darcy to the fact they were no longer alone. Dropping Anne's hand as though it had burned him, he looked towards the door.

Elizabeth stood just within the room. One of her hands clutched the door handle; the other was twisted in her skirts. She was even more beautiful than he remembered.

Darcy drank in the sight of her as his heart pounded in his chest.

Neither moved.

Neither spoke.

Neither so much as drew a single breath.

After what seemed a small eternity, Elizabeth wrenched her eyes from his. "Forgive me," she murmured. And then she left.

CHAPTER 6

> Pray, pray be composed, and do not betray what you feel to every body present.
>
> — Elinor Dashwood, Sense & Sensibility

The book Elizabeth had intended to retrieve from Lady Catherine's library was forgotten. She all but ran from the room, intent upon putting as much distance as possible between herself and the intimate scene upon which she had intruded. Any emotional distance would prove impossible. In her mind's eye she saw Darcy—again and again—bestowing a tender kiss upon Miss de Bourgh's hand.

Miss de Bourgh's smile as she gazed at him had been radiant.

Darcy's smile had been less so, but that he had smiled at all pained her exceedingly.

For months Elizabeth had known he was lost to her, regardless of his generosity to her sister and all that entailed. He did not accompany Bingley when he returned to Netherfield. He did not attend Bingley's wedding to Jane. Through his avoidance, he had made clear he wanted nothing further to do with her. However much it hurt, Elizabeth was forced to make her peace with that. She was not so naïve as to believe that Darcy, to whom honour and duty meant so much, would live the rest of his life as a bachelor when his estate required an heir. Eventually, he would need a wife; but his choosing his cousin in her stead—a woman for whom he had shown no prior inclination or attachment in April—was as distressing as it was shocking.

Darcy was no simpleton. He was a man of the world—highly intelligent, discerning, and industrious. Beneath his staid exterior, he had a quick, dry wit and, Elizabeth suspected, a tightly reined passion. She had glimpsed that passion; she had seen evidence of it in his eyes at Pemberley. The recollection of that look alone was enough to convince her that Miss de Bourgh, frail and cross and so different than herself, could never make him happy.

But the private little smile Darcy wore in the library suggested otherwise.

How different he looked on this day than on the day he had proposed to her! Then, he had entered the room in such a fit of agitation Elizabeth had not known what to expect. She had certainly not expected his ardent declaration of love or the bestowal of his hand; nor had Darcy expected her swift refusal or her subsequent castigation.

Apparently, that was not the case with Miss de Bourgh.

Willing herself to keep her composure, Elizabeth hastened through a maze of rooms she barely recognised. All had garlands of rosemary, laurel, fir, and ivy strung across the mantels, and festive kissing boughs suspended above the doorframes. The faint sound of a pianoforte carried to her from the drawing room as Miss Darcy and Lady Josephine played a lively duet with more skill than she could ever hope to possess. She felt the hot prick of tears in her eyes, and moisture on her cheek. Irritated and impatient, she brushed it away with her hand.

Had her path never crossed Darcy's at Pemberley, where she had been granted the opportunity to see the man he truly was, his transferring his affections to his cousin would have been easier to bear. But Elizabeth *had* seen him at Pemberley. She had gotten to know him at Pemberley. There, she had watched him conduct himself with perfect ease as he spoke with friends and neighbours and servants and villagers —many of whom had known him his entire life. At Pemberley, Darcy went from being a man Elizabeth had misjudged terribly to being a man she resolutely admired. Once she learned what he had done for Lydia, her admiration became much more—it swelled to love; a love that was now firmly fixed, for better or worse.

She entered the main foyer, where the grand staircase rose in all its glory from the centre of the space to the very top of the manor house. Its gleaming mahogany banisters, wrapped with bows and evergreens and boughs of prickly holly, loomed just ahead; but the purposeful staccato of approaching footsteps—a gentleman's footsteps—echoed through the hall behind her. Elizabeth quickened her pace and practically bolted up the carpeted stairs. In her haste to gain the second floor, she managed to tread on the hem of her gown. She pitched forward violently, landing hard upon her forearms, her knees, and the palms of her hands. The suddenness of her fall forced a sharp, startled cry from her lips. Her nose was mere inches from the Axminster carpet.

Darcy's distressed voice rang through the foyer. "Miss Bennet! Good God!"

Horrified that he, of all people, had witnessed her spectacular exhibition of clumsiness, Elizabeth's cheeks flamed. She attempted to stand; as her feet were tangled in several yards of her morning gown, it was a task easier said than done. Unequal to meeting him with even the appearance of equanimity, Elizabeth untangled her gown with shaking hands and leapt to her feet. By the time Darcy reached the second-floor landing, she had reached the safety of her rooms.

Hours later, Elizabeth remained within the confines of her bedchamber, too affected and embarrassed to even venture downstairs for tea. She could only imagine what Darcy must think of her after such a ridiculous display. As if falling on her face was not humiliating enough, she had run from him as though harm would have befallen her had she stayed.

Emitting a short, humourless laugh, Elizabeth contemplated her plight. By all appearances, Darcy was an engaged man. How was she to face him with any degree of composure? Worse still, how was she to face Miss de Bourgh? The thought of seeing them together and wishing them joy when her own felicity would never come to pass made her heart constrict. If Darcy had not already announced their news to his relations, she suspected he would likely do so at supper. How in the world would she bear it?

In that moment Elizabeth longed to return to the parsonage. As Charlotte and Mr Collins remained confined to the village, that was an impossibility, not only presently, but for some time to come. She had received a letter stating as much from her friend that morning. Retrieving it from the little silver salver beside her bed, she opened it for what felt like the tenth time and read:

Dear Eliza,
All is well at the home of the Harkers. After passing a near sleepless night, Mrs Harker was safely delivered of her babe. Her labour was as long and

arduous as we expected, but I am pleased to report her discomfort was quickly forgotten the moment she beheld her son. He is a hale, lusty boy, and both mother and child are doing well.

Now, I must beg your forgiveness, not only for my absence, but for abandoning you to shift for yourself in such dreadful weather as we have lately seen! Please convey my heartfelt appreciation to Colonel Fitzwilliam for having the foresight to insist that you accompany him to Rosings Park yesterday evening. (Mr Collins received word early this morning). I shall not mention my husband's opinion on the subject, other than to say that you, more than anyone, are aware of his sentiments regarding Lady Cather-ine's condescension. No doubt, he shall have much to say in the future, but I urge you to spare no thought for it now. Presently, the business has already been forgot.

Be not alarmed, but in his determination to hasten to Rosings this morning, Mr Collins happened to slip on a patch of ice while climbing into his gig and broke his ankle. Mr Harker, with the aid of his sledge and mule, was instrumental in pulling him out of the drift in which he landed. Mr Gooch, the apothecary, has since been to see Mr Collins and has authorised him to be transported no farther than his own home here on High Street, where we shall be forced to remain for some weeks until the ankle is healed enough to return home.

Do not worry for us, for Mr Collins and I have both been made very comfortable by our friends, as I suspect you have as well. Dear Eliza, do take every opportunity to enjoy yourself in our absence, especially if a certain gentleman from Derbyshire is in residence at Rosings for the holiday, as I suspect he may well be. You can be in no doubt to whom I refer, nor as to what my sentiments are on that score. Pray write to me when you can tell me all. Call it faith, call it hope, but I have every confidence I will see you happy and settled at last.

I am as ever,
Your devoted friend,
Charlotte Collins

Elizabeth flopped onto the bed and expelled a harsh breath as the pages of Charlotte's letter fluttered through the air and landed beside her pillow. Unless Lady Catherine banished her from the house in a fit of pique, her stay at Rosings would be of some duration. She stared at the canopy above her head and thought wistfully of Longbourn.

It had seemed like such a good idea at the time to come to Hunsford and spend Christmas with Charlotte rather than remain at home, where Bingley had whisked Jane off to Scarborough to meet his relations mere days after their wedding. Though gratified to see her dearest sister happily married to the man she loved, the newlyweds were not expected to return to Netherfield until after the New Year, when they would stop in London for a fortnight to visit their aunt and uncle Gardiner. Having never been parted at Christmas, Elizabeth missed Jane exceedingly.

The Gardiners, who usually came to Longbourn for Christmas without fail, decided against making the journey to Hertfordshire a second time in as many months and headed south instead. Mrs Gardiner's aunt was aging and longed to spoil her young nieces and nephew before they grew too old to be spoilt. After closing their house on Gracechurch Street, the family had set off for Surrey.

Then there was the matter of Mr and Mrs Wickham, who were expected in Newcastle months ago, but who had come to Longbourn just after they married and had yet to leave. Despite a lieutenancy that awaited Mr Wickham in the north, the couple had been in no hurry to depart. Daily did Lydia make calls and receive her friends as though she had never disgraced herself and her family by running off with a lying reprobate. Her husband, as fond of society as ever, appeared content to avoid the responsibilities of his profession so long as he was able to gratify the vanity of his new mother, his sisters, and their neighbours. His condescension and false flattery, coupled with her intimate knowledge of his reprehensible treatment of Mr and Miss Darcy, made Elizabeth sick.

It went without saying that Mrs Bennet rejoiced in having her youngest daughter returned to her—and 'dear Wickham', too. Mr Bennet held a very different opinion; but to Elizabeth's vexation, her father proved remarkably disinclined to exert himself. He made no enquiries as to why they remained at Longbourn, nor did he issue any demands that they leave. Instead, he acted much as he always had by ignoring his household in favour of his book room and bidding no one disturb his peace.

When Charlotte had written that her parents could not travel to Kent for Christmas due to Lady Lucas having a bad cold, she had all but begged Elizabeth to come in their stead. Having no pleasure at home with the Wickhams in residence and Jane and Bingley from Netherfield, this scheme appealed to Elizabeth like no other. She sent her friend a favourable reply, packed her trunks, and was off within a se'nnight. Mr Collins's obsequiousness would be a welcome reprieve from Mr Wickham's insufferable presumption and Lydia's crowing about being a married woman.

Now, she was staying at Rosings Park instead, Mr Collins was injured, Charlotte must remain in the village to nurse him, and Darcy had transferred his affections to Miss de Bourgh. Only Shakespeare himself could have devised a more wretched comedy of errors!

When a sharp knock sounded upon her sitting room door a moment later, Elizabeth wiped tears from her eyes with a tired exhalation before hauling herself from the bed and smoothing her skirts. She had barely exited the bedchamber when Lady Carlisle appeared unbidden in the sitting room. Startled, Elizabeth blinked at her.

Without ceremony, her ladyship took her firmly by the arm and steered her to the nearest chair. "I understand you have suffered a fall, Miss Bennet. Sit down at once. You are pale."

"Your ladyship is very kind," Elizabeth replied as the countess claimed a seat beside her, "but apart from a headache and a slight rash from the Axminster, I am unharmed."

Lady Carlisle regarded her with a penetrating look that reminded her much of Lady Catherine. "You may be unharmed, but I daresay you are not yourself, my dear. If you were, you would have come downstairs, or at least taken tea in your rooms. You have done neither."

"Have you been spying on me, your ladyship?" she enquired, yet uncertain as to whether she ought to be amused or perturbed.

A complacent smile appeared on the countess's lips. "I have no need for such tactics when my nephew is apparently devoted to performing that office himself." She folded her hands upon her lap. "Darcy has been beside himself with concern for you."

Hearing Darcy's name caught her completely off guard, as did hearing he was concerned for her. Elizabeth's heart skipped a beat, but reason soon prevailed over whimsy.

He alone had witnessed her fall.

He alone had seen her distress.

Despite the fact Elizabeth had retreated to her rooms without assistance, Darcy had no idea whether she was injured or not. And, of course, there was her connexion to Bingley. He was Darcy's oldest friend. Elizabeth was now his sister. If an accident befell her while she was at Rosings and Darcy did nothing to promote her comfort in its aftermath, Bingley would be displeased with him. Elizabeth also knew Darcy's staunch sense of duty would revolt against shirking any such responsibility, real or imagined. Both his honour and his character would never permit it. She said, "Mr Darcy is the very best of men."

"On that we are agreed. There is nothing Darcy would not do for those he loves. There is no distance too far, no expense too great. If it affords them comfort, whatever it is, he shall see that it is done." Lady Carlisle paused and made a slight adjustment to one of her rings. When she returned her attention to Elizabeth, her demeanour softened. "He is very upset, Miss Bennet. I have never seen him more so. He obviously cares for you very much. In fact, given his behaviour, I am inclined to believe him in love with you."

Coming from his aunt, such a statement was not only surprising, but impolitic. Elizabeth was at a loss as to how to respond. Though Darcy had once claimed to have loved her, she could hardly say as much to Lady Carlisle, nor could she mention anything of his involvement in restoring her family's respectability, nor of his avoidance in its aftermath. Feeling all the frustration of her predicament as well as the full weight of her disappointment, she shook her head. "I fear your ladyship has mistaken responsibility and duty for affection. I have never known a more honourable gentleman than Mr Darcy. His friendship with Mr Bingley, who is lately married to my eldest sister, is of long standing. Naturally, such concern for me stands as a testament to the fraternity he feels towards my brother."

This seemed to try her ladyship's patience. "I have met Mr Bingley, and though I happen to know his friendship does mean a great deal to Darcy, my nephew's present concern amounts to much more than you merely being the sister of his friend! As I mentioned last night, I have known Darcy all his life. I have seen him with women—I know how he behaves. To my knowledge, he has never shown any lady the interest—nay, the preference—that he has shown you. Yesterday, when Richard informed me that he believed Darcy admired you, I was sceptical. Today, I am sceptical no more. Not ten minutes ago, my fastidious nephew all but pushed me out of the drawing room and up the staircase in a fit of agitation the likes of which I have never seen. He marched me to your *door!*"

A heated blush suffused Elizabeth's countenance. Chagrined and peevish, she turned towards the hearth, where the warmth of the fire crackling in the grate posed a stark contrast to Lady Carlisle's mien. She inhaled a slow, measured breath, all the while reminding herself no good would come from losing her temper and making an enemy of Darcy's aunt.

"Tell me this much, Miss Bennet. Do you care for my nephew at all?"

Elizabeth's spine stiffened. Not only was the question intrusive, but inappropriate. "Whether I care for Mr Darcy or not is inconsequential. I will say this much—despite what your ladyship believes, Mr Darcy's interest does not, in fact, lie with me, but in another quarter. As of this afternoon, it is firmly fixed."

The countess huffed in annoyance. "While I agree Darcy's interest is indeed firmly fixed, I disagree it lies in any other quarter."

Other than Lady Catherine, Elizabeth had never known a more officious woman! Clearly, Colonel Fitzwilliam inherited his stubbornness and intractability from his mother. Annoyed herself to be submitted to an inquisition by one so wholly unconnected to her, she blurted, "Since your ladyship claims to know Mr Darcy so well, she must also know he has lately proposed to his cousin."

"His cousin? Do you mean that business with Anne?" Lady Carlisle laughed. "That is nonsense! I thought you were smarter than that, Miss Bennet. You cannot possibly believe they are intended for each other. That is my sister-in-law's wish, certainly not Darcy's."

At this point, maintaining even the appearance of equanimity was a lost cause. Arguing had gained her nothing. Elizabeth's patience had reached its end. "I am well acquainted with Lady Catherine's wishes. It is generous of Mr Darcy to honour them. You may rest assured when he announces his betrothal to Miss de Bourgh that I shall wish them both every happiness." Her hands, like her voice, trembled. Abandoning her chair with an abruptness that caused the countess's eyes to widen, Elizabeth squeezed her fingers into fists and tucked her traitorous hands behind her back. "I must beg your ladyship's pardon. The hour has grown late, and I ought to dress for supper."

Lady Carlisle gaped at her with something akin to alarm. Elizabeth was surprised to learn it was not the result of being so rudely dismissed by an insolent girl of inferior birth. "You cannot mean to say that Darcy has an understanding with Anne! Upon my word, he would never consent to such an arrangement."

Perilously close to losing what little remained of her composure, Elizabeth tamped down the urge to give way to tears. "I should not have mentioned it. It is, after all, not my news to relate."

Lady Carlisle rose from her chair and said with some distress, "You are not well. You must calm yourself at once, my dear, or you will surely look a fright at the supper table!"

It was such an absurd thing to say that an incredulous laugh bubbled up from Elizabeth's breast. She quelled it at once and offered her ladyship a brittle smile. "My having a red nose at supper will not bother me half so much as it shall likely offend Lady Catherine. You need have no worries in that regard. By the time the dinner bell is rung I shall be myself again."

The countess regarded her with a cautious, somewhat dubious look, as though she believed Elizabeth was on the verge of losing her mind. "Be that as it may, I shall send a maid to assist you as soon as may be."

"Considering my rudeness, that is generous of you. Thank you."

The countess inclined her head. "If you were rude, Miss Bennet, it was because I was officious, insufferably so. I am afraid it is a Fitzwilliam family trait, inherited through marriage as well as blood. As far as I am concerned, all is forgot. I shall see you in the dining room at six o'clock and not a minute later." She turned and made to leave but stopped short of the door. "Do make sure your maid applies a bit of powder, my dear. Should you actually appear at the supper table with a red nose, Darcy shall likely send to London for his personal physician!"

When Lady Carlisle had gone, Elizabeth sank to her knees on the carpet and wondered how she would ever survive another moment, never mind an entire evening, at Rosings Park.

CHAPTER 7

Every moment had its pleasures and its hope.

—JANE AUSTEN, MANSFIELD PARK

"I SHALL NEVER UNDERSTAND HOW YOU CAN PACE THE length of a room for half the day, Darcy," Emerson drawled from the comfort of a wingback chair. He propped his feet upon a footstool fashioned from the foot of an elephant, crossed his ankles, and took a sip of tea. "It is dreadfully tiresome."

Darcy paused before his cousin's chair. "And I shall never understand how you can spend day after day, week after week, being idle. You have an estate, Emerson. You ought to ensure that it is running smoothly every so often, and that you are not bankrupting yourself."

Emerson shrugged. "I have a steward to see to that bothersome business. He does well enough. As of this moment, I am not destitute… at least, I do not believe that I am." He squinted at his teacup and pulled a dissatisfied face. "Good God," he muttered. "Are these wretched looking creatures supposed to be monkeys?" He shook his head. "Who in their right mind would ever paint such abysmal specimens on fine bone china?"

"Lady Catherine painted them," Darcy informed him as he resumed his pacing, "before she married Sir Lewis. The figures depicted are human, by the way." At least he thought they were human. It was an appalling effort—the worst he had ever seen. A proficient painter her ladyship was not.

"Upon my word, I do believe these two are tupping…!"

"They are dancing, Emerson," Darcy replied in annoyance.

Slowly turning his cup in his hands, Emerson frowned. "I say they are monkeys, and monkeys do not dance." He tilted his head to the left, and then to the right. "Is that a pineapple or a goat?" He appeared truly perplexed.

"There is no telling what it may be, dear," Lady Carlisle told him as she entered the drawing room with alacrity. "Catherine has no eye for composition, no talent, and hideously bad taste." She glanced at Darcy and pursed her lips. "Tell me you have not been pacing the length of this room the entire time I have been gone, Nephew."

Emerson snorted and lifted his teacup in the air. Before he could provide his mother with a detailed account of his interpretation of Lady Catherine's artistic endeavours, Darcy crossed the room and said to his aunt in a low, serious voice:

"How is Miss Bennet?"

"Miss Bennet claims to have a headache and a few minor abrasions from the Axminster. I doubt they are serious." She walked to the fire, where the tea things were laid out on a lacquered table and proceeded to pour herself a cup of tea. Her lips lifted and she exclaimed, "Singlo! Thank goodness for small miracles. I cannot abide oolong, especially the way you take it, Darcy."

Darcy shook his head in consternation. He could not care less about tea; he cared about Elizabeth. "Do you have anything further to relate after speaking with Miss Bennet, madam?"

The countess settled herself on a chair next to Emerson's and regarded Darcy over the rim of her teacup. "She was upset, but that is to be expected when one sustains a fall, not to mention the humiliation she must suffer for having been observed. She was also quite stubborn and impertinent. That, I did not expect." She took a sip of tea. "By the by, Darcy, Miss Bennet claimed you intend to marry Anne."

Emerson, who had just taken a sip of his own tea, choked on it.

"What?" Darcy blurted ineloquently.

Lady Carlisle rolled her eyes. "Really, Nephew. I did not mumble. I daresay you heard me well enough."

Darcy sincerely doubted he had. Elizabeth knew better than to think he desired a union with his cousin! It was not Anne to whom he had proposed last April. It was not Anne to whom he had professed his love.

"You must be mistaken," he insisted. "I cannot believe Miss Bennet said any such thing."

His aunt regarded him curiously. "What cause would she possibly have to believe otherwise? I doubt Catherine has kept her opinions on the subject to herself. She could barely keep her countenance at breakfast this morning."

"I assure you Miss Bennet knows better than to believe any such claims from that quarter. She is neither impressionable nor stupid."

"She may well be both," Emerson observed unhelpfully, "if she believes you have set your sights on Anne. What a pity. I rather liked her. Oh well. There are always the sisters Birtwhistle." The smirk he wore was insufferable.

Darcy glared at him.

His aunt clucked her tongue in admonition. "Not only was Miss Bennet adamant you are to marry Anne, but she was also equally adamant regarding your concern for her. She believes it is owed to your friendship with her brother—born of your fraternal affection for him rather than any notion of fondness you may harbour for her." Lady Carlisle shrugged. "I did attempt to enlighten her, but she appears to be as obstinate as you are, Darcy, and would not hear a word I had to say on the subject." She took another sip of tea.

Agitated, Darcy walked to the window as he contemplated all his aunt related and what it meant. By the time the setting sun had sunk well below the snow-covered horizon, he had arrived at two conclusions—either Elizabeth Bennet hated him with a passion, or she cared very much what he thought of her. Darcy fervently hoped it was the latter. If she cared what he thought of her, then it stood to reason she must also care what he felt. The very notion of Elizabeth caring for him brought a smile to his face. His dearest wish—to have Elizabeth, whom he had loved for so long, as his wife—may yet be within reach.

He envisioned her at Pemberley, teasing him from across his supper table, smiling at him as she played his pianoforte, and welcoming him into her bed once they retired for the night. Children would come in time—intelligent, happy, dark-haired children as beautiful as their mother. Darcy could think of nothing that would bring him more joy.

Suddenly impatient to be gone, he turned from the window and addressed his aunt. "Pray excuse me. I have recalled a matter of significant import to which I must attend without delay."

Emerson stared at him as though he had grown an extra head, but Lady Carlisle smiled almost smugly. "For such an educated, industrious gentleman, your discernment in this regard has been embarrassingly slow. Do get on with it."

The hint of a rueful smile played at the corners of Darcy's mouth as he bowed to her. He was not inclined to disagree.

After dressing for dinner, he waited by the grand staircase for what felt like a small eternity for Elizabeth to emerge from her rooms. When at last she appeared, she looked tired, but still every bit as lovely as she had hours earlier. He straightened, tugged at his tailcoat, and walked briskly through the hall to meet her.

Though she blushed at the sight of him, her steps did not falter.

Darcy's heart pounded in his chest. There was so much he wanted to say to her, so much he wanted to do. He knew that he should greet her, or compliment her, or enquire after her health, but after passing much of the last four-and-twenty hours in nervous anticipation of this very moment, all rational thought had left him. Instead of a proper greeting, he blurted, "I am not engaged to my cousin."

Elizabeth stared at him, blinked, and then performed a perfunctory curtsey. "In that case, Mr Darcy, I shall say 'good evening' instead of wishing you joy."

He was mortified by his total lapse of proper deportment but heartened by her flippant reply. Did he imagine her eyes widened slightly in surprise? Did he imagine a flash of scepticism crossed her face? Darcy had no idea. He was far too distracted by her presence to be certain of anything. He bowed to her and apologised to her and then he simply stared, intent upon absorbing every detail—her fine eyes, her blushing countenance, her pleasing figure, her lovely gown. Finally, he remembered himself, but instead of speaking sense to her this time, what came out of his mouth sounded far more like an order. "Speak with me, Miss Bennet. Now, before we suffer any further misunderstandings between us."

Elizabeth's cheeks flamed as she averted her eyes, no doubt as embarrassed by his untoward behaviour as she was by his suggestion. She glanced behind her, down the hall from whence she had come, and then towards the staircase. "I do not know where we can possibly go together without being interrupted or overheard. For such a large house, there is little privacy to be had within these walls."

"There is a parlour on the third floor. It is rarely used and full of furniture my aunt has deemed insufficient for her tastes. If you are amenable, we may go there now. The rest of my family has already gone down for their supper. We shall not be disturbed."

"Surely, our absence will be remarked upon by someone."

"If anyone does happen to enquire, it is likely my aunt, Lady Carlisle, shall take it upon herself to relate a close approximation of the truth—you chose to remain upstairs, and I have pressing business which demands my attention. No one except my aunt shall ever suspect anything else. Lady Carlisle is the soul of discretion."

Worrying her bottom lip between her teeth, she regarded him in silence for some time. "It appears you have given this matter some consideration, sir."

"I have thought of little else other than seeing you, of speaking with you, for many months."

Elizabeth inhaled sharply. This time, her incredulousness was plainly visible, and remained long enough for Darcy to take notice.

It was then, after months of denying himself the pleasure of her society—of looking upon her and speaking with her—that he felt a pang of desperation in his breast that proved difficult to dispel. He angled his body closer, far closer than was deemed permissible, and quietly, but fervently, said, "Please, Miss Bennet. Will you permit me the honour of a private audience?"

Elizabeth held his steady gaze for some duration before slowly inclining her head. She did not comment on the double entendre of his words. She did not even raise her brow. "If you are assured of our secrecy, then I shall consent to speak with you, Mr Darcy. There is something I would say to you as well."

Relieved she would hear what he had to say—that she trusted him enough to meet with him alone—Darcy offered her his arm.

After a slight hesitation, Elizabeth accepted it and they began their ascent to the third floor of the house in silence. It was darker there, with only one sconce out of every three or four having been lit, likely to conserve the expense of purchasing new candles.

The parlour was at the very end of the hall. Darcy paused to remove a candle from one of the sconces, then opened the door. There was no fire burning in the grate. There were no candles glowing in the chambersticks on the mantel. Without the candle Darcy had procured, the room would have been as dark as pitch. And cold.

While the satin evening gown Elizabeth wore was elegant and flattering, it provided insufficient protection from the chill in the air. Shivering, she rubbed her hands over her arms to generate warmth. "I had not imagined it would be so chilly, but in retrospect I suppose I ought to have known better if this room is rarely used."

"It will not remain so for long," Darcy assured her. He moved to the hearth, lit several candles and lamps on the mantel, and then knelt to tend to the business of starting a fire. With hundreds of servants at his disposal to perform every household duty, it had been years since he had cause to build a fire at Pemberley, but he was more than up to the task. Soon, a small flame flickered in the grate. Slowly, methodically, Darcy fed it pieces of kindling. When it was well established, he added larger pieces and several well-placed logs, and the little fire roared to life, radiating warmth and light throughout the room.

Elizabeth lauded his efforts and moved closer to the hearth, extending her hands towards the flames. "I did not realise building fires was a talent of yours, Mr Darcy."

Dusting a bit of ash from his hands, he rose to his feet. "My father taught me the proper way to build a fire when I was a boy. It is a skill that has served me well over the years whenever I have found myself seeking refuge in abandoned hunting cabins during sudden storms. The weather can turn quickly in Derbyshire, especially in winter, and one ought to be prepared for every contingency."

Elizabeth glanced around the little room, where sofas and chairs and tables and all manner of trinkets and paintings were arranged in poor order. She indicated a table that had been shoved in a corner on the opposite side of the room. It was piled with books—atlases and encyclopaedias by the look of them. "If we only had some supper, I daresay we would be very cosy indeed."

Darcy silently reprimanded himself for his lack of foresight. He could have prepared a picnic for the two of them. They could have dined here together, on a soft rug spread upon the floor before the fire. "Miss Bennet," he began, but the look in her eyes and the expression on her face made Darcy fall silent.

"Please allow me to thank you first. For the unexampled kindness you have shown my poor sister. Ever since I learnt of it, I have been anxious to tell you how gratefully I feel it. Were it known to the rest of my family, then I should not have merely my own gratitude to express."

It was the last thing Darcy had expected her to say. He was stunned—nay, he was horrified—to discover Elizabeth knew of his involvement in the preservation of her family's good name. Deeply agitated, he turned from her and strode to the window, running his hand across his mouth as he fought for composure. If he were to propose to Elizabeth now, he had no doubt she would accept him. They would have a life together, and children, and everything Darcy desired—everything except the knowledge that her acceptance of his hand was born of affection for him rather than a debt her father could not possibly repay. "I did not think Mrs Gardiner was so little to be trusted."

Elizabeth crossed the room to stand beside him. "Do not blame my aunt, sir. Lydia's thoughtlessness first betrayed your concern in the matter and, of course, I could not rest until I knew every particular."

Bitter with disappointment, Darcy briefly shut his eyes. Before he could tell her that her family owed him nothing, that he had thought only of her and of restoring her happiness—he felt the weight of Elizabeth's hand on his arm. It was a brief touch, a gentle touch, but it seared his skin through his coat sleeve and the fine lawn of his shirt like a spark from a fire. He extended his own hand, wanting only to prolong the exquisite novelty of her touch, but she withdrew hers immediately and increased the distance between them to one infinitely more respectable.

"I know it is considered improper for a lady to raise such matters with a gentleman, but, taking into account your own candour on the subject, I can no longer remain silent." She took a fortifying breath and, with some effort, confessed, "This evening, Mr Darcy, you informed me you are not engaged to your cousin, but I cannot see how that is the case. Though my intrusion upon your privacy was most unconsciously done, the unguarded moment I witnessed between you and Miss de Bourgh in the library was one of intimacy. Based on that—on the emotions revealed on both your faces, as well as the hand you held and pressed and kissed—I was certain you had formed an attachment and meant to marry."

Darcy was about to object, to tell her that she was mistaken and that he could never marry Anne—that he did not love Anne; but the words lodged in his throat when he saw Elizabeth wipe tears from her eyes and turn aside her head.

It was not the first time his thoughtlessness and impatience had made her cry. The urge to comfort her—to embrace her—was overwhelming, but Darcy would not risk incurring her anger or losing her trust. Patience, not impatience, would best serve him now.

"Forgive me." The corners of her mouth lifted in a smile, but her smile was fragile, and her voice sounded brittle and thin. She was far from composed.

"Of course," Darcy murmured. He dared not say more.

Twisting her fingers together, Elizabeth expelled a tremulous breath. "Mr Bingley returned for Jane, but you did not accompany him. You did not attend his wedding. Your subsequent avoidance made clear your opinion that our society—*my* society—was no longer acceptable to you. While I did not come to Rosings by design, I had hoped we could at least meet each other as common and indifferent acquaintances."

Darcy had heard enough. He would hear no more. "No," he said, shaking his head vehemently, appalled she would ever believe he could think of her as anything but his *wife.* "Never. There is no one's society I find more acceptable than your own—no one whose friendship I have longed for as I have longed for yours these many months. I did not accompany Bingley to Hertfordshire, Miss Bennet, because I believed you blamed me for your sister's elopement. Had I disclosed but a small portion of my dealings with him to your father, your sister would not have been so easily persuaded and preyed upon by Mr Wickham. She would not have been permitted to go to Brighton at all. Nothing less than my belief of your indifference could have kept me from you. Elizabeth," he said with no little emotion, "did you truly believe that my love for you was so fickle? Or that you are so easily replaced in my heart as your statement implies?"

Elizabeth stared at him in wonderment. She opened her mouth as though to speak, but her lips formed no reply. Darcy noticed further evidence of tears upon her cheeks. She brushed them away with an impatience he remembered well from his time in Hertfordshire. "I thought you wanted nothing to do with me. I thought you had proposed to your cousin…I thought…I thought you had proposed…"

"No," he told her gently, reaching for her hands and grasping them tightly in his own. "I did not propose to Anne. When you happened upon us in the library, it was after Anne had confided her engagement to a local gentleman. No one knows of it. I was congratulating her this afternoon. I did not propose." Unable to bear her tears a moment longer, Darcy released her hands and drew her into his embrace, comforting her the way he had wanted to comfort her that summer, in Lambton. He pressed his cheek to her temple and shut his eyes. Her scent nearly overwhelmed him—orange blossoms and ginger and something sweeter. Something headier. Something uniquely Elizabeth.

When her hands slipped beneath his coat and found purchase around his waist, a lump formed in his throat. He swallowed it with some difficulty and said, "You must know the only way I shall ever be truly happy is to spend my life with you. If need be, I will drop to my knees and beg, but make no mistake—I love you as I have never loved another." So powerful, so fervent, were his feelings in that moment, his voice shook. "Dearest, loveliest, Elizabeth! Do me the honour of consenting to become my wife."

A tearful, breathless little laugh, and then a soft, but impassioned, "Yes," was all the reply he was to receive, but it was the perfect reply, and the only reply Darcy knew in his heart that he needed to hear.

CHAPTER 8

Family squabbling is the greatest evil of all.

— Edmund Bertram, Mansfield Park

HAND IN HAND THEY MADE THEIR WAY FROM THE cluttered parlour on the third floor down to the dining room. Elizabeth could hardly believe the miraculous hand fate had dealt her. Not only was Darcy not engaged to Miss de Bourgh, but he was as deeply in love with her as ever. It seemed incredible that, in a matter of hours, she had gone from a state of hopeless despair to one of incandescent joy. Beaming, Elizabeth acknowledged she had never been happier. Judging by the smile on Darcy's face, and the way he seemed unable to bear taking his eyes from her, she knew he felt the same.

When they reached the second-floor landing, Elizabeth let go of his hand, but Darcy snatched hers back again and raised it to his lips for a kiss. "Are you so eager to relinquish me, madam?"

Elizabeth shook her head at him, even as the corners of her lips lifted in a smile. "Hardly, but it would not do to appear so familiar before your family when they know nothing of our happy news. Poor Lady Catherine would likely suffer an apoplectic fit."

He laughed. "Indeed, but I have confidence in Anne. No doubt, she will soon do what is right to be done and announce her own engagement. Ours, I fear, will not disturb Lady Catherine nearly as much as her daughter's shall."

"Let us hope that is the case. Her ladyship has had much to say regarding the subject of Lydia's marriage. I do not relish hearing what she will likely have to say regarding my own."

Darcy's brow furrowed with an expression of concern, and he slowed to a stop. "Was she unkind?"

"She was frank."

"Meaning she was rude, condescending, and officious," he remarked irritably.

Elizabeth squeezed his hand. "Calm yourself, Mr Darcy. I would not have you give over your joy to anger. In truth, I cannot blame your aunt for holding such a low opinion of my sister, not after what she has done. Lydia was indulged and spoilt all her life. She showed no restraint, either in Brighton or Hertfordshire. Not only was she a willing participant in Mr Wickham's debauchery, but she left Brighton with him—she left the protection of the Forsters and all her friends—to elope!"

Pitching his voice low, Darcy muttered, "And my own sister, whose manners were everything they ought to be, nearly did the same."

"'Nearly'," she replied as quietly, "is by no means the same as having done so. Georgiana may once have been deceived herself by Mr Wickham's duplicity, but she has since seen the error of her ways. I can tell you with certainty my own sister has not. Neither has her husband. He flatters and flirts and makes love to us all, much the same as he ever did. I thank Heaven for Charlotte's invitation to spend Christmas in Hunsford, for I could not have tolerated spending another day in his presence. Rest assured, I will bear Lady Catherine's judgment and enquiries with fortitude if it means I am spared Mr Wickham's insincerity and lies."

Darcy stared at her with a look of incredulous disbelief. "You cannot mean to say that he is in Hertfordshire now, at Longbourn!"

"They have been there for months." She then related all she had seen and heard from Mr and Mrs Wickham since they first arrived in her father's house. Darcy was livid, understandably so. He had paid an exorbitant amount of money to bring about their marriage. He had purchased Mr Wickham's commission. He had even settled a dowry upon her sister. In return, the couple had agreed to go to Newcastle, where Mr Wickham would report for duty a fortnight after their wedding. Instead, they had made themselves comfortable at Longbourn.

"He has likely sold his commission or lost it at the gaming table," said Darcy, his countenance dark. "I shall send an express to Bingley this evening and ask him to look into the matter."

"That is all well and good, but Mr Bingley and my sister are currently in Scarborough visiting his relations. They will not return until after the New Year."

"Then I shall go to Longbourn myself. I must speak to your father in any case."

"That, too, is well and good," said Elizabeth tartly, "but shall we not have some supper first, Mr Darcy? When your fancy carriage slides from the carriage shed into a snowdrift, I will be quite cross should you be forced to walk back to the house through a foot of snow in the dark on an empty stomach." She linked their arms and tugged him towards the staircase with a teasing smile. "Besides, I believe Lady Metcalfe would take offense if you were to go to Hertfordshire in lieu of attending her ball. I hear the Misses Birtwhistle, all three of them, shall be in fine form and desirous of a handsome partner to invite them to dance."

As soon as Elizabeth mentioned the Birtwhistle sisters, Darcy looked as though he had tasted something sour. Elizabeth made a concerted effort to conceal her amusement, but Darcy looked so dissatisfied and put out by the prospect of dancing with them she soon abandoned all pretence and gave way to laughter.

With an expression of hauteur that she had not seen him assume since the last time they were in Kent together, he said, "Laugh all you like, Elizabeth. The Birtwhistle sisters shall soon be family, yours as well as mine." He inclined his head towards hers until his cheek brushed her hair and said, "It is their brother, Thomas, to whom Anne is betrothed."

She could not have been more surprised had he confided Anne meant to marry the butler. "Goodness!" she cried and laughed again.

By the time they made an appearance in the dining room, two courses had already been served. Lady Catherine was displeased by their lateness, Lord Carlisle was displeased in general, a gentleman whom Elizabeth had not met but understood was Colonel Fitzwilliam's younger brother appeared half in his cups, and Viscount Emerson was rattling on about a horse he had purchased. Everyone else stared grimly at their food, pushing what Elizabeth surmised had once been a chicken around their plates with their forks.

It was nothing like Longbourn.

The gentlemen stood, and the viscount ushered Elizabeth into an unoccupied chair next to his own with a broad smile.

Rolling his eyes at his cousin's gallantry, Darcy claimed the only available seat at the table, directly across from them.

The viscount settled into his own chair and spread his napkin across his lap with a dramatic flourish. "As I was saying, Miss Bennet. I had never seen such a beautiful horse in all my life. I simply had to have him. He is a stubborn animal, to be sure, but uncommonly fast and clever. The gentleman I purchased him from would not agree to part with him at first, but eventually I wore him down." He winked at her. "I named him Napoleon."

Colonel Fitzwilliam gaped at him. "Why on earth would you name your horse after Bonaparte?"

The viscount stabbed an overcooked carrot with his fork and shrugged. "Why not? It is as good a name as any other."

"It is a *terrible* name," the colonel cried indignantly, "not to mention unpatriotic! Bonaparte is the sworn enemy of the Crown and a clear and present danger to all of England!"

"Semantics," his brother replied with a dismissive wave of his hand.

The murderous glare Colonel Fitzwilliam levelled at his elder brother would likely have felled a lesser man. "It boggles my mind," he said harshly, "how I can possibly be related to you, Arthur."

"And yet you are," the viscount replied equitably, reaching for his wineglass and sniffing the contents within. "You must admit that of the two of us, I am by far the handsomest." He took a generous sip of wine. "Would you not agree, Miss Bennet? Surely, you have noticed how I stand out in a crowd."

"Surely, my lord," she replied archly, "you have heard the adage 'pride goeth before a fall'."

With the exception of Lady Catherine and the earl, all at the table erupted into laughter at the viscount's expense, even the viscount. He raised his glass to her with a lopsided grin. "Well met, Miss Bennet. Well met, indeed."

"I see you have not changed overmuch since you were last here in the spring, Miss Bennet," said Lady Catherine. "You are still every bit as impertinent as ever. I would have thought your family's recent misfortunes would have taught you some humility, not to mention respect for your betters. I see I am mistaken in that regard."

A heavy, uncomfortable silence settled over the room as a violent flush of heat spread from the neckline of Elizabeth's gown to the top of her head. In that moment, she could not decide what mortified her more: Lady Catherine's allusion to Lydia's impropriety or Lydia's total lack of regard for anyone other than herself. One glance at Darcy told her all she needed to know of his own feelings: he was furious.

"Madam," he said sternly; but her ladyship was in no humour to be gainsaid and provided no opportunity for him to say more.

"I trust, Darcy, you have solicited Anne's hand for the first two dances tomorrow evening."

Darcy's angry countenance revealed he had done no such thing, nor was he liable to do so. Before he could articulate as much, Miss de Bourgh announced, "Everything is settled with Darcy, Mama." She did not so much as lift her eyes from her plate.

Lady Catherine looked smug with satisfaction while Darcy glared at Miss de Bourgh and silently seethed. Apparently, his confidence that his cousin would do what was right to be done regarding her engagement to Mr Birtwhistle was sorely misplaced.

Colonel Fitzwilliam sputtered and coughed as he choked on his wine while his younger brother snickered into his hip flask. If the occasion required it, Elizabeth doubted Mr Fitzwilliam would be capable of walking from the dining table to the drawing room without falling on his face or into a wall.

"Stephen," Lady Carlisle hissed at him, "you are at the dinner table, for God's sake. Sit up!"

Glaring at his youngest son, Lord Carlisle slapped his hand heavily on the table, causing Georgiana to flinch. "Sit up, boy!"

"Anne," Lady Catherine commented as though nothing untoward had occurred, "has perfect posture. Do you not think so, Darcy?"

"Have I mentioned my new horse?" Viscount Emerson asked no one in particular.

Lady Carlisle rolled her eyes. "Yes, Arthur. You mentioned your horse, several times in fact." In that moment, she looked so much like Darcy when his patience had been tried to its limits by Mr Collins, Elizabeth nearly laughed.

"I acquired him in Brighton, you know," said the viscount. "Have you been to Brighton, Miss Bennet?"

The moment the word 'Brighton' left his mouth, Elizabeth wished she could disappear.

Lady Catherine, in contrast, looked as though she had been handed a boon.

The viscount noticed nothing. "I daresay you would enjoy it immensely! Brighton is a ripping place. Very exciting. The races are simply marvellous! I plan to go back there come summer. Perhaps we ought to form a party." He turned to Lady Josephine, whom he had ignored for the entirety of the meal, and said brightly, "What do you say, my dear? Shall we have Miss Bennet to stay with us in Brighton next summer?"

Lady Josephine gawked at him, likely as taken aback by his suggestion as she was his address.

"That is very generous of you, my lord," said Elizabeth, "but I must decline. I fear the delights of Brighton hold little amusement for me."

"Nonsense," he insisted. "Brighton is nothing but amusement! There is sea bathing and horse racing. There are balls and parties every night, and the society there—"

"Is superficial and overrated," Darcy interjected with a terseness that made the viscount scoff. "Despite its manifold attractions, Brighton would not be to Miss Bennet's liking."

"By God, Darcy. You are a dullard," his cousin told him peevishly as he turned his attention to his dinner. "Should you ever marry, I daresay your poor wife will be bored to death."

"Anne shall hardly be bored at Pemberley," said Lady Catherine. "Will you, Anne?"

In lieu of a reply, Miss de Bourgh shovelled a spoonful of peas into her mouth.

Darcy's lips were little more than a thin, angry line.

Oblivious, Lady Catherine said, "I understand that you have been to Pemberley, Miss Bennet. This summer in fact, while your youngest sister was off cavorting in Brighton."

"Yes, ma'am," Elizabeth replied, making a concerted effort to remain civil.

"And how did you find it? Was it to your liking? Of course, it was to your liking," said her ladyship imperiously. "Pemberley is one of the most vast and prosperous estates in all of Derbyshire! It is a shame you were called home so abruptly and did not see much of it. Pemberley is very grand, though I have never liked that Darcy keeps it so wild. That will change once Anne is mistress."

Miss de Bourgh stared intently at her plate. This time, she had the decency to blush.

Darcy, it seemed, had finally had enough. "Your presumption astounds me, madam!" he told his aunt in a tone as grave as his countenance. "That you persist in your efforts even after I have told you—repeatedly and in the plainest terms—that they will never be realised is incredible!"

"There is something to be said for persistence," Elizabeth remarked, drawing the attention of the entire table, "just as there is something to be said for allowing nature to have its way. At Pemberley, I found there is so much to see, so much to please, not only in the grounds but within the house itself." She looked to Darcy then and held his steadfast gaze with an earnestness, a warmth—an affection—so deeply and profoundly felt she had difficulty containing it. Her lips lifted in a small, but heartfelt smile. "At Pemberley, I found much to admire."

An infinitesimal smile played at the corners of Darcy's mouth as he returned her gaze with equal warmth and feeling. "Do me the honour of granting me the first two dances tomorrow evening, Miss Bennet, and the supper set as well."

Lady Catherine raised her voice in protest, but her disapprobation was drowned out by the murmurs and exclamations of surprise and delight from the rest of her relations.

His forwardness was entirely unexpected and made Elizabeth blush; but in that moment, nothing mattered more to her than the expression of unadulterated joy in Darcy's eyes. "They are yours, Mr Darcy."

He rose from his chair and rounded the table to stand before her. "Marry me before the year is ended," he said, holding his hand out to her, "so that *you* may be mine."

She slipped her hand into his palm, and he tugged her to her feet. "My heart has been yours for many months now, sir. I would marry you tomorrow, but I suppose marrying you before the year is out will do nearly as well."

Without ceremony, Darcy kissed her hand. His smile was brighter than she had ever seen it, and the steady, ardent look in his eyes was entirely familiar. Elizabeth could not be more pleased as he drew closer to her—as close as he dared in a room filled with his family—and refused to relinquish her hand.

Colonel Fitzwilliam leapt from his chair wearing a wide grin as he slapped Darcy's back, then embraced him with sincere affection.

Georgiana abandoned her chair so quickly it was knocked to the floor. Throwing her arms around Elizabeth in a fierce embrace, she confessed her joy in gaining a sister.

Viscount Emerson followed suit, as did Lady Carlisle and Lady Josephine, all offering congratulations and good wishes for a lifetime filled with love. The earl looked on with something akin to confusion while Mr Fitzwilliam, who was by this time well and truly foxed, raised his flask a few inches into the air and blinked at them. It was likely all he could manage.

Over the din, Lady Catherine's imperious voice demanded order, but no one obliged her. She grabbed her cane and raised it high above her head, but quickly lowered it as a gentleman Elizabeth had never seen before was shown into the room and announced by a footman.

Silence settled over the room.

"Mr Birtwhistle," said Miss de Bourgh in a breathless voice, rising from the table with alacrity. Her entire countenance suddenly appeared as though lit from within, and Elizabeth knew Darcy's dour cousin not only admired this man but loved him.

Thomas Birtwhistle's lips curled upward. "Good evening, Anne," he said warmly.

Lady Catherine gasped in outrage. "What insufferable presumption you have, Mr Birtwhistle, coming here and addressing my daughter in such a familiar manner! Such insolence and disrespect shall not be tolerated at Rosings Park."

By then Miss de Bourgh had crossed the room to stand before her betrothed, who not only accepted her proffered hand, but placed a tender kiss on the back of it before pressing it against his chest, directly over his heart. Both wore identical expressions of adoration.

And then, before anyone could so much as utter another word, Lady Catherine muttered an unladylike oath and fainted face first into her supper for the second time in as many days.

CHAPTER 9

I will only add, God bless you

— Fitzwilliam Darcy, Pride & Prejudice

"Good lord," Emerson said loudly over the din of the musicians once Lady Metcalfe had taken her leave. Wrinkling his nose, he watched her push and shove her way through the great press of bodies packed into her ballroom. "That woman is worse than Lady Catherine! She prattled on so long my arse fell asleep!"

Fitzwilliam snorted into his cup of negus. "You have been standing on your feet the entire time, Arthur. What does your arse have to do with anything?"

"Damned if I know," said Emerson with a shrug of his shoulders.

"Behave yourselves," Darcy warned, averting his eyes from a group of young ladies whose flirtatious glances and tittering not only made him irritable but uncomfortable. They could not be more than sixteen or seventeen years old. "Your mother and Lady Josephine are somewhere in this ridiculous crush with Georgiana. Emerson, if your wife happens to hear you speaking uncharitably of our hostess, she will drag you home by your ear."

"Heaven forbid," Emerson drawled, rolling his eyes heavenward as the music swelled.

"Speaking of being dragged home by one's ear," Fitzwilliam enquired, "has anyone seen Stephen? I have lost track of him entirely."

Darcy inclined his head towards the long line of energetic couples dancing 'The Young Widow' in the centre of the room. "He is presently engaged with my future wife."

Fitzwilliam's brows rose to his hairline. "I am all astonishment."

"As am I," Emerson remarked, raising his hand and gesturing to a servant bearing a tray laden with glasses of elder wine. "Miss Bennet is too good by half!" He selected a glass and gave it a subtle sniff as the servant hurried on his way. "Have you told her about him yet? Someone ought to tell her about the infuriating little fop before his hands find their way to her—"

"Emerson," said Darcy in frustration. "Do not try my patience tonight. It has been worn thin enough as it is."

Between Lady Catherine, who blamed him for driving Anne into Mr Birtwhistle's arms, the Misses Birtwhistle, who were as wild to see him as they were made desolate by the news of his betrothal, and Stephen, who had taken a sudden, alarming interest in acquainting himself with Elizabeth, Darcy's patience had been tried to its limits. His one consolation, aside from the fact that Elizabeth loved him and had agreed to marry him as soon as may be, was that Stephen was sober for once. It was more than Darcy could say about the youngest Miss Birtwhistle and her insipid friends. "By God, the society here is tedious," he muttered.

Fitzwilliam tilted his head towards Darcy's. "As much as I hate to agree with Arthur, he is correct. You really ought to caution Miss Bennet before my brother does something untoward, such as shocking her by recounting his assignations with courtesans, a certain lady patroness of Almack's, or the sisters of his friends."

Darcy sighed. "Elizabeth is neither blind nor stupid. Stephen was dead drunk at supper last night, and little better this morning. But he did make an appearance at the breakfast table," he admitted, albeit grudgingly, "and his apology for his behaviour sounded relatively sincere. As far as his dancing with her, I made every attempt to discourage it, but Elizabeth did not take kindly to my interference. She has a generous heart, a strong constitution, and a love of dancing. As much as I would like to do so, I cannot dance every dance with her myself."

"Whyever not?" Emerson asked with a shrug of his shoulders. "She is your betrothed. There would be talk to be sure, but hardly a scandal."

Fitzwilliam agreed. "It is Christmas Eve, Darcy. In less than an hour, Christmas will be upon us. You are newly engaged and in love, and this crowd is half in its cups. Save for Lady Catherine, I would wager most everyone in attendance is more inclined towards forgiveness than not, that is if they even take notice!" Smirking, he inclined his head towards one of countless boughs of mistletoe suspended over the windows and doorways. "Go, find your betrothed, drag her off into a dark corner, and give her a proper kiss!"

Though his cousin's suggestion was hardly proper, Darcy felt the familiar stirring of desire. The prospect of holding Elizabeth in his arms and tasting the flavour of her lips tempted him like no other. There had been no opportunity to do so the night before, nor had preparations for Lady Metcalfe's Yule Ball afforded them time alone that day.

A servant approached, carrying a tray overloaded with cups of negus. Darcy beckoned to him.

Emerson raised his glass aloft. "To Miss Bennet!" he announced with a broad smile. "May she fill Pemberley's nursery with your children, teach you to laugh at yourself, and, above all else, make you happy!"

"Hear, hear!" Fitzwilliam cried, and both men drained their glasses at once.

Shaking his head at their antics, but smiling despite them, Darcy drank his negus at a more respectable pace.

Emerson spied another servant and waved him over.

It was nearly midnight, the room was filled to bursting and unbearably hot, and Elizabeth had reached the end of her patience with Mr Fitzwilliam. While he had proved an adept partner, he was without doubt an abysmal conversationalist and, she suspected, a libertine. If his eyes did not stop wandering to the neckline of her gown, she could not be held accountable for her actions!

Their dance ended and Mr Fitzwilliam bowed to her. His gaze, as it had for most of the night, darted to her décolleté.

Performing an impatient curtsey, Elizabeth forced a smile to her face. Before she could bid him a good evening, he brazenly reached for her hand. She evaded his grasp and tucked her hands behind her back, wanting desperately to be rid of him. He was the son of an earl, handsome, persistent, and young—no more than eighteen or nineteen at most—and likely used to having his way. Subtlety had proved ineffective, as had reminding him she was engaged to Darcy. Sending him on an errand seemed like the quickest method by which to accomplish her goal. "If it is not too much trouble, Mr Fitzwilliam, I should like a glass of punch. If you would be so kind as to procure one for me now, I would be appreciative."

He inclined his head to her. "It would be an honour, Miss Bennet. Allow me to escort you to the refreshment table. I should like to hear more of your sisters in any case, especially your two unmarried sisters."

It pained her to admit such a thing, but Elizabeth had liked him better when he was drunk. "Mary and Kitty?" she replied, repressing her annoyance as she feigned a congeniality she did not feel. "Whatever for?"

"Kitty," he parroted, lifting his eyes to her face as he snickered like a schoolboy. "Surely, that cannot be her name."

"Her Christian name is Catherine, Mr Fitzwilliam."

"And you call her Kitty?"

"Yes."

"How singular!" He laughed outright, but his laughter abruptly faded, and he frowned. "Miss Kitty does not resemble a cat, I hope." He appeared perfectly serious.

Elizabeth stared at him in disbelief. "No. Of course, not. She resembles my mother."

"That is very good to hear," he replied, and offered her a winsome smile.

Elizabeth wondered whether he had been imbibing, or had suffered a grave illness, or had been dropped on his head as a babe. She was still attempting to make sense of his odd behaviour when several very young, very attractive ladies emerged from the crowd, smiling and giggling and batting their lashes.

Mr Fitzwilliam's eyes followed their progress with interest.

As the ladies drew closer, their giggling grew louder and their looks bolder. Judging by the bright flush of colour on their cheeks, Elizabeth suspected they must have been in the punch pot while their chaperons held court in a corner or the card room, gossiping and sipping sherry.

Elizabeth was forgotten as Mr Fitzwilliam singled out the prettiest, brashest young lady in the bunch and tipped his non-existent hat to her. The girl's eyes widened, her smile widened, and she nearly tripped over her own feet. She blushed and smiled like anything as her friends laughed.

The entire scene reminded Elizabeth too much of Lydia and Mr Wickham. She was of a mind to depart and leave both parties to their absurdity but knew from experience that no good would come of pawning the rakish Mr Fitzwilliam off on a bunch of foolish young ladies who appeared to have had more wine than sense between them.

"Mr Fitzwilliam," she said sweetly but firmly, recalling his attention to herself.

He appeared startled to see her standing beside him, her brow arched impertinently. "Miss Bennet," he stammered, then bowed to her. "How do you do?"

He was, without doubt, the strangest young man she had ever met; as she was cousin to Mr Collins, such a distinction was not awarded lightly. "I am thirsty, sir. I shall feel much better after you fetch the aforementioned cup of punch."

"Oh, yes! Of course, Miss Bennet. Your servant," he replied and departed at once, dodging several dozen couples as they formed the next set.

Shaking her head at his retreating back, Elizabeth wondered if he would, in fact, do as he promised and return with a cup of punch for her, or whether he would simply forget her entirely after becoming distracted by something or, more than likely, someone else. She decided it did not matter, turned on her heel, and set off in the opposite direction in search of Darcy.

After wandering the length of the ballroom, then the card room, and evading several gentlemen who were too inebriated to stand on their own two feet, she came upon Darcy in the Great Hall. A massive Yule Log crackled and popped in the hearth as flames danced and curled around its sides. It was the largest she had ever seen, a colossal bough of freshly felled oak that more closely resembled a tree trunk than a log. It was adorned with decorations—symbolic offerings and gifts—and smelled of green wood and a hint of elderberry wine as it burned.

Darcy was bent low over a table, scribing what looked to be a letter on a thick sheet of paper. Except for the two of them, the enormous hall was empty and blessedly devoid of the chatter and loud, raucous laughter that persisted in the other rooms. French windows bedecked with boughs of holly and ivy lined the outer wall, and music—a few lively strains of 'Sir Roger de Coverley'—ebbed and flowed from the ballroom as happy couples danced and clapped and cheered.

"Shall I compliment you on your elegant hand, Mr Darcy, or the length of your letter?" Elizabeth quipped as she approached. "Or perhaps your pen requires mending. It is a shame Miss Bingley is not in residence to oblige you, for I hear she mends pens remarkably well."

Darcy started at the sound of her voice and immediately laid aside his pen. "Forgive my inattention, Miss Bennet. I did not notice your approach." His bow was formal, but his smile as he gazed at her was welcoming and warm.

Elizabeth returned it, but the sheet of paper on the table piqued her curiosity. She peered over his shoulder and read:

Arrogance

Conceit

Selfish disdain for the feelings of others

Improper pride…

Her smile slipped from her face. “What is this?”

Darcy snatched the paper off the table and quickly folded it in half, then repeated the process thrice more, seemingly embarrassed. He cleared his throat. “It is as you see,” he replied, staring fixedly at the little square of paper in his hand. “As tradition dictates, I have comprised a list of my personal faults, and the poor choices I have made throughout the year. I had thought to begin the New Year—and our life together—with a clean slate.”

Many years had passed since Elizabeth had last honoured that tradition herself. Neither her mother nor father had thought much of writing their faults and offenses upon a slip of paper and tossing it into the Yule Fire on Christmas Eve. ‘Codswallop’, her father had called it, before pouring himself a glass of port and settling into his chair. He told stories instead, and drank too much, and Elizabeth and her sisters played the pianoforte, sang Christmas carols, and danced. At Longbourn, no one dwelled on their shortcomings at Christmas—or any other time of the year for that matter.

In silence, Darcy stood before her, his posture erect and his countenance impenetrably grave.

No, Elizabeth decided. *Not grave, but penitent.*

Chagrined, she recalled much of her own conduct over the last twelve months and coloured deeply. Darcy was not the only one who had faults to acknowledge, nor was he alone in making poor choices. A stack of paper, an inkwell, and several pens had been set upon the table for the use of Lady Metcalfe’s guests. Elizabeth approached the table, pulled a sheet from the top of the stack, and selected a pen. “It is an admirable way to acknowledge the wrong we have wrought,” she told him softly. “I have much to atone for as well.”

Though Darcy had remained standing as he wrote out his list, he insisted upon fetching a chair for Elizabeth’s comfort.

She thanked him as she sat upon it, dipped her pen into the ink, and wrote:

Vanity

Prejudice

Accusation

Blindness…

By the time she finished writing, her list extended halfway down the page, much like Darcy's. She folded it as he had done—until it was small enough to fit in the palm of her hand—and rose from her chair. "Let us both begin our life together with a clean slate."

They walked to the fire as the Chippendale clock in the corner of the room began to chime the hour.

By the time it had chimed four times, Darcy had relegated his faults and offences to the fire.

By the time it had chimed six times, Elizabeth had cast hers in with his.

They watched the little squares of paper burn until both were nothing more than tendrils of ash and cinders amidst a host of bright flames.

When the clock chimed twelve times, Elizabeth slipped her hand into Darcy's, and he kissed it. Then they made their way to the French windows, where they could see the wide terrace and the garden just beyond the house had been meticulously cleared of snow. Beyond that, torches flickered brightly on each side of the snow-covered drive. A long line of sleighs pulled by sturdy, matched pairs stretched the entire length of it, awaiting the return of their mistresses and masters.

Elizabeth opened the door.

Outside, the air was as fresh and crisp as the night was dark. Darcy found it oddly, gloriously peaceful. There was no moon in the sky, no stars; the only light to be had shone through the windows—the incandescent glow of hundreds of candles in the ballroom and the Yule Fire crackling in the hearth in the Great Hall. He turned to Elizabeth and the corners of his lips lifted in a gentle smile. "Happy Christmas, Elizabeth."

"Happy Christmas, Mr Darcy," she said with quirking lips and sparkling eyes.

Darcy shook his head at her formality, even as he laughed. "We are alone for the moment. When will you dispense with calling me 'Mr Darcy'?"

"When you give me leave to do so," she replied as her teasing smile grew.

She was truly beautiful this evening. He had no idea where she had acquired the ball gown she wore—perhaps from Georgiana or Lady Josephine—but it flattered her figure in ways he dared not consider. Her hair, too, was arranged more elaborately than he was used to seeing it.

One rebellious curl had come loose from the rest, likely while dancing, and brushed against her cheek. Darcy wrapped it around his finger. "Call me by my name, Elizabeth, please. I have longed to hear my name on your lips for a very long time."

"As you wish, Fitzwilliam."

Her voice was incredibly soft, as soft as her hair—as soft as the expression of her lovely, dark eyes and the sensual shape of her mouth. All had a profound effect upon Darcy. "May I kiss you?" he asked as softly, settling his hands on her hips and drawing her close.

She came willingly, sliding her own hands along the lapels of his coat until they rested on his shoulders. "You might have done so before."

"There was no mistletoe," he teased.

"Nor is there any now, but I do not believe we have need of it." Her bottom lip was caught charmingly between her teeth.

"No," Darcy agreed, gently running the pad of his thumb along her lip and tugging it free. He swallowed thickly and urged her closer, barely able to credit she was truly his. He was grateful, and humbled, and nearly overwhelmed by his love for her. The hand that remained on her hip urged her closer still, so close that Elizabeth was nearly pressed against the length of him. His other hand cupped her cheek, and, with unexampled tenderness, Darcy slowly trailed his fingertips along the column of her neck and the supple skin of her shoulder.

Elizabeth's eyelids fluttered closed, and she shivered.

"You are cold," he murmured, mentally chastising himself for failing to see what should have been obvious: Elizabeth ought not to be out of doors in such weather wearing only a ball gown.

"I am well," she insisted. She withdrew her hands from his shoulders, slipped them inside his coat, and pressed herself flush against his body. "Kiss me."

Darcy's breath hitched.

Elizabeth had embraced him in much the same manner the previous night, but they had been hidden away in an unused room at Rosings then, and she had been distressed and overcome with emotion. Now, they were in public, in full view of the house and Lady Meltcalfe's guests. If someone were to look out the window and see them, Elizabeth would be utterly compromised.

"You are overthinking this, Fitzwilliam," she whispered as she gazed at him, her entire countenance overflowing with acceptance and love.

A lump lodged in Darcy's throat as he returned her gaze with equal feeling. She would be his wife. In his heart of hearts, she was already his wife, and had been for some time. Let the naysayers and gossips say what they will; there was no one in the world Darcy loved as he loved Elizabeth Bennet.

She was fearless, she was guileless, and she had told him to kiss her.

Darcy desperately wanted to kiss her.

He should kiss her.

He would kiss her.

And then he did kiss her.

Many minutes later, when he reluctantly withdrew from the pleasure of her lips to catch his breath and cool his ardour, Elizabeth cupped his jaw with her hands, pulled him close, and kissed him again.

The End

About the Author

Susan Adriani is a graphic artist turned storyteller. She cannot imagine a world without books, Google maps, copious amounts of tea, and Jane Austen.

Also by Susan Adriani

Misunderstandings & Ardent Love

The Truth About Mr Darcy

WELCOME HOME

MARY SMYTHE

CHAPTER ONE

Pemberley, December 18__

FITZWILLIAM DARCY SANK INTO THE SQUABS OF HIS carriage and closed his eyes, only to open them again as the beguiling face of Elizabeth Bennet once more invaded his mind. As was always the case, she had been smiling in that arch way that he found so tempting and her eyes, so delicately framed by the fan of her lashes, were challenging him. Over what, he could not say, but Darcy was inclined to answer that challenge with a kiss to those impertinent lips.

He groaned and rubbed his face with both hands as if trying to scour the image away. He could not have her, he should not want her, and he wished she would stop haunting him. *She is unsuitable. She has no fortune. Connexions to trade. Her family is crass and vulgar, and I cannot marry her...even if she is everything I have always wanted.*

And it was true. He had met scores of women, some of whom were even desirable in one way or another—either in suitability or attractiveness, though rarely were the two combined into one lady—but none had struck him the way Elizabeth had. However, it was neither her beauty nor her cleverness which had ensnared him in her spell.

No, the real reason he was in love with Miss Elizabeth Bennet was that he yearned for her tenderness. When her sister had fallen ill at Netherfield, she had tramped through fields full of mud and dirt to nurse her back to health. Bingley's sisters had scoffed about her 'scampering about the country just because her sister had a cold', inadvertently proving their lack of loyalty to one another, but he had found it more than simply charming. He had longed all his life to be treated as such by someone, anyone other than Mrs Reynolds who, for all her wonderful qualities, was a servant and paid to be in his service. He did not doubt her affection for him, but it was not the same thing. There would always be some measure of propriety between them.

Elizabeth loved without reservation or condition; she had arrived in the breakfast room with her petticoats six inches deep in mud, her hair dishevelled by the wind, and sweat dotted along her brow from her exertions. This had invited scorn from Miss Bingley and Mrs Hurst, yet between her flushed cheeks and the brightening of her eyes, Darcy had been enraptured. And he had then been aware for the first time that he was in great danger of succumbing to his infatuation with this country girl.

Having witnessed for himself Elizabeth's capacity for loving tenderness, Darcy wished to be the object—nay, the primary recipient—of her affections. What would it be like to be held in warm regard by such a woman? He ached to know.

The carriage stopped unexpectedly, and Darcy jerked forward, bracing himself by the leather strap affixed to the wall to prevent himself from falling into an undignified heap on the floor. He heard a rap on the door and opened the window blind to see his coachman, Marley, standing just outside. His man held tightly to his hat as it was buffeted about by the wind and pelted constantly with sleet. "Beggin' yer pardon, Mr Darcy, sir, but the weather is takin' a turn fer the worse. Lambton is just ahead an' we could stop fer the night, or we could press on to Pemberley."

"What is your opinion?"

Marley stamped his feet and rubbed his hands together against the nipping cold. "It would be safer to stop, o' course, but then we'd like to be stuck o'er Christmas. Might be worth the risk to make fer Pemberley."

That settled the matter; he could not very well stay at an inn for the foreseeable future. Snowstorms in Derbyshire had the tendency to last long and keep the residents of the county trapped within their own homes for weeks at a time. If they failed to make it to Pemberley tonight, they might very well start the new year in a rural inn.

"Press on," Darcy said to his driver, who tipped his hat to his employer. A short time later, they rumbled cautiously down the lane once again.

Outside the walls of the carriage, the wind screeched and howled in warning to anyone stupid enough to be out of doors in such weather. Had they not been so close to their destination, he would have taken immediate pity on the men and gone to the inn, no matter how long he expected to be trapped there. They would all be more comfortable at Pemberley.

Darcy waited for and finally felt the turn that would take them onto the long drive of his ancestral home. He held onto the handle above the door again, steadying himself as the coach tilted precipitously, and anticipated the moment his world would right itself once more. If only he could expect such a shift in his feelings for Miss Elizabeth Bennet. He felt a jabbing pang, like the merciless thrust of a knife in his chest, as her fine eyes rose again in his imagination, warm and full of welcome. For him.

"Please, God…" Darcy murmured, angling his face towards the roof. He squeezed his eyes tightly shut as he pleaded, quietly but earnestly, "Tell me what to do."

"*Whoa!*"

Darcy heard the shout of his coachman just as the carriage jerked hard, sending him sliding across the slick leather seat beneath him. His gloves lost their grip and…

Later…

Darcy rubbed his temple to assuage the pounding ache in his head as he mounted the front steps of his home. He had been very lucky to escape significant injury, he knew that, but he would feel more gratitude for this once the pain subsided. He would retire to his study with a hot toddy, put his feet up by the fire and allow the comforts of home to soothe his head-ache, all the while likely pretending that he was under Elizabeth's tender ministrations.

Miss Elizabeth Bennet, he reminded himself silently but firmly. Snow peppered his shoulders and seeped into his greatcoat as he squinted into the swirling whiteness, careful of his footing with each step. He longed to reach the warm comfort of his home quickly but measured his speed for safety instead. Slipping and falling into a snowbank would be an inauspicious end to an already nearly disastrous day of bumpy travel.

The double doors opened ahead of him and his butler, Griswold, greeted him in the usual manner. "Welcome home, sir. I trust your journey was comfortable?"

A throb in Darcy's head reminded him of just the opposite. "Indeed."

He entered the great hall of Pemberley and released a breath that rose around him in a cloud. Griswold closed the doors behind them, keeping the cold weather firmly outside, and turned to accept the articles Darcy was struggling to remove. First his cane, of course, then his hat and gloves, everything removed in the order of ease.

Darcy required assistance to remove his greatcoat, soaked by the brief time he spent struggling with the obstinate wooden roadblock. Griswold, standing behind him, grasped it at the shoulders and pulled sharply to peel it away from the clothing beneath.

Darcy tugged at the bottom of his dark green coat to straighten it back into position. "See that Marley and Jacobs are given a hot meal in the kitchen after they have seen the horses and carriage to the stable. And please send word to Mrs Reynolds that I have arrived. I shall be in my study."

Griswold bowed and carted the greatcoat away himself, disappearing into an antechamber to the side of the hall.

"Fitzwilliam!"

Startled, Darcy jerked his head around towards the grand staircase as someone cried out in joyful greeting. He was surprised that Georgiana would be so enthusiastic about his return, but—

Darcy's mind and heart stopped in the same instant when his sight arrested upon a light and pleasing figure on the upper landing. It was not his sister's, but rather the woman whose image tormented his every moment with longing.

"Elizabeth!" he exclaimed as none other than Miss Elizabeth Bennet rushed down the staircase and hopped off the last step onto the marble floor of the entry hall. She did not pause at the base but instead gathered up her skirts and all but sprinted towards him across the distance that remained between them.

When she reached Darcy, Elizabeth spread her arms wide and launched herself at him, her laughter echoing throughout the room like silver bells chiming. He reached out on instinct and caught her around the waist, drawing her to his chest. Upon contact, Darcy could feel his heart begin to pitter-patter against the inside of his ribs in time with each peal of her laughter.

As in each and every one of his dreams of her, Elizabeth clung tightly to him and weaved her fingers into the hair at the back of his head, holding him to her, as desperate for him as he was for her. Darcy could feel his heart pulse with the affection he had been trying so desperately to keep at bay.

But...what was she doing there? It could not be proper for her to come all the way to Pemberley, to the household of an unmarried man, and throw herself at him—no matter how much he was enjoying it.

Over Elizabeth's shoulder, Darcy warily scanned the hall for signs of miscellaneous Bennets and curious servants, but all appeared to be in order. There were no other visible guests and his servants carried on as they always had, paying the couple in the entryway no mind save for a few secret smiles as they went about their business.

What had he missed? Did they all somehow know Elizabeth, know how Darcy felt about her? Why would they all look the other way as their master was accosted, however amiably, in front of them?

Darcy felt Elizabeth shift and pull away from him, returning her heels to the floor and leaning back to look him in the face. Instantly, Darcy was enchanted by the sparkle of joy in her lovely green eyes. Her cheeks were glowing with health as she said, "I am so glad you are home, dearest. How was your trip? Were you able to assist Charles?"

"I..." Darcy knew not how to answer that. The last he was aware, he had been travelling home from London and had not seen Bingley for a month, at least. "Charles?"

Elizabeth flashed her impertinent smile at him and arched a brow in that way he liked. "Did he and Jane like our gift? I do hope they fit little Holly, for she grows so fast!"

"Holly?"

Elizabeth shook her head at him with what he thought looked like exasperated fondness, a few wispy curls that were dangling around her face swaying with the motion. "You did not even ask, did you? I shall have to write to my sister, then, and get her opinion directly."

"Uh..."

"Oh!" Elizabeth suddenly exclaimed, reaching up to tenderly touch his forehead. Darcy felt a sharp stab of pain and hissed in response, causing her to recoil slightly. Elizabeth's lips, the ones he had imagined kissing many, many times, were curved downward as she said, "You are hurt!"

"Am I?"

Elizabeth lowered her hand to show him the blood smeared on her fingertips. "What happened?"

"It was nothing." Darcy tried to demur, though he was beginning to wonder if he had not struck his head more forcibly than he had originally thought to bring about this extremely wonderful dream. Was he unconscious right now, bleeding to death in the snow while he revelled in one last fantasy of his beloved Elizabeth? Was he already dead? He could imagine heaven exactly like this.

"It most certainly is not 'nothing'!" Elizabeth exclaimed. "You are *bleeding*."

Darcy shrugged, feeling his cheeks heat at her ire. "Not much."

"Come." Elizabeth urgently took hold of one of his hands with both of her own and tugged him towards a hallway that led them deeper into the house. As they passed the staircase on their way, she turned to issue an order to the housekeeper. "Mrs Reynolds, please fetch some warm water and clean towelling. We might also require the services of the physician."

Mrs Reynolds, who had scuttled down the stairs at Elizabeth's exclamation over his injury, hovered only long enough to accept these instructions before dashing off towards the kitchens.

Darcy arched his neck so that he could watch his most faithful servant rush away to see to the commands of a lady who was not her mistress. Wait, was she? Had he married Miss Elizabeth Bennet and then somehow forgotten?

Much as he enjoyed this image of an Elizabeth who was apparently his wife—for who else had the power to order his servants around besides the master and mistress?—and who was fussing over him just as an affectionate lover would, Darcy was mightily confused as to how it had come to be. Was it real? Or was it merely some combination of his desperate love for an unsuitable country maid and a powerful strike to the head? Had his mind been addled?

Elizabeth steered him into his own study and directed him to sit in his favourite chair by the fire. The olive green leather squeaked beneath him as he sank into the seat and shifted into a comfortable position. His beloved Elizabeth sat on the matching footstool before him and began removing his boots. Darcy watched her intently, his eyes fixed upon each twisting curl caressing her cheek, the thick, dark lashes that shielded the colour of her eyes, and that sweet button nose dusted with cinnamon freckles even in December.

Her task completed, Elizabeth left his boots on the hearth where they could be dried by the blazing fire and then returned to his side. She spread a blanket across his lap and tucked it beneath his thighs, leaning over him at an angle which allowed him to see down the front of her dress. Darcy told himself that he should look away, but his inner voice reminded him, *she is your wife, fool.*

Was she?

Elizabeth settled herself back onto her ottoman and smiled at him. "There now. All warm."

Darcy did not respond other than to stare at her. He still could not fathom this...this...was it reality or illusion? Was she his wife or an unmarried country miss he had left behind?

If Darcy had to guess by her looks alone, he would suppose that she was his wife. Her physical charms, always lovely, were exactly as he had remembered, but she was dressed very differently than he had seen before. Elizabeth could look charming in a potato sack, but the gown she wore was fashionably cut and constructed of a deep burgundy red satin trimmed in ivory lace—just a touch at her neck and cuffs, but clearly expensive all the same—and was accented with a green sash beneath her bust. It was very becoming on her, especially the way it dipped in the front to expose the tempting swell of her bosom to his gaze.

"A-*hem*." Elizabeth coughed, interrupting Darcy's perusal of her person. He raised his gaze, his face tingling with embarrassed warmth. "I believe *that* shall have to wait for later, sir. For now, we shall see to your injury."

That? Could she mean...?

Darcy shifted in his seat to adjust his blanket, disguising his burgeoning response to the most tantalising thought of Elizabeth upstairs in his—their?—chambers, just as Mrs Reynolds entered the room with the fresh towels her mistress had requested. A maid trailed behind her with a steaming kettle, while yet another followed with a ceramic wash bowl.

Mrs Reynolds addressed Elizabeth directly, "How is the patient, ma'am?"

Elizabeth smiled gratefully at the housekeeper and accepted the towel. The basin was settled onto a small table that always rested beside his chair and one of the maids poured steaming water from the kettle into it. "Stubbornly refusing to admit he is injured, of course. Has a note been dispatched to Mr McCallister yet?"

"Of course. I am sure that he will be here directly, though the weather might delay his arrival."

"I do hope he shall be more careful out there than my husband," Elizabeth replied. "It would not do to have him injured or ill when he is the one who is supposed to ride to the rescue! When he arrives, please direct him to the study and see that he is offered something warm to eat and drink before he leaves again."

With this, Mrs Reynolds was dismissed, and she left closing the door to the hallway behind her.

And so Darcy was left alone with his wife. *My wife*. What could he say to the woman whom he had apparently married, when he had no recollection of having done so? He was not about to look a gift horse in the mouth and demand an explanation, but he was a bit stymied as to how to begin a conversation with someone he felt he knew, yet knew not at all. Not in these circumstances.

Luckily, he did not need to ponder for long as Elizabeth turned back to him, her eyes crinkling with warmth as she observed him. She reached out her hand to stroke again at his forehead, just barely skating over the tender skin with even more tender fingertips, and Darcy felt a pleasant tingle rushing over him at her contact. "My poor love." Elizabeth dropped her hand so that she could caress his cheek with the backs of her fingers. "Does it hurt?"

Not when she cared for him so sweetly. "No," Darcy replied hoarsely.

Elizabeth's mouth curved softly, her eyes sparkling like evergreens dusted with fresh snow. "My brave man. I trust you will be good whilst I clean your wound?"

Unable to resist this charming vision, Darcy turned his face so that he might brush his lips against the hand that was caressing his cheek. "Perfectly well behaved."

"I love you, Fitzwilliam."

Elizabeth bent towards him and bestowed upon him a small kiss, one that felt as though it had been given many times, and then leaned back.

"And I you." The response felt natural. He reached out, cradled her face between his palms, and brought her back to him, pressing their mouths together where they belonged. He deepened the contact, sweeping his tongue out to meet hers for a moment before withdrawing. Darcy allowed their lips to separate but pressed his forehead to hers in order to linger over their embrace for a few moments longer.

"I missed you," Elizabeth whispered, her breath tickling his cheeks. With a sigh and a final peck on the lips, she leaned back and reached for the cloths Mrs Reynolds had brought, dipping one into the basin of warm water poured by the maids. She wrung out the excess and brought it to his wound, dabbing lightly at the tender spot. When the rag came away, it was splotched with crusty blood, but not much. It had likely stopped bleeding some time ago.

"I believe you will live, Mr Darcy," Elizabeth teased, rinsing the cloth and putting it to use again. "It does not look so bad now that the blood has been wiped away. Merely a scratch. But what happened?"

He had yearned to be precious to another his entire life, petted and coddled as if he were treasured. Elizabeth's ministrations were more than his fantasies had even suggested, soft and loving with a healing warmth that was as much a balm to his soul as to his body. Darcy had imagined being treated this way many times over the past decades—by his parents, his sister and, most recently, by this woman who had captured him with her kindness—but there was no comparison to the reality of devotion. Darcy felt his heart swell as if it had grown three sizes, so full of love that it threatened to burst within his chest.

Belatedly, the expression of anticipation on Elizabeth's face reminded Darcy that she had asked him a question. "I, ah…I cannot recall."

"You cannot recall?"

"I think I bumped my head as we turned into the drive and must have blacked out. The next thing I knew, we were approaching the house and…I saw you."

"What is the last thing you remember before that?" Elizabeth asked.

"I, ah…" What should he tell her? Darcy remembered leaving London two days ago, but she seemed to think he had been visiting Bingley at Netherfield where his friend was supposedly married to her sister, Jane. Well, at least *that* was not terribly surprising; Bingley had been more than usually infatuated with the eldest Miss Bennet during the autumn and Darcy could hardly fault him for his choice when he, apparently, had married the younger sister. "I feel…a bit confused. I remember leaving London to come here for Christmas to see…where is Georgiana?"

"Georgiana?" Elizabeth was looking increasingly worried. "At Bedford Hall."

"Oh…of course."

They were interrupted by a knock at the door before Elizabeth could interrogate him further. Mr McCallister came into the room and bowed to his patrons. He was a youthful man of middling height, still relatively new to his business, with strikingly blond hair and blue eyes. His collar and cravat were both damp from melted snow and his boots were dotted with moisture. "Apologies for the delay, Mrs Darcy. I was at the Cratchit farm seeing to little Timmy. The poor lad has injured his leg again."

Elizabeth's expression and tone were infused with deep sympathy. "I hope he will be well."

"He will," Mr McCallister assured her, a touch brusquely. He then moved on to the matter currently at hand without further pleasantries. "I understand Mr Darcy has suffered a bump to the head, madam?"

Elizabeth spun around on her ottoman to address the physician directly. "Yes, and it seems his memory is a little faulty, as well. He cannot seem to remember his journey today nor some of the things that came before it. Should we be concerned?"

Mr McCallister indicated with the wave of a hand that Elizabeth should move aside so he could assess the patient. She stood and removed to Darcy's side, placing herself between him and the fireplace, as Mr McCallister seated himself upon her vacated seat. "Perhaps. I shall examine him and give you a more definitive answer. Please feel free to make yourself comfortable elsewhere, Mrs Darcy."

"Very well." She pressed a soft kiss to the crown of Darcy's head. "I shall be in the library."

As Elizabeth moved towards the door, Darcy felt himself gripped by a sudden surge of panic. If she left the room, would the illusion dissolve? Would she disappear and take this perfect life of warm affection with her? Darcy snatched at her wrist and held it firmly, tugging her back towards his chair. "I would prefer you stay."

Elizabeth looked at him in surprise but consented easily enough. "Of course, if you wish." She loosened his fingers with her free hand so that she could slip her palm into his and hold it properly. Elizabeth then resumed her station at his side, out of the way of the physician's work yet still within her husband's line of sight.

"Very well," conceded Mr McCallister, though the turn of his mouth convinced Darcy he was displeased and only humouring his wealthy clients.

Mr McCallister then proceeded with his examination, asking after the severity of Darcy's pain, whether he had fallen unconscious after the accident, or if he felt nauseated. Darcy replied to each query with his usual stoicism, faintly annoyed to be sharing what should be his and his wife's private moments with this brusque little man.

"Your wife says that you have been experiencing memory loss. Can you tell me the last thing you *do* remember?" Mr McCallister asked after inspecting the cleaned wound.

Darcy explained what he had already told Elizabeth and watched the physician's brow furrow deeper with each revelation of conflicting facts.

"Can you recall the date?"

"December the twenty-fourth," replied Darcy. He could feel his wife squeeze his hand and looked up at her to see alarm writ across her face.

"Very close." Mr McCallister leaned forward to peer into Darcy's eyes. He held his forefinger up and waved it slowly in front of Darcy's face, the patient's eyes following dutifully. "It is indeed December, but only the eighth."

"I see."

"And you believe that you arrived today from London?"

"Yes."

"Your wife tells me that you have just returned from your brother-in-law's estate. Do you recall anything like that?"

"I suppose I might perhaps have stopped at Netherfield—"

"Netherfield!" Elizabeth exclaimed anxiously. "Whatever would you be doing there? The Bingleys have not lived at Netherfield since this past summer when they moved to McClane Manor. And you could not have gone so far as London, for you have only been away since yesterday!"

"I would not worry overmuch, Mrs Darcy," soothed Mr McCallister, "confusion and memory loss are fairly common with bumps to the head, though I would not have suspected a minor scratch such as this one to cause it. He will likely recover over the next few days. Otherwise, he seems in good health and shows no alarming symptoms."

"He is well?"

Mr McCallister shrugged and then stood. "As well as can be expected considering the situation. His pain is tolerable, he does not complain of impaired vision or nausea, and he can walk without stumbling. Aside from his faulty memory and the cut on his head, I would say he is perfectly well. If he complains of anything else, send me a note and I shall return and render my opinion."

"Thank you, sir," said Elizabeth, walking with him to the door. "Please see Cook for something warm to drink and a bite to eat before you leave us."

Mr McCallister bowed to Elizabeth. "Thank you, Mrs Darcy."

"Oh, and I was sorry to hear your office had been broken into recently. Did they catch the thieves?"

"Oh, yes." Mr McCallister's lips curled into a smile that could be considered nothing if not mischievous. "And I can guarantee you that these particular criminals will think twice before breaking into another person's property again."

Elizabeth laughed aloud and congratulated the physician on his cleverness. "So I have heard! Please, let us know if you require anything to fix the damage. You are such an asset to the neighbourhood that we do not wish you to be without anything you need."

Mr McCallister thanked Elizabeth again and then left, probably to accept his meal from the kitchens. She closed the door behind him and returned to her husband. But this time, instead of seating herself on the ottoman, she propped her hip against the arm of his chair and leaned into him, her head resting upon the top of his. Elizabeth sighed. "Oh, Fitzwilliam, what am I to do with you? I thought *I* was safely considered to be the wild one in our little family."

Darcy reached out and crept his arm around her waist, pulling her closer and into his lap directly. He buried his face in Elizabeth's neck and inhaled the rich scent of cinnamon and evergreen boughs. "Forgive me, my love. I shall do my best to worry you less."

"See that you do," she scolded playfully, twining the fingers of one hand into his hair and scratching his scalp in comforting circles. Darcy closed his eyes and enjoyed the sensation.

This morning—well, he thought it was this morning, though perhaps he was wrong about that—Darcy had woken up unmarried and pining for the woman reclining across him. Now, he was growing ever more relaxed with the thought of Elizabeth as his wife, though the concept had been foreign to him only an hour ago. It had not been difficult; even before his accident, Darcy had known that he was in love with her. He had merely forbidden himself the pleasure of it.

Of course, considering the words of the physician, perhaps Darcy simply was not remembering things correctly. It was possible, maybe even probable, that the reality known to Elizabeth and all the other people around him was the true one, and he had been trapped in an old, bitter memory of his time before marrying her. And how could he have ever tried to deny himself this? It was more perfect than Darcy had even dared imagine.

There was one detail that still plagued him, however. "Elizabeth?"

"Hmm...?"

"You say that I went to visit Bingley, yes?"

Darcy felt Elizabeth's cheek graze against his hair in a nod. "Yes, yesterday morning. You were due back around midday, but I suppose the weather prevented you." It sounded reasonable to him.

"Why did you not come with me? I would have thought you eager to visit your sister." He need not add that he would have preferred to keep her at his side.

"I have been so ill in the carriage recently that you felt it best I stay behind." Elizabeth leaned away from him so that they could meet eyes. "Do you not remember that, either?"

Darcy shook his head in the negative. "I am afraid not. You have been ill?"

Elizabeth stroked his hair as she answered, "It is only natural at this time, my love. Remember what Mrs Clausen said?"

She laughed at the blank stare he gave her. "She said that the nausea would get better soon, but that carriage rides might be uncomfortable until the end, and that it was nothing to be concerned about."

"The end...? The end of *what*?"

The motion of her free hand drew his attention downward, and he observed her rubbing at her belly, which, now that the fabric of her skirts was pressed against it, he could see was swollen into a moderately sized bump. Elizabeth petted her stomach the same way she did his head and he made the connexion.

"You...you are...?"

Elizabeth frowned at him, the motion of her hand stilling at the crest of her swollen abdomen. "You do not remember that I am with child, either?"

The joy simmering within him ever since his realisation that Elizabeth was his wife came to a full boil at this new information. He was to be a father! Elizabeth was carrying his child! What did it matter if he remembered or not?

His wife emitted a tiny squeak as Darcy wrapped both arms around her and pulled her tightly to himself, cradling Elizabeth as they would soon cradle their son or daughter. "I love you so!"

Elizabeth settled into his arms and wrapped her own around his neck, nuzzling down into his embrace. Despite her worries, she was apparently not unwilling to share this moment with him. Darcy kissed her hair, so delightfully scented with the aroma of Christmas spice and greenery, and revelled in the happiness that he desperately prayed was real. God had granted him his answer.

Elizabeth did not break their embrace for a long time, half an hour or more, but finally she did pull back and kiss him before entreating, "You must be famished after such a long day. Come upstairs to our rooms and I shall have trays brought up."

Their rooms. "Perfect."

Late that evening, Darcy and Elizabeth lounged by the fire in their rooms and discussed some of the things he had apparently forgotten. They both agreed not to be concerned about his damaged memory for now, as it changed nothing about the happiness of their present. And though their shared past had surely brought him much pleasure that he could not recall, he would not disdain this holiday gift by questioning it.

"When can we expect to meet this little one?" Darcy gently stroked the convex slope of Elizabeth's stomach as he spoke. They were seated upon the rug in front of the fire, she leaning into him with her chest against his back as he propped them both up with one arm. His other was wrapped around his wife, caressing the bump that was his future child.

Elizabeth smiled down at her belly and tangled their fingers together on top of it. "In the spring. Mrs Clausen expects him or her to arrive around Easter."

"So we shall not visit Lady Catherine this year."

Elizabeth laughed and he felt as much as heard the jingle of bells as she did. "As if I were invited!"

"No, I suppose not," Darcy said, deciding that sounded much like his aunt. Anne would never have agreed to marry him even if he had asked, so her mother's hopes for a match were in vain, but there was never any convincing Lady Catherine of anything. It was likely that, even though he and Elizabeth were long married, his aunt still somehow expected him to send his wife away and come crawling back to wed her daughter. Poor Anne was deathly terrified of childbirth, knowing as they all did that she would likely die in the attempt, so he made himself a promise to rescue her from any further attempts of her mother's to matchmake in the future.

Outside their window, the sky had grown dark, but the sheer whiteness of the snow still piled up on the sill as it continued to float from the heavens to earth. Knowing Derbyshire as he did, Darcy expected it to continue all night and into the morning when it might cease, if they were lucky.

In the meantime, Darcy decided as he pulled his lovely wife closer to him, he did not mind the frightful weather outside as long as he was snowed in with Elizabeth. They could read to each other by a delightful fire in the library, play chess or cards in the parlour, go to the music room for some seasonal songs, or simply stay in bed all day while the world was at a standstill outside. The last prospect seemed most promising to him. Darcy closed his eyes, chin propped against the crown of Elizabeth's head. The cinnamon scent was intoxicating by the warm fire.

"Shall we go to bed?"

Darcy's eyes flew open and he looked down at Elizabeth. Her lips were curved into the kind of smile he had never seen—well, never *remembered* seeing, in any event—on her face before, but one he could appreciate as a man in love.

Though she struggled a bit to flip over, Elizabeth was soon on her feet with his aid and she reached out to him. Darcy took her hands and got up to follow her into his chambers.

CHAPTER TWO

DARCY AWOKE WITH A YAWN AND A STRETCH, ARCHING HIS back until his joints popped like a crackling fire. After loving his wife quite thoroughly, he had slept better than he could ever remember. Not that his memory was faultless lately.

He rolled over without bothering to open his heavy eyelids and reached across the mattress for the warm body he knew was nearby, but his grasping fingers found nothing. Darcy rolled onto his other side and groped around in case she had for some strange reason decided to move elsewhere, but found nothing there, either. Where was Elizabeth?

Opening his eyes, Darcy squinted around the confines of his four-poster bed and found himself alone and with no sign of another person's recent presence. The blankets were only rumpled on his side of the bed, the pillows had no indentations other than his own, and there was a distinct lack of cinnamon and evergreens wafting through the air. Moreover, he was wearing a night shirt, and he clearly recalled his wife tossing it aside during their amorous activities the previous night. Where was Elizabeth?

"Elizabeth?" Darcy called out as he sat up, his voice hoarse as it generally was upon waking. "Are you here?"

There was no answer.

Wariness began to creep into his mind and Darcy grappled for the opening in the bed curtains. *Elizabeth must have gone back to her bedchamber. She always was an early riser.*

Finally finding the divide, Darcy shoved the curtains apart, the metal rings hissing angrily against their pole as they slid along it. He looked about his chamber and found nothing amiss, everything just as he usually left it, even a fire crackling merrily in the hearth on the other side of the room. But something was missing. Some*one*. Where was his Elizabeth?

"Elizabeth?" he called out, louder this time, and with a note of panic in his tone.

He heard a rustling inside the dressing room and felt his shoulders release their tension. She was still here. Darcy waited with impatience as the door opened.

"Did you call for me, sir?" It was Bailey, his valet.

Disappointment crashed over him like an avalanche. "No. Where is Mrs Darcy?"

"Mrs Darcy, sir?"

"Yes. Where is she?" Darcy's tone became increasingly irritable as his fear mounted.

Bailey stood there for a long moment, clearly unsure how to answer. "You are not married, sir."

No. No, it could not have been a dream! It positively could not!

A sick feeling rose in his gut as he pushed back his blankets and placed his feet upon the floor. It was chilly to the touch, even with the thick carpet surrounding his bed, but then everything felt cold.

"Sir?" Bailey's voice recalled Darcy's attention to the present and he looked up at his valet, who continued to stand at attention a few feet away. "Are you well? Is your head paining you?"

Darcy reached up to his forehead to feel for the injury from yesterday and to assure himself that something was as he remembered it and that his marriage to Elizabeth was real. But he found no unbroken skin at all. He probed around until he found a tender lump deep within his hair, but it was certainly not the wound he remembered.

What *did* he remember?

Darcy nearly collapsed in grief as he realised it had all been a dream. A wonderful, impossible dream. His face buried between his palms, he fought mightily against the compulsion to sob.

Dimly, Darcy heard the door to his bedchamber open and Bailey's voice instructing a footman to tell Mrs Reynolds she must summon Mr McCallister. Bailey returned and helped Darcy to his feet, then guided him back into bed, tucking him in as if he were a child.

"What has happened?"

"You arrived home yesterday after a carriage accident. We all thought you were well enough, acting as you usually do, but perhaps the injury was more severe than we had thought."

"I…I have been asleep since yesterday?" he asked. He could remember none of what had transpired after the accident, yet his mind had filled in the blanks with the most wonderful flight of fancy.

"No. You complained of a head-ache but insisted that it was nothing to be concerned about. You did not wish us to call the physician."

"Then what?"

Bailey was puzzled by his questions but would never deny him answers. "You went upstairs to greet Miss Darcy and then retired to your study for a bit. You had your dinner on a tray there, as Miss Darcy had retired early."

"And I behaved as usual? Nothing strange at all?"

"No, sir. Nothing peculiar at all, to my mind."

Darcy lay back again until his head sank into his pillow. He had come home. Behaved as he always did. He had not been unconscious and dreaming since the accident. He had slept all night, one must assume, but it was strange that the day he should be missing had been filled with something entirely different.

What was real?

Though tempted to use his injury as an excuse to remain above stairs all day, it was not Darcy's way to loll about when he could be up and working. Moreover, his bedroom and sitting room now reminded him of the hours he had spent—or, rather, had not spent—with Elizabeth in his arms, loving her just as he had always wished. Thus, after assuring his servants that calling for Mr McCallister on Christmas Day was not necessary and would likely be an unkindness, he ordered Bailey to dress him for services.

This holiday was spent much like the ones before it—largely in silence. Darcy escorted his sister to church in the sleigh for the annual reading of Christ's birth, though it was so poorly attended he almost regretted the bother in going. That is not the point, he reminded himself, though his bitterness still left a disgusting flavour in his mouth. Just before his dream, or whatever it had been, he had humbly asked God to give him an answer to his dilemma with Eliz—ahem, *Miss Elizabeth Bennet*—and had been taunted with an illusion instead. The Almighty was not only merciless, but cruel.

Upon returning to Pemberley, the Darcys shared a hearty, yet awkwardly silent breakfast of fresh pastries, steaming piles of eggs and bacon, and hot drinks. Darcy ate little of it, and Georgiana not much more before excusing herself to practise on her new pianoforte in the music room. He grunted his acquiescence to her intention and continued to look out the window at the piles of snow blanketing his grounds in white. Georgiana skittered away, clearly fearful of his black mood.

Darcy deliberated where to go next as his study, his usual haven, was out of the question; one look at his favourite chair by the fire would have him awash in misery again and force his servants to bother McCallister after all. No, he could not go to the place she had tended to him so lovingly, rested upon his knees, and told him of their impending child. It was out of the question.

The library? No, that would not do. Not only was it connected via internal door to his study, but libraries reminded Darcy of the *Miss Elizabeth Bennet* he had met in Hertfordshire. She had claimed not to be a great reader and rather to take pleasure in many things, but it was nevertheless clear that she enjoyed the pursuit much as he did. It was one of the things he had always hoped to share with someone special to him, and he had no doubts that the Elizabeth who was his dream wife would have spent many hours in the library with him. Besides, the furniture was very similar to that in his study and would hardly keep his mind from the room next door.

There were numerous parlours and the like where he might go, but what was the point in sitting in an empty space meant for attending to guests on a day where none could possibly be received? It would only compound his loneliness in the wake of his crushing disappointment. Moreover, he would be forced to tear one of the servants away from their duties to light a fire or be made to suffer the December chill while he indulged his melancholia. Should he wish to do that, he could save everyone the trouble and time and go outside to lie in a snowbank…and he was not yet so downcast as to be tempted by *that*.

Unless I intend to visit the kitchens, I suppose I shall play billiards. Strange how in a house this large my choices should be so limited.

An hour later, Darcy had given up on billiards with a frustrated huff and haphazardly tossed his cue upon the felt. A solitary game held no appeal for someone overwhelmed with his own miserable solitude. It made him remember the occasion when Miss Elizabeth Bennet had accidentally wandered into the billiards room at Netherfield where he had been playing a lonely game, much like the one he had been partaking in presently. That was the end of it; he could bear it no more.

"God rest ye, merry gentlemen
Let nothing you dismay..."

As he walked out into the hallway, the soft swell of his sister's voice and tinkling of piano keys caught Darcy's attention. Georgiana was still in the music room, it seemed, playing song after song as was her wont. Without much thought on the matter, Darcy turned his footsteps in that direction.

Only a few doors down from where he had been whiling away his time, Darcy reached the open doorway within moments and peered inside. There was Georgiana, seated primly on the bench before her instrument, picking out a pretty Yuletide carol.

Darcy crept quietly to a chair closer to Georgiana so that he might listen without disturbing her, settling in to let the music waft over him like a soothing and gentle snowfall. He stayed in this attitude for over half an hour as she practised, playing the same part of the same piece over and over again, and he listened appreciatively to her talent. There was another lady who, while not so technically proficient, was very—

"Stop it!" He castigated himself harshly. Darcy glared at the hands in his lap as they fiddled with the ring on his little finger, a nervous habit he had developed since inheriting the jewellery five years ago.

A moment later, he realised the room had quieted and looked up to see Georgiana still on her bench, but turned to look at him. Her eyes were wide and wary as she gazed upon him and he was certain that she had heard him muttering under his breath as a madman would. Darcy straightened his posture. "I apologise for interrupting you, dearest. Do not allow me to disturb you."

"It is well," Georgiana said, folding her hands upon her lap. She continued to stare at him as if deciding something. "Are *you*?"

"I beg your pardon?"

"Are you well?"

"I—" Should he lie? "I am..."

Georgiana, now biting her lip and staring at her lap where her fingers irritated a ribbon on her gown, pressed on. "You can tell me, you know, if anything is bothering you. I shall listen."

Ever uncomfortable sharing of himself with others, Darcy initially declined the favour she offered, unsure of how even to begin describing what ailed him. "I thank you for your concern, but I am well enough."

"Brother," she ventured again, timidly raising only her eyes to look at him, "I know that I have disappointed you, but I would like to…that is, I feel that…" She gave up on what she was trying to say and lapsed into silence.

Darcy leaned forward and, forgetting his own misery for a moment, reached out to pluck one of her hands away from its activity and hold it gently between his own. "Georgiana, dearest, look at me." She obeyed, albeit reluctantly. "Do not think that I consider you less than you were before. I am not pleased by your past behaviour with—" He paused to grimace as if suddenly tasting something vile, "—that man, but it does not necessarily follow that your value to me as my beloved sister has been tarnished. I would wish you to learn a lesson from your mistake, that is all, not chastise yourself for being duped by a practiced seducer."

Darcy had given this speech in various forms before, but he hoped that she would believe him this time. She gave no indication of appeasement, however, and so he continued, "Moreover, I am also proud of you."

Georgiana looked up at him fully at this remark, stuttering, "P–proud of me? But why?"

"Because you may have initially erred in judgment, but you then revealed the whole to me and allowed me to save you from your folly. Do you recall that letter you sent me, begging for my attendance at Ramsgate on an urgent matter? It proves to me that, in your heart, you knew what you were doing was wrong. It was very brave of you to ask me for help, knowing that the outcome was unsure."

His sister resumed her downcast gaze, though this time it focused on their joined hands in her lap. "I…did I ever tell you I sent you that letter because of a horrible nightmare?"

Darcy started. A nightmare? "Indeed?"

"Yes," Georgiana agreed with an unsteady nod. "The night before I sent you the letter, I had just accepted Geo—*that man* and was greatly anticipating the beginning of our lives together as husband and wife. He just needed a week to settle his affairs and then we could be off to Gretna Green."

Darcy managed to regulate his fury as she told this tale, though it was difficult.

"But that same night I had doubts about whether or not our plans were honourable, and so I prayed to God, asking Him for an answer. I went to sleep and had a terrifying nightmare, a vision almost, of what our future would be like should I elope with him."

"What kind of nightmare?" Darcy swallowed to wet his suddenly dry throat. His own plea to God in the carriage as he approached Pemberley reverberated in his mind and he tried desperately to disregard it so that he could hear the remainder of his sister's story.

"It seemed so real!" Georgiana continued, raising her head to look him earnestly in the eye, her brows raised high on her forehead and her mouth animated. "I dreamt that we had been married—I know not for how long, but it seemed well into the future—and were living in London. Oh, Brother! How awful it was, the house we were living in. It was dirty and smelled dreadful and..."

As Georgiana recounted the details of her vision and the indignities her dream-self had suffered at the hands of George Wickham, Darcy became strangely excited. To think that they shared a similar, albeit mysterious, experience that had given them a glimpse of their possible futures!

And that was precisely what it was, Darcy realised...a *possibility*. Perhaps God had not given him the vision of Elizabeth as a torment, but rather as an impetus to go forth into the future and make her his own. Giving him a peek into the utter happiness that could be theirs had been intended as encouragement for Darcy to give up on his ridiculous arguments against the match so he could pursue the woman destined to be his wife.

"...and so, at the end, I *died*, frightened and alone with no husband and no money. The dream was so terrifying that the next morning I sat down and wrote you that letter. What do you think it meant?"

CHAPTER THREE

THE WEEKS DRAGGED ON IN DERBYSHIRE AS, MUCH AS DARCY had predicted, most of the residents in his part of the county were confined by heavy snow for the entirety of the winter. For the greater part of January, they were kept indoors with only a few fleeting hours of weather allowing for outdoor activity. The days were long and the nights almost unbearably so, and therefore Darcy had much time to think on what he had experienced. And, indeed, whether he had experienced it at all.

The physician had come at Mrs Reynolds's beckoning after the holiday to examine Darcy but, as in his vision, found nothing to be amiss with his patient other than a lost day. Memory loss was not uncommon, Mr McCallister had said in a moment that caused Darcy's head to swirl with dizzying recollection, and not necessarily something to be concerned about. He had prescribed headache powders, readily available through the local apothecary, for any lingering pain, then told Darcy to rest and call on him again if other concerns arose.

Darcy had pondered his vision at length since his sister had divulged her own cautionary nightmare to him and, though still confounded by the mystical workings of a universe which might condescend to take pity on a pair of lonely souls struggling to make a life-changing decision, he was nearly convinced that it had been a gift from God. After all, he could not very well call it a dream because it had felt entirely, excruciatingly real. The pain in his head while Elizabeth, as his wife, had dabbed at his scrape had been real. The pleasure of taking her to his bed had been real, as well. Most of all, the swelling of love within his heart had been achingly real—and continued to be so.

No, it was not a dream. Was it a hallucination? No, that was truly no different from a dream other than its tendency towards lunacy. There had been too much rationality at its core to write it off as a hallucination. Was it truly a premonition? Perhaps he had been given a glimpse into his future life. Darcy rather hoped that this was the case as he then had something to look forward to. It was still possible that he was simply going mad, as he had feared in the carriage on his journey home, but he had nearly persuaded himself that was not the case.

Well, no matter what it had been, Darcy was absolutely decided on one thing: he would marry Miss Eli—Elizabeth. He would marry *Elizabeth*.

A month later, soon after the roads had reopened for travel, Darcy sat before the fire in the study of his London town house, sipping at a cup of steaming coffee as he watched the flames leap and crackle before him. It was bitterly cold outside, and the winter air seemed to seep into every corner, forcing him and everyone else with sense to remain by their hearths where they might maintain some semblance of warmth.

It was still early—well, early for those who resided in the capital, at least—but Darcy had hopes that Bingley would soon receive the note he had sent and come calling that same day. Though happy to see his friend on any occasion, today he was particularly eager; he hoped to convince Bingley to re-open Netherfield.

"Brother?"

Darcy looked up to see Georgiana standing in the partially open doorway of his study and he smiled, inviting her to enter his refuge. It was not as if she were interrupting anything other than his scheme to go back to Hertfordshire, one which he had thoroughly considered for many weeks already. "Come, sit."

Georgiana entered and took the leather chair across from his. It squeaked as she sank into the cushion. "How are you this morning?"

"Very well. Why do you ask?"

"You were so very unhappy while we were still at Pemberley, I worried that something was wrong."

"I had a…rather, I was concerned about something, but now that we are returned to town, I hope that it shall all be resolved soon." He had been tempted to share his own vision with Georgiana, as she had shared hers with him, but he was not yet so free with his innermost thoughts that he felt confident in describing them to a sister many years his junior. Moreover, he could not yet be certain that the vision in question truly was prophetic in nature and, perhaps superstitiously, he felt that to share it with someone else might prevent it coming true even if it were.

"I see," she said. "I hope whatever trouble you have had will be resolved. Is there anything I might do to assist?"

Darcy raised his cup to his lips to avoid answering directly, blew upon the hot surface of his beverage, and took a tentative sip. When he had swallowed, he set it upon his saucer and returned it to his lap. "I am afraid not."

"I see." Georgiana dropped her eyes to her primly folded hands. She then raised her chin again so that she might look at him directly and boldly requested, "Will you not speak of it with me? I wish to help to you, even if in just the role of a caring listener."

Darcy, though a touch startled by her plea, found himself pleased at her willingness to be his confidante. Perhaps he had been unfair in his assessment of her as yet another relation with whom he could never achieve closeness. Still, he was not sure how to broach the topic; should he tell her of the vision, as she had experienced something similar herself?

"I am honestly not sure where to start. I have developed an…affection for someone. A lady."

Georgiana's eyes widened and she clapped her hands together. "Miss Elizabeth Bennet?"

Darcy could feel his brows shoot up. "How could you possibly know that?"

A tiny curl of her lips, one that indicated how pleased with herself she was, appeared on Georgiana's face. "You mentioned her in two—no, three letters last autumn while you were staying in Hertfordshire with Mr Bingley. As you have never written, or spoken, of any lady before her, I rather assumed that you might hold her in some esteem. So, I was correct?"

Darcy nodded, still rather stunned that he had been so transparent when he had been at great pains to conceal his infatuation.

"How wonderful! I shall have a sister at last! But, why would such a thing make you melancholy?"

Darcy shifted in his seat and prepared himself to admit the crux of his previous consternation regarding the potential alliance. "Miss Bennet, while a charming young lady, is not of our circle, nor does she possess a fortune. She would be considered unsuitable by most." *Including myself, at first.*

"Is she not a gentlewoman?"

"No, her father is a gentleman. The Bennets have lived at Longbourn for many generations, I believe."

"Then Pemberley is in some sort of financial trouble? Do you require a large dowry to keep it solvent?"

"No, of course not."

"Then what is the problem? Does she not like you?"

"She..." Wait, *did* she like him? Surely she did; their debates were fierce, but enjoyable, and she teased him almost constantly while they were together. And Darcy's vision told him that they were destined to marry. Elizabeth must like him. "I suppose."

"Well, I do not know what the great fuss is about," Georgiana declared rather uncharitably but with such an adorable pout that Darcy was inclined to laugh.

"I agree, though I bow to your superiority in seeing it much more quickly than I did. I have decided to offer for the lady, though first I require Bingley's help."

Georgiana's look of puzzlement had returned. "I hardly see how the addition of another gentleman will assist your proposal, Brother!"

Darcy could not help chuckling outright at this assessment, correct as it was. "No, dearest, Mr Bingley will likely be wooing his own Bennet sister. I shall suggest he open Netherfield again, that we may both stay there for the duration of our courtships. It is but three miles from the Bennet estate and therefore ideally placed for our needs."

"Excuse me, sir." They were interrupted by the butler, who bowed and held out a silver salver with two cards placed upon it. "Mr and Miss Bingley have just arrived. Are you at home?"

Darcy could not hide his distaste at the thought that Miss Bingley had accompanied her brother to his summons. "Please show them to the green parlour. I shall be in directly."

Darcy huffed in aggravation, forgetting for a moment that his sister was there as an audience. She brought his attention back to herself when she giggled.

"I assume you are not so pleased to entertain Miss Bingley?"

"I apologise," Darcy said. "I should have hidden it better."

"I hardly disagree with you!" cried Georgiana, wrinkling her nose as if she smelled something awful. "She is rather intolerable much of the time and clearly believes that she will be the next mistress of Pemberley. I shall not feel much pity for her when your engagement is announced."

"You should not speak so."

"Perhaps not, but it is the truth and I abhor deception. Besides, I wish for you to know what a great favour I am doing you when I distract her so that you might speak to Mr Bingley without interruption later."

"I shall buy you a new bonnet if you do."

"Make it a parasol and we have an accord."

"Done."

It was, unfortunately, more difficult for Darcy to have a private word with Bingley than he had anticipated, as his friend's disagreeable sister seemed more than usually intent on speaking to him. Miss Bingley interrupted Georgiana each time she tried to suggest that they retire to the music room, as had been the Darcys' agreed upon plan, rattling away about everything and nothing at once.

"...and what do you think happened next? Why, she trod on her own frock and tore it, right in the middle of the dance floor! I should have died of embarrassment, had it been me. Of course," Miss Bingley paused dramatically for a moment and fluttered her eyelashes in Darcy's direction, "I should never be so ungraceful. I have always been lauded for being light on my feet."

"Indeed," was all Darcy could say to that which would not be rude. He would make sure to impress upon Bingley at parting that, the next time he came to call, he should leave all of his relations at home.

Darcy was quite anxious to have a few minutes alone with Bingley to make his communication about Miss Bennet, how mistaken he had been to try to divide them when it had been none of his concern, but Miss Bingley was monopolising the entire visit. His vision had told him that not only was his own happiness tied up with Elizabeth, but also that Bingley and Jane Bennet were destined to marry and make a happy home themselves. It was not a great logical leap from there to assume that his previous belief in the elder Miss Bennet's reserve had been a mistake on his own part rather than a true disinclination of the lady's. If nothing else, Darcy supposed that she might later fall in love with his friend because, in his vision, they had been mentioned as cheerfully settled with a baby daughter on an estate close enough to Pemberley to be visited during short day trips. He owed it to Bingley and the mystical forces that had given him a glimpse of a joyful future to make right what he had put asunder.

But first, he must somehow speak to Bingley without his sister's interference.

"And I am sure that dear Georgiana," Miss Bingley turned to the girl and rested a hand upon her upper arm as if they were the greatest of friends, "would have been the belle of the ball! She is so delightful and sweet that all the gentlemen would flock to fill her dance card. Is that not right, Charles?"

Bingley, who had been forced into silence by his sister's monologue, startled at being addressed. "Ah, yes, of course, Miss Darcy will be much admired when she comes out."

Miss Bingley winked at Georgiana as she said, "I believe she is admired already."

Bingley shifted on his seat as if it had suddenly sprouted needles, and Darcy could not blame him. Had anyone insinuated that *he* was attracted to a sixteen-year-old girl, a mere child, it would have driven him to discomfort, too.

"She is not out yet, so it hardly matters. All things in their proper time."

Both Bingley and Georgiana cast Darcy grateful looks. He coughed into his fist to mask the bark of laughter that threatened to burst from his mouth at their matching expressions.

Miss Bingley would not be deterred. "One never knows…"

"Well, this was a fine visit, but I think we should be going, Caroline," Bingley said, leaping up from his seat as if pricked by one of the invisible needles. "We should not trespass on the Darcys' time."

Miss Bingley gripped the arms of her chair as if she intended to brace herself against being dragged from it. "Oh, but we were having such a lovely time and we are such close friends…"

Bingley, showing the small amount of courage he could occasionally call forth, insisted more firmly, "I am due at another appointment in an hour. We must depart."

Miss Bingley's frown was deep, but she acquiesced. "Very well, Charles. Mr Darcy, would you be so kind as to see me to the door?"

Trapped by civility, Darcy walked over to her chair and offered an arm which she rose to take. Miss Bingley grabbed hold tightly and held his appendage to her person with the force of possession as she steered him out the drawing room door and into the hall.

Once they were alone, Miss Bingley glanced over her shoulder as if making sure there was no one around to eavesdrop. "Mr Darcy, I must speak to you on an urgent matter. When I heard that Charles was coming here today, I took my chance that we might steal a private moment."

Darcy leaned away from her, apprehensive about what she could possibly wish to say to him. Should he be concerned about a wilful act of compromise right here in his own house? "And what might that be, Miss Bingley?"

She dropped her voice to a whisper that echoed about the empty hallway. "I have seen Miss Bennet here in London."

Darcy swallowed as a lump solidified in his throat. "M-Miss Bennet?"

"She called at Hurst's town house, presuming upon our friendship, just to throw herself in my brother's way again! Can you believe the audacity?"

Darcy's thrumming heart slowed its pace, his confusion receding; she meant Miss *Jane* Bennet. "You were friendly with each other in Hertfordshire, and it would be natural for her to call upon you when she visits town."

Miss Bingley rolled her eyes. "That is beside the point. What should we do? We spent so much time directing Charles away from her and now she is here! I have not returned the call yet, and I rather think I should not, but what else is to be done? Charles can never know that she is in town."

"I am not inclined towards deception, Miss Bingley."

The lady placed a hand upon his upper arm as if to soothe his ire. "Not *deception*, merely an omission. I had hoped that you might help me persuade him to leave town, just for a little while, to avoid her. Should he come across her accidentally in his current state, he might become as besotted as before and do something rash!"

A thought occurred to Darcy and his lips curled at one end, just a touch. "Very well. Tell him to meet me at our club tomorrow at three o'clock and I shall say what needs to be said."

"Darcy!" Bingley announced his presence in his usual fashion—loudly and from across a room full of people.

Darcy raised a hand in response and watched as his young friend wove through the room and stopped in front of his table. "Bingley, good of you to come today."

"What can I do for you? If you are looking for a fencing partner, I warn you that I have only just barely recovered from the last time. I much prefer riding, if there is a choice to be had. Of course, it is colder than preferable—the weather outside has been positively frightful!"

Darcy shook his head, amused. "Nothing of that sort. Your sister wished for me to speak to you on an important matter and, as it happens to conveniently correspond with my own plans, I was happy to oblige her."

Bingley's good cheer dimmed immediately. "Oh?"

"I wished to inform you that Miss Bennet is in town and appears interested in continuing your acquaintance." Darcy steepled his fingers against his chin, resting his elbows upon the arms of his chair as he regarded Bingley.

Bingley stared at him with his mouth open. "I thought you believed her indifferent to me."

Darcy, having prepared himself for this query in advance, allowed no emotion to slip past his hauteur. "I believe I was mistaken."

"So…you think she loves me?"

Darcy shrugged. "I am not the best judge of the lady's feelings. I think it worth the while to find out, however."

"And what made you change your mind? I suspect that the Bennets are no more wealthy, connected, or proper than before. Why should Miss Bennet be a suitable match for me now?"

"Those are still considerations, of course, but I have pondered the situation further since we departed Hertfordshire and have come to the conclusion that these things do not necessarily lead to a man's happiness in marriage. Would you prefer a wife with connexions and dowry but no affection for you?"

"No, certainly not!"

"That is exactly what I have been considering." Darcy allowed his eyes to lose focus as Elizabeth darted across his mind again. She beamed at him, as if proud of his efforts.

There was silence between the two gentlemen for some time, both lost in the labyrinth of their thoughts. Every time a bell rang for one of the servants in attendance of the club's members, Darcy remembered his beloved's jingling laugh.

It was Bingley who broke the quiet, gently, as if cracking open an eggshell. "So…what should I do?"

Darcy sighed and lowered his hands to fold over his chest. A malleable friend was an asset, though it did not fail to strike him that he was, in part, manoeuvring Bingley to his own ends. "It is my suggestion that you visit her. She is at number twelve Gracechurch Street as we speak and likely thinks that the connexion between you is dissolved because your sisters failed to return her call."

"Miss Bennet called upon my sisters? And they did not tell me?"

"Miss Bingley asked me just yesterday to conceal the fact of Miss Bennet's presence in town from you, though I informed her that I have an abhorrence of deceit." Darcy's slight smirk revealed that he appreciated the irony of deceiving Miss Bingley rather than her brother as she had intended.

Bingley, after a moment of slack-jawed consideration, guffawed at his sister's expense. "And so you promised to speak to me, did you?"

"I did," Darcy admitted. "I did not, however, affirm that I would tell you what she wished me to say. It was her scheme to keep Miss Bennet's stay in town from your notice and persuade you to go elsewhere to avoid an accidental meeting."

"She really thinks me a child, does she not? Trying to push me towards ladies of whom she approves and caring nothing of my opinion on the matter. Your sister—who is a lovely girl, mind, and will make someone an excellent wife one day—is her current mark and much too young for me! Do not misunderstand me, but I wish to marry a woman, not a girl."

Darcy waved away Bingley's apology. "If, say, you had shown interest in her a couple of years from now, I would have considered it a possible match, but she is barely sixteen. *Your* sister would do well to remember that *mine* is not ready to be married."

"So I should call upon Miss Bennet," Bingley reiterated, mostly to himself. "See if she still loves me—or if she ever did. How will I know?"

Darcy refused to own an opinion in this instance. "Only you will know that, Bingley. It is a matter between yourself and Miss Bennet—no one else can be a proper judge."

Bingley stood from his chair, nearly leaping from the seat in his eager haste to leave. "I think I shall yet call on her today, Darcy, if you do not mind my abandoning you here."

Darcy offered his friend a lopsided smile and stood, holding his hand out. Bingley grasped it firmly and shook it. "Not at all. Let me know how you get on."

"I will, I will," Bingley agreed, still pumping Darcy's hand vigorously in thanks. "What can I do to thank you?"

"When you return to Netherfield," said Darcy, "take me with you."

CHAPTER FOUR

As Darcy and his cousin travelled towards Rosings in March, he relayed an outline of his plan to woo Elizabeth. Now that Bingley was on the precipice of proposing to his own Miss Bennet—the work of a few weeks of regular visits to her relations' house in Gracechurch Street—Netherfield Park would be re-opened at last. As soon as the lady returned to Hertfordshire, her suitor would follow, likely as an engaged man. As Bingley had promised that day at White's, Darcy had recently received an invitation to join him there in May, and he had not looked so forward to anything in his life.

In the meantime, he was obligated to visit Lady Catherine.

"What do you think?"

Colonel Fitzwilliam was sitting across from him, arms folded against his chest, staring at Darcy as if he had grown an extra head that had turned out to be a clucking chicken. "I think you are daft."

Darcy was comforted that he had not told the colonel about his vision as the mockery was less severe without it. "How so?"

"Lady Catherine is going to murder you for this."

Darcy smirked. "Nonsense. She needs me alive."

"Very well, then, she will murder this Miss Elizabeth Bennet of yours."

"That does seem more likely."

"Secondly, what are you about, marrying a country nobody with no fortune? Since when have you decided to marry for something so unreasonable as love?"

This point Darcy took more seriously. "My parents married for material considerations and were not happy. I could not say they were *un*happy, yet I believe they lived without a fundamental element of life that many take for granted. Not only did they not love each other, but they were indifferent to the children created from their union. I do not wish the same for myself or Georgiana."

"Very well. What of this young lady? Possessed of little dowry and no worthwhile connexions—I assume she must be a great beauty to have captured your interest."

"I should certainly never deny it, but that is not what drew me to her. She is…witty. Intelligent. Clever. We could debate on a subject for hours, and she would change her true opinion simply to make the conversation more interesting. She did not defer to me just to gain my good opinion. More than that, though, she is kind and affectionate. Loving…"

Fitzwilliam raised his eyebrow. "And you know this because…?"

Darcy flushed as an image of the Elizabeth from his vision swam before his eyes, stretched across his lap as she tenderly stroked his hair, but provided his cousin a less fanciful explanation. "When we were at Netherfield, her sister was caught in the rain and became ill, requiring the hospitality of the Bingleys during her convalescence. Eliz—that is, *Miss* Elizabeth walked three miles across muddy fields so that she might tend to the ailing lady herself. She was very diligent and cared nothing for the approbation of the household, only her sister's well-being."

"I must say that is very…bold, yet impressive. Most young ladies would not go so far, even for a favourite sister."

"Elizabeth would do anything for someone she loves."

Fitzwilliam nodded. "And I suppose you want to be on the receiving end of that loyalty?"

"I do."

"Fair enough." A grin spread across Fitzwilliam's face, an expression of equal parts amusement and playful condescension. "You have grown so much, little cousin."

Darcy told him to go do something to himself that was not appropriate to repeat and the colonel guffawed, warning him playfully to watch his language so as not to offend his fair lady. Darcy rolled his eyes and redirected his attention to the passing scenery; they would be at Rosings within a quarter of an hour.

Up ahead along the dusty lane, a slender figure walked in a pale green muslin dress that seemed familiar to him. Darcy leaned towards the window and squinted at her; his heart-beat stuttered as they came closer and the figure became clearer to him.

"It could not be...why would she be here?"

"Who?"

"Ah..." Darcy hesitated, searching for any detail that might confirm his suspicions. The young woman was the correct height and build, there were a few dark curls coiling beneath her straw bonnet confirming her to be like in colouring, and, though as a gentleman he would never admit this to anyone, there was a notable familiarity in the way she walked, something he had observed surreptitiously from time to time.

"Oh, I see," Fitzwilliam said, leaning forward and blocking Darcy's view of the young lady in the road. "Do not tell me that you have thrown over your lovely Miss Elizabeth already!"

Darcy shoved him away. "Of course not!"

"Good! Because I require some entertainment whilst we are here attending to dear Aunt Catherine. Since your heart is already spoken for, I may feel free to flirt with whomever I wish."

Darcy took no notice of the colonel, instead resuming his close observation of the young lady outside the carriage. As the team of horses ahead of them came upon her, she removed herself from the roadway to avoid their stamping hooves and stood in the tall grass to the side of the packed dirt of the lane. Her face remained hidden by the brim of her bonnet as the conveyance passed, but at the moment Darcy's window drew level with her, the lady raised her head, and he saw her face.

Elizabeth was in Kent.

Though Darcy was in a rage to find Elizabeth as soon as their carriage stopped in the drive at the front steps of Rosings Park, his duty to attend his aunt took precedence over any other task. Thus, full of nervous energy, he entered the gilded dwelling of Lady Catherine de Bourgh and willed her to be generous with information regarding his beloved's presence in her county.

The usual pleasantries were conducted with all the ceremony his aunt demanded, including the usual tripe about his supposed engagement to Anne. As soon as he could interject, Darcy asked, "I understand that you have some new residents in the parish?"

Lady Catherine narrowed her eyes at him, a silent promise that she would not be deterred and that they would revisit the subject of his engagement to Anne later. "My parson, Mr Collins, has recently married."

Darcy's stomach clenched and he struggled to breathe for a moment. It could not be...could it? Elizabeth would not marry such a toad as Collins, surely! "I see."

"She is a remarkably sensible young woman," continued Lady Catherine, seemingly ignorant of her nephew's distress. "And very wise to take my direction."

The tightness within Darcy eased a bit, though it lingered still. His Elizabeth would never capitulate to the various whims of his eccentric relation. She would be far more likely to laugh and then do as she pleased...unless she were beaten down by the strictures of an illiberal husband.

"Mrs Collins currently has guests staying at the parsonage, a younger sister and a good friend from her home in Hertfordshire. I understand that they may claim an acquaintance with you."

Darcy heard a badly concealed snort of laughter and flicked his eyes towards his cousin Fitzwilliam, who was seated across from him with a fist pressed against lips and straining not to smile.

"I spent some time in Hertfordshire in the autumn with my friend Bingley, who had leased a house in the area. May I enquire as to the maiden name of Mrs Collins?" Darcy prayed silently that Elizabeth had not been taken away from him by Mr Collins, of all men.

"Lucas. She was Miss Charlotte Lucas."

Any apprehension remaining over the issue was now dissolved. "I recall Miss Lucas. A very sensible young woman, as you say."

"Yes, though I do not know how much I approve of her friend Miss Bennet." Lady Catherine gave a disparaging sniff. Darcy struggled to hold back a smile, though the idea of his beloved Elizabeth crossing verbal swords with the cantankerous old woman was mightily amusing. He was certain that his love would come out on top in every skirmish, though he doubted that Lady Catherine would realise it. "She is a pretty thing, I suppose, but so full of impertinence and opinions. I do not envy her mother in trying to see her married."

It was becoming increasingly difficult to contain his amusement at Lady Catherine's expense. Not only would Elizabeth be married, but she would be married to *him*. Before summer, if Darcy had his way. Unable to think of anything he could say both to agree with his aunt and to retain the truth of his sentiments towards Elizabeth, Darcy said nothing.

Lady Catherine, however, needed no such encouragement to continue. "Do you know that headstrong girl refused Mr Collins? Well, now her friend has married him, and she has lost her chance. To think that she would not have him because she could not like him! Utter nonsense!"

Having met Mr Collins, Darcy thought it spoke more to Elizabeth's credit than her detriment that she would not have such a man for her husband.

"...not even one-and-twenty and such opinions! I suppose you have seen these younger sisters she tells me are all out already? I have never heard of anything so ridiculous—"

Lady Catherine carried on about the defects of the impertinent miss visiting down the lane for as long as she had about the cradle betrothal between himself and Anne. It seemed his beloved had made quite an impression on his aunt, much as Darcy had imagined.

"I think you shall have a champion in Lady Catherine," Fitzwilliam teased him later as they ascended the staircase to their assigned chambers, having finally escaped the drawing room to refresh themselves post-travel. "She seems quite enthralled by your lady—it *is* your lady to whom she refers, is it not?"

"Do you recall the young miss we encountered by the roadside as we entered the lane to Rosings Park?"

Both of Fitzwilliam's brows rose in response. "Truly? That was your Miss Elizabeth? By Jove, you were not exaggerating when you said she was pretty!"

"Had you expected otherwise?"

Fitzwilliam laughed. "I suppose I had expected someone more...fashionable."

Darcy halted at the top of the staircase and affixed the colonel with his most withering scowl. "And what do you mean by that?"

"Do not look so fearsome, Darcy!" Fitzwilliam cried, slapping his dour relation on the back so hard that Darcy stumbled forward a step. "I mean no harm by it. She is a lovely thing, to be sure, simply not a creation of the fashionable world. Though, now I consider it, such a lady would hardly suit you at all—you despise London."

"I do not *despise* London."

"But you do not love it, either."

Darcy could hardly argue with that conclusion. "So how much trouble do you think Lady Catherine would cause should I attempt to pursue Elizabeth here?"

Fitzwilliam guffawed at Darcy's plan. "As I was saying, I think our aunt might surprise you. Your Miss Bennet was all she could talk about!

Aside from your supposed engagement to Anne, of course," he teased. "I think she likes the young lady, despite all her censure."

"It would not surprise me were that the case. Lady Catherine has ever been known to be contrary to her own opinions. However, I doubt she would encourage my intentions towards Elizabeth."

"She will never relinquish her dream of seeing you matched with Anne, even after you marry. Warn your bride never to eat in our aunt's presence. Just to be on the safe side."

Though not certain whether his cousin was jesting or not, Darcy laughed and promised to heed his advice.

Darcy's yearning to head directly to the parsonage and throw himself at Elizabeth's feet was destined to be delayed by the demands of his aunt, though the happy news that the residents of that abode would be joining them for tea the next day kept him from doing something foolish and rude. He anticipated her arrival upon his aunt's doorstep as a child eagerly awaits gifts on Christmas Day.

"Do sit down, Darcy!" Lady Catherine scolded as he paced before the windows of the drawing room, his eyes seeking the arrival of the party from the parsonage through the glazed glass. Their arrival was imminent as teatime was nigh upon them. "You are making us all dizzy with your pacing back and forth. Come, sit next to Anne."

With a discreet flick of his eyes towards the ceiling, Darcy acquiesced and turned to walk back to the seating area surrounding his aunt's chair at the centre of the room. He took his assigned place next to his cousin Anne, who greeted him with the barest of nods as she raised a handkerchief to her perpetually dripping nose, and resigned himself to staring at the door to the entry hall instead. Across from him, Fitzwilliam grinned, no doubt mocking Darcy's impatience.

After many more minutes of restless waiting, the butler entered the room with four people trailing behind him and announced them. "Mr and Mrs Collins, Miss Bennet, and Miss Lucas."

Darcy rose perhaps a little more quickly than the rest of the household and bowed to the group. Mr and Mrs Collins stood at the front, the husband babbling away at Lady Catherine for some ridiculous condescension she had performed and the wife forbearing his soliloquy in silent patience, while a mousy young girl of about Georgiana's age lurked behind them. If his memory served him, it was Miss Maria Lucas, the younger, sillier sister of the parson's wife. But he cared for none of *them*.

Elizabeth came into the room right behind her hosts. He saw her eyes survey the room, lingering on each face for a few moments before skipping to the next. When Elizabeth came to him, her expression shifted a touch, but he could not say whether she was pleased to see him or not. She did not smile, merely nodded her head in affirmation that she had noted his presence and acknowledged their acquaintance. Then, she looked away.

Darcy swallowed as anxiety began to rise in his throat. He knew that she was not yet his wife, but he had seen no trace of that warm welcome his vision had portrayed in her gaze. Her eyes were as lovely as ever, but they seemed to hold him in no special regard; was she too embarrassed to look at him with open affection in his aunt's presence?

"...and so, I told my dear Charlotte of your recommendation and she immediately—"

"Yes, yes, do sit down, Mr Collins." Lady Catherine interrupted the clergyman's monologue with an impatient wave of her bejewelled hand towards the chairs to her left, where Fitzwilliam was seated. Darcy returned his cousin's impish grin with a glare as Elizabeth settled herself close to him. "Fitzwilliam, come here. I wish to introduce you to the Collinses."

The visit, so keenly anticipated by Darcy, was turning out to be a rather dismal one. Perhaps his expectations had been too high, but between Lady Catherine directing the conversation and Mr Collins's ceaseless flow of undeserved compliments to her ladyship, there was no opportunity for Darcy to speak to Elizabeth at all. Worse, she had given all her attention to Fitzwilliam as he entertained her with his various exploits, most of which Darcy was certain had been either exaggerated or entirely fabricated for her enjoyment. Though he had bantered with Elizabeth in his vision, he had never seen her light up in that way in his actual, undisputed presence and it chafed to see her bestow such a gift upon another man. And Fitzwilliam, that scoundrel, was as much enthralled with her vivacity as he was with teasing Darcy over his supposed triumph. The colonel sent a few sly looks in his direction, silently conveying his smugness at their respective positions.

Anne, having essentially dozed off beside him, made no objection when Darcy stood and walked over to where Elizabeth was awarding Fitzwilliam another merry rejoinder. He could stand it no more! She would give *him* some attention now.

"What think you, Darcy?" Fitzwilliam asked as Darcy stepped close enough to join their conversation. "You were there. Was it not the finest hour of horsemanship you have ever witnessed?"

Darcy hardly knew to what his cousin referred, but supposed it must be some bragging tale that had but a fleeting relationship with the truth. "I suppose you left out the part where you fell off your horse and into the pond?"

He heard Elizabeth's laugh chime for a moment, but she stifled it quickly with a demure press of fingers to her smiling lips. Her eyes sparkled like the deepest part of a smooth, clear lake. "He failed to mention that bit, yes."

"Darcy, how could you?" Fitzwilliam exclaimed, a hand pressed dramatically over his heart. He turned his teasing focus to Elizabeth and said, "You must not believe him, Miss Bennet, for my cousin Darcy is the most disreputable liar I have ever had the misfortune to meet."

"Oh?" She turned to Darcy, her expression pertly challenging.

Darcy scowled at Fitzwilliam and suppressed the impulse to give him a swift kick. "I believe *you* are the one in the family with the reputation for telling tall tales, Fitzwilliam."

"Wounded again!"

Elizabeth darted her eyes between them as if appraising the scene before her. After a moment of consideration, she observed, "It seems the pair of you have shared many youthful exploits."

Fitzwilliam nodded. "All teasing of him aside, he is like a brother to me. Speaking as a younger son with three others that came before me, perhaps this is not an exclusive position, yet I prefer Darcy to any of *them*. He is far more tolerable a companion."

Darcy winced at Fitzwilliam's poor word choice; tolerable, indeed! A quick glance at Elizabeth showed her to be amused, yet he perceived a touch of teasing reproach in her eyes when she turned to face him. "High praise, indeed. Tolerable."

Touché. "Ahem, yes, well..."

"What is that you are saying, Fitzwilliam? What is it you are talking of?" Lady Catherine suddenly interrupted; he could hear the rap of her cane against the floor as she demanded their attention. Darcy closed his eyes to prevent them from rolling upward in exasperation. "What are you telling Miss Bennet? Let me hear what it is."

Fitzwilliam winked at Elizabeth and announced to the whole room, in a display of his own whimsically lax relationship with the truth, "We are speaking of music, madam."

"Of music! Then pray speak aloud. I must have my share in the conversation if you are speaking of music. There are few people..."

After enduring a rattling speech from his aunt and defending Georgiana's habit of continual practice upon her own instrument, Darcy found himself lucky enough to see Elizabeth seated at the pianoforte across the room, ready to play for company.

Unable to resist, and of no mind to do so in any case, Darcy waited until his aunt was once again absorbed in giving unwanted advice to someone else and followed Elizabeth thither where Fitzwilliam was assisting her by turning pages. If only his pest of a cousin would disappear and leave such a task to him! But at least he was free to watch her without the impediment of reading the music.

Elizabeth glanced up at him as he approached and offered him an arch simper. "You mean to frighten me, Mr Darcy, by coming in all this state to hear me? But I will not be alarmed, though your sister does play so well. There is a stubbornness about me that never can bear to be frightened at the will of others. My courage always rises with every attempt to intimidate me."

"I shall not say you are mistaken," Darcy replied, easing his features into a smile which seemed to surprise her, "because you could not really believe me to entertain any design of alarming you; and I have had the pleasure of your acquaintance long enough to know that you find great enjoyment in occasionally professing opinions which in fact are not your own."

Elizabeth laughed heartily at this picture of herself and turned to Fitzwilliam, whom she must suppose to be a conspirator in her teasing. "I see that it is now my turn have my honour maligned! It is, indeed, most ungenerous of your cousin to share his unfavourable opinion of me with all his acquaintance. I had hoped to pass myself off with some degree of credit whilst I was here."

Unfavourable opinion! What could she possibly mean by that? Darcy had thought many things of Elizabeth over the past few months, not all of them justified or fair, yet could she truly believe that he disliked her in some degree? Darcy could think of nothing to say in response to her sally.

Fitzwilliam, bless him, stepped in with a defence. "I believe you mistake him, Miss Bennet. I have heard nothing but praise of yourself since Darcy informed me of your acquaintance."

Elizabeth looked truly startled now and turned to fix Darcy with a puzzled gaze. "Oh?"

"Indeed! He was quite—"

But here they were interrupted again by Lady Catherine, and Darcy was called back to Anne's side, though she was now fully asleep with her chin resting upon her chest. Elizabeth resumed her playing and continued to chatter amiably with Fitzwilliam until their visit came to an end a short time later.

❄

Darcy dismounted his horse and tossed the reins to a tall, almost skeletally thin man dressed in black who waited by the front door of the parsonage. This fellow was the manservant of the Collins household, a Jack-of-all-trades who worked both in and outside of the house, and familiar by sight, though Darcy could not claim to know his name.

"Thank you," Darcy murmured absently. "Are the ladies within?" Darcy's eyes flicked to the closed door at the front of the house.

"Indeed, sir." The manservant's mouth spread into a toothy, unsettling grin; Darcy found that he preferred the stoic expressions of his own help.

A maid in a patchwork dress led him down a hallway dark with shadows, pausing at a room at the very back of the house. She knocked lightly at the wooden door blocking her entrance, and received a muffled bid to come inside.

The cosy parlour within was flooded in bright, warm sunlight, a stark contrast to the darkened corridor just beyond the door. Darcy was announced and moved forward on eager, quick feet, his gaze darting around the parlour, searching for the face he most wished to see. First, he spied the trembling Miss Lucas standing by her chair near the fireplace. Mrs Collins was next to her sister stowing some embroidery out of sight and smiling placidly at her unexpected guest. And Elizabeth…

…was not there.

"Mr Darcy, welcome," said Mrs Collins, waving him into the room with a slight gesture of her hand. Though gravely disappointed, Darcy knew it would be intolerably rude to turn around and leave, so he stepped fully inside and bowed to the two ladies within.

"Mrs Collins, Miss Lucas," he muttered, rising to stand erect.

"Will you not sit down, Mr Darcy?" offered Mrs Collins with another slight indication of her hand.

While Mrs Collins asked the maid to bring tea, Darcy claimed a seat on the sofa nearest her. As he sat, Mrs Collins offered, "I am sorry that Eliza is not here to greet you as well, Mr Darcy. She has been out walking this morning and should return any moment."

Darcy started at this statement which, though it had not been excessively bold, had cut directly to the heart of what he had wished to ask. Had he been so transparent? "I see."

"Eliza is very fond of walking, as I suspect you already know. She often ventures out before breakfast, though today she delayed so that she might wait for the post."

This was good information that Darcy tucked away into the back of his mind. He would make a new habit of walking out in the mornings in hopes of accidentally stumbling across his beloved in the wilderness. "Walking is very beneficial exercise."

"Indeed, it is," agreed Mrs Collins. "I admit that I encourage my friend to walk out as much as possible while she is here. There is no knowing when she might leave Hertfordshire again."

The tea arrived, and Darcy accepted the cup Mrs Collins poured for him. "Kent is lovely this time of year."

"Quite."

Several more minutes of strained conversation passed between Darcy and Mrs Collins as he lingered, hoping every minute Elizabeth would return. The appropriate time for ending a visit was drawing near and he hated to leave without seeing her, but perhaps his efforts would be better spent roving the lanes and groves in search of her.

Before he could form a resolution to rise and excuse himself, the door swung open and Elizabeth entered. She was radiant standing there in a patch of warm sun, her cheeks brightened by her exercise and her fine eyes gleaming like emeralds. A long ringlet of dark hair had escaped from the simple knot at the back of her head and bounced against her collar bone, springing up and down with each of her movements. In one hand she held a letter aloft. "Charlotte! Wonderful news from Jane!"

Elizabeth stopped speaking suddenly as her gaze came to rest upon Darcy. He felt himself flush and stood slowly, depositing his teacup upon the tray with the other refreshments as he rose. "Miss Bennet." Darcy bowed his head but kept his eyes trained upon her lovely face.

Elizabeth's cheeks deepened in colour and she lowered the letter to her side, her own gaze riveted upon him as she returned a curtsey. "Mr Darcy."

"What news, Lizzy?" asked Miss Lucas, the only words she had spoken in Darcy's presence at all since he had arrived.

Elizabeth hesitated, darting her eyes in Darcy's direction for a brief instant, before seeming to steel herself for her communication. She straightened her spine into a rigid posture and, with a grave look in his direction that he could not interpret, said, "She is to be married."

Miss Lucas clapped her hands with marked enthusiasm. "Oh, that is wonderful news!"

Mrs Collins agreed, albeit with more decorum than the younger lady. "So Mr Bingley has proposed?"

Elizabeth continued to look at Darcy, her eyes narrowed. "Yes, he has. He has already gone to my father for permission and they hope to marry this summer."

"That is excellent news." Darcy's joy for his friend was sincere.

Selfish motives aside, he was glad that Bingley's suit had been successful; he deserved every happiness.

Elizabeth came forward into the room and took a seat by the window, almost as far away from Darcy as she could get, which disappointed him greatly. Perhaps she was wary of allowing herself to hope?

He would not leave her in suspense. Darcy left his cooled tea behind and strode over to where Elizabeth was settling and took a chair closest to her. She looked startled to see him sitting across from her, which Darcy did not doubt stemmed from the same place her anger at him did. She was sceptical of his intentions and wished him to know that she was on her guard. "I am sure that there is a letter waiting for me at Rosings with the same news. When did Bingley propose?"

Though apparently surprised by this line of enquiry, as indicated by the astonished rise of her eyebrows, Elizabeth answered, "A week ago. She waited to send me word until Mr Bingley had received my father's blessing."

"And they hope to marry in summer, you said?" With any luck, their own marriage could take place soon after—or even at the same time! A double ceremony would suit his feelings very well, indeed. "A lovely time of year for a wedding."

"Yes," she agreed slowly. "They hope for June, a month or so after we return home. I would be sorry to lose her so soon if she were not going only three miles away."

It smarted to know that he would be taking her much further than three miles from her home and beloved elder sister, but his vision had indicated that the Bingleys would move to Derbyshire sometime in the future. Elizabeth would be satisfied then, surely. "But you would not wish to always be near Longbourn, I think?"

The surprised arch of her eyebrows was back and Darcy reined in his feelings. Though he knew how it would be, Elizabeth was as yet ignorant of the path their future would take. He needed to remember that, vision or not, many things were still undecided between them, and he should not get ahead of himself. She would surely surmise that relocation to Derbyshire was imminent once he made his offer. "I shall have to write to Bingley and offer him my congratulations."

"Indeed?" Elizabeth's head tilted ever so slightly to one side as if she were trying to puzzle something out.

Darcy felt heat rise in his cheeks and coughed, clearing his throat. "He has long admired your sister and I am sure it will be a happy match."

Elizabeth continued to look at him, her eyes roving his face as if looking for weaknesses. Apparently finding none, or at least nothing she could consider definitive, she said, "I shall tell her you said so."

A week later, Darcy strolled about the grounds on foot, musing over his interactions with Elizabeth in recent days. That she had been polite and charming as always was indisputable, but her response to him was rather troubling. He had led himself to believe that she would be as eager to see him again as he had been her, yet her glances lacked the warmth that had characterised their interactions in his vision. Darcy understood that an unmarried woman could not openly display her feelings for a man before he decidedly revealed his own, particularly in the presence of said man's relations, but he had hoped for some discreet hint of affection in either her eyes or tone that would encourage his suit. Did Elizabeth believe his departure from Hertfordshire indicated that he would not offer for her? It was a reasonable assumption, Darcy supposed—and, if he were to be honest, the one he had intended to inspire at the time—but he had rather hoped that his Elizabeth would wish to resume their flirtation even so. Or perhaps he had hidden his feelings too well, and she was unaware of his affections for her?

And what of her interactions with Fitzwilliam? Was Elizabeth so animated with his cousin to punish Darcy for his abandonment of her in the autumn? Or was she just being mischievous in that sweet way of hers? Could she simply be attempting to bring herself closer to his relatives in anticipation of an offer from him? She would not prefer Fitzwilliam...would she?

Darcy had paid a few visits to the parsonage after their initial reintroduction at Rosings in hopes that being away from his aunt might ease their way, but these interactions had not been any more satisfying than the one they had engaged in under the nose of Lady Catherine. She remained courteous but distant as if their acquaintance were but a trifling one, and Darcy could not understand it.

Even when he had paid a call upon the parsonage without Fitzwilliam in attendance, their meeting had been awkward. He had done his best to convey his delight at her sister's and Bingley's engagement, but she continued to treat him with what he would almost call suspicion. Darcy surmised that she was not unaware of his efforts to separate the couple initially, but surely his further attempts to bring them back together mitigated his original error. Was this the source of Elizabeth's cold distance from him? Did she mistrust him? Or, worse, did she doubt his feelings towards her because of his previous meddling?

Darcy knew none of his concerns could be resolved without speaking to the lady privately, but he could not imagine how he might obtain such an audience with her. Between his intrusive aunt and her ridiculous cousin, they could never find uninterrupted time for such a discussion whilst in company at the manor house. He could call at the parsonage again, but there were too many people there, too. He had taken Mrs Collins's subtle advice to look for Elizabeth in the early mornings while she went out walking, but so far he had been unsuccessful.

Looking up to the clear blue spring sky, Darcy murmured a prayer. "Lord, please guide me."

A sharp crackling sound drew Darcy's attention to the brush up ahead of him and he was astonished to see none other than Elizabeth emerging from behind a bush, a half-plucked wildflower suspended between her fingers. She picked another petal from it as she hummed a sweet tune and watched it float down upon the grass like snow flurries.

With another flick of his eyes upward, Darcy silently thanked the Almighty for such quick service and then returned to the ethereal form of his lady love walking in the dappled light beneath the tree canopy. He took a breath and called out to her, "Miss Bennet."

Elizabeth stopped, another petal falling from her fingers only to be carried away by a passing breeze, and looked up to stare at him. He still could not tell if she was glad to see him.

Tossing the ravaged flower to the ground, Elizabeth bobbed a curtsey. "Good morning, Mr Darcy. I see you have found my favourite walk. I often tour the grove in the mornings."

That is good information. "Indeed? Would you please allow me to escort you from here?" Darcy held out his elbow, inviting her to take it.

Elizabeth bit her lip and cast her gaze all around, skimming over Darcy and fixing upon everything save him. "You need not feel obligated, sir. I would not wish to interrupt your stroll."

"'Tis no inconvenience." When she still did not accept his overture, he added, "I would be most happy with your company."

Tentatively, Elizabeth laid her gloved hand upon the arm he proffered. "If you insist."

They began walking together, feet moving in tandem as if engaged in a dance, perfectly in harmony with one another. How well they suited! Even in the way they strolled through a grove, they were flawlessly matched. Two pieces joined together into one whole. And she was so lovely…

Lost in contemplation of how entirely enchanting she was, Darcy almost jumped when she broke their silence after a few long minutes. "I am actually glad that we met this way, Mr Darcy, as you are owed gratitude and I mean to give it to you."

"Gratitude?" Darcy repeated, befuddled. He gazed into her eyes, which glimmered as though set afire from within, and a haze of distracting affection settled upon his mind.

"As you know, your friend Mr Bingley has recently become engaged to my sister Jane," she began. When he nodded in confirmation of this premise, she continued, "I understand from her letters that it was *you* who had encouraged Mr Bingley to call upon her while she was still staying with my aunt and uncle in London—and, I suspect, in spite of his sisters' disapproval. After you left so abruptly last autumn, I confess I was surprised to hear that you had directed your friend to Gracechurch Street to renew an old acquaintance."

Darcy awkwardly shuffled his feet in the grass. "Miss Bingley mentioned to me, in passing, your sister's being in town. I am sure she...forgot to tell her brother herself."

Elizabeth's smile thinned into one of sceptical amusement. "No doubt. In any case, I wished to thank you for your intervention, sir, for you have made Jane the happiest creature in so doing. She and our entire family shall ever be grateful that you have taken it upon yourself to reunite them, as she has been very unhappy since he left Netherfield last November."

Darcy gulped, not quite sure what to say. Certainly, he had told Bingley of Jane Bennet's presence in town, but he had also had a hand in separating them to begin with. She should not thank him for correcting something he, himself, had done to cause so much pain. Guilt gnawed at his stomach as he said, "You need not thank me."

A gentle touch to his arm, one that felt so achingly familiar he could have sobbed, brought Darcy's attention back to Elizabeth's face. Her eyes were softer than before, though not quite in that warm, welcoming way of his vision, and a light smile touched her lips. "But I do. No matter our personal feelings for one another, Jane's happiness means everything to me, and I shall not forget your generosity in encouraging your friend to return to her. You have my gratitude, whether you would accept it or not."

Darcy stopped suddenly, causing her to stumble forward a step before regaining her balance. He could take no more of this! Spinning so that he was facing her directly, Darcy grasped both of Elizabeth's hands and spoke fervently. "If you *will* thank me let it be yourself alone. That the wish of giving happiness to you might add force to the other inducement which led me on, I shall not attempt to deny. But your sister owes me nothing. Much as I respect her, I believe I thought only of *you*."

Elizabeth looked nothing short of astonished at his speech and said nothing in reply.

"I know not why you suggest there is ill-will between us, but let me tell you now that nothing could be further from the truth. Indeed, though I admit to having struggled, my feelings will not be repressed. You must allow me to tell you how ardently I admire and love you."

Though a piece of him wished to enumerate all the obstacles he had overcome in order to reach this inevitable conclusion, Darcy found himself unable to continue and simply waited for her response.

Eventually, Elizabeth, staring at their clasped hands which hovered between them, spoke. "I…I know not what to say. I thought you heartily disliked me, as I—" Here, she broke off with a blush and bit her lip. "You like me?"

"Love, actually," he corrected, somewhat desperately. "I *love* you, Elizabeth."

She said nothing immediately in response, apparently struck dumb by his confession, and Darcy's heart, so swollen with love for her these past months, shrivelled. She…she did not love him. Worse, she apparently did not even *like* him.

Elizabeth closed her eyes and inhaled deeply through her nose. She raised her eyes to his face, a look of tender pity in their depths. "Forgive me, I should not have said any such thing. My feelings for you have become more favourable over the past week since I learned what you had done for Jane. It was so contrary to what I believed about you in Hertfordshire that, at first, I did not quite accept it, but Jane was so in earnest about what Mr Bingley had told her that I could not continue thinking so ill of you as I had before. I do not return your…your feelings for me," Elizabeth glanced down at their hands, squeezing his as she said this, "but I…oh, I do not know what to say!"

Neither did Darcy. Should he beg her to marry him anyway? No, she would only accept him out of obligation, and he could never countenance knowing that any affection she had for him would be artificial, a pleasant lie. Darcy wanted what he had seen in his vision, an Elizabeth who was genuinely happy to see him and missed him when he was away even for a short time. He wanted her to kiss him and stroke his hair when he was ailing. To love him at night with all the passion she embodied. He could never accept a shadow of her as his wife.

With his jaw clenched tight in an effort to control the emotion that was struggling to spill out of him, Darcy released her hands and took a few steps away from her, back turned. "I think you have said everything, madam. Please accept my best wishes for your health and happiness."

Having said this much, Darcy directed his steps back towards Rosings, though he hardly intended to return to the house in such a state. Perhaps he could master himself enough to go to the stables and ready his horse for a long, punishing gallop through the fields.

"Wait! Mr Darcy, *wait!*"

As ever, Elizabeth's wish was his command and Darcy halted a few yards away, though he did not turn to face her. He could hear the rustling of her skirts as she hurried to catch up with his longer stride, the soft panting of her breath as she exerted herself to reach him. She was suddenly before him again, having placed herself directly in his line of vision, and the pain became fresh; she was so enchanting in her rose-coloured muslin gown, dainty green sprigs of vines etched across the fabric. The cut was modest, as it should be, but the way her chest heaved as she spoke to him reminded him of his more immodest imaginings and he darted his eyes to the side.

Elizabeth, however, would have none of that and leaned over so that she might look him full in the face again. "Pray, sir, do not leave. I have no wish to cause you pain and am sorry to have done so."

Darcy watched as Elizabeth bit her plump bottom lip while she apparently considered what to say. "Do not make yourself uneasy. I perfectly comprehend your feelings and am only ashamed of how I related my own to you. I beg you to forget I said anything to make you uncomfortable."

Elizabeth released her lip, slightly reddened from its abuse, and Darcy desperately wished he could give in to his desire to kiss it. He would happily be the cause of its heightened colour.

"You mistake me. I…I do not dislike you, though I admit I did at one time. You must admit that our acquaintance did not begin in the most auspicious manner." Elizabeth fixed him with a significant look, a reminder of his cruel faux pas at the assembly where they had met.

Darcy winced and began his apology in halting tones. "What I said then was rude and unspeakably untrue. Indeed, it has been many months since—"

Elizabeth shook her head and pressed her gloved fingertips to his lips to halt his latest repentant speech. Darcy's eyes widened at the action and she blushed in response, withdrawing her hand to her side. "No, I have understood for some time that my beauty is hardly anything to my elder sister's, whom you correctly marked as the only handsome lady in the room."

"But you are wrong!" Darcy interrupted, offended on her behalf that she would think so cruelly of her own appearance. Was this what his thoughtless comment had wrought? "You are the handsomest woman of my acquaintance! I have thought so for some time now."

Elizabeth flushed more deeply, reminding him of the time she had appeared at Netherfield in muddy petticoats looking to nurse her ailing sister. She had then been infused with a healthy pink brilliancy, much as she was now. "That aside," she said, apparently not wishing to dwell on the topic further, "I feel that I have largely misunderstood you over the length of our acquaintance and, whilst I cannot yet admit to any tender feelings for you, I am not averse to knowing you better. I feel that I have been ungenerous in my characterisation of you, though there is still much about you that puzzles me exceedingly."

"Such as?"

"Such as…" Elizabeth hesitated a moment to abuse her lower lip again with her nibbling teeth; it was driving him mad with the desire to kiss her. "Your relationship with Mr Wickham."

Darcy could feel his own flush creeping up the back of his neck, though his was not out of bashfulness; it was anger that infused him now. "You take an eager interest in that gentleman's concerns," he accused.

Elizabeth's brow folded down in her own show of petulance. "Who that knows his misfortunes can help take an interest in him?"

"His misfortunes!" Darcy turned away from her to begin pacing. He moved back and forth across the grass, muttering, "Oh, yes, his misfortunes have been great indeed!"

"According to him," she snapped, "of your infliction. I am inclined to think that a man who would be so kind as to reunite two lovers would not be so cruel as he has accused you of being, though his story is quite condemning. What have you to say in your defence?"

Darcy stopped a few feet away from her, struggling with what to say. Were she his wife, he would, of course, divulge the truth of the matter, but marriage now looked an increasingly unlikely prospect. Nonetheless, he loved her still and trusted her not to condemn an immature girl who was much the same as her own younger sisters, at least in naivete.

And so, Darcy found himself revealing the whole of the matter to her, holding back his ire for the man so as not to offend her further. With any luck, revealing Wickham's perfidy would cool her infatuation with the scoundrel. Darcy watched Elizabeth's expression shift from challenging to aghast as he told the tale regarding his and Wickham's shared history. He hesitated only a moment to tell Elizabeth of Wickham's worst sin, though it was no reflection of his trust in her discretion. No, it was simply difficult for him to speak of and filled him with such shame at his inability to protect his sister from Wickham's machinations. Darcy ploughed on, however, to reveal Georgiana's plight from last summer. He even told her of the nightmare which had instigated her letter to him, and his subsequent rescue of his sister from that reprobate's greedy clutches.

"I know not by what falsehood he has imposed himself upon you," Darcy concluded, his fists clenched behind his back, "but this is a faithful narrative of all my dealings with Mr Wickham."

The grove was nearly silent save for the distant twittering of birds and the rustle of green leaves overhead. Darcy stood at rigid attention, watching Elizabeth's face as it shifted between different shades as she considered his story. Her expression, usually so open and sweetly arch, was fixed in a stony visage that was more familiar to Darcy's face than hers. Only her deep evergreen eyes showed any animation as she stared at him. They stood there in tormented silence for some time.

"I feel so foolish," Elizabeth eventually admitted, blinking rapidly as tears formed on her lashes. "To think that I believed…forgive me."

Darcy stepped forward, the toes of his boots kissing the tips of hers, and raised his palms to cradle her cheeks. He tilted her head back so that he might look directly into her eyes, so remarkably fine even tainted with self-reproach and sadness, intending to offer her words of comfort. Instead, his eyelids fluttered closed, and he bowed his head to brush their lips together, like the lightest touch of a butterfly landing upon a wildflower.

Darcy swallowed and drew back, a tremor of anxiety shooting down his spine when it occurred to him just what he had done. He had imposed upon her! If Elizabeth's opinion of him had been growing in esteem before, it surely would return to all its former dislike now. He opened his eyes to survey the look of disgust that must surely be writ across her face. "Forgive me, I…"

What he saw instead startled and thrilled him in equal measure. Elizabeth's eyes were relaxed and soft like a patch of fresh grass warmed by the afternoon sun.

"There is nothing to forgive," she assured him with an embarrassed smile.

"Elizabeth…"

She moved back a step, shaking her head and chuckling at his expense. "I think, perhaps, it is too soon for *that*," Elizabeth teasingly scolded. "You forget, *sir,* that we truly know little of one another. I think it best we improve our acquaintance gradually for now."

Darcy's heart began to swell again, ever so slightly, with hope. "I believe I can grant you that."

CHAPTER FIVE

Bingley bounced down the front steps of Netherfield, arms thrown wide. "Welcome back to Netherfield. How was your trip to Kent? Was your aunt well?"

Darcy accepted the hand offered to him and shook it, laughing at his friend's ebullient greeting. His mood was similarly light now that he was returned to the county of his lovely Elizabeth—at her invitation, no less. "It was a good trip, and Lady Catherine is as she ever was."

"Sounds like my own dear mother," replied Bingley. "Now, come inside and make yourself comfortable. Your rooms from your last stay have been prepared. I daresay if you can manage to find your way about Pemberley, you can remember the route to your rooms here at Netherfield."

The two friends ascended the front steps of Netherfield and entered via the double front doors. As he quickly strode across the entrance hall, Darcy darted his eyes towards the parlour that had been in use most frequently during his previous stay. After a slight cough to clear his throat of a disagreeable tightening sensation, he broached a question he felt forced to ask. "Have your sisters accompanied you into the country?"

Bingley tugged at his cravat in the way he did when he was nervous. "At first, Caroline did not wish to return, but then she happened to see some of my correspondence and—"

"Why, Mr Darcy!" The shrill tones of Miss Bingley's voice echoed around the entrance hall. Affected cultured accent or no, the lady was no more delicate at times than Elizabeth's mother. Miss Bingley had managed to catch Darcy by surprise by arriving from exactly the opposite direction he had expected, probably the breakfast room, and had used this advantage to pounce. "I had quite despaired of seeing you today! I was certain that you had been overset by highwaymen in this savage backwater!"

Mrs Hurst, standing to the side and just behind her unmarried sister, agreed immediately. "Oh, yes, it was quite disconcerting."

Darcy forced himself to suppress his eye roll, but Bingley allowed himself the privilege. "It is barely two o'clock! I daresay any highwayman worth his salt would wait until closer to dark before attacking any unsuspecting victims."

Miss Bingley disregarded her brother entirely and moved forward to latch herself onto Darcy's arm with both of hers. Her perfume tingled his nose and threatened to make him sneeze. "I am so glad you have arrived here in safety, sir. I do not know what I should do were some terrible fate to befall you."

Darcy extricated himself from her grasp as gently as he could. "Yes, well, I believe I shall retire to my rooms for now to refresh myself. I shall return directly."

A knock on Darcy's bedchamber door half an hour later caused him to glance up from fastening the chain of his watch to his fresh waistcoat. Bailey opened the door to reveal Bingley standing just over the threshold. Bingley murmured a quiet thanks to Darcy's valet as he came into the room and walked directly towards his friend.

"Apologies about Caroline, Darcy. I have tried to dissuade her from pestering you, but she is as incorrigible as Mother."

Darcy had met Mrs Bingley—the current one, not the future Mrs Charles Bingley—on a handful of occasions and could not dispute the resemblance between mother and daughter; they shared the same light brown hair, beaky nose and undeserved hauteur. If Darcy ever needed yet another reason never to offer for Caroline Bingley, seeing her future on display in the form of the widowed Mrs Wallace Bingley would suffice. The woman might be more subtle than Mrs Bennet, but she was twice as cunning and three times as ruthless in pursuit of climbing the social hierarchy. Fortunately for the men of England, she was presently making an extended visit to her sister in Ireland after some...unpleasantness the previous Season involving an insult to a countess. Bingley, Darcy supposed, must have taken after his late father.

"What can I do for you, Bingley?"

"I wanted to talk to you before you came downstairs for tea," said Bingley, his face shifting into a pointed look. He continued unnecessarily, "Without Caroline and Louisa."

Darcy slipped his arms into the sleeves of his coat as Bailey presented it to him and flexed his muscles to slide it up onto his shoulders. As he was tugging at his lapels, adjusting the garment into its proper place upon his form, he replied, "Was there something particular you wished to discuss?"

"Yes, but it is rather...awkward."

Taking that as a hint for further privacy, Darcy dismissed Bailey, who quickly disappeared into the dressing room, shutting the door behind him.

Once they were assuredly alone, Darcy swept a hand towards a pair of chairs that were placed before the empty fireplace and invited Bingley to sit.

"It is about Caroline," said Bingley. "I assume that you have not changed your mind about proposing to her?"

Darcy could not withhold his frown at the suggestion and Bingley chuckled.

"I thought as much," he said with a crooked grin. Bingley then coughed, straightened, wiggled in his chair, crossed and recrossed his legs, and generally moved about until Darcy encouraged him to proceed with an impatient look. "Right, well, I have told her many times that you would never offer for her, but nevertheless she persists in all her schemes and plots. As I hinted downstairs, she learned of your visit here by going through my correspondence. I thought that I had left her behind in London, but she arrived a week later with the Hursts in a hired carriage. Hurst later told me that she has been scheming with Louisa ever since she learned you were to be here."

Darcy was beginning to feel a touch unsettled by the direction of this narrative. "And?"

"And," Bingley let out a long, deep breath. "And I do not know what Caroline might do whilst you are here. She is growing desperate, and I clearly cannot control her any longer. I would rather not cast her out of my house, especially when all I have are suspicions and no actual proof of poor conduct."

Darcy had been the target of such designs before, but admittedly never while living under the same roof as the predatory lady in question. Occasions to provoke a situation in which he would be required to offer marriage had been few and far between before this, but Caroline Bingley now had nearly unlimited access and opportunity to effect whatever plan she wished. Increasingly desperate in the face of her brother's engagement to a lady of lower consequence than Miss Bingley had hoped for, and also probably nursing some lingering suspicions about Darcy's affection for this same lady's younger sister, she might prove dangerous. He would have to be especially on his guard during this visit.

Bingley quietly added, "I would like to think she would not disgrace me, but I shall understand if you wish to leave."

Darcy could not afford to leave. He was so close to receiving acceptance of his suit from Elizabeth and making his Christmas vision into a reality that he absolutely could not abandon the quest. As his beloved was back home with her family at Longbourn, Hertfordshire was where he needed to be.

"That will not be necessary." Darcy settled back into his own seat with his elbows propped on the arms of his chair and one ankle crossed over his knee. "Moreover, I have business to attend to while I am here that should dissuade your sister and her machinations."

"Oh? What kind of business? You do not intend to donate your fortune to orphans and become a blacksmith, do you?"

"No, I am not yet that wretched," he replied. "However, I have recently begun pursuing Miss Elizabeth Bennet and hope to tender my proposal forthwith. It should only be a matter of weeks before I lead her to the altar—assuming she will have me, of course."

By the expression on Bingley's face, one would think that Darcy had just announced his intention to not only give up his fortune and apprentice himself to a blacksmith, but also embrace the daily habit of frequent nudity. The former he had no interest in doing, but the latter would not be so bad; at least within the confines of his bedroom and with Elizabeth as his equally naked partner. All Bingley actually said, however, was, "No."

Darcy could not help it—he openly laughed at Bingley's bewilderment. "I assure you, it is the truth. I reunited with Miss Elizabeth in Kent while visiting my aunt, and she has agreed to allow me to call on her."

"But you dislike each other!" Bingley countered. "No, you must be playing a joke on me. Well, it is not funny! Elizabeth is soon to be my sister, you know, and I shall not have anyone—even you—besmirching her reputation."

Darcy flinched at the reference to Elizabeth's previous dislike for him, despite her recent assurances that those feelings were now done away with. Indeed, though she had not expressly told him that she was in love with him, her shy smiles, gentle teasing, and generally welcoming demeanour before their parting in Kent had indicated a reversal of her prejudice against him. Darcy had carefully, and discreetly, begun wooing Elizabeth whilst still under Lady Catherine's nose, and he was pleased with his inroads into her affections thus far. He believed her frank enough to tell him there was no hope directly rather than allowing him to follow her back home and continue their association in a more public arena.

No, she liked him now. Or...did she?

It was Darcy's turn to fidget as the insecurity he had been repressing since that first meeting in the grove with Elizabeth broke free of its bonds and rushed to the surface of his consciousness. Was he fooling himself? Had the vision really been only a concussed dream after all?

An image of Elizabeth on the day he had bid her farewell at the Hunsford parsonage rose in his mind and his anxiety calmed. The smile she had presented him then, one that was not simply arch and sweet, but also tender, had not been the workings of a troubled mind; it had been entirely, miraculously real. Darcy would cling to that.

There had been a long pause in conversation whilst Darcy had contemplated the plausibility of his having gained Elizabeth's affections and then tranquilised his feelings. Finally, he was ready to address Bingley's concerns.

"Perhaps we did not always get along, but my feelings for Miss Elizabeth have been growing for some time. Since last autumn, as a matter of fact, though I had at first tried to talk myself out of wanting her. Eventually, it occurred to me that my happiness was not dependent upon what others wished for me, but what I wished for myself. I intend to make Elizabeth my wife, and I shall do whatever it takes to convince her to accept me. I assure you, Bingley, that I shall not dishonour her in any way."

Bingley's surprise had not diminished, but his sympathy now appeared to be engaged. "Forgive me, Darcy, I really thought you were joking. So, you are in love with Elizabeth, then?"

Darcy gulped and focused his eyes upon his signet ring, which he absently twisted around his little finger. "I am."

"I must say that I still can hardly believe it. Who would have thought...? You and Elizabeth...? It boggles the mind."

Darcy began to see some of the humour in this situation, as his Elizabeth might. "This is a wretched beginning, indeed," Darcy teased with a smile. "My sole dependence was on you and I am sure nobody else will believe me, if you do not. But, indeed, I am in earnest. I love her and intend to make her my wife."

"Well then, let me be the first to congratulate you."

Darcy stood as well and accepted the proffered hand from his friend, shaking it heartily. "Do not congratulate me yet, my friend. She has not accepted me."

"She will," said Bingley with confidence. "You are one of the best men I know, and she will surely see that. If not, I shall have a word with her—or, rather, I shall have Jane do it. That sort of thing is probably better coming from a sister."

A bright flare of happiness bloomed in Darcy's chest; Bingley was convinced that Elizabeth would accept him for himself, not his fortune. "You are a good man, yourself, Bingley. Miss Bennet is a lucky woman."

"*I* am the lucky one," Bingley disputed as his eyes glazed over and his grin became dreamy. "She is such an angel…"

Darcy shook his head at his besotted friend but had not the heart to tease him. Fitzwilliam had spent endless hours tormenting him at Rosings over the same behaviour that Darcy had reportedly exhibited towards Elizabeth. It would be ungenerous to torture his friend over something Darcy himself could not hold back.

"You do realise that this will make us brothers, yes?"

"Of course," replied Darcy. "I am looking forward to it."

"It is only that Caroline has been pushing me at your sister for so long with that aim in mind that I find it amusing she will, ultimately, have her way—just not in the manner she intended."

Darcy joined his friend in roaring laughter. Happy thought, indeed.

"Now, I suppose we cannot avoid joining your relations for tea any longer. Shall we?"

"We shall." Bingley likewise stood and followed his friend across the room towards the door which led out into the hallway.

As they approached it, Darcy thought that he heard a soft shuffling and the patter of feet on the other side of the door. Suspicion mounting in the back of his mind, he grasped the brass knob and pulled with some haste, revealing the corridor beyond. There was no one immediately visible over the threshold, but Darcy could almost taste the scent of a lady's cloying perfume in the air.

A queasy feeling of unease filled Darcy's stomach. Precautions would need to be taken.

"Darcy?" Bingley broke into Darcy's contemplation, voice lilting in enquiry. "Is aught wrong?"

"No," Darcy replied, though his brow furrowed."Come, let us go down."

Darcy jolted upright in his pallet as a scream rent the silent night, throwing all that was calm into chaos. Casting his coverings to one side with a single sweep of his arm, Darcy lowered his stockinged feet to the floor and leapt up. Within two strides, he was at the door and wrenching it free from its frame.

"Unhand me, you lout!" Two forms squirmed fitfully on the large bed before him. A candle flickered on the end table next to the woman, illuminating her face and that of the sleepy man stretched out beside her upon the mattress.

"I assure you, madam, that I have no pretensions to—"

"*Be silent!*"

"Bailey, Miss Bingley—what is going on in here?" Darcy called out, his voice raised so that he might be heard over Miss Bingley's continued complaints and whines.

Miss Bingley whipped her head in his direction, her expression transforming from one of disdain and anger into that of whimpering fear. Darcy was hardly convinced of her sincerity, considering the rapidity with which her emotions seemed to shift. "Oh, Mr Darcy! This brute has attempted to attack me! I am innocent—"

"And yet here you are in my bedchamber in the middle of the night," Darcy interrupted, his eyes flicking about the space significantly. It was a large, luxurious guest apartment at Netherfield, and right in the centre of the space was the four-post bed which she currently shared with his valet. "I do not suppose you found yourself lost on the way to your own rooms tonight, Miss Bingley?"

Before she could respond to his veiled accusation against her virtue, a loud banging against the door which led out into the hallway startled them all. "Darcy! Are you well, man? I heard screaming."

"Come in, Bingley," said Darcy, feeling that this situation could only be improved by the addition of one of Miss Bingley's male relatives. If the horrified, open-mouthed look on the lady's face was any indication, she disagreed completely.

An instant later, Bingley was inside and holding his candle aloft as if searching for the source of the disturbance. "What is the—*Caroline!*"

"Charles, this is not what it appears." It was a mystery to Darcy why Miss Bingley even bothered attempting to justify her presence. It was perfectly clear what she was doing there, though it was also evident that her plans had somehow gone awry with Bailey in the bed next to her and Darcy on the other side of the room with his arms folded across his chest.

Darcy fixed his attention on Bingley and, with his tone as cold as his expression, began his recitation of events. "I suspect that your sister had intended some scheme upon my person, but I took your warning to heart, my friend, and slept in my dressing room tonight. 'Twas Bailey she found instead."

"Is this true, Caroline?" asked Bingley, though there could be no other explanation.

Miss Bingley held the sheets up to her chin, scowling at her brother as she plotted what to say to get herself out of this situation. Ultimately, nothing seemed to come to her so she remained silent.

Miss Bingley broke the stalemate, an unnerving smile stealing across her face. "Charles, I believe we both know that I would not be here were I not...*invited*. I cannot account for why his *servant* was in his place when I arrived, but I assure you that I was here upon Mr Darcy's request."

"You most certainly were not!" Darcy's denial exploded from his mouth on the heels of a snarl. "I would never—"

Bingley's raised hand prompted Darcy to halt the words that he was ready to hurl at Miss Bingley. "You do not need to explain yourself. I warned you of my sister's increasing desperation, and I have no doubt that she has taken it upon herself to arrange this little rendezvous without your input or consent. I simply wanted to give her an opportunity to tell the truth of the matter—not that I expected it."

"Charles! How could you say such a thing about your own sister?"

"Look around you, Caroline!" countered Bingley, waving his free hand around to indicate the room in which they stood. Darcy ducked out of the way of one of Bingley's passes, nearly backhanded by his friend's irritated enthusiasm to make his point. "You are in the bedchamber of a man who is not your husband in the middle of the night with the clear intent to seduce him! How could I think otherwise?"

"This would not have been necessary had you assisted me in gaining a proposal from the beginning." Miss Bingley's upper lip forked upwards in a sneer as she spat this accusation at her brother. Her fingers were clenched like claws in the duvet as she continued. "But no, you have clearly been working behind my back to prevent it!"

Darcy felt compelled to interject, "Forgive me, madam, but on that point you are incorrect. Your brother forewarned me of your potential plans—and, if I do not miss my guess, spoke to you on the matter at various times, as well—because he knew that I would never offer for you and hoped to prevent a scandal. I would caution you, however, lest you think to try something similar in the future, that this will be the only reprieve you are given, and I shall not hesitate to cut you from all association with my family in a most public way should you not heed me in this."

Miss Bingley looked nothing short of aghast at his declaration. "You have led me on for these many years of our acquaintance and now you tell me that you never would have offered for me? What of your honour?"

"You are mistaken again, Miss Bingley, if you think you could have presented yourself to me in any possible way that would have tempted me to offer for you. From the very beginning, from the first moment I may almost say, I have attempted to impress upon you my disinclination for your company, my abhorrence of your manners, and my disapproval of your presumption as regards both myself and my sister. Only my fondness for your brother has ever tempted me to be to be in the same room with you for any length of time, and as such I have never, not once, considered you for the position of my wife. Indeed, I am sorry to cause pain to anyone, but in order to put this matter to rest once and for all it must be done; you are the last woman in the world whom I could ever be prevailed upon to marry."

After a long stretch of furious quiet, during which only the short, harsh breaths of Miss Bingley could be heard, she finally gathered herself enough to speak. "You have said quite enough, sir. I perfectly comprehend your feelings—as senseless and short-sighted as they are—and have now only to be ashamed that my brother would count a dishonourable, foolish man such as yourself amongst his friends. However, these bitter accusations might have been suppressed, might never have existed, had *Miss Eliza Bennet* not turned your head from me. Do not bother to deny it! I heard everything that you told my traitorous brother this afternoon."

Darcy felt the muscles in his back, shoulders, and neck seize with tension as Miss Bingley crossed a line from which there was no turning back. "Do not bring her into this."

"And why should I not, pray?" Miss Bingley scoffed, crossing her arms over her small bosom and leaning back into the pile of pillows against the headboard. "It is clear that she has stolen my future husband from me and, as such, is a party to this little discussion. With her pert opinions and 'fine eyes', she has no doubt performed the type of seduction I am currently accused of. Tell me, Mr Darcy, did you find *her* in your bed the last time we were all together at Netherfield? Is *that* why you have overlooked the more appropriate candidate for your wife in favour of a country nobody?"

"Caroline—"

Darcy cut his friend off, his body rigid with anger. "You will never dishonour Elizabeth's name again with your innuendos, or I shall see to it that all of London knows of your grasping, scheming attempts to snare yourself a husband. Do not think that you will be welcomed back by any of the *ton*, that any of the best drawing rooms will remain open to you. I can and I shall ruin you if you so much as breathe even a single libellous whisper about her virtue. Do I make myself perfectly clear?"

Miss Bingley, for all her petulance, eyed him with wariness as Darcy issued his threat, probably gauging how serious he was in his intent to follow through with it. At length, a single word was forced through the gaps between her clenched teeth. "Perfectly."

"Come, Caroline," Bingley broke in, severing the connexion between their glaring eyes by drawing both pairs to himself, "back to *your own* bed with you. We shall discuss the ramifications of your behaviour in the morning."

With a sniff, Miss Caroline Bingley rose from the bed and swept from the room, the light of her candle bobbing along the walls in her wake.

Once a door—he assumed that of Miss Bingley's chambers—had slammed shut somewhere along the corridor beyond Darcy's suite, Bingley released an enormous sigh of exasperation and weariness. "Propose to Lizzy quickly, Darcy, and save us all any further trouble. The sooner you are off the marriage mart, the better it will be for the rest of us."

Darcy allowed a smirk to crack his stony visage. "I cannot agree more."

CHAPTER SIX

THE FOLLOWING DAY WAS FILLED WITH A PALPABLE DISQUIET amongst the residents of Netherfield Park. The servants, save for Bailey, were thankfully unaware of the turmoil they had missed overnight, minimising the scandalised whispers to only the gentry in residence. Mrs Hurst, who denied any part in what her sister had allegedly done, was visibly nervous around her brother and his house guest, speaking only when spoken to. Her husband, by contrast, seemed to care not a whit about what had happened so long as it did not interfere with his meals. Miss Bingley herself kept primarily to her chambers, though more likely as a petulant display of her belief in being ill-used than due to any shame she might—and should—feel over her actions. Another likely motive was a desire to avoid her intended victim at all costs.

Bingley, as portended by his manner during the initial confrontation with his younger sister in Darcy's bedchamber, was uncharacteristically sullen and frustrated with the situation. He had, as promised, gone to Miss Bingley's rooms upon rising that morning to confront her further over her actions and then left her with all the satisfaction of having finally pushed him too far.

Bingley's wedding to Jane Bennet was planned for early June and his mother was due to journey to Hertfordshire for the event, after which the elder Mrs Bingley would take her youngest daughter into her custody. Until then, Caroline insisted she be able to behave as was customary amongst her neighbours in Hertfordshire.

"What would you have me do, Darcy?" Bingley had asked in a tone of exasperated defeat. "I could lock her in her room, but she would simply abuse the servants, make outrageous demands, and otherwise be intolerable. It is easier to give her some small concession and have done with it. Besides it would seem strange to our neighbours—and might raise speculation—if she were suddenly confined to house-arrest."

Darcy could not help but disagree, feeling that to bow once again to Miss Bingley's whims reinforced the old, dangerous precedent, but it was not his place to tell his friend how to arrange his affairs. He had already come near to disaster for them both by attempting to separate Bingley from Jane Bennet in the autumn and would not make the mistake of meddling again. Additionally, Bingley's secondary thought relating to the suspicions of the neighbourhood had some merit. "Very well, but I shall not be held responsible for my actions should Miss Bingley carry out her threat and malign Elizabeth with scurrilous rumours. I mean to keep my word should even a single insult to the lady's honour pass through Miss Bingley's lips."

"And so I have reminded Caroline. She will say nothing against Elizabeth's virtue or suffer the consequences. It was made very clear to her by us both."

Darcy bowed his head to his frustrated friend, only minimally satisfied by their conversation. "Now, I shall leave your company so that I might dress for the evening. I hope to depart on time tonight, for the sooner we do, the sooner I might see my Elizabeth again."

Bingley, his hand still shading the upper portion of his face, chuckled a bit at Darcy's expense. "I shall have no more of your teasing about my besottedness after this, Darcy, for you are as bad as I ever was."

Admittedly, it was so. Darcy left the room to submit himself to Bailey's ministrations with a rueful grin upon his face.

After many vexatious delays by Miss Bingley, the Netherfield party arrived at Lucas Lodge for the planned dinner party. They stood clustered in the entryway, Darcy tugging at the deep burgundy waistcoat he had worn in hopes of impressing Elizabeth, as their host approached with arms spread wide. They were late but Sir William welcomed them heartily.

"Welcome, welcome!" Sir William crossed the room with a grace his girth should not have allowed. When he stopped in front of his esteemed guests, his belly continued to wobble like a bowlful of jelly for several seconds. "We are so glad to have you here at Lucas Lodge, Mr Bingley, and all your party. Mr Darcy! It is excellent to see you again, sir."

Darcy bowed to his friend's neighbour. "Likewise, Sir William."

Sir William Lucas was a right jolly old soul who considered everyone his friend, even those as standoffish as the Bingley sisters or, Darcy was forced to admit, himself. It was humbling to be received with so much generous cordiality after their previous encounters, when Darcy had been prickly with impatience. It was of no little concern to him that his reception in Hertfordshire might be somewhat subdued after what Elizabeth had told him of the impression he had left behind him. But a wink of Sir William's eye and a twist of his head let Darcy know that his reception might not be so dreadful after all.

Sir William beckoned them further into the house with a flapping hand. "We have just now sat down to dinner. This way, this way."

Darcy trailed just behind Bingley as Sir William led them into the dining room. Almost everyone present was familiar, if not by name, then by face, as they all looked up from their soup to greet the newcomers. He searched for one in particular and found her at the far end of the room, seated between one of her sisters and an older man whom Darcy recognised but whose name he could not recall. Gordon? Goldman? Goulding? Something to that effect. This same gentleman was leaning towards her and speaking softly of something Darcy could not hear from his distance.

Elizabeth, however, seemed not to notice the efforts of her dining partner as her attention was directed at Darcy. In the glow of the candles scattered along the table, her eyes twinkled as she regarded him, her lips spreading into a wide smile. Before Darcy could subdue the flutterings of his heart long enough to return this welcoming gesture, he felt Miss Bingley tugging sharply upon his arm in the opposite direction.

Her audacity freed Darcy of the spell the sight of his beloved Elizabeth had cast over him and he whipped his head around to narrow his eyes at Miss Bingley, who met his glare with affected innocence. Darcy snatched his arm free of her clutches, not inclined to show her any favours after her behaviour the previous night, and edged away from her. Her expression froze as if she were working hard to maintain an outward pretence of calm, but he could feel Miss Bingley's offence at his rejection of her overture. Well, she should have known better than to attempt further familiarity with him; Darcy would not indulge her, even in public.

Before he could whisper any sort of verbal warning to the presumptuous and quietly fuming Miss Bingley, Darcy heard Sir William address him. "We have a seat for you here, Mr Darcy."

Darcy looked to his host who was indicating a pair of vacant chairs at the end of the table nearest to them, immediately to the right of where Sir William himself would sit. Apparently, he was being afforded a place of honour.

"And please allow me the privilege of escorting you to your seat, Miss Bingley." Sir William presented his bent elbow to the lady. She eyed it with some distaste, but, without Darcy's arm to replace it, apparently decided that she would allow her host to perform the task. Laying her hand as lightly upon Sir William's sleeve as was possible while still technically touching him, she followed his lead around the table and allowed him to plant her in the chair right next to the one assigned to Darcy.

Darcy baulked at the idea of sitting next to that wretched woman and looked to Elizabeth. She smiled weakly as if she understood his frustration, and Darcy suppressed the impulse to sigh. As he pulled out his chair, he again glanced down the length of the table and met Elizabeth's surreptitious gaze. Knowing that her attention strayed in his own direction made Darcy feel slightly better. And at least he could see her without obstruction from his current position.

As they moved through the courses, Darcy struggled to be more sociable, his taciturnity a fault Elizabeth had encouraged him to correct before they left Kent. According to her, he was considered proud and above his company in Hertfordshire—which, in all fairness, he was—and the neighbourhood had responded badly to this perception. Elizabeth, herself, had thought him cold, aloof, and disapproving, which had led to her to belief that he had disliked her for many months. Only his confession of his love and devotion, a great surprise to her, had disabused her of this notion.

Still, it was difficult to keep his thoughts on Sir William and the various guests on his end of the table when his eyes were drawn so frequently to his heart's desire at the other. Elizabeth returned his glances frequently, which only encouraged his inattentive behaviour to his dining partners. She would tilt her head at him, raise an eyebrow and nod towards the person he was *supposed* to be talking to in playful admonition. His own lips ached to respond in a large grin, but he withheld all but a small, silly one so as not to draw attention to their flirtation.

"I think I can guess the subject of your thoughts," Miss Bingley whispered close to his ear.

"I should imagine not."

"You are thinking how insupportable it is to be here, surrounded by these *savages,*" Miss Bingley sneered.

How she could entertain any such notion contrary to all evidence before her eyes, Darcy was unable to imagine.

"And I am of your opinion on the matter. However, I believe it shall be much the same from now on since my brother has engaged himself to one of the natives. At least until I can convince them to move to town and abandon this dirty little village. In the meantime, it will be nothing short of intolerable! Especially when in company with our future in-laws."

Darcy followed the direction of Miss Bingley's nod and saw Mrs Bennet crowing loudly at Elizabeth's end of the table about Jane's recent triumph in attaining Bingley's hand. She carried on and on about the details of the wedding, when it was planned for, how many new things Jane would need before she could be married, etc, etc. It was unbecoming, Darcy could not deny it, but another flick of his eyes to Elizabeth and his feelings shifted.

With his eyes still upon the flushed cheeks of Elizabeth, luminous in the dim light cast from the candles, Darcy replied, "Their enthusiasm is understandable. It is no small thing to see a daughter married."

"And so *advantageously.*" Miss Bingley's resentment was simmering close to the surface now, no doubt fuelled by the bitterness inspired by his outright rejection of her advances the night previously. "I always knew that Charles was lacking in common sense, but to be caught by a family of fortune hunters..."

"Bingley has done quite well for himself. Not all landed families would so warmly welcome a man whose origins are in trade."

Miss Bingley's jaw clenched, and her eyebrows descended low over her eyes, clearly angered by the implied insult to her own standing in society.

Darcy watched as Miss Bingley smoothed the anger out of her expression, reverting to the condescending air she typically affected in company. "Landed they may be, but the Bennets lack any sort of social refinement. A family estate cannot make up for the total want of propriety and crass behaviour exhibited by so many of them."

Darcy declined to respond to this paltry attack against the Bennets. He would not be drawn into disparaging his future family as he had done in the past.

"Take Miss Eliza, for example," continued Miss Bingley, immediately inciting Darcy's ire. "I have always thought that, in her air, there is a self-sufficiency without fashion which is intolerable. She scampers about the countryside, unaccompanied, covering herself in mud and Lord only knows what else and brandishes her opinions about with no consideration for her station in life. I am sure you recall how impertinent she can be." She tittered gratingly.

In an effort to prevent himself from responding, Darcy reached out and plucked his wineglass up off the tablecloth and took a deep swig to occupy his tongue while Miss Bingley persisted with her tirade.

"I remember," she said, leaning towards Darcy in a conspiratorial manner, "when we first knew her last autumn, how amazed we all were to find that she was a reputed beauty! Though I suppose she is tolerable enough for *these* people, even if she is nothing to the ladies of the *ton*."

As Darcy lowered his wineglass back to the table, he noticed that his grip was straining the delicate crystal and forced himself to release it before he shattered it.

Darcy raised his eyes towards Elizabeth again as he gathered the frayed ends of his equanimity and willed himself to calm. She looked up from her conversation, almost as if she sensed him watching her, and frowned slightly at what she saw. *"Is something wrong?"*

Before he could force a smile he did not feel to assuage Elizabeth's concern, he heard Miss Bingley reach the crescendo of her waspish speech. "And I particularly recollect your saying one night, after they had been dining at Netherfield, 'She a beauty! I should as soon call her mother a wit'."

Miss Bingley cackled at this memory, drawing the attention of several people surrounding them who had previously been ignorant of their conversation. The chatter of the other guests became muted for several long, awkward seconds before it started up again, harried and harsh whispers that rasped against his ears and disturbed the flames lighting the dining table. Darcy could feel the shadows skirting across the walls looming over him, accusing him, as his ugly words were bandied about the room upon the lips of others.

His eyes darted around him from one face to the next, absorbing the scorn he was attracting. Sir William, jolly happy soul though he was, was frowning at the pair of them in offended censure, his ruddy cheeks inflamed with indignation on behalf of his friends. Bingley, from across the table, looked ready to melt into a puddle of embarrassment at his bride's feet, either due to the scene his sister was making or the slander she was repeating. Probably both. Jane Bennet, sitting next to him, looked equal parts discomfited and confused by what she was hearing. From the other end of the table, Darcy could hear Mrs Bennet castigating him as a 'proud, disagreeable man' and exclaiming 'Lizzy does not lose much by not suiting *his* fancy'.

Darcy looked towards Elizabeth. She was across from her mother, pretending not to hear Miss Bingley. Her head was lowered, and she did not venture to connect her gaze with his. Darcy turned back to Miss Bingley who was still tittering maliciously over the pain she was causing. Wickham aside, he had never despised another human being more.

"Lower your voice, madam," scolded Darcy. He might have said more, but anything else would have exploded from his mouth in flames of rage and fury.

But Miss Bingley was insensible to the rebuke—or perhaps simply delighted in it—and carried on as before. "I thought it quite apt. *I* never saw any beauty in her. Even her eyes, which I have sometimes heard called so *fine*, have a sharp, shrewish look which I do not like at all. I could never see anything extraordinary in them. But afterwards she seemed to improve on you, and I believe you thought her rather pretty at one time."

"Yes," replied Darcy loudly, rising from his seat and throwing his napkin onto his plate when he could contain himself no longer, "but that was only when I first knew her, for it is many months since I have considered her as one of the handsomest women of my acquaintance."

Miss Bingley was finally silenced by Darcy's outburst and sat with her head tipped back to look up at him towering over her, eyes and mouth wide with either shock or affront.

"Further, in the future I shall thank you to hold your tongue in reference to her—and to each of the four-and-twenty families of Meryton, but most particularly the Bennets."

A heavy silence hung over the table. Every face was pointed in his direction, each pair of eyes widened with astonishment—or perhaps disgust. Swallowing thickly, Darcy bowed low to his host, a paltry attempt at an apology. "Excuse me."

The last was said as he stalked out of the dining room. Darcy could hear the fevered murmurings of the collected guests as he made his escape and his name, as well as his own terrible words, rang in his ears as he departed. He did not even bother to glance back at Miss Bingley… or Elizabeth.

Darcy stood outside in the yard, breathing deeply and attempting to force his heart into its usual rhythm. The anger, humiliation, and shame coursing through his veins, however, made that impossible. The rising moon watched his struggles with an impassive face, and the stars winked as if laughing at his expense.

Had Elizabeth heard what Miss Bingley said? She must have—everyone else certainly had. Even if she had somehow been fortunate enough to have missed Miss Bingley's gleeful recounting of his insulting words, she would not remain in ignorance for long. Her family and her neighbours could all repeat it for her. As if the initial snub he had delivered at the assembly were not enough—and *that* she had held onto as proof of his dislike, using it as the impetus for her own for many months—Elizabeth now had further evidence of his ungentlemanly behaviour. All because he had once stubbornly refused to acknowledge her ability to tempt him! Would she return to hating him now?

If she did, Darcy would not blame her. He had slandered her to her face, to his friends, treated her coldly and then abandoned her. How could he have been so surprised by her admission of dislike in Hunsford? He had never courted Elizabeth's good opinion, never bothered to, and had instead relied upon his wealth and social standing to gain her favour, despite how much he told himself that he wanted to be loved for the man that he was alone. It was a miracle that she could even stand the sight of him. Only by God's intervention had he been shown the error of his ways and been given a second chance; one that was likely now squandered by the jealousy of a shrew.

No, that was unfair. As disgusting as Miss Bingley was to him, it was Darcy's own hateful commentary that had come back to haunt him. It was his insufferable pride which had struck the final blow to all of his hopes. Elizabeth's inevitable fury towards him would be the retribution he deserved.

"Mr Darcy?"

Darcy's heart seized for a moment. He thought that he heard Elizabeth's voice—the Elizabeth from his vision who so tenderly spoke his name—beckoning him softly in the twilight.

"Are you well?"

Darcy, upon again hearing the phantom voice of the wife from his dreams, slowly turned away from the darkening sky. There, in the open doorway of Lucas Lodge, haloed in escaped lamplight, was the Elizabeth of the present. The one who had heard those despicable things Miss Bingley had reported to the entire party. The one who must surely despise him again.

Darcy ached to touch her but knew he would not be allowed. Instead, he attempted to commit her image to memory, the last he would likely have of her before he left in the morning for Derbyshire, something to treasure within his withered heart for the rest of his days.

As always, his—no, no longer *his*—Elizabeth was everything lovely.

She was wearing an evening gown of deep, dusky rose with a sash of burgundy satin cinched beneath her bust, delightfully matched to the hue of his own waistcoat as if they had planned it together. Her hair, often wild and barely tamed, was pinned in place with only a few well-crafted ringlets allowed to dangle against her temples and the back of her neck.

Overwhelmed by a surge of feeling, Darcy tore his eyes away from her and redirected them at his own feet. He wanted to say something, to apologise and swear that he would never bother her again, but the tightness in his throat constricted his words. Darcy felt as if he were choking on his own shame.

The feel of tender fingers on the sleeve of his coat startled Darcy and he opened his eyes to find Elizabeth standing beside him. "Please say something."

Darcy was rather astonished, and it took him longer than usual to form a response. When he did, it was halting and tentatively hopeful. "I am surprised you should wish to speak to me at all."

"Because of what Miss Bingley said?"

Darcy nodded only once, which was more than enough to acknowledge her guess.

Elizabeth sighed softly, closing her luminous eyes for a moment as she gathered what she wished to say. He hoped she would be gentle, even if he did not deserve such consideration. "Can I assume that you actually said those things?"

"To my shame, yes, I did," Darcy confessed, clenching his jaw. "I am more sorry than I can say, both for the insult and for the embarrassment it has caused you. I shall leave tomorrow and—"

"You have just arrived! Why would you leave?"

Darcy stumbled over his words in confusion. "I—I would have thought you would not wish to see me again after—that is, because of what I said—"

"You mean when you defended me to the entire neighbourhood and called me 'the handsomest woman of your acquaintance'?"

"I—well—"

"I shall not lie and say that I was not offended by Miss Bingley's recollections," said Elizabeth, both eyebrows now raised high and her lips drawn in a stern line; then her mien relaxed again, her brows lowered to their natural position and her mouth softened. "But I was more than impressed by your reply. It very clearly negated any previous opinions you might have expressed in the past."

Was he having another vision? Was his brain on fire, hallucinating an Elizabeth who was ready to forgive him? "But your neighbours, your family…I have mortified you…"

Elizabeth shrugged in a way that was not strictly lady-like but that nevertheless struck him as endearing. Humour emanated from her countenance as she said, "One benefit to having a family such as mine, sir, is an increased *tolerance* for humiliation. What just occurred was not comfortable for me, of course, but I have experienced worse."

Darcy winced at the notion that Mrs Bennet and her youngest daughters could somehow behave more reprehensibly than Miss Bingley had. He must not have hidden this thought successfully, however, because Elizabeth laughed.

"Oh, yes, you will have to build up your own *tolerance* for their ways," she teased, squeezing at Darcy's forearm with the fingers that still dallied upon his sleeve, "for my mother heard what you said very clearly and is now telling the entire neighbourhood that we must be secretly engaged."

"Engaged?"

"I am afraid there is no escaping it now." Elizabeth's words were playful, though Darcy detected a flutter of anxiety in them. "Unless, of course, your feelings have altered since we were in Kent?"

"Only in that I love you even more than I did before," he replied quietly, all but breathless. "Elizabeth, I am ashamed of how I have behaved but, if you can find it in your heart to forgive my many blunders, I shall spend the rest of my life making amends to you. I beg you, please agree to be my wife."

When she raised her face to answer, he could see the welcome in her eyes. "I will."

CHAPTER SEVEN

DARCY STRUGGLED TO CATCH HIS BREATH, COLLAPSING upon the bed next to his bride. He and his dearest, loveliest Elizabeth had been married three days before and were at last returned to Pemberley after a long journey, taken as quickly as possible but still interminable for the newly wedded couple. Their trip had been filled with uncomfortably crowded inns where they were forced to dampen their enthusiasm whilst consummating their union, and the freedom to express how much they were enjoying the more intimate aspects of married life was one of the many advantages of being home.

Home.

"I am so glad to be home, my love," Elizabeth said, her head resting upon Darcy's chest with her wild curls spilled across his shoulder and their shared pillow.

"As am I," he agreed after another moment. Darcy's heart was finally beginning to settle, but it remained swollen three times its usual size with love for his new wife.

They lay together in the most perfectly contented silence he had ever experienced, regulating their breathing patterns and heart-beats into a more sedate pace, and enjoying one another's touch. The back of his fingers skimmed the skin of her bare shoulder, the tickle of her hair upon his chin, her thigh pressed against his stomach as his other hand stroked her knee. They were tangled together in sublime embrace.

The past weeks between their engagement and actual marriage had been an agony of waiting for Darcy and, he suspected, for Elizabeth as well. Thankfully, the Bingleys had been amenable to sharing their wedding date, thus sparing him and his bride from further delays. Mrs Bennet had been initially opposed to the idea, preferring instead to plot two separate occasions at which she could preside as the mother of the bride, but her husband had convinced her that one grand occasion rather than two smaller ones was the better choice. She had contented herself with this and Mr Bennet had been relieved to spare himself prolonged discussions about lace and finery.

The banns had been read on three Sundays, and the couples had been married the Monday immediately following the last. As it had been Darcy's idea to conduct the ceremony so soon after the conclusion of the necessary rituals, Elizabeth had teased him mercilessly about his impatience to ensnare himself in the parson's mousetrap. He had admitted this readily, further confessing that he hoped to carry her off to Derbyshire directly after the wedding breakfast. She had laughed at his haste but not objected to the scheme, possibly—or even probably—weary of her mother's planning, Miss Bingley's sneering remarks, Lady Catherine's vehement disapproval of their match, and the attention they had garnered from the community. They had silently agreed that some peace and solitude was something to look forward to at the conclusion of their nuptials.

The response of others had been something of a surprise to Darcy. A few had been expected—Caroline Bingley's petulant complaining and increasingly direct insults towards Elizabeth—and others—Lady Catherine storming all the way from Rosings to Longbourn in order to make her disapproval clearly known to her nephew and future niece—were more than he had bargained for. The Bennets, always excitable and a mite uncouth, were true to form, with the matron flurrying about after wedding details, the younger sisters giggling and whining by turns, and the father hiding from it all in his book room. Georgiana, as she had intimated to him in the winter, had been pleased to gain a sister, and Fitzwilliam, the loveable blackguard, had impishly flirted with Darcy's bride. The militia, and Wickham along with it, had thankfully departed the county not long after Darcy had entered it again, and so that scoundrel's opinion was blessedly not shared—at least not with him.

These things Darcy had braced himself for, at least in part, but his astonishment had been great when the couple had received numerous heartfelt blessings from the neighbourhood at large. He had predicted that Miss Bingley's outburst at Lucas Lodge would turn the community against him for his ill-considered words, but the response was exactly the opposite. As Elizabeth had pointed out to him just before his proposal, his defence of her had mitigated whatever terrible thing he had reportedly said in the past and turned him into something of a romantic hero. Once the tale had spread far and wide, many of the young ladies of Meryton and the surrounding area had given over lamenting the absent redcoats and instead sent their sighs in his direction. It continued to baffle him, but Darcy was not averse to being considered acceptable as Elizabeth's future husband.

The candle at their bedside guttered low, casting flickering shadows upon the walls. He should reach over and snuff it, but Darcy felt both disinclined and unable to move from his present position. At this hour of the night—or, very likely, early morning—everything was quiet and still; not a creature was stirring anywhere, not even a mouse, and all were snug in their beds. He sincerely doubted that any of the rest were as satisfied in this moment as he was, though. Well, he amended to himself with a smug little grin, perhaps Elizabeth.

"What are you thinking?"

Darcy strained slightly to look at his wife, still nestled against his chest. Elizabeth's face was turned away, so he contented himself with nuzzling the soft curls along her forehead.

"I can see you smiling," she accused with a teasing lilt to her voice. The hand that had been resting upon his stomach stirred into motion, her fingertips tracing tickling patterns around his navel, and he closed his eyes to enjoy the sensation. "What has you looking so pleased with yourself?"

His grin expanded as images of the past few hours rose up in his memory: carrying his bride across the threshold of Pemberley and taking her directly up the marble staircase, kicking the door to his chamber closed with the heel of his boot and then tumbling immediately into their bed, clawing at the ridiculously tiny buttons knitted together down the back of her dress, her own hands grasping desperately at his hair as she responded to his kisses with wild passion, her curls falling in a cascade of shimmering waves around her shoulders…

"I think you can guess."

The tickling fingers on his stomach gave him a playful swat. "And here I thought you were prideful before! You are going to be impossible to live with."

Darcy laughed in a fit of irrepressible joy. "It is far too late for regrets, *Mrs Darcy*. You cannot be rid of me now."

"I suppose I shall have to learn to *tolerate* your swelled head, then." Elizabeth heaved an exaggerated sigh of exasperation before lifting herself up upon the elbow that rested beneath them. The blanket of her hair followed her movement, sliding across his shoulder and sweeping against his jaw before settling in a pool of dark curls between them. She was smiling at him in that mischievous way which delighted him as she settled in to look at him, one eyebrow raised high.

Darcy lifted the hand that had been skirting along her shoulder and upper back to brush some of her hair away from her face. His fingers lingered against her cheek once this task was completed and tenderly appreciated the lines of her expression. "So long as I am *tolerable,* then."

"Speaking of 'tolerable'," Elizabeth said, leaning into the hand stroking her face, "I have been wondering how you came to fall in love with me to begin with. I can comprehend your going on charmingly, when you had once made a beginning, but what could set you off in the first place?"

Darcy's mind had been so filled with Elizabeth for such a long time that he honestly could not say. "I cannot fix on the hour, or the spot, or the look, or the words, which laid the foundation. It is too long ago. I was in the middle before I knew that I *had* begun," he admitted.

"My beauty you had early withstood, and as for my manners—my behaviour to you was at least always bordering on the uncivil, and I never spoke to you without rather wishing to give you pain than not. Now be sincere; did you admire me for my impertinence?"

She asked the last with such an arch look that Darcy laughed again and pulled her in for a lingering kiss, his fingers tangled in the curls at the back of her head. "For the liveliness of your mind, I did."

"You may as well call it impertinence at once," Elizabeth replied, nuzzling at his jaw and earlobe in the most distracting way. "It was very little less. You were disgusted with the women who were always speaking and looking, and thinking for your approbation alone. I roused, and interested you, because I was so unlike *them.* Had you not really been amiable you would have hated me for it; but in spite of the pains you took to disguise yourself, your feelings were always noble and just; and in your heart you thoroughly despised the persons who so assiduously courted you."

Darcy said nothing in response to Elizabeth's speech, his attention divided between her words and the way she was slowly working her way down his neck. From what small amount his pleasure-seeking mind was able to absorb, however, he was unable to disagree with in her theory.

"There. I have saved you the trouble of accounting for it; and really, all things considered, I begin to think it perfectly reasonable. To be sure, you knew no actual good of me—but nobody thinks of *that* when they fall in love."

"Was there no good in your affectionate behaviour to Jane, while she was ill at Netherfield?" Darcy knew it had been *this* event which had fixed the attachment he had unsuccessfully tried to deny. He had witnessed her affectionate care for her sister and coveted it for himself, thus falling more sincerely under her spell. Before that, Darcy supposed that his inclination for her could have been considered a weak, transient thing, and, had he left Netherfield before that, he likely never would have fallen so deeply in love with her. To see her standing there in the breakfast parlour, eyes brightened by exercise and clothes spattered in mud in the service of attending her ailing sister, had awakened a longing within Darcy that he had not experienced since he was a boy. The longing to be loved.

Of course, with his lovely bride sprawled across him so provocatively, Darcy was now longing for something…else. His lips began searching for the spot on her neck that caused her to squirm, and he used the hand he had captured to draw her nearer.

Elizabeth allowed his ministrations for a few seconds but was apparently determined to finish their conversation. "Dearest Jane! Who could have done less for her? But make a virtue of it by all means. My good qualities are under your protection, and you are to exaggerate them as much as possible; and, in return, it belongs to me to find occasions for teasing and quarrelling with you as often as may be; I shall begin directly by asking you why, if you loved me back in the autumn, did you leave Netherfield? It was above four months until we saw one another again, and I suspect that you did not know of my presence in Kent until you arrived."

Darcy did not answer directly, his ever-present smile of the past month slipping into a frown. "I confess that it does not speak well of my character when I admit that I once thought you unsuitable to be my wife. I despised your connexions and your family's behaviour. Added to that your lack of fortune, I had determined after no more than a month of struggle that I could not have you. And so I left."

"I surmised as much myself. Do you recall my surprise when Jane wrote to tell me you reunited her with Charles? I assumed then you had whisked him away from Netherfield to keep them apart, and likely in concert with his sisters."

Darcy allowed that was the case. "But I was a fool, Elizabeth. I love you as I have no other. When I realised what I would be giving up by not pursuing you, I knew what I had stolen from my friend. Once I knew that, the natural thing was to reunite them."

"Of course, that is just like you. Too good and honourable to allow an injustice to stand, even when you yourself have brought it about." A tender and indulgent smile curled at the corners of Elizabeth's lips. "But what happened to change your mind?"

Darcy considered what to tell her. He had told no one of his premonition at Christmastide—not Georgiana, who had experienced something similar, nor Fitzwilliam, who had always been his closest confidante, nor even Bingley, whose own future was a feature in the vision—out of both a sense of privacy and a concern that others would declare his mind addled. Should he share it with Elizabeth, now his closest kin and confidante? "You may not believe me…"

"I believed your last confession, Mr Darcy," Elizabeth reminded him with a touch of asperity, tucking her chin down and raising one brow up. "Let us try for the same success now."

Reaching out to tangle their fingers together and joining both sets of hands above his heart, Darcy began, "Very well, though I do not truly understand it, myself. Last Christmas Eve, as I was on my way home to Pemberley…"

CHAPTER EIGHT

December 8, 18__

DARCY STARTLED AWAKE WITH AN EMBARRASSING SNORT. HE was confused for a moment, unsure why he was sleeping anywhere other than beside his beautiful wife, but then his sleep-befuddled memory stuttered into function again. He was in his carriage on his way back to Pemberley after visiting the Bingleys.

There was a rap at the carriage door and, after a shake to clear away any remaining mental cobwebs, Darcy lowered the window panel to peer out. "What seems to be the problem, Marley?"

"There's a tree branch in the road, sir. Me and Jacobs, we'll try and clear it out quick, but it's a big one. Likely fell from a rotted tree on account of the weather."

Darcy leaned forward a few inches to survey the landscape outside, finding it dusted in sparkling white. Though there had only been flurries in the air when he had left McClane Manor an hour or so ago, Jack Frost had apparently been more enthusiastic here. "How far are we from Pemberley?"

"Likely only about three miles or so, sir," replied Marley. "We passed through Lambton a bit ago and are already in the park."

Darcy felt a thrill of anticipation in his stomach; he would be with his Elizabeth very soon. "Do you require assistance with the removal?"

"Oh, no need to trouble yourself, sir. I'm sure me and Jacobs can handle her."

But Darcy was eager to see his wife and, therefore, unwilling to wait patiently in the carriage whilst his men struggled with a rotted log in their way. The task would be more quickly accomplished with three and then he could hold Elizabeth that much sooner. "I would prefer to assist. The sooner we clear the road, the sooner we can be home."

Marley sputtered a few more protests as Darcy unlatched the carriage door and jumped out without bothering to take out the step. His boots crunched in the fresh, crisp snow as they hit the hard earth.

"Stop fussing, Marley, there's a good man," Darcy said, halting the coachman's stream of obsequious words with a friendly pat on the shoulder. "You sound more and more like Mrs Reynolds every trip. Next you will be fretting that I shall somehow 'shoot my eye out' during a hunt."

Marley guffawed at this image, which was faithful to Mrs Reynolds' character. "She be a worrier, that one, no doubt about it."

A few yards ahead, the horses stomped fitfully in the snow as they waited to be guided into motion again. Jacobs stood in the middle of the road before them, surveying the debris in their way.

"What do you think Jacobs? Is it too fragile to move as one?"

"Not if we lift it real careful like," Jacobs replied, nodding at the offending branch. "But me 'n Marley can take care of it, sir."

"Nonsense. It should be nothing for the three of us."

The men worked in tandem to heave the heavy obstacle out of their path which was, indeed, much easier with a third strong pair of arms to assist. Darcy's overcoat might be a touch dirtier for the effort, but Bailey would surely forgive him. Eventually.

"Heave ho!" grunted Jacobs as they all lifted the branch and hefted it towards the side of the road. Darcy's muscles strained but it was nothing he could not handle; he had always prided himself on being an active master and not merely directing his servants and tenants from his study.

They had successfully released the beastly log down the embankment beside the lane and were congratulating one another on a job well done when...

Whack!

Later...

Oh, how his head ached! Darcy rubbed his throbbing temples with the thumb and middle finger of his left hand, attempting to assuage away the pulsating pain that was building between his ears. Cursed tree branch had come out of nowhere! He was quite lucky he had not lost an eye when the blasted thing struck out at him so violently and without provocation.

Remembering his conversation with Marley about Mrs Reynolds's mollycoddling made him chuckle, albeit somewhat wryly and with a slight wince. Perhaps the old dear had something of a point if Darcy could be felled by nothing more than an offended tree.

The snow was coming down heavier now and the men were all thankful to be back at Pemberley where they could hide themselves away from the increasingly inclement weather, warm by the fire. Darcy tramped through the thickening blanket of snow accumulating on the ground as he made his way to the house.

Home. At last.

The double doors opened ahead of him and his butler, Griswold, greeted him in the usual manner. "Welcome home, sir. I trust your journey was comfortable?"

A throb in Darcy's head reminded him of just the opposite. "Indeed, though I am glad to be home. Where is Mrs Darcy?"

Griswold proceeded to relieve his master of his dirtied apparel. "Mrs. Darcy has been awaiting your arrival all morning, sir. I believe she will be relieved to see you home safe."

Darcy required assistance to remove his greatcoat, soaked by the brief time he spent struggling with the obstinate wooden roadblock. Griswold, standing behind him, grasped it at the shoulders and pulled sharply to peel it away from the clothing beneath.

"Thank you, Griswold." Darcy tugged at the bottom of his dark green coat to straighten it back into position. "See that Marley and Jacobs are given a hot meal in the kitchen after they have seen the horses and carriage to the stable. The weather is abysmal today."

"Of course."

"Oh, and please send word to Mrs Reynolds that I am arrived."

Now, to go find his wife. Darcy clapped his chilled hands together, rubbing them to warm his numb fingers and turned his steps towards the library where he was sure to find her; it was Elizabeth's favourite room in the entire house.

"*Fitzwilliam!*"

"*Elizabeth!*" Darcy's boots squealed against the marble floor as he skidded to a stop and whirled around. He watched, full of warm delight, as none other than his beloved wife rushed down the staircase and hopped off the last step with energetic joy. Elizabeth did not pause at the base but instead gathered up her skirts and all but sprinted towards him across the distance that remained between them.

When she reached Darcy, Elizabeth spread her arms wide and launched herself at him, her laughter echoing throughout the room like silver bells chiming. He reached out, ready to absorb her into his embrace, and caught her around the waist, drawing her to his chest. Upon contact, Darcy swept her around in a wide circle, her gown flaring about in a whirl of burgundy silk and ivory lace, while his heart beat against the inside of his ribs with each peal of her laughter.

Setting Elizabeth down, Darcy bowed his head and kissed her, long and eagerly. She dug her fingers into the waves of his hair and responded with all the vigour he could hope for. They were awhile in parting, but finally their heaving chests required more air than such a passionate embrace could allow, and they pulled back, panting.

"Have you missed me, my love?" Darcy asked, his face beginning to ache from the grin that split it apart.

Elizabeth's laugh jingled again as she pressed her forehead against his and closed her eyes, seemingly savouring their reunion. "I confess I did."

"And have you been well in my absence?" Darcy moved his hand around to her front to rub at the bump that was not yet visible through the heavy layers of her clothing. He was rewarded for his consideration with a tiny kick.

"We have *both* been well," replied Elizabeth, pecking him on the lips. "The nausea has not been so very bad and I almost wish we had come with you."

Darcy shook his head and stroked her belly. "Nonsense, the motion of the carriage is too much for your stomach."

"I suppose you are right," she said. "I am so glad you are home. How was your trip? Were you able to assist Charles?"

Darcy rolled his eyes, and her laugh rang out again. "The dispute was settled before I arrived. The land deeds were belatedly discovered in an area that Bingley had neglected to search."

"Allow me to guess—they were in the library?"

"You know our brother well," replied Darcy drily.

"Perhaps better than you do if you did not previously suggest he search there." Her hands stroked gently at the small of his back.

"I did!" Darcy protested, speaking with a petulance he did not truly feel. He drew her closer by the hands that rested upon the crests of her hips and pressed a kiss to her forehead. "Nearly a month ago, via letter. He claims he never got it, but I suspect that it is lost somewhere on his desk."

Elizabeth grazed the tip of her nose against his jaw. "Or in the library?"

Darcy snorted. "Only if someone else placed it there. I am convinced he only enters the library one time in a month, if that. I have instructed him to hire a secretary."

"Jane performed that role admirably before the babe was born, but I suppose she will not have time to do so now," Elizabeth said. "Which reminds me, did they like our gift? I do hope they fit little Holly, for she grows so fast!"

"I did not ask."

Elizabeth shook her head at him with what he thought looked like exasperated fondness, a few wispy curls that were dangling around her face swaying with the motion. "I shall have to write to my sister, then, and get her opinion directly."

Darcy began to lower his head towards Elizabeth's again, observing, "You would have done so anyway, I suspect."

Just as his lips were about to touch hers, Elizabeth jerked back from him and exclaimed, "You are hurt!"

Her brow crumpled with concern as she reached up and tenderly touched his forehead. He felt a sharp stab of pain and hissed in response, causing her to recoil slightly.

"Am I?" Darcy had rather forgotten about his accident. Had not, in fact, been aware that he had sustained an injury from it at all other than a slight headache.

Elizabeth lowered her hand to show him the blood smeared on her fingertips. "Yes, you are. What happened?"

"It was nothing."

"It most certainly is not 'nothing'!" Elizabeth exclaimed. "You are *bleeding*. Come."

Elizabeth urgently took hold of one of his hands with both of her own and tugged him towards a hallway that led them deeper into the house. As they passed the staircase on their way, she turned to issue an order to the housekeeper.

"Mrs Reynolds, please fetch some warm water and clean toweling. We might also require the services of the physician."

Mrs Reynolds, who had scuttled down the stairs at Elizabeth's exclamation over his injury, hovered only long enough to accept these instructions before dashing off towards the kitchens.

"I am perfectly well," Darcy said, though he did not attempt to slow their progress through the corridors. He allowed Elizabeth to pull him along in her wake, watching the bounce of her curls against the back of her neck with appreciation. And, though he would complain throughout, as was his habit, Darcy knew that he would not protest in any sincere way as she fussed over and coddled him. Indeed, he was rather looking forward to it.

Darcy staggered as the floor beneath him quite suddenly seemed to pitch upward and throw him off balance. He heard Elizabeth exclaim and felt her hands tighten upon his arm, straining to keep him on his feet. Her small frame, however, was no bulwark for his weight, and so all she could really do was guide him to the wall nearest to him so that he could collapse against it.

"'Perfectly well,' he says!" Elizabeth cried, one hand still grasping his elbow as the other reached up to tilt his chin in her direction. Once she had positioned him where she liked, he could see the concern carved into her features, the frightened panic glinting deep in her eyes, though the image of her dear face had become sporadically indistinct. Darcy tried to force himself to focus, but he was still quite dizzy. Everything seemed to be filtered by a pervasive fuzziness, as if he were looking at the world through a frosted window. "Can you hear me?"

"Y–Yes, I can hear you." Darcy shook his head back and forth to dispel the distortion at the edges of his vision. Doing so only made his head spin more, however, so he stopped and squeezed his eyes shut. The world heaved and spun around him.

"Can you stand?"

Darcy attempted to right himself and, finding his feet solid beneath him, raised himself gingerly into a sitting position. "I believe so."

"Come with me, very slowly," said Elizabeth, her voice echoing lightly like ripples dispersing to the far edges of a pond. It began at her normal volume and faded into the barest whisper as it seeped into his mind.

Darcy shuffled his feet forward and kept his eyes shut against the swirling, tilting world. He could still feel the floor shifting around underneath him, but with his wife's guidance was able to navigate his path.

"This way," Elizabeth said, cooing sweetly in that ethereal echo. The sound of her voice was split by the sharp squeal of a door hinge and he felt a relaxing warmth reach out for him, welcoming him into whichever room she had chosen.

A few more steps and she halted him with an order to seat himself. Darcy lowered his body downward, his knees bending and his back arching, and he heard the soft creak of buttery leather and felt a cushion sink beneath his weight. Once he had settled himself against the back of this familiar chair, Darcy felt secure enough to open his eyes again.

They were in his study, which he probably could have surmised earlier had the earth not been shaking so unsteadily along their route. Elizabeth sat on the matching stool before him and pulled his boots off, tugging at the heel of his right foot to force the Hessian to relinquish him. Darcy watched her intently, his eyes fixed upon each twisting curl caressing her cheek, the thick, dark lashes that shielded the colour of her eyes, and that sweet button nose dusted with cinnamon freckles even in December.

A strange, wistful feeling of familiarity washed over Darcy as he surrendered himself to her ministrations. She made him comfortable, and then, once Mrs Reynolds had arrived with the towels, examined his wound with loving solicitude. It tugged at the deepest recesses of his memory, tickling his conscious thoughts persistently. He was sure that there was something about this scene that he ought to recognise.

Darcy felt as if everything unfolding before him had already happened before, though he could not say why. There was a specificity to this scene which tugged at his recollections.

Elizabeth turned back to him, her eyes crinkling with warmth as she observed him. She reached out her hand to stroke again at his forehead, just barely skating over the tender skin with even more tender fingertips, and he felt a pleasant tingle rushing over him at her contact. "My poor love." Elizabeth dropped her hand so that she could caress his cheek with the backs of her fingers. "Does it hurt?"

Not when she cared for him so sweetly. "No," Darcy replied, leaning into her touch. The familiarity still tugged at him, stronger than before.

Elizabeth's mouth curved softly, her eyes sparkling like evergreens dusted with fresh snow. "My brave man. I trust you will be good whilst I clean your wound?"

Darcy turned his face slightly so that he might brush his lips against the hand that was caressing his cheek. "Perfectly well behaved," he assured her.

"I love you, Fitzwilliam."

"And I you."

Elizabeth bent towards him and bestowed upon him a small kiss, one that had been given many times, and then leaned back. He reached out, cradled her face between his palms, and brought her back to him, pressing their mouths together where they belonged. He deepened the contact, sweeping his tongue out to meet hers for a moment before withdrawing. Darcy allowed their lips to separate but pressed his forehead to hers in order to linger over their embrace for a few moments longer.

"I missed you," Elizabeth whispered, her breath tickling his cheeks.

Truly, Darcy was certain this *had* happened before. Perhaps late last spring when he had scraped his hand against a splintered fence post? Elizabeth had tended him then, soothing his torn skin with ointment and healing kisses. But…no, that was not it.

Yesterday had been their first true separation since their marriage the summer before last, so he could not be remembering another welcome after a long absence. Elizabeth had only remained behind at Pemberley because the swaying motion of the carriage upset her stomach in her condition. That could not be the source, either.

What was striking his memory so forcibly? The answer to this question was elusive, skirting just out of his reach whenever he attempted to capture it, like a skittish sparrow. Teasing, teasing recollections!

Elizabeth began to clean the wound, the warm water and her gentle touches immensely soothing. "I believe you will live, Mr Darcy. It does not look so bad now that the blood has been wiped away. Merely a scratch. But what happened?"

"It was nothing at all," replied Darcy absently, the feeling of remembering and yet not remembering continuing to niggle at the back of his mind.

"I shall have to disagree with you there. You nearly collapsed in the hall."

"Marley and Jacobs stopped the carriage just outside of Lambton to remove a fallen log in our path, and I got out to help. After we had rolled it down the embankment, a tree branch struck me across the face. That is all."

"You could have lost your eye!"

Darcy laughed and she scowled at him, her nose wrinkling adorably. "You have spent too much time with Mrs Reynolds, my love. I was in no danger of losing any portion of my body and, as you see, have arrived home nearly unscathed."

"Except for your dizzy spell."

"Except for that," he conceded, the strange sense of faulty memory washing over him again. He pursued it deep into his mind, but it flew out of his reach once again.

They were interrupted by a knock at the door before Elizabeth could interrogate him further. Mr McCallister came into the room and bowed to his patrons.

"Apologies for the delay, Mrs Darcy. I was at the Cratchit farm seeing to little Timmy. The poor lad has injured his leg again."

Elizabeth's expression and tone were infused with deep sympathy as she said, "I hope he will be well?"

"He will," Mr McCallister assured her, a touch brusquely. He then moved on to the matter currently at hand without further pleasantries. "I understand Mr Darcy has suffered a bump to the head, madam?"

Elizabeth spun around on her ottoman to address the physician directly. "Yes, and he has experienced some kind of episode, as well. He became very suddenly lightheaded in the hall, so much that he had difficulty walking. Should we be concerned?"

Mr McCallister indicated with the wave of a hand that Elizabeth should move aside so he could assess the patient. She stood and removed to Darcy's side, placing herself between him and the fireplace, as Mr McCallister seated himself. "Perhaps. I shall examine him and give you a more definitive answer. Please feel free to make yourself comfortable elsewhere, Mrs Darcy."

"Very well." She pressed a soft kiss to the crown of Darcy's head. "I shall be in the library, my love."

As Elizabeth moved towards the door, Darcy felt a sudden swirl of dizziness and an aching need to keep Elizabeth close to him. Darcy snatched at her wrist and held it firmly, tugging her back towards his chair. "I would prefer you stay."

Elizabeth looked at him in surprise but consented easily enough. "Of course, if you wish." She loosened his fingers with her free hand so that she could slip her palm into his and hold it properly. Elizabeth then resumed her station at his side, out of the way of the physician's work yet still within her husband's line of sight.

"Very well," conceded Mr McCallister, though the turn of his mouth convinced Darcy that he was displeased and only humouring his wealthy clients.

Mr McCallister then proceeded with his examination, asking after the severity of Darcy's pain, whether he had fallen unconscious after the accident, or if he felt nauseated. Darcy replied to each query with his usual stoicism, faintly annoyed to be sharing what should be private time with his wife with this brusque little man.

"Your wife says that you had a fainting spell. Can you tell me what brought it on?" Mr McCallister asked after inspecting the cleaned wound.

Darcy scoffed at the physician's description, picturing his mother-in-law waving her handkerchief around as she wailed about her poor nerves. "I did not have a 'fainting spell'. Just a moment of dizziness in the hall."

"I see." Mr McCallister's lips were drawn taut in scepticism. "And are you prone to dizziness, sir?"

"Not at all."

"And what were you doing when you fainted?"

Darcy glared at the physician as a reminder that he had not, in fact, fainted.

Mr McCallister inhaled a deep breath through his nose and released it harshly through his mouth, as if it were *his* patience being tested by this interview. "Very well. What were you doing when you became dizzy?"

"Walking."

"Strenuously?"

"Can a person walk 'strenuously'?" Elizabeth laid her free hand upon his shoulder for a moment, a silent plea for him to be polite.

Mr McCallister disregarded Darcy's testy question. "And has this symptom repeated itself?"

Darcy darted his eyes at Elizabeth whose expression warned him that he had better tell the truth or else face unspecified consequences. "Once, just a moment ago. As my wife was about to leave."

"And how do you feel at this moment?" Mr McCallister leaned forward to peer into Darcy's eyes. He held his forefinger up and waved it slowly in front of Darcy's face. His patient followed it dutifully.

"Well enough."

There were a few more enquiries about what day it was, where he had travelled recently and why, as well as questioning him on names and facts he should know which his wife was able to verify. Mr McCallister concluded his interview with a noise at the back of his throat that Darcy presumed was some kind of acknowledgment.

When he did not appear to be inclined to say anything further, Elizabeth pressed Mr McCallister, a slight tremor in her voice, "Should we be concerned, sir?"

"I would not worry overmuch, Mrs Darcy," soothed Mr McCallister, "dizziness is fairly common with bumps to the head, though I would not have suspected a minor scratch such as this one to cause it. He may or may not experience it again over the next few days and, if he does, he should sit down immediately lest he fall and injure himself more seriously. Otherwise, he seems in good health and shows no alarming symptoms."

"He is well?"

Mr McCallister shrugged and then stood. "As well as can be expected considering the situation. His pain is tolerable, he does not complain of impaired vision or nausea, and his memory seems intact. Aside from the fainting—excuse me, *dizziness*—and the cut on his head, I would say he is perfectly well. If he complains of anything else, send me a note and I shall return and render my opinion."

"Thank you, sir," said Elizabeth, walking with him to the door.

"Please see Cook for something warm to drink and a bite to eat before you leave us."

After a few more comments back and forth in which Elizabeth asked after a recent break in at the physician's office, Mr McCallister thanked her and left, probably to accept his meal from the kitchens. She closed the door behind him and returned to her husband. But this time, instead of seating herself on the ottoman, she propped her hip against the arm of his chair and leaned into him, her head resting upon the top of his. Elizabeth sighed. "What am I to do with you? I thought *I* was safely considered to be the wild one in our little family."

Darcy reached out and crept his arm around her waist, pulling her closer and into his lap directly. He buried his face in her neck and inhaled the rich scent of cinnamon and evergreen boughs. "Forgive me, my love. I shall do my best to worry you less."

"See that you do," she scolded playfully, twining the fingers of one hand into his hair and scratching his scalp in comforting circles. Darcy closed his eyes and enjoyed the sensation. His idle hand found the bump at her middle and began mimicking the circular movements of hers. The child inside wriggled beneath his palm and he grinned.

Elizabeth settled into his arms and wrapped her own around his neck, one set of fingers still rubbing the tingling skin beneath his hair, and nuzzled down into his embrace. Despite her worries, she was apparently not unwilling to share in this moment with him. Darcy kissed her hair, so delightfully scented with the aroma of Christmas spice and greenery, and revelled in the happiness that he desperately prayed he would never have to live without again. God had answered his prayers.

Perhaps it was this reminder that the Almighty had graciously pushed him onto the right path, or maybe it was the soft scent of his wife tickling his nose and provoking his memories, but Darcy jerked out of his comfortable stupor as his previous sense of unattainable memory suddenly resolved itself.

The vision. He had not thought about it for so long, not since telling Elizabeth of it that first night they had returned to Pemberley as man and wife. But *that* was the source of the intangible, prickly sense of having already experienced some of the events of today. When he had been walking down the hall earlier, his dearest, loveliest Elizabeth leading the way to this very room and his favourite chair, it had provoked a recollection so strong that it had been literally staggering. He was now living the events of his vision, albeit as a man who belonged in this life rather than as one who had been dropped into the middle of it with no notion of how he got there.

"Fitzwilliam?" Elizabeth sat up an instant after he had jumped in the wake of his epiphany. Her voice was edged in concern, her forehead crinkling. "Are you well? Should I call Mr McCallister back? He might not have left the kitchens yet—"

"No, no, my love." Darcy shook his head, rubbing a palm up and down the length of her back. "It is nothing like that. I simply…realised something. Something rather remarkable."

"Oh?"

"Do you recall the night we arrived at Pemberley?" he asked. "Do you remember what I told you about the vision that led me to forget all of my concerns over our match and pursue you for my own?"

"Yes…"

"Well, I think it has finally come true…"

The End

About the Author

Mary Smythe is a homemaker living in South Carolina with a rather useless BA in English collecting dust in a closet somewhere. Mrs Smythe discovered the works of Jane Austen as a teenager and has since gone on to read everything written by Ms Austen at least once yearly, always wishing that there were more.

Also by Mary Smythe

Dare to Refuse Such a Man

THE PINK DAFFODIL

ELIZABETH RASCHE

chapter ONE

Mary Bennet bustled into the Meryton church heedless of both its dank interior and the holiday decorations waiting to be hung on its walls. She was on a mission, and such details were beneath her notice. The young man dallying in the entryway of the church might have been beneath her notice, too, had she not run into him in her haste.

"Oh! I am sorry." Mary ducked her head in apology, though a note of reproach in her voice suggested the human obstacle had himself to thank for the collision. She sidled around him, too intent on finding the vicar and saving the poor of Meryton to mind any bruised elbows, hers or otherwise.

Mary's polite, plastered-on smile deepened into a real one when she saw the vicar. Old Mr Weathering was pottering about the pews closest to the altar, his aged limbs creaking along with the benches he scraped across the floor. Just seeing him made Mary's breath slow with contentment and friendship.

"Let me do that, sir," Mary said, joining Mr Weathering in shifting another pew.

The young man stepped inside the church and hesitated before asking, "May I be of assistance as well?"

Mary looked at him askance, still annoyed at him for bumping into her. She could see now that he was of about her age, perhaps a bit older. His figure was tall, thin, and straight, but his clothes were all confusion: he wore a gentlemanly waistcoat, linen shirt, and fine fawn breeches, but they were spattered with dirt and dotted with loose buttons and rents in the fabric. His boots were covered with enough dust to give Hill the vapours before banning him from Longbourn forever. The man's face was another awkward mishmash. His ears stuck out from the sides of his face in awkward projections, just as red hair sprouted in untidy directions above them. His blue eyes looked kind, though, and the man's crooked smile made Mary forget what she was doing for a moment.

He apparently took her pause as permission to join her and Mr Weathering in moving the pews about and worked with them in silence even as he observed them falling into what was evidently a friendly argument of long standing.

Mary returned her attention to the vicar and helped him position the next bench. "I do not see why you need to move them every week," she said.

"They seem to move around of their own accord." Mr Weathering's eyes crinkled deeply, the evidence of a lifetime of good-humoured expressions. "Well, Miss Bennet, how may I help you?"

She disliked the question. It made it seem as if she had come to the Meryton church to obtain something for herself, when really she was there as a benefactor. "Have you thought more about my proposition?"

The genial smile on Mr Weathering's face wavered. "Oh…"

"The Meryton Widows and Orphans Society."

"I remember, child. I had not forgotten." As Mr Weathering rubbed his face in thought, Mary's heart warmed. Of course, Mr Weathering had not forgotten. He had not forgotten anything that was important to her, not since she was nine years old and had run crying into the church. She had had a terrible day, as children count them—her sisters had plagued her, her mother had forgotten her, and her father had laughed at her as if she were a dancing bear. Dashing into the church had simply been a means of annoying them, proving her value by hiding until they noticed she had gone.

Except that they never had noticed, and Mary had discovered a source of solace that satisfied her more than if they had. Mr Weathering had listened to her tale, wiped her tears, and encouraged her to face it all with Christian fortitude. She had felt understood and important for the first time in her life. She had found herself returning to the old man's smile again and again after that, eager to please him with her piety and to prove herself worthy of his regard. Mr Weathering was always friendly and sympathetic, and Mary found she could be helpful to him—even more so as they both grew older. Mr Weathering's stiff, thin height eventually bent into an elderly hunch, while Mary's meagre nine-year-old figure grew into that of a woman. She knew she had a little stoop herself, which she attributed to near-sightedness and which Lizzy claimed had more to do with lack of exercise. But Mary paid as little attention to her posture as she did to her dark hair, which Lizzy likewise claimed would have been lovely with a little more effort. It was all vanity a pious young lady would disdain.

"Then what do you think of my endeavour?" Mary asked. Moving around the young man shoving pews, her shoulders straightened with self-conscious pride in her piety. "It will be a great boon to Meryton. If I may say I have your approval, it will encourage more people to donate." A note of stubbornness entered her voice. "I can do it without your public acknowledgement, of course, but I do not see why—"

"It is only that there are already so many charities in the world," Mr Weathering said, still breathing heavily from his brief exertion.

"A strange complaint from a clergyman!"

Mr Weathering could not help but smile. "True, I do not mean to discourage charity, exactly. It is only that I hoped to see you engage yourself in other pursuits for a time, Miss Bennet. Why not attend some of those agreeable house parties at Netherfield? I hear the Bingleys will stay there this winter after all."

"House parties are not agreeable to *me*." Mary wondered if the stranger could hear her from where he now stood judging the alignment of the back rows. She hoped so. She was sure she sounded the epitome of Christian rectitude. There was some degree of allure in a party at Netherfield, of course—she could play her music to the company, for example—so even Mary had felt glad when a broken carriage wheel had delayed the Bingleys and Mr Darcy from going to London. Mr Bingley, given another day to weigh his intentions, had suddenly insisted on remaining at Meryton for the winter. Jane's face had brightened when she heard the news, and all the Bennets had been pleased that Jane might have more time with Mr Bingley. Lizzy, however, had looked dangerous enough to rout a French army when she learned Mr Darcy was to stay as well.

"You have so little time to enjoy yourself, my dear. Youth does not last forever. I would be better pleased to see you sporting a fine gown and chatting with your friends than devising another charity for Meryton."

What friends? Mary felt cross that Mr Weathering did not seem to understand. "Such frivolity is not nearly as important as helping the poor."

"There must be balance in any life, Miss Bennet. Did not Christ accept a gift of scent rather than have it sold for the poor?" Mr Weathering made another effort. "I had hoped to officiate at your wedding before I retire. Surely there must be a fine young man somewhere in Meryton to dance with?"

Now Mary flushed at the stranger's presence and hoped he did *not* hear. No one acquainted with Meryton society would expect any such thing for Mary, except the kind old vicar. *No one thinks me pretty when they see Jane. Or Lizzy, or Lydia, for that matter. People will laugh if he goes on saying things like that.* "I have no intention of finding any beaux," she said, her chin lifting.

"Well, then, why not help Meryton in some way than another society? This old church will need decorating for Christmas. I was thinking of inviting all the young people to help, making a party of it, of sorts." He scratched the wiry white hairs of his beard.

"Of course, I shall help you decorate," Mary said, taking out a little book and making a notation in it. "I shall do that as well." Her expression, blankly efficient in accepting another duty, must have discouraged the vicar, for he sighed as he watched her write and obediently stated the date for it. "Now, do I have your permission to express your support for the *Meryton Widows and Orphans Society*?" She could not help pronouncing the name with emphasis, hoping it carried to the stranger adjusting the pews, and to anywhere else someone might hear.

"If that is what you wish, Miss Bennet."

"Excellent. Thank you, Mr Weathering." Mary turned quickly enough to bump into a pew, which she conscientiously readjusted before sailing off. As she passed the red-headed man, he bowed slightly. The bold blue eyes in his face were lit with appreciation, and his ready smile coaxed one from Mary in return before she could school her features.

How strange. The smile felt so natural on her face, like she was brimming with warmth on the inside that spilled out without effort. Mary did not smile often. *There is not much to smile about. This world is a vale of tears, after all.* When she did smile at the visitors to Longbourn or the shopkeepers wrapping her purchases, her mouth pursed into a prim courtesy that showed she knew what was due to society. The gentleman —if a man in such dishevelled attire could count as a gentleman—made his own smile look easy, as if he were delighted to see Mary. And her response of heedless joy surprised her.

Perhaps he was very pleased with the idea of the Meryton Widows and Orphans Society. Although he had smiled at her before mention of that, now that she thought of it. *Well, no doubt I have impressed him further with my conscientious adherence to duty.* Perhaps some ladies would only have accepted the duties of holiday decoration and charity work in order to make themselves pleasing to a gentleman. *But not I.* Reminding herself of her own righteousness made Mary stand tall. As she passed through the door into the street, the moist air felt still and cold, as if the skies, like the people of Meryton, were holding their breath for snow. Mary moved with brisk assurance to the millinery on the high street, where Kitty and Lydia revelled inside with ribbons and bonnets. Some ladies would have dived into the merchandise with them, seeking some frippery to catch the eye of a beau. *But not I. Does not Fordyce warn us against 'the levity of dissipation, the vanity of parade'?* Mary's self-satisfaction buoyed her as she stood on the sidewalk waiting for her sisters, watching the passersby and considering possible strategies for seeking donations. The clammy air clung uncomfortably to the skin exposed between her gloves and the sleeves of her pelisse, but she welcomed the sacrifice of her comfort for a greater good.

All around her, signs of Christmas lit up the high street, but Mary scarcely noticed them. Garlands of crimson ribbon hung in the milliner's window, and gold-painted acorns dotted the display of gloves underneath. Mary cared nothing for such décor or potential gifts. An errand boy hefted a plucked goose down the street, his arms straining to enfold it, but Mary's gaze skipped past him as an unlikely source of donation. She looked more thoughtfully at Sir William Lucas, who wore a sprightly green waistcoat under his jacket and a sprig of holly pinned to the lapel of his gaudy overcoat. But it was not the festive garb that caught at her. *Yes, I must call at the Lucases', or else speak to them when we are all at Netherfield. Sir William is sure to donate.* As she watched the genteel passersby and a few well-to-do farmers stroll past, the particulars of how she might approach them began to form in her mind. Her ruminations busied her until she spied a tall, lanky fellow wearing awkward clothing and an even more awkward smile.

Him again. Though he was too far down the street to notice her, Mary could still feel the smile the red-haired fellow had bestowed upon her in the church, and she found herself smiling back. *Perhaps there is a* little *bit to smile about. It is Christmastime, after all.*

While Netherfield's edifice might not be imposing to some, Mary admitted to herself a sensation of smallness as the Bennet carriage rolled up to it. Though Lydia's bonnet blocked much of the sight through the carriage window, Mary saw enough of Georgian pillars, immaculate lawns, and expansive, glittering windows to make her squeeze the subscription book on her lap in nervousness. Though it was not her first visit to Netherfield, she had still not grown used to the grandeur. *Suppose Jane really does marry into all this.* Mary would find it hard to adapt to such a shift in fortune, but Jane was more malleable. Perhaps even a bit *too* malleable sometimes.

And beautiful. Glancing at Jane's smooth, angelic features and soft fair hair, Mary could acknowledge that her sisters belonged in such a place.

Not *all* her sisters, however. Lydia waved her arm through the window and halloed at Mr Bingley, who gave a swift bow before walking up to the carriage, his smile broadening as he spotted Jane. Mr Darcy followed him but offered only a nod as Lydia clambered out of the carriage.

"We are here at last! And we shall pick your forest bare of everything that can be used to decorate," Lydia said. She danced out of Mr Darcy's way as she made room for the others to alight. Now that Lydia's head was not blocking the window, Mary could see Miss Bingley hanging back behind the gentlemen, her expression blank. Clearly Miss Bingley was not delighted at the prospect of a ramble through the woods with the Bennets to find greenery for Christmas decorations. Mr Bingley's enthusiasm would have to do for all their side of the party, for Mrs Hurst and her husband had declined to stray from the fireside, and Mr Darcy's stern expression raised profound questions about why he had agreed to participate in the festivities at all.

"Move along, Lydia, and let us all out." Mama descended from the coach with the help of Mr Bingley, who quickly turned to aid Jane next. Mama's bonnet was tugged tight over her head to block the wind. After days of still, cold air and an overcast sky, the weather had turned enough to boast a clear winter sun and a brisk, rollicking wind. It remained, nevertheless, quite cold. Mary flexed her gloved fingers and hoped they need not ramble out of doors long. If her fingers grew too cold, they might not thaw out enough to play the Netherfield pianoforte.

As Mr Bingley was fully immersed in chatting with Jane, Mr Darcy made up for his deficiencies in politeness by assisting Mary, who gripped her subscription book with eagerness to fill its pages, down from the carriage. As she stepped into the sunlight, she spotted a gentleman even farther away than Miss Bingley—the red-haired man she had seen in the church. It might have been Mary's nearsightedness, but his clothes appeared tidier than before, if not by much. The fraying seam in his nondescript overcoat and the stain on his linen shirt showed the improvements had not gone far enough. The smile was the same, though.

"Are you well?" Mr Darcy's low voice was probably meant to be reassuring, but Mary's chin jerked up.

I only stumbled a little. And it had nothing to do with seeing that young man. "Of course."

Satisfied, Mr Darcy turned back to the carriage, where Lizzy was next to descend. As Lizzy reached down to him, their two clasped hands wavered a little in the air, an unsteadiness to them that seemed caused by more than the motion of climbing down from a coach. As Lizzy's feet touched the ground, her hand fluttered slightly but then relaxed in Mr Darcy's, as if she had tried to pull her hand away and been resisted. It was only a moment, and then Mr Darcy released Lizzy's hand, the two stepping awkwardly apart. But Mary had seen it.

So, too, had Miss Bingley. Though Miss Bingley had been standing with primly correct posture on the steps of Netherfield, now she drew one hand weakly to her forehead and hobbled down the remaining steps emitting a faint "Oh, dear."

"Is something the matter, Caroline?" Mr Bingley's brow wrinkled with concern.

"I fear I am not at all well." Miss Bingley's voice was breathless. "I am so sorry! We shall have to postpone our excursion. Mr Darcy, will you assist me into the house?"

Though Mr Darcy was prompt in joining Miss Bingley at the base of the steps, his glance at Lizzy showed his disinclination to leave.

"What a pity! Poor Miss Bingley, I am all compassion for you," Mama said. "I have such spasms myself—so many ladies are prone to them. But we shall do very well without you, you know. Mr Bingley will show us the forest whilst you rest. Jane particularly wants to see every bit of it." Mama's red cheeks might have hinted shame at her insistence, but Mary knew it was only the sharpness of the wind.

Miss Bingley threw a look of appeal at her brother. Mr Bingley's uncertain expression showed his inner conflict, but after a moment, he made a polite bow to Mama.

"I regret that we shall not have the pleasure of taking an excursion today, Mrs Bennet. I am sure my sister will feel better soon, and then we can proceed as planned." With a gentle but firm touch, he guided first Mama and then Jane back into the carriage. Mary glanced back at Miss Bingley, who leaned heavily on Mr Darcy's arm as they climbed the steps of Netherfield. Miss Bingley had lowered her voice, but Mary still caught whispers of her remarks: 'six in one carriage!' and 'crushed and vulgar both.' The red-haired gentleman fell in with the pair but spared a smile for Mary as they all went inside.

He remembers me. Mary felt her cheeks heat. She had had neither the time nor the presence of mind to smile back at him, but she felt her lips pulling into a smile now. *And he is a gentleman.* With his unkempt clothing, she had been afraid he might be a workman or servant with a gentleman's castoffs. *Not that we are not all equal in the eyes of the Lord—or rather, we are judged according to…something or other? Hearts?* Her thoughts felt oddly confused as she climbed back into the carriage. Something about the man's smile made her head muddled. *What a pity we were not introduced! We would have been, if Miss Bingley had not been so spiteful in preventing the excursion.*

"What a spiteful woman! Anyone could see she was not ill at all," Kitty said, as the carriage door was shut. And though not a moment before, Mary's thoughts had been just the same, she sniffed and shook her head in sententious disapproval.

"You ought not say that, Kitty."

Mama threw up her hands—a dangerous manoeuvre when there were so many ladies crammed into one carriage. "And to think, she did not even ask us in for tea after we drove all this way! I cannot say I like her manners. I daresay Kitty is right; she is spiteful, indeed." Viewing Mary's nose wrinkle in distaste, Mama tossed her head, another risky venture in the crowded coach. "We are all disappointed, Mary. Do not argue with your sister when we are in such chaos."

"I am not in chaos, Mama." Mary thought her own serenity godly and magnificent.

"Yes, what does Mary have to be disappointed about? She hates tramping about in the woods," Lydia said. The wide muslin bonnet on Lydia's head now blocked the view again, so only the scrambling sound of gravel under wheels and the bumping of the carriage told Mary they were headed home.

"It is not that I have no disappointments, Lydia," Mary said, trying to keep the sharpness from her tone. "I merely regulate my feelings so that I am not in chaos. I might have asked Mr Bingley and Mr Darcy for donations if we had been able to go on our excursion." She lifted the subscription book as if to illustrate.

"Oh, the Old Ladies Society." Lydia's scornful tone suited her smirk.

"The Meryton Widows and Orphans Society."

Lydia remained unimpressed. "Meryton cannot have more than, say, three widows. Two who are fine and fat, and only one who has any need at Christmas—that dreadful Mrs Cranby. And I believe the vicar has already provided very well for her."

"And the only orphans are the Roberts' children," Kitty said, eager to second Lydia, "who have gone to live with their aunt, the one who runs a dairy. Last I heard, they were eating so much butter they were making themselves ill."

"It was a sign of grief, Kitty."

"Either way, I do not see why I should give them my pocket money. You only want a charity to harp on and groan about." She and Lydia giggled.

Mary folded her arms, a difficult task with her sisters pressed against her on either side. "You admit Mrs Cranby is a poor widow. You both are simply weak in Christian spirit. Those of us who are strong in spirit—"

An annoyed expression flitted over Lizzy's face, and she joined the discussion with a dry tone. "Mrs Cranby is, I believe, always in strong spirits—gin, mostly."

"Only you would make sport of a widow, Lizzy." Mary's indignation was keen.

"A poor joke, I admit, but I must say I do not like Mrs Cranby's tastes in recreation, and I do not care to finance them." Lizzy turned to her own window, frowning. The worried lines in her brow showed some other disappointment than wasteful charity and carping sisters. Mary wondered if Lizzy was thinking of Mr Darcy's hand pressing hers, or Miss Bingley's arm clinging to Mr Darcy's. *Is she so susceptible? I thought she did not even like Mr Darcy.*

"You see? Not even Lizzy will countenance your horrible widow," Lydia said.

"She is not horrible."

The squabble might have continued had Jane not intervened to redirect the conversation. "Have you any idea who that other gentleman was, Mama?"

"What gentleman? I should think you had eyes for no one but Mr Bingley, dear Jane," Mama simpered.

Lydia leaned back, her bonnet smashing against the window as if she wanted to erase the view altogether. "She means the ugly fellow standing near Miss Bingley."

"Ugly?" Mary's confusion provoked her sister, though Lydia misunderstood the reason for it.

"Oh, do not preach at me for calling someone ugly. If he is ugly, then he is ugly, and it would be a lie to say otherwise, would it not?" Lydia nodded at her own logic.

But this time, at least, Mary was not trying to criticise their speech. *Is he ugly?* She supposed the over-sized ears, chalky skin, and bulbous nose must count as ugly, but she had never seen them that way. The man's smile had lit up all the world, and she had been too dazzled to make out individual features. *Well, if he is ugly, he is still pleasant to look at, somehow.*

The others debated the possible identity of the newcomer, and the debate degenerated into dispute as the carriage veered in unsteady progress to Longbourn. Though Jane entreated them to make peace and Lizzy sat in abstracted silence, the other ladies poured forth speculation in contradiction to each other. Mary surprised herself with her declarations in favour of the young man when Kitty asserted he most likely was a ne'er-do-well cousin or a pitiable hanger-on.

"I am sure he is a worthy young man," Mary said, though she privately admitted she had little evidence to support the idea. When Lydia and Kitty grew even more outlandish in their supposed explanations for the man's presence at Netherfield, Mary felt overheated enough to change the subject and so appealed to Lizzy to aid her cause. "Lizzy, will you ask Mr Darcy to donate to my society? He seems to like you."

"He certainly does not." Lizzy's blush might have passed for indignation with the others, but Mary remembered the way Lizzy's hand had rested in his.

She is lying. She must know he feels something for her. Mary's lips twisted as if she tasted something sour. *Lying, to her sisters! How far Lizzy has fallen already, all for a trifling hint of romance.* Mary had hoped Lizzy's cheerful wit might aid in cajoling the inhabitants of Netherfield for money for the Meryton Widows and Orphans Society, but it seemed flirtation had diverted Lizzy from the path of usefulness and charity. *Thank goodness I am not angling for a gentleman, nor am I susceptible to any man's charms.* A flash of unease went through her. She had felt uncommonly interested in defending this newcomer to Meryton. *But that is not romance. It is Christian benevolence to think the best of others. I am immune to the silly romance Lizzy seems to be contemplating.* What would become of her life's work—for she had determined her Society would no doubt burgeon into an impressive life's work—if Mary were so easily entranced? Her resolve strengthened. *I shall never fall into such a foolish flirtation.* Her fingers stroked the subscription book on her lap, its pages an unambiguous symbol of purity—clean, white, and completely empty of subscribers.

chapter THREE

"...AND SO, WILL YOU GIVE TO SAVE THE WIDOWS AND orphans?" Mary completed her well-rehearsed speech to Mrs Burnell, who had smiled a welcome when she first encountered Mary on the high street and now wore the pained expression of patience stretched thin. *Was it too long an explanation? But surely people will want to know exactly why giving at Christmas is so important.* Mary forced a smile, hoping it looked as welcoming as Mrs Burnell's once had.

"I am afraid I am rather in a hurry right now," Mrs Burnell said, stepping around Mary to enter the millinery. As Lydia spotted yet another potential giver escaping Mary's clutches, she grinned at Mary through the millinery window and then went back to debating ribbons with Kitty. Lydia and Kitty were snug enough within the shop, gossiping and choosing presents for sisters, parents, and very likely themselves, while Mary stood in the frigid air, her breath puffing into a mist that slowly faded away in the afternoon sunlight.

I shall not *go inside,* Mary said firmly to her feet, bidding them to stay still. In truth, she could have approached people she knew inside the millinery almost as well as outside, but she did not want to miss even one person passing by who might contribute. And the additional martyrdom of chapped lips, wind-stung cheeks, and frozen toes made Mary's chest swell with pride. Mr Weathering would be impressed with her devotion to duty, no doubt. Others, as well. A small physical pain was often the fate of those who chose duty.

Mary could remember the one occasion her mother had actually made much of her, five years ago. A maid had slapped Mary for lecturing her about dangling for men, and Mama was shocked and grieved at poor Mary's suffering. She fussed over her for once, though Papa thought the *contretemps* more amusing than not. The mark left by that slap was Mary's own personal stigmata, physical proof she was marked as one of those seeking holiness, a beacon of virtue in a fallen world. Mary's ceremonious forgiveness of the maid had been equally satisfying, though her sisters seemed to have too much sympathy for the maid and not enough for their sister. "To be sure, we should all like to slap Mary," Lydia had said. She had only been ten at the time, but Mary felt it indicative of the woman she would become. Lydia's making faces at her through the window of the shop did nothing to dispel the memory.

Mary tried to refocus on her task.

"Mr Walcott, a word—"

"You have already asked me, Miss Bennet." Mr Walcott strode by with a brisk air that would have detained a less dutiful young lady, but Mary neatly stepped close enough to make passing farther rude.

"You said that you would consider a donation. Christmas is but two weeks away! In order to provide the generous aid so due to our Meryton widows and orphans, a timely donation is of the essence." She edged farther in front of him, making a dash forward impracticable for him.

"I, um, shall think on it quickly, then." He muttered an excuse that a passing cart's rumble made unintelligible, and, when Mary was distracted with the scent of roasted nuts emanating from the cart, Mr Walcott retreated back the way he had come.

That blasted cart. Mary forgave herself the unchristian thought. The street merchant had wound his way back and forth down the streets of Meryton all afternoon, wafting mouth-watering scents and drowning conversation in squeaking wheels. Mary's stomach grumbled as if to second her dismay. *I am not going to waste money on treats when I can give it to my Society,* she told it. It was simply another admirable sacrifice for her cause, though one that shook her composure more than stiff fingers and chilled breath.

The people of Meryton clearly needed an example of forbearing compassion in order to bring their cold hearts to life. She had not garnered much in coins for the purse or many promises in her subscription book, but perhaps that would change as people saw that Mary's determination did not fail her through the cold. Mary retraced her steps to her spot outside the millinery and readied for another assault, gazing on the passersby with a gimlet eye. The milliner, pausing in the window to adjust the display, frowned at the barrier now raised in front of her shop before responding to Kitty's beckoning.

A stab of guilt went through Mary. It was true that people did seem to be avoiding the millinery now that she had been stationed outside it for a few afternoons. *But Kitty and Lydia will not stand out here with me, and I cannot be altogether alone.* Their compromise was that Mary stood on one side of the window while her sisters shopped on the other, but they had not accounted for the milliner's own ideas of what was appropriate. Mary had a feeling the milliner would not allow her many more afternoons of canvassing here.

All the more reason to make today count. Mary squared her shoulders and stared down the street, hoping for a better prospect. A lanky figure ambled towards her, a shock of red hair poking out from under his beaver hat. Mary's face flushed in self-consciousness. *Him again.* They had not been introduced, so she could not speak to him, but she watched him while pretending to cast her gaze over red-brick walls and grimy lampposts.

"Miss Bennet!" The man stopped in front of Mary, his face lighting up as if seeing her were some sort of unexpected treat.

Mary did not know what to do. She did not wish to be rude, but she could hardly disobey the proprieties and respond. She settled on a slight jerk of the chin and turned away.

"Miss Bennet, do you remember me?" The fellow persisted, his long legs easily planting himself in front of her. Mary felt as outmanoeuvred as Mr Walcott must have done earlier. "I saw you first in the church—that is how I learned your name—and then we met at Netherfield, when we were supposed to pick greenery." He had a rolling Scottish accent, light but unmistakable.

"We did *not* meet at Netherfield." Her desire to correct him overcame her disinclination to speak. "We have not met at all, for no one has introduced us."

The blue eyes blinked in surprise. "Oh, I suppose we did not receive a formal introduction, exactly. But Bingley was on the brink of it, only you had to go away." His friendliness had such enthusiasm to it that, although Mary was well aware a gentleman ought to know better than to press in this way, she found herself smiling. "I am Arthur."

Her smile disappeared. "Arthur?"

Her flat tone must have shown she once again disapproved, for Arthur scratched at his temple. "That is to say, you can *call* me Arthur," he said weakly.

"I certainly cannot. A lady call a gentleman by his Christian name!" Her lips pursed, and he hurried to correct her.

"No, it is not my Christian name. I go by 'Arthur' these days." His cheeks were already ruddy from the cold, but now redness spread more thoroughly over his face. "Ask Bingley or Darcy. They call me Arthur. They like it."

"*Mister* Arthur, since we have not been introduced, it can matter nothing to me what anyone calls you." Mary started to turn away again, but Arthur took a step towards her, apparently casting about for a way to keep her attention.

"You are canvassing for the Meryton Widows and Orphans Society, are you not?"

It was the first time anyone besides Mary had given it the correct name. She hesitated.

"I would be very pleased to make a donation," Arthur said, folding his hands in a gentlemanlike way. "Will you write me down for fifty pounds?"

Mary's mouth dropped open. *Fifty pounds!* She had hoped for such munificence from Mr Bingley or Mr Darcy but had hardly expected it. And now a stranger wished to give her all that! *It is too good to be true.* Still, if Mr Arthur intended to aid her society, she could hardly insist on distance until they received a formal introduction. She permitted herself to smile at him now, and though she assured herself the warmth in it was only for the good of the Society, she could not help her breath catching at the light in the gentleman's eyes. "How very generous, Mr Arthur! The widows and orphans of Meryton have found a protector, indeed."

"I am glad it pleases you." Again, the squealing cart passed by, forcing a pause into their conversation, but this time the interruption became a source of pleasure rather than of trepidation. Mr Arthur raised his voice and asked, "Shall I buy us some roasted nuts to celebrate, Miss Bennet?"

Mary's stomach rumbled in appreciation of the idea. It was hardly proper etiquette to accept treats from a gentleman to whom one had not been properly introduced, but Mary decided a fifty-pound donation had its perquisites. "I would like that very much. Thank you."

Mr Arthur hailed the cart, which ceased its squealing to rest heavily on the road outside the millinery. "Two bags, please," Arthur said, and the street merchant handed one bag to Mary. Mary popped a toasted nut into her mouth. The heat and salt danced in heavenly bliss on her tongue, and she took another bite before Arthur even had his own bag in his hand.

"Is it good?" Arthur watched Mary's enjoyment with a satisfaction that said he knew it was. He accepted a bag from the cart and tried them himself.

"Very," Mary chuckled, but the street merchant interrupted with a curt demand for his money.

"Oh, yes. I beg your pardon." Arthur dug into his coat pocket and fished out a net purse. His face fell.

Mary glanced down at the purse. "What is it?"

Arthur flushed. "Um, there is a hole in my purse. I fear the coins have slipped out and are nowhere to be found."

"And what about my money, then?" The nut-seller pounded a fist on the surface of his cart, thumping loudly enough to make even the customers within the millinery jump. His eyes narrowed at Mary, clearly suspecting a similar trick from her.

Mary's cold fingers extracted some coins from her reticule. "I suppose I shall have to pay for them." Her tone was cool and haughty. She paid off the man and then turned away from Arthur to dismiss him.

"I say, I am exceedingly sorry, Miss Bennet. I shall pay you back."

Her sarcasm created no illusions about her thoughts. "I am sure you shall. Thank you so much for your generosity, *Mr* Arthur." *Fifty pounds! I am a fool, to have believed that. Why would such a man be invited to Netherfield? He must be taking advantage of Mr Bingley's good nature.* She marched into the millinery to evade his spluttered apologies, and though he gazed through the window at her with a mournful look, she made a point of turning away so as not to meet his gaze. The warmth of the toasted nuts made a pleasant sensation in her middle, but Mary refused to take another bite even as the scent wafted through the millinery.

"Can I have some, Mary?" Kitty asked. Mary thrust the bag at her, hoping Mr Arthur saw her disdain for his gift, but when she peeked back at the window, he had gone.

So much the better. I do not care for people who make pretences about their means in order to impress others. How prideful! She sat down on one of the milliner's benches, grateful for a reprieve from the wind and cold. The milliner's relieved look said she, too, was grateful Mary was having a respite, and she peered out at the street as if to hasten customers in while the shopfront was unguarded.

"These are lovely! Thank you, Mary." Kitty grinned as she dug into the bag again, and Mary felt a momentary pang at the loss of her treat. *I suppose I ought not to be too hard on Mr Arthur. He does have such a nice smile. Perhaps he did not mean any harm.* But as Lydia and Kitty giggled over a lieutenant striding past the window, Mary felt vexed at their delight, and she remembered Lizzy's blushes over Mr Darcy. Why did ladies become so foolish over gentlemen? *I must not let his smile dazzle me. The fact remains that he is impecunious and would not admit it.* Nodding to herself, she tried to disregard the scent of the salted nuts still hanging in the air, and the 'nice smile' of Mr Arthur.

chapter FOUR

THE DRAWING ROOM AT NETHERFIELD WAS SPACIOUS enough to host quite a large party for tea the following evening. Sir William, Lady Lucas, and Charlotte Lucas had been invited to dinner, while the Bennets had been asked to join them for tea afterwards. While Charlotte and Lizzy gossiped together in a nook of blue wainscoting and japanned tables, Mr Hurst huddled by the fire, dozing after the heavy meal despite his wife's attempts to rouse him. Sir William trod back and forth over the blue fitted carpet as if pacing to keep warm, but it was only his way: eager to engage in every conversation, restless in his movements. The drawing room fire roared with a cheerful blaze, warming even those on the other side of Mr Hurst's bulk splayed in a wingback chair.

Mary had hoped for an opportunity to play the pianoforte, but the order of the day appeared to be mere chit-chat and tea drinking. Miss Bingley, whatever her other failings, treated her guests with great generosity: the tea was strong and hot, an array of gingerbread scented the air with spice and tempted the palate, and the fire was stirred up to make the whole room cosy and bright. Mary accepted a cup of tea and listened to the conversations swirling around her. Miss Bingley related her opinion of the latest novel, Mama nodding vehement agreement despite having never read it. Mr Darcy and Mr Bingley discussed the relative rents around Meryton, and Kitty informed Mrs Hurst of all the militia officers' names, ranks, and relative skills in dancing.

Though she had tried to fool herself into thinking otherwise, Mary had to admit she had hoped to see Mr Arthur at Netherfield—if only for the purpose of lecturing him to improve his behaviour, of course. He had been at the dinner, but he had been out of the way when the

Bennets had arrived, and now Mary searched for him in vain. They had still not been formally introduced. Mary found herself craning her neck out the drawing room doorway and was only called back to propriety when Sir William, still roaming the room, approached her.

"A very pleasant evening, is it not, Miss Mary?"

"Very pleasant, Sir William. I had hoped to have some music rather than mere idle conversation, however. Perhaps we could persuade the others, and I could play for you all."

Sir William's smile slipped for a moment. "But, uh, conversation has its own joys, has it not?" The smile suddenly returned. "I am most delighted to have an opportunity to discuss all the latest events with you."

"Indeed?" Mary's eyes lit up. "I have grave news of Meryton to relate, Sir William. It is about Christmas, and the worthy widows and orphans who cannot celebrate it as we might hope…" She had learned to shorten her speech, and whether it was due to her greater circumspection or Sir William's pure generosity, he readily agreed to subscribe for five pounds. Mary wrote his name down with a flourish, and they beamed on each other with equal satisfaction.

"Capital! Capital! Mr Bingley, you must hear what our kind-hearted Miss Mary Bennet has been doing." Sir William called over Mr Bingley and made much of Mary's charity, and Mr Bingley nodded and made noises of agreement.

Finally! Someone recognises the importance of my work. Mary lowered her head, closing her eyes in what she hoped looked like humble appreciation. When Mr Bingley spoke over her shoulder to someone behind her, however, her head jerked up and her eyes opened wide.

"Arthur, where on earth have you been?" Mr Bingley's voice held its usual good humour, even when he tried to scold. "Darcy thought you had been kidnapped by the elves."

Mr Arthur stepped into the drawing room, Mary moving aside to let him by. Her eyes glued to him, she could not help feeling a thrill of satisfaction that he must have overheard her being praised for her Society.

"I cannot imagine Darcy saying anything at all like that," Mr Arthur said, wryness twisting his lips. "Will you not introduce us, Bingley? Miss Mary seems to put a high value on the proprieties." His eyes were like the ocean, an ever-changing blue—melancholy and stormy only yesterday, now merry and sparkling like waves in the sunlight. Mary dipped a curtsey as he bowed.

"Miss Mary, this is my old schoolfriend." Mr Bingley's expression wavered, as if he were suppressing amusement. "We call him Arthur, Darcy and I. Arthur, this is Miss Mary Bennet."

"And now the introduction is complete, and you must be satisfied," Mr Arthur said, brushing back the red hair that had fallen into his eyes. His clothes appeared in the best repair Mary had seen so far. Indeed, only one dark stain mottled the waistcoat, and there were no tears or loose seams at all. *Apparently he makes more of an effort for dinner. Perhaps Mr Bingley's valet accosted him and forced him into looking presentable.*

"I cannot be satisfied with so meagre an introduction." Mary turned her enquiring expression on Mr Bingley. "You have said nothing of where he comes from. You did not even give a full name."

The corners of Mr Bingley's eyes creased, and she could see he had some joke he was enjoying. "That is all the introduction I am at liberty to make, Miss Mary. Now, shall I make a donation to your Society? Write me down for twenty pounds, please."

Though the sudden gift seemed intended to distract her, Mary could not pass up the change in subject. "Twenty pounds! That is so generous, Mr Bingley."

Sir William marked the occasion with more exclamations of 'Capital! Capital!' and resumed his pacing about the room, and Mr Arthur looked bemused by Mary's expressions of gratitude. Mr Bingley bore them with a bow and sidled off to sit with Jane as Mary wrote down his name.

"But Miss Mary, my name is not there." Mr Arthur's tone held reproach. He had leaned forward far enough to read the names in her subscription book.

Mary looked up, disconcerted. "I beg your pardon?"

"You did not write down my name, with fifty pounds. Do you not remember?" His brow fell in dismay, and Mary felt a strange stab of guilt at his disappointment.

Surely he is not serious. He does not have fifty pounds. Does he? "I…was not sure…"

He shrugged. "You are to be congratulated on your caution, Miss Mary. The poor of Meryton have an able defender in you. It is only right that you imagine a fifty-pound donation from a man such as me to be made in jest." He forced a chuckle, but as his gaze shied away from her, Mary thought she detected a flash of hurt. He strode off to be introduced to the other Bennets, and Mary watched him go, a feeling of shame blooming in her chest. Did Mr Arthur really have fifty pounds to give? She supposed if he had gone to school with Mr Bingley and now visited him, he must be a gentleman with *some* income. *Perhaps he really did just have a hole in his purse.* Heat flickered at her cheeks as she realised she must have misjudged him. *It is not my fault. Why does he look so untidy and poor if he is rich enough to donate* fifty pounds *to the Society? It is as if he is purposely confusing me.* The reasoning fell flat even in her own mind, and she hastily scribbled Mr Arthur and the amount in her subscription book. Whether he would in fact follow through with the sum or not, she supposed she had to give him the benefit of the doubt. It did make the little list look much more presentable. Perhaps such a large donation would inspire other visitors to Meryton. Mary remembered she had not yet asked Mr Darcy to give, but when she surveyed the room, she saw he had disappeared. The library was only a few steps away from the drawing room; probably he had gone to fetch the book Miss Bingley was raving over.

Mary settled on a sofa to await his arrival, but after a moment, she realised Lizzy was missing as well. *Did they both go to fetch the book?* It would not be proper to disappear with a gentleman, even only to the next room, but Mary wondered if the hot blushes Lizzy had suffered from were signs of a greater foolishness than Mary had guessed. Uneasy, Mary rose and slipped out into the hall.

The library door was wide open, and the bitter voices drifted out of it clearly. "You would have dragged Mr Bingley away to London, and what would have become of my dearest sister?" Even from the hall, Mary could see the scornful lift of Lizzy's eyebrows. "Thank heaven something put a spoke in your wheel."

"Something? Or someone?" Mr Darcy's voice was dark, dangerous. "Perhaps your desire to catch your sister a husband—"

"I did not break your carriage wheel, Mr Darcy. Though had I known the outcome, I might have been tempted to. As it was, I fully expected your influence to win out over Mr Bingley's inclinations. I am glad to be wrong." Lizzy folded her arms over her chest.

"You paint me as a bully, only focused on my own whims, rather than on Mr Bingley's good." Mr Darcy stepped closer to Lizzy, his height towering over her, but she showed no sign of intimidation.

"Why are you to be the judge of your friend's good? To force his choice *is* to bully."

"I am trying to choose better for him than I would for myself." His voice dropped lower, and Mary had to strain to hear it. "Temptation does much to a man. Do you wonder that I try to help him escape the longings I feel myself?" His hand reached out to caress Lizzy's cheek, and in a flash his lips had pressed hers.

Mary froze where she stood. *Oh, Lizzy!* Her first impulse was to call for help, but in a moment she saw that would only make matters worse —for Lizzy was *returning* the kiss, though she did break it off suddenly and step back in flustered dismay. "Mr Darcy!" Lizzy's breathless reproach made them avoid each other's gaze.

"I apologise."

Lizzy turned, and Mary realised she was intending to leave the library. *Finally doing what you ought to have done at once! How foolish, Lizzy.* Mary retreated to the drawing room, eager to relate what she had seen to her mother if she could get her alone, and heard Lizzy's quick steps behind her. As Mary resumed her seat, Arthur immediately joined her on the settee. Mary fleetingly noticed her own relief that he held no grudge against her before hurrying to take up her teacup and sip intently as if she had been seated there all evening instead of creeping about surreptitiously observing her sister. She spied Lizzy's face as her sister passed by, and what she saw made the cup tremble in her hand.

Though angry lines still marred Lizzy's brow, something in the curl of her lips showed a mix of wonder— and satisfaction. Mary blinked, studying her sister further, but there was no mistaking it. Though Lizzy claimed to hate Mr Darcy, and no doubt she felt annoyance at his effrontery, she was also cherishing their moment of wantonness. Mary gave her head a tiny shake as if to banish that most improper moment from her memory.

It is my duty to tell Mama what I saw. Mary was quite sure on that point, but perhaps she owed it to Lizzy to warn her beforehand, to give her a chance to prepare what she was going to say. If she crept into Lizzy's room tonight, she could say what she had seen. Catching sight of another glimpse of her sister's face, Mary found herself oddly sympathetic. *Perhaps Lizzy can explain it all away, and I need not tell Mama. No! Of course not. There is no way to 'explain away' anything so serious.* She tried to push the topic from her mind for the moment and focus on Lady Lucas's description of a new tippet. Next to her, Mr Arthur was leaning towards the lady, nodding with vigour, but Mary had the impression he had little understanding of the subject matter.

"Are you fond of tippets, Miss Mary?" Mr Arthur asked, when Lady Lucas had finished.

"Am I—I beg your pardon?" She had not expected so inane a question. "Um. I wear them sometimes. When it is cold." She realised she sounded just as witless herself. "I take pride in dressing respectably." She gave a pointed look at the stain on his waistcoat, and he reddened.

"I spilled something earlier."

"And the day before, and last week, I suppose."

His forehead wrinkled with annoyance. "Yes. I spill a great many things. I cannot help it."

"But your valet could help their remaining soiled."

He looked down at the stain doubtfully. "I suppose, if I had one."

The perplexed look suddenly shifted into a grin. "I used to have a valet, once, but I gave him the horrors, and he gave them to me as well. We horrified one another."

Mary found herself laughing. "I think I can understand that."

"He always looked so stern when I came home, like an old aunt who is very, very disappointed with what one has done with one's life and has nothing to do but look reproachful about it. So now I have no valet at all, and I am a great deal happier." He adjusted his cravat as if to show he did not need one, either.

"Happiness *is* more important than worldly appearances," Mary said. For once she did not like the sanctimonious sound of her own voice, and she stared into her teacup.

"That is what I think, as well. But too much of the world insists on the outward trappings, the pomp and show. It gets very tiresome. My mother says I need to behave with more ceremony, and I suppose there is truth in that, but I should like to be natural with people all the same." Only the lightest Scottish accent burnished his words; clearly his time in public schools had softened it.

"You mean talk to ladies without proper introduction, for example." Mary sipped her tea to hide her smile.

"Well, yes. Among other things." He took the barb in good humour. "You are glad to have met me, all the same, are you not?"

She realised she was. "Of course."

"Then perhaps my appearance will not give you the horrors, the way it did my valet." He leaned forward and dropped his voice. "Or Miss Bingley. She detests me."

"I am sure she does not."

"Watch her face when she looks at me, and you shall see I am quite right. It is not only that she winces at my untidiness. I spilt tea onto one of her gowns—a grave offence, I admit—and then I said the Earl of Gainsborough was a fool." He grimaced.

"That is not very polite, but why should Miss Bingley be so offended by it?"

"She said she was sure anyone with such a heritage could not be counted a fool and rattled off what his ancestors had done. I do not care what *they* did. He is a fool and no mistake." His brow furrowed. "You are not like that, are you, Miss Mary? Insisting rank or family makes a man good when he is nothing in himself?"

Mary drank her tea, considering. "Such an idea seems inconsistent with Christian principles, Mr Arthur. We are judged by our actions, or our hearts, by the One who is wisest of us all."

He gave a sharp nod. "I thought you would agree."

"Not that rank is meaningless." She tilted her head. "But I think it compels the bearers to more duties, not more excuses."

The frown on his lips showed he did not like this perspective. "Perhaps."

Their conversation wandered from descriptions of the places in Meryton Mr Arthur had not yet visited to fanciful sketches of Scotland where he had grown up, though he still mentioned no place name nor family name exact enough for Mary to place him anywhere precisely. The evasions ought to have made her suspicious, but she found her distrust ebbing away as they chatted. After half an hour, she realised she had been engaged in chatter no more weighty than that of the rest of the company—yet she had not minded. *Somehow, Mr Arthur is easy to talk to.* The recognition left her nonplussed, as if she had lost something by not insisting on religious topics or moral epigrams. *I must not let myself slip into a different kind of worldliness. Mr Weathering would be so disappointed for one of his flock to stray.* She tried to keep her serious state of mind even as the Bennets bid their hosts good-bye and clambered into the carriage. While the others gossiped on the way back to Longbourn, Mary resolved what to say to Lizzy.

That night, when Lizzy's bedroom door closed after Mary, she delivered her speech at once, fearing that she would lose her nerve if she delayed even a moment. Lizzy was already looking perplexed by the visit; she had let down her hair and removed her gown but had got no further before Mary begged entry. Mary imagined that had it been Kitty or Lydia, Lizzy would have expected an appeal for the loan of some item. Had it been Jane, she would have expected a sisterly chat. She evidently had no idea what to expect from Mary.

"Lizzy, I saw you with Mr Darcy in the library. I saw him kiss you, and I must tell Mama first thing in the morning."

Lizzy frowned and turned away to hang up her gown without answering.

"Do you hear, Lizzy? What you did was very wrong, and I must tell Mama." The silence encouraged Mary to indulge in a lecture. "The virtue of a lady is both beautiful and brittle, Lizzy. No woman dare risk it, and all must act to defend it. Your own conscience will give you sufficient warning of what may occur, if you but consult it—"

"It was, indeed, very foolish of me, Mary."

Lizzy's sudden capitulation took the momentum from Mary's speech, and she paused. "Y-yes. It was." She could not help relishing the moment a little. It was so rare for Lizzy to admit Mary had the upper hand in anything.

"I was caught up in the moment, but you need not fear that I shall do so again. Mr Darcy is—" Lizzy seemed at a loss to describe him. At length, she merely finished, "Mr Darcy is not for me."

Now that wrong had been assigned, Mary's curiosity welled up. "You always said you hated him, Lizzy. Why did you kiss him back?"

"Oh, I do not know." From the way Lizzy averted her face, Mary guessed she did know, at least a little. "I hated him partly because of what I thought he had done to Mr Wickham, but that has proved false, and—"

"What does that have to do with kissing him?"

Lizzy spread her hands, unable or unwilling to explain. "Suffice it to say that I can take care of myself, Mary. You need not worry for me."

Mary toyed with a stray ribbon on Lizzy's dressing table. "I must tell Mama. It is the right thing to do." She said the words as if hoping to be contradicted. She was beginning to like this change in Lizzy, a relaxation from prejudice, a willingness to treat Mary as—well, more as an equal than a meddling little sister.

"You must do what you think best." Lizzy's level gaze met Mary's, until Mary's dropped.

"I suppose, if you are sure you will be careful..." Mary flicked the ribbon, unsure what more to say.

"I shall be at least as careful as you are with your Scottish fellow," Lizzy said, with a hint of an impish smile.

"*My* Scottish fellow!" Mary let go of the ribbon, and it curled in on itself in lazy swirls.

"Well, if he is not yours, he makes enough calf's eyes at you to be so. It seems you have your own suitor to defend yourself against." Lizzy loosened her stays and prepared for bed. "Will you tell Mama about that, too? She is so intent on watching on Lydia and Jane, she noticed nothing of the matter."

"There is nothing to notice." Mary tried to return to her lecture, but she found she had lost the thread of it—and the spirit for it—entirely. "We shall both be careful, shall we not, Lizzy?"

"Indeed." Lizzy climbed into bed, throwing a look at Mary that dismissed her. Mary backed out of the room, shutting the door behind her, and crept back to her own. Though she left her sister on the other side of Longbourn, the vision of Lizzy and Mr Darcy kissing stuck in her mind. There must be something truly tantalising about romance to make Lizzy so foolish as to kiss and not tell. Perhaps Mary ought to report her sister's indiscretion—yet she could not bring herself to do so.

My Scottish fellow? Ridiculous.

But her dreams that night made it seem quite natural.

chapter FIVE

THE EXPEDITION TO THE FOREST GROUNDS OF NETHERFIELD to pick greenery had been postponed to a bright Wednesday afternoon, the December sky mottled like an ill-powdered lady. Though Kitty and Lydia dallied on the Netherfield lawn to make snowballs from the patchy snow and the Hursts continued to huddle by the fireside, the others dispersed into the forest to gather plants suitable for Christmas decorations. A few hundred yards into the forest, the shouts and laughs of Kitty and Lydia dwindled, and the spiky scent of pine suffused the air. Not much of the snow had filtered through the treetops, so the branches and dried grass crackled under Mary's feet, occasionally snapping with enough fervour to startle her and make her freeze where she stood.

Bah! Mary clutched the tiny knife Mr Bingley had lent her and wished she could plunge it into the metaphorical heart of the forest. She admitted that Christmas greenery looked very cheery near a hearth, but she saw no reason why she should be entangled in the business of collecting. While Jane rhapsodised about the beauties of nature to Mr Bingley and Lizzy strode the wood paths with confidence, Mary hung back, eyeing the dead vines stringing the gaps in the trees with distaste and trying not to step on anything too noisy.

"This is most unpleasant," Mary said, though she did not think anyone was close enough to hear her now. It did not hurt to announce her martyrdom now and then; people were so likely to forget how much she suffered. Mary looked about and noticed a holly tree that Jane and Mr Bingley had already picked over thoroughly. Perhaps she could still scavenge some of the leaves. But that would hardly demonstrate her commitment.

She chose instead a pine bough. The sap would make her gloves sticky, but so much the better for displaying her martyrdom and her gentle Christian sufferance for the enjoyment of others. Mary worked at the bough with the knife, but even prolonged sawing only made a shallow mark in the wood. Mary tried twisting the branch, heaving her weight on it, but that did not produce much more of a break. *Earth does not want to cooperate with the festivities of heaven. I always knew these greenery traditions were not Christian.*

"Here, Miss Mary, let me." The Scots accent told her who it was, even if the gangly shadow looming over her from behind did not. Mr Arthur crossed to the pine branch and used his own knife on it. "I do not think we need one so thick, but seeing as you have already hurt the tree a little—"

"Hurt the tree! It has hurt me." Mary nursed her finger, just visible through her torn glove.

"Well, you ought not to have chosen this branch. It will be too thick to bend into a wreath, in any case." His matter-of-fact tone disarmed Mary, and she watched him work in thoughtful silence. "We can use it at the church, perhaps, if the Bingleys cannot make room for it here."

"That is a good idea." She was grateful to him for making it possible to use her ill-chosen branch. *So much for my martyrdom. I appear only to have caused trouble.*

"I like your Mr Weathering. Even though I am new to the area, he has invited me to help decorate the church for Christmas." He spoke as he cut, his voice carrying easily over the rough burr of his knife on wood. In the distance, occasional cracks and pops signalled others of their group moving through the forest, but Mary could not make out their conversation. "He speaks very highly of you, you know."

Praise from Mr Weathering was usually Mary's delight, but she found herself strangely embarrassed. "He is a good friend of mine. It is not surprising that he should speak of me kindly." The words tasted odd on her lips. It was exactly the sort of thing she would have said to try to sound humble, but now she found she meant it in real humility.

"Well, I believe him." His head remained bent to his task, but Mary sensed it was more an effort to avoid her gaze than to saw more evenly. "I have seen you about, sometimes, and you seem just as he says. I saw you the other day in Meryton, helping that little girl."

"What little girl?"

"I do not know her. A little girl had been teased by her brother and was crying, and you stopped and wiped her tears and comforted her." He paused long enough to throw a look back at her, one that seemed intent, but she could not read the feeling in it.

"Oh, Sally. Yes." She had forgotten. In a family of five sisters, there were always tears that needed to be wiped away. Mary had grown accustomed to doing so, and it did not seem remarkable to her to practise it on other little girls.

"It was kind of you, Miss Mary."

"I suppose." It was not the sort of thing Mary took pride in; that sort of impulse was too well-practised to feel remarkable or saintly.

"I have two sisters, myself, both younger. I do not think I ever dried their tears, though—I was more likely to cause them!" He chuckled and shook his head, as if the memory both pained and soothed him.

"What are they like?"

He spoke of their playful Scottish childhood games and of their eagerness for gowns and anything English as they grew older. Mary listened, feeling the strain in her shoulders loosen as he talked. She forgot about the sap sticking the fingers of her gloves together, the dead brush pushing awkwardly at the soles of her feet through her soft boots, the chill of the air. She entirely forgot she was in a forest and fell into comfortable conversation with Mr Arthur, exchanging stories and venting opinions with a naturalness that surprised her.

He had just finished describing his sister Hattie's enthusiasm for dogs and watercolours when he posed Mary a question. "And what do you like?"

"What do I like?" She hesitated. "I go to church, and I help with household matters, and sometimes Kitty and Lydia like for me to—"

"No, I mean what do you *like?* What do you do for enjoyment, for no reason other than enjoyment?" He had finished sawing now and broke off the remainder of the branch with an ease that Mary envied.

"I...do not know." It was a strange admission, one that made Mary uncomfortable. It was not that she had no enjoyment in life; it was that all her pleasures were those of pride. She brought charity baskets to people in Meryton; that was enjoyable, but mostly for the feeling of superiority that her generosity created in her heart. She played the pianoforte, but that was more for the pleasure of hearing herself praised, not because she liked the music. She helped Mr Weathering with the church and did so out of a feeling of love for the old man, but she could not deny her sensation of pious self-righteousness threading through it. *Why, there is almost nothing I like for its own sake, nothing I would do without the desire to satisfy my pride.* She bit her lip, thinking, trying to reassure herself. *It simply means I am intent on living a pious life. A little excess pride is natural enough in such a case. I would not want to be any less devoted to piety.* Betraying her devotion to piety would be like betraying her friend the vicar, and she did not want to do that.

"Well, you will have a great deal of fun finding out. Hattie tried ever so many hobbies until she found what she liked." Mr Arthur took Mary's confession in stride, despite the sidelong look he gave her. He stepped back from the pine tree, adjusting the branch he had cut, and then he stepped back again so that he stood side by side with Mary. His hand swept upward. "Do you see that?"

She looked up. A small plant grew entangled with the branches arching over them from the tree behind. Mary could not make it out clearly through the fog on her glasses, but it seemed a mass of feathery leaves and white berries. "What is it?"

"It is mistletoe."

Mary stood there, staring blankly up at the tangle of vegetation. "Oh."

Mr Arthur reached for her, his hand wrenching her face towards him in a gesture that would have inspired Lizzy to make sly jokes about broken necks. But Mary's consciousness was taken up by the warmth of his hand through his glove as he turned her head. Unsteadily, his lips touched hers, and though for a moment Mary thought her feeling of falling must come from an imminent swoon, she soon realised Mr Arthur's oversized feet were slipping on the snow and ice and tilting them both dangerously far over. He regained his balance and caught her to him to steady her, and though Mary supposed they must look ridiculous to any onlooker, she could not help but feel his recovery of her—despite his making it necessary in the first place—thrillingly heroic. When he released her, she swayed, confusion welling up within her, her cheeks heating.

"There! You are pink as a daffodil now." Mr Arthur smiled down on her.

"I—you—" Mary spluttered, flailing about for composure. She stepped back from him, stumbling on the churned-up snow of the forest floor. "How dare you! You have insulted me! You have imposed yourself upon me when I was alone and defenceless."

The happy look on his face drained away. "I thought…" He began again, slowly, as if he knew what he said might offend her. "I told you it was mistletoe, and you did not move. You know the tradition?"

"A heathen tradition, for scullery maids!" Mary's hands balled into fists as she realised he was right—she *had* stood there, woodenly, after he said it was mistletoe. "I was not waiting to be kissed! It never occurred to me that you might kiss me, that anyone might—with no one about—alone and defenceless—" She was not terribly coherent and was becoming less so. "I was merely looking at it." The words sounded like an excuse, and she could not explain how true they were. Why should Mary think of kisses under the mistletoe as having anything to do with her? All of Meryton knew her for her strict propriety and her piety. None would dare to suggest a kiss even in jest, not even when others were doing it. But Mr Arthur could not have known that. "You have compromised me, Mr Arthur!"

"Nothing will compromise you so much as shouting about it," he said, testiness entering his voice.

"What if someone had seen you kiss me? Anyone could have passed by!"

"A moment ago you were angry because I kissed you when you were 'alone and defenceless'."

"Well, either way, it is horrible!" Her hands pulled at her skirts, as if she were grasping at straws. "And to make facetious remarks about it—"

"I have said nothing facetious." There was a stubbornness to his voice now, and, although this new side of Mr Arthur fascinated her, she could not let it distract her. "I have been as respectful as I could be, given…" His chin trembled, but soon his jaw hardened in resolve. "I did not mean to offend you by kissing you. Now that I know you do not like it, you need fear nothing from me."

"But I—" She could hardly admit now that she did like it, not when she was upbraiding him for his discourtesy. But it pained her to leave him thinking that she found something amiss with the moment itself. *It is only that it is not proper. Why can he not see that?* "I must go back."

"If you wish." He moved to accompany her, and she glared at him.

"You cannot think of walking with me!" Mary gestured at dead leaves tumbling in the wind, scattering over the worn path through the Netherfield forest. "There is a path. I shall be perfectly safe returning to Netherfield."

"I walked behind you on your way in, and you certainly did not keep to the path," he said sourly. "Indeed, it is so overgrown, I do not think anyone could keep to it wholly. I shall walk with you until Netherfield is in sight, at least."

Mary huffed, unwilling to lower herself to engage in an argument she sensed she would not win. With a prim delicacy, she loosened her tight grip on her skirts and gently raised them instead, stepping over dried brambles and trying to skim gracefully between the tangles of brush. She remained in haughty silence for several minutes, until her frustration spilled out again.

"You should not have done what you did."

"I gathered that much." Mr Arthur's tone was rueful, but when Mary peeked at him, his expression looked suitably chastened.

She walked in silence a few minutes more, digesting his submission yet feeling dissatisfied. "And daffodils are not pink."

"Not pink?" His wide blue eyes gazed at her fully now, though he had averted his glance often enough before.

"Certainly not. They are yellow or white."

He rubbed the side of his face. "I am sure I have seen some pink ones. At Easter. Big, goblet-looking things."

She pursed her lips. "You are thinking of tulips, I believe." Seeing he meant to continue the conversation, she remembered she was supposed to be righteously indignant. "It does not matter what sort of flower you liken me to in pretty compliments, for your behaviour belies it all."

"I rather thought my behaviour emphasised how pretty I think you." Mr Arthur was smiling now, as if he sensed some weakening of Mary's anger.

But I have not weakened! I am just as angry as ever. I am. If it was not true, she had to *make* it true. Mary could not risk losing her reputation, and Mr Arthur's attentions had done more to upset and unbalance her than anyone or anything she knew. When they stood at the edge of the forest and Netherfield's stone façade glinted in the afternoon sun through the treeline, Mr Arthur gave a formal bow and paused, showing he meant to keep his word and let her proceed from there alone. Mary strode forward with as much hauteur as she could muster and did not look back.

But though her actions suggested she had erased the entire event from her mind, inwardly her thoughts tumbled in a thousand directions. She wondered if anyone could have seen them, if anyone at Longbourn guessed Mary had had her first kiss, if Mr Arthur thought much about the matter or if he had moved on to tease someone less prickly. And while Mary shoved mistletoe from her thoughts, flowers crept in, despite the December frigidity—a remembrance of a hothouse bouquet Mr Bingley had sent to Jane, tulips bowing over an Easter celebration, and a daffodil that remained intractably pink despite all her efforts at correction.

THE DRAWING ROOM AT LONGBOURN WAS OFTEN UNTIDY, but on the wintry morning after the expedition to the Netherfield woods, it was even more cluttered than usual. Lydia and Kitty had gone for an early walk to Meryton, and now their discarded mittens, scarves, and stockings dried by the fire while they gossiped upstairs over what they had seen. The sharp scent of woodsmoke mingled with that of wet wool, prickling Mary's nostrils as she sat with a book near the window. Lizzy, usually careful with her books, had somehow found each of the novels she picked up tedious in some way and left them in a tottering stack while she rested her chin on her hand and gazed into the crackling flames. Jane had had to abandon her mending in order to help Hill with some sudden household catastrophe—such disasters often following their mother's haphazard orders—and the whole drawing room bore the look of irresolution and incompletion.

Mary raised her eyes enough to watch Lizzy over the pages of her book. Since coming back from Netherfield yesterday, Mary had worried that one of her sisters might have seen Mr Arthur kiss her, but her fears gradually eased. If Kitty and Lydia had seen, they never would have been able to keep from teasing Mary about it for so long, and Lizzy seemed too wrapped up in daydreams and silent speculations for the subject of her thoughts to be Mary. *Mr Darcy is the more likely subject.* Jane was calm enough to appear inscrutable at most times, but when their eldest sister made no effort to speak alone to Mary, Mary felt reassured that Jane had not seen, either. Mr Darcy had been too intent on Lizzy to see anything even if he had been nearby, and likewise Mr Bingley, on Jane. That only left Miss Bingley.

I am sure Miss Bingley would disapprove if she had seen—who would not?—

but she is much too ladylike to gossip about it if she did. I think. Mary did not know her well, but Miss Bingley's elegance was undisputed, and she appeared the very model of an upright young lady. When the Bingleys first came to Meryton, Mary had hoped to win Miss Bingley's friendship, but so far Mary had not had a chance to impress her. Mary lacked fashion, to be sure. But she felt certain Miss Bingley would appreciate her piety and skill on the pianoforte if only that lady had the chance to witness them. Of course, if Miss Bingley had seen Mary and Mr Arthur under the mistletoe, those dreams were useless now. Miss Bingley would not want to associate with a loose young woman.

Mary found herself going over that moment over and over again, telling herself she was examining the memory for any sign someone might have been near—the snap of a twig or a flash of colour. Though she found none, her thoughts dwelt on the memory nevertheless. It gave her a thrill of pleasure to close her eyes and pretend she could feel the pressure of Mr Arthur's warm lips on her own. It felt so strange to have a source of enjoyment to recall at will, one that depended neither on pride nor approval. *I suppose Jane and Lizzy have all kinds of enjoyments like this, pleasures of the mind and such. Even Kitty and Lydia must have happy memories they dwell on.* But for Mary it felt new and enchanting. Just thinking of Mr Arthur made joy swell in her chest, even as she scolded herself for it. She knew she ought not to forget the impropriety of his behaviour, but somehow she found she had forgiven him without even wanting to. *Perhaps I am a better Christian than I thought. Forgiveness comes so naturally.* But the giddy feeling bubbling within warned her this forgiveness had another cause.

"Oh, girls! I have such news! Everyone must come and hear it at once." Mama often insisted the dull facts she collected at Mrs Long's were thrilling news, but as she bustled in from her trip to Meryton, her cheeks looked more flushed than the bitter wind could explain, and her eyes were wide with suppressed emotion. "Come at once!"

Mary listened to the distant stamping of Kitty and Lydia descending the stairs, and Jane soon appeared and obediently took up the mending. Lizzy shifted in her seat by the fireside, lifting her gaze to her mother but for once too listless to joke. When all the daughters had assembled, Mama spread her arms as if she were on the stage.

"Only think—a gentleman has been in disguise amongst us!" Mama's voice was breathless—no doubt largely from her hurry to get to Longbourn to deliver the news—but it added a hushed importance to her words nevertheless.

"In disguise!" Kitty's eyes grew as large as her mother's. "What do you mean?"

"It is Denny," Lydia said. "He is on the run for pig-stealing." She erupted into giggles, and Kitty joined her, but for once Mama had no patience for them.

"It is *not* Denny. There is a lord amongst us, girls! Hidden for his own purposes, and Mr Bingley and Mr Darcy in on the secret." Mama could wait no longer to build suspense and spilled her secret fully. "The man we have been taught to call Mr Arthur is no other than *Lord MacArthur* of Scotland!"

Mary's heart squeezed, and she froze in place, only to drop her head a moment after. *A lord? Impossible!*

"Imagine!" Jane's habitual calm was too great to let her eyes pop like Kitty's, but she did look surprised.

"He is truly a lord?" Lizzy finally stirred from ruminating on whatever deep thoughts were monopolising her attention. "His attire certainly hid him well. I do not think I ever saw him dressed in a gentlemanlike fashion."

"Someone had best have a ball, so that I can dance with him," Kitty said. "Imagine being able to say you danced with a lord!"

"We can do better than that." Lydia tossed her dark curls. "I shall make him a Christmas present. You can help me, Kitty."

"Perhaps I want to make a present for him myself!"

"Well, it will not be as nice as mine."

"You do not even know what to give him, I wager!"

Mary listened to their dispute with a growing despondency. Though her sisters had received the discovery with glee and interest, for Mary it brought only pain. *I shall never get near him, now.* Ladies all over Meryton would be seeking him out, eager to display their advantages of charm, beauty, or wealth. *And his kiss must truly have meant nothing.* No lord meant anything good by kissing a poor gentlewoman. The best she could hope for was that it was a thoughtless act of the moment. Indeed, Mr Arthur had kissed her in such a practised way, even catching her when they had both nearly fallen in that clumsy way. At least, he had seemed debonair to her. For a moment, Mary considered she might not be the best judge of such matters, but the remembrance of Mr Arthur's entrancing blue eyes drove doubt from her. Of course, he was a dashing gentleman, probably heedlessly kissing dozens of ladies who swooned at his feet. She could imagine Mr Darcy swooping Lizzy up if he ever took a tumble while kissing her, just as Mr Arthur had done with Mary. No, Mr Arthur must have acted on a whim, as lords and rich men from the North were wont to do. It doubtless meant nothing at all to him.

"But why did he hide his identity, Mama?" Lydia asked. "What is wrong with being Lord MacArthur?"

"Nothing at all, my love. Mrs Long says Mr Bingley thinks it a great joke that Lord MacArthur tries to hide his title when he comes into new company. Lord MacArthur wants to be known and admired for himself, not his rank, apparently, though why he thinks we should not give full credit to his good qualities without this disguise I do not know. Certainly I always sensed something noble in him, some greatness of character that could not be explained." Mama did not find it necessary to say why she had never come to mention such an intuition before. "You must finish trimming your new bonnet tonight, Lydia, for I intend to invite Lord MacArthur to our Longbourn festivities this week."

"Longbourn festivities?" Lizzy's dry tone showed she had finally been roused enough to participate in the conversation fully. "Do you mean our cutting up gold paper into stars, and the snap-dragon, and dusting our faces with flour from bullet pudding? That is not much for Christmas, for a lord."

"They are country activities, Miss Sauce, and it is exactly the sort of thing Lord MacArthur wishes to see in Meryton. Their Scottish games may be very different, you know."

"At least we know he will not complain if flour gets on his clothes." Kitty smothered her giggles.

"He is a very nice young man." Though Mary agreed about the unkemptness, she could not help speaking up to defend him, even as her spirits sank.

"A very nice young man!" Lydia scoffed at the faint praise. "He is a great deal better than that. He probably has more thousands a year than Mr Darcy."

"Not so much as that, Mrs Long says," Mama said. "These Scottish titles often do not have much by way of livelihood attached to them. But he is nearly as rich as Mr Bingley, and there is the title, you know. I am sure he will get over this youthful embarrassment of it, with a steady young wife to guide him."

"Well, I would help him be proud of it," Kitty said.

Lydia danced round her sister, deftly avoiding Lizzy's tottering stack of books. "What fun! Just when you think Meryton is going to be dull all winter. There may be lords all round us, for all we know. Lizzy, what should you think if Mr Darcy turned out to be a lord in disguise?"

"Mr Darcy is proud enough to be *ten* lords in disguise," Lizzy said, her smile wry. "The only surprise would be his willingness to let any advantage of his own go unacknowledged."

At that moment, Mr Darcy was announced, and the Bennets had the unusual pleasure of seeing Lizzy overcome with embarrassment. Papa emerged from his study to greet the visitor, and Mama wrung her hands and sat on the edge of her chair looking like a flustered pigeon perching next to the intimidating hawk of Mr Darcy. "Why, Mr Darcy, I was just telling my girls about your Lord MacArthur. What a funny joke he played on us all!"

"I confess I find no humour in it." Mr Darcy refused to sit, his long legs pacing irresolutely through the drawing room, slowing whenever he neared Lizzy's chair. "A foolish and unnecessary omission of the truth, and false pretences. I would not have acceded to it had not Bingley persuaded me."

"Mr Bingley seems to have greater powers of resistance and persuasion than we granted him," Lizzy said, her chin lifted in challenge, but Mr Darcy did not respond.

"Mr Darcy, you knew all the while? Did you know him at school?" Lydia leaned forward.

"Both Bingley and I did. He had a great many friends at school, but many of them turned out to be mere tuft-hunters. I suppose that is why he likes to pass as a mere gentleman of leisure, now that he is thinking of marriage."

"Marriage!" Mama's scream of delight needed no explanation. "A worthy goal, indeed."

Mr Darcy's frown suggested he disagreed with her sentiment, if not her statement. "His mother and sisters wish it. His family favours early marriages, and, as the only son, of course he prefers to secure an heir as soon as possible."

"Secure an heir? That is not a very romantic description of the purpose of marriage," Lizzy said.

"I imagine it is what is most required." Mr Darcy's tone was so haughty, Mary could almost forget that he had ever looked on her sister with the glow of attraction.

"Perhaps Lord MacArthur finds other purposes equally enthralling." Lizzy's eyes met his, and though her voice remained calm, something intense passed in her gaze. "He may desire a companion for his pursuits, or a helpmate in his tasks on his estate. Or perhaps—" her tone turned rueful—"he may even engage in the egregious folly of falling in love."

"It may be." The words seemed to come from Mr Darcy unwillingly, and he sat down next to Lizzy, almost in defeat. As they conversed, Lizzy's wit sparkled, turning Mr Darcy's remarks about end over end, and he seemed alternately provoked and charmed. Mary watched, wondering what was to come of it all.

Mr Darcy kissed her. Whether it meant nothing in the moment or not, Lizzy has the wit and beauty to attract him, perhaps even into marriage. Lizzy was captivating, whether she meant to be or not. Mr Darcy certainly felt the force of her charms. Though a marriage between the two would appear lowering for a Darcy of Derbyshire, it was nothing compared to how a lord—even a Scottish lord—would be lowering himself to think of wedding a Bennet. Particularly a Bennet not so witty nor so beautiful as Lizzy.

A Scottish peer would never think of meaning anything serious to a lady such as me, Mary thought. *His kiss was either a whim, or an intention to seduce.* Either way, the only sensible course of action was to avoid Lord MacArthur. Kitty and Lydia might delude themselves into thinking a lord would marry a Bennet, but Mary knew better.

When Mr Darcy had gone, Mama set out pen and ink in great state to write her invitation to Lord MacArthur. Though Mary was able to keep silent and maintain her seat near the window, she could not bear to go farther, anxious to hear what she could of her mother's chatter.

"I cannot invite him to Longbourn for Christmas Day, of course," Mama said, "since we shall be going to Netherfield for dinner that day in any case. And why lose a moment? We can easily have our games this week, a few days early."

"The Bingleys have invited us to Netherfield on Saturday, remember, Mama. There is to be a musical evening." Jane's gentle reminder made Mama smile upon her.

"I would never forget dear Mr Bingley, Jane. Very well, we shall invite him on Friday. That will just suit. Now, how shall I phrase it?" Mama pursed her lips in thought.

"You ought to let Mary write it," Lydia said, laughing. "He seems to like her well enough. Remember how he dragged that great pine bough all the way in from the woods, just because Mary chose it? And he had it hung in the passageway when it was clear it would not fit on the mantel."

Mary said nothing, though her heart beat hard at Lydia's words. She had avoided Lord MacArthur the rest of their visit at Netherfield and had not thought what had become of the branch he had cut off for her. *It only means he was trying to make amends, in his way. Politeness for his misstep.*

"Mary, write? I think not, Lydia. It will be most proper coming from my pen. We must do things as the nobility do now, you know." Mama bent over her page.

Except all that fuss was exactly what he was avoiding. Mary wondered that her mother could not see it, that Lord MacArthur would much rather be treated as an ordinary gentleman. But her mother's aptitude for taking hints was never very good. *At least the Christmas games will please him.* There was no way the Bennets would all remember the obligations of etiquette in the frolic of bullet pudding and snap-dragon. Mary hoped Lord MacArthur would enjoy himself, even as she resolved to have as little to do with him as she could. *I can watch him from afar and wish him well.* At least, so long as she felt sure he had meant no real harm to her, that it had only been an idle kiss. By behaving coolly to him, she would show him her dignity and keep herself from losing her head over his bright blue eyes and awkward grin. She would not let herself fall in love, and that meant she must hold him at bay.

The deep unfairness of it, though, stung her. Had her heart treasured the kiss less, she might have allowed herself to smile on the man more.

chapter SEVEN

THOUGH MARY HAD ASSURED HERSELF SHE COULD FACE Lord MacArthur with equanimity, when Friday came and he was stood on the Longbourn doorstep, Mary found the task harder than she had imagined. As Lord MacArthur hastened in from the chill wind buffeting the trees, his gaze sought Mary out and latched onto her, and she could not help flushing. She tried to make her curtsey stately and cold in response to his greeting.

"I cannot believe Bingley will be missing this," Lord MacArthur said, his grin spanning from ear to ill-shaped ear as he addressed Mrs Bennet. "Had he not your two daughters to amuse him, I think he would be running pell-mell to join us here." He broke into a laugh. "I am not so surprised Darcy will not be joining us, of course." Whether as an excuse to avoid any ungenteel merriment or simply by coincidence, Miss Bingley had fixed a card party for the same day as the Longbourn festivities. That Jane had chosen to go had been no surprise to anyone. That Lizzy was also for Netherfield…Well, Mama was shocked and claimed it unfilial, but Mary suspected Netherfield had its own attractions for Lizzy.

"I cannot imagine Mr Darcy playing bullet-pudding," Lydia said. "He is so stiff and dour."

"*You* are not dour, Lord MacArthur." Kitty fluttered her eyelashes. "I am sure we shall have great fun." She led him to a table where slips of gold and silver paper were arrayed with several pairs of scissors. "Mama says we must start with the decorations, and when they are all hung, we can play our games." She sat down and beckoned him to the seat beside her, but Lord MacArthur threw a glance back at Mary, as if in appeal.

"I am…busy helping my mother." Mary forced the excuse from her lips, and she felt only disappointment when it was accepted. She wandered around the kitchen, receiving only a scolding from the cook for her help, and nearly received the same from Mama when discovered there.

"Mary, do go and help your sisters! You do not want Lord MacArthur to think my daughters have anything to do with the kitchen, do you?"

"I had much rather go upstairs, Mama."

"Go upstairs? You may turn your nose up at a lord, Mary, but the least you can do is set off your sisters' charms a little to help *them* catch him. Go and say how becoming Lydia's bonnet is, as I have done. Or hold Kitty's scissors for her while she is choosing paper."

"I do not want to hold Kitty's scissors." The mere idea felt insulting, and Mary knew her tone was testy.

"Well, find *something* to do in there!" Mama waved her hands at Mary, as if to herd her into the drawing room. Accustomed to obedience, Mary stalked back into the room, where her eyes met the vision of Kitty balancing on a chair to hang a string of gold stars, Lord MacArthur's arms stretched out ready to catch her.

"Miss Mary!" Lord MacArthur turned from Kitty, leaving her to balance as she might, her brow wrinkling with annoyance. "We have finished a whole cascade of stars, fit for the heavens."

"They *shall* cascade, if you do not help me hang them up," Kitty said. "Do hold up this other end, my lord." The appellation made her brow smooth out, and her voice returned to good humour, as if remembering he was a lord mended everything. Lord MacArthur took up the other end, and between the two of them they made a presentable loop over the mantel.

"They are lovely." Mary pretended to focus on the decorations while she tried to gather her wits. It was difficult to maintain her stoicism when Lord MacArthur was so cheerful and friendly. "The cook says we may stir the Christmas pudding, if we wish."

"Stir the pudding?" Lord MacArthur cocked his head.

Lydia leapt up to explain, guiding him into the kitchen. "We do not *make* the pudding, of course. The cook does that. But we each close our eyes and give the pudding a stir clockwise and make a wish. Then, when the pudding is ready for Christmas, perhaps your wish comes true! But you must not say what it is." Longbourn's kitchen had been given a good scrub-down for the occasion, and the cook stood by with a pleasant smile for the lord visiting it. Lydia gave the pudding a stir with a flourish, whirling currants deeper into the dark mass. "There! Now, do not ask me what I wished for, because I shall never tell." Her saucy smile at Lord MacArthur showed he might be connected to it, however. "Now Kitty."

Kitty complied, and then Lord MacArthur took a turn, his brow furrowing in thought as he considered his wish. *What does a lord have to wish for? He has a title, and freedom, and enough money to get along.* Mary watched him release the spoon with regret, as if his wish were far happier than his real life.

"Now for the snap-dragon!" Lydia clapped her hands.

"But Miss Mary has not had her turn yet." Lord MacArthur turned to Mary. Though he stood apart from her, as if to show his respect, his expression was as coaxing and friendly as ever. "Well, Miss Mary?"

His attention made her shift her feet. "Very well." She moved to the bowl and gave it a quick stir, closing her eyes as she wished. *I wish I truly could be friends with Lord MacArthur.* She had not had his friendship long, but already her life felt painfully lacking without it. Mary laid the spoon aside and followed the others into the dining room, where the raisins had been soaking in brandy for the game of snap-dragon. Apparently Lord MacArthur was already familiar with the sport of snatching burning raisins from the basin, for he lit the brandy without comment while Kitty shaded the window to give the snap-dragon a ghostlier glow. Although they all took turns in decorous fashion to begin with, soon Kitty and Lydia were snatching raisins left and right, giggling over their conquests, and Mama came in to exclaim over their dashing exploits.

"Oh, Lydia, I am sure you shall lose all your fingers!" Mama said, but she was clapping her hands as well. In the noise and tumult of the game, Lord MacArthur hung back a moment, drawing closer to Mary.

"Are you still angry with me, Miss Mary?" he asked in a low voice.

Mary trembled. She could not lie, but admitting she had forgiven him might reduce the distance between them. *Now is the time to be strong.* "I must see if the cook has the bullet pudding ready." She escaped into the kitchen, her heart fluttering in protest. When the cook put her off, Mary slowly walked back towards the dining room, only to find Lord MacArthur waiting in the doorway, his profile lit by the snap-dragon flickering behind him. His face was too shadowed for Mary to read his expression, but she somehow sensed her chance for dissimulation had gone.

"Miss Mary, many people snubbed me when I was simply 'Arthur'. Shopkeepers, the Hursts, Miss Bingley." He tilted his head. "You are the only one who snubs me as Lord MacArthur."

"I am not—" It would be a lie to say she was not snubbing him, and Mr Weathering's training had gone too deep for that. "That is, I—" Suddenly she felt as though she could not bear to hurt him again, even if it protected her heart. "I was trying to make sure you understood that —what happened—should not have happened."

"I apologise again, Miss Mary. I shall apologise a thousand times, if you like. Can we not be friends again?"

She knew she ought to say no, but the pleasure of his friendship was too keen, too new. It was a joy so unlike the prideful satisfactions of duties done and praises won. *My Christmas wish is coming true early.* "I suppose we may, if we are, um, respectful." She did not know how to put it more delicately, but he nodded vigorously as if he understood. They retreated together to the blaze of the snap-dragon, and soon Mary found herself shouting with the rest, tasting the sweet brandy on her fingers as she sucked her burned fingertips, hot raisins scorching her tongue. Though they did not speak to each other, she felt Lord MacArthur's companionable presence beside her. Lydia grew noisier and noisier with the fun, and though she occasionally called on Lord MacArthur to watch her reckless grabs, at last Mary had a chance to speak to him without being noticed.

"Why did you hide who you are, Lord MacArthur?" Mary asked. The name sounded strange in her ear, and she pronounced it awkwardly. She had thought of him as 'Mr Arthur' for what felt like forever. *And Mr Arthur is a much friendlier name.*

"It was only a bit of fun." He barely glanced at her, as if he were accustomed to the question.

"It was very misleading."

"That is rather the idea." Humour tinged his nonchalance now. His hand darted forward for another raisin, and Lydia applauded briefly before returning to her own efforts.

Mary's lips pursed as she saw the unruffled expression on his face, caught in flashes of light from the basin. "Our bishop says wilful deception is against God's will. You may not have lied, exactly...but you were certainly deceitful." The sanctimonious tone in her voice irritated even herself, and she was not surprised to find it did not sway Lord MacArthur.

"My conscience is clear enough." He shrugged his shoulders, but the tension in his brow showed his annoyance.

"Perhaps it should not be."

His thin shoulders straightened as he turned to her. "A little playful prank is nothing to regret. Being a lord is hardly easy, you know. Everyone expects things from me. Of course, I want some time away from the estate, just to relax and not think so much." He turned back to the table to snatch another raisin, deftly swallowing it. "Besides, I want others to know the *real* me."

"Pretending to be what you are not is hardly the way to do that. Part of what makes us who we are is our duties and our ties to others. Hiding those does not show who you really are." Though part of her winced at bringing up so serious a topic in the midst of their merriment, she needed to understand.

"Yet Christ asked people to sell everything and even leave behind their families. Does that not suggest he thought their true selves did not involve those things?" Lord MacArthur replied.

Mary bit her lip, thinking hard. Apparently Mr Arthur had considered the matter with more depth than she had thought. "I cannot agree with you. We are also supposed to honour our mother and father and render to Caesar what is due to him." Though she felt disgruntled with his objections, Mary also felt pleased he was arguing by using scripture. No one in her family felt inclined to discuss such things with Mary. "It is clear we have great duties given to us, whatever our true selves are, and a life lived without acknowledging duty is nothing."

"Be that as it may, you seem to live upon nothing *but* duty. That is another way of concealing a true self. You hide your frivolous side, the side that does things simply because you enjoy them." He gestured at the flickering light of the snap-dragon. "This is the first I have really seen of it, your playfulness here." Though it was hard to tell in the shadows, Mary thought she spied a wink. "Not that it has lasted long."

"I-I find it difficult to forget other concerns." She took a deep breath. "But you avoid the main point. Hiding that you are a lord means hiding important parts of yourself. God ordained you for the position, and you defy his will by trying to shirk it, even in reputation. Deceiving others keeps them from knowing you entirely." She had to raise her voice to be heard over Lydia's hooting laughter and her mother's clapping. "Think of my sister Jane. She has many good qualities, but she is also the daughter of Mrs Bennet and the sister of Lydia. She cannot change those aspects of herself, nor would she wish to. Mr Bingley seems to like her, but if he marries her, he marries the daughter, the sister." Kitty dropped a raisin, and when it stung Lydia's arm, she shrieked and banged against the table, spilling brandy from the basin. Mary tilted her head at the fracas with a smile, as if she had prepared the demonstration.

"I think I see what you mean about Miss Bennet." Lord MacArthur looked thoughtful, although he brightened and nodded at Kitty when she boasted of her latest catch. His expression clouded again when he turned back to Mary. "But I am not altogether convinced that I have done anything so very wrong. Perhaps it is a bit unfair of me to expect people to judge me only by who I am apart from the title, when the title will demand so much from me in behaviour. But it is difficult for a young man to be the master of an estate all by himself. I tire of all the responsibility, so I hide from it a little." His brow had furrowed further as he spoke, but now it suddenly smoothed. "And Miss Mary, I still think you hide a part of yourself as well."

Mary reached for another raisin, the last one. She had to snatch it from Lydia's outstretched fingers, and she popped the prize into her mouth, the juice and brandy squeezing sweetness onto her tongue. Making an elaborate curtsey to Lydia's indignant protests, Mary smiled. "Perhaps I do," she said to Lord MacArthur, and walked to the window to push the curtains apart to let in light for the bullet pudding.

A maid carried in the pudding, in fact a mound of flour with a bullet delicately balanced atop it. Each of the players took a butter knife and made a slice into the pudding. When Lydia's slice wound up disturbing the bullet, everyone groaned and laughed.

"Now I am in for it," Lydia said. The rules demanded she retrieve the bullet with her mouth, so she pressed her face into the flour, searching for it. By the time she acquired it, flour stuck to her eyebrows and dusted the front of her hair. Kitty replaced the bullet, and they began again, this time Mary disturbing the bullet and having to duck her head into the mass. Lord MacArthur was the next to err, and soon all were covered in flour and laughing at each other. The scent of burned brandy trickled through that of the flour pasted over Mary's nose, and she found herself grinning at Lord MacArthur. *He is right. I do keep the part of myself that just* enjoys *too bottled up.* It seemed a mark of their deepening friendship that he had criticised her in so pointed a way, and she accepted the point. *And I truly believe he is reconsidering his childish way of hiding his rank.* The idea that he might take her advice seriously made her heart swell.

Mary found herself more talkative than she could remember, chattering at Lord MacArthur and taking his jokes with good humour. Though Kitty and Lydia still made weak efforts to capture his attention, they seemed to resign themselves to the fact that Mary had the best chance of winning the lord's favour. Seeing her sisters withdraw for her sake made Mary both proud and uneasy. She had never put herself forward in attracting a gentleman, and to be placed in that position by her sisters' retreat made her second-guess herself. *They do not understand. They think a lord could think seriously of a Bennet for marriage. They do not see that it is only friendship.* As the day progressed, however, Mary grew accustomed to being left clear to chat with Lord MacArthur, whatever unwarranted conclusions her family might draw from it.

"I shall see you at Netherfield tomorrow for Miss Bingley's musical party," Lord MacArthur said as he left Longbourn. Mary watched him go with warmth in her heart. She wished she could do something for him, to show him how much his friendship meant to her. *Kitty and Lydia talked of giving him a Christmas present. He is not family, but perhaps it would not be too improper.* A gift would show she had truly forgiven him the indiscretion of the kiss.

Mary wiped a trace of flour from her gown, considering. "Lydia, do you wish to go to the shops?"

"Lord, what a question, Mary! I dare say I try to go every day of my life. Let me find my mittens. If we hurry, we can leave Kitty behind, and how vexed she will be!"

Mary waited, dawdling sufficiently to enable Kitty to join them. In town she bought enough red and green thread to make the milliner's tight-lipped, polite smile turn to a real one. *I suppose she was still cross about all the time I spent canvassing here.* Guilt pricked at Mary, but not for the milliner's sake. She had not thought of the Meryton Widows and Orphans Society since Lord MacArthur had kissed her. *At least now I know Lord MacArthur can actually pay his subscription.* Her plan for the Christmas present would require time, time she must subtract from her charity efforts. *Is that wrong? Am I becoming a worldly woman, caring more for one rich man's gift than helping the widows and orphans?* But she remembered Mr Weathering's exhortations to lessen her duties a little, and Lord MacArthur's friendly criticism. *I shall try enjoying myself more this Christmas. I can always return to strictness later if it turns out badly.*

Tucking away the green and red thread, she strolled back to Longbourn with her sisters with a new spring in her step.

chapter EIGHT

Netherfield was bedecked with greenery of every sort, some carried in from the forest just outside, and other parts selected by Miss Bingley's taste and purchased by Mr Bingley's wealth. Some of the lighter pine boughs had been twisted into wreaths with rosemary and bay leaves wound into the circles. Laurel and ivy were hung in loops and clusters on some of the walls and mantels. Apples and oranges dotted the greenery with bright colour. The enormous pine bough Mary had chosen ornamented the main passageway, and Miss Bingley had deftly transformed its bulk with sprigs of holly and painted acorns. Though the ornaments could not alleviate the heavy scent of pine from the branch, they eased the eye, if not the nose.

The drawing room had more Christmas allurements than just decoration: mulled wine threw steam into the air, apples bobbing in the spiced brandy like treasures cast up from a shipwreck. A plum pudding crusted with sugar had been neatly sliced and waited to be sampled. Lydia was already tasting the candied oranges. "How pleasant this all is, Miss Bingley!" she cried, popping another sugar-coated slice into her mouth.

"I am glad you like it." Miss Bingley presided in queenly decorum in the centre of the room and managed the assortment of treats with gentle glances and gestures at footmen and maids. Her smile declared she was in her element and proud to be displaying her skills of hospitality in front of Mr Darcy. Mrs Hurst no doubt had her share in the business, but she gracefully permitted her sister to appear the sole manager.

"How is the mulled wine, Mr Darcy?" Miss Bingley's duties did not prevent her from keeping an eagle eye on her prey, and she immediately called for his attention the moment he bent his head to speak to Lizzy.

"It is quite well flavoured, Miss Bingley." Mr Darcy was in good enough humour to satisfy Miss Bingley's need for praise, but Mary doubted his happiness came from the wine or the hostess. It more likely came from Lizzy's nearness. Lizzy sat on the sofa with Kitty, and Mr Darcy leaned towards her with an interest that suggested whatever quarrels they had engaged in were ended.

"Everything is so cosy and Christmas-like," Lydia said, wiping the sugar from her fingers. "All we need to be perfectly jolly is Mr Wickham! It is too bad he is not in Meryton."

Lizzy's tone was cool. "Mr Wickham's absence is no detriment to *my* happiness."

But Lizzy always favoured Mr Wickham. Whatever her past preferences, Lizzy clearly did not like him now. Mary wondered what had caused the change. Mr Darcy's contented smile suggested he might have something to do with it.

Mary sipped her tea, burned her tongue, and then sipped at it again. *Can we not get to the important part of the evening?* All this eating and drinking was pleasant enough, under ordinary circumstances, but Mary wished she could hurry them all to finish their food and begin the music. A stack of carols waited in her lap, and she was eager to display her talent before Miss Bingley and Lord MacArthur.

At last the dishes were carried off and Miss Bingley nodded Jane an invitation to play. Jane's performance was simple and pleasing, an old ballad that made Mama hum along and Mr Bingley sigh—more with romantic thoughts than musical appreciation, Mary thought. *It is not a very complicated piece.* Mary's arrangement of *God Rest Ye Merry, Gentlemen* would require much more skill.

Though Mary sat bolt upright when Jane finished, signalling her readiness to go next, Miss Bingley asked Lizzy to play instead. Lizzy's performance improved on her sister's, and though her rendition of *Shepherds Watched Their Flocks by Night* was no more complex, it was more expertly played. Mr Darcy showed his appreciation of the piece—and the player—by hovering alongside the pianoforte and turning the pages for her, whilst Miss Bingley searched the room for a reason to prevent a second piece from Lizzy.

"Perhaps you will entertain us next, Miss Mary," Miss Bingley said. Mary hurried to the pianoforte. Her fingers quickly picked out the tune, splaying into chords after a moment, and Mary's thin, quavering voice began to sing.

"God rest ye merry, gentlemen…" She could not see much of Miss

Bingley, not while she was trying to keep up with the complicated chord progression, but the few glimpses she caught showed rolling eyes and a strained expression. *She is not impressed yet.* Mary sang louder, her notes unsteady as her throat strained for the high notes. Now she caught sight of Lord MacArthur, and he looked stunned. Ordinarily Mary would interpret such shock as admiration for her skill, but her sensitivity to Lord MacArthur's opinions made a new hypothesis flash into her mind. *What if it is the other kind of stunned? What if...he does not like it?* She put more effort into her song, now frantically seeking out Miss Bingley's response with every moment she could spare from her playing. *Miss Bingley looks disapproving. But perhaps she is simply jealous of my skill.* With her new hypothesis in mind, however, she could not delude herself for long. *No, Miss Bingley thinks I play and sing ill!* The realisation made her voice shake so hard that her distress must have been evident, for suddenly Lord MacArthur burst into song with the next verse, and the rest of the group joined in. Their combined voices drowned out Mary's exhibition, but she was grateful for it nonetheless.

When the song ended, Mary trembled and collected her music. Usually she would have remained planted on the pianoforte bench as long as possible, playing as many airs as she could before someone defied the demands of politeness enough to force her out. Today she scrambled off the bench as if it burned her. *What a fool I am! Of course I knew there were places my fingers did not quite get it right, and of course I knew my voice sometimes did not hit the right notes, but somehow...*Somehow she had always convinced herself that these were minor faults, ones easily overlooked given the complexity of the pieces she favoured. *I practised so hard! And it was all for nothing. Miss Bingley thinks ill of me, and Lord MacArthur—well, his friendship is indisputable, concealing my shortcomings in that way, but I still wish I could have pleased him.*

Mrs Hurst played next, choosing a selection from Handel's *Messiah* that put Mary's little piece to shame. Mary sat in miserable silence on an elegant mahogany chair that jabbed her in the back, unable to persuade herself that there was anything lacking in Mrs Hurst's musical finesse. Mary had not realised how much she had hoped Miss Bingley and Mrs Hurst would single her out after hearing her play. She had watched them select Jane from the Bennet sisters for special treatment, and part of her clung to the idea that they would do the same with Mary, if only they knew more of her. *Knowing more of my music did not help anything.* But there was still Mary's piety and her devotion to charity. Perhaps that would make her worthy of their attention.

Mr Darcy's frequent smiles at Lizzy encouraged Mary. She had still not asked Mr Darcy for a contribution to her society; it was the perfect chance to bring up the matter in front of Miss Bingley. If Mr Darcy were impressed, Miss Bingley would be, too. Now Mary waited as impatiently for the end of the musical portion of the evening as she had waited for its beginning.

Lydia and Kitty had no interest in performing, but Jane and Lizzy took another turn, and Miss Bingley herself played an intricate medley of carols that happened to repeat—and improve upon—the ones Lizzy and Mary had played. When Miss Bingley finished, Mary hurried over to Mr Darcy, who had seated himself near Lizzy after dragging a chair close to the sofa where she was ensconced.

"Mr Darcy, would you be so kind as to donate to my Meryton Widows and Orphans Society? It is a great benefit to Meryton. Mr Bingley and Lord MacArthur have promised to give." Mary had not realised how sudden and impertinent her demand was until she saw Mr Darcy's irritation.

"A charity?" Mr Darcy spoke slowly, as if he were struggling to comprehend her request.

"It is the only charitable society in Meryton providing for widows and orphans," Mary said. She hoped she sounded business-like and competent, but she feared a note of entreaty had entered her voice.

"I suppose I can give you a pound or two." Mr Darcy's dissatisfaction with the request was clear. He took Mary's subscription book into his hand and Mary hurried to snatch a pen off the writing-desk and dab it in ink for him. "I cannot say I have great hopes for the outcome. How deplorable it is of humankind, so often do we succumb to the impulse to give money rather than alleviate the real causes of misery. I know a great many landholders who shower gold on the poorer tenants without lifting a finger to change the conditions that *make* them poor."

Mr Darcy wrote down his name and an amount and then gave the book back to Mary, saying, "The real work of Christmas is to do good. But we do more good by ensuring that general conditions are fair, real, honest—not handing out coin to placate the people suffering real injustice."

"But none of those changes can be made without coin," Lizzy shot back in Mary's defence.

"And will this society actually make these changes?" Mr Darcy shook his head. "With all respect to your sister, Miss Elizabeth, I rather think not."

"True, Mary's society cannot reshape the conditions under which we all live." Lizzy's colour rose as she grew more animated. "But we women are not much permitted to work towards altering the foundations of the English way of life. We cannot change the political climate, nor re-make how buying and selling are done—but what we can do as women, Mr Darcy, is exactly what Mary is doing. We can help individuals with the little purchases we make with collected coin. Mary is exerting herself to help as best she can. Her devotion to duty is admirable, especially in a society that gives her no place in effecting larger changes. She gives up her time and her pleasures to help others, again and again."

Mary listened to Lizzy's vindication with mixed feelings. She was grateful to Lizzy for speaking up for her work and agreed with her in principle. Yet somehow hearing her life described as a series of sacrifices and duties, however noble, made her sad. *I have never felt that way before. What Lizzy says is exactly what would have pleased me most a few weeks ago.* How had she changed so much in so short a time? *I know what it is like to be happy for better reasons, now. I know how to feel joy without pride.* Her next thought humbled her. *I know what I was sacrificing now, and it is not so easy to give up.*

"Miss Elizabeth makes some very good points, yet I cannot say that all a lady can do is collect and distribute money," Lord MacArthur broke in. "Why, take my estate in Scotland. It needs a school for the children. And the young mothers there could use some sort of cottage industry—something to do to bring in a little money while remaining at home. Active womanly management could bring about these things, and not merely by gathering coin and paying it out." He glanced at Mary as if for her approval, but she stared blankly at him.

Lizzy rose to the occasion. "I admit a partial defeat then, Lord MacArthur. You are right, there is more room for a lady's beneficial interference than I suspected." She smiled. "I ought never to undervalue the power ladies have to interfere, ought I?"

Miss Bingley, sensing Lizzy was getting the better of the conversation, waded in with a view that happened to coincide exactly with Mr Darcy's, but as Mr Darcy admitted some points of Lizzy's, she was left to defend the position alone, and soon abandoned it. Mary drifted from the conversation, moving to stare out the window at the scattering of fat flakes dusting the bushes.

"I congratulate you on the vindication of your way of life," Lord MacArthur said, joining her. "Mr Darcy has turned his colours, and Miss Bingley is routed."

"Yes." Mary continued gazing on the flakes as the wind stirred them up and then left them to drift down, again and again.

"You do not seem pleased."

"I am, a little. It is only—" She finally turned her gaze on him. "I suppose it was akin to hearing my eulogy, and finding it wanting. All duty, no real life lived, no happiness."

"None?" His head bent closer. Their backs were to the company, and though there was nothing scandalous in looking out the window together, Mary felt oddly intimate with him.

"Well, a little. Now." Her lips were moving of themselves, forming the heedless smile that had covered her face the first time she met him. This time, the naturalness of the smile did not surprise her. *It feels right because it is real joy, not self-aggrandisement.* "Now that I have your friendship."

"I hoped that might be so." His hand moved, hesitantly sliding over Mary's hand on the sill. Her breath caught.

It is an accident. She tried to excuse him, but then his hand squeezed hers, and her dreams collapsed. *A lord does not squeeze a poor gentlewoman's hand for any good purpose. He does not kiss her for any good purpose. What a fool I have been!* She backed away, pulling her hand away. Though the keenness of her voice made it difficult to keep its volume quiet, she did her best. "I am not that sort of woman, my lord. Pray do not play the fool with me." Stumbling, she retreated to her mother's side and sat in prim silence, ignoring the company for the rest of the evening and refusing to meet Lord MacArthur's gaze.

He is toying with me. That is not friendship. That is not even respect. Mary wanted to feel righteous anger thrumming through her body, but instead she felt weak and bereft at the loss of the one pure joy she thought she had found. *I must put him out of my mind entirely.* The self-respect of any lady would demand that much. Mary would not be the victim of seduction, however much she liked the lord. *But what if he meant no seduction? What if it is just his way?* Thoughts swirled in confusion. *Or what if—he meant it differently?* The prospect of a joy too bright dazzled her, and she pushed the idea away, lest it delude her. *I must talk to someone. I must have advice. And pray.* Lizzy was too wrapped in her own romantic dreams to be dependable. But Mr Weathering was old, experienced, and kind. He would know what to say to put Mary at ease. *He will help me put Lord MacArthur out of my mind completely.*

But who would help her put him out of her heart?

chapter NINE

THE CHURCH STILL SMELLED DANK AND LOOKED BARE WHEN Mary arrived the next day, but stacks of greenery in the corner and bundles of ribbons heaped on the seat of a pew showed Mr Weathering was ready to have it decorated. The young ladies and gentlemen of Meryton were supposed to help him that afternoon, and thus the vicar was unsurprised to see Mary there in the morning, early as usual.

But I am not here to help this time. She could remember a thousand visits to the church, her head held high as she planned how to aid the elderly vicar and the people of Meryton. Though she had told herself she was humble, now she saw how arrogant she had become, assuming she would always be the pious one distributing aid and never the forlorn supplicant seeking advice.

"Miss Bennet!" The vicar's warm smile greeted Mary, and already a soothing feeling seeped through her chest. "If you can sort the ribbons, then—"

"Actually, I am here because I need your advice." Mary ducked her head, suddenly embarrassed but still craving the peace she sensed he could give her. "May we talk awhile?" She glanced around the sanctuary, ensuring it was empty, and felt a pang as she remembered it was where she first saw Lord MacArthur.

"Certainly." He moved slowly to a pew and eased himself into it, his rheumatism no doubt acting up in the chilly, damp weather. "Is it about the Meryton Widows and Orphans Society?"

Guilt washed over Mary as she sat down beside him. She had forgotten her charity work again and again. "No, nothing like that. I was in the forest gathering greenery with Mr Arth—Lord MacArthur." The discomfort of saying such things aloud halted her, and she squeezed her hands together until she felt the courage to go on. "And he kissed me." Mary expected to hear an exclamation of shock or dismay, but Mr Weathering only rested his chin on his hand as he propped his arm on the pew in front of them.

"I see."

"I was very angry with him, and he apologised, and I thought we were friends again." Now the words came in a rush, all tumbling over each other. "But he pressed my hand yesterday, and now I cannot help but think I must be an object of seduction for him. I suppose I must avoid him from now on." But even as she said that aloud, she realised she was hoping Mr Weathering would contradict it all. *He knows much more of men than I do. What if I have misunderstood everything?* She gulped, trying to compose herself lest she begin to cry.

"And have you any feelings for Lord MacArthur?" The vicar's voice was carefully neutral, but it did not reassure Mary. To her, it sounded the practised non-judgment of a holy man, coaxing out the full story before delivering a verdict.

"I—we—" She hardly knew what to say. "I thought we were friends. I like him." Her cheeks heated. "Of course, I do not expect any foolish fairy tale things. He is a lord, and I shall be lucky to have fifty pounds settled on me, if that much."

Mr Weathering's expression gave away nothing. "I see. No expectations."

"What shall I do, Mr Weathering? If I keep seeing him, perhaps he will try again, and—" her distress wrung the confession from her—"I may not be strong enough to turn him away, next time."

"Certainly you must preserve your chastity, my dear." Mr Weathering's tone was absent as if he were deep in thought. For a moment he ruminated in silence, still leaning on his arm. When he sat up straight, Mary knew he must have reached a conclusion. "Miss Bennet, you have long disclaimed your own charms. I have spoken with Lord MacArthur several times, and he has always seemed sensible and earnest. It is true that he ought not compromise your dignity by kissing you, but it may be that Lord MacArthur is a sincere suitor."

Mary's heart pounded in erratic—and unreasoning—joy. "A lord marry a Bennet? That would be ridiculous."

"If his intentions were honourable, would you allow him to court you?"

Mary shook her head. "Of course, but it cannot be as you say. I have nothing to give him, nothing." Though the prospect he dangled in front of her dazzled, she pushed herself to stick to hard facts. "He has given me no reason to think he will propose, Mr Weathering. He has simply talked with me and kissed me and held my hand. For a Scottish peer to marry a woman such as I—it is impossible." She shifted in her seat. "I thought you would give me advice, not tempt me with fantasies. What am I to do? Shall I risk offending him by avoiding him markedly? Or gently avoid him and hope that is enough?"

"I always think prayer the best first step in obtaining guidance," the vicar said, humour tinging his voice. Mary lowered her head in obedience, and as the vicar spoke a prayer, she tried to arrange her thoughts into an attitude suitable for such things. *But I am still so confused. I almost wish Mr Weathering had been angry and told me never to speak to Lord MacArthur again.*

"...And help Mary to know her true heart, and her true desires, with Your guidance. Amen."

The ending of the prayer unsettled Mary further. *Why does everyone harp on about discovering what I want? It is not relevant, certainly not now.* Though dissatisfied with the prayer, Mary thanked the vicar and rose.

"You are leaving us?" Mr Weathering looked disturbed.

"I cannot stay and help with the decorations. Lord MacArthur will be here." She picked up her reticule. "I shall take the basket I prepared to Widow Cranby. It is not Christmas yet, but perhaps it is good to deliver it a little early."

"Such a charitable heart." This time, the vicar's praise gave her no satisfaction, though it had been one of her dearest pleasures in the past.

*I do not seem to care much for anything anymore. Except...*Mary pushed the thought away. The failure of the vicar's praise to cheer her boded ill for her future life. *That is all I shall have once Lord MacArthur leaves. The empty satisfactions of pride and self-righteousness.* It would never be enough to make her happy, not now. *I shall have to find some other interest, some pursuit as Lord MacArthur's sister found.* She had not tried many things. Perhaps she could learn to draw, or press flowers, or read Shakespeare. *I do not even know what I like.*

The lane to Mrs Cranby's house angled off the main street and crept into a patchy jumble of cottages and gardens. Mrs Cranby's house had once been tidy. But now the shutters dangled awry on their hinges, and the path to the door was mottled with dead weeds poking through the dusting of snow. Mary knocked, breathing a few last gulps of clean air before Mrs Cranby welcomed her in.

"Miss Mary Bennet! Do walk in." Mrs Cranby stood back to let Mary by, and Mary passed into the swirl of tobacco smoke and haze of gin that permeated the cottage. Mrs Cranby often had visitors, and each left their mark in scent: pungent tobacco, unwashed bodies, and alcohol. This morning, though, it seemed Mrs Cranby had not had a drop herself, and Mary proffered the basket and delivered the speech she had prepared on behalf of the Meryton Widows and Orphans Society.

Mrs Cranby received the basket with delight, her eyes glued to the pouch of money inserted among the fresh bread, new mittens, a receipt for coal purchased and ready for delivery, and other winter necessities arranged in the curve of the wicker. "How very kind! You've a Christian heart, Miss Mary." Mrs Cranby settled the basket on a table and gestured Mary to sit near the hearth. "I hope you can stay a bit and have a cup of tea."

"Thank you." As Mrs Cranby heated the water, Mary's gaze drifted over the dust coating the shelving and the sticky grime collecting around the floor near the hearth. For years, every time Mary had entered the cottage, she had felt a burst of superiority. She had felt sure she would never descend to such habits of slovenliness in home and dress. Now Mary found herself wondering—if she found herself forlorn and alone, would she really care so much about tidiness? Or would she cling to whatever momentary peace she might find, whether it be self-righteous sermon-books or cheap gin?

"Stir up the fire a little if you choose, Miss Bennet. Or add a few coals—I can afford to, now you say the coal-man shall bring more." Mrs Cranby busied herself stuffing tea leaves into a pot. "Do you see the coal scoop there? My husband made it for me." Wistfulness entered her tone. "It was a little joke between us."

Mary looked at the coal scoop poking out of the scuttle. It was unusual enough to demand notice: made of wood rather than metal and carved into the shape of a tortoise below the handle. Though she had heard the story many times already, Mary let Mrs Cranby continue.

"He always said I was as slow adding coal as a tortoise. Every time, he said it. And then, a year before he died, he whittled that coal scoop for me, saying I might as well have a scoop that matched me. How we laughed, Miss Bennet!" Mrs Cranby paused over the tea leaves, as if to steady herself. "He was the best of men."

Mary wondered how she had never caught the glimpse of vulnerability in the woman's face before. She had borne the tedious tale of the coal scoop a thousand times and had congratulated herself on her patience with an elderly woman who repeated herself. *How did I miss the pain in her voice? And the happiness when she speaks of her late husband?* Though Mary usually scorned to touch much in the cottage, today she picked up the scoop to examine it more closely. It was really not the right sort of thing to move coal; the lumpy back of the scoop, mimicking the pattern of a tortoise-shell, made it awkward to push it into a pile of coal, and the wood was worn and stained with soot. But though it was impracticable, it had been used with love for years. Mary found herself admiring it.

"It is nice, isn't it?" Mrs Cranby sounded pleased that Mary was taking a closer look. "Ah, now the water is boiling away! My Sam always said I talked the water away, because half of it would boil off before I minded it. I just love a good chat, that's all." And though she was chastising herself and repeating the reproaches of her husband, Mrs Cranby bubbled with warmth. "How troublesome he was, sometimes! Did I tell you that once he wore his dirty boots to bed?"

"Yes." Mary glanced at the brightness in the woman's face. "But tell me again, Mrs Cranby. I have forgotten the details."

The widow obliged, successfully readying the tea despite her stream of talk. As she told Mary more about her memories, Mary found herself confronted with a feeling that surprised her. She had always felt sorry for Mrs Cranby; she had both pitied and disdained the woman's scant resources, her tendency to drink, her incessant talk. But when she saw the gleam of happiness in the woman's eyes as she described her Sam, Mary felt something new: envy.

Whatever her current life, she has known love. Real love, real affection. Mary found herself forgetting to sip her tea as she listened. How strange it felt to envy Mrs Cranby anything! Mary had spent her life looking down on her, and now she saw that Mrs Cranby had had something precious that Mary had not dreamed of. *She believed in love, and had it.* Mary wondered if some of the yearning for escape into liquor had come from believing that no such love would ever come again. *If she believed she could find such love again, would it make a difference? If she felt Sam near her in some otherworldly way, or if she thought she could find a new man she loved as much, would she be happier?* Mary tried to dismiss the thoughts as unholy or unfeasible, but they drifted through her nevertheless. *And what about me? Could I ever hope to find a husband to love as dearly as Mrs Cranby loved her Sam?* She did not know. She had assured herself there was no hope so often that she had grown accustomed to thinking of love as a foolish pursuit. She had derided Lizzy for exploring romance. *But Lizzy believes in love. She hopes for it, risks her heart on the idea that things might turn out well.* Lizzy could be wrong, of course: Mr Darcy might ride off to Derbyshire without glancing back. Or Lizzy's heart might one day be broken by her lover's death, as Mrs Cranby's had been. *But they both believed in love. What if I could, too?* It was too frightening to think of Lord MacArthur, or to apply any of the new thoughts to him. But Mary rested her chin on her hand and met Mrs Cranby's gaze. Mary did not dare risk her heart yet, but she craved some new knowledge, some perspective to help her.

"What else do you remember?" she asked, her smile gentle.

chapter TEN

"And I can never say enough how delighted I shall be to have a son-in-law such as you, Mr Bingley!" Mama said for the third time, as if determined to prove the remark. Mama's effusions over Mr Bingley's proposal to Jane had lasted most of the day, never mind that Christmas Eve ought to have demanded her attention in a hundred ways—placating an overwhelmed cook, preparing the baskets to be given on Boxing Day, or purchasing a gift for her husband at the very last moment. Instead, it was Mary who was inspecting lists and filling the baskets in a corner of the drawing room while her mother crowed her appreciation to Mr Bingley and Jane.

Mr Darcy and Mr Bingley both had arrived unplanned on Christmas Eve, shortly after noon. Mr Bingley's flushed request to see Jane alone had set off knowing glances from one Bennet sister to another, and the result had been as everyone hoped: a real proposal, complete with a visit to Mr Bennet's study for his approval. Mr Darcy had volunteered to take the remaining Bennet sisters on a walk, discreetly leaving Mr Bingley to Jane and her parents. Mary had chosen to remain at home instead. She still felt a pang of guilt for having set aside so many of her duties in her fixation on Lord MacArthur, and the gifts for Boxing Day needed to be completed. From the way Mr Darcy's smouldering gaze had fastened on Lizzy, she imagined he would find a way to make his own proposal during the walk. He would doubtless welcome having one fewer Bennet sister to evade in doing so.

Mama's praise, though exuberant, wearied the others over time. Mr Bingley began glancing out the window as if for an escape, and Jane's gentle hints to her mother to let them be alone were too subtle for Mama to discern.

"Perhaps we might catch up with the others on their walk, if we hurry," Mr Bingley said to Jane. It was an improbable project; Mr Darcy, Lizzy, Kitty, and Lydia had been gone for nearly an hour, but it was a good excuse to be alone. Jane rose immediately, brightening at the suggestion, but again Mama failed to catch her meaning.

"I shall accompany you as far as the main road," she said. "I simply must tell you how pleased I am at having such an upright, gentleman-like suitor for our dear Jane—" as if she had not been doing exactly that all day. The three disappeared out the door in a flurry of scarves and gloves, and Mary hoped Jane might be able to shake their mother off at the main road as promised. Though Mama loved to chatter at her daughter's suitor, she was not much for walking, and the feat might be possible.

Longbourn was swallowed by silence once they had gone. Papa was immured in his study, and Hill had rounded up all the servants to help prepare for Christmas—and to stay away from where Mary worked on their Christmas baskets. Mary breathed deeply as she finished arranging the little gifts and treats. The memory of chatting with Mrs Cranby came to mind again and again, fundamentally challenging her idea of who she wanted to be. *I have been prideful and insincere. But now I sincerely wish to help people, to understand them—and I want to believe in love.* Though it disturbed her, she turned over her memories of Lord MacArthur, examining them for any hope of real love and a happy ending. Part of her still insisted it was not sensible to think he might truly wish to marry her. *But part of me believes. And perhaps that is enough.* Even if she were wrong and her dreams fell apart, she felt brave enough to dream them anyway. *Thank you, Mrs Cranby. Thank you, Lizzy and Jane.*

A knock came at the door, but with all the servants scolded away from the drawing room, Mary doubted any of them had heard. She answered it herself, and the vicar bowed before her.

"Mr Weathering! Please come in." Mary led him to the drawing room. He received the good news of Jane's engagement with a smile and proper congratulations and then marvelled at the Boxing Day gifts. But his creaking frame moved restlessly, as if he had not yet come to the point of his visit. He held a flat package in one hand.

"Would you like to see Papa?" Mary asked.

"Indeed not, Miss Bennet. I came for a particular purpose. I am a courier today." Mr Weathering proffered the packet, and Mary took it with a puzzled look.

"What is this?"

"I have come on behalf of Lord MacArthur, my child." Though he tried to smooth his features into one of stately importance, a smile crept over his lips. "When he first came here and seemed," he coughed delicately, "appreciative of your merits, I made enquiries with a friend who is visiting London this winter. He is from that part of Scotland and was able to tell me a great deal about Lord MacArthur and his family." Mr Weathering rubbed the sparse hairs on the top of his head. "Apparently, Lord MacArthur's reputation is much as you would expect. Good-hearted, kind to tenants, no significant debts, but a little flighty. A young lady of a responsible bent would complement him admirably."

Mary looked down at the brown paper package, hardly able to digest the vicar's words. "But how did you know who he was?"

"Lord MacArthur confided in me one day—the day you first saw him, it must have been. He wanted guidance. I suppose he felt torn between the demands of his rank and the other parts of his life. He told me who he was and why he concealed it, and as I knew he was staying at Netherfield, I agreed to keep his secret. But I decided to find out more about him, and I have." He nodded at the packet. "That is the result of my enquiry, as well as a gift from Lord MacArthur himself. He says he would have given it to you at the decorating party, but you were not there."

Mary's hands began to tremble, crackling the paper as it moved. "Do you mean...he might be seriously inclined towards me?"

Mr Weathering no longer tried to hide his smile. "It would be most unusual to make a vicar a go-between for an illicit affair." He turned up the collar of his coat, preparing to go, but Mary stopped him.

"But Mr Weathering, what am I to do?"

"Do?"

"Am I to write to him, or go to Netherfield, or wait for him here? Will he come and—propose? Or does he wish for us to know one another better?" The questions began piling up in her speech, and they were nothing to the questions heaped in her brain.

"My child, I have no notion. I am just the messenger." His eyes crinkled with amusement at her eagerness.

"That is all?" Exasperation clutched at her, and she shook it off. "Wait a moment, if you please!" Dashing up the stairs, she retrieved a small parcel, wrapped in gold paper left over from the stars cut out for decoration and tied with a red ribbon. "Please take this to him, then. It is his Christmas present." Her cheeks heated. *Does being in love always make people feel foolish?* "You might as well be *my* messenger, too."

"Very well, Miss Bennet. A trip to Netherfield will do me no harm." He tucked the parcel into his pocket, and Mary escorted him to the door. She watched him go down the walk in his slow, steady way, and felt an impulse to rush behind him and speed him along.

He will get there soon enough, she told herself, but her foot tapped of its own accord. She pulled open the packet. The letters from the gentleman in London she skimmed hurriedly; they did not give much detail beyond what the vicar had already said. But the last page in the packet was a watercolour, Lord MacArthur's gift. It was a picture of a daffodil, its petals curled in exquisite detail. But the daffodil was painted neither white nor yellow, but pink, a rosy, flushed pink that made Mary laugh with appreciation. He must have hunted through Netherfield's botany books to find a picture to copy and complete the joke. *No one has ever given me something like this.* She wished she could tell him right now how much she loved it. *I am pink as a daffodil all over again just looking at it.* Of course, it was a bit embarrassing to have a moment—a kiss—that, strictly speaking, ought not to have happened, memorialised in such a fashion. *And Mr Cranby ought not to have criticised his wife for shovelling coal so slowly—but they turned it into a joke, a warmth between them rather than a reproach.* Perhaps that was what love did, transform the awkwardness and errors of life into beautiful moments. This shift in perspective, the idea that she did not have to spend the rest of her life making herself and Lord MacArthur feel shame about that day under the mistletoe, made her heart flutter with joy. Mary hurried upstairs to place the picture gently by her bed, nudging it this way and that until the angle was perfect. It took the strongest effort of will and reminders of Christian charity to go back to the baskets and resume her work, wondering what the picture might mean and hoping it signified what was in her own heart.

chapter ELEVEN

CHRISTMAS EVE HAD NEVER PASSED SO SLOWLY, AND Christmas morning was not much better, despite the pleasures of exchanging small gifts with her family and observing their ebullitions of joy and surprise. The Longbourn hearth was too small for a proper, monumental Yule Log, but a makeshift one wrapped in hazel twigs burned there with a merry dance of lights. Lydia had begged the cook to let her sample the Christmas pudding, and she shared it with her sisters in an unusual generosity of spirit. As Mary tasted the currants and heavy sweetness, she could not help thinking of the wish she had made as she stirred it. Now she had not only Lord MacArthur's friendship, but perhaps more.

It was my first attempt at daring to dream, she thought, *and it has turned out well.* And now Mary's dreams of love were sparked into life and blazing as joyfully as the Yule Log on the hearth. Even if it all came to nothing, she knew a new part of herself, one she had never suspected existed underneath her pride and piety. *I can love with a true heart.*

As she had expected, Mr Darcy had proposed to Lizzy on their walk, and now he was nestled in the family as one of their own, though Mama still cast glances at him making clear that disbelief and intimidation had silenced her tongue only for the moment. Mr Darcy had come to Longbourn to walk with the Bennets to church and now sat on the sofa beaming at Lizzy, though, for reasons Mary could not fathom, he threw a few curious glances at her as well. His attention mostly reserved for casting smitten glances at Lizzy, he rambled on about the jellies, puddings, trifles, ragouts, and other dishes being assembled for the Netherfield Christmas dinner.

"Miss Bingley has driven the housekeeper to exhaustion," he said, and though he spoke to Mama, his gaze drifted back to Lizzy, his smile deepening as it did. "Mr Bingley would have accompanied us on the walk to church as well, but his sister seemed to think some of the servants required a dressing-down, and she claimed she had no time for it."

"Scolding the servants on Christmas! I hope Mr Bingley will not do it on her behalf," Lizzy said.

Mr Darcy's smile deepened under her attention. "There is no fear of that. He is meek as milk to them at the best of times, and any reproaches he tries to deliver on Christmas Day are likely to turn to praise and humility within seconds."

"And Lord MacArthur? Will he be joining us?" Mary's cheeks felt as fiery as the Yule Log, but she could not help asking.

Mr Darcy's look of curiosity returned, as if he were reconsidering his opinion of her. "He will be along presently," was all he said, however, and the conversation turned as the Bennets began the arduous and noisy process of seeking out their pelisses and scarves. Before the full complement of mittens and bonnets could be assembled, however, Lord MacArthur was announced.

The maid who brought him in stumbled over her words, as well she might. For the first time in their acquaintance, Lord MacArthur was dressed as a lord should be. His greatcoat was new, every seam tidy, and not even a dusting of snow to mar its smoothness. The superfine coat beneath it was spotless, and his boots shone with good care.

After making his Christmas greetings, Lord MacArthur bowed to the family. Then he looked meaningfully at Mary and gave an even deeper second bow for her alone, one likely intended to astound with its stately elegance. Indeed, he bent so low that Mary reached out in worry that he might topple over, but he righted himself at the last moment, the only sign of his near miss the holly sprig pinned to his lapel having gone awry. "If you will pardon me, I must speak to Miss Mary about the Meryton Widows and Orphans Society."

"But that is all over," Kitty piped in, and Lizzy quickly hushed her.

"Perhaps we can lead the promenade to church." The Scottish accent rolling on his tongue had never sounded so friendly. Mary hurried to join him, wrapping her scarf tighter around her neck. The brush of cold air on her cheeks as they went outside did nothing to dispel the heat in them. Mary and Lord MacArthur soon outpaced the rest of the family.

Lord MacArthur drew a new purse from his pocket, one netted unexpertly yet with unmistakable care from red and green thread. It was the Christmas present Mary had given him. Lord MacArthur gently rubbed the workmanship with his thumb. His appreciation was so clear that

Mary doubted he even saw the asymmetry in its width nor the awkward, tangled loops of netting at one side. *I suppose there are advantages to having an untidy beau,* Mary thought ruefully. She hoped the gift signalled her contrition for assuming the hole in his old purse had been a ruse when he offered to purchase roast nuts for her.

Lord MacArthur's gaze lifted from the purse. "Thank you for my gift, Miss Mary."

"Thank you for mine. I love the watercolour. Did you paint it yourself?"

His awkward smile still made her heart beat fast. "I did."

"I am sorry I presumed you were poor. And I am sorry for assuming you meant—well—something not… *right* by kissing me." Mary took a deep breath. "It seems I have much to learn about kindness and charity. Perhaps you wish to discuss the Meryton Widows and Orphans Society, after all." The humour in her voice betrayed her.

"Only to say that I hope a branch may be founded in Scotland." He reached out to grasp her hand, and she savoured the feel of his gloved fingers around hers. "I see how it is. You want to be loved for your virtues, but it is just as likely that we are loved for our faults. Or what we think of as our faults. I love you for your kindness, charity, and honesty, Mary. And I love you for your little foibles as well—your wish to be noticed and not overshadowed by your sisters, your penchant for instruction. The latter of which I greatly need, by the by." He grinned, tilting his head. "You like some of my faults, do you not? There is a little of the angel in me, and a little of the devil as well. Can you love the devilish side, the side that stole a kiss from you?"

"I already do." Mary ducked her head.

"Then marry me, Miss Mary."

Now she could not help lifting her head, gazing into his eyes with a new sort of pride, one mixed with wonder and gratitude for a dream fulfilled. "I shall."

"Then it looks as though I shall get my Christmas wish." Snowflakes began to sift through the air, silvering his red hair. For once his locks were smoothed down in Byronic waves rather than sticking out in every direction. Mary nearly reached out to tousle it to reveal the awkward young man she had first known.

"You are not supposed to say what your wish was before it comes true," she said, a new playfulness entering her voice as her heart brimmed with joy.

"I shall take the risk." He tucked her arm in his, pulling her closer. "Will your mother weather a third engagement this holiday?"

Mary giggled. "She will manage."

As they walked, Mary could almost picture the happiness to come: the delight of telling her news to her parents and Mr Weathering, the new plans to be made for a new life, and, best of all, Lord MacArthur's company through it all. That moving to Scotland might involve a little hardship pleased her. She supposed she would always have a streak of martyrdom in her nature. She simply had to make sure that part of her was used to good purpose, rather than annoying others with it to little effect. *And I must make sure life is not all martyrdom. I must pursue my own enjoyment as well.* Smiling up at her awkward Mr Arthur, she felt she had already found one source of pure enjoyment already.

And throughout the Christmas service of the freshly decorated Meryton church, though it was not botanically correct to do so, Mary pictured pink daffodils in every cluster of holly, each wreath of pine boughs, and every sprig of mistletoe.

EPILOGUE

Mary was wrong; her mother did not manage the news of a third daughter engaged at all well—at least, not if 'manage' meant behaving with any degree of decorum or rationality. When Mama learned that Mary was to be Lady MacArthur, she sat in stunned silence for a good minute, then burst from her chair in wordless noises of joy. Then she grabbed her pelisse, called for the carriage, and shot out the door to deliver the news of three daughters engaged—three!— to her every acquaintance with an almost gibbering glee. And though her mother's ecstasy pleased Mary, she found herself far better pleased by Mr Weathering's calm smile and simple words:

"I always hoped you would live a happy life, Miss Bennet. And now I think you are beginning to know the way of it."

Though the Darcy and Bingley weddings were accomplished swiftly and with great éclat, Mary found she had to wait for hers. Planning a wedding necessarily took some time, and furthermore, as Lord MacArthur at first told Mary sheepishly, his mother wished for an engagement of a sober enough duration that all could be assured the couple's attachment was no passing fancy. It seemed his doting mother had, as mothers are wont to do, not forgotten a particular incident in Arthur's youth when he had become enthralled by a horse he had seen at auction, only to discover an even better, faster, more beautiful beast moments after purchasing the first. Once Lord MacArthur explained to his mother that the present circumstance was not at all the same thing because Mary was not a horse but rather a lovely, accomplished, delightful, witty young woman whom he would love ardently till the day he died, the lady graciously acquiesced, and planning for the wedding began in earnest. Letters flew back and forth to Scotland, improving

Mary's acquaintance with the ladies who were to be her mother and sisters there. Though Mary felt some regret that she would be far from her own family, she was relieved to discover her new mother's letters had a sweetness and patience she was sure she would like. Lord MacArthur's sisters both seemed kind and genteel, while his favourite sister Hattie had a droll sense of humour that made Mary eager to meet her. The time was also spent in getting to know Lord MacArthur better, and Mary found herself delighted with the pastimes of an engaged woman. Though she spent many an hour sitting in a cosy corner with her husband-to-be, she spent others studying her new duties and resolving to blend good conduct with playfulness in her role of Lady MacArthur. Her serious streak remained, fitting for the solemn accomplishment of Christian and civic pursuits, but a light-heartedness and steady belief in love tinged it, like a rosy warmth added to a pale daffodil.

It was no surprise that Mary's new favourite colour, fated to bedeck many a room in the halls of MacArthur House and many a gown swirling in Highland reels, was pink.

The End

About the Author

Elizabeth Rasche has a doctorate in philosophy and lives in Arkansas. When she has a Jane Austen novel in one hand, a cup of tea in the other, and a cat on her lap, her day is pretty much perfect.

Also by Elizabeth Rasche

A Learned Romance
Flirtation & Folly
The Birthday Parties of Dragons (as Lisa Rasche)

MISGIVINGS & MISTLETOE

KARALYNNE MACKRORY

CHAPTER ONE

Darcy

It was insufferably cold. The air had been crisp with the slight scent of snow when we boarded the carriage at Darcy House in London. The sky painted white with grey veins of chimney smoke weaving upwards into the heavy clouds. I ought to have waited out the little winter burst of weather. I expected it was like any at this time of year, a temper tantrum from Mother Nature. A short torrent of heavy snow to be shortly followed by a weak sun and pale blue skies once again.

I ought to have waited. I should have allowed Georgiana the pleasure of a snowy walk in the park near our London home on Brook Street and only embarked northward towards Pemberley when the roads were less likely to be bogged down by the weather. She would have enjoyed that and yet the selfishness I seem unable, or perhaps unwilling, to root out of my character prevailed again.

It was useless in the extreme to think of the ought tos and should haves. I had been plagued enough by them as it was. Lord knew I had many regrets. They have been my constant companion these many months and dwelling on them has served me ill as I continue to play them across my mind as if I could direct a different outcome by simple will of mind.

In a word, I was a coward. That was the reason even now Georgiana was huddled under several heavy carriage rugs and tucked in with all but one of the hot bricks. I looked towards her and found her eyes on me.

"Are you quite warm, dearest?"

"Yes, Brother. I thank you. But are you not cold? Here, have one of the blankets. It was kind of you to give them all to me, but you must be positively frozen."

I stayed her hand with my own gloved one, adjusting the rug more snugly around her shoulders once again.

"I am perfectly comfortable, I assure you."

My sister frowned at me, her doubt writ plainly on her beautiful features. Well, there was nothing to it. Her comfort was paramount, and no number of fur rugs would change the cold I felt anyway as it originated from within rather than without.

Our original plans to journey northward for the Festive Season were purposely kept flexible as experience had taught me one could not control the weather and the further north we travelled, the more treacherous the roads could become. However, it was folly in the extreme that I insisted we begin our journey today.

And why the ill-judged departure? Mr Gardiner had said she would be journeying to London to spend the Festive Season with them. Lately, I purposely pushed her name from my thoughts whenever possible.

His eye twinkled with just such a glint as I had oft seen when either of the Gardiners occasioned to speak of their niece. I suspected they had known the wishes of my heart for some time now. Perhaps as early as our first detestable negotiations regarding the business with Wickham months ago.

I had come to respect both of El–...her esteemed relations during those torturous three weeks spent discovering Miss Lydia and Wickham, bringing the lady to safety, and arranging the marriage. Revulsion shivered through me at the word.

Matrimony had been a short-lived dream in my mind. It had been enlivened by the sunlight streaming through the windows of Pemberley, weaving through her mahogany locks, as she stood near the window and turned pages for Georgiana at the pianoforte. That dream grew from a spark to a raging inferno. Hopes I had not dared allowed myself to reach for, seemed within my grasp. She had looked at me then, a slight smile upon her rounded lips. Her eyes warm and bold, dared to hold my own captive longer than was perhaps proper. It was then that the blasted word marriage danced across my heart, spurring beats to skip.

In that moment, I could have bet all that I owned that she did not hate me as she did at Rosings Park when I had insulted her so abominably. Encountering her at Pemberley later in the summer had felt like an unexpected boon, a gift from God. It was a chance to do all I could to show her that I was not so mean a person as to ignore her perfectly aimed barbs of criticism so expertly deployed at Hunsford. I would show her I had taken her strictures to heart and had attempted to right myself and become a gentleman worthy of the hand of such a lady. No, in my home in August, she did not hate me.

Back then the word marriage did not taste bitter.

The business with Wickham and Lydia Bennet changed all of that, for it stole all the sweetness the word had held just as assuredly as it had stolen any chance of happiness in such a state for me.

While I had gained a trusted friend in Mr Gardiner from the distasteful job of saving the reputation of those who had little enough care for it in the first place, I had lost so much more in the process and had not even known it. That understanding would come later when I had returned to Hertfordshire with Bingley after Wickham had taken his obnoxious bride to their new posting in Newcastle.

Elizabeth had been grave, indifferent, and withdrawn. Her eyes never held mine long and any attempt I made to converse with her was thwarted by others. It was as if she had formed a confederacy with her friends for protection from any attention from me. I could not even return my tea cup to the table set aside for such a purpose at Longbourn without Elizabeth's friends surrounding her and spiriting her away. It was then that the hope of marriage burned through its flame and dissolved to ash.

Of course she could not forgive me for failing her sister in such an egregious way. My selfishness had prevented Wickham's character to be rightly understood before it was too late. And Elizabeth—I winced at the lance to my heart, deserving the pain of it—could not forgive me. I understood it perfectly too, which was the worst of it. How I hated that I forced her to call him brother.

My only comfort was that she did not know of my actions to save her family's reputation. Her heart was too good, and I did not wish for affection built on a foundation of gratitude.

So I retreated to London and did not even return for my friend's wedding to Miss Jane Bennet that followed so swiftly afterwards. It pained me to think of Bingley's disappointment. I could provide no right excuse not to stand up with him. Good natured as he was, he did not hold such a slight against me, but extended a welcome invitation to spend Christmas with him and Mrs Bingley. That too I declined. At the time, I had not known she would go to her London relations, and the temptation to see her was too great. I told myself I was sparing her feelings, but I begin to believe I was only thinking of my own.

When Mr Gardiner had disclosed she was for London and would not spend the Festive Season at Longbourn or Netherfield, a dark cloud surrounded and suffocated me. She was to arrive in but a day. My chest pounded at the idea of her being so close. I began to persuade myself with any manner of ridiculous arguments that I could encounter her without the lancing slice to my heart that the past had brought. And then I remembered her indifference when last we met.

I nearly laughed bemusedly to think that I had experienced her approbation, albeit briefly, at Pemberley, and had endured her abhorrence at Hunsford. How tragic that I should almost wish for her hatred over seeing her indifferent to me. I was not foolish enough to believe I could ever regain her approval.

Mr Gardiner had begun to extend the invitation to dinner after her arrival when instinct had prompted me to inelegantly cut him off.

"I thank you, but it will be impossible to accept. Georgiana and I leave for Pemberley tomorrow. I apologise, I had meant to mention it earlier."

Mr Gardiner had been taken back by my quick refusal, unused as he was to anything less than convivial conversation between the two of us these many months. He hid his surprise well, and it was a testament to his good breeding—better than my own at present—that he did not give voice to the change in my tone either.

The possibility of seeing her had seized a great claw about my throat, squeezing the life out of me while dragging that ever present yearning to the front with powerful force.

"I am sorry to hear it. Can you not postpone a day?" Mrs Gardiner entreated kindly.

My expression felt brittle and apt to shatter. "I wish I could, but sudden business carries me northward."

The sudden business was undoubtably my self-preservation. We spoke no more of my travels, sudden though they were, and I took my leave of them soon thereafter. Truth be told, I was sorry for it too, for their company had been a source of contentment for me. I had anticipated another week of it at least before departing for Derbyshire. They were intelligent, well-spoken, and good people and I shudder to think that I had once cast aspersions upon their worth last spring.

Informing Georgiana of our departure was the work of a moment thereafter. She had never questioned my arrangements for our travel before and did not start then. I had said I would travel north, and I would not dissemble to the Gardiners just to avoid her and so upon returning home, I informed my valet and the housekeeper of our new plans and set them in motion.

Turning towards the window, I saw that what had begun in London as the stray dusting of snow had become a swirling wall of white. Thick flakes of snow swiped past the near-frosted glass of the carriage window. Beyond, the ground had been blanketed several inches due to the diligent winter storm. The world was a spinning, white abyss.

However, I could feel the horses were setting a good pace and the wheels felt secure. I wondered briefly if she was travelling in this weather, and I hoped to God she was not. It did not feel as if we were in any danger—my groom had our conveyance well in hand; however, I could not help but distrust any other driver. None would be as careful as my own. If she were travelling even now to her relations in London, I prayed fervently for her safety and the good judgment of her driver. And the soundness of her carriage. And the warmth of the rugs about her. Surely her father would have advised against travel on such a day.

We slowed at a turnpike, to allow a passing carriage to make its way in the path we had just come. Curiosity propelled me to the other side to peer out that window to see if I might recognise the carriage. My interest was quickly lost when it was nothing more than a farmer's cart, loaded with goods draped in oil cloth.

Eager to drive past this unaccountable feeling of disappointment within me, I anticipated the feel of the carriage regaining its previous speed but realised that John had slowed for another carriage. I heard his muffled voice exchange a greeting and a few indistinguishable words with the other driver. Soon, however, the other traveller passed our carriage window. It was an unremarkable grey carriage, not her family's equipage.

"I am worried we shall find ourselves trapped in this snow."

Georgiana drew my attention from the lumbering carriage, slowly being swallowed up by the swirling flakes.

"Be at ease. John is well skilled and would deliver us to safety long before we could be marooned anywhere."

As if summoned, my groom appeared at my window, startling me with the realisation that we had not continued on after passing the last carriage, but stopped altogether. Had I been so transfixed with scrutinising the other carriage for recognition that I had not noticed we were still?

Opening the window, I greeted my head groom.

"What is it, John?"

"I took the libe'ty, sir of speakin' with that passin' carriage. The roads be passable now, but I wondered at the stretch ta come."

"That was wise of you. Tell me, what did he say?"

"He's as much as said the northern road is right swallowed up, sirah. I think 'twould be best if we sought our berth for the day and let the heaven pass its fury."

I was nodding before he had finished, for I trusted his judgment and knew he would not delay our travels without good cause.

"Where about are we?"

He rubbed his jaw through the thick muffler about his face and pulled his hat off briefly to scratch his crown as he evaluated his answer.

"I'd say we are aboot sixes to Hatching Green or your friend, Mr Bingley's house."

"Where are we, Brother?"

"John says we about equal distance between Hatching Green and Netherfield."

"I hate to think what Mr Bingley's new bride would think of us to land so unceremoniously at their doorstep without warning."

As little as I wished to stay at Netherfield, due to obvious reasons, least of which were the haunting memories, I could not allow her to persist in worrying on that regard.

"Mrs Bingley is the soul of kindness and would not for a moment find you the least bit of a burden, Georgie. I have no doubt she would be a most gracious host."

I was pleased to see the crease leave her brow and turned once again to tell my driver to stay our course and find us an inn in Hatching Green.

"In that case, if you do not mind, Brother, I should very much like to stay at Netherfield. Mrs Bingley is the sister of Miss Elizabeth Bennet who visited Lambton and Pemberley last summer, is she not?"

What was this rock that suddenly lodged in my throat? Instinctively I wished to dissuade her from this choice. The storm would likely pass by the morning and if we were already on our route, we might return to it all the sooner. Besides, I was certain my friend would attempt to entreat me to stay longer. Although she would be in London, I was certain that the ghost of her memory would haunt me at Bingley's home. It had been such when I returned last fall with hope in my heart only to have it dashed by her pervasive reserve.

Georgiana smiled sweetly at me, unaware of the turmoil her request stirred inside me. Her gentle opinion, spoken so sweetly, forced my hand. I answered her question with a nod, unable to confirm verbally that indeed, Mrs Bingley was her sister. With a mind growing numb despite the fervent beat of my heart, I turned to my groom.

"Take us to Netherfield then, John."

"Yessir."

Georgiana shivered at the cold air that had entered the carriage through the window. I closed it quickly, marvelling at the ability of my limbs to act without command, for there was simply no way my stunned mind controlled them. To Netherfield we would go. I thanked God she would not be there. In all likelihood, if she had not already left for London, she would be required to prepare for her journey at home. I comforted myself with the notion that I might enter her county silently and rob it of a night's sleep with impunity.

Who was I fooling? I was not likely to sleep a wink.

CHAPTER TWO

Elizabeth

A SHIVER RAN UP MY SPINE LIKE A GHOSTLY HAND, AND I pulled my cloak more securely around me. The brutal winds had died down about half an hour ago, and the snow now fell in peaceful, languid swirls to the ground. With my head tilted up I watched the spinning white crystals as they fell, unhindered or unhurried by the wind. This was the exact kind of quiet I had sought when venturing into the garden paths behind Netherfield. In this weather, not even small animals were scurrying about. The world had gone silent and still, and my heart beat a little calmer at the reprieve. A flash of colour drew my attention to the side where a Redwing trotted across a barren branch and up to another where it stilled and seemed to assess me.

I watched the little bird, admiring the way his plume blended into the white, brown, and grey branches while the tuft of rust painted feathers under its wings drew the eye. A proud noble bird, it seemed to me. It stayed still, quietly looking all around me, its head making small shifts in graceful though sudden movements. In that moment I felt envious of the creature. Its ability to withdraw into the background, without losing its very essence. The way it calmly perched as if content in its life.

My life had seen little contentment for months, and any certainty I had felt in myself had been gone the better part of the year. Not since before I had received the letter from Mr Darcy after his proposal at

Hunsford had I felt the peace of the assured. Until the moment that I read his letter, I had never known myself. I had been chasing that contentment since.

For the span of a few brief days, I had felt as if I had found that longed-for feeling. I felt certain that he would answer my every desire and fulfil all that I could hope for in a life's partner. During those stirring days at Pemberley, I felt whole and content. That all changed though.

The Redwing twitched its head to the side and in a flash flew off to another tree down the lane. At his departure, disappointment seeped into my bones like fire smoke. The soft sound of boots on snowy gravel drew my attention and I saw my sister Kitty, accompanied by Mr Gordan, making their way to where I stood in the gardens.

I stifled a sigh. No wonder the bird had fled. My moment of quiet was about to be interrupted as well. Mr Gordan was a kind man, handsome and amiable even. He was a cousin of my new brother Bingley. Mr Gordan and his friend, Mr Simons, had been invited to spend the Festive Season at Netherfield by Bingley. I had nothing with which to complain about Mr Gordan or Mr Simons, though the latter had hardly spoken a word in my presence in the whole of the two days I had been settled at my sister's home.

Mr Gordan was not as clever or quick witted as one gentleman, formerly known to me. It was difficult to find anyone who matched Mr Darcy's intelligent conversation. However, Mr Gordan was pleasant, politely interested, and often sought my company. I did not notice any particular regard from him; rather I had begun to suspect perhaps it was not strictly me he was seeking either. In fact, his companion, my sister, was often the recipient of his distracted gazing.

However, Kitty was full young still and, after Lydia had left our parents' home in the manner that she did, was made less confident without that sister's constant influence. I could not but be glad for the changes in Kitty, for she had long been too attached to Lydia's side and her character had begun to be tainted with the same impulsive recklessness.

Without Lydia, she was still prone to bouts of silly childishness but never with any of the selfish malice that marked Lydia's behaviour. I was pleased to see the changes in her and anticipated more would become apparent the longer my sister Jane and I fostered her comportment. I had not anticipated sharing the task with Jane for the next several weeks, though.

I ought to have been in a carriage to London had it not been for a number of factors, the primary of which was the very same approaching gentleman. My mother, always the matchmaker, declared I could not escape to London to my aunt and uncle's house—not when Mr Bingley was hosting a number of eligible bachelors. How overset she would have been had I told her I no longer intend to marry so it mattered little if my new brother were to have one hundred fine-looking cousins invited to Netherfield.

I am certain my father would have heard my protest and allowed me to keep to my plans. However, before I could appeal for his support against Mama, Jane entreated me sweetly to come to Netherfield. It was to be her first house party, and she was discomposed to host it without her dearest sister. My mother I could have withstood; my dearest Jane, I could not.

The letter to Mr and Mrs Gardiner with my regrets was sent early this morning by post. Given the weather, I guessed it would arrive late. I regretted the need to disappoint both myself and my aunt, who had written with anticipated excitement of her intentions to host a few dinner parties. It must be said that I suspected my aunt saw my low spirits at Jane's wedding and her efforts to cheer me with social parties both garnered my gratitude and stirred my discontent. At any other time, I might have welcomed such social gatherings, for I dearly loved to laugh. Of late, I had been feeling rather disinclined to be in society.

Events being what they were, I was forced to admit that any hope for Mr Darcy had long fled and any tender feelings he might have once harboured would have now long been dissolved. I could not live day to day on the bread of disappointment. Whether it was London or a winter house party at Netherfield with Jane, it mattered little enough; I must get the better of this hopelessness.

With that reminded determination, I greeted my sister and Mr Gordan with a smile.

"I see you have caught me in my little hiding place."

Mr Gordan bowed, smiling broadly as he replied, "We do not wish to interrupt your musing, Miss Bennet, and will depart post haste if you so desire. Say the word and Miss Catherine and I will take another path."

"I should like a bit of company as it is. Shall we walk along the tree line? The ground is mostly unhindered by snow, and it is easier to traverse."

Kitty latched onto my arm and we began walking side by side, Mr Gordan following a few paces behind us. Our path curved along those same trees the Redwing had taken, where he had flown from branch to branch and eyed the snow-covered garden below for any morsel of nourishment. Before long, it curved around to a small decorative lake.

"Do you remember, Lizzy, when the pond at Longbourn froze over and we could slide in our boots across the surface?"

My mind drew forth the memory instantly: pink cheeks, warm muffed hands, and the exhilaration of gliding across the bumpy slick surface of the frozen pond. We ran as best we could, our arms and legs swinging for purchase of a little balance and then slid across the ice. Without any ice skates, we were forced to make do with our boots.

I squeezed my sister's arm. "Indeed, I do. I also recall the frequency with which we lost our footing and ended on our backsides on the ice. I believe none of us returned home that day without a surfeit of bruises."

"I can picture it perfectly," Mr Gordan cut in, "and am only sorry I had not stumbled upon you winter fairies at your play that day."

"Hardly that, sir!" Kitty's retort was full of laughter. "We looked closer to a bunch of ragamuffin urchins than some delicate winter fairies. Our hair a fright and our cheeks windburned, and I believe, Lizzy, you tore your skirt. Mama was not best pleased to see it either."

Humour bubbled through me, releasing tension and filling me with sweet bliss. That was the winter after the gentlemen from Netherfield had left the area after the Netherfield ball, and we sisters were all feeling more than normally cooped up. Jane was broken hearted, Lydia and Kitty upset over a series of training days that kept the militia from our threshold, and Mary often felt melancholy during the long winter months. Lydia had been provoking our middle sister as it was, Kitty complaining of her boredom, and even gentle Jane was terse in her replies that day.

With determination, I had dragged all my sisters—one or two very much displeased at the notion—out into the weak winter sun for a walk. When we had come upon the pond, which must be said is not too distant from the house as it is, my younger two sisters were already complaining about the cold and wishing to return. On impulse I declared that the first one to reach the other side of the pond could determine when to return to the house.

Upon this edict, I had attempted to cross it, thinking I would easily reach the other side before any of the others could so much as step out to follow me. The slick surface soon bettered me, and I came swiftly and humbly to my backside, though sliding some feet with the momentum of my start. The shock and pain of the fall pulsed my back and silenced for a minute, my open-mouthed expression matching those of my sisters at the shoreline. Then I laughed. My hilarity could not be subdued, and I laid there a few mere feet onto the pond, with my sides pinching in a stitch at the uncontrolled humour. Soon all my sisters were enjoying a little reprieve at my cost. Lydia even going so far as to declare her ability would far surpass my own at crossing the pond.

She had attempted and, to her credit, had made it a few feet further than I when she lost her footing. The comedic relief then turned palpable. It became a breathing thing, pulling from each of our breasts the discontent of the day and replacing it with sweet release. Eventually all my sisters had tentatively joined Lydia and I on the pond. We did manage to balance a little as we slipped our boots across frozen water.

"And who was it that won the prize?" Mr Gordan asked with a chuckle.

Kitty's smile faded and she tilted her head as if in thought, turning towards me. "I do not believe anyone did. As I recall, we all spent an hour at the pond spinning each other and trying to master our gliding."

"You are correct, sister. By the time we had our fill of bruises and freezing spills, we rushed back to the house for a warming cup of tea."

"'Tis too bad that my cousin's lake is not frozen, for I should have loved to see who would win the challenge this time."

He had said it to me, though his eyes had glanced at my sister. Oblivious to his attention, Kitty had bent to scoop up a patch of fresh snow. She brought it to her face and inhaled deeply.

"You will think it sounds strange, but I love the smell of fresh snow."

"Snow is only water, it has no smell," Mr Gordan countered, charmed.

Kitty opened her mouth to protest but seeing the glint in his eye, rolled hers in a gesture I had hoped she had quit when Lydia left. I looked about while my companions bantered about the smell of snow. I might have joined in their debate, as I believed snow did have a scent: it was the scent of hope and new beginnings. When it snowed, everything on the ground was covered in fresh white softness. Dead hedges, broken stones were all the same to the master of the skies. All made beautiful after a fresh blanket of snow. It did not snow in Hertfordshire as often as other parts of the kingdom, but every time I felt as if it was a gift.

My eyes found my careful winged friend. He was perched once again high on a nearby branch. I nodded my head in acknowledgement to him, stopping short of a curtsey. The freedom and grace of the bird was a source of admiration, and, in that moment, I promised with determination to seek my happiness in whatever measure was still left for me.

"You are quite mistaken," Kitty said with a laugh. "Here try it for yourself!"

Of a sudden, I felt the cold sting of snow spray across my face, melting and sliding down my cheeks. When I cleared the flakes sending stinging sensations over my skin it was to see Kitty standing wide eyed and tense, her gloved hands covering her gaping mouth.

"Miss Bennet, are you alright? Here, take my handkerchief."

The gentleman's voice must have pulled Kitty out of her shocked state, and she rushed to me, full of remorse.

"Oh Lizzy! I am terribly sorry. The snow was intended for Mr Gordan."

With the help of the linen, I wiped the remainder of the melting snow from my brow and embraced my sister in a fierce hug. Laughter once again built low inside me, pulling with it any melancholy I had ventured outside to banish in the first place and expelling it into the cool breeze.

I assured her no harm done and while she looked at my laughter a bit awkwardly, as if she did not quite know how to take me, she accepted my assurances with a relieved sigh.

"Well, I am not so quick to forgive, I fear. As I was your intended target, you may wish to run, Miss Catherine, for my arm is surer than yours."

Kitty once again was struck dumb at the notion, disbelieving that Mr Gordan meant to retaliate at all. He raised a brow at her hesitation and scooped up a bit of snow in his gloves. Kitty eyed it and I saw the fire of defiance enter her eyes. She feigned nonchalance as she dusted off the snowflakes that were accumulating on her cloak.

"You, sir, do not scare me. You would not dare."

Mr Gordan raised his hand as if to throw it, only to pause when Kitty shrieked and with a laugh took off down the path towards the house.

"You had better take after her, Miss Bennet."

"Oh no, I shall be no part of this."

Mr Gordan turned towards me, a genial smile upon his lips. In that moment, he looked quite handsome. "Aye, she might have started it, but that does not necessarily follow that I mean to be fair. Go now, Miss Bennet, catch up to your sister."

Swiftly I reached up to the nearest branch above where we stood and shook it. Snow came tumbling down around Mr Gordan, catching only the edge of my cloak as I chased Kitty. My Redwing bird took flight too at my actions, flying higher into the heavy, laden sky. I heard his warbled call mingled with Mr Gordan's surprised laughter. A quick look over my shoulder confirmed the gentleman, covered in snow, was beginning his pursuit.

When I reached Kitty, we turned and saw that Mr Gordan had indeed followed. She latched upon my arm with a gleeful scream and turned her back as he tossed his ammunition at us, landing purposely near our feet. In unison, we turned towards the house again, our laughter trailing behind us in our wake. My sister pulled me determinedly towards the nearest doors to the house, the ones leading into the parlour.

I hoped my sister and new brother would forgive the unconventional entry into their home since in a moment it would be too late anyway. I pulled at the knob, thankful it was unlocked, and with rumbling laughter pulled her through before shutting the door behind us, our backs pressed against the glass.

My chest was heaving, my hand resting upon the cold skin above my dress as the warm woollen cloak I had worn had been tossed behind me in our escape. The heat of the parlour was welcome, and I felt the snowflakes about my shoulders and on my hair—which was in a ghastly mess as pins had escaped haphazardly—begin to melt into tiny droplets of water.

Kitty was laughing too, in a way I had not heard in many months. She turned to look through the door window as Mr Gordan approached. When he came through the door full of good humour as well, she hid behind my shoulders, her cold nose pressing into the back of my neck. Her childish glee spurred more laughter from me. The gentleman too seemed compelled to laugh at it.

It all happened so quickly then. Beyond our laughter, I recognised a silence in the room and that we were not alone. I first saw Jane and Mr Bingley sitting on a settee together, lips pressed together in amusement at our spectacle. Mary, with a book in the corner, looked quite disapproving and Mr Simons stood looking shocked nearby, with his eyes fixed upon us. A movement to my left caught my eye and I saw a trim figure sitting in an armchair near the fire.

My eyes travelled up her beautiful copper velvet travelling clothes, to the elegant cut of her coat. The laughter so readily upon my lips faded as I first recognised the figure to be Miss Darcy. Without the ability to stop them then, my eyes travelled from near her shoulder where a masculine hand rested tensely on the back of her chair.

There was little I could do to prevent my eager eyes then in seeking more of its owner. First a broad chest led to a cravat as white as the snow outside, then a familiar jawline pressed tightly closed, and finally to fathomless eyes bearing down upon me as if I had been conjured from the ether. That gaze stole through me, like the rapids of a raging river washing havoc as it cut through my senses. My wits were scattered, and my heart battered by the cold water running now viscously through my veins.

The expression on his face stilled my heart and stifled what was left of the good humour from our unconventional entrance. His face was cut from stone and pale with disapproval. What a sight I must have made, rolling into the parlour in a swirl of snow with Kitty and Mr Gordan. Bitterly did I regret the indulgence of a moment ago, not if it would further sink me in his eyes. But what was he doing here? I was certain that Mr Bingley had said he would not attend.

Belatedly I dipped a curtsey to both Darcys. His returned bow was perfunctory at best, though his sister's welcome was all that could be called warm as she rushed towards me with hands outstretched in pleased reception of renewing our acquaintance.

Numbly I returned her welcome. Though I believe I asked what brought her to Netherfield, I could hardly hear her reply. Not when every nerve was attuned to the movements of her brother. He had not stepped forward to greet me but had retreated to the mantel, his back to us, the muscles tense under his jacket. He stared at the flames within as if his very life depended upon it.

CHAPTER THREE

Darcy

BINGLEY PASSED ME A GLASS OF BRANDY AND TO MY CREDIT I neither spilled the dark liquid with trembling hands nor gulped it down heedlessly. Instead, I lifted the glass to my lips and partook a regulated, proper slip. The tumult of my senses would have me finish the glass and refill it once more. Ingrained gentlemanly restraint kept that from happening.

Mrs Bingley had gathered her sisters like a hen gathers her chicks and, with laughing rebukes, led them upstairs to change out of their wet, wintry attire, and invited Georgiana along to show her to a room to change out of her travelling clothes. She had only been within the room briefly, like a flash of lightning in the night, then the room went dark again.

My friend had asked if I wished for something stronger than the tea offered upon my arrival and, once the ladies had departed, I accepted, and we too left the room to the quiet of Bingley's study.

With unseeing eyes, I gazed into the swirling glass in my hand, the slow, churning movements a sort of comforting repetitive act. My mind, however, was still in the room I had just departed.

She was like Chione, the Greek goddess of snow, as she entered the room so abruptly, the icy wind spinning in behind her, snowflakes swirling along the dancing tune of her laughter. The sight of her at first seemed a wild dream. My eyes devoured every inch of her.

Her skin was either translucent ivory or rose pink, there was no in-between. She was alive and wild with energy and my heart stuttered to a stop at the glorious sight of her. Tendrils of hair blew around her until the door was successfully closed to the elements without and I watched as they gradually drifted around her face once more.

Everywhere she had sparkling crystals of snow clinging to her clothing like a night sky full of stars. Her laughter still drifted around the room, bouncing and touching each surface until every measure of it landed upon my heart.

How was it that I had gone so long without a drink of this effervescence, this *joie de vivre*? I drank in every aspect of the picture she presented, knowing at any moment she would become aware of our presence. Dreading and yearning with equal measure for her eyes to alight upon me.

The door had opened once more behind her and in came a figure in a dark great coat. The winter fairies' glee doubled at once. Reluctantly my eyes left Elizabeth and travelled to the newcomer. It was an unknown gentleman—his focus on my heart's desire, his lips lifted in pleasure. I disliked him immediately and wished him back into the snow from whence he came.

Dismissing the stranger most happily, I returned my eyes to her. A moment later our eyes connected, and a shock went through me, viscerally and painfully through every nerve of my body. I watched the rose bleed from her cheeks as all expression of pleasure drained out of her. Her fine eyes, so alive and spirited, dimmed. I watched it all, as anguish tore through my heart. Her delight had melted like the snowy stars upon her cloak and hair upon seeing me.

Numbly, I acknowledged her with a bow, wishing I could go to her and shake some life into her again. How repugnant my presence must be to her now after all that Wickham had done to her family. I burned with hatred for the man. For the blasted snow outside that had marooned me here and forced such torment upon her. For how nearly impossible it felt to resist going to her, even when her cheeks lost their pink loveliness. I wanted to take her up in my arms and beg her to have me. I needed to hold her to me and see if she smelled like the snow. To press my lips to the cold skin near her neck and warm her cheeks with my hands.

My sister stood and walked to her in greeting, the movement snapping me out of my head once more. Georgiana was now in possession of the embrace I so desperately desired. It was too much and forced me to retreat to the fireplace rather than follow with my own greetings. My mind raced and struggled through the shock of her presence to formulate plans for our departure. Every possibility was presented for evaluation, every option considered. Still all my senses were attuned to her voice, the sound of her welcome towards my sister. Her voice sounded higher, slightly strained to my ears, and I winced for the reason.

Jealousy burned within me as my ears caught the sound of the unknown gentleman speaking with Bingley. His voice was merry. The sound grated in my ears. Who was this man? And why did her eyes, those fine eyes that I had long admired, sparkle when he came through the door and shutter when she encountered me?

"Come now, Darcy. You must drink the brandy to be warmed by it. Staring does little good."

Bingley's carefree voice penetrated my review of the cascading memories from moments ago. I nodded at his jest and succumbed to what I had wished to do from the start and downed the glass in one gulp. Ignoring the disbelieving laugh of my friend, I refilled my glass with another measure and brought it to my lips. My back was to the room, and I paused planning to finish it off as well.

It would not do. I lowered the glass halfway, grasping at the edges of my composure and when I felt myself in good regulation, gently placed the glass without partaking further on the sideboard. With a deep breath I turned to my friend, every tumbling emotion within disguised.

"I thank you, Bingley, for allowing us to trespass upon your hospitality so unexpectedly. Had I any other choice, I would not have intruded."

"Nonsense, my friend. Jane and I are pleased beyond reason that the weather forced you to stop at Netherfield. We were both disappointed when business prevented your attendance at our nuptials. And you might recall, I invited you to holiday with us."

I acknowledged his words, careful not to allow the growing tempest within to show. Panic began to churn and grasp at my insides. Bingley had invited me to come to his house party but believing it likely his new sister would be there and, not wishing to darken that festive season, I had declined. Now that we were here at Netherfield, and the snow had prevented us making good on my excuse to have Christmas at Pemberley with Georgiana, I was growing ever more certain by the minute that Bingley would renew his early invite and entreat me to extend our stay.

Temptation burned within and, I daresay, a lesser man might have succumbed to it, but I had a greater resource within me to resist. She would not wish me here, and I would sooner give my life than bring her pain.

Bingley did not disappoint me; my friend spoke the words I had begun to expect and renewed his wish for us to stay for the entire season.

"I appreciate your kindness, but I am afraid—"

"Darcy! What pressing matter forces you northward in this weather?" Bingley half-laughed, half disbelievingly pointed to the window. The snow was still coming down heavily and the sky was darkened with the late afternoon. Soon the sun would set. Daylight was short in the winter.

"In the morning the roads will soon be passably frozen, and we ought to go on with our plan."

"I would not place my bets on that. With how quickly it is covering the roads, it would be foolish to think the roads could be traversed in several days' time, say nothing of tomorrow."

I was already shaking my head. "It is impossible that I stay, Bingley, and that is the truth of it."

"Is it Caroline? Darcy, she is not here. She did not wish to return to Hertfordshire and opted to stay with the Hursts in London. You will not have to endure her fawning."

"Miss Bingley does not factor in my decision to depart again tomorrow."

His lips pressed together in displeasure, and I hated myself for it. My friend had always been easy mannered and pleasant. I was disappointing him and being unreasonable, but he could not know it was all for her.

He turned his back to me and walked a pace to the mantel. Though he was still, I sensed he was agitated as his hands, which he held behind him, were pressed into fists.

Truth be told, I had never seen Bingley so displeased. My spirits sunk further, and I knew I had no justifiable reason to refuse. It was even prudent to stay as I could very well see myself that the snow would not let up soon enough for a continuance of our journey north. However, it must be attempted.

"When you came to me in September and told me you were mistaken regarding Jane's regard, I believed you. When you had expressed remorse for extending our separation when she was in London by not telling me of her presence, I believed you."

Bingley slowly turned around and solemn, almost accusatory eyes pressed upon me. "You returned with me to Meryton when I came to press my suit with her. And left just as swiftly when it became apparent that, much to my everlasting good fortune, Jane would soon be mine. I begin to see now that perhaps I was too hasty in believing you when you offered your congratulations at our betrothal."

I opened my mouth to refute what I could see easily he had begun to suspect because of my actions of late. But the words died in my throat. I could not explain that every blessing he had garnered had been my heart's desire for myself with his bride's sister. It was a bitter, slashing slice to my heart.

"You missed my wedding, for God's sake! I begin to wonder...do you disapprove of my wife so much that you cannot even stomach her hospitality?"

"No! God's teeth, Bingley, no. She is a worthy woman and a most excellent lady."

Bingley scoffed, again turning his back to me. I began to pace, burdened with this new pain. As my closest friend, I could not allow him to go on believing as he did, yet how could I tell him that it was not his wife's presence that troubled me but her sister's.

"If foolishness over friendship is your desire, so be it. But know this, Darcy, I am heartedly ashamed that it has come to this. For I am married, and God help me I do not regret it even if..."

He did not voice the last, but I could easily finish it. Even if he and I could no longer be friends as a result of it. My pacing grew more fevered, and I ran my hand through my hair repeatedly. I could not stay, yet I could not go. Her words from Hunsford broke into my depressed thoughts. I was selfishly disregarding Bingley's feelings by keeping my own counsel. It would not do.

"I love her," I blurted.

At Bingley's outraged and shocked countenance, I laughed but quickly corrected his misguided assumption. "I love Miss Elizabeth."

My shoulders shrugged and my hands fell open in supplication to my friend. I could hear my voice was ragged, shaky with resignation. "I love her, and she hates me."

Though the confession poured out of me in painful, though relieving purges, it had cost me too and I sunk into the nearest chair and covered my face with my hands.

"Darcy—"

I did not wish to hear his pitying words, so I filled the air with my own. I told him of my long-held admiration, about encountering her at Hunsford, and about the dagger my pride had forced into my own heart at her rightful refusal. He had been at Pemberley this summer when she had been there and countered with her obvious approbation there. That had been the worst of my confession. I had to acknowledge how much hope had been grown there in those few days. Bingley did not know the particulars of Miss Lydia and Mr Wickham's elopement. I had only approached him after that matter was settled.

If Mrs Bingley had informed him of the irregularity of that union taking place, I did not know. I certainly was not going to tell him of the imprudence of his wife's youngest sister. Thank heavens, I had made the Gardiners promise not to share my part of it. Bingley's wife could not have known any more than Miss Elizabeth that I had a part in securing the marriage.

I did however explain how little Miss Elizabeth seemed pleased with her new brother-in-law, Wickham. And how she likely blamed me for not warning the neighbourhood last year when her family might have been protected from such a regrettable connexion. Bingley admitted he had not noticed Elizabeth's demeanour when we returned to Meryton in September. His focus had been on the eldest Bennet daughter. It was painful to admit aloud what had tortured me within.

"She could hardly countenance the sight of me, Bingley. Gone were the teasing words and playful smiles of Pemberley. I might have once held her affection, but by September, I had lost it. She hates me."

Bingley smirked at me, and my brows lowered in disgust. Regardless of his amiable temperament, I saw nothing of humour in it.

"Clear that brow of yours. I am only thinking that you simply must stay now."

Exasperated, I stared at him. "Have you not been listening at all? She does not wish for my presence, and I would not force it up on her."

Bingley laughed. He laughed! Shaking his head as he walked to his desk, I watched him leap in the air behind it. It took another similar jump for him to reach and grasp what he aimed for. My eyes travelled to what he captured in his hand and flinched as he tossed it to me. Instinctively my hands raised to catch it. It was a kissing bough, a tightly woven bundle of mistletoe.

Confused I tossed it back at him and stood to leave. I had not expected Bingley to be so obtuse or uncaring. The damned mistletoe bundle was lobbed at my shoulders again and expertly I plucked it from the air with a frustrated groan.

"Will you stop it? Is this all the reply I am to receive when I tell you that I have no hope?"

Bingley smiled wider and I swear my hand twitched with the temptation to take the greenery in my hands and gag him with it, our long-lasting friendship be damned.

"Calm yourself, Darcy. I have a plan. And you shall have more than hope by the end of it." His head nodded towards the mistletoe in my hand, and I did attempt to gag him as I aimed right for his face this time in returning it.

I was nearly to the study door, out of humour and more than ready to seek my chambers above. I would need all the respite I could get if I were to endure dinner in the same room as her this evening. Say nothing of that smirking unknown gentleman eager to pay her his attentions. What torture awaited me!

"She does not hate you."

Bingley's words froze my legs and I stood still, my back to him and my chest immobile, lest any breath might remove the words from the air or prevent me from hearing more.

"She does not hate you, Darcy. I cannot break a confidence, mind you. But I can tell you that Miss Elizabeth most certainly does not blame you for her sister's union to Wickham."

I turned at this, pressing my lips together lest they speak the hopeful words raging through my head. Bingley smiled at me, shrugged and tossed the mistletoe in the air above him, catching it easily.

"I cannot believe—"

"Believe it. I will say no more than this. Woo her and win her, Darcy. And I daresay, you may find it not as impossible a task as you think."

My head bent, my eyes were certain to be wild, searching, as my thoughts, disjointed and confused, tried to settle into any semblance of order. Could Bingley speak the truth? My thoughts went swiftly to Hunsford once again and how mistaken I had been about Jane Bennet's feelings for my friend. Elizabeth had known her sister better. Conversely, might Mrs Bingley know Elizabeth better too?

It was not a short jump to assume then that Mrs Bingley would then share with her husband the truth of it. Hope surged within me and for the first time in weeks I wondered if I might still have a grasp at happiness.

"When does she depart for London?" Now my mind was tentatively formulating possibilities, but I had to know how much time I would be allowed with her.

"How did you—It does not matter. Her plans have changed. Mrs Bennet would not countenance her missing Jane's house party when she learned there would be eligible bachelors in residence."

My mind's eye returned to the exquisite picture of Elizabeth as she entered in from the snowstorm. Her beauty was staggering, and the cold rose of her cheeks begged to be warmed with kisses. Then the picture was spoiled by the addition of a third of her walking party.

I frowned and said, "And what of this gentleman suitor of hers?"

Bingley looked puzzled so I clarified. That gentleman had produced her laughter, while the sight of me had stolen it from her breath.

"My cousin, Mr Gordan?" Mr Bingley, laughed. "I think not."

"I saw the way he was looking at her, and she at him, Bingley."

Bingley's face turned contemplative. He shook his head finally and replied without concern. "Perhaps you have some competition then. However, if you choose to forfeit the match and carry on to Pemberley, then you may."

I growled out my response. "I will not forfeit."

Bingley's smile stretched wide. With one hand he slapped my shoulder and with the other he pressed the mistletoe into my chest. My hand came to catch it.

"Then you had better tell your valet that you will be staying at Netherfield." Bingley walked out of the room and stopped to turn once more to me over the threshold. "She does not hate you."

'She does not hate you'. The words echoed in my head, growing stronger with every turn. Still, I could not act without my own proof. I looked at the mistletoe in my hand and briefly allowed my imagination to take hold the thought of a stolen kiss. Warmth spread through me, and I promised myself I would watch for any sign from Elizabeth. If she gave me any hope at all I would latch on to it and never let go.

With renewed purpose, I tucked the mistletoe into my breast pocket and headed to the stairs to inform my valet, Wilkins, of our change of plans.

CHAPTER FOUR

Elizabeth

BEFORE I COULD ACCOUNT FOR IT, I WAS PRESSED INTO MY bedchamber by Jane, and a maid was helping me out of my wet clothing. All the while my body made the necessary movements to remove the sodden dress, replace my boots with warm woolly slippers, and adorn another dress, I found other parts of me were elsewhere. My heart was still someplace below, probably lodged in Mr Darcy's pocket where it leapt out of my breast the moment my eyes connected with his. My mind—there was no determining its location for I had yet to gather enough rational thoughts. I had lost my wits entirely, to where I did not know. I suspect they might have abandoned me likewise when my heart did.

Though I could not fathom his being here at Netherfield, I had no trouble recalling the last time I had seen him. He was grave then and gave me no encouragement. When last we saw each other, I thought of little else than that I wished to fall up on his feet and give my gratitude for all he had done for my poor undeserving sister. I intended to express my family's thanks, little though they knew they owed them to Mr Darcy; however, every attempt to speak to him had been thwarted by my own cowardice or the perversity of my neighbours in wishing to speak to me at the most inopportune moments.

Jane and Charles's wedding flashed before my eyes. His absence was acutely noticed, at least, by the bride, the groom, and me. Jane had tried to assure me that his reasoning for missing it was business and not personal. She did not think, after all I had described at Pemberley, that Mr Darcy would have lost all affection for me. It was the last we spoke of it since we saw the outcome quite differently.

A tentative knock sounded on my door and given the maid had completed her duties some time ago, leaving me to warm by my fire, I stood to answer it. I glanced at the mantel clock and was dismayed to see how quickly the hours had been eaten up with my useless musing, for it was nearly time to go down to dinner.

My visitor was none other than Miss Darcy. Delight and trepidation surged within me as I pulled the door aside and welcomed her in. She was timid and uncertainty sat on her shoulders; she kept her words quiet as she asked if she might visit with me a while until it was time to go down.

"Of course, I should like to hear how you passed these last months since we were together last."

Miss Darcy smiled then, presumably relieved at my words for her eyes brightened and the oppression about her shoulders flitted away. Impulsively I reached for her hand and led her to sit with me upon my mattress. I did adore this creature. Her sweetness was the greatest proof of the worthiness of her brother, for it showed me what tender care and love she had daily received.

My familiarity released some last reserve within the young girl for she at once spoke in a flood of words, in such quick succession I hardly was able to follow them. She had enjoyed the rest of the summer at Pemberley. After my party had left, soon thereafter the Bingleys went northward for her brother had sudden business in town as well. Miss Darcy unknowingly answered every one of my unspoken queries over the past months regarding where he had been and what he might have been doing. I hungered for every answer. How often had I tried to picture him, wishing I had the right to know how he had occupied his time?

After his visit to Hertfordshire with Bingley in September, he had returned once again to Pemberley. My heart sank a little at this, knowing how his departure from my county had affected me.

"I was glad for his return for he works himself too hard. He was often tired and out of sorts in the weeks after he left Netherfield. It was good to have him at Pemberley with me again, where I might be sure he did not overtax himself."

This little revelation spun threads of hope round and round my heart, squeezing ever tighter. Mr Darcy was unhappy when he left Hertfordshire. Why might he have been unhappy? My mind whispered that he might have regretted me, cared for me even then. It was a heady feeling, particularly as I had been treading through the thick waters of misgivings and doubt for so long.

"We spoke of you often."

My head snapped up at this. I pressed her hand and opened my mouth to speak any one of the multiple questions flying about my mind when the dinner gong sounded, and my heart lodged in my throat. What I would not have pledged to the universe for five more minutes!

With a sigh of disappointment, I said, "We are expected below. I am well pleased you sought me out in my chambers, Miss Darcy. More than you know, I have longed to renew my acquaintance with you."

It was the right thing to say, for my companion beamed with pleasure. On impulse I implored her to use my Christian name, and she returned the offer with happy compliance. Together, we exited my room and made our way to the stairs. All the while we spoke of intimate nothings, the pleasure of Georgiana's company filled me. I might have called her sister at one point, had my own sister not stolen that happiness from me.

"Brother! Look who I have found!"

My heart stuttered at the sight of Mr Darcy waiting for his sister at the bottom of the stairs. A string connecting me to him pulled, my limbs moving with greater purpose. I could not free myself from the look in his eyes, nor did I wish to. It was searching, contemplative, yet warm in a way I had not expected. The warmth was unexpected but not unfamiliar. At his estate, I had been fortunate to be the recipient of such a look. His lips lifted in the slightest of smiles, and my own mirrored it unbidden.

"Miss Bennet." The low tones of his words drifted up to me, stirring my insides as he bent for a reverent bow.

It was the first time he had officially acknowledged me since our unexpected meeting earlier this afternoon, and I was not too lost to realise it. I became caught up in every review of that moment in the parlour searching for understanding in this newer, more welcoming Mr Darcy. As a result, my toe caught upon the last step, and briefly I lost my balance.

Steady, warm hands held me secure against a broad chest before I could humiliate myself by falling literally at his feet. I blinked up at my saviour and found his gaze warmer still, though only a heartbeat later he carefully untangled our limbs and set me back on my feet.

"I thank you, Mr Darcy," I murmured as I took an additional step backward, the movement contrasting drastically with what I wished to do, which was step once more into his embrace.

I felt someone loop their arm through mine and the spell was broken; I turned to see Kitty asking after my well-being. Without so much as a moment to answer, another voice further sobered my mind.

"Ah ha! What good fortune is this? I have caught not one, but two lovely ladies under the mistletoe." Mr Gordan was descending the stairs while indicating above our heads. Kitty and I looked upwards in unison and found indeed there was a kissing bough directly above us.

The jovial gentleman stepped forward to claim his prize, and I presented my cheek with an awkward laugh. He pressed swift chaste kisses to both Kitty and me. My cheeks were on fire, especially when I chanced a look to see how Mr Darcy bore it. His countenance was severe and his displeasure readily apparent, though his focus was directed at the back of Mr Gordan.

I stepped away from the hanging adornment, and closer to Georgiana again, my hope would be that her brother might then look at me. I could not account for my boldness, I had no real proof of his regard, but I hoped. And that hope propelled me recklessly onward.

I was rewarded then with the full measure of his attention. It felt blissful, intimidating, and intoxicating. Deliberately I shifted my eyes up to the mistletoe above me and to my side now, and then, with all my insides pressing into my heart, returned my eyes to him with the same kind of steady focus he had presented to me. The thought of kissing Mr Darcy drifted through my mind, and my eyes dropped to his mouth. He stepped nearer and my eyes nearly closed.

"Might I have the honour of escorting you into dinner?" The baritone of his voice wrapped around me. Mesmerised still by the shape of his mouth, I watched its movement more than I had attended his words. I became lost in the spell of his voice, and I might have happily stayed all night in such a blessed state had not Georgiana's voice broken into it.

"Elizabeth, are you well?"

Mr Darcy was as startled as I was at his sister's words. My eyes pressed closed in order to focus my thoughts. Upon opening them, I saw that his surprise was at her use of my name. I credit myself with enough understanding of his expression to garner that he did not disapprove of our new familiarity.

"Thank you, yes I am well." I turned from Georgiana and lifted my hand and eyes to her brother. "The honour would be mine, sir."

He took up my hand with a smile and those strings of hope around my heart pulled tighter. Soon enough, if Mr Darcy did not have a care, he would thread enough of them to bind all the broken pieces of that organ together once again.

CHAPTER FIVE

Darcy

THE LAUGHTER THAT DRIFTED THROUGH THE WALL TO ME IN scattered wisps propelled me to finish the business at hand and complete the necessary correspondence to notify my staff at Pemberley of our change of plans. *Letters, how odious indeed, Miss Bingley!* I thought with a wry smile. The rest of the party were assembled for festive games this morning as the snow had not abated all night. The laughter and merriment drew my attention, and I searched the sounds for hers.

"Darcy, you must join us in the parlour."

"I am nearly finished and then I shall be at your command. Believe me, despite my natural inclination to hide away from society, I am eager to compete in the festivities."

"Compete?" Bingley's humoured query had me lifting my eyes to him with a smile. "Do you not mean participate?"

I shook my head and eyed him with all seriousness. "I told you yesterday that I shall not forfeit. I aim to win. Thus, I stand by my earlier response."

Bingley's smile was wide as the Thames. He bid me to hurry and left to return to his party. I bent my head with a smile to match his and did as I was told. With a flourish I finished the missive, noting my handwriting was not as even or meticulous as it usually was but not caring enough to produce a respectable copy. Another volley of laughter drifted through the wall to my ears and with impatience I sanded and sealed the letter, dropping it atop the others I had completed this morning.

There! I was free to enjoy the games. With less dignity than I was raised to display, I dashed out the study door and down the hall to the parlour. Upon entering the room, my eyes sought and found the source of all my pleasure. She was standing in the middle of the room, surrounded by smiling and laughing participants. Her eyes were covered with a pale pink scarf, tied securely amongst her chestnut curls in the back. They were playing Blindman's Bluff. I had always despised the game, knowing it was just an excuse for bending propriety's rules for contact between individuals. The game was played with one individual in the middle, blindfolded, while others surrounded them. The person in the middle must try to catch one of the outside players and then feel blindly who they are. If they guess correctly, then they are free from the circle's imprisonment.

For moment I was caught up in the vision of her. Below her blindfold, her smile was radiant, and I felt its warmth all the way to where I stood at the doorway. My eyes devoured the curve of her jawline, the slope of her neck, and the beauty of her figure as she darted from side to side with her arms out, attempting to find someone.

Bingley was behind her, and he lifted his arm to hail me. I entreated him to silence though and relished in more of my shameless observation. Every time she stepped towards someone, they darted out of her way, and her musical laughter floated about the room. She nearly found Mrs Bingley, and that woman squeaked as she stepped aside into her husband's arms.

The pleasure at the scene was spoiled when Mr Gordan said something, Miss Kitty beside him laughing in response, causing Elizabeth to twirl around at the sounds. He was directly in front of me, and so she stepped tentatively in our direction. The closer Elizabeth stepped with outstretched arms towards Mr Gordan, the less I wished to simply enjoy watching her.

With a silent bow and brittle smile, I stepped abreast of the gentleman and gestured he allow me space amongst the circle. My timing was such that though he did not seem best pleased at my intrusion, it served to distract us both from Elizabeth's continued progress nearer.

Her hands fluttered to a stop as they landed softly upon my chest, and all concern or attention for the gentleman to my left vanished.

My heart squeezed almost painfully at the contact. She breathlessly murmured her triumph at having caught someone, then I watched as her lovely cheeks pinkened further as she realised it was not one of her sisters. It was now her role to determine correctly who she had captured.

My role was to manfully resist pulling her into my arms and kissing her senseless. Between the two of us, I believed I had the more difficult task. Especially as her warm breath poured over me from her embarrassed laugh. Did I once foolishly say I detested this game? Interesting how quickly my feelings changed with Elizabeth's slim fingers tentatively exploring the breadth of my shoulders and cut of my jacket.

It was a most heady experience especially when her fingers brushed against my collar and feather light over my face, exploring the contours of my jaw, nose, and forehead. Where had all the other members of the party gone? In the deepest recesses of my mind, I registered their glee and laughter, though I swore it felt as if Elizabeth and I were alone.

I watched her smile freeze, her features bloom with added colour as I believe she determined my identity. Her delicate frame then seemed to lose balance and my hands instinctively came to steady her at her upper back.

Elizabeth's hands left my cheeks, to my displeasure, and reached for the scarf hiding her eyes from me. My heart leapt when upon lifting the side of the scarf to clear her vision her lips formed my name silently like a prayer. My Christian name. Fitzwilliam. The vision of her lips forming the syllables captured me entirely.

She blinked, her eyes losing the lovely, glazed look about them when they had first encountered mine upon the removal of the scarf.

"Mr Darcy," she quickly asserted to the group. Applause and chaos soon followed as Bingley quickly drew attention away from Elizabeth and me to appoint a new recipient of the blindfold that had been retrieved by Mrs Bingley from Elizabeth's hands.

It was then that I recalled enough of myself to realise I still had my hands about her. Reluctance such as I had never experienced made pulling them to my side nearly impossible. Still, though I no longer held her in my arms, my eyes connected with hers and held.

With gentle persuasion, I entreated her to step away from the grouping with me. Every nerve in my body was soring with hope and eagerness. Though I could not assume anything with this woman, so worthy of the very best.

"Will you not say it again?" I breathed, shocked at first at my own audacity, then terrorised by it.

Elizabeth blushed again but steadfastly returned my gaze as her lips opened to reply.

"Fitz—"

"Fitzwilliam!" Georgiana's voice cut across the room and silenced my companion. Before lifting my head to address my sister's entreaty, I gazed heatedly at Elizabeth, hoping to convey my dismay at the interruption and acknowledgement of the moment.

With difficultly, I swallowed the desire to ignore my sister, the room, and all of England in favour of rewarding Elizabeth's sweet lips for the gift she had been at the cusp of bestowing up on me.

Looking away felt nearly impossible, though I had to. "Yes, dearest."

Georgiana was beaming, half laughing as she walked towards Elizabeth and me. She pointed above our heads and giggled. "You are standing below the kissing bough, Brother!"

The attention of the room was now again upon Elizabeth and me. I felt her stiffen beside me and cursed Bingley who was smiling like a monkey at the circus. When I placed my lips upon hers for the first time, it would not be for an audience and not under compulsion from some silly traditional Christmas garnishment!

Still, I knew if I withdrew, I would embarrass her more, and quite probably send her the wrong message about my suit.

"So it is, Georgiana. Well, Miss Bennet…" Her eyes flashed to mine, and I smiled tenderly at her. "Might I claim my prize?"

How beautiful she looked as she attempted to hide how my words affected her, still I admired the way she lifted her jaw with determination and gave me the slightest of nods.

With a dramatic flair I knew she would not expect, I captured her hand in mine and bowed low as if for the queen.

"My lady," I breathed across her knuckles, pressing my lips upon the satin skin of her hand for a prolonged moment.

The pleasure in her expression confirmed to me that I had chosen my prize wisely. She might not have objected had I placed my lips elsewhere, but I could see she disliked our audience as much as I did. I briefly wondered the logistics of carting her off to places unknown so that I might repeat the deed—though her hand was not the locale I had in mind.

CHAPTER SIX

Elizabeth

THE SENSATIONS PULSING UP MY ARM AT THE CONTACT OF Mr Darcy's lips might have been imagined and entirely fantastical. That such a small point of contact should affect the rhythm of my heart or the clarity of my thoughts was illogical. Yet, such was the case. Thus, when he unbent himself after, I was still in a drunken stupor from the swirling cordial of stimuli.

Mr Darcy took my silence in stride, politely excused my stupid manner, and entreated me with quiet words to a pair of chairs nearby. How fortunate my legs still seemed to know their place for they obeyed without any conscious direction from my head. On the short journey of just a few feet I blinked in quick succession, expelling the delicious fog that had been soaking my brain in all manner of pleasant ruminations. Though I had no wish to leave that pleasant state of mind, I did not wish for Mr Darcy to misinterpret my actions.

I had lost him before with my sister's thoughtless actions and, though my family's absurdities had not disappeared north to Lydia's new residence, I did not desire to waste this unexpected moment to express my gratitude to Mr Darcy for his actions. How fortunate for me that the reminder of the new Mr and Mrs Wickham effectively drained any remaining heady results of the kiss under the mistletoe with Mr Darcy.

Our first attempts at conversation fell flat after just a few moments;

it seemed every topic felt either tedious or uncomfortable. I could not speak of Pemberley without thinking of what took us so swiftly from there, and safer topics such as the weather were uninspiring and dull. Our initial silence brought with it the weight of awkwardness and unfortunate memories. I feared after a time that we would each be forced into silence and despaired of those moments where conversation seemed to come more easily when we had encountered each other at his estate in August.

At length, and with a clearing of his throat, Mr Darcy asked after the health of my aunt and uncle Gardiner. I had my chin tipped to my chest at the time, my fingers playing with a fringe upon my dress. I suppressed a smile; I believed his question was a desperate cast for something for which we could speak easily. Only I had knowledge of his actions in finding Lydia and, therefore, knew he had more recent interactions with my relations then I had. Though I could not be certain, there were lines in my aunt's letters that made me suspect that, despite the ghastly situation with the Wickhams having been resolved long ago, the gentleman occasioned a visit or two in the few weeks after discovering the couple. He had no need to ask me of their well-being; I was certain he could account for their health just as well as I could, if not with more recent knowledge.

I ought to have taken the opportunity to express my gratitude for his actions, but I hesitated. It was not cowardice that stopped the words from passing my lips, but a feeling that now was not the time for such a disclosure. I did not wish for any interruption or to have my sincere thanks be lessened by the joviality around us or the brevity of the moment.

At the same time, I was amused by his enquiry and, feeling a familiar spirit of impertinence rise within me, I could not help but to tease him a little.

"I believe that they enjoy good health, sir. Though I understand my uncle has rejected the *au courant* sedate colour styling of Mr Brummell and has instead opted for some atrociously detailed waistcoats and cravats." A brief glance at Mr Darcy's confused expression had me dipping my head down again with mirth. "My aunt is aghast and can have no explanation. She feels as if she cannot be seen in public with him though he…"

It was a mistake to dare another glance at the gentleman, for his quirked brow and knowing glance had me losing my composure and dissolving into laughter.

"I think Mr Gardiner looks rather dashing in the puce waistcoat with canary embroidery."

This bit of idiocy had my eyes glittering with humour. I ought to have known he was too clever to be long confused by my ridiculous statements. His words gave clear indication he realised his question was an unnecessary one. The way he glanced at me caused me to wonder if he understood that I knew of his recent interactions with my relations.

"Well deserved, Miss Bennet. Given your fondness for the Gardiners, and theirs for you, I ought to have realised that they would have told you of my visits to them in London."

"Yes, I heard of them from my aunt."

The smile on my face seemed to hold, becoming brittle. My heart surged with feeling as I again battled with whether to speak of his actions for Lydia now that he had acknowledged having seen my relations in London. Good heavens! He had all but introduced the topic himself. Fear that I could not express my gratitude with the measure it deserved in such a public setting stole over me now that it seemed I simply must.

"I believe they said last week that you were to holiday with them, so it was a surprise to see you at Netherfield when I arrived."

Now I was the one to not understand. His visits to my relations in London had been in August on Lydia's behalf. I had not made plans with my aunt for the Festive Season until a few weeks ago. I had believed his visits were more distant than that. Did Mr Darcy frequent my uncle's house? With the unhappy business of Lydia's recovery and wedding long in the past, what need did he have for continued acquaintance with my relations?

The weight of these questions felt to have tangible power over my features for I could not raise my eyes to look at him for several moments. The pattern and texture of my dress held my vision captive while my mind grappled with the unknown. My lack of response must have given Mr Darcy discomfort. He shifted uneasily next to me and cleared his throat a number of times. Then Mr Darcy went still, which had the unexpected power to draw my eyes to his. They seemed to be wide with fear, though almost as soon as our gaze connected, they shuttered, and Mr Darcy's expression was as inscrutable as always. The moment was so swift that it seemed unreal, and I convinced myself I had imagined it all. The gentleman's next words were given in so casual a manner that I became convinced I had misread his earlier discomfort.

"Your uncle seemed a man of intelligence and discernment so when I...happened to encounter him in town, I desired to further the connexion. I hope you do not mind."

"Of course not. I am happy you found them as pleasing a couple as I do."

I was filled with the curious desire to know what prompted his visits, how often did they occur, and why. A seed of hope began to sprout within my breast that, perhaps, if Mr Darcy could look kindly upon my relations in trade after what my sister had done, he would not cast me out of his sphere so readily either.

"If not for this weather, and my mother's desire for my exposure to a bit of society..." I absently looked towards where Mr Gordan was standing among the rest of the room's occupants. Mr Darcy's gaze had followed mine and narrowed. Looking away, I continued, "The plan was to travel to London for a few weeks."

"I am relieved you did not venture into the storm then, Miss Bennet."

"Your sister did say it was dreadful." I hesitated, the question I wished most to ask clawing up my throat before I could stop it. "And you have business with my uncle?"

Mr Darcy did not say anything at first and his silence prompted me to lift my eyes to his, in hopes of discerning his thoughts. His eyes were soft, gentle, and contained within something rather appealing that I could not quite name.

"No business. I hope Mr Gardiner might count me as one of his friends, though I know not what he may say about me to his dearer connexions."

With a smile, I assured him that I had heard nothing for which he ought to be worried. "Though they have not spoken much of you—" *My aunt ought to have said more!* "—I can assure you, sir, that both of the Gardiners think well of you."

Mr Darcy acknowledged my information with a nod, then dipped his head to the side in a manner I found quite striking.

"I wonder if their good opinion carries much weight with their relations."

I could not help the fullness of my smile then. For his curious and hopeful expression rendered his already attractive features quite beyond handsome. A vulnerable Mr Darcy was, it seemed, appealing to me.

"I suppose I know from our visit to your estate that you enjoy angling. However, I never expected to see you fish for compliments." A darker hue filtered into his cheeks, and I laughed. "The Gardiners' good opinion carries a great deal of weight, though their thoughts only add to impressions already held by many of their relations."

"Indeed?" Mr Darcy queried with a slight upturn of his lips. That my heart fluttered at the turn of his countenance was hardly a surprise at this point, though I did wonder and worry at the power his full smile might have on me.

"I am relieved to hear it. Quite relieved."

The feeling behind his words had me caught off guard. Surely Mr Darcy knew his worth, for never had a better man existed in the whole of my acquaintance. He had no need to blush at relations that skirted propriety with ruinous actions. The fact that he would question and desire my good opinion gave me much pause for thought. Why did he avoid me these many months if he desired my good opinion?

"I wonder that you could doubt it," I whispered

Though Darcy shifted upon my words, given the number of other guests in the room, I did not think they were heard. With a deep breath, I turned more fully to him, determined to savour any moment I had with him before either of us were called back for another game.

I also planned to seek my answers from my aunt for the frequency and reasons for Mr Darcy's continued acquaintance with them. At present, I ventured another topic. We had now successfully spoken of my relations without any painful reminders of my sister. Perhaps we could likewise speak of our time in August.

"When I was touring Pemberley grounds in August, your head gardener informed me that there were well over twenty different species of roses cultivated at Pemberley. Like the library, I must assume it is the work of many generations as well."

"It is. The rose garden was a particular favourite of my mother's. She alone brought more than half of those to Pemberley in her time."

The softness about his eyes when he spoke of his mother drew me in and, though my heart felt full and my mind scattered on occasion with just one piercing gaze from him, I continued the topic for some time. I listened at times for the pleasure of the sound of his voice, so little used in the past. He had a pleasant baritone that seemed designed to comfort. Mr Darcy's face softened, and the expression of endearment and love transformed it. Envy of his mother crept into my heart, but I was warmed by the trust he was bestowing me by sharing such memories.

CHAPTER SEVEN

Darcy

THE COOL WATER SLAKED MY THIRST MOST SATISFYINGLY. I lifted the glass to my forehead to feel the cooling relief before handing the tankard to the waiting footman and retrieving the towel he held out for me. Blotting the perspiration from my face and neck, I felt my friend slap my shoulder as he retrieved his own towel from the footman.

"I thank you for the match, Darcy. Though it cannot have been much of a challenge for you, I appreciated the chance for exercise."

"You are not unskilled, Bingley. You ought to take up with my man Woolings at the club."

Another footman presented our fencing foils tucked within the velvet folds of the travel case for approval and, once granted, closed the case, and exited the ballroom presumably to return them to our rooms. We were secluded there where we had set up for our exertions. Last evening, the weather had turned wet once again, precluding any outdoor activities for the gentlemen of the house. This morning I noticed the rain had turned quickly into another heavy snow, brushing the landscape all the same stark white.

"Perhaps I may when next Mrs Bingley and I travel to London."

While Bingley did have some talent in the fencing that I had long enjoyed, as he said himself, he was no challenge. We were matched well enough to provide the desired release of energy; however, that was the extent of it. A part of me had hoped Mr Gordan might be up for a match when Bingley presented it to the gentlemen of the house this morning. It might not have been entirely sporting of me for I was certain I could best him. Truthfully, I had wished to trump him most thoroughly, but the gentleman had not seemed interested in taking up swords for exercise. I could not, without revealing sentiments I hoped to keep hidden, appear too eager to match him by repeated requests.

To my way of thinking, Mr Gordan paid far too much attention to Elizabeth and her sister than was proper. At times I was relieved to see him focusing his charms on Miss Catherine, only to be incensed that when her back was turned, or she became occupied elsewhere, he would immediately pay Elizabeth his attentions. Frankly it was appalling how capricious he was with his interest, and I could not like him for it.

My valet would not thank me for the damage I might have done to my shirt as I tore it off over my head rather forcefully. My thoughts were perhaps readily apparent as I grabbed the clean replacement handed to me and jerkily pulled it over my head to cover my bare chest once more.

Jealousy, plain and simple, was the root of my problem with Mr Gordan, a man of mild temper and witty repartee. It tasted bitter and clouded my mind of rational thought. I envied how easily he conversed with the ladies and detested every beautiful smile he stole from Elizabeth in the process.

Feeling the need to once again rid myself of ill humour, I took back the glass of water and drank the rest all at once, letting the cold water sooth my temper as it flooded my throat.

"How well do you know Mr Gordan?" I hid the tension in my jaw and spoke the words through the towel as I blotted once again at my face.

Bingley smirked at me and shook his head. "He is my cousin so I should think I know him quite well."

The amused tone of my friend's voice did not escape me. So, my disguise was not as well fixed as I had hoped. I dropped the towel and glared at Bingley.

"Do you not think it curious that he spends an inordinate amount of time courting two of your sisters by marriage?"

"To be truthful, I had not noticed his preference."

"Not noticed?" I sputtered. "Come now, man! He simpers and preens and makes love to them both. One minute he is all smiles to one and when she leaves the room, he quickly makes his way to the other. It is ungentlemanly."

Bingley looked at me contemplatively, then handed his towel off to the footman. He pulled off his sweaty shirt and replaced it with a clean one as I had done moments ago, his gaze purposely avoiding mine.

"Do you object to his attentions to my sisters as a whole or do you perhaps only disapprove of his attentions to one of them?"

I growled and turned to my waiting valet as he began reassembling my cravat at my neck. "I believe you know my sentiments and thus no answer is necessary. Regardless, it is not right that he should attempt to raise hopes in both ladies."

Bingley did not answer, and I clenched my jaw hard enough it felt as if it might snap. When we were both once again properly attired to venture into the rest of the house, Bingley turned to me.

"Darcy, what is this with Gordan? He is a good man. And I should think with all the time you are spending with Elizabeth that you might not feel so threatened by his smiles to her."

Envy that he, as her brother, was granted the privilege of addressing her by her Christian name surged within me, pulling and twisting my heart most painfully. I thought of all the morning walks I had spent with Elizabeth and the easy way we had begun to interact. Gone were the halting speeches, and forbidden topics. When we walked together, I felt the heady tonic of hope fill me. Several times, I almost stopped our steps to beg for her hand, to plead that she overlook all my many faults and redeem me by becoming my wife.

Almost as soon as the hope budded on those walks began to comfort me, the image of encountering Elizabeth in his company just a few days ago came crashing back into my memory. Mr Gordan had beat me to her one morning, and the two were walking arm in arm around the barren winter garden. Her cheeks were flushed, and I dared not guess if the source was her companion or the bracing wind that morning. I knew what I wished to be the cause. In that moment I had been filled with uncharacteristic caution. I turned before they might encounter me and returned to my chambers, like a coward.

When I was with her, I did not feel threatened by Mr Gordan at all. When *he* was with her, I did. Was it simply that I had become a horribly spoiled child regarding her, unwilling to share her sunshine with anyone else?

When I was with Elizabeth, I was convinced that the particular glint in her eye and the way her crooked smile turned just so was just for me. Indeed, even with Mr Gordan, it seemed her alluring lips did not turn up quite the same way as they did for me, although I could not be entirely certain of that. I had been mistaken in her feelings before. I was haunted by our past with every step we took together.

Disregarding Bingley's statement, I simply, if not a trifle petulantly, said, "I cannot like the way he pays them both attention. And you can wipe that smile off your face, Bingley. I should think you would feel the same way had another man been applying his charm to Mrs Bingley while you attempted to court her prior to your marriage."

Bingley's eyes narrowed and he nodded sympathetically. He soon shook it off, presumably remembering no such phantom suitor existed and he had already achieved his happiness in securing his lady as his wife. Lucky man.

"Why do you not take advantage of the mistletoe I have been hanging about the house?" he queried, back to speculating on my troubles. "I have seen you purposely skirt around it when Elizabeth is within even a few feet of one."

I had been avoiding even the small chance that we might be caught under a kissing bough again. My friend had instructed his servants to repeatedly rearrange the garnishments to catch as many as he could by surprise. Far from suspecting Elizabeth to be cunning enough to place herself under one, I could not help but purposely look about her whenever I approached.

Did I wish to kiss her sweet lips? What a ridiculous question. Did the Romans build the Pantheon? Did the sun rise in the East? Every moment of every day I wished to capture those tempting pieces of flesh. But I refused to allow that delicious heaven's reward more than space in my thoughts. The temptation was too great to waste our first kiss upon festive obligation. I hoped that Elizabeth would one day welcome my kiss and, when that day came, I wanted her to be certain I bestowed it most willingly and not under duress from some Christmastide tradition.

Thus, I did keep my distance whenever she was anywhere near one of Bingley's blasted mistletoes.

"Speak to your cousin, Bingley. He cannot have them both, and he ought not to be so obviously courting one under the other's nose."

Yes, I had avoided answering his question about the mistletoe.

Chuckling and shaking his head at me, Bingley once again slapped my shoulder as we approached the ballroom doors to exit. "Shall I tell Mr Gordan to make up his mind then?"

I admit I rolled my eyes at my friend, bemused and irritated in equal measure.

"Though you might dislike his choice if you do not choose to act yourself, Darcy." Bingley slowed his steps and turned to me, speculation and challenge in his eyes. "Tonight, Jane's parents will be dining with us, as it is Christmas Eve. They plan to stay the evening in one of the guest quarters. I am thinking it is time for you to forget Mr Gordan and make your move!"

My friend laughing, then added, "And while Mr Bennet is here, you can gain his consent for the best Christmas gift of your life."

CHAPTER EIGHT

Elizabeth

WHEN MR DARCY RETURNED TO THE PARLOUR WITH MY NEW brother, I felt the heat in my cheeks I had hardly suppressed for the past half an hour surge into a full-on inferno. Though his clothes were neatly arranged and properly adorned now, in my head all I saw were the sinews of solid mass flex and bend to their master's will under the thin lawn of bare shirtsleeves.

I had returned from my walk this morning, taken later due to the snowy weather, a goodly measure disappointed. Mr Darcy had not joined me this morning and though I was rational enough to presume he might believe the snow would keep me from venturing out of doors, still I could not help having missed our almost daily routine.

Of course, we did not arrange to take our constitutional together; however, I had mentioned the first day I encountered him that I preferred to walk at this time of day and often took myself on the wooded path. That small hint had felt bolder than I had ever been. I was pleased and relieved when Mr Darcy began encountering me on my walk almost every day since. That began nearly a fortnight ago.

Those walks fed the little spirit of hope within me. Nourishing her and strengthening her until I had begun to allow her to whisper in my heart that all might be well. I had promised myself I would speak of his actions regarding Wickham and Lydia today. I would express the gratitude that had fostered in my heart from the first moment I learned of his actions. Except today, due to the snow, I was delayed by more than half an hour dressing in the appropriate warming attire, and he did not come. Foolish creature I was, I allowed my disappointment to turn to discontent which ate at my confidence in his affections. Why, if he still cared for me beyond that of friendship, did he not declare himself?

Upon my return to Netherfield, tired rather than refreshed by my walk, I passed near the doors to the ballroom. Upon hearing shuffling and strange sounds, I allowed myself to be pulled by curiosity to the gap in the double doors.

The sight seized all thought and froze every limb: two gentlemen, dressed in just shirtsleeves, breeches, and boots in the rapid volleys of a fencing match. My eyes drew immediately to one with dark curling hair, little wisps pressing into the perspiration on his brow. My head acknowledged his opponent, but he held no fascination.

Mr Darcy had the grace of a lion and the predatory movements to match. The muscles of his arms flexed under the shirt, and I could see the beat of his heart at his neck. His muscled legs coiled and strode forth with ease and confidence. Just then he executed some manoeuvre, and Bingley was bested. Mr Darcy's face split then in a wide smile, his straight, even teeth, stark white against the glow of his face. He was magnificent and every part of my insides felt stirred about and lodged in my throat at the sight.

When the two turned towards the doors where I shamefully stood peeking, I squeaked silently and dashed down the hall, fearful they would soon emerge and see me.

Though now he was fully and impeccably attired, I could not help the images that flashed before my mind's eye upon seeing the dampness about his hair and the flushed healthful radiance to his countenance.

He hesitated in his approach to me, and I saw to my right, near the mantelpiece, a branch of dried mistletoe bound in red ribbon. My heart sunk a little, which I might have counted a good thing considering how it had previously been lodged in my throat at his entrance into the room, but I had begun to suspect a pattern to the way Mr Darcy acted near me with regards to those blasted little garnishments.

Feeling a little overwarm suddenly and a disheartening return of the disappointment earlier from my unaccompanied walk, I stood when I saw him change direction to pick up a book at a nearby table.

I do not know how long I was at the window, watching the swirling snowflakes spin past the pane, when I felt a warmth at my back and knew instinctively that it was Mr Darcy. Though my suspicions that he was avoiding being caught under the mistletoe with me were confirmed, as I had chosen this window for its lack of such a festive adornment, I felt only a measure of happiness that he had come to me. That he would not wish to kiss me would have to be mourned at a later time.

Turning towards the gentleman, I stepped aside to allow him space in the window well with me. When he stepped into the smaller space beside me, my heart once again crept up into my throat. My eyes glance at his hands, now hanging inactive at his sides. Moments ago, I witnessed those hands grasp assuredly the hilt of his foil, extend towards his opponent, and…

I blinked, having missed what Mr Darcy said.

"Pardon me, sir. I was wool-gathering. Can you repeat yourself?"

His lips lifted into the briefest of smiles, though nothing as wide as they had in the ballroom, and he said, "I mentioned that I loved the way the ground looks covered in snow."

I turned to the window, grateful for the cold air near the glass to cool my cheeks. "It is several inches deeper than it was an hour ago even. My parents may not be able to traverse the distance if they do not leave soon."

"You did not venture out in it, I hope." Mr Darcy moved a fraction closer to me or was it that I swayed towards him?

"I did. You know how much I love to walk out of doors. However, have no fear, a little exposure to the elements did me no permanent ill."

"I can see that. I hope you were wrapped warmly. It must have been cold, for your cheeks are still flushed from the exercise."

I nearly choked out a laugh at this statement. What would he think if he knew that I had long since warmed from my wintry walk? That seeing him about his exercise had thawed me quite satisfactorily.

I know not how it came about, but I was successfully able to steer the conversation to other topics. While I cannot say that I did not occasionally lose my train of thought to pleasant images passing through my consciousness, nevertheless I spent a rather enjoyable thirty minutes in conference with Mr Darcy before the tea tray was wheeled in.

When all were comfortably sated by the midday repast, sitting about in lazy whispered conversation about the room, I stood to retrieve my sewing basket where I had left it near an armchair in the corner. No sooner had I grasped the basket and turned around, but that I almost lost the contents of it in fright at the unexpected appearance of Mr Gordan behind me.

With a stifled shriek, I fumbled to keep the contents of my basket from spilling about the floor. Mr Gordan apologised for surprising me and helped steady the small burden in my arms.

Nervous laughter soon followed, as my heart settled into a steadier rhythm. I smiled and shook my head in mock reprimand.

"Miss Bennet, I do apologise," Mr Gordan grimaced good naturedly. "I thought you saw me stand when you did, and I did call out a greeting."

"It is nothing, sir, but my own absent-minded temperament today. How are you today, sir?"

Mr Gordan flashed a handsome smile, though his eyes remained unaccountably serious. "I am well, thank you. I wanted to take this opportunity while you are not otherwise engaged, to speak to you on a matter of great importance to me."

I suspected at once what this matter of great importance might be, and I beamed at him with understanding.

"I wonder if this matter involves a certain sister of mine."

The gentleman coloured slightly yet was pleased by my intuition. Mr Gordan had been quite clear on his sentiments and without any disguise in his admiration towards Kitty. He spoke to me of her often, recalling bits of their conversations or sharing a humorous encounter to me. I did not think he realised that he and I had not spoken much of any other topic in days. Indeed, I am sure he did not know how often our conversations drifted towards my sister, although until now he had never started a conversation specifically about her.

"How may I be of service to you, Mr Gordan?" I asked, my lips parting in good humour and happiness for Kitty. Unbeknownst to this gentleman, my sister suffered under the same ailment. Though at first, she seemed oblivious to his attentions, she soon began to speak to me only of him.

My eyes drifted about the room, until I saw that Kitty was not present. I recalled that she had left with Georgiana at that lady's entreaties to see my sister's drawings. Since Lydia had left for the north, Kitty had once again taken up the favoured pastime that her little sister often teased her about.

In surveying the room, my eyes caught sight of Mr Darcy. His face was stern and disapproving, and he was glaring a hole in the back of Mr Gordan's coat. I wondered briefly what Mr Gordan could have done to displease the gentleman so.

"Not here, Miss Bennet." Mr Gordan drew my attention back to him. He pulled out his pocket watch and checked its face. "I need to speak freely and fear being interrupted or overheard. Will you meet me in the conservatory twenty minutes before the dinner gong?"

He took up my hand and pressed it in gratitude when I agreed, and I smiled inwardly at the dramatics of it all. He ought to have simply asked Kitty to meet him and speak his heart directly to her. I imagined Mr Gordan lacked the confidence he needed for such a step and that my assurances would be all that he needed to make it. Of Kitty's feelings I felt certain, for she had expressed them to me in the dark of night a few days previous when she climbed into my bed one night feeling a need for a sisterly talk.

A commotion at the door drew both our attentions. My parents had arrived safely from Longbourn for the festive activities this evening. I was pleased the roads remained passable and relieved for their safe arrival. Though I disliked the thought of them alone at Longbourn on Christmas morning, I winced at the loud complaints my mother was even now listing to the room at large regarding the weather, the cold, the carriage and the roads.

Mr Gordan then took himself off to change for dinner after speaking briefly with the new arrivals, and I, seeing as the time was well spent, realised I would not have time to do any sewing after all and replaced my basket where it had been. I kissed the cold cheek of my mother and likewise bestowed a kiss on my father's face.

"Hello, Papa. I am pleased you were not detained by the snow."

"Or trapped in the carriage with your mother," was his wry reply, to which I laughed.

Jane stood and went to show them to their room, and I left to repair upstairs to change as well. Mr Darcy, I noted, had already left the room.

CHAPTER NINE

Darcy

"YOU HAVE NO IDEA HOW MUCH HAPPINESS YOU HAVE brought me, Miss Bennet."

I doubt that a day will go by in my life where I will not hear those words reverberate through my head and infect every place of light within me. It had been a mere half an hour since I first heard them. Thirty minutes of torturous repeat across the backs of my eyes and in painful swells within my breast. It was just a series of words, yet they had the power to erase days of hope.

I blame that hope. Hope had led me to believe that she had come to care for me just a little. She had said herself that she no longer thought ill of me but, arrogant lout that I was, I had allowed hope to convince me that a good opinion was the same as affection. As love.

Hope had been a third companion on our walks.

I had been walking by the open doors to the conservatory when I heard those hated words. The door was ajar and inside, just around the partial cover of a bench under fern cover sat Elizabeth with the spectre of Mr Gordan standing in front of her. I could not see her face as her back was to me, but my memory was seared with the vision of Mr Gordan saying those words and his expression of joy.

It seemed I was too late and that Elizabeth—no, I must not think of her as such—Miss Bennet had made another choice, had secured her future with another gentleman. My brain felt sluggish and stupid just thinking about it. It felt worse than when I had believed her lost to me after Wickham had seduced her sister.

I wanted to hate Mr Gordan, but I could not. My heart simply beat too slowly to waste any emotion on him. All the passion I could gather for him was that he had better treat her as she deserved. He had better give her the world.

Bingley asked me a moment ago if I was well. I assured him I was perfectly well. He went away sceptical and has not since ceased glancing my way. Blast it all! I was not well. A man sliced in half could not rightly be believed to ever be well again. I wished that my friend would stop looking at me, for his concerned glances were a reminder that the ghost of anguish I tried to keep hidden was haunting my visage.

"I love the lighting of the Yule Log," a voice next to me said.

Blinking, I forced my thoughts out of the black and to attend my companion, only to find her there beside me, looking up at me with those effervescent eyes. Her heart shaped lips were bowed in a smile. I felt my spirit long for her.

"It always brings me joy for the what the year ahead may bring."

A man who felt less might have said more, but I could not utter a single word. Miss Bennet smiled as she turned her countenance towards the actions of the footman near the hearth. The Yule Log had been brought in, and cheerful voices echoed off the walls around me, each hitting my ears like canon fire. Bingley began a speech about the year behind us and the year to come. In truth I heard one in every five words, for my traitorous mind was filled with her perfume and the question as to why she stood beside me while her betrothed spoke in hushed tones in the corner with her father.

Oh good God! He was likely in conference seeking Mr Bennet's blessing. What sin had I committed to be required to endure the purgatory of standing witness to both the proposal and her father's interview. By the looks of it, Mr Gordan would be successful.

"Excuse me, Miss Bennet," I croaked and gave a perfunctory bow and was gone from her side.

Miss Bennet's back stiffened and those damnable eyes lifted at the gruffness of my tone. I could see that my manner had been abrupt and unfeeling, but escape was essential. Else I would not be accountable for my next actions. Every part of me begged to take her in my arms and speak some sense to her. I had loved her longer than he; I would spend my life devoting every energy to her happiness. These were things I could vow to her. He could not even devote the whole of one evening, for even now that he had completed his conference with her father, I saw him beaming down upon Eliz—Miss Bennet's sister.

I could provide the world to her—certainly more than Mr Gordan could—but Miss Bennet had already soundly rejected my temporal advantages at Hunsford. She could not care for them now.

I spared a thought for Georgiana who was ensconced next to Mrs Bingley, before leaving the room. She was smiling shyly at the antics of my friend has he expounded upon the traditions of the Yule Log. I wondered if every Christmas would now be filled with painful remembrances.

I knew that before long Bingley would invite us all to go into the dining room for the feast the servants had been preparing the better part of the day. I would not offend and insult their efforts by asking for a tray, though I wished dearly to avoid society the rest of the evening. However, I needed a moment to compose myself for I would be expected to attend and present to the world that I was well, that my heart had not shattered at those words from the conservatory that never left my thoughts.

I miscalculated the time; instead of arriving at the dining room among the party's migration, I found that I was a few minutes late and everyone had already been seated. I apologised to Bingley for my tardiness and looked for an open chair. It was the result of careful study that I avoided discerning her location. I might have done myself a service had I looked for her location for then I would not have been caught off guard to find the chair with my name place was directly beside her.

With a murmur of further apologies to my dinner partners, I took my seat. Energised currents ran the length of my arm where it sat mere inches from hers. Other than acknowledge my general salutation with a civil nod, she said nothing to me at all. I had a weakness for her voice and knew not if I desired it more or prayed for her silence. In the end, she would give me silence for the majority of the meal.

To this day, I could not tell you anything about this meal, except to say that it all tasted like sawdust.

When the craving for her attention could not be overcome any longer, I turned to her and manfully squelched the claws of that beast of anguish within me to choke out the following words.

"May I offer you my congratulations, Miss Bennet."

She sat back only a fraction and seemed surprised. I saw her glance a second across the table to where her betrothed sat before leaning towards me in a whisper. The scent of her perfume wafted into my senses, numbing them and making me barely catch her words.

"I did not think my father had made the announcement."

I took a sip of my wine, blushing slightly at the truth of her statement. I would have to admit to learning of it by accident. I swallowed, hoping it would dislodge my heart where it sat perched in my throat. "I must confess that I happened by the conservatory earlier this evening."

The confusion left her eyes and they filled with pleasure. Every sparkle felt like a sliver to my already beleaguered heart.

"Then you know." Elizabeth smiled again in the direction of Mr Gordan and my teeth clenched painfully. "It is a good match. I confess, I am quite happy."

I sat up straight, painful swells of yearning lapping along every nerve of my body. Before long I would be swallowed up by the sensations and hoped one day to become numb to them. I loved her and would always love her. Had it been the Christmas spirit that had swept me away in a tide of hope? Had I allowed myself once again to be blind to her real feelings and only see that which gave me pleasure and gratified my every dream for us?

I wished to God I had never been caught in the snow and deposited upon Bingley's doorstep. If I had never left London, I would never have encountered her again and allowed myself to believe that approbation could equal or at least lead to love.

However, she had stated that she was happy, and, though I was sinking into a never-ending mire of torment, that was the last whole and unblemished desire of my heart. That I had hoped to be the source of that happiness could not be questioned; however, she deserved to have that life's blessing. If Mr Gordan could make her happy then I would have to live a sort of half-life of contentment with that.

"Happiness. In the end that is all I ever hoped for you."

Her brows furrowed and I suspected she might soon feel some compassion for the feelings I expressed back in April. Any caring, compassionate soul would, and Elizabeth was among the most feeling of ladies in my acquaintance. I hoped she would not waste even a moment of her happiness worried about how her once misguided and mistaken suitor felt towards her. Though it felt as if I was cutting into my own heart to speak the lies, I knew I would have to relieve her of that burden.

"I hope you will not be made to feel uneasy by this, Miss Bennet. Given your sentiments last April, I had no real expectation, and I have since endeavoured to overcome my own. I shall always value your friendship, and, in the future, we can meet as indifferent acquaintances and you may be at ease."

"Oh!" her eyes lifted and held mine for but a moment before shuttering and looking to her lap. Before they were cut off from my view, I detected moisture gathering in those fine eyes that first lead my heart to her keeping. *Elizabeth!* Compassionate and feeling Elizabeth—of course she would feel sorry for me no matter how convincing I attempted to be.

Her hand trembled as she pulled her glass to her lips. I watched the liquid stain them and had to look away. For her happiness I would get the better of these feelings. I did not wish for her pity, but I loved her all the more for having it for me.

Before I could even contemplate the words coming from my mouth, they were there, and I hoped they would restore her equanimity.

"I shall only add God bless and my best wishes for a Happy Christmas to you. I will be leaving for London in the morning and will be unlikely to have a chance to take my leave of you then."

Her breaths seemed to come in staggered steps, though her voice was steady.

"I am sorry you feel the need to leave so suddenly."

"It is business, nothing more, that calls me to London," I lied. More and more lies I would heap upon the space between us if it eased a little of that remorse and pity creasing her brows, causing her to bite her full lower lip and to chafe her hands as they lay at her lap in a knot of fingers.

We were silent for a time, and I wished I could see inside her mind to know that I had eased it with my assurances. I did wish her happy. I looked to where Mr Gordan was and found him in animated conversation to his dinner partner, Miss Catherine. Though he seemed to speak with affection towards her, I must now see he did so in the attempt to develop that brotherly connexion that would soon be his.

"And will you return?"

Her question brought my attention from across the table back to the lovely woman beside me. It puzzled me that she should ask such a thing. Surely she did not wish to be subjected to my return during those happy weeks of her betrothal. Something about her tone made it sound almost hopeful but that could not be.

"I cannot say. My plans are not yet fixed."

Her shoulders seemed to deflate with relief. She ate very little and said even less for the rest of the meal. Though every moment with her tore me into ever smaller pieces, my heart sunk to the floor when Mrs Bingley cheerfully invited the ladies to withdraw to leave the gentlemen to their port and follow her to the parlour for music and festivities.

I stood and allowed myself the privilege of holding Elizabeth's chair as she stood. As I grasped the back of the chair, my fingertips inadvertently brushed her skin at her bare shoulders, which felt was silk under them. In the candlelight she looked beautiful to me, as lovely as she had ever looked, if a trifle pale. My eyes never left her as she walked, without so much as a look back, out the dining room door.

Mr Gordan, I noticed spoke briefly to Bingley before leaving right behind the ladies. Whatever excuse he could give was transparent to me, given I knew of his triumph already.

When the footman brought around glasses of port, I asked for a brandy instead. He brought it to me moments later with a small decanter. Without shame, I asked he leave the tray beside me rather than stand about to pour.

It would not do to become foxed, and it had not been my intention to imbibe excessively, no matter how my mind yearned for absolution. In April I had indulged in that temptation one too many times and had certain knowledge that the memories and longings did not fade. While the alcohol brought minute oblivion, I was often trapped in a prison of my own making wherein sentiments ricocheted around my breast in ever more powerful rounds made more poignant by the brandy rather than numbed by it.

I spoke little and only caught bits of the conversation around me. Mr Bennet, I found, was so odd a mixture of quick parts, sarcastic humour, reserve, and caprice that despite my heavy heart, in a word, he was amusing. Had I been in a better frame of mind, I might have wished to know him better. However, he reminded me of her, and I poured myself another glass.

CHAPTER TEN

Elizabeth

'*I HAVE SINCE ENDEAVOURED TO OVERCOME MY OWN*'. HE SAID IT IN SO subdued and emotionless manner, I might have thought we were speaking of the weather, not of the ardent love and admiration he once expressed for me but had since 'overcome'. He was not intending to be unfeeling or to reach inside my soul to remove my every wish housed there and crush it. He was incapable of wilfully setting out to injure another. Which made his words all the more devastating.

I reached for my glass and brought it feebly to my lips. I still marvelled at the place he chose—between the second and third removes during the Christmastime feast—to make his sentiments clear. Had we not often walked in private around the grounds at Netherfield and might that have been a better setting for such a private disclosure?

And therein lay the answer. For Mr Darcy, such sentiments having been 'overcome'—how I was beginning to loathe the word—might not have considered the topic required a more secluded setting. Clearly, he had no fears of being overheard and if he were, he might not be embarrassed to have another discover he once admired me. In the past. But no more.

Oh, good heavens! I felt suddenly as if I might become sick all over Jane's lovely wedding china. I replaced my silverware and held my hands clasped together at my stomach, attempting to regulate my breathing. Nausea swelled within me.

How did we transition from speaking of Kitty and Mr Gordan's betrothal to Mr Darcy's own discarded marital ambitions? Perhaps I had been too unguarded in my feelings. He must have discovered them and thought to warn me. I ought not to have let his tender eyes lead me into the tempting belief that he still cared for me. The saying often says with one marriage, soon others follow. Perhaps Mr Darcy did not wish me to continue in unfounded expectations.

He had been uncivil and cold in the parlour before dinner. Then I had felt the unease of foreboding that carried me through the earlier parts of the meal in silence. Good gracious, I could hardly acknowledge his whispered greeting upon seating himself beside me for those feelings of unease. I ought to have allowed that foreboding to shore up my heart so that it could not now be so injured.

His words filtered through the haze of my torment to register in my mind. He was leaving for London tomorrow. It was proof of how far I had become infected with this unrequited love that despite knowing for a certainty that he did not desire my affection, I still could feel something like desolation with regards to his upcoming departure.

My heart lurched, skipped a beat, then painfully bounded along at the thought of him going away from here. When might I see him again? Did I desire to subject myself to such a torment?

"And will you return?" I winced inwardly at my plaintive question. Surely he could hear the pathetic yearning dripping from each word.

"I cannot say. My plans are not yet fixed."

With that, I vowed not to pain him further with my conversation or to subject myself to further mortifications with every word that passed my lips carrying with it the scent of my disappointment and revealing the depths of my anguish.

When Jane stood to invite the ladies to withdraw, I nearly leapt up and bounded across the table with such haste to escape. Every muscle felt taut and ready to snap to my indecorous desires until his fingers brushed the inner curve of my shoulder.

My heart stilled. My soul surged. Heat tore through the sensitive skin there and burned a path through it down my spine and inward to my heart. It was a marvel that I did not turn then to instead leap into his arms and beg him to reconsider, shamelessly embarrassing us both in front of the assembled party. It took a great deal of effort but instead I stiffly walked with the other ladies out of the dining room, my heart singing to stay behind with Mr Darcy as my legs propelled me further away.

In the parlour, Mary was entreated to play some carols and a few of the ladies began to sing the merry songs of the season. This was usually my favourite Christmas tradition, but I could not even find the words for the songs within the growing empty spaces of my mind.

Time was elusive and I have no notion how much time had passed before I was brought out of my numbed state by the effulgent smiles of Kitty and Mr Gordan.

"Thank you, thank you, Lizzy! Mr Gordan—Anthony—told me of your encouragement."

Kitty blushed, her eyes straying to lock with the gentleman at the use of his Christian name. So, he had mustered up the courage to speak after all. I know that he had sought my father's permission to pay his address to Kitty earlier in the evening when I saw them speaking before we were called to dinner. It seemed Mr Gordan, once finally convinced of a successful outcome, did not hesitate a moment. Had it really only been a few hours ago that he had begged me to help him win her heart?

The conservatory had been pleasantly warm, and I remember feeling anticipation for the evening as Jane had told me she placed me near Mr Darcy at dinner. When Mr Gordan came, pleading for me to help him win Kitty's heart and vowing his devotion to my younger sister, I did not feel any worry about breaking Kitty's confidence to tell him she would welcome his suit with a gladdened heart already his.

"Then might I assume you are betrothed? It is official?"

Kitty replied through a giggle, "Papa has not announced it but that is only because he has not yet left the other gentlemen in the dining room."

Mr Gordan kissed Kitty's hand, prompting another blush and a weak cough as she tried to suppress her reaction to his attentions.

"Miss Bennet, I had no notion that in asking for your aid, I would gain the knowledge that my dearest Kitty was already mine in heart. I thank you and am pleased to be gaining such a sister."

Before I could say anything in response, the doors opened and a few of the gentlemen began to trickle in. Kitty and her intended had distracted me pleasantly from the drowning I was experiencing but now every cut sung again with aching anticipation of Mr Darcy's return to the parlour.

When the door did not open again for any additions for some minutes after the last, I forced myself to acknowledge that it was a blessing. Mr Darcy had not returned with the other gentlemen. Where he was in the house, I knew not. Perhaps he was instructing his valet on the packing of his bags.

I went through the motions of the next several minutes as my father stood up and address the group, "If I can have your attention, I would like to announce the engagement of my daughter…"

My mother shrieked, and many other audible proclamations of delight filled the room such that my father was forced to pause his speaking until the room had settled once more.

"... my daughter Catherine to Mr Anthony Gordan. May you see her grow less silly, and she make you always youthful."

The room now become unbearably loud with congratulations to the couple. My brother summoned a footman to retrieve some punch to celebrate the occasion. The torment of my mind was now becoming unbearably great and after expressing my delight once again to my sister and her intended, I made my way to Jane to say goodnight.

"Lizzy, you do not look well. How can I bring you comfort?'

My eyes swelled with tears that I could no longer suppress and upon seeing them, she quickly tucked me under her arm and issued me out of the door. Upon reaching the safety of my bedchamber, she turned me about to face her and simply looked at me, her eyes full of feeling.

"It is as I had feared. I am too late," I whispered, pulling away to sit inelegantly at my dressing table and begin pulling pins from my hair. Tears dripped heedlessly down my cheeks one by one as silent testaments to my pain.

"I feared your dinner conversation was not to your liking. What did he say, what did Mr Darcy say?"

She took up the job of removing my pins for me and I was glad for my arms felt too heavy to command. How I managed to repeat those hated words to Jane of his overcoming his love for me, I know not. The void where I might have felt their sting was growing wider and I counted that a good thing.

"Oh Lizzy..." she cried, and then I was enfolded in the comforting embrace of her arms where I openly wept at the loss of a man I only learned to love too late. Eventually she helped me to dress for bed, stirring some headache powders into a glass of water, both of which arrived at the door from a maid I do not recall her summoning.

All the while, Jane mumbled and shook her head in disbelief. She had assured me after Mr Darcy and his sister were stranded by the storm that I had nothing to fear in his staying. Her confidence had led me to believe that all might be well, and this might be a Festive Season I would not soon forget. Indeed, there were moments like that first evening at the stairs, under the mistletoe and along our many walks that I felt as if every Christmas wish I could desire would be mine.

Well, the truth of it was, I would not soon forget and that was entirely the problem.

CHAPTER ELEVEN

Darcy

I LINGERED A MOMENT BEHIND THE OTHER GENTLEMAN, wishing to slip into the parlour when the brandy had sufficiently burned through the riot of my mind. When I neared the partially open door my tardiness was punished suitably to hear Mr Bennet begin to announce the engagement of his daughter. Convinced I was not in good enough regulation to stand witness to that, retreat was imperative. Pivoting on the soles of my boots, I left before I would be forced to hear Mr Bennet connect her name to Mr Gordan's.

Without much thought for my destination, I exited the front doors and stood upon the entry steps. The cold blasted against my cheeks in a way that felt both right and soothing. The sky was pitch except for the swirling white spots falling effortlessly down around me and catching the light of the torches on either side of the doors.

Tilting my head up I allowed the snow to fall unheeded upon my face. Every thought drained from my head bit by bit, down my limbs and, I imagined, down the steps of Netherfield. All I felt was the whisper soft touch of the snowflakes melting against my skin.

As the cold of the night began, in careful measures, to crawl past my skin into my body, I welcomed the numbing sensation. Echoes of cheerful voices and festive songs would occasionally pierce the silent stillness with their taunting sounds. Each wave of sound seemed to collect and form around me, becoming a cursed companion on those snowy steps.

When I feared I would be swallowed up by the feeling of being just outside of happiness the rest of my days, I turned haltingly to return inside. My limbs moved in jerking movements, a testament to the effect of the cold on my muscles. Their cry of pain at being used after the cold immobility of my earlier attitude surprised me. How long had I been lost in the winter wasteland of my suffering?

Though the corridor was often cooler by several degrees than any of the principal rooms, it felt pleasantly warm upon my cheeks. By measure they begun to thaw, heat flooding into them in painful pinpricks.

When I felt composed enough to face her, I entered the parlour. I would make as short of a stay as would be proper, express my desire to retire, and notify Bingley of my departure the next day. I had decided to importune Mrs Bingley to allow Georgiana to stay some weeks longer. I would return to London alone, get the better of my disappointment and sweep through the county on my way to Pemberley later and collect her then. She would find the occupants of Netherfield far more enjoyable companions than I would be in the coming weeks.

The cheerful feel of the room permeated every surface and combined its scent with the pine and spice from the decorations. The spirit of pleasure lingered though the singing and laughing had since ended. Glancing about I noticed only a few occupants still milling about late into the evening, others having retired I presumed. Mrs Bennet slept against the side of a settee, looking as if she ought to have sought her bed long ago.

I felt like a dark cloud in a room full of warm sunshine. I worried my mood would begin to dispel the cheer and was careful in my steps to not disturb any of the muted conversations around me. My eyes swept the room briefly for her; I doubted I would ever learn to keep my gaze from straying in her direction.

Disappointment had a taste and I detected it now, seeing that she was not there. Why I longed to see her when every glimpse sent shards of pain through me, I know not. Still, I was forced to admit that a part of me came in from the snow with the express hope of seeing her once more before I left for London.

I saw my host and hostess seated together in a corner, close in conference to each other and though I was sorry to interrupt their cosy tête-á-tête, without the chance to see Eliz...Miss Bennet, all energy to hold back the oppression of the room's quiet serenity was gone and I longed only for my bed.

I walked slowly across the room. Mr Bennet looked up from his book as I passed him and acknowledged me with a nod then just as swiftly bent his head again to the text. There was a couch with its tall back facing me with two occupants I neither cared to know nor be pulled into conversation with, so I kept my head held high and with purpose strode to the darkened corner where my friend and his wife sat.

Bingley stood upon seeing me, his hand reaching behind him in an unconscious manner to maintain the hand of his wife.

"Darcy! Where the devil have you been? I supposed you had retired."

I bowed to the lady and addressed Bingley, "I ought to now, but I wished to thank you both for your superior hospitality. I know I may speak for my sister in saying that we have been made to feel quite at home."

Mrs Bingley spoke then, her voice tight in a way I had never heard. "You are welcome, Mr Darcy. I am sorry the weather forced you to change plans."

Bingley's head shot around to look at her briefly, though she did not meet his eye, rather kept her gaze directed at me. Her eyes were not unkind, though there was a searching quality to them. I had never thought she and her sister looked much a like before. Mrs Bingley was fair with blue eyes and golden hair where her sister was dark, with chameleon eyes that changed from deep green to brown with golden flecks depending on the angle of the sun. But looking at Mrs Bingley now, I detected similarity in the slightly questioning brow and disconcerting steadiness of her gaze. Mrs Bennet had never taught her daughters to be demure.

I cleared my throat, and for some shameful reason felt compelled to look away from her fixed gaze.

"I wonder if I might importune you both further and ask if you might take Georgiana under your care for a few more weeks, allowing her pleasure not to be suspended once more on the whims of a much older brother, for I must away to London on the morrow."

Bingley startled at this and fumbled, "Of course, Darcy. Georgiana is always welcome here. But must you really depart so soon? I had begun to believe your plans were fixed to...that they were fixed at present at Netherfield."

There was an accusation within his words, and it stirred my torment into a pyre of smouldering irritation. Surely, he could see that to stay now was impossible.

I opened my mouth to respond, planning to carefully regulate my tone so as not to allow that burning inside my chest to escape.

"Charles," despite my efforts, the reprimand was in the use of his Christian name. It had slipped out and I rushed to ease the sting I saw in his rearing back. "Plans change, and I must…"

Of a sudden, the sound of a gentleman's laugh drew louder than the soft currants of conversation that had floated about us previously, and, in my already perturbed state, I allowed its piercing interruption to add coal to my already burning anger within. I turned to know its source only to see Mr Gordan seated quite inappropriately close to Miss Catherine.

She smiled at him, and he imprudently tucked a curl of her hair behind her ear.

My temper sparked and my vision blurred. My veins thrummed with the pulsing injustice quickening in my blood. This was the gentleman to whom Elizabeth had been entrusted? Was I the only one to see the way he acted when her back was turned or, as now, when she was not in the room?

A fresh swell of justified rage rose within.

"That bloody…"

My arm was restrained, and I looked to see what impeded me from moving towards the dastard making love to his intended's sister, at the very start of his engagement. Bingley held firm to my arm and attempted to persuade me to return to the corner with him. I had already traversed half the distance, my fists ready for use upon completing the other half. The insult to Elizabeth was more than I could allow and if Bingley would not forestall it, I certainly felt no compunction to stand back.

"Darcy, are you out of your mind?"

"Unhand me, Bingley, or so help me I shall strike you too."

"I shall not unless you regulate yourself and act in a more rational manner."

Mrs Bingley had now stood, staring at me in with those exasperatingly unfathomable eyes.

I looked between the two of them, my teeth clenched near to breaking. "I only seek to do what one of her relations ought to have done but apparently will not."

"For God's sake. Lower your voice—or better yet stay your tongue—before you cast insults that cannot be returned."

Mrs Bingley continued to look at me searchingly and though I had yet to ever raise my voice to a lady, felt every impulse then to shout at her stop her staring. I had no desire to curb my righteous need to defend Elizabeth's honour, especially when her nearer relations would not. I did not wish to be exposed to Mrs Bingley's evaluation at the same time.

I returned my attention to the couple at the couch only to see that Bingley's forestallment and my burst of anger had gone unnoticed, and they were standing with Miss Catherine's father who had roused his wife. The whole party were speaking quietly together, probably preparing to retire. I readied to pull my arm forcefully from my friend's grasp, knowing myself to have greater strength. I did not intend for Mr Gordan to bid good evening without a confrontation.

"You were not here earlier, Mr Darcy, when my father made his announcement." Mrs Bingley's calm voice drew my eyes back to her.

"I believe I am well enough informed despite it, Mrs Bingley." The despair within swelled above the fury for a moment and closed my throat with anguish.

"Then I am sure you will wish to extend your congratulations to my sister Kitty and Mr Gordan before the evening comes to an end."

My mouth opened, searing words clawing up my throat and turning to dust. My arm went limp in the hand of my friend, my brain void of any coherent thought. By rote, I replied, every word pushing my heart to beat slower as if it needed to be silent or else her reply would not be heard.

"Did you not mean to say Miss Elizabeth?"

I could not look at her for the answer, instead keeping my gaze carefully above her head. I was too cowardly to meet her eyes. If she corrected her mistake, then she would see the turmoil in my own as hope barely sputtering to life died again.

She laughed, puckering my brow but still I could not lower my eyes.

"Is this what the matter is?" Bingley's tone now lost all its earlier firm offense, and he dropped my arm. I could not have left that corner of the room had it been on fire though. I needed to know what caused Mrs Bingley to laugh.

"I assure you. I speak correctly. My sister Catherine has just this evening accepted the hand of Mr Gordan."

The air whooshed out of me and for a moment my vision felt hazy. Could it be? But Elizabeth had confirmed it at the table. My mind, sluggish and shocked, slowly repeated the evening. With every review of it, I began to hope that I had mistaken Elizabeth's confirmation at the table.

"I believe Mr Gordan asked Elizabeth for some assurances that his suit to Kitty would be acceptable before he proposed. He is a naturally modest man and relied heavily upon her opinion."

This time my eyes met Mrs Bingley's and though they were no

longer assessing, neither did they seem open and friendly as they usually did.

My thoughts returned to earlier this evening, and the words I said to Elizabeth crashed into my remembrance. Actual weakness had me stumbling into a nearby chair. Bingley exclaimed, and in the edges of my vision I saw his wife forestall any further action on his part.

I had told Elizabeth that I no longer cared for her. In an attempt to preserve my heart, I had damned it. My head fell into my hands and unfathomable torment filled me. I recalled the way she reacted to my words. Her lovely face paling and the sparkle in her eyes sputtering dark. Could she have returned my feelings? I might never know now. I thought her lowered spirits were due to pity for me in her new engaged state. But could they be the evidence of her disappointment? The thought that Elizabeth could only have been injured by my words if she returned my feelings caused my heart to soar only to plummet once again. Good God! Elizabeth! I only wanted her happiness, and by my own hand I had crushed her soul.

I looked up now at Mrs Bingley, "Where is Elizabeth?"

Too late I noticed my slip but could care not that I had broken with propriety to call her by her given name.

"She retired some time ago, Mr Darcy. I believe she suffered terribly from a sick headache."

Every word added to my agony. Each a stone of weight upon my breast so that I could hardly draw breath. I had caused that pain for Elizabeth.

All this time Bingley had remained silent. Though his amiability often caused people to believe him to be slow at times, he was rather the opposite.

After some minutes, he leaned down and patted my shoulder, whispering, "Pull yourself together, Darcy, for the Bennets approach."

I did as he said, his words spurring my limbs into action, though they felt numb all over. I stood erect, my face, I hoped hid what was inside.

We bowed to Miss Catherine and Mrs Bennet and nodded to Mr Gordan and Mr Bennet. They bid goodnight to their hosts, and while they exchanged pleasant nothings about the meal, the evening's festivities, and the Christmas day to follow, I looked upon my once rival and was surprised I still felt a tincture of jealousy. Though I now knew that his intentions were not fixed upon Elizabeth, he had secured his future to the woman he cared for—while I had allowed myself to be blinded by misgiving, imprudence, and jealousy that drove mine away with piercing untruths.

Enough! I was a gentleman and decided it was time to begin acting as one. I offered the couple my sincere congratulations at the next moment of pause in the conversation. I did wish them well and was pleased at their future union. Obviously, their union meant that Elizabeth was free. Doubt whispered it did not matter as I had been the means of destroying that chance, but to preserve my display of calm, I suppressed the haunting thought.

When the party retired and I was left alone with the Bingleys, I felt myself finally beyond the initial shock of Mrs Bingley's revelation. Desolation lapped at my heart, causing it to sputter now and then like a candle left near an open window during a rain.

Desperation loosened my usual reserve and I nearly begged Elizabeth's sister to ease my mind. "I had hoped to prevent her concern for my feelings. I told her things, Mrs Bingley…I spoke untruths so that she would not suffer a moment's remorse for her once suitor and instead be allowed to enjoy the bliss of her new engagement. I swear to you that I had believed she would not be injured by my words, rather relieved."

Mrs Bingley did not answer, and I could not blame her silence for I knew it protected her sister. I pressed on, regardless.

"Please tell me I am not too late. That such tender feelings as I had hoped were mine, before jealousy and imprudence clouded my observations, are not destroyed by my untruths. And falsehoods they were, every word, for I have not ceased to love Elizabeth from the moment she blazed across these fields to your care in this very house last year."

"I cannot ease your mind for I do not know what all Elizabeth feels or suffers. I can only say that I shall not countenance seeing her as she was this evening ever again, Mr Darcy. Despite your long friendship with my husband, my allegiances must always be with my sister."

I nodded, feeling her reprimand only combine with the many castigations I was already hurling at myself.

"Though 'tis the season of charity and love," her tone had softened, and I met her eyes with my own glistening, "the spirit of this time can heal all wounds."

I thanked her for the sentiment, and, with a few whispered words between them, Mrs Bingley retired, leaving me with her husband. Bingley settled into the chair beside me and allowed my thoughts the silence they required. Usually wanting solitude, I could not help but feel gratitude for his presence that prevented me from drowning alone in my thoughts. I spent a while in quiet contemplation and fervent prayerful supplication. After a time, and very late into the night, I bid my friend to find his bed.

"You may leave me now, Bingley. I thank you for staying with me. I have not been good company as I have been plagued by my thoughts. Even still, I was glad not to be alone with them."

Bingley slapped his thighs and leaned forward as he prepared to stand. "Shall you wish to review any sentiments with me prior to speaking with her..."

I smirked, amazed that I could feel a moment of light-heartedness. "Do you mean, should I wish to practise professing my love, as you did with me in September prior to speaking with Mrs Bingley?"

Bingley laughed, and his cheeks pinked slightly. "Precisely. A little begging for forgiveness, I learned, likewise works magic on the ladies."

"Duly noted." I chuckled, then sobered. "I have much to atone for."

Bingley smiled kindly at me and stood then to shake my hand. "It has been interesting seeing you in love, my friend. It is far more dramatic and unpredictable than I had anticipated. Please tell me I was not such a changeling as you have been."

My brow raised by way of response, and he shook his head in amusement.

I thought back to his beaming countenance in the autumn, leading to the morose sombre miens of the winter in London after leaving Netherfield. A tinge of remorse for having a hand in that passed through my thoughts, though I knew I had long been forgiven for it now that Bingley had secured the hand of Jane Bennet.

I laughed, as I expected he hoped I would, and he nodded, bidding me a good night. I told him I would remain a while longer in the parlour before retiring, and he did not question me. He did, however, stop at the doorway and reach up to pluck the mistletoe bundle hanging there and toss it to me.

"And if all else fails, maybe kiss her."

I caught the garnishment easily and laughed, though this time there was no cheer behind it. Tucking the little bundle into my breast pocket, I spent the rest of the night burdened with thoughts and determination. I did not sleep. At times I paced the carpeted rooms, at times I sat staring at the remnants of the large Yule Log, still burning warmth into the early morning hours. When dawn stretched its light across the sky like limbs after a long sleep, I felt my heart begin to firm up in resolution.

I would beg for her forgiveness and not waste another moment in cowardly misgivings. I would declare my feelings for her. I resolved that should she grant me the gift of her love on this Christmas morning, I would never again allow her a moment's heartache if it was with in my power.

A sound outside the parlour doors drew my attention, and I stepped into the hallway. My hope was rewarded by the sight of her slim form accepting her cloak from the waiting footman and pulling on a pair of gloves. Her face was still pale, and shadows surrounded her eyes. I was dishevelled, my cravat long discarded and crumpled in my pocket. I ought to leave her to her walk and use the time to make myself more presentable, to ensure a greater impression. But my heart yearned and could not be repressed.

"Miss Bennet, might I have a moment of your time?"

CHAPTER TWELVE

Elizabeth

THE AIR LEFT MY LUNGS, AND I FELT A WEIGHT INSIDE DROP to my soles. For certain, he would see from my wan countenance that I had not slept, and I could not bear the thought that he would know why. There was nothing for it; I had been seen and must acknowledge him. Slowly I turned around and with a nod began to remove my gloves, using the action as an excuse not to meet his eyes.

"No, you are prepared for your walk, and I do not wish to suspend any pleasure of yours. Might I be allowed to join you?"

"If you wish, sir." My voice cracked only slightly, and my eyes darted up to his for only a second. The connexion, though brief, tore through me and sent my heart fluttering. I doubted I could pretend serenity for long in his company and hoped our conversation would be short. I remembered with a tincture of pain that he planned to leave for London today and, though the thought of his departure tormented me, I took relief from the thought that I might not need to hide my feelings long.

He dispatched the footman to retrieve his cloak and before too long we were walking along the outdoor path around the house. Snow had fallen during the night, but it was only a dusting. The cold was significant because the sun had yet to break through the grey clouds.

After a time, I found we had ventured to the path along the trees that I preferred, and I looked about for my Redwing friend. Though my eyes were diverted in the task, every other nerve and sense were attuned to the gentleman beside me. My thoughts were scattered by his disordered attire and the remembered sight of his bare neck when I encountered him this morning. His hair had a wild look that I felt certain mirrored the look in my eyes. It was obvious to me he had not gone to bed all night. Any of his possible reasons for not so doing haunted me.

"I shall not trouble you long. I shall say my piece and if you wish it, shall leave you to the rest your exercise."

His tone drew my eyes, though I had avoided such an action prior. I ought to have said something, but my lips felt unresponsive.

Mr Darcy slowed our walk and in time we stopped under the branches of one of the trees. Inside I felt as if I were on the edge of a cliff, waiting for his words to push me over it.

"What I wished to say to you deserves a great speech, full of descriptions of sentiments and heartfelt expressions. I spent the night through contemplating what to say and could not find the words other than to simply say to you that I love you. Still and with all my heart. I beg you—I beg you to forgive my imprudence yesterday."

The silence that followed roared in my ears. I tried impossibly to hold onto the unbelievable words that fell from his lips, but I could not. Insecurity was a difficult foe to defeat. Had I not really awoken? Was this all a dream? The wind bit my cheeks, and I knew it was not, yet it seemed incredible that such joy could be mine after such anguish as I had felt.

Mr Darcy lowered his head and began to press at the buttons of his coat. His voice had grown flat, no longer imbued with the warmth of his earlier words. "If however, you cannot forgive me—"

"Please, sir…I…can you repeat what you said?" I interrupted, perturbed by his bleak tone. I was desperate to prove to my doubts that I had heard him correctly earlier. He must have felt something from my plea that bolstered his confidence, for he lifted his eyes once again to mine. There they stayed and I never wanted him to look away, especially when his voice lowered and he said the words I had worried were merely a dream.

"I love you, Elizabeth."

I felt myself sway towards him as surges of emotion flowed through my body. He steadied me against his chest just as tears made his countenance blurry. Wishing to see him once again, I blinked rapidly to clear them. He crooned his love once more near my ear.

"I love you," I whispered back, or my heart did. I knew not which, but he must have heard regardless for he sighed a great sigh and pressed me to him where I was soon engulfed in the strength of his arms.

He murmured words of regret in my ear, each sentence coming quicker upon the last. He had never stopped loving me, he had longed for me all this time. He had only spoken the words the day before that brought me such misery because he had thought I was engaged to Mr Gordan. This made me laugh, and I pulled out of his warmth a little to see his face at such a ridiculous speech.

My laughter melted into a heartfelt smile at the sight of his face. He had been anguished at the thought of me with another. As absurd as his mistaken assumption was, I could not laugh at that for I knew that pain of loss when I thought he no longer cared for me.

"Who is Mr Gordan to Mr Fitzwilliam Darcy of Pemberley," I scoffed, tenderly teasing him.

"Precisely my thoughts!" was his pretended arrogant reply. His face went flat again, his brows creasing. "When you said you were happy, I forced myself to accept that, though it left a bitter taste. At the same time, I observed he was always paying such attention to your sister too. I felt he did not deserve you!"

I apologised for what it must have looked like to him to have Mr Gordan constantly seeking my company whenever Kitty was otherwise occupied. Mr Bingley had done the same when he and Jane were engaged. I had thought nothing of it, seeing as every moment was in conversation about my sister.

"No, do not lessen my guilt. I allowed my insecurities to colour my view. After Wickham…"

He stopped, obviously unhappy to speak of such a topic, however, I knew it was time that I expressed my gratitude. I slipped out of his arms, unhappily. I knew that I could not rightfully express my thoughts as they were in constant disorder caused by the feel of his arms about me.

"I know of the role you played in securing the safety and reputation of my sister, thus saving my whole family. I cannot express to you how such benevolence and sacrifice has affected me. Were the rest of my family aware, I would have more than my own gratitude to express."

I took up his hand and bowed my head over it in thanks.

Mr Darcy hesitated and then said, "I did not wish you to know. I did not think Mr and Mrs Gardiner to be so little trusted."

"Your faith in them is not misplaced. My sister Lydia's imprudence revealed it to me many months ago. After, I urged my aunt to tell me all, for I had to know it."

"I see. I am sorry he was ever allowed access to her. I ought to have…in any case it is done, and I know my culpability in it."

"Which was nothing!" I cried. "They alone made their choice and anyway enough of this." I stepped closer to him again, eager to return to the warmth of our previous declarations. Admiring his handsome face, I said, "We were speaking of more pleasant things earlier."

I smiled coyly at him and thrilled when the smile returned to his features as he pulled me gently into his arms. His hands ran the length of my spine, sending cascading delight. My hands rested upon his chest, where I boldly settled my head against the firm muscles there. For a time, I listened to the thump of his heart and exalted in the happiness I felt.

"Elizabeth, after all the misgivings and misjudgments plaguing our acquaintance, do you think you could forgive me mine enough to accept my hand in marriage? It is still yours for the taking after these many months."

I lifted my head, wishing there to be no more confusion or doubt, and whispered, "Yes."

Then his hand caressed my wind-chapped cheek, the look of pleasure on his face quite becoming. He pressed me to him once more and that is when I felt the crunch of something in his pocket. Apologising, I pulled away quickly and he chuckled, pulling out a piece of mistletoe that had not borne its time in his pocket well.

I eyed him, amusement bubbling up within me. That he would carry it about with him…My brow raised in question, and he blushed.

"Bingley said if all else fails—" He cleared his throat, an endearing blush stole across his cheeks. "Never mind that. It did not fail."

Darcy tossed the flattened leaves to the ground beside us and took up my face again, this time pressing his lips to mine in a glorious riot of feeling. My eyes closed to the sensation. His lips were warm against mine, and I soon felt all the cold around us dissipate. The passion that brewed and built within me felt freeing and all encompassing. I would not have been surprised to find after that the surrounding snow had melted at its force.

Alas, the snow had not melted, for a clump of it fell upon our faces causing us to startle and pull back from one another. While we both sputtered and laughed, I caught a glimpse of my Redwing friend hopping off the branch above us to another before pausing and looking back at me. The pleasure of that moment increased at the sight of that bird. I had promised him to seek my happiness in whatever measure was still left for me and, to my greatest contentment, I had.

Looking at my betrothed wipe away the sopping mess from his hair,

I felt that bliss travel along every part of my body, filling and renewing by the very beating of my heart. My soul laughed; my heart soared as high as that Redwing's as he took flight at the sound.

EPILOGUE

Darcy

I WATCHED HER STRETCH AS HIGH AS SHE COULD ON HER slippered toes to secure the piece of mistletoe to the mantel, the swell of her belly more pronounced in this posture. A miracle in the making. Without thought, my legs propelled me to her. I had been admiring her figure from the comfort of my chair near the fire.

My arms slipped around from behind my dear wife of ten blissful months, who now carried our child. My hand ran along the curve of her abdomen as I bent my head to kiss between her shoulder and her neck. A spot where I knew often worked to my advantage. She melted into me, and a burst of pleasure stole through me.

My evening stubble soon tickled her skin though and she squirmed, laughing as she tried to move away. Devilishly I wiggled my chin against her neck to tickle her further and relished in every squeak and laugh that resulted.

"Stop, I beg you," Elizabeth breathily pled.

I lifted my face to meet her gloriously fine eyes, marvelling that just a year ago I had despaired of ever seeing them look upon me with the love that shone in them daily during this past year. The baby moved beneath my hand and we both looked down in wonder at it. A child. Mine. Last Christmas I had been given the gift of her love. This year I would be given the gift of becoming a papa some weeks after the New Year.

With this sentiment cascading through my thoughts, I bent my head and kissed my dearest wife. She responded to my affection with equal passion and for a time we were lost.

I begged her to let me take her upstairs, but she declined, laughing as she said, "I have more mistletoe to hang!"

I looked at the basket by her feet. She had been hanging mistletoe all over Pemberley, and I did not grumble at it as I had when Bingley had plagued his house with it last year. I certainly did not avoid them either.

Georgiana had gone to spend the Christmastide with our aunt and uncle, leaving us to spend the time alone together—her gift to us, knowing how much Christmas meant to us now.

"Then I will help you," I growled suggestively.

Elizabeth laughed and bent to retrieve the small basket. I quickly relieved her of the burden and began following her out the door.

She chuckled and threw over her shoulder at me, "If you help, it will likely take twice as long!"

"Oh, my dear, I very much hope so!"

The End

About the Author

KaraLynne Mackrory lives in a fantasy world where the characters of books charmingly shock, amuse and altogether delight her constantly. She is frequently forced to write their stories lest they stage a coup in her mind and send her to Bedlam.

Also by KaraLynne Mackrory

BeSwitched
Blinded by Prejudice
Bluebells in the Mourning
Falling for Mr Darcy
Haunting Mr Darcy - A Spirited Courtship
Yours Forevermore, Darcy

Subscribers to the Quills & Quartos newsletter are the first to hear of new book launches, bonus content and sales. We invite you to sign up at www.QuillsandQuartos.com or by scanning the code below with your phone.

www.ingramcontent.com/pod-product-compliance
Lightning Source LLC
LaVergne TN
LVHW010625110826
845149LV00014B/2777